Other Books by Steven Brust

To Reign in Hell
Brokedown Palace
The Sun, the Moon, and the Stars
Cowboy Feng's Space Bar and Grille
The Gypsy (with Megan Lindholm)
Agyar

THE VLAD TALTOS NOVELS:

Jhereg
Yendi
Teckla
Taltos
Phoenix
Athyra
Orca
Dragon

THE KHAAVREN ROMANCES:

The Phoenix Guards
Five Hundred Years After

Other Books by Emma Bull

War for the Oaks
Falcon
Bone Dance
Finder
The Princess and the Lord of Night

FREEDOM
&
NECESSITY

STEVEN BRUST & EMMA BULL

TOR
fantasy

A TOM DOHERTY ASSOCIATES BOOK
NEW YORK

DISCLAIMER

The extracts from *The Times* of 1849 are genuine. The authors cannot warrant the reliability of the articles' reported facts or their freedom from such errors of interpretation as arise from that periodical's political sympathies.

This is a work of fiction. All the characters and events portrayed in this book are either products of the author's imagination or are used fictitiously.

FREEDOM & NECESSITY

Copyright © 1997 by Steven Brust and Emma Bull

All rights reserved, including the right to reproduce this book, or portions thereof, in any form.

Cover art by G. Wappers, detail from *Episode des journées de Septembre 1830 sur la Place de l'Hôtel de Ville de Bruxelles*. Courtesy of Musées royaux des Beaux-Arts de Belgique, Bruxelles-Koninklijke Musee voor Schone Kunsten van Bulgië, Brussel.

Edited by Terri Windling and Patrick Nielsen Hayden

A Tor Book
Published by Tom Doherty Associates, LLC
175 Fifth Avenue
New York, NY 10010

www.tor.com

Tor® is a registered trademark of Tom Doherty Associates, LLC.

ISBN: 0-812-56261-5
Library of Congress Catalog Card Number: 96-27428

First edition: March 1997
First mass market edition: December 1997

Printed in the United States of America

0 9 8 7 6 5 4 3 2

THE AUTHORS WOULD LIKE TO THANK:

Will Shetterly and Pamela Dean for courageous Scribbliness, Patrick Nielsen Hayden, Terri Windling, and Delia Sherman for daring editorship, Jean Brust for political savvy, the Fabulous Lorraine and Liz Cooper for cheers and wolf whistles, Jim Bird and Dawn Celeste for rendezvous points, refreshments, and clothes, Coffee & Tea Ltd. for that life-giving first cup of the day, the Fantasy Shop in St. Louis for the impromptu writers' retreat, Wilson Library at the University of Minnesota for the chance to read the classified ads in *The Times* circa 1849, Betsy Stemple for authenticating the damage, Victor Raymond for Prussian government intelligence, and Neil Gaiman, Charmaine Parnell, and Micole Sudberg for troubleshooting and accent-checking.

If the authors got anything wrong, it's no fault of the above-named people. Being contrary sorts, the authors might have done it on purpose.

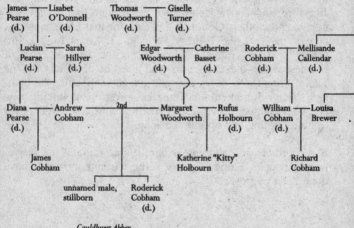

James Pearse (d.) — Lisabet O'Donnell (d.)

Thomas Woodworth (d.) — Giselle Turner (d.)

Lucian Pearse (d.) — Sarah Hillyer (d.)

Edgar Woodworth (d.) — Catherine Basset (d.)

Roderick Cobham (d.) — Mellisande Callendar (d.)

Diana Pearse (d.) — Andrew Cobham — 2nd — Margaret Woodworth — Rufus Holbourn (d.)

William Cobham (d.) — Louisa Brewer

James Cobham

Katherine "Kitty" Holbourn

Richard Cobham

unnamed male, stillborn — Roderick Cobham (d.)

Cauldhurst Abbey

THE COBHAM & VOIGHT FAMILIES IN THE AUTUMN OF 1849

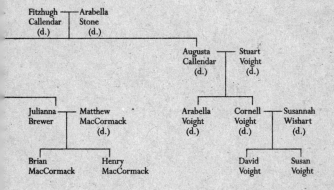

Fitzhugh	Arabella
Callendar	Stone
(d.)	(d.)

Augusta — Stuart
Callendar   Voight
(d.)   (d.)

Julianna — Matthew   Arabella   Cornell — Susannah
Brewer   MacCormack   Voight   Voight   Wishart
           (d.)   (d.)   (d.)   (d.)

Brian   Henry   David   Susan
MacCormack   MacCormack   Voight   Voight

Melrose Hall

When the content of the interest in which one is absorbed is drawn out of its immediate unity with oneself and becomes an independent object of one's thinking, then it is that spirit begins to be free, whereas when thinking is an instinctive activity, spirit is enmeshed in the bonds of its categories and is broken up into an infinitely varied material . . . because spirit is essentially consciousness, this self-knowing is a fundamental determination of its *actuality* . . . the loftier business of logic therefore is to clarify these categories and in them to raise mind to freedom and truth.

—Hegel, *The Science of Logic*

FREEDOM
&
NECESSITY

... I don't know whether in Switzerland you have an opportunity of following the English movement. It has started up again at exactly the point where it was interrupted by the February Revolution. As you know, the peace party is nothing but the Free Trade party in a new guise. But the industrial bourgeoisie now acts in an even more revolutionary way than during the Anti-Corn Law League agitation. For two reasons: 1. Having weakened the basis of the aristocracy at home by the repeal of the Corn Laws and Navigation Acts, the bourgeoisie now intends also to ruin the aristocracy in the sphere of foreign policy by attacking its European ramifications. It reverses Pitt's policy and turns against Russia, Austria, and Prussia, in short it supports Italy and Hungary. Cobden has openly threatened to proscribe any banker who should lend money to Russia and has begun a veritable campaign against Russian finances. 2. Agitation for universal suffrage in order to achieve the complete political separation of the tenants from the landed aristocracy, to give the towns an absolute majority in parliament and to nullify the power of the House of Lords. Financial reform in order to cut off the church and deprive the aristocracy of their political advantages.

Chartists and Free Traders have joined hands in these two propaganda campaigns. Harney and Palmerston have apparently become friends. O'Connor was in agreement with Colonel Thompson at the last meeting held in London.

There is no telling what consequences this economic campaign against Feudalism and the Holy Alliance will have ...

PART ONE

APPEARANCE

Mr ROEBUCK also begged to enter his protest against this ill-considered and crude piece of legislation, which he described as the result of a species of cant which was almost as dangerous as vice.

Mr MOWATT had also felt himself obliged to oppose the bill, because it was calculated to mislead the people for whose benefit they affected to legislate, namely, the parents of females in humble life, by teaching them to dispense with the moral education and training of their children, and lean only on the legislature. (Hear, hear.)

LATEST FROM PARIS
By Electric Telegraph

The sentence of death pronounced by court-martial on four privates of the 7th regiment of Light Infantry for having resisted the arrest of Sergeant-Major Boichot, and a similar sentence passed on a grenadier of the 15th of the Line, for having deserted his post in presence of the insurgents of the 13th of June, were confirmed by the Council of Revision held on Tuesday.

A Socialist writer, named Louvet, has been sentenced by the Court of Orleans to imprisonment for two years and to pay a fine of 4,000f for having published an incendiary address to the people, exciting them to revolt against the established Government.

THE POSTING-HOUSE THE GREY HOUND
LANGSTONE, NEAR PORTSMOUTH
9th OCTOBER, 1849

My Dear Cousin,

I wonder how you will greet these words; indeed, I wonder how you will receive into your hands the paper that bears them, as I think you cannot be in expectation of correspondence from me. You have always been a hardy soul—body and mind—and so I don't imagine you the central figure in some Gothick tale, clutching at these pages and your disordered locks and changing colour six times in a minute.

I am sorry; I am too frivolous; I shall begin again, taking care to keep better governance of my near-ungovernable fancy. But truly, what ought I to anchor my senses to but nonsense, in a situation so out of common, so utterly outside of the natural, as the one I've got myself pitched into?

In short, I have been given to understand that I am believed dead by all my family and acquaintance—that I was seen to die, in fact, or at least, was seen to sink beneath the water a last time, and my corpse never recovered, though long and passionately sought for. You may imagine the fascination with which I heard this account, though you will imagine, too, that my fascination was accompanied by horror, which is far from the case. I cannot tell how it is, but though I know the thought of myself as a corpse should by all rights cause me distress, I find it holds only the interest, raises only the feelings, that such a thing might in verse or fiction.

What should distress me yet more, and what may, as my sensibilities recover somewhat from the curious flattened state they are now in, is that, for all I can recall, I may indeed have drowned. I have no knowledge of any act, any word, any thing at all that occurred between the conclusion of that pleasant luncheon on the lake shore, and my discovery—rediscovery—of my wits and person at the bottom of the garden behind this respectable inn at an hour when almost none of the respectable inhabitants of it were conscious. I have read, I suppose, too many fables and fairy-tales, for the first thing I asked of the good landlord, upon gathering my straying thoughts and finding my voice, was the month, day, and year. How relieved I was to find I had not been whisked away for seven times seven years, but for a scant two months! And yet, how and where were those two months passed? For anything I could tell, I might indeed have spent them happily in Fairyland, but for sundry signs about my person that it might not have been an unalloyed happiness.

You must choose how you, and even I, proceed now, for I

confess I cannot. I have trusted in that natural reserve and discretion that I know to be so strong in you, that others of our family have wrongly termed coldness or even slyness, to keep the source and contents of this letter from the knowledge of any other, unless the time and company be such as to recommend their revelation. Cousin, re-introduce me living to my family, or do not, as seems wise to you. I know you are wise; and though I may be clever, cleverness owes something to experience, and the experience of returning from the dead has not come much in my way previously. If it is best that my existence and abode be known only to you at this time, I shall keep silence—very like the grave, I suppose.

I fall into nonsense again—I am heartily sorry for any distress it may cause you; it is meant only to fend off any of my own. Weigh this matter for as long as you will, knowing I am very comfortable where I am. The landlord and his wife are kind people and disposed to be uninformative about curious doings, as I suppose must be often observed of those who run public houses near the coast. When you write or come, make your enquiries for Jack Cobb, as I have chosen that for my *nom de discrétion*. You will laugh—at least, I believe you will laugh—I am employed as the new head groom. Were you to share that fact with my Aunt Louisa, I know that the rôle in which I could not cast you, that of High Gothick tragedian, would be quite satisfactorily filled after all.

I cannot write more; you know, I hope, how much I would wish to say, what a multitude of questions I would ply you with, which of our mutual acquaintance I would most urgently enquire after. I trust you to do what you can for me, as you always have done, in good fortune or adversity. Merely addressing you on the page has served to clear away some of the fog which besets my thoughts, and to give me greater resolution altogether. Though my gratitude is beyond any measurement, it is still less than you deserve, and you will, as a result, find me always

Your most faithful relative and friend,

James Cobham

MELROSE HALL
THURSDAY

My Dear James:

So you have cheated death once more, proving that the child
is, indeed, the father of the man. Well, I am delighted, but I
cannot pretend to be surprised. Each time I would receive a
letter from Aunt Margaret, she would seem more persuaded
that you had perished beneath the waves, and Mother was positively hysterical; whereas I would remark to Kitty, "James
cannot drown, however drunk he got himself." And now I
find that I am right.

And yet, you have lost two months of your life? My dear
James, that is excessive. A day or two now and then I would
say nothing about, but two months! If you continue, you will
become a greater blot on the family name than I—what would
my uncle your father say? And what of my reputation? I
should have to pay off my debts and marry Kitty and become
respectable, God forbid!

But you say nothing to imply that this missing time could
have been the result of a debauch, instead making ironic comments about Fairyland—a subject, my cousin, that is best not
treated lightly, whatever your own opinions are. My dear fellow, if it is not simply the result of a debauch, then we have
a regular mystery before us, do we not? I can imagine that,
were it I who had lost two months of my life, I should have
some curiosity about how I had passed the time.

Ah, James! Do not be fooled by the complacent tone of my
words. Truly, I am relieved and moved; but you have asked
what action to take, and it is to action I must address myself.
Let me be as cool, dispassionate, and rational as David Hume
himself, assess the facts we know, and see what is to be done.
It seems that there are only two possibilities: you have either
been the victim of a freak accident on the part of nature, or
the victim of an enemy; and until we know which of these it
is, I think it imperative that you remain hidden. As for finding
out, that is more difficult. What enemies do you have who

could treat you thus? You speak of signs about your person, but what do these signs indicate?

Another matter to consider is this: habits are ingrained in us without our awareness, so examine your habits—are you finding them altered? If so, in what way, and what can they tell us? Also, if your last memory is of that luncheon, what exactly do you recall about it that may be significant? Did anyone say anything that struck you as unusual? Especially, did you eat or drink anything worthy of note? My memory will be of no use to you, because all I remember of the affair is the pleasant haze from the port I consumed, and a few words I exchanged with David that would have led to me putting a ball between his piggish little eyes had not someone—was it you?—jumped in to prevent it.

Other than those few suggestions, I have no idea how to proceed. Shall I come out there and join you? Or are there useful investigations I could make from here? I repeat, you should not show yourself until we know more, and yet I am, frankly, at a loss as to how we can learn anything.

There is little to tell of doings here, James. Thomas was set upon by footpads and beaten soundly a couple of weeks ago, but, aside from some bruises and embarrassment, seems none the worse for it. Susan has dropped from sight, and there is speculation by some (including, I confess, your humble servant) that she harboured stronger feelings for you than she cared to reveal. David is living at Cauldhurst in your father's absence, which makes me grit my teeth, but I can hardly prevent it (of course, you could, should you wish to resuscitate yourself). He says it is only until repairs are completed on the rectory in Dunston, but I think he must have hired the slowest carpenters in the south of England. Brian continues his studies, and I begin to believe we really will have a solicitor in the family before too much longer, but it leaves him with little time for anything else. Henry lost an appalling amount of money to a pair of sharps at the Locket and had to send home for his expenses. Waters has settled down to a sort of life not unlike what Mother would wish for me; you may have predicted it, but I am surprised. He periodically asks me over for billiards, and I am running short of excuses. Powers is travelling on the Continent. His claim is that the journey is merely for pleasure, but I have never believed anything he says of himself; on the other hand, I admire him as much as I ever have and cannot suspect him of malice. Calvert makes trouble for everyone around him, but not, I think, this kind of trouble. But the big news is Johnson, who has actually purchased a naval commission and gone off with a ship whose name I forget. The timing of his departure may appear suspicious to you, and if so we can investigate it, but that seems to me to be grasping at phantoms, if I can send your own phrase back at you (and if you have forgotten the occasions on which you used to say that to me, be assured I have not, you casuistic scoundrel).

James, you must believe that, insofar as I can do anything useful, I am entirely at your service, and, if I have not explicitly said so, I am delighted to learn that you are still among the living—and I am more than a little anxious that you should continue in this condition, and until you give me a more clear idea on how I can be of help to you, I Remain, my Dear Fellow, Your Cousin and Friend,

                                                    Richard Cobham

THE GREY HOUND
14th OCTOBER, 1849

Faithful Richard,

And that's for you, for flourishing Hume at me; here's the Devil quoting Scripture, indeed! You must give my rationality its due now, however. Were I of a mystical bent, my present condition might drive me to madness. Failing that, it would certainly cause me to write the most tiresome sort of letters. Or do I pride myself on a reticence I have not achieved? Beside your letter, as empirical and sensible as any Rationalist might pen, mine seems full of "a host of furious fancies." Well, I am resolved to let our mystery spin itself out as a philosopher's experiment. If I am a madman in a rational world, I have the consolation of sound philosophy; and if I am sane in a world of supernatural morality and intangible motive force, I will at least have my wits to treasure.

That I entertain the latter idea at all will suggest to you that I am in a weakened state, that I am not myself; and you will be exactly right if you suppose it. I have a shocking bad head. Apple brandy is the cause—No, if I am dead and my character to be reformed by it, let me at least be honest (as temperance has been forestalled)—an *excess* of apple brandy. My host makes his own. I sampled it last night in the taproom, after full dark had made it unlikely I should have any more travellers' rigs to tend, and after I had seen the nags baited, the mucking-out done, and the harness properly oiled and stored and *not* flung over a rusty nail or dropped on a bench as if it were an old shirt. I may have mislaid two months of my life, but I am more careful with the property of others. (When reading the above scold to the boy who helps in the stable, I nearly said, "as if it were a spoiled cravat," but I recalled, barely, who I was supposed to be. I am trying to be careful with my secret, on the chance—the likelihood?—that it is someone else's as well.)

No, I am not done with the brandy, or the subject of it at least, though I wish I were done with the stuff itself. I sampled it, as I say, and meant only to sample it. It was quite good; it hadn't the refinements that an upbringing in a French monastery will give a brandy, but it was rustic and mellow at once, and had not forgotten the orchard. I said some of this to the landlord—Coslick is his name. He looked at me rather sidelong and sly, and said, "Do ye fancy yourself a drinking man, then?"

I was much struck, as I could not recall Coslick putting a direct personal question to me before. I allowed that I did, on occasion, imbibe.

"Well, ye'll drink with me, then, and if ye fall out your chair, I'll see ye wake safe in your own bed."

Richard, I was put up for membership at my clubs while still at Oxford. If I cannot recognize a challenge of that sort when it is made to me, then I have not profited by the education given to young men of our class. Besides, there was something in the nature of a test about the business, a whiff of initiation, though I could not tell you at this remove what gave me to think so. I rolled up my shirt-sleeves—figuratively, for the literal ones were already up—and set to work.

Coslick is a large man, of the complexion common to men to whom excess is only just enough. But when his watch (mine is lost with my two months) had told off an hour past midnight, he was face down upon the table and snoring mightily, and I was able to rise from my chair and stay on my pins. I would have got him to his bed, as he had promised to get me to mine, but that I wasn't sure I could lift him, and didn't think Mrs Coslick would care to find me in her boudoir at such an hour even if I could. I made the poor man as comfortable as might be, and proceeded, slowly, to my room above the stables. If it was a sort of initiation, no high Hermetic secrets have been imparted to me today as a result, and in my present ruinous state I am heartily glad of it.

Today is Sunday, when other people's scruples offer inn-keepers all the holiday they can claim. I am especially blessed, since "travel" may not include the use of one's own legs, but certainly describes taking out a horse. My heart goes out to poor Coslick, if his head is half so bad as mine, for the locals have come to the taproom after morning service, and he has no recourse but to stand and smile and serve them. The heavy, mizzling weather of the last week has finally gone, leaving us with one of the bright, cider-like days that October sometimes brings, which make one cry out against the prospect of winter. Fresh air is physic to the ailment brandy leaves behind; I have taken command of a bench in the shade of the stable wall, where I am trying to move as little as possible, while writing this on pages from my note-book. Yes, I found it still on my person when I came to myself after my abbreviated death. It was much the worse for water, as you can tell somewhat from these sheets, but it received still harder treatment somewhere in our travels, for half the pages were torn roughly out. You will want to know what was written on them, and call it a clue, but I am afraid that with the best will in the world, I could not tell you. I'd got the thing from Burkitt's in Bond Street barely a week before I went down to Melrose to meet my doom, and might have noted down a dinner engagement and a reminder to buy a dozen pocket-handkerchiefs, but nothing more than could occupy two or three pages. The rest are no doubt scattered upon the swells of the River Styx, fouling poor

Charon's oars, and if he chooses not to read them, I think no one ever shall.

This is a surprisingly congenial way of life, Richard, in spite of a few pin-prickings of restlessness, of uncertainty, over my past and future. I have always been good with horses, and I find I enjoy this work that I had been accustomed to leave to others. I possess very little, but I delight in all of it. My wardrobe is much transformed, of course, from that of the young fellow who'd been in the hands of a valet practically since he'd left the nursery. I have two linen shirts, which I wash myself—yes, very finicky, I'm become a veritable beau with my two shirts—and a neckcloth, for if I need to smarten myself up a bit. I've a pair of buckskins, unfashionably loose but very easy, and a good moleskin waistcoat, in a comfortable shade between grey and brown. (You will please not trouble to remind me of the periwinkle blue silk brocade one that I wore at dinner that first evening at Melrose, of which I am quite fond, not least because it served its intended purpose of annoying Aunt Louisa and David. In fact, if my luggage is still at Melrose, I give you leave to wear it. Tell Aunt Louisa I came to you in a dream and said as much.) My boots are my own, thank Providence, and have made a gallant recovery after being filled with lake water. Last week I found my most treasured item of clothing, one of disreputable aspect and questionable pedigree but so suited to my present humour that I would not give it up if paid. It is a vast and possibly antique driving coat, rusty black, with deep turned-back cuffs and a highstanding collar, and a pair of pockets so large that I could drop one of Mr Colt's pistols in each and hardly grudge the room. It swallows me up nearly to the ankles. I discovered it on the seat of the gig Coslick rents out, after one of its trips, and the most diligent questioning has not brought forth anyone who'll admit to owning it. As his boots were to Puss, so this coat is to me. I assure myself that I seem a latter-day Dick Turpin when I've got it on, though I may in fact look a quite modern scare-crow.

My room above the stables has a large casement window, a fire with a well-drawing chimney, a bed with a good straw tick, a chair, a table, and both a lamp *and* candles. In addition to bed and board, I draw a salary here sufficient to cover my needs and give me no pause about spending tuppence mailing fat letters to you. Coslick takes the *Gazette*, probably more for the convenience of his patrons than for himself, and I have it when it's made the rounds. I regret only one great lack, and that's books; there's no bookshop closer than Portsmouth, and no way for a dead man with a false name and no credit to order from Hatchard's. If you can see your way clear to sending the occasional volume along without attracting too much attention, you would make my present life a Paradise.

I have begun to learn the rites and rhythms of the village, to recognize what is ordinary and what is worth commenting on over porter in the taproom. This is not so wide a field as it might be in many a village of this size, for, as I think I mentioned, discretion here is raised to nearly religious dignities; too much curiosity about one's neighbours is like unto heresy. I can think of nothing to account for it but a long history of smuggling, which is more than likely. But I take much pleasure in examining the comings and goings of the citizenry (which I am in the ideal position to observe), and in attempting to deduce what I cannot see from what I have seen. I've gone ambling about the countryside, a little farther each time as my strength returns, taking surveys of roads, houses, cottages, pasturage, cultivated land, stands of timber and wilderness. Now, when I hear coach-wheels on the Portsmouth road (which is the only real highway through Langstone), I can tell you if it is the mail-coach, or only the stage; when the rector's gig passes, I can make a fair guess at which cottage houses an ailing parishioner for him to visit; when a smart claret-coloured phaeton drawn by a pair of broken-winded greys swings into view, I know that the squire at Chesford is tooling into Portsmouth for some amusement. I can still be stumped, however; on Friday I saw a very fine rig, a large closed coach with dark green panels and four admirable matchbays to draw it ("admirable" is sadly milky in this case; you might pay five hundred pounds for that team at Tatt's and think yourself a clever fellow). The coach and cattle were much splashed with mud, as if they'd come far over heavy ground, and the whole turnout had come down the lane that leads to Ryder Hill village, where I would have sworn there was no manor house nor rich squire to account for them, but the horses seemed fresh and eager. The driver was holding them in strongly as they trotted through the village, or they might have careened through the rain like a runaway and not stopped until they reached Portsmouth and the sea. The more I think on them, the more I admire those horses. I shall see if Coslick will lend me one of his hacks on my next holiday, and I'll ride out that way. Someday I may be a live man again, and a man of property, who might buy a new team if their present owner could be induced to sell.

Oh, Richard, on re-reading your letter I find it so energetic, so sensible and to the point when compared with this one! You want to untangle this mystery, to pick up one clear end of the string and follow it to its end. You want to act, to solve, to resolve. I think I would have been the same, not so long ago; I think I would have. But for me, here, this is no string but a fog bank, and I live in it, a state of positive living, of continuance, as if it has no ends or edges. I am not passive, I am not sitting idle and stupefied until stirred, but I cannot feel the urgency I should over the blankness of my own recent past, as a problem to be solved. It really is as if I had died, and returned Hindoo-like as someone else; for death is hardly a thing to be fixed or striven over after the fact. Am I misleading myself about my true nature, my past self? I would, wouldn't I, have actively pursued the solving of this puzzle? I would have railed against the injustice of two months lost, perhaps stolen, burned over the suspicion of some wrongdoing, laboured to assemble clues and hints. Instead I can burn and labour over any matter but this one, and over this one there is only a cool and featureless pall. I am strange to myself, Richard, sometimes, and when I think on that, I feel the beginnings of fear.

But I will marshall facts for you, to answer your questions, and by so doing perhaps awaken the part of me that ought to ask more. I cannot say I have no enemies, for it seems as if growing to manhood in the possession of wealth, or its expectation, produces one or two, earned or not. But none of them, I think, would have the energy to hurry my death, expecting not unreasonably that I will manage it for them at my present pace. Halliwell hates me for that piquet game, and because I have money and he has none he thinks it unreasonable of me to object to his plucking some of it. If he likes to cheat he should learn to do it well. Stone's enmity I earned, and I regret that one still; I was a child and a fool, and if I could have the clock turned back, I would do better by him. He was not guilty, Richard, and I knew it, and I should not have stood by and let him be expelled. There, I have never admitted that to a soul, and should not have done so even to you, but every man should have so good a chance to clear his conscience after he is dead. I wish that you could publish it, but you would then have to say how you knew it, and it's too late to give Stone any relief if you did. Tournier resents me on Stone's behalf, and I cannot but honour him for that, whatever I may think of his other dealings. I had forgotten Calvert until your letter, but if my present difficulties are rooted in my dealings with him, I shall die of repugnance straight away and save everyone the trouble of sorting this out. If there are other men who would do me a wrong, I think it would be not a personal but a public wrong, and one not done only to me, but to the nation—but that much, any of us could say. I hope I have not earned the hatred of any woman, though I am not such a coxcomb as to claim that they all love me. And my family? Brian could not want me dead, since he rarely can distinguish me from any dozen other of his male relations. David would certainly not want me dead, as it would rob him of an opportunity to wax censorious, which is the only time he's truly happy. You could want me dead, of course, for the inheritance; but as you say, it is a legacy fraught with responsibilities and the peril of a respectable middle age. Perhaps Kitty wants me dead, in the hope that you'll come up to scratch. I love her dearly of course, but I also grew up with her, and Richard, I will be a friend to you and tell you now: Be resolute and give her the slip! She's sharp-tongued and hot at hand, and damnably expensive to boot, and the two of you would be fighting like cats before you'd got out the church door. She also gets her way in the end, always, and so if she tells me she will have you, I shall resign myself to the traditional work of getting you to the church and holding the ring, if you call on me to do it.

Why is it that this family seems incapable of anything short of extremes? On reviewing that hasty, partial summary of the motives of my relatives, it stands out so. Brian pursues extremes of scholarship; David, of priggishness; Kitty, of self-indulgence (I crave your pardon, it is only a step-brother's natural freedom); I, of politics; and you, Cousin? I, at least, cannot fault you, for you do me too great a service now, merely in reading these lines.

My habits are so uprooted by circumstance, abode, and change of fortune that I can hardly say what is strange and what is merely necessary alteration. I have no clubs to go to, no money to gamble away there, no horse to hunt and no pack to hunt with, no carriage to drive; and though I may still drink—woe to him who may still drink, and has a good capacity for it—I have no occasion to drink out of simple idleness or boredom. I have never used tobacco. In short, I do a great many things I was not used to do, but I take leave to doubt it is because I got into the habit of being an hostler.

As to my physical condition, in particular upon my arrival here, it was not so bad as a dead man might expect. I had, from the evidence of scars, received several wounds, most of them trifling. There is a long mark, still reddened and puckered, on my right forearm that might have been a burn; my wrists were somewhat chafed; and my shoulders and upper back are marked with an irregular collection of scratches, which I discovered from the itching they produced as they healed. Those were the worst of my brands—of a different character than I might have got in any two-month period, but certainly no more alarming. My other afflictions were likewise moderate. I had, at first, some inflammation of the lungs, which is surely to be expected when one has been breathing water. I was also rather weak, and for the first few days could almost have wished I had not returned to myself, for I was beset by racking pain in my head, stomach, and all my limbs, strange visions awake and asleep, and frantic starts and terrors, and could keep no food or drink down. It must have been some fierce but short-lived fever, for after a few days, in which I think the Coslicks must have debated whether to put me out of the house as a lunatic or a plague carrier, these miseries faded away, and I was left with only the weakness, which is all but banished.

Did you quarrel with David that day by the lakeshore? I don't remember it—but then, you and David have been quarrelling for so long, and so bitterly, that it would be a wonder if any of us noticed. When we were at Harrow, and I stayed at Melrose for holidays, you fought then; you once threatened him with the nursery toasting-fork, do you remember? I was terrified. He'll be a bishop someday, you know, and may the Church of England have much joy of him. His parishioners should bring suit against my father for giving him the living at Dunston.

What has become of all the people and possessions that came to Melrose with me? I hope that Wye gave his notice promptly and has found another employer, for he's far too good a valet to be out of a place for long. He was rather wasted on me, but you could never have told it from his manner; he always behaved as if he had the dressing of the Prince Consort. If my step-mama sacked him, I must do what I can to make sure he has not suffered for it. Hatcher's position will be secure; he is my father's employee, in fact, though I have never had nor never wanted another groom since I was breeched. Did he take my horses back to the Abbey, or are you by some oversight left with them eating their heads off in the stable at Melrose? If so, send 'em packing at once. I wish I could have Cavalier with me, but head grooms at out-of-the-way taverns do not keep blood-horses. I can imagine anything happening to my cases after my disappearance, from Aunt Louisa having them burned, to my step-mama insisting that my every stocking is sacred and must be returned to her at once, to everyone but the maids forgetting their existence entirely. If they're still in your charge, do as you please with them.

It does not surprise me that my step-mama should have me already buried. She was formed to be one of those stalwart Mediæval gentlewomen who held household at the castle, facing hardship and siege, while her husband rode to the Holy Land. Placed as she is, with my father's man of business and his bailiff keeping the estate in perfect order, her talents have festered. She can only invent sieges to bear up under, and unleashes all that store of resignation and fortitude on her fancied ailments, fancied slights, and enlarged disasters. My drowning must have been her moment of shining glory. I only wonder that she has not yet planned an exquisite funeral for me, for I cannot think that so small a stumbling-block as a missing guest of honour would give her pause. Which reminds me: For how long do I remain, by law, missing and presumed dead, and achieve actual legal quittance? The courts, like God, must measure time spent in Purgatory; in cases like this, where the deceased-to-be is the heir to property, there must be some provision. Brian could certainly tell you, and you may ask him outright without fear that he'll think you greedy. I doubt he would connect any question of law with anything so concrete as your situation *vis-à-vis* my inheritance.

You do not mention my father. Some word of my accident must have been sent to him; has there been any response? If matters were still at sixes and sevens in Jamaica, or if conditions for sailing were poor, he could not have returned to England yet, but a letter might have made better time.

Poor Thomas! You don't say if he was robbed, though I know that he rarely has much on him to steal; his watch is in pawn more often than in his pocket, poor devil. If there is any way you can apply my resources to help him, please do so. He is so honest, and always so very cheerful, that one forgets—*I* forget—how he must struggle to get along. He won't let me buy a great many of his paintings—says he knows quite well I have no respectable taste along those lines, and will only prop them against a wall somewhere and ignore them. He wrongs me in that much, but it is true that he deserves a great deal more than philanthropy. I had rather his brilliance be discovered before he died, but I cannot think of any assistance I could offer that he will accept, other than the occasional loan of ten pounds, and I hate to think what shifts he goes to to pay me back. May his genius prevent him from becoming fashionable for the sake of his comfort. Has he ever shown you the portrait of the two little Lancashire children, the one he finished last spring, that he calls "The Spinning-Room Door"? His work is unsettling; but England has asked for a great deal of unsettling which she has gotten in very little measure. If Thomas can do what other men of more violent emotion could not, I will stake him to my last penny.

Miss Susan Voight never made any effort to disguise the strength of her feeling for me: she considers me the greatest waste of three decades' worth of meals and an Oxford education that ever stood in shoes, and will tell anyone so at the least provocation. Don't, by your hope of heaven, give her cause to dislike you; she will read Engels to you. Perhaps if you took her fancy, she would read Engels to you by moonlight. But by what feat of stage magic has she disappeared? Or do I take "dropped out of sight" to mean that she has finally taken some scholar's lodgings in London with the necessary respectable older lady to play propriety, and has ceased to write to Kitty? For she couldn't very well write to you, you know, or to Brian. For all her advanced notions, Susan Voight is very well bred and brought up, and I could as soon envision her with a waistcoat and a cigar, like the French *lionnes*, as conducting a correspondence with a young man who is not her brother. Did she learn the propriety, or the advanced notions, from Great-Aunt Augusta, and if the latter, what was Great-Aunt Augusta in her salad days?

Henry is an unlicked cub, a yet-unformed lump of clay; but in the name of mercy, can't he have the wits to stand off from the same foolish conduct that we indulged in at his age? We did, you know, and I still remember more than once helping you get back over the wall and past the proctors when you'd had a skinful of the Locket's hospitality. He'll do, in the end, but it makes me feel old and grey only to think about him, so I won't.

I wish Johnson the best of luck in his new state, and think he may do well, if only his ship is not ordered to some port in Australia. There are those who would give him a warm welcome there. (Discretion, Jamie, discretion. These are not your belongings.)

Richard, it would be a comfort beyond expression if you would join me here, and one I must deny myself. I would have to explain you, at the very least. If I am under any suspicion or watch, it would cause alarm; and if I am in any danger, you would be as well. And how would you account to family and friends for a sudden urge to trot down to Portsmouth? The romantic lure of the sea? Bathing, for your health? No, I won't put ideas into your head, or you'll do it merely to lacerate everyone's sensibilities. They don't value you as they should; perhaps they don't know that there are kinds of seeds that will never germinate unless their hard skins are scratched and tumbled.

There are two things you could do for me, if the opportunity presents itself. First, I agree with your reasons for keeping me dead for now. It may be that later on we can use the revelation of my miraculous recovery to force some stubborn hidden fact into the light, but at this time there may be as much to be gained in leaving everyone's expectations intact. Having agreed, however, I am in no position to canvass any of my usual haunts to discover if I was ever sighted during my two missing months. Can you take such a thing on? Going up to Town is not so hard to explain as down to Portsmouth. I think you know, or know of, most of them—the haunts, that is— and are not likely to be shocked upon discovering the wonderful variety of my acquaintance. Be a little careful of that sharp tongue of yours, and I believe they'll take to you. But be alert, too, and carry your revolver in case of unfortunate misunderstandings. Richard, I cannot make my meaning more plain, so I must rely on your natural inclination to distrust everyone and say nothing you do not have to. Take care.

The other service you can do me is to describe as much of my accident and what led up to it as a port-tinted cloud may have allowed you to witness. Of all the strange and villainous dreams I have had these last weeks, not one that I can recall has touched on any matter that might relate to it. I have dreamed of water, and of things in it that I cannot clearly remember when I wake, except that it seems a mercy to me to have forgotten them, but nothing that could have taken place anywhere but in dreams.

I revise my estimate upward; this will cost fourpence at least to send. If I go on in this fashion, I shall be required to practice a few economies in order to keep up my correspondence. (That was a joke—if you send me a guinea under the seal, I shall plant you a facer when I see you next.) I would ask you to offer my best to your mother and mine, but under the circumstances, I think you ought not. You are better than I deserve, Richard, to endure all this; it cannot be an easy burden. Which gives me a twinge of conscience for twitting you about faith. Though I cannot share yours where it touches upon things you defend as unknowable, I do pledge you mine, and my duty to keep it. If there should be a God, or any other supernatural force at work upon us, I would desire it to defend you from all harm.

Yours devotedly,
James

BRIGHT'S HOTEL, KENSINGTON
15 OCT 1849

Dear Kitty,

At last I have got something that convinces me that I'm not chasing wild geese. *You* won't be convinced, but you never thought I ought to embark on this anyway, and won't drop a kind word about the project until I have something quite extraordinary to tell.

Do you recall, two years ago, your step-brother's trip to Blackpool? Well, he was there. The address he wrote from, during his stay, is a very low tavern on the outskirts, with one shabby room to let; and the wicked old fellow who owns it confessed, after a little persuasion and a few aids to his memory, that James had been there for four hours. Before he left (which was after dark, just by the way), he gave the man a great deal of money and a packet of letters to mail at specified intervals. I will wager you anything you like that they were addressed to the Abbey. *Such* a faithful correspondent! If your mother had ever written back, the deception would have been undone. James must have known it was unlikely. How could he have guessed that I would write to tell him that Grandmama had died, and be puzzled all this time by his silence?

I won't tell you how I got the information in the end, for you would swoon dead away. But I mean to continue, now that I have some scrap of encouragement. Can you recall any other journeys he made, no matter how well-documented they seem to have been? Didn't he take a whole year's leave from university in '38 or '39? Where did he go then? And if you tell me you can't possibly remember and anyway you were still in the schoolroom at the time, I'll say that I was, too, and didn't live in the same household, and I remember more than you. Don't turn proper on me, Kit darling, or I shall say it's just funk and that falling in love has wrecked your nerve.

As to why I'm doing this, I'm not certain I know, really, now that I've been at it for a while. I have a lowering presentiment that I'm about to expose my late cousin James as a rogue, and I'd rather not. It will hurt so many people, and it surely can't matter now that he's dead what he was. It may be my odd form of grieving. If his body would turn up, I might stop.

Oh, no, Kitty, I think I'm venting my rage on this, for what else *can* I turn it on? Such a horrible, *horrible* waste! James was nothing short of brilliant, and spent three-quarters of his time in the effort to drown it, stupefy it, waste it, and hide whatever was left. I used to watch him, evenings in the drawing room at Melrose, or across the table at dinner, or at rout-parties and balls in London. You teased me about being in love, but it was a scientific sort of attraction. I watched to see what he'd react to. Polite and attentive about horse racing, agricultural principles, social gossip, the stories of Poe or the essays of Ruskin—oh, almost anything would engage his polite interest, it was no wonder he was the darling of every fashionable London hostess, you could seat him next to *anyone*. But sometimes he failed to guard himself. Sometimes a subject was raised that would bring his head just a little up and around, as if he'd heard a trumpet in the distance, and bring a sharpening of his features, a wakening in his eyes. Suddenly there would be an ardent look there, a passionate intellect gazing out from inside that pretty skull. David held forth one evening in the drawing room, I recall, about the excellence of the new Poor Law, how it had rooted out the criminally lazy men and women who had been living on the kindness of the Crown, and forced them to labour for their own welfare. James got his eagle look, and more besides, a kind of cold fire that I thought ought to have been visible to everyone. With his sweet ballroom smile he began to describe to our charitable man of God the conditions of the workhouses, the soft, easy comfort of them before this last brave reform, until Aunt Louisa cried out for her hartshorn and for him to hold his tongue, silence at once! how dare he speak so crudely before ladies! This lady should have cast her manners aside and sprung to her feet applauding, as she wanted to. How I wish the Lords and Commons might have been there, to shout for their hartshorn!

Perhaps I was in love: I was in love with his *mind*, with his capacity for brilliance, and I envied it and wanted it for mine. I would not have tossed it away at every opportunity like an old newspaper! Had I been given his brain, and his sex, I would stand for Parliament tomorrow, and do my part to turn the Poor Law and all the rest of it upside down. Instead of doing anything, *anything* at all, he is dead, and I am so full of fury that I have to turn it on some outward object, or it will tear me to bits.

I am grieving and raging, and exorcising, too, that poor little intellectual love that makes me smart so. I mean to find out the true extent of the waste of James's mind, so that I'll have no taste for making a hero of him later. If I learn that he descended to roguery and outright crime, I'll be done with him, won't I? And perhaps some more deserving, if less clever, fellow can give me a new and more mature outlet for my passions, and fill the place in my affections that I will empty and scrub clean of any trace of my sad, strayed relative.

The devil's in it that I can't settle to anything else until I'm done with this. My project for the working women's schools has been left to languish, but not forever. I promise, Kitty, that if by Christmas I've learned nothing that even you will admit is momentous I'll abandon my study of the history of James in one slim volume. Promised three times on the little red leather pony saddle, and you know how sacred that is, darling.

Continue to forget to give my love to everyone. They'd all want to know where I was and what I was doing, and whose house I was coming to live in next for months at a time, as any good unmarried female ought to be glad to do. Thank heaven for an independent mind and means!

Your loving cousin,
Susan

From *The Times*
October 17, 1849

Yesterday, Mr W. Carter, the Coroner for East Surrey, and a jury, assembled at the King John's Head, Abbeystreet, Bermondsey, for the purpose of inquiring into the circumstances connected with the deaths of George Barlow, aged 46, William Barling, aged 22, James Barling, aged 4 years, and Thomas Barling, aged 18 months, who lost their lives at the explosion of fireworks which occurred at the premises of Mr W. Barling, No. 4, New Brook-street, Bermondsey New-road, on the night of Friday last.

STATE OF SAXONY
DRESDEN, Oct. 10.
(From our own correspondent.)

... The Government tolerated too much and too long; from an unwillingness to use its powers it looked on quietly on repeated violations of the right of the public association, which was flagrantly abused by the formation of revolutionary clubs, central committees of the Democratic party, with the almost avowed object of repeating here the scenes of Vienna and Berlin, and even the ridiculous farce of clubs of women; and the Chambers and the National Guard discovered too late that in endeavouring to force on the Government an acceptance of the phantom of a German Constitution, they had only played into the hands of the Red Republicans, who soon pushed both out of sight and left the Government literally to fight the battle for the preservation of social order, nay, for the existence of society itself, alone, while the scale was turned in its favour only by the late assistance of Prussia. ...

MELROSE HALL
WEDNESDAY

My Poor, Dear, James:

The more I think about it, the more convinced I am that you and Susan would make a fine pair—she covering her passion with the language of the intellectual, you hiding your rationality behind a façade of emotional raving, each insisting you are despised by the other. And you both think you have everyone fooled. I mentioned this to Kitty (speaking only of Susan), and she gave me one of those looks that says she knows more than she is willing to say and, with an accompanying smile, she said, "Might I trouble you for the salt?"

I recall the lecture we attended by the scholar with the unpronounceable German name—you know, the son of the man who wrote so well about intimidation in law versus vindictive punishment. At the lecture, the scholar said (I wrote it down): "Sensuousness is the true unity of the material and the spiritual, a unity not thought up and prepared, but existing, and which therefore has the same significance as reality for me." What people like Susan deny is the sensuousness of existence—as you, dear James, deny the rational *in practice* even while insisting that I "give it its due"; and what we are all striving for is to integrate the sensuous with the rational. If I go a step beyond this, and wish to integrate the unknowable with the rational, then that is only part of the same thing.

All of which has nothing about it that is irrelevant to our predicament. The more I consider the matter, the more convinced I am that there is an agency at work here: an agency that has had some use for you and now no longer needs you; or from which you escaped before its use of you was complete. If the latter, beware! for it may be hunting you still. James, acquire protection in as many forms as you can; in forms you trust as well as forms in which you do not believe but will nevertheless carry about you as a favour to me. Have with you, at all times, iron that cuts, polished silver (a coin will not do), a sprig of mistletoe, and a loaded pistol. And if your emerald has not been lost (better, perhaps, if it has), put it somewhere safe but do not carry it upon your person.

James, I do not rave. Attend me, out of friendship if for no other reason.

Consider the change in your own character that you discuss—that is, your lackadaisical attitude is itself a clue.

Consider the marks on your wrist, which can admit of no explanation other than restraint.

Consider that, as near as I can tell, you were *nowhere* during the mysterious two months—I have spent the last week looking into this, James, and you were as missing as if you were indeed under a lake.

Consider your exhaustion—physical as well as spiritual.

Consider the mark on your forearm, which fills me with foreboding although I cannot claim to know what it represents.

What agency, then? I hope we can exclude the family for the reasons you give: the last thing Kitty wants is for me to become respectable. James, she does not *want* to marry me, any more than I want to marry her. You do her an injustice, I think. I treasure the sharpness of one side of her mouth, for it amuses me as much as the mystical nonsense that pours forth from the other; and provided I refrain from mocking the latter, I never feel the former—all of which may cause you to laugh, because I know you perceive no difference between Kitty's "mystical nonsense" and my own. If so, laugh away. My argument is that I am looking for evidence that would convince any rationalist, while she looks only toward her own feelings. And at that, you know, she may be more rational than either of us.

Of those others you mention, none fills the bill with the possible exception of Tournier, who has the least motive. Halliwell is ineffectual and trivial; he always was and he always will be. As for Stone—well, laying aside my opinion that you do yourself an injustice (he knew very well what he was getting involved in, and if he was not guilty that time there were plenty of other occasions, and in my opinion he deserved worse than to be sent down; had you been honest with the authorities he would have been in gaol a dozen times)—he has never left the area, and he drinks to such a degree these days that he could not plot his way to the next tavern should the Blackbird close.

But if Tournier hates you, for any reason, that is another matter. He is a solid friend, and I think could be a relentless enemy. And he has a brain that would cause me fear, and he has friends that extend his reach to places of which Kitty speaks but does not understand. Yet to conceive of him using you in such a manner on Stone's behalf, and Stone nothing but a common drunkard, requires a strain on the imagination. Still, I think I may pay him a visit, and drop your name and see if he reacts. I shall do so before the Sabbath and let you know if I have learned anything.

The only other news, which just struck me at this instant, may be more sinister, or it may mean nothing: Your old acquaintance Barlow has been killed in some sort of explosion. I know nothing of the details, having heard it only from Waters, who said something like, "First James, and now Barlow. They're all going, it seems," but then would say nothing about what he meant. If you wish, I will knock him up and try for more details, even though this may mean an afternoon in his insufferable company.

We are, indeed, a family of extremes; yet I must take your question to be rhetorical. How could we be anything else? We are, all of us, the seed of a man who nearly tore the Earth apart with his passions and a woman who held it together with her thoughts. That no one has heard of us is thanks only to great good fortune and the excesses of the rest of humanity. The explosions on the Continent last year were to us merely the notes of a symphony, although, indeed, one we each listened to from our own box. You (aye, and Susan) hear the trumpets of a great future. Brian listens from the most distant box, making copious observations that no one will regard, for he is too passionate about his dispassion. David sneers at any concert that has the improvement of Man as its theme. I listen eagerly for the spaces between the notes which will, perhaps, allow me to hear more of what is always there but never played.

I do not, by the way, recall the incident of which you speak, but I recall plenty like it. James, I would gladly puncture David's skin for him if I had the least excuse, and at Cauldhurst he very nearly gave me one when he launched into that sanctimonious lecture on incest. Incest! I could, perhaps, have pointed out to him that the blood-ties between Kitty and me are rather more distant than between a Mohammedan and an Irishman, but that would have been stooping to his level, so instead I merely asked him how he had come to study incest so closely, and inquired if he had some special interest. He took it as I knew he would, but stopped short of giving me reason to call him out. A pity.

But on to practical matters, James: I have consulted our solicitor about your estate, and have arranged for the affair to be delayed; all the easier because no one seems in a hurry to settle it. I don't know whether this circumstance ought to make me happy or suspicious, but I suspect it is because Aunt Margaret, who should be most concerned, has gone off on another of her journeys. Kitty seems undisturbed, but I place the emphasis on *seems*. You may be right about Brian, but I did not wish to take the chance by speaking to him; not yet. As for your father, I know that a letter was sent some weeks ago; beyond that I cannot tell you.

I do not know about Susan. I have never given Kitty any cause for jealousy, and I fear that asking about Miss Voight will give her one. But Kitty says nothing about her, and she has not appeared in any of her usual haunts in some little time.

As for me, I believe that, after visiting Tournier and learning what I can, I shall invent a pretext and pay a visit to Portsmouth, during which I shall stay at a convenient inn, at which time my rig will develop some minor problem, which will require long conversations with the hostler. Look for me in two weeks, and, James, take all precautions in the meantime. Until then, I remain your devoted cousin,

Richard

P.S. I have hired Wye myself, and I am glad of it. He is a treasure, that fellow. I took the opportunity to pension off old Cutter, so Wye has been promoted to butler. Your horses are all being well cared for, and if I have the use of them, believe that it is only from respect for your memory.   —Richard

P.P.S. On your behalf, I have purchased one of Thomas's paintings. It is a simple study of a woman's face against a black background, which I chose because the lines on her forehead intrigue me. He does have some talent, I think.   —R.

P.P.P.S. I enclose volume 1 of *Lives of Eminent Men* by Mr Aubrey on the basis that I have found it amusing; in particular his sense of humor corresponds well with yours, I think. I also enclose a copy of Hegel's *Science of Logic*, and if you do not know why I have sent it, you are not the man I thought you were.   —R.

MELROSE HALL
OCTOBER 1·8th

Dear Susan,

I think you overestimate my ability to swoon and underestimate my imagination, because, dear, there is little you could do that would shock me, I think, which you will realize if you recall that I was the only one in the family who was not shocked by your remark to Mrs Stephenson at the Christmas party, not that Mrs Stephenson didn't deserve it, as I told you then, and I still laugh wickedly when I think of it, and I thank you for bringing it to mind.

This mania of yours about James does not shock me, and it no longer amuses me either, because I think it an obsession, and as I despair of your ending it, I merely hope it will run its course quickly, although once it does run its course, what then? You will be back to Projects, any project, so long as it leads you away from your spiritual side, in other words, from yourself as you have done for so long, and which has led you to use yourself, the family, and those you love as if they were political studies, or else you will make yourself unhappy while accomplishing nothing. You say you have found some something? Well, I shall not ask what, but rather, why? No, do not answer me, but ask yourself, because in your letter you address the question, and then drop it without a tenth part of the effort

you'd have given to any question that didn't require introspection. Susan, *if you do not admit to yourself that you were
in love with James, you will never grieve, and if you do not
grieve you will never recover.*

Heavens, I do not know what it is about you that makes me
lecture you as if I were Aunt Louisa, unless it is that you are
the only person who treats me as if my advice should matter,
except for Dick, and even he has lapses which require re-
minders from time to time.

By the by, I think you, and, for that matter, Dick, are wrong
about David, because you do not realize that he is an honest
man, and of more importance, he is a man looking for the
Truth, rather than, as you seem to think, one convinced he has
found it, though to be sure, he sometimes thinks he has found
a large piece of it, and that makes him annoying, if not down-
right dangerous, but I do not think this happens as often as
you think, and soon enough he is himself again, in which state
he is less belligerent than you pretend, until you or Dick light
his train, as you are wont to do. I believe, in fact, that David
trusts his instincts as much as the rest of us trust our own, and
his only error is in failing to realize that his instincts are those
instilled by your dear mother, rather than, like the rest of us,
the instincts we developed in trying to survive Aunt Louisa.
Think of it, Susan: had you not been sent to Melrose, you
might have turned out like David, and even if you had met
James when you did, you might not have fallen in love with
him, as I will maintain that you have until I am dead, and
perhaps longer than that, for neither David nor Dick truly
knows what lies on the other side of the Long Wall. I do miss
James, but yet I know he is still with us, for I feel his presence
all around, and I am reminded of him often for I can tell that
Dick is still grieving, though that part of him remains closed
to me. It is odd, you know, how Dick and I seem to have made
an agreement to share pleasure but not pain, an agreement that
cannot last, and that I suspect he knows as well as I cannot
last, but he *will* insist on playing the rogue, a rôle to which he
is not suited. The fact is, I love him as much as you loved
poor James.

My studies, Susie, are continuing, which I tell you with evil
spite in vengeance for all you tell me of which I disapprove.

Yesterday I took a piece of red silk and on it I dripped the wax from a yellow taper, then I took only the smallest amount of opium to prepare my spirit, and when I looked through the silk out into the garden at noon I saw the Shimmering Gate, if only for an instant. This is the second time I have seen the Gate, and the first time when I was fully awake, and I know that I heard the voices calling out for me to accept my birthright, and I long to go to them, if I only knew how, but I know that it will come to me, and not by any of the horrid means the men of the Trotter's Club use. The power is *not* evil, not of itself, whatever use it is put to.

I know, Susan, what you think of my studies, but I cannot talk to Dick about them, or we'll be at it, so who else do I have? Besides, it is my fascination with the Other Side that allows my sensualism on this side, and without that, what would we have in common? I know you deny being a sensualist, at least in the way Mr Shelley and I use the word, though you might admit to it the way Mr Hume and Richard use it, but I believe your denial as much as I believe what you say about James.

Ah, poor James. I sometimes think he saw what I see, and refused to believe it, and that is what led him to the sort of life that ended beneath the lake.

It is quite night out, and I am tired, and Dick is off somewhere, so I believe I will go to sleep and resume tomorrow, and for now I shall remain your affectionate

Kit

RICHARD COBHAM'S JOURNAL

OCTOBER 19

Visited Tournier with no results. Good news, I suppose. I am trying to remember my previous dealings with him, and think I have only come across him once or twice; a pleasant enough man with eyes that bespeak intelligence and awareness of his surroundings—two characteristics that do not always march in company. He did not strike me as deceitful, though I suppose a truly deceitful person wouldn't. When I mentioned J, T said,

"It's hard to believe all those secret dealings and plots are gone for ever." Odd comment, that Stone echoed some time later, when I looked him up. He was too drunk to have sensible conversation with, and smelled bad. Mentioned J anyway, and Stone gave me a funny look and said, "He never tells you everything, you know. And that is just a way of lying." Told S that J was dead but do not think it got through. Then went to the Academy and saw a very good, quite passionate work by some Italian, and some fine studies by Brown, as well as the usual drudge.

OCTOBER 20

Must have had dream, but do not remember it. K said I woke up saying, "Where the devil has Susan got to, and what does she know?" then went back to sleep. K seemed amused. Riding all day until rain started. Clipper entirely recovered and seemed to enjoy ride as much as I did. Relief! Fox hunting season soon, perhaps I should buy a spare shotgun so foxes can shoot at dogs. Thought about J during ride. It is peculiar how expectations affect one; it is J's conviction that I am cool and rational that makes me wish to be so, at least when acting on his behalf. Odd. Must give this some thought.

DEERLEAP MANOR, NAVAN, CTY. MEATH
20th DAY OF OCTOBER, 1849

Bella Mia,

Darling Susan, at last you write to your poor old Dilly! It was so long since Horace and I had heard a word from you. Only that sad little scrap of a note so long ago—I think it must have been August, or even the end of July, for I think the Sunday just after was when they blessed the new loaves—about the death of your poor cousin James. Oh, and I have missed you so much! It was a great treat to come to the Metropolis last spring, but it only served to remind me how used I am to seeing you often. Do you remember what lovely times we had when you were in Venezia, and how you would visit at our dear little villa there? Poor little house, how it must look now, all over-run! I cannot be so concerned as you over who has the governance of Italy, but I do miss my little villa, just a bit, and if only things could be more settled! But you must see our sweet manor-house here, *bella*, it is just what a gentleman-farmer's residence ought to be! I have re-papered and re-draped everything, and it is quite splendid now. Horace visits the mills once a month, of course, and is gone a week at a time and I miss him terribly. But when he's at home, he takes to country life amazingly well, and rides or drives around his "lands" and meets with the bailiff and oversees so many things! I am so glad we have an estate of our own at last, though I love the Manchester house, of course, it is so new and everything of the best! But a man of real substance ought to have property, some land that can belong to his family, not like a house in town, however nice. A house in town may be an ornament to Mr Horace Talbot of Manchester, but there is something not quite proper about Sir Horace Talbot, Bart. and his Lady having no settled country residence. You'll think me very high in the instep, dearest Susan, but you know all the real sticklers would say the same, and I couldn't bear to be pitied by people like Lady Wolburn, whom we all thought a perfect scrub when she was only Sylvia Parks! Horace was afraid, when we first came, that I wouldn't "take to" Ireland, and I confess, I had hoped he might find a place in the Shires, where we might have lots of visits and house-parties for the hunting and go up to London twice a year. But his agent found this place, which is a very old estate, only a little broken up and somewhat hurt by this last terrible failure—but that, of course, was what made it possible for us to get it, because Horace says the Land Laws would never have been changed otherwise. Oh, pardon, pardon, *bella*, I wrote those words, but they're quite the first appearance of "Horace says" in this whole long page, so please forgive me! I wonder what you'd think of him now. He seems much changed to me, though still so sweet to his Darling Dilly that I wonder if I shall ever stop being the happiest, most thoroughly spoilt creature in the world. He had an Irish manager at first, which seemed wise to me, for one ought to have an Irishman to tell one how to go on in Ireland, shouldn't one? But after a few months Horace turned him off and got another fellow, a rather intense young man from somewhere in Scotland, who has put up a house on the estate, and he and Horace have their heads together at every turn. It was before the old manager went that Horace came to me one evening in the drawing room before supper. He was still in his outdoor things, and I was so shocked, because Horace is very careful in his dress. He stood upon the hearth for some little time, and I began to think he had some dreadful news to break to me, and I asked him what it was. And he burst out, "They have no plows." I was terribly confused then, you may imagine. But Horace sat down with me that evening and tried to explain all the things he had seen and learned, and they seemed to make him so sad, *bella*, you would hardly have known him. He said (there it is again, but he did say it, truly) that the whole way of farming here has forced people to live on the edge of starvation, and that they have no proper leases for their little huts and scraps of ground, and that it was no wonder that the rates had gone unpaid everywhere, never mind rent, and that he meant to do something about it, at least in so far as he could, on his own land. That was when he dismissed the local man and got the other. He's set himself very systematically at this, just as he goes about the manufacturing, and the breakfast-table half the time is covered with plans for cottages and corn-mills, notes on the cost of feeding horses vs. oxen vs. mules, and charts of the price of wool for the last ten years. I am so glad for this, not only because it keeps him happy, but because I can see now that the constant improvements at the mills are not because he feels he has to advance—goodness, he's richer than ninety out of a hundred men in England already! It's because building and improving are positive delights to him. He can't explain himself to me, poor lamb, because with a few exceptions like the evening he came in to supper in all his dirt and told me about the tenants, he really hasn't any great flow of talk. So I must learn his heart by his actions, and I have never been disappointed. Susan darling, I suppose nothing but a clever man would do for you, but I think Horace is quite clever in his own way, and is exactly the husband to make me happy. So I wear my most fetching thread-lace cap to breakfast and smile at him across his plans, and he turns all rosy and beams and clasps my hand (if there's no one else at table, of course!) and says, "There's my own Dilly!" He has built three cottages so far, with two rooms downstairs and a loft above, and good fire-places with ovens and chimneys, and moved three families in. Our tenants are all so friendly and lively, with such easy ways and so polite, that it's difficult to have any idea what they really think. But I hope Horace will not rush upon this too quickly, even though I think all his ideas are quite right, for it would hurt him very much if his improvements were rejected. These are not Englishmen, who welcome progress and inventions and fresh notions. The Irish seem very backward—the women all had to be taught how to use the ovens, as they had never had any—and not inclined to accept new things with any good grace. They also seem to have no notion of being too proud for charity, which given their wretched state I suppose is a fortunate thing. They are all very beautiful, though, many very dark and striking, especially when they are in a passion about something, and of course, being Irish, they are very nearly passionate about everything all the time. And the land itself is like them, not cozy and charming like the English countryside, but striking and beautiful, and just when you think it's most open, it proves to have been hiding some secret dell or chasm. The Manor itself is, as Horace puts it, "a fine old pile," all of light grey stone and roofed with slate. When he first saw it, Horace says, he grumbled about the window tax, but now he declares it a fine light place inside, and wonders that other houses haven't so much glazing. You must come to visit, *bella*, and you shall have the green suite, which is the very best in the house after my own and Horace's, and hear me greet you with "*Céad míle fáilte*," which I do very well.

We did see a little of your poor cousin James when he last came to visit his mother's family. Yes, that would have been '47, because Horace was already thinking about property in Ireland, and we were visiting a few of his business connexions in the north, and down the eastern coast. I was afraid to travel because of all the rumours of risings everywhere, and rebellion being talked by the Young Ireland people, and everyone said there would be so much hard feeling against the English, but the north seemed safe enough, and even between Belfast and Dublin there was nothing to alarm me—except the dreadful

roads, in places! And of course, I knew Meg Hillyer from her
come-out, which was the same year as mine, and her cousin
Carlotta Pearse was engaged to poor Mr Brookings who was
such a great friend of my brother's, and so we were invited to
several delightful parties and dinners at the time of James's
visit. Such a beautiful young man he was! Very like some of
the handsome Irish men, but with more refinement of feature.
And almost fragile-looking, though of course he was no such
thing. He lifted me down off my horse after a ride once, and
held me up around my waist for a moment without the least
trouble, even smiling a little, as if he could have stood that
way an hour. I blushed like a poppy, you may be sure. It makes
me so sad to think of those fine dark eyes closed forever! He
flirted ever so gracefully with all of us ladies, and the men
seemed to get on well with him, too, which is a thing you
hardly ever see in the same person, the ability to make himself
agreeable to both sexes. And everyone praised his lovely open
manners, though that surprised me a little, because I always
thought that, though he was outgoing, he was not so *open*,
which was again very Irish of him. But he was always a delightful companion, always ready to hold one's parasol or ad-
vise one on the matching of ribbon or notice when one had
got new gloves on, and in such a way that it never made
Horace in the least jealous. It was quite an idyll for just under
a fortnight, in fact, but then he put Carlotta out of temper with
him, and found it more pleasant, I suppose, to take himself
off. I won't speculate on what he did, but Carlotta has become
so sour and prudish in recent years that it might have been
anything, and I can't but be sure that it was some piece of
intolerance on her part. At any rate, that was the last time I
saw him. Meg told me that he'd gone back to England immediately after, when I asked after him, because a month later
I thought I'd seen him in Dublin. I'd gone up to visit a *cor-
setière* that Meg recommended, but she was quite out there,
the woman was nothing like so good as the one in Belfast who
makes my stays. I saw the fellow only for a moment in the
street, but the hair was very like, and his height and carriage,
and something about a gesture reminded me of James. But the
man was wearing a coat the color of old mustard that hung in
such a sack-like fashion, dressed like an under-clerk, in fact,

and James was always so elegant, so it was nonsensical of me to wonder. Dublin is not what it used to be altogether. Half the shops are shut, and what is there is sadly out of fashion. There was a good show scraped together for the dear Queen's visit in August, but after that the poor old city returned to its workaday clothes. Belfast is quite smart, however, and is the only place for good lace since Paris is in such confusion. And I have found a shoemaker there as good as any in Italy, and you know how I used to dote on my Roman dancing-slippers. I do wish you could see your way clear to visit, *bella*, for I could show you such lovely things, and we could get up all manner of splendid amusements for you. Riding here is really unequalled, and the horses are very fine. Horace has got me a chestnut mare that outshines anything I ever had before. There is always a great deal of rain, but whenever the sun does shine, someone can be counted on to mount a pic-nic expedition. And there are dinner parties, and musical evenings, and dancing, and shopping of course! Do say that you might come, darling, and make me even happier than I am now!

The boys are with us, of course. Sebastian is his father's joy, and it is so sweet to watch him tease his Papa for a look at his watch, or a ride on his knee in the evenings after dinner, when the nurserymaid brings him down before his bed. The baby Robert is still not so stout as I would like, but Nurse says that he's much improved by Irish buttermilk and Irish air, which would make me love this country if I didn't already. I am hoping that I may be increasing again, and if I am I wish ever so much for a girl, for though the boys are delightful, it would be so lovely to have a little daughter to dress and play with.

My candle is burned quite low, and Horace has looked in on me twice already, the second time saying that I shall lose my looks if I stay up so late all the time, which of course made me blush. I will close by sending you all my love, and kind wishes to all of your family. Write me soon, dear!

Yours devotedly,
Delilah Talbot

THE GREY HOUND
21ˢᵗ OCTOBER, 1849

O Most Obliging Richard,

I do not think I have ever received mail that pleased me half so much as your improving reading. If you'd sent me novels, I would have been grateful; but I would also have known that you expected to hear nothing much more about them, besides a hearty "thank you." Herr Hegel sends a quite different message: that you agree to conduct an impassioned dispute by the kind offices of the mail-coach. I am restored in my every faculty and cell, like a watered plant. Hegel is perfect food for disputation, since it is possible to defend almost any position on Earth with a well-sharpened quote from him (*vide* Herr Strauss and Herr Göschel, who might, without Herr Hegel's kind philosophic intervention, have been moved to do each other a mischief).

My happy state is not solely due to your kindness nor to the judicious application of German philosophers, I am forced to admit. Now promise me that you will not come pelting down within hours of receiving this, abandoning all pretence of stealth, caution, and good management of my horses (and I will come back to that, you post-scripting wretch) in the hope of finding the same for yourself when I tell you—Well, the truth is, I was seduced last night. It was a passage of extraordinary sweetness and, I think, unalloyed good will on both sides, with a lass named Rose. She is housemaid to the rector. I had not seen her before this evening, but it seems she had seen me, and when she came to deliver a message from her employer to Mrs Coslick, she remained afterward in the twilight of the inn yard on some pretext until I came out of the stables.

The most distracted and melancholy man in the world might have been knocked flat were he to come unexpectedly upon a trim little creature with a mass of curly black hair, bright eyes black as hawthorn berries, a white bosom, tiny waist, and a sudden cherry-coloured blush that he himself had caused. I am not so distracted and melancholy on my worst days. She bobbed and smiled and asked, in a pretty Irish voice, if I wasn't the new hostler Jack Cobb then? I admitted to that. Well, I'd be a busy man, surely, but might I do her a great favour, and it not taking much of my time? She had a new leather belt from Mrs Coslick, she said, but it was too big around, and if I had an awl to hand in the harness room it would be the work of a moment to put a new hole in it.

I felt as if I'd fallen into a rude old song, right down to the awl, and I was hard put to it not to laugh out loud. But there was no harm in it, I decided, since she could trust me not to take advantage. She'd get her belt fitted, I'd get a fine new ingredient for the *ragoût* of my imagination, and neither of us would get one thing more. But in the dim light of the harness room, she drew the belt snug around her waist and said I'd have to mark it, since she couldn't hold it and see it both; and when I bent down to do it she kissed me on the mouth, and carried my hand to her breast. I think she'd expected me to tumble her there, but I carried her up the stairs to my room over the stable and made a good thorough job of it instead, and she, far from objecting, gave me substantial assistance. She was delighted to hear my stumbling Gaelic (my mam, I told her, was Irish; I neglected to mention that she was a Pearse, of the Leinster Pearses) and gave me a lesson in it, and a lesson or two else. The sky was growing pale outside my window when she stood by my bed with her shift in her hand, smiled wistfully over her bare white shoulder, and said, "Let's have a last one, Jack, *a cushla*, to warm ourselves on." And so we did.

It was false pretenses, I know, and I'm sorry for that, but not for anything else. I was not her first, and when I raised the question of pregnancy, she laughed and told me she was "a clever girl, and sharp to catch yourself on in a stillroom." I have no idea if I will see her again, but I doubt either of us could avoid it if we wanted to, with the rectory half a mile away.

Now surely this is not something that attaches itself automatically to this job and this station, or every man in England would want to be a working-man, and a groom, too. Nor was I handed such kindnesses when I was a fine young gentleman of property (though to be fair, when I sought them out they were usually given). (What a strutting, plumage-spreading thing to say! But there's nothing to be puffed-up about in it—a fellow with passable looks, nice manners, a lot of money, and generous habits has a better chance of getting a "yes" from women who are inclined to it. And when I got a "no," I left it at that, and that I *am* proud of.) I think Rose would never have approached me if I'd worn a silk hat and a gold watch-chain, because inequity of class poisons the easiest and most natural dealings between people. It would have been commerce, even if no money had changed hands. As it was, we had an exchange of attraction and pleasure, and if it was a little enhanced on her side because her partner might almost have been taken for a gentleman in uncertain light, there's not too much harm done.

Never, never let my letters fall into Saint David's hands, Cousin—the last opens with drunkenness, and this with whoring! It would make him the happiest man alive.

You know perfectly well that your German is rather better than mine, and that even if you couldn't recall Ludwig Feuerbach's name, you could certainly pronounce it when reminded. I am the last person in the cosmos who can be made to fall for your ignorant rake charade. I have very little quarrel with Feuerbach, who asserts that religious belief is a stage that humanity passes through on its way to wisdom and self-knowledge, and that God originates in Man. I know It must originate somewhere, since the name is so often bandied about, and that, Diccon my dear, is nothing but the evidence of my eyes and ears. But tell me that God is a great Unknowable, and I will, sensibly I contend, ask why then should I trouble myself with the business? There is so much Knowable in the world (however yet unknown to me) that it seems criminal to waste time on something that, if it has indeed any more reality than Coleridge's Xanadu, will not be revealed to me no matter how I conduct myself. Nor am I interested in some great revelation after death. I have seen death; it is where things stop. And if some straggling, tormented bit of consciousness should survive such a cataclysm, I cannot imagine it being of any effect on the living world or use to itself thereafter, poor shattered hypothetical thing. Never mind reconstitution as a sexless, perpetually ecstatic being clad in a fresh-laundered bed-gown flitting to strains of endless music.

I believe in the spirit of Man as well as the matter. I have seen great courage in men, and women, too; seen them do great things for each other, for their nations, for the world, with a kind of selfless vision that cannot be accounted for by the base, brute self-interest of the body. But why that greatness must spring from some supernatural source, some origin beyond our most subtle sense and understanding, is more than I can see. I respect and revere the spirit of Man all the more because it is of earthly origin. We have a purely natural potential for good that owes nothing to the Archbishop of Canterbury and a thousand thousand parish *raconteurs* belabouring poor half-awake souls of a Sunday morning with the potential wages of their ranked and catalogued sins. If you would make a planet of saints and angels, begin by seeing that no person need struggle against his fellow, nor steal from him, nor even kill him, for his food and his shelter. Give him the means to communicate with others, and to read and hear what they would communicate to him. Let him seek the work that suits him best, work that he can see in a moment is of benefit to himself and his fellows. Let him combine with others in his community and his nation to shape and revise the laws he will then live under, so that he knows they serve him, and he them. And give him, at last, leisure to rest, to love his spouse and children, to make, if he chooses, something of beauty only for its own sake. Then you will see Paradise, Richard; then you will see the New Jerusalem, and you will never need to call upon a god to ratify it.

Do I claim, then, that there is no sin? Not at all. As I believe in the spirit and natural goodness of Man, so I believe in natural sins against it. Hypocrisy is a sin against Man. So is cruelty, and if I had a shilling for every faithful servant of the Church of England who'd kicked a dog or struck a donkey, let alone abused his fellow human beings with tongue or hand, I could buy India. Any man or woman who will watch another suffer or starve without stretching out a hand is a sinner; and though Jesus said the same, the church that claims him connives at shifting paupers from the parish rolls to the government workhouses, that its tithing and rate-paying citizens may be spared their direct upkeep in righteousness.

There are men who could almost make a believer of me by their example; but I revere them for their Earthly acts and principles, and not for their dedication to an artificial night-watchman of morality. Such men do not weigh the social place of curates, deacons, and deans, but see their own faces in the face of every man and woman they meet. They know that any suffering is not an individual but a universal evil, and any struggle against it the business of every living person to advance. Are these principles granted by a belief in a supernatural agency of goodness? They are not solely in the gift of a Christian deity, at least, since you may find them in Bedouins, Chinese, Polynesian Islanders, and the aborigines of North America. You may find wickedness in those populations also, the wickedness of my definition; but if you apply any scientific method to your study, comparing equals and maintaining controls, I doubt you will find a correlation between wickedness and unbelief.

As to Feuerbach's "sensuousness," that is part and parcel of the natural good, the inherent and entirely knowable spirit of Man. Our hearts leap in us at the sight of a hedge of may-blossom, of a thoroughbred's dash across a field, of a loved one's sudden smile; at a breath of sandalwood or the smell of turned earth; at the cool smooth touch of silk, or the sturdy weave of canvas, or the tickle of cat's fur; at the taste of a familiar apple, or the heat of ginger; or the sound of a hundred voices raised in unison, or the sweet falling notes of a piano-forte. Divines will tell you that our hearts leap because they recognize the presence and products of God. But why should that be even likely, to say nothing of inevitable? If I cannot know God, I cannot recognize it, nor feel kinship with it, nor expect any intercourse with it whatsoever. My heart is more likely to leap at the appearance and works of the Prime Minister, and I assure you it does not. No, we glory in these things because what is good in us knows its own kind. We are made by nature and evolution to receive these pleasures, and we are disposed, by the spirit that grows out of our great powers and potential, to appreciate them in their glory. The spirit can be stunted and deformed; but search for the cause and you'll find the hand and will of another human being, or a convocation of human beings who name themselves governors of their fellows. You will not find a hornéd Devil nor a vengeful God.

So, on what basis do you say I deny the rational? Ah, here's the answer, at the bottom of your page. You would fling your fancied "unknowable" into the category of rational things, like a codfish into a currant-cake, and then chide me for refusing to swallow the whole. I, on the other hand, see no need to *strive* to reconcile—pardon, integrate—the sensuous with the rational. The substance of reality is gathered for me by my senses, which is presented to my consciousness as evidence and example to form my knowledge of the world. It is a world, therefore, both rational and full of sensuous delight, and to deny the latter would be to deny the former, by the very process of perception.

Have we a dialectic, Cousin? Will you try a synthesis now, and give me the pleasure of building another antithesis? I hope you can imagine my furious joy, scribbling away in the lamplight, sometimes surprising myself with what I think, and how I have chosen to express it. If any thorough sensualist or glutton should claim that there are no delights outside those of the senses, I will challenge him with this example, a near-ecstasy of the intellect.

Does Susan deny the sensuous? Perhaps her heart leaps up at the works of the Prime Minister. But we may wrong her; she was all but raised by Great-Aunt Augusta, recall, who was no prim colourless dried-up creature. It is damnably difficult to deny sensuousness in the south of France, or anywhere in Italy, or on the coast of Portugal, and Augusta travelled with Susan in tow to all of them. Morocco, which I remember hearing something about, would have been before Susan's tenure. What a vision that is—Susan as an *houri* in spangled silk, with kohl on her eyelids! Is there room in this world for an *houri* in stout footgear and Serviceable Stays? Forgive, please, that great blot and unsteady hand—I shall try not to laugh again with a pen full of ink.

Though Susan in spangled trousers is not more strange than your correspondent in a moleskin waistcoat. I have been earning my keep quite successfully, Cousin, despite pretty distractions and my initial worn-down state. (Mrs Coslick still makes clucking noises and presses food and cordials on me, but her standard for manhood is, after all, Coslick. I feel sometimes as if I were still in the nursery.) I had a chance to show off or get myself killed on Thursday, and for a few really horrid moments I thought it would be the latter. Mr Bincham, who I think I mentioned in my last letter—he is the squire at Chesford—was bringing home a stallion to add to his stud, and stopped at the Grey Hound on the way to get the road-dust out of his throat. (I expect he wanted to show off his new prize.)

The animal was just what I would have imagined: very showy, barely sound, and, as it fell out, a lad of questionable character. He was being led by a groom on horseback. Bincham, driving his rubbishing high-wheeled monstrosity, rattled into the yard barely ahead of them, brought his team 'round sharply before the inn-door, and pulled them up in that insufferable way that idiots will, because they think it makes them look dashing—with a great whip-crack and a yank on the ribbons. His team went back on their hocks, which they must be used to, poor brutes. But the worst damage lay with the stallion, who was quite close in once Bincham turned his rig. He heard the whip, and saw the point flying, and the high wheels lurching before his nose, and the team in distress, and reared. The groom was taken unawares and pulled clean out of his saddle before the stallion tore the lead from his hands. The horse kicked out behind and might have dashed the groom's brains out if the fellow hadn't been quick. Then the beast began to clatter and scramble across the inn-yard bricks, looking for a way out. Two farmers managed to get a hay-cart across the gate to block it. For a moment I thought he'd try to go straight through that, but at the last instant he changed direction and headed for the double doors to the stable. Then he saw me, standing in front of them.

I must have looked a deal easier to go through than the hay-cart. And I think he'd had bad treatment, from worse than Squire Bincham, for it only takes a little of it to make a high-strung horse hate the whole race of Man. He went for me, rearing, teeth bared, lashing out with his shod front hooves. It was like watching a tree fall on me. At the point at which the stallion occupied the whole of my vision, I realized I was calling out, not loud, in that foolish language that I can only just remember Grandfather using to his horses, that random mixture of French and Gaelic and Latin. I was thinking that I was about to die, and I was speaking gentle nonsensical things to a horse with my last breath and being amazed at how easy and calm I sounded.

The hooves came down, I swear, no more than a finger's length from my nose; the stallion took one startled step back, his muscles bunched to run; and stayed to stand trembling before me, his eyes rolling and his hide steaming with sweat. I continued to talk nonsense and watched his ears swivel furiously, from me to the rest of the yard, and back to me. I held out my hand, palm up, and he laid his ears back and made as if to bite. Then he as quickly thought better of it and let me touch him. I saw him taking in the smell of me; after that he seemed to give up the whole quarrel. A few more cautious overtures and I could pass my hands all over his head and neck as he stood drooping with fatigue and something that, had he been human, I might have called shame.

The groom's arm was dislocated, and I doubt anyone could have got the stallion close enough to Bincham's carriage to tie him in back, so Coslick let Bincham board the horse overnight in the stable. Another groom came in the morning to fetch him. I hope the brute gets fair treatment; but few stud owners, or coachmen or grooms, have the patience or inclination to cure a horse of viciousness caused by fear. It's more likely that he'll be put down in a year or two, poor devil. At any rate, everyone here now thinks I'm at least a gipsy. My most fatuous utterance on equine behaviour and conformation meets with solemn agreement, and is instantly transmitted by word of mouth 'round the parish. If I had the faintest notion how I gentled the horse, or even some assurance that I really had anything to do with it, I would be terribly proud of myself.

To return to your letter: On the chance there is an agency at work in my temporary death, I will certainly be as careful as you would wish me to be, but I will continue to assume it is a corporeal one. It's more likely; and how would we look if I were permanently killed because I had split my efforts at self-preservation between natural and supernatural wards and thus slighted them both? At any rate, I wouldn't know where to begin to assemble the latter. Your list is not very practicable. I think the coastal air disagrees with mistletoe—I haven't seen any that I recall. If I had not lost my emerald—which I have, be comforted—I could have pawned it to buy something in polished silver, but without it my resources don't extend to these little vanities. Iron that cuts seems a very good idea for either sort of danger, but I also found, on returning to myself, that my pocket-knife was missing. I've had two since then, cheap ones but decently sharp and handy in my work; but managed to lose them both. Will a nice folding hoof-pick do? That I have in my pocket at the moment. It might cut if it attained sufficient velocity—say, if attached to the front of a locomotive. Horseshoes, they say, are very lucky, and I'm surrounded by those. As for the loaded pistol, I think it a splendid notion, and if I had one, I would certainly carry it. Richard, do you have the faintest idea what an hostler's wages *are*?

I promise to carry a sharpened stake; in that way I'll also be prepared to be of use if anyone wishes to bury a suicide.

Indeed, Richard, there's no need for panic. I did suffer from a certain emotional torpor, but the most ready explanation for it is shock, and it is fading away rapidly. And I was not *nowhere*, as you suggest so vigorously; I was simply not in any of the places you have scouted. If it makes you feel better, you may certainly ask Kitty to scry in a bowl of water—if you can think of a way to ask her to do it without telling her I'm alive and currying horses eight miles from Portsmouth. Failing that, you must resign yourself to relying on my sense of self-preservation. I have a reasonably well-developed one, you know, and if what I escaped was an attempt on my life, then I have the advantage of a warning this time.

Which reminds me—Richard, have done, won't you? If I agree to believe, absolutely, that you have no interest in marrying Kitty, or she in you, will you agree to stop telling me so at every opportunity? It makes me feel as if either I have overestimated your brains or you have underestimated mine. Or have you also hesitated to ask *me* about the whereabouts of distant relations, for fear of making me jealous? I dreamed of Kitty a few nights ago, perhaps because your letter brought her so much to mind. She was standing in a doorway with tear-tracks on her face; then she seemed to notice me for the first time, and her expression as good as said, "What are you doing here?" the way she always used to when I'd caught her showing some strong emotion that she hadn't intended to put on display. That was all; but it was the first dream I've had in weeks that I could remember the whole of, and that didn't seem, fragmented and uncertain as my recollection might be, like an unwise experiment with the laudanum bottle.

In the matter of Stone, you do not have all the facts in the case, and I cannot give them to you. You can afford to think more generously of him, now that we have ruled out the possibility of him having done me this disservice, and I hope you will.

Richard, for once and all: You cannot call David out. To shoot him properly with all the attendant ceremony you would have to go off to the Continent, and David would refuse to go. Then you'd be forced to shoot him here after all, where it would be murder, and you'd get Newgate, Queen's Bench, and a nice hemp cravat, in that order. Think of the unutterable satisfaction it would afford David, as he expired, to know that he had been Wronged, by God's law and Man's! That you had considered him of enough moment to wreck your life getting in the last word! A shocking uneven contest, a real brain against a bag of wind. Don't do it. (And anyway, why didn't you just tell him you have no intention of marrying Kitty? Well?) It seems very odd of him to rant about incest; you and Kitty aren't even connected, let alone related, unless someone, somewhere, did something indiscreet in a prior generation and was then quite amazingly discreet about it afterwards. But Kit has no look about her of Cobhams, Callendars, or Brewers, so unless David has gone to a great deal more trouble than it would be worth to dig up unpleasant tales about the Woodworths or the Holbourns, I'd have to say he'd been drinking. (What a happy possibility!)

Bless you, Richard, I know you only mean to come here to give me the rare treat of grooming my own horses. If you ruin their mouths I shall roast you alive, you cow-handed rattle. I hope you already knew that you must put Juno between the shafts first, because if you didn't, you've probably learned it from getting soundly kicked by Minerva. Or your groom has— but no, Hatcher would have told him about their crotchets.

Mind you treat them as works of art, for they very nearly are. Are you quite sure it's wise to come? It would reassure you, I suppose, that I'm really here, and in passable health and spirits. But there's not much else to be done here. I'm increasingly convinced that, wherever I was during those two months, it was not here, or even in the immediate vicinity. And wherever I was, someone has to have seen me; the evidence of my own body tells me that I was not close-confined for two months. I had exercise—I may even have had rather hard work, for although I was weak with illness and exhaustion when I arrived, I had a reserve of muscular strength that seems greater than I remember. I think it's time to pursue inquiries in Portsmouth itself. If all else fails, I shall wander up and down the streets asking strangers if they know me. But unless I hear otherwise from you, I shall keep an eye out, in about a fortnight from the date of your letter, for a counter-coxcomb driving the finest pair of greys that ever ate corn.

That, in its turn, reminds me of my elusive team of bays; I have seen them again. They were drawing the green travelling-coach as before, and as before seemed quite fresh—their coats were dry, and from the length and eagerness of their stride and the tossing of their heads they might have been positively restive. But this time, as they trotted past down the Portsmouth road, it was sunset! If they were nearly home, travelling so late, why were the horses fresh? And if they'd only just set out, why set out when darkness was certain to overtake them? If they were only going a few miles, why in the name of sanity travel in a coach and four? Unless it was a larger party of travellers—and particularly if they preferred to travel in a *closed* carriage. Would you like to wager anything on the possibility that this is one of the sorts of things that my hosts and their customers do not discuss in the taproom? No, you may trust me to keep my mouth closed and my ears open. Perhaps the opportunity may arise to do the owner of that coach some service—one that could only be repaid with a four-horse team. One should be open to possibility.

Your unwarrantedly hopeful cousin,
James

Dear Kitty,

Your letter was waiting for me here when I returned. I don't know on what day it arrived, since I haven't been here since I left London on the 17th—well, of course I haven't. You'll think I'm feverish after a beginning like that, but it's only that I've just come from the station. What is it about unpacking that seems to set one's mind so nicely back in order? *My* bag, as you can tell very well, is still full, dropped upon the sitting-room carpet to wait while I write to you.

Perhaps you'll think better of my "mania," as you call it, when I tell you that I've realized a lifelong ambition because of it. I have attended a lecture at Oxford. In fact, I've attended two, and if I hadn't got a sudden reminder that my masquerade wouldn't hold up for so long as that, I might have stayed until the end of term. In short, darling, I've been larking, and I would have loved to have had you with me. But what a figure you'd cut in trousers and a fashionable coat! Madame Blanche used to call you "the little Venus" out of your hearing, at fittings, your first Season in London. I've enough of the boy about me that, though I'm an elegant lady, I make a really splendid young Town beau. The hair caused me a moment's hesitation, but only a moment. Once the deed was done, I revised my entire opinion of my looks, and I don't believe I shall ever grow my hair long again. As you can see, I saved you a lock. You may tie it up with a white ribbon—for a wasted maidenhood, of course!—and frown at it in lieu of me.

There are Fellows at James's college who recall him well. Some of them were classmates, in fact. They have no reluctance to talk about him, or *anything* else, as long as you're willing to take your turn standing the round. Oxford, from the evidence, will teach one to drink if nothing else. I contrived to empty my glass into things other than myself as often as not, and still I had an uncertain morning or two. It was worth the trouble, however, if for no other reason than to find out

what men are like when they think there are no women present.
What silly creatures! They reminded me sometimes of elon-
gated versions of ten-year-old boys, squabbling and punching
at each other, swearing just to hear the sound of it, arguing
furiously about things no one present knew the facts of, only
to see if one of them could carry the point through sheer force
of personality. And the things they believe, and will pronounce
on quite solemnly, about women! I *couldn't* keep from laughing sometimes, and had to make something up quick when
they wanted to know what the joke was.

In the service of my mania, too, the mornings were worth
it. Before '39, James was something of a skyrocket in those
parts—one of the most promising undergraduates at his college, the odds on him taking a First and a Fellowship so short
that it was considered not worth wagering. Was that why he
got the year's leave so easily? James, it seems, didn't discuss
it particularly before he left, but the stories that circulated after
he was gone made up in part for the lapse. The official reason
for his leave, according to Billy Harkness (now, I understand,
a sought-after tutor in classics, but probably still much the
same little round-faced chap who shared rooms with James
over Hilary term of '38) was that he had endangered his health
through overmuch study, and required a year of rest and gentle
climate, at doctor's insistence. Harkness was charitable about
it, but when pressed, admitted that James had seemed pretty
stout to him. Stevenson (I don't know that I ever got his first
name; a handsome fellow of excellent address, but rather sly)
declared that he knew positively it had been no such thing. A
lady, he assured us all, older and of uneven reputation; and a
gentleman who might even have been her husband. There was
a near-general outcry over that last, all 'round the table at the
Cat With Two Tails. The lady, said Wilson DuMont, was
pretty widely agreed upon, but Cobham had a regular revulsion
for adultery. At any rate, it had been fixed upon that he'd gone
to the Continent, and whether with or without the lady, his
pistols, or the other gentleman formed the topics of discussion
for a tedious half of an hour.

It was DuMont, much later, who raised the matter again. By
that time we were alone at the table. He was drinking gin, and
I was drinking water as if it were gin, and we had progressed

from convivial to philosophical. "But d'you know, none of it was true, in the end," he said, as if he had just noticed the fact. "For I never saw a chap come back in such state from a year's running wild in that way. At first you thought that now he really *was* sick, whatever he was when he'd gone. And then you thought, no, he was just sort of pared away, and all the free-and-easy parts of him gone. He'd make a show of being sociable, but that's all it was, show. And he was always good for a drink, but you hated to take it from him, because for every one of yours, there'd be two go down his gullet. You wouldn't have known," he said, blinking his rather protruding blue eyes at me, "I suppose you'd still have been on your pony then. But he wasn't much for the bottle before '39, only what a gentleman might do any time.

"He'd got a knock, had Cobham. He'd got a right hard knock, and whether from a woman or from some other thing there was no finding out from him."

At that moment Harkness came back, to fetch DuMont for something, he *said*, but I suspect he was more concerned that DuMont might be telling wild stories to James's young relative. I repeated to him what DuMont had said, about James on his return. At first Harkness claimed not to have noticed a change. That raised a protest from DuMont: "You did, too, Billy. It was you who said so to me, and you were damned peevish about it, too." Harkness looked disapproving, and said that he hoped he wasn't so Methodistical as to object to what was no business of his.

DuMont had drunk just enough to make him careful for the truth and a bit blind to the intentions of those who weren't telling it. "Rubbish. You said you had nothing to say against dropping the acquaintance of chaps like Stone and Tournier and Johnson, but that he was a damned fool to cut his old friends who'd never done him anything but good."

I'm glad that people's ears aren't as expressive as those of cats or dogs or horses. With my hair cropped and no hat on, I could never have disguised my interest if they were. "Rubbish yourself," replied Harkness, rather short. "Why would I have cared what company the man kept? Now come along, we're to meet MacDonald in half an hour. Go with us as far as the gates, Vaughan?" That was to me; in trousers I'm Stephen Vaughan. I agreed to go along with them, thinking there might be more to be got out of Billy Harkness, with careful handling. Besides, it was getting dark, and a slightly-built gentleman, alone, might be a target for the sort of footpads who watch for drunk and foolish young men to come out of taverns.

We were barely a step out the door when Nemesis fell upon us—or upon me, I should say. The next establishment down the street, its primary entrance opening on the corner, was a rackety boozing-ken called the Locket. It's a noisy place any time it's open for business, but the commotion seemed a little augmented as we approached. Harkness was in the middle of suggesting we cross to the other side, and I was getting a better hold of my walking-stick, when a figure burst out of the passageway between the two buildings and cannoned into us.

Harkness was knocked off the pathway. I had my stick drawn back ready to jab into the man's belly, when his grip on my shoulder tightened. He must have thought he was three sheets to the wind, but not so bosky that he wasn't mindful of the embarrassment should he prove wrong. So he didn't bellow, at least, when he exclaimed, "Susan?"

DuMont was busy picking Harkness up, and Harkness was busy objecting to bloody fools who can't look where they're going, so they both missed it, thank heaven. I looked straight into Henry's shocked face, beamed my widest, thrust out my hand, and cried, "Henry, you dog! I never thought to see you here. By the devil, haven't they rusticated you yet?"

Bless his silly thick head, he realized *something* was up. He stammered, and I clapped him on the shoulder and introduced him to the others as "my damned idiot cousin, Henry." The insult was enough to make him behave naturally—that is, to protest in terms rather stronger than he would use in front of a lady—and I stepped on his foot to silence the apology that followed. After that the crisis was passed. Still, we were both conscious of the wisdom of separating quickly from the other two. Henry linked arms with me and in the most inelegant style imaginable mumbled something hasty about "family business—beg your pardon—pleased to make your acquaintance," and swept me down the street and back into the Cat With Two Tails.

I'm sure you can imagine much of the subsequent conversation, in which I told him it was none of his business and that my reputation was in no danger as long as cloth-heads like him didn't name me out loud in the street. After that he seemed quite pleased to see me, and began even to appreciate my masquerade, especially after I admitted that I could, indeed, let him have five pounds until next quarter-day. Then the reason for his sudden appearance on the street came out: the proctors' bull-dogs were in the Locket. Henry had come pell-mell out the back, leaving behind a card-game he bitterly resented interrupting, since, he assured me, he could feel his luck about to turn.

It occurred to me, on hearing this, that the bull-dogs were likely to fall upon the whole row of drinking-houses now they were there. Henry behaved as if he thought himself quite safe, but I knew how much reliance to place on *that*. I rose from the bench, about to suggest we repair to my rooms; that, of course, was when the two large gentlemen came in, looking about them for the likes of Henry. He sprang up and in a fine, brainless excess of chivalry commanded, "Out the back! I'll delay 'em!" There was no turning him, no chance to point out that, as I was not an enrolled student, I was in no danger of being taken up for breaking the college rules. I could, however, be taken up by the town watch for participating in a disorderly incident, which Henry seemed determined to precipitate. I left by the back way, after all.

I'm terribly afraid the result will be that he's been rusticated on my behalf. You'll say he's been accused of nothing more than he was guilty of, but he'd have *got away with it* if it weren't for me, and so I feel responsible. If he has been rusticated (God forbid he's actually been sent down—if he has, there's nothing for it but to come forward and confess the whole thing), be kind to him, Kitty, for my sake, and don't let the Legion of Aunts have their way with him. It was lack-witted of him, but the impulse was so very selfless!

Once I returned to my rooms, I had leisure to assemble my new collection of facts, rumours, innuendo, *et cetera*. Now what, Kit, will burn out a shooting star, and that in the course of a year? Drink? Opium? The whole family would have known. A fortune-hunting female? That could have been kept from you and me, but Richard would have known; Uncle Andrew would have enlisted him to help rescue his feckless cousin, since Uncle Andrew always got on rather better with Richard than he did with his own son. And once it was over, there would have been no reason to keep it so quiet as this. Gaming debts? James plays high, I think, but not compulsively, and anyway, *that* rumour couldn't have been kept out of the schoolroom, either. The fact is, if James got himself in some great scandal and the family found it out, we would have got wind of it. And if he *had* got into a mess, how could the family—*this* family—*not* have found out?

It could have been a woman, and not a scandal; if he did go to the Continent and fell in love and was jilted, say. He might have successfully kept something like that from everyone. (Though unless the woman were overwhelmingly ineligible, you would still think it would have to have taken place in Mongolia; *someone* ought to have heard of it.) But I'm inclined to think that cock won't fight, and not because I'm blinded by passion, Kit, you ninnyhammer. Perhaps some of the milk-and-water misses we knew at Miss Trevelyan's believe that a man can reach the age of 29 without any feeling for a female other than a pure and distant longing. *I* have red blood in my veins, thank you, and a genuine brain between my ears, and know that men are allowed to act on their passions in a style that women are not. As well as cutting a modest swath through the ranks of females of easy virtue, James fell violently in love with at least six young ladies to my certain knowledge, and probably with as many more I've heard nothing of. All this to disabuse you of the notion that I would refuse to accept the possibility that James Gave His Heart Elsewhere. If James gave his heart, it was certainly elsewhere, since there was never any evidence that he gave it to me.

No, the Mysterious Lady theory just doesn't seem strong enough to support the events. I won't dismiss it entirely, but I can't help thinking there's something else behind that year's leave of absence. For someone like James, there are a great many more ways to get your heart broke than would ever occur to sensible people. Oxford has given me some new ideas (and that's more than can be said for some people who are properly enrolled and attend lectures). Call it one of my hunches, darling; in fact, call this whole foxhunt one of my hunches, and perhaps you'll have a new respect for it. Remember my hunch about Harriet Cox's love-notes? And the one about the house on the river? Well, this is another. If it makes you feel better, I'll even endeavour to attribute it to my mostly unacknowledged fey sensibilities.

Now I'm back in London and in my skirts, and the concierge has sent up the coffee-pot, thank God. All's right with the world. Along with your letter, there was an invitation from Mrs Overshot to a musical evening tonight, and I'm feeling sufficiently refreshed that I may go. Mrs O. actually knows one note from the next, as well as a composer or two, so I'm not unreasonable in hoping for a passable string quartet. She hasn't, to my knowledge, yet imposed on her guests to the extent of a yodelling soprano, and so I feel quite safe. Besides, I have a new sea-green glazed poplin that shows off my shoulders, and I've had no chance to wear it. I shall drape myself over one of those spindly gilt chairs and distract everyone from the music, whatever it is.

Let me first properly answer your letter, or at least the parts that require it. I shall ignore all of your trolling for impassioned declarations of my True Emotional State, and only remind you that *I* don't prod at *you* to tell me your every intimate feeling. Some of us don't necessarily say everything we feel, which doesn't mean that we *don't* feel, or that we aren't aware of what we feel. What I admit to myself is my own business, and I may have admitted a great many things to myself that I may not have seen fit to tell you about. Oh, dear, I'm sorry, Kit, that sounds as if I don't love you, and you must know that's not true. *If* I preferred to talk about these things, I would talk about them to you before any other. But I have a great love of physical and intellectual and emotional privacy; it's why I'm at Bright's instead of battening myself as a houseguest on someone. No one here would *think* of doing anything so impertinent as wondering aloud how I spend my time. And when I'm denied physical privacy, the emotional and intellectual equivalent sustains me. I can make small talk to a hundred silly people at a hundred insipid parties during the Season, secure in the knowledge that my refuge is no further away than the quiet back rooms of my mind, which are furnished only I know how. My skills and inclinations suit me to a career in diplomacy or political life; it's a pity that my habits and beliefs make me entirely *un*suited to be the wife of a diplomat or a politician. Also, however many social situations I may ride into armed only with the figurative jawbone of an ass, I am a coward in the matter of public humiliation. If I feel strongly, and nothing comes of it, I would rather my unrequited feelings die unrecognized by anyone but me. I *hate* to be gossiped about.

As for public suffering, I hate that, too, that parade of black bombazine and yards of veiling and sable-bordered handkerchiefs. Yes, I have suffered a loss. I don't choose to have my hand patted over it, even by my friends; and no amount of weeping or solicitous utterances or speaking looks on the part of others can touch the grief inside me, can lessen or change it. Only time and my own efforts, of thought and feeling, can work upon it. We live isolated at the heart of it, at the true heart of life. We can't know each other as we know ourselves, however much we love or care. I love and care for you, Kitty dear, and I know you love me, and care for me. I know that your determination to make me declare everything I feel grows out of your love for me. But it's not in my nature, and my nature is one of my comforts at times like this. Leave me my comforts, Kit, and know that if there's anything I need that I can't supply from within me, I promise to turn to you, or to whomever can best give it.

I hope that's sufficient introspection for one sitting, for, given what I've just said, I think you can imagine what an effort it cost me! Not least because I would never have you think me ungrateful, or unfeeling. You are the dearest creature in the world, and you know I would forgive you scores of lectures and scolds. I only take leave to ignore the ones I don't deserve.

You shouldn't feel any obligation to think well of David, you know. He's forfeited the courtesy dozens of times at least. And he's not looking for Truth. He's looking for Justification, which looks exactly like Truth in the eyes of a man like him. And though I knew Mama for only a relatively short time, I can't think she'd approve of David as he's turned out. I think his instincts were more likely honed at school, where he learned to be a pompous bully because it was easier to make himself feared than liked. You may be as charitable about David as you like, if it pleases you, but for heaven's sake don't *act* on any of your charitable assumptions! You've already gone one further in selfless kindness than I would and let him run tame at Melrose, where he repays you by abusing your choice of living arrangements. If you find that no one will come to a house-party there for fear of finding my brother at it, don't say I didn't warn you. Doesn't he ever have parish business at Dunston? Can't he find satisfaction interfering in the lives of his parishioners and browbeating them into feeling obliged to invite him to dinner? Heavens, I thought that was the first duty and concern of clerics everywhere!

Oh, dear, I *have* made you angry; you never call me Susie unless vexed. I don't object to your studies, darling, and shan't in future if you will only forego that unspeakable "ie." Congratulations on your progress, if you'll accept the congratulations of someone so utterly ignorant as I'm afraid I am. Except, you know, if you took "only the smallest amount of opium," I'm surprised you didn't see six waltzing Cossacks and an elephant playing the cello, at the very least. I had some once, in Italy; I saw and believed the most ludicrous things and then went to sleep. Grandmama claimed it was educational stuff, used in moderation, but that it always caused her to wake afterward with a devilish headache. Perhaps it's of some use when coupled with the proper actions and places and things, the way a cannonball is of most use if you also have access to a cannon and powder. And pardon me again if I'm speaking in hopeless ignorance, but have you any notion what sort of birthright it is that you feel you ought to accept? Oh, dear, again. I really do feel as if I ought simply to hold my tongue—or rather, my pen—on this subject, because I'm sure you'll think I'm being disapproving, but I'm only trying, in my hamhanded, literal-minded way, to learn. I've always wanted to think of myself as a scholar and an educated woman, and I'm too little educated to declare some subjects not worth the study. What a dreadful thing it would be to make the declaration, and discover later that I'd denied myself something like astronomy!

Which leads me to sensualism. Well, I certainly prefer to do only pleasant things (wear new clothes, eat strawberry ices

and curry, have someone else brush my hair—but I haven't
had a chance to test that one under new circumstances yet—
argue with clever people who don't cheat, swim in the Mediterranean) and will avoid unpleasant ones if at all possible
(being shouted at, travelling by the stage-coach, sleeping on
the floor, being bored), but I wouldn't say I live only for pleasure. It happens that a lot of life gives me pleasure, and that
much of it that doesn't is easily avoided without calling down
any public or private censure (which, after all, is one of the
things I *don't* like). But if you mean that I believe that anything that's good for you is pleasant, or that anything pleasant
must be good for you, you must be thinking of someone else,
Kit dear. There have been several times in the last few years
when I thought a general election would be very unpleasant
but a splendid and necessary thing to have, and though there's
been no opportunity to test my theory, I still hold it, and a few
stronger ones besides. And on the other hand there's marriage,
which I believe a great many women say they like, but which
as presently constructed I claim to be a great evil. (Richard,
that pretense of a rake, will ask you to marry him, if he hasn't
already. Say no, Kitty; the advantage is all on your side while
you live in sin!) There's another example: any effort to pro-
mote women's suffrage and some equality of the rights of
women will be met with damned unpleasant responses; but I
think any such effort is a positive good.

What *did* James see, all his life? What did form him and
drive him? We're asking the same question, Kitty—you must
see the justice of it, or you wouldn't have brought it up yourself. You think it was magical. His Oxford friends think it was
female. But I'm not satisfied with either of those guesses, not
yet, at least. I mean to test a few of my own, and see how
close I can get to the truth by my own literal-minded, dogged
methods.

There—done just in time to change for dinner and my musicale. Perhaps I shall meet some handsome freedom-fighting
general from some embattled Balkan enclave at Mrs Overshot's, who will admire the revolutionary fire burning in my
eyes and carry me off to help him win his war, each of us
with one arm around the other and rifles in our free hands.

(But if he were embattled, however would he reach London? Hmm. I think I shan't depend upon him.)

Yours, in skirts or trousers,
Susan

P.S., later: Never mind generals. I met Thomas Cavanaugh instead. Do you remember him? Good antecedents, poor as half-a-churchmouse, quite good painter, friend of Richard's and James's? He took me aside at the intermission, fairly dragged me, I wondered if he'd gone mad and nobody'd told me. But he said, once we were out of earshot of everyone else, that he'd heard I was rummaging about in James's past, and was it true? He was terribly agitated. I tried to fob him off, but he insisted on a straight answer. Stop at once, he told me—well, the quote was, "For your life, stop at once." I pretended to be very cool about it, though how I jumped inside! I smiled and asked him if he was threatening me. No, he said, but someone else was bound to if I kept on. He drew my attention to several ugly bruises on his face and a few half-healed cuts, likewise, and said, "This is what happens when you talk about him in the wrong places, to the wrong people. He's dead, it's over. Leave it." It was my turn to drag him—he turned to go and I gave his arm a stout yank, which I'm afraid hurt him. "What's over? Leave what?" I asked, and he went rather white, and well he should. Then, as the wildest stab in the dark, I said, "Has this got something to do with Stone and Tournier and Johnson?"

Kitty, I've never seen anyone stand so still. It was as if I'd killed him, let him stiffen, and propped him against a wall. "I don't know," he whispered, after a moment. I shook his poor arm and said, "You're lying." "I'm not," he replied, a little stronger. "I *don't* know." Then, unfortunately for me, he got some of his wits back, because he looked at me pretty sharply and said, "What do you know about that lot?"

My wits hadn't ever been lost. "Some things," I answered him, quite cool and steady. "If you're going to ask questions, so am I."

He didn't like that a bit. But we went 'round in that fashion a few more times before I told him that he could come to see me at Bright's Hotel at one o'clock tomorrow, and I'd let him try if he could do any better at frightening me off than he had so far.

It had never occurred to me that it might be possible to simply poke about the fox's earth with a stick and see what happened. Write soon, darling, heaven knows where I'll be. Don't be alarmed. I have a lovely pistol, and I'm a wondrous good shot. Tally-ho!

—S. V.

RICHARD COBHAM'S JOURNAL

OCTOBER 22

Sent J a horse pistol, powder & shot, mistletoe, & medallion as well as a bit of money so he can get useful knife. Hope he uses them. I worry for him & wonder if I should tell K that he is alive.

OCTOBER 23

Sent for some books on the history of the Portsmouth area. Wrote to J. More cautions, more arguments. He will no doubt respond vociferously to the latter and ignore the former.

MELROSE HALL
TUESDAY

Dear James:

Do you know, I always used to be able to tell when you had just enjoyed a fresh dalliance: your conversation became smug, your attitude self-satisfied, your confidence in your observations grew, and your demeanour was generally that of the cat perpetually cleaning its whiskers. All of which, I know, sounds censorious, but somehow you manage to make it charming (although, to be sure, it was at such times that Susan always seemed most annoyed at you). In any case, it seems you retain this characteristic, for which I salute you, in spite of the barbs sent in my direction. In addition, of course, I congratulate you on your good fortune; pleasures of the flesh may not bring us the sublime joy of spiritual delight, but they are certainly a better way of passing the time than whist.

That said, a caution: we both know you are a fine-looking fellow, and one with a pleasing manner to the ladies, yet such transports as you describe, when they come too easily, make me think of Irish songs about stolen watches; and under your present circumstances this is more true than ever. Please be careful, and be suspicious.

But good heavens, my man. How you go on! I do not speak of life after death, upon which subject I hold no position except the desire for indifference. Nor yet do I ask you to consider as the Unknowable that which never crosses our paths nor has any effect on us. When I sent you Hegel, my dear cousin, it was no more an endorsement of the "absolute idea" than it was in order to claim that our society "must be rational because it exists," to quote those who misquote the fellow. Again, I have no dispute with your attitudes toward goodness or sin; I have committed both, by any standards, and will do so again, hoping only that the former acts should outweigh the latter (sins existing only in the mind are not sins, David's opinion to the contrary).

Rather, I argue, the Unknowable is that which lives in the cracks between the known and the irrelevant; between the hard edges of the world and the shadowy figments of waking dreams; between the mundane world and the ignorance of superstition. *Between* Hegel's absolute idea and Feuerbach's sensuousness. The unknowable lives in a pack of cards after it has been fairly shuffled but before it has been dealt, when all the possibilities are open, and when each possibility *matters*.

Jamie, each man makes many choices, and each of those choices matters. I know you are not one of the sophists who would deny us free will (perhaps in order, as Brian says, to justify the most atrocious acts); well then, for what do we *use* this free will? And above all, what of the will (free or otherwise) of those forces that live among us, and whose influence we cannot believe in because we have never seen them, nor deny because they permeate our lives? There lies the Unknowable, cousin, and if you have never considered this matter before, then do so now, because your life, at least, depends upon your doing so.

Are you blind, James, or suicidal?

You think Grandfather spoke "nonsense"? That nonsense saved your life, James. Think on your own words. I speak of the Unknowable as something that has an effect on our lives, and you have just lived it! A ton of horse nearly landed upon your head, and you reach into the very place of those forces I have determined to understand, and so preserve your astoundingly thick skull, and yet you say, "Nonsense." That, my cousin, is veritable nonsense, and I beg you to consider the matter.

No, I do not expect you to believe me, but I hope to move you enough to be careful; until we know more, that is all we can do. I have spoken with Tournier, and I am inclined to think him guiltless. He did not start when I mentioned your name, merely giving me condolences in a tone that suggested he would not speak ill of the dead. He is a sharp one, James, but I suppose he isn't pointing at you. As for Stone—well, I will stand mute, then. I understand and respect your discretion, even when I wonder at its wisdom.

Speaking of wisdom, I have no intention of calling David out, still less of assassinating him. But do not deprive me of my dreams. (Besides, I think I would look quite dashing standing up on the gallows and giving a speech about sanctimonious vicars, with a few quotes from Hegel, Hobbs, and Hume to add spice.)

Your horses are well, James, as you will soon see, and you sound like Mother when you fret about them. In the meantime, guard your health, remain alert, enjoy the touch of your housemaid and the sight of your bays (although, should you suddenly imagine that they are giving off a soft glow, as of phosphorus, I take no responsibility for the consequences!), and look for me soon, ere the waning of the moon, or something equally poetic, when you shall have your hand firmly shaken by your cousin,

Richard

MELROSE HALL
OCTOBER 26ᵗʰ

Dear Susan,

You know, do you not, that I am possessed by jealousy because you, for reasons good or bad, and I will not go into that
now, have dressed yourself up like a man and got away with
it, which I have wanted to do for as long as I can remember,
only I have never got 'round to it, which is another way of
saying I have never been brave enough, and then I find you
actually attended a lecture! How was it, for heaven's sake?
What was said, and what did you learn? My goodness, the
things you leave out of your letter are enough to make me tear
out my hair, not that I have ever been so awfully proud of my
hair to begin with, because I have always wished I had thick,
dark, glorious hair like yours, and now you have gone and cut
it! It is enough to make me start underlining words, like Aunt
Louisa in her letters, which never say anything interesting because she never does anything interesting, but you do and you
will not tell! Oh, I know you have told me a lot, Susan, but,
well, for heaven's sake, you heard men talking about women,
and you talk about their foolish notions, but you will not say
what those foolish notions *are*, which is what I most want to
know. There, now I have underlined a word, and it is all your
fault.

Did I really call you Susie? I am sorry, I was vexed, but I
did not think I was as vexed as all that, but it was really an
accident, because I know how much you loathe it.

Well, the fact is, I am absolutely thrilled with your adventure, and I wish I could have been there too, and I do not
believe that Madame Blanche said any such thing about me,
because I do not and never have had a figure like that and she
never spoke of such matters anyway, because all of her conversation was about the Court, and where Her Majesty might
appear, and who was marrying whom, for heaven's sake, but
I do hope Henry does not get into any trouble, he has always

been a dear, if a little, well, slow, at least compared to you and Richard.

As for sensualism, Susan, you know very well what I mean, which is that we do what brings us pleasure, whether physical, spiritual, or emotional, and without regard to whether it is frowned on by the Right Reverend Most Honourable Lord David Voights of the world or not, so do not be coy. I am living in sin, and you are running about wearing men's clothing, and we are both doing these things because we want to, and not doing those things the Legion of Aunts would have us do.

And my dear, adorable, silly old Susan, of course you do not prod at me for every intimate feeling, because you need not, I tell you what they are almost before I get them, and *please* do not think that I want you to violate this privacy you treasure from some vulgar curiosity, nor even from some well-bred curiosity, but because I worry about you, and there, I underlined another word, and now I really do sound like Aunt Louisa, but yes, we live isolated, but we do not live as isolated as you chose to, and sometimes those who love us can help ease our pain if we let them, but instead of letting me help, which God knows you are not obligated to, you talk and act as if you were denying that any such feelings exist which makes me mad with worry for you, because if you do that, and you mean it, you will end up in one of those upstairs rooms here at Melrose with no one talking about you, so, dear, I am being selfish and asking you to reassure me that you are all right, but really you do not have to, because, reading between the lines, I think you have, and I thank you because I feel better already.

I still think you are wrong about David, but that is because I have known him in other frames of mind, but I will concede that you are right that I ought to be careful around him, and I certainly do not want to talk about him any more, because he makes me sad, and I wish I knew what had ruined him, because something tells me it is not his fault.

I really was in quite a taking if I let slip that comment about my birthright, I had not meant to say that, and I would prefer not to talk about it, either, and with all the things I do not want to talk about I am starting to sound like you, but I will say that there are stories about Great-Grandpapa Woodworth that have haunted me for as long as I can remember, and I have dreams of him talking to me, dreams in which he seems to be a sweet, kind man, and he is telling me that I am the only one left who, well, it all sounds like nonsense and I should not have said it, even if I do believe it, sometimes anyway.

Do you know, I cannot for the life of me remember Cavanaugh, perhaps we never met, but that is neither here nor there. You will notice that I have written all this without saying a word about James and your quest, and that is because I am afraid I have to admit I was wrong, and that is not easy for me as you know better than anyone, if you remember that I spent weeks insisting that Harriet was having an affair with that awful Billings fellow after you had proven that her beau was that beautiful young man from India, and I knew you were right, and I just could not admit it until they had actually gotten on the boat together, but now I am admitting that you are right about James, so I hope that is some atonement. It is not your "hunch" that convinced me, or even the dire warnings from family, acquaintances, and strangers, it is something that happened to me, right here, and I must take a deep breath and tell you about it.

This morning while taking coffee with Richard on the terrace, and thinking about your letter and wondering how I could convince you to leave it alone, it occurred to me that I might enlist Richard's unknowing help in explaining some of these strange things you talk about, so I casually mentioned that I had not heard anything of Tournier in a long time and I wondered how he was getting along, and Richard nearly bolted out of his chair, saying, "Why do you ask about him?" "Why, no reason," I said, "why does it matter?" "Nothing," he said, "it is nothing," although any fool could see it was something, which I think means it is something, and Tournier is a member of the Trotter's Club, which makes me afraid.

So you are right, and I will say it again, you are right. There is something going on, and I do not know what, but it is positively the most intriguing intrigue since the matter of the Vicar's dormouse.

My goodness, Susan. We are involved in a *mystery*, which is enough to make me underline a third word in the same letter!

Something did happen to James on the Continent, or wherever, it must have, and there is a reason for his death, and there are things going that give me a shiver that is half fear and half excitement, like when we broke into Aunt Louisa's jewelry box. Richard knows something about it, Susan, and I must find out what, for I am now your confederate, and you must tell me everything you learn, and I will tell you everything I learn, and I will help you in any way I can. There, is that enough? And I am glad that you are a good shot and have a pistol, and, whatever you think, I am going to dig up the old grimoires that are buried behind the dictionaries in the library and read them because that is my way of carrying a pistol, too, and I must stop now and get this into the post because I am already dying to hear from you, so you must write at once to your excited and affectionate,

Kit

Postscript: I found the most amazing letter tucked into one of the old grimoires, so I have copied it exactly and am sending it along, and I will not say one word about it because I want you to form your own opinion without undue influence by

K

WINFIELD ABBEY
THIS NINTH DAY OF AUGUST
IN THE YEAR OF OUR LORD,
SEVENTEEN HUNDRED AND SIXTY-ONE

My Dear Sir James,

I must suggest that you Immediately break off those Studies of which we Spoke when you were Kind enough to allow me to Visit you last Month. I Dare not Speak more now, but will reveal All when next we Meet. For now, I can only say that there are Powers at work of which I had not Known, and of which you cannot Know, and our Choices are to Leave it Alone or to Attack Head-on.

From the Letters of yours I have Read and the one time I had the Pleasure of your Company, I think I know which way

you would Choose, and if so, as God is my Witness, I am
Willing to help you, but we must not Rush in, for it would be
Rash and even Foolhardy. Allow me, then, to make some Prep-
arations, which will take me the remainder of this Month, and
after that I will come down to Melrose and we will speak in
more Detail. Until then, Sir, I Beg you to be Circumspect, and
to do Nothing, but trust your recent acquaintance, but, I assure
you, your Good and Loyal Friend,

Sir Thomas Woodworth

THE GREY HOUND
27th OCTOBER, 1849

Dear Richard,

There was music in the taproom tonight, a travelling fiddler,
and though most of the tunes were merry, I found myself unaccountably melancholy amid the good cheer of my neighbours. Have you ever suffered from that species of perversity
that makes you long for company, though you cannot bear to
converse with anyone? To seek out lively music, though your
heart cannot take any part in it? No one, I think, could tell
anything more than that I was quiet, but then I am often quiet
here, as there is so much I must not say. I sat in my corner,
and responded to the greetings of my fellow men with a smile
or a nod, and felt a stranger to everything, myself included.

I am sunk in a fine Celtic gloom, and ought not to be spending paper and ink sharing it with you. I ought not to have
shared anything at all with you, in fact, and am a bloody fool
to have started now. All my clean, cold habits so suitable to
the thin air where I once dwelt are overturned [two lines
crossed out and unreadable here]. I have never kept a journal,
Richard; it would have been a madness whenever it wasn't
merely an indulgence. But these letters to you have become a
solace, an indulgence, a madness so much like journal-keeping
that I think I must stop them, for my own safety, and disappear
properly until such time as this pretense, and all pretenses, may
be abandoned. Then I think that I cannot stop, that that first

impulse to tell you that I lived was my whole secret self reaching out for a life, however short, in the daylight. Do desert-dwelling creatures feel a longing to sit atop their rocks as the sun rises, to forego the life-saving darkness of their burrows at noon and watch, just once, the clanging, remorseless advance of their assassin?

[Three lines crossed out.] But I never did keep a journal then; I wrote no clandestine letters; how did I deal, in that arid past, with these bouts of pain and self-loathing? I drank, of course. I drank a great deal. And unlike most men, I wash my secrets down my throat with wine, drown them utterly until the morning when they return to lay their burden on my spirit, as the wine has laid its burden on my body. If I could command myself better I would not send this, but commit my writing to the post-office burning in my grate. I am not drunk, Richard. If I were drunk I would never write such things, for the torrent of feeling that hurries my pen along now would be decently re-channelled.

The cholera is in Portsmouth and Southampton; Langstone has a good chance of escaping it altogether, the farmers tell me, because of better airs. I have seen Portsmouth, and though Langstone's air is infinitely more agreeable to breathe, I am inclined to think we shall be spared for lack of crowding and squalour and filth. By whatever reasoning they reach it, others share the conclusion, and the traffic of waggons, riders, and pedestrians from the south has increased uncomfortably. Two days ago—Thursday—two burly fellows came from Portsmouth, on foot, to the Grey Hound. Something about them suggested the sailor; they may have been travelling inland to escape the fever, or the press, or the law. They were nearly civil when they arrived, though it seemed to require some effort. Strictly speaking, since they weren't mounted, they weren't my business. But there had been some anxiety chafing at me all day, and I had been prowling the premises like a sheepdog, hunting for something that needed setting right. Traffic on the road had dropped to an unaccustomed trickle, perhaps because of the pouring rain, so the place had no other custom. They called for food and drink, and then more drink, but neither was so much as part-disguised when they began some ugly-sounding banter with Coslick about what a fine, prosperous-looking tavern he had, and how he must have laid up a deal of blunt against his old age. The progress from that to attempted robbery was very quick; had it taken a few seconds more, Coslick might not have got hurt. But by the time I came through the taproom door, one of them had produced a great knife and had laid Coslick's hand open with it, and the shock of it had sent him staggering back, his face like tallow.

You have never seen me do what I did then, Richard. You have seen me reverent before the Marquess of Queensbury, most excellently sportsmanlike; you have never seen me face my man, considering nothing but efficiency, expediency, and the benefits of a truly lasting outcome. You should, I think. If you had, you might have hesitated to answer that first letter.

If I had had your pistol by me, I would have shot to kill. I'd had no chance to buy another knife. So I did the things one can do, barehanded, that will disarm a man and bring him down, and keep him from getting back up. There are a good many of them, if you don't care how much and what kind of damage you do to the other fellow.

Once I am out the other side of that state, it sickens me. It is not honest rage. It is a kind of machine-life, limited to machine-thought, cold and passionless. Cause and effect, action and result, result viewed without any moral colouration. The ideal result being that your enemy can never strike you again. One of these men will never strike anyone again, unless he has someone to tell him where to aim the blow. The other may strike someone, but not while standing. Neither of them would have been concerned again with the matter of good or bad air had not Mrs Coslick asked me to give her the knife I had taken from the one who had cut her husband. At that point I noticed that it was still afternoon, that I was indoors, that there were four other people in the room, that I could hear the rain coming down, that I could smell bread and beer and old candle smoke and sweat. I let go of the man I had blinded, handed Mrs Coslick the knife, hilt-first, and walked out through the rain to the stables, to vomit, and to wash the blood, theirs and mine, off my hands. Then I went into the stall with Coslick's brown cob, Dutchman, and made a pretense of combing out his mane, until my fingers shook so much that I couldn't hold the comb and only stood there, my face in the coarse hair, breathing the honest smell of warm horse and thinking of nothing at all.

You will say that the intensity of my reaction, after my outburst of violence, is my mark of grace, the proof that I am better than my actions, the assurance that violence is unfamiliar and unnatural to me. How comforting that reflection was, the first time I had it! But you see, Richard my cousin, my reaction has been equally intense on every previous occasion. The tide of action recedes; I come back to myself; I cast up my accounts; I tremble like a palsy victim. Trust me always to be scientific—my sample is large enough to make the experiment valid. Would you like to know *how* large—how many times— or would you very much prefer not? Rest easy, I am not going to tell you. You are not quite yet my journal, or my rock in the sun. The two men were taken up to be held for the assizes. I was not. I wonder at that. Had the two attempted to rob Coslick and been felled by the sudden collapse of part of the taproom ceiling, he would have to fix the ceiling, wouldn't he? His customers would refuse to drink there, in fact, until he had inspected the timbers for rot and made all safe again. Yet tonight those customers nodded and smiled at me, and some even gave me a companionable thump on the shoulders. Am I less dangerous than dry rot? Or only, less dangerous to *them*? I should love to know how they can be so sure.

I thought of the possibility that the two sailors had not chosen the Grey Hound at random, that they were meant, ultimately, to attack me. If so, it was a half-hearted attempt; or it may be that this unseen enemy is less effective than either you or I might fear—in fact, if I ever thought you were behind my misfortune, Richard, you would be cleared entirely by this. Or it may be that what happened was directed at me, and was conducted precisely as planned—but then, why? What a foolish waste, to maraud about Coslick's taproom, when a blow with that fine big knife between the shoulders, at twilight, in one of these little farm-lanes, would have done such an admirable job. Wouldn't it be an excellent thing to be able to ask those two men about their motives? If you think of any way to suggest all of the appropriate questions to the magistrate, without drawing any attention to myself, my imposture, or indeed *my* motives, do please let me know.

More on my bays and the green coach, and possibly the end

of the matter, though an odd and somewhat unsettling one. We have been infernally busy for the whole of this cold, wet week, what with the increased traffic from Portsmouth. Today it was nearing dark, but we had custom still; in times of plague people will behave like fools and court more likely danger to escape it, such as driving into a ditch in the dark and breaking their necks. I had just sent off a post-chaise north with a fresh near-side leader, and was checking the spent one's lame foreleg for heat, when something bade me look up. Down the road, heading against the direction of nearly all the other traffic on the Portsmouth road, was the coach, in its usual style.

I watched it come, expecting it to go past. But the coachman hauled his team down to a walk and directed them into our yard, and I handed the reins of the lame horse to Emmett, the local lad who helps in the stable.

I don't suppose you are in the habit of looking other people's coachmen in the face, Richard. I know I never was, in my old life. But if you are taking a man's horses into your keeping, you look to his face. It will tell you, often, more about the state of his cattle than his tongue will. And so I took hold of the leaders' bridles and looked up to take this man's measure.

He was the ugliest human being I have ever seen. To look at him was a kind of blow, a paralysing shock like a great sudden noise or a slap. I retain very few details of his features—they were so outlandish that at first I could not fit them to a model of human physiognomy, and I had no time to accustom myself in whatever measure I could, for after a good scowl at me he leaped down off the box and strode off into the inn. I remember only skin tanned to greyish-brown and fissured like tree bark, and hard black eyes that caught the last light like jet beads, and the whole face seeming pinched between brow and chin, as if those two promontories meant to squeeze out every other feature. I had forgotten the lame horse behind me, until it flung up its head with a deep, warning snort, and nearly tore the reins from the boy's grasp. That set the team of bays to sidling.

As I quieted them and sent Emmett off to the stable with his charge, the coach door on the inn side opened and a lady stepped down. She made no protest about the muddy pavers, and did not seem to expect anyone to assist her down the step, but she was a gentlewoman; her pelisse and the breadth of skirt that showed beneath it, her shallow-brimmed bonnet, were costly, elegant, and exceedingly fashionable, and her way of carrying herself suggested that she was not used to thinking twice of any of those things.

She would have drawn anyone's eye, I think. Her figure was compelling; but when she turned her face to me, I felt a moment's unreasonable shame at having thought of her as a man might think of a woman, for her face was so like a child's that I could nearly forget the evidence of her form. The hair revealed inside the bonnet-brim was fine and nearly white, like a very blonde child's, and her brows and dense lashes were the same. Her eyes were the blue of an unweaned kitten's, round and open and clear. Her mouth, too, was kitten-like, and the whole face might have spent no more than ten or twelve uneventful years in the world. Then she smiled, her lips parting over small, even teeth, and she said in a resonant, sweet voice that seemed almost familiar, "Jim, isn't it?"

"Jack, ma'am, begging your pardon," I replied, and used all the force of my will to control my face and voice. I believe I spoke without hesitation, but the moment between her words and mine seemed space enough for a hanging. "May I help you with aught?"

She blushed and continued to smile; her skin was so transparently white that the rush of blood under it was instantly visible. "I am sorry. Jack. Will you fetch down one of my cases for me? The smaller one."

She showed no sign of disbelieving me. I think it was only a heart-jarring coincidence—she knew the new hostler's name was a short one beginning with J. But that was another question: how did the subject of the new hostler's name arise in the presence of such a piece of refinement?

The case was small, but heavy. I tipped it a little as I brought it down from the top of the coach; the contents did not shift. "I'll carry it in for you," I said.

"Oh, no, I'll carry it." I doubted she could. "But this is for your trouble."

And instead of a coin, she held out a ring, a rather handsome, plainish one of plaited iron. I looked swiftly into her face, and she laughed, and said softly, "The parson's girl sews for me. She asked me to give it to you, from her."

"She can't do the giving herself?" I asked.

"I expect she had work to do," said the lady, coolness creeping into her voice. It reminded me of what I was supposed to be, and how little I was entitled to question gentlewomen. "Hold out your right hand."

Surprised, I did as I was told, and she slipped the ring on the third finger herself, sliding her cool little fingers along mine. She looked up at me with a quirk of those short pink lips, a knowing expression on her child-face, and I suspected that the parson's girl gossiped as well as sewed for her. Then she took the case two-handed, but not labouring, and went into the inn in a rustle of taffetta skirts.

She was not gone a minute before her coachman was back on the box, and she followed close behind. Neither of them looked at me then or as they rattled out of the yard, headed south. I went inside, but seek where I might, I could not find the case she had carried in.

Somehow, I think I will not muster the unmitigated cheek necessary to ask that woman if she would like to sell her horses.

Gideon Johnson's ship is the *Cormorant*, and she berths in Southampton, if you are interested. I find I am not, particularly. Among the precipitate travellers from Portsmouth this week were a captain's lady and her brood, and they had with them one of the journals that covers Naval business in tedious detail. Johnson's name appeared just above the fold, and sprang out at me. It gave me a cold shock, but that passed quickly. I hated that man, once. Now I only wonder if his deeds will catch up with him as I expect mine to draw level with me, one day; or if perhaps he'll live to be the mechanism of my atonement. You will be wondering if he was behind the two sailors in the taproom. No, he wasn't. He is infinitely delicate in these matters, profoundly tidy. I would know one of Johnson's little contrivances if I saw it acted out in Baghdad or Peking. If you should learn that Gideon Johnson is the author of my difficulties, do me a great favor and pick me out a nice box. Preferably trimmed in brass, to match my manners.

Tonight I ought to hold off from our argument; my impassioned defences of the strictly rational world leave behind them very little comfort for their wielder. But the world is not made for my comfort, and beguiling my intellect into a kind of perceptual drunkenness with fancies of a shadow-world and shadow-beings cannot help me. Lies do not heal. I have faith, however, in the healing power of truth, and I am profoundly ill tonight, Richard. So let us have a little tilting, after all.

What shall I make of your Unknowable, which can live in a place that does not exist? I believe in possibility, in Chance, but not as a deity or a property of metaphysics. By Hegel's furiously all-inclusive system, the logic of Being comprises being, nonbeing, and becoming; Chance, I suggest, is created by the latter, a product of reality journeying toward its resting configuration. Much superstition has been invented to account for the appearance of reality in motion, but it is still perceivable concrete reality, even if temporarily a little blurry to the unaided eye. (The dialectical process suggests that identifying the logic of Being as "becoming" is more accurate than the thesis, being, or its antithesis, nonbeing, but Hegel seems to me to suggest that all three are in place simultaneously, which I like. Or is this only a case of the finer points of German verb tenses escaping me? The quality of your German is up to philosophy; mine may not be, quite.) But because it is a product of a changing state, Chance is at its own mercy, as we are at the mercy of Chance. The presence of sweet, blind possibility is in the pack *before* the shuffle; after it, when the cards lie mute in the suspense before the deal, they are Being, stilled, complete. The money is already won or lost in a faro game, once the cards are shuffled—pity the players, who are only a little behind on the news, and believe the delay has room to contain a change in their fortunes. We should rub our rabbit's feet long before that point, if they are to be effective.

But if we want to change the outcome of our hypothetical card game, Diccon, we must move on to Hegel's logic of Essence, mustn't we? This is a matter for his categories of actualisation—no, *die Wirklichkeit* would be "actuality," not "actualisation," and besides, Herr Hegel would never use such an active word. He is a good and noble philosopher and would never suggest that the sciences of thought had any more to do than sink firmly down on their broad buttocks and Be. So, actuality, the outer expression of inner essence. Substance in the matter of the pack itself, accident in the shuffle; cause in the play, effect in the transfer of guineas, player to player; action and reaction over and over again. Each thesis and antithesis reflects on and mediates the other. This is the basket in which Hegel places forces in conflict, and the power of one object in the universe to make a difference on another. Think, dear Richard, of the objects in a card game that have that power! Surely Hegel was a gamester? They should install a perpetual table of piquet as part of the curriculum at Oxford and Cambridge.

Gradually we draw back from the pack, through the actions of and transformations on the pack, to the hands themselves, and reach at last the logic of Concept. Let us contemplate immediacy, those characteristics which each object has by virtue of Being—hearts and spades, court cards and that tidy alignment of pips that were laid down at the Beginning by the Creator, a painstaking and ink-smudged printer. Let us contemplate, as well, mediation from outside. Another player discards, one begs another card from the dealer, and look! Reality, our hand, is transformed, weakened or reinforced. Now, at last, we must deal with free will, which Hegel identifies as the ability to change one's own nature, self-mediation. Can I be permitted to slip here from the hand to the player who holds it? He does not wait for Chance to rule his hand, but discards, judges the wisdom of his fellows at table, does what he can to turn Chance up sweet.

The players, indeed, will serve as well as their hands to illustrate Concept. They have immediacy: the gifts of heredity, personality, diet—what, you say diet is irrelevant in a card game? Honest, earnest Richard, you are not enough of a gambling man after all. They have mediation from outside: well, perhaps I should have saved food and drink for this category; and does any man at the table hate another? Revere him? Bed his sister? Do any of the players struggle under an injunction against high play laid by a beloved papa on his deathbed? Self-mediation I have addressed.

All of existence encompassed at a card-table; there's a comfort for those of us who thought we had wasted the hours of our youth! Perhaps I should test Hegel against cock-fighting as well, and see if the system is truly universal. The actualization of the idea is every fool's downfall. If Hegel had had the least interest in applied philosophy, instead of philosophy unsullied by use, he might have had the kindness to warn us of it. Any gamble seems like a fair one before the shuffling of the cards. Any risk seems likely to yield a grand outcome, before the pieces at risk fall into their final order. Sometimes Becoming is a cruel false promise, to lure one into the cell of Being, and all the rest is the sound of the key turning in the lock.

[Two lines crossed out] No, Jamie. The topic is philosophy, which exists outside of time. Now there is a metaphysical position for you! Other than as it relates to Hegel's self-change, free will is not a matter I will discuss at any length tonight, or perhaps ever, save to say that I believe in it without reservation, and am thus robbed of consolation from that quarter. But to what "forces," besides ourselves, do you allot free will? I won't pretend to believe you refer to animals, though we could have an interesting time of it, perhaps, discussing whether dogs and horses have free will and choose to obey us, or whether we only play on their instinctive reactions to control them. And I dangled God in front of you, a Supreme Being, and you only sidled off, muttering about Hegel's absolute idea (which, it still seems to me, is a conjuring trick of Hegel's to allow him to discuss God under the guise of general philosophy—the man goes to such uncommon and suspicious lengths to avoid being identified as a theologian). Here, too, we could have a debate, if I would only admit to the existence of the subject under discussion. Does God have free will? There's one that poor old Billy Harkness would have loved to get his teeth into, back at Oriel. No, better not to bring up the good Billy, either. I'd no notion philosophy could hold so many pitfalls for the memory.

Caution be damned, I shall wrench the lid off the thing. Are we approaching a discussion of, among other things, fairies, ghosts, demons, djinn, and all manner of teeming spirits of Nature? You will please hold me excused. I mean this, Richard. I might indulge you over a decanter of port by the fireside in the Melrose library, as a form of telling ghost stories on All Hallows' Eve. *I will not do it now.* I am worn down and reduced to essentials; the excess of spirit that once allowed for charm and civility and tolerance in the face of the tedious baggage of my fellow men is all used up in me. When you sent the pistol, you sent the perfect gift for the man I have become. I apologise for the previous pages, in fact, for looking back on them I can see that the gift of Hegel, which you thought to send to the James you knew and had last seen in flesh and blood, has gone astray and been profaned.

I cannot send this. Richard, you have become my journal after all, for having said these things to you, I find I cannot countenance saying them at all. I wish I did not have them to say. I will burn this when I finish, but having begun the excavation of this particular ruined city, it seems a shame not to at least finish revealing the outlines of the walls.

Discretion triumphs. I have sat with pen poised over paper, unable to begin the sentence, for perhaps three-quarters of an hour. I have set down the pen and gone to poke up the fire three times, each time returning to the table with renewed purpose, and *cannot write a word.* Never mind knowing how to keep a secret—I can't remember how to give one up. Someone should, in all decency, just break my neck and be done with it.

I hadn't yet told Richard—told *you*, don't abandon a perfectly good conceit—about the squire's poor stallion. He still lives, but not, I think, for long. He bit a groom quite badly, and kicked down a stout oak partition in the squire's stable. He is vicious out of fear. Strange, how we take that for granted in men, but in horses consider it grounds for execution. The knacker may as well sharpen his knife now. There, that is a suitable bauble to ornament my mood and the document informed by it.

Good-bye, Richard. [Part of a line crossed out.] What will you think when you realise that there will be no answer to your last letter but a windy silence? I started to write, "How

will you feel,'' but I don't want to ask after feelings, even in
a medium as private as this. I know when I am giving pain.

James

If you have ever wanted to call me a great many unforgivable names, please do so now. You may also say you told me
so. The rector doesn't have a housemaid.

I could have found this out had it ever occurred to me to
mention the matter to Mrs Coslick. That this letter was not
burnt yet is a happy chance. There are things in it that I wish
you did not have to see, but it saves a deal of time to merely
send it, and let you sieve from it the useful information—my
coach takes on a slightly different complexion, no?—and hope
that time will eventually dull the pain and mend your memory
of me, a little.

On the small chance that you haven't guessed it yet, I shall
be explicit: I must now disappear. If you need to respond to
this, do it, please, with the greatest circumspection and no hope
of a response. I shall not be here, but I will try to arrange for
some kind of forwarding of one last letter. After that you will
not hear from me, nor I from you. The danger is too great,
Richard, for both of us. You don't know the nature of the
intrigue I might have—may have—involved you in, and it was
monstrous of me to have drawn you in, blind, for the sake of
my own comfort. You *have* been a comfort, for what it may
be worth to you. I have been cruel in the foregoing pages,
which was no desert of yours but only what I am: sometimes
cruel, without justification. Even to those I love most, and you
are of that number.

Each man makes many choices, indeed, and each one matters. You forgot to add that, once the first choice is made,
another invariably follows on it, resulting from the first; and
another on that, and another. They all matter. I believe I am
nearing the last link of a chain of choices, and the outcome it
will fasten me to is impossible to predict from here. Understand that this, too, is my free choice. I am not driven to this,
except by that most tenacious of instincts, even stronger than
the determination to keep a secret: the will to survive, even
separated from everything that is dear to me.

All lives are abbreviated; nature puts a period at the end. I have been dead once to you, Richard. Let me die again, and celebrate my funeral, at least in the privacy of your own mind and heart. It won't be so hard, now that you've had the practice.

With regret,
J.

PART TWO

ESSENCE

From *The Times*, October 27, 1849, pg. 3
RAILWAY ACCIDENT

On the arrival of the London and North Western train, which left Leeds at 11 o'clock yesterday morning, at the Phillips Park station, several passengers got out, and amongst others a young lady named Howard, who had booked at the Droylsden station. Just as they got out a luggage train belonging to the Lancashire and Yorkshire Company, on its way to Ashton, was seen approaching at a very great speed, and directly its whistle was heard. At the Park station there is a crossing, and on the opposite side of the line, to the booking-office there is a gate and turnstile leading to a lane. The young lady before mentioned, either not knowing of the approaching train, or thinking she could get out of the way before it reached the station, was walking across the line in order to go through the turnstile, when the train came up, and one of the buffers striking her, threw her with great violence in a slanting direction about four or five yards in advance, into a corner, near a gate; her umbrella was thrown behind her. Her head came into contact with some paling at the side of the line near the gate, with such force as to cause a large wound of the scalp; and she was so stunned as to be quite insensible. A surgeon was procured; an engine and carriage were brought up from the Miles Platting station, and the young lady was conveyed home to Droylsden. On our inquiry last evening we learned that she still remained in a state of insensibility, and it was thought she would not recover. The only external injury which she appeared to have received was the large contusion on the head; but she must have been considerably injured by the sudden shock. We have since learned the chief injury was concussion of the brain, and but slight hopes are entertained of her recovery. It is a piece of highly reprehensible neglect on the part of the porters and other servants of the company at the station, who must have known of the approach of the luggage train, and of the existence of the lane on the other side of the line, not to take care to see that no passenger attempted to cross the line until the luggage-train had passed. Since the above was in type, we have received the following account of another accident, apparently caused by the engine and carriage which conveyed the young lady home. It seems that the engine and carriage, proceeding forward to Ashton, came in contact with a horse and cart, the property of Mr. Barlow, of Ashton, whose driver was crossing the line at Rynal's-lane, which is a level crossing, when the horse was knocked down and killed, and the driver was severely crushed, but no bones appear to be broken. Mr. Woolven immediately proceeded to the scene of the accident, and made every arrangement for the removal of the carriage thrown off the line, and there are hopes of the man's recovery.

—*Manchester Guardian.*

THE POSTING-HOUSE
THE GREY HOUND
WEDNESDAY

My Dearest Kitty:

Should I ever again have to travel without you, I will remember to take along a sample of whatever soap or ointment you use in your hair, for nothing about this journey is as painful as waking up without the scent of you; my first waking thought is the recollection that you are not with me, so quickly have you become part of my existence. Indeed, last night I dreamt that I was searching for you desperately, and I awoke this morning with the dream vivid in my mind, and disappointment was my accompaniment, so you see that you are in my thoughts both waking and sleeping.

As for the business that brought me here, well, I cannot report much luck, and I do not wish to speak of it to you—it is enough that it has taken me to this forsaken corner of England without requiring that it occupy my conversation with you as well. I arrived safely after a foul but mercifully brief stint on the train and a long but rather pleasant journey by coach, and found the inn to be really a charming old place, where everyone is fat and friendly, the food good if rather thirstier than I would prefer, the only trouble being in the stable, which I am told the hostler has recently left rather abruptly; but this has no direct effect on me, having brought no horses; it does seem to make up a great deal of conversation among the staff, however—they use it an excuse for anything that may be wrong, a trait I find more charming than irritating.

Most of my time is spent in the common room, which term I use advisedly: it is a big, plain room with a large hearth and long tables, and one can imagine Cromwell's Ironsides coming through the door demanding to know where the King is hiding, thus forcing each man to decide if he favours dash, flair, romance and a well-cut costume over the forward movement of history. Fear for one's skin? Surely such mundane matters never entered one's thoughts in those days—at least, they never enter my daydreams of those days! And then the door opens, and it is not Cromwell's troops, nor yet a disguised Scotchman seeking a place to hide the Pretender, but only a short, husky farmer with his fat wife stopping on the way to Portsmouth where they hope to sell a few sows for bacon to the Naval yards. My business is of the sort that involves long periods of sitting, so I have much time for such reflections, and for missing you even more, because your observations of the place would be a delight to me; when this is over, you must allow me to bring you here on holiday.

Apropos, forgive me if I sound mysterious and even sinister about my "business" here. My departure, although I mentioned the possibility two weeks ago, may have seemed abrupt, but really, there is little enough to talk about; I am following some clues that I hope will gain me some advantage, and there is nothing of questionable legality or morality about it. I do not choose to go into detail, but I assure you I will tell you all about it soon enough. In the meantime, you would be doing me a great service if you could search the library and see if you can find the origin of the curious device I have traced on the enclosed sheet. I suspect it will appear in one of the editions on Heraldry, as it is a Coat of Arms—Welsh, if I am not mistaken. In addition, please reassure your Charming and Delightful Aunt about my continued well-being, and make the proper noises about the estate as such noises are needed, and write to me as soon as you can, for I miss you.

You are wondering, no doubt, how long I will be away. The fact is, I cannot be certain. I ask questions, and I get partial answers, or lies, or glances that hold so much confusion it threatens to spill to the floor, yet every once in a while I learn something useful. I may be chasing around a bit, so I do not know how quickly I will get your letters, but I will arrange to have the letters chase me as required. I do not know, Kitty, but I hope that within a fortnight you will once more be holding in your arms your affectionate, adoring,

Richard

RICHARD COBHAM'S JOURNAL

OCTOBER 29

Arrived at Grey Hound, settled in. No sign of J, but place still in uproar over his leaving and the fight he spoke of in last letter. Have decided to use my own name, maybe stir something up. Will start asking questions tomorrow.

OCTOBER 30

Figured out some crossed-out phrases from J's last letter: "... six   years ... Ice-cliff ... admirably ..."; "... close, and   because   I   fear ... Engels ... interrogated ..."; and, "... Stone to the wolves ... cunning ..." Does no good at all for finding him, and damned little for understanding him, or this. Spent time dodging questions while asking my own. Am not very good at this. Everyone wants to know how I know "Jack." And I thought I was being so subtle!

OCTOBER 31

Saw J's mysterious coach go by! I wonder why he never mentioned the odd coat of arms. Wrote to Kitty. Walked around the area. People suspicious of me, will not speak. Cannot blame them. Damn James anyway.

1 Nov 1849

Kitty, my dear,

I've been a busy girl. I haven't shot anyone yet, you will be pleased to know (mostly, I suppose, because you'd be mad as fire not to have been there if I *had*). Nor has anyone shot me, and I hope you're pleased about that on its own account.

I apologize for the pen; its home is an inkstand in an hotel near a railway station, and in consequence it's a poor hired-hack of a pen. My own I absent-mindedly consigned to the care of the concierge along with the rest of my hand luggage. I am waiting for yet another train. I've been on such a lot of them of late, and waited in so many stations and hotels, that I genuinely cannot remember which one this is.

I'll take up the story the day after I wrote last. Kitty, you heartless unrepentant little flirt, you *do* remember Thomas Cavanaugh. He's the man you danced with three times at the Irvine's ball in Hampstead in order to make Richard jealous enough to fall into your hand like a ripe peach, if I remember the quote. Yes, *that* man, you wretch. He remembers *you* very well, though for the sake of your vanity I hesitate to tell you so.

He arrived for our meeting precisely on time, and was a little taken aback to find that he'd entered a private sitting-room at Bright's occupied by a young unmarried lady without chaperone. But I was charming at him, pulling out the "vivacious" and "delightful" stops nearly as far as they'd go, to try to smooth over the fact that I hadn't given him much choice about whether to come or not. He was rather haughty at first—blackmail affects some people that way, I understand. He sat on the edge of the settee and stiffly refused any tea.

"How wise of you," I said. "I'm having sherry, myself. Will you take a glass?"

He blushed to the roots of his hair—you'd think I'd asked him to undo my buttons. Gracious, after everything else I'd done, and what I now know he suspected I'd done, the spectacle of me taking spirits ought not to have made him blink. I poured us each a glass, set his in front of him, and sat back to study my guest. He's a nice-looking man, ignoring the bruises. Rather angular face and a longish aquiline nose, very noble Roman. Well-spaced hazel eyes, and a wing of brown hair that tends to fall forward into them when he looks down, which he does often. His linen was very neat, but his coat was shiny at the cuffs and collar, and his boots, though polished, had been re-sewn along the tops of the soles. He was turning the sherry glass between his fingers without drinking, and seemed to be working up to saying something difficult.

I thought I should forestall it, whatever it was. "Who gave you that beating?"

He started; then he replied warily, "I couldn't be sure. It was dark."

"Rubbish. You were certain enough last night that it had to do with my cousin, and that I was in danger of something like it because of what I've been up to. Who told you, by the way, what I'd been up to?"

Billy Harkness, it seems, had been active in the letter-writing line. He'd described a young *male* cousin of James's, however, who didn't correspond to anyone Cavanaugh had heard of. "But when I saw you, last night, with your hair all cut off, I realized that you could have matched the description Harkness gave. Though I couldn't credit that you might . . ."

"Don't be upset," I suggested, "I'm sure no one else could, either." Then I reminded him of his reaction the night before, when I had mentioned the names of the three men DuMont had said Harkness objected to. The short of it is that after a *lot* of dedicated browbeating, I got him to tell me how I could find the three men. I had to specifically assure him that I didn't mean to trip up to their front doors, bang the knockers, and ask, "Excuse me, but do you know anything discreditable about the past of the late James Cobham?" I might be unconventional, I said waspishly, but I'd never heard any connexion drawn between that and actual idiocy.

He was made terribly unhappy by the whole thing, poor fellow. I'm glad you didn't break his heart, Kit; he's quite a nice man and deserves better.

Information in hand, I had to plan my next foray. How *does* a well-bred lady of marriageable age intrude herself into the presence of a single gentleman with the intention of filching secrets? If one is very cold-blooded, one might choose to get herself in between his sheets. Or one might merely acquire the responsibility for changing them. .... But single gentlemen, especially single gentlemen of exhaustible fortune, don't keep large establishments. On yet another hand, *their lady friends often do.* Mr Gideon Johnson, for starts, had a *chère amie* who must have got a number of awfully nice presents in the course of her career, and who was in need of a superior sort of upstairs maid, since I'd just bribed her old one to go to Bournemouth for a fortnight. Heavens, if at this point my trunk fell off the baggage-waggon and came open, they'd be sure there was an entire theatre troupe travelling through by train! Another assortment of clothing required, as well as a glowing set of references which I had a grand time forging. You'd have done better, I know, but I tried to make you my inspiration in the task of writing four different hands.

Mr Johnson is on a ship somewhere, it seems, according to Madame's dresser. His lady had a letter from him during the two days I worked for her. He is too discreet to write more than his name in the corner of his envelope; but Madame was not too discreet to leave the envelope where a really determined servant might get a look—though the woman might well have *eaten* the letter itself, for all I could find it. This meant that when Madame began to pack in a hurry, your correspondent proceeded to do likewise, and was on the same northward-bound train. One carriage back, in fact.

Our destination was Manchester, where I am ashamed to say I eventually lost Madame. But I don't think it was a coincidence that Hugh Stone was also in Manchester. He escaped me and the whole rest of the world, darling: Stone took his own life in Manchester before I could even begin to study him. He was a shocking drunkard, according to the people who knew him there (who are few—he was only visiting), and none of them seem surprised that he did it. Poor man. Mr Cavanaugh said he'd been sent down from Oxford, and regarded him as untrustworthy at best. Still, I don't believe he deserved his end.

Which leaves Tournier, and since you think he might be dangerous, I shall approach him—or rather, the neighbourhood of him—with the greatest caution, and plenty of advance preparation. I know it must seem as if I haven't learned anything at all, but I have some hope of that turning around; I haven't given up. After all, if I stop now, what a sad waste of my curious new wardrobe!

Now, regarding your clue: this is perfectly maddening. Who the devil is Sir James? The only one I can think of with any connection to the family is James Pearse, who was our James's Irish great-grandfather. It can't be him, though—what would he be doing at Melrose in 1761? For that matter, I thought that your mother's marriage to Uncle Andrew was the first time there was any link between the Woodworth and Cobham families. Yet here's a Woodworth plotting furiously—what? a French invasion? Catholic emancipation? the summoning of succubi?—with Melrose Hall as a projected setting. Though it's true that gentility in Britain automatically conveys a certain amount of inbreeding, in acquaintance if not blood.

Still more confusing: I made a rather dusty search through the land records of the parish (I'm sorry, dear—yes, I *was* within a few miles of Melrose and didn't come to see you. I really couldn't; it would have weakened my resolve) and discovered that in 1761 Melrose Hall was one of the properties owned by the Callendar family, whose head at the time was Fitzhugh Callendar, who is Richard's and my (and was James's) great-grandfather. It certainly now belongs to Richard, but I could find no record of a transfer from Callendars to Cobhams. When Roderick Cobham married Mellisande Callendar, was it part of her dowry? Still, I'd think there would be paper on it somewhere.

It's funny that you should mention the Vicar's dormouse. Because it wasn't a dormouse scratching at all, was it? It was that foolish and unbelievably valuable little Chinese dog, and nothing was what it seemed to be. I shall take that as your instincts speaking, and remind myself not to accept the first explanation for anything.

Well, one of the things I was assured in the taverns of Oxford was that women have no carnal desire, that they cannot want physical love for itself because they have no erotic impulse to awaken, that they only *submit* to their husbands and lovers, and that only out of pure affection and a desire to please. Thus, you see, we are angels, and our greatest gift to the world of men is self-sacrifice. My, at least we're allowed the desire to *please*. And, of course, this means that men need not go to the time and trouble of pleasing *us* in that way, or learning anything of our individual pathways to delight, since we can be neither pleased nor delighted. Well. I suggest you go and find Richard now, twine your arms around him, and do whatever you think will serve to wrench his thoughts from business, literature, history, philosophy, or the racing news. You will be striking a blow for the freedom of our sex, darling.

Madame Blanche did indeed say many such things, pet, generally accompanied by lamentations that young ladies in their first season were not permitted *décolletage*. Self-knowledge is one of the keys to power, so you must simply come to terms with having a Shape.

My dear, what you describe isn't sensualism, only the pure obstinate determination to have our own way. And isn't it funny that anyone who knows us, socially at least, on hearing that one of us had gone haring off on an adventure like this, would assume it was you? and would be taken aback to learn that it was Miss Voight of the perfect manners and upright carriage and unruffled, rather stern demeanour? Not for me to explain to them that always knowing what to do with one's hands is an asset, not a liability, in a venture like this.

I must go: my train is due in ten minutes. Perhaps I should invest in more railway companies. Please write to me at Bright's, Kit, and don't fret about delays in my reply, since they'll only mean that I've gone out of town *again*.

> All my dearest love,
> Susan

SUSAN VOIGHT'S JOURNAL
(WRITTEN IN CIPHER)

Nov 1

In a railway carriage. I just wrote the cheeriest letter to Kitty; it makes me feel an awful hypocrite. Probably a waste of effort—she'll smoke me out in spite of it, I can never keep anything from her for long. And after her last letter, with her vowing us confederates—oh, my dear, my dear, I *can't* tell you all of it. You'd order me home, and I'd know you were right to do it. But if I turn my back on this horror now, what's to stop it from arriving on the doorstep at Melrose someday?

Until now, my letters to Kitty would do for tracking everything back to its source if anything happened to me. But having started to shade the truth, I'd better provide some documentation Just In Case. That's what this is. If Kitty doesn't remember our old cipher from the days at Miss Trevelyan's, I shall come back from the dead or out of durance vile and kill her.

We all have our talents. Kitty summons visions—at least, she believes she does, and I suppose I must accept that. Mine is memory, of conversations and events and faces and numbers. So I have considerable faith in the accuracy of the text that follows—*that* to anyone reading this later who thinks I must have made much of it up, since I couldn't have remembered it.

I mentioned blackmail in the letter, but didn't tell Kitty the extent of it. Cavanaugh wouldn't do anything but insist that I leave it lie, until I asked him if he'd seen anyone from the hotel on his way to my room. Yes, he said, one of the maids. Had anyone seen me greet him at the door? Was anyone in the passageway? No, he said, which I knew, but I had to make sure *he* did. And did he speak to any of the hotel staff at the desk? "You know I didn't," he answered me, becoming rather short. "You told me to come straight up and speak to no one." "Then," I said, "if I were to say that you weren't here at my invitation, but had forced your way into my room—for whatever purpose—is there anyone who could testify that it wasn't so? Besides yourself?"

He turned quite white, though I think he'd begun to see where I was headed before I got there. I didn't let him answer, but continued, "Artists, like ladies, are accepted on their reputations. Would a charge of either attempted rape or attempted robbery interfere with your getting commissions? I believe the members of the Royal Academy would hesitate to hang your work."

The sherry glass was motionless in his hands as he said, "I would manage somehow, I think. But you would be utterly ruined."

"I believe so. I hope you won't make that necessary." He didn't reply immediately, and I hurried to fill the breach. If I'd known my opponent, I'd have picked a better set of weapons; Thomas Cavanaugh was quite clever enough to push his way through my cobweb threats. The only reason he hadn't yet was because he was a little blinded by principle and convention. If I gave him time to think, he would use it. I said, "I'm sorry to have to play on your chivalry. It does you credit that I can."

His long mouth, which had always seemed so kindly and inclined to smile, was set thin and hard now. "I see," he said at last, "that there was more than one bloody-minded high-handed devil in your family."

"My cousin was the other?"

"He ... was always kind to me. But he was not an easy man to be friends with, nor even, at times, to be in company with. He had an instinct for finding the weak places."

I set that aside for later thought. "But he's dead now. What harm can there be in finding out how he lived?"

"I think that depends on how he died."

Well, one of us had to say it out loud, and it seemed Cavanaugh wouldn't. "You believe he was murdered?"

"I don't know that he wasn't."

"He was alone in the boat," I said. "It's a spot where the river widens out, just before it joins the Medway; we call it a lake, but it's not, really. And it's quite deep there, with a cross-current. He capsized."

Cavanaugh said, "He swam very well."

"He'd been drinking."

"For much of the time I knew him, he'd been drinking. It never made a great deal of difference. I sometimes wondered why he bothered."

"He was alone," I repeated, "and there was no one near him."

"Who saw it, actually saw it happen?"

I thought about it. "None of us saw the actual fall. My brother and my cousin Richard had been quarrelling on and off all day, and they'd reached rather a pitch. They were about to come to blows and Henry—another of my cousins—had stepped in to stop them when we heard the splash. He—James—was already underwater, but he surfaced for a moment immediately after, and we all saw him then. He *was* a good swimmer, we knew that. Both Richard and Henry were headed for the bank, to go in if he needed help, but not in any great hurry. And then he never came back up.'' I realized that I was sitting very straight and stiff and not looking at anything, so I stopped speaking.

''If he'd fallen in and struck his head,'' said Cavanaugh, ''he would either have come to the surface and stayed there, or not come up at all.''

Well, there. It wanted only that, I suppose, to put this whole project entirely out of my league. Except that I think I must have suspected, all along; I've behaved throughout as if I was conducting an inquest. Kitty was right when she wrote asking me to question my motives.

Cavanaugh was alarmed to find that I still didn't mean to draw back. I had to press him to get the full names and directions of the three men, and something about their characters and modes of life. ''Hugh Stone's a drunkard,'' he said, ''has been ever since he was sent down. I don't know what for, but it had something to do with James, and there's bad blood there. I don't think he'd do anything but weep at you, but a man with a jugful in him is unpredictable. Alan Tournier is another story. If his brain and James's had been horses, you could have got up a match-race worth wagering on. Clever lad, but fiery, short on self-control. He may have learned some, though, and if he has, watch out! He's Stone's friend, and won't hear a bad word about him.

''I'd tell you to stay clear of Gideon Johnson altogether, but that kind of thing doesn't weigh with you, it seems. I don't know anything against him, really. Except his manner, and that he keeps some shady-looking company, the sort of men you see hanging about on the fringes of prize-fights—well, that wouldn't mean anything to you. And he's never short of the ready, though he hasn't any employment and his family property, what there was, was more mortgage than bricks. Keeps a woman—'' He stopped short, blushing furiously, until I said,

"Of course he does. I am more than six. Go on."

"—a woman named Betty Howard, rather a bird of paradise, used to all the best. She has a house out near Waltham
Forest, and another place in Chelsea. Johnson's in and out of
town, but she stays put, and she always seems to know when
he's due back."

Those were the high points (or the low ones, depending on
one's outlook) of the conversation with Thomas Cavanaugh.
I'll continue to feel guilty about using him until something
worse comes along to feel guilty about, and maybe after. If I
survive all this, I shall spend a great deal of money commissioning paintings from him, in an effort to atone.

And so I became Betty Howard's upstairs maid, and it all
still seemed like a lark, even after I discovered that she carried
a little pearl-handled pistol with her everywhere, that she faithfully burned every letter she received, even the ones from her
dressmaker, and seemed desperately afraid of something that
never materialized. Until the letter from Johnson, that is, when
she terrorized her little French dresser with an outburst that
was half angry, half frightened, and largely unintelligible to
me, lurking in the passageway.

I didn't "lose" her in Manchester, in the sense that I let
Kitty believe. She went to a lodging-house in Droylsden,
where she stayed the night, leaving only once to go to a chemist's. The next morning, *very* early (I nearly missed her, and
had to scramble into my pelisse and dash when I saw her come
out) she left her lodgings and walked a good mile and a half
to a shabby inn at Fairfield, where she went straight upstairs
without seeking out any further direction, or even being seen
by anyone but me. The room next to the one she'd entered
was unoccupied, and I pressed my ear to the wall to eavesdrop.
(And thought, of course, of Kitty at Miss Trevelyan's, determining that a water-glass didn't conduct sound any better than
the plaster wall itself.)

Still, I could only hear perhaps one word in three. One voice
was male, and difficult to follow; a few words of a sentence
would be loud, the rest inaudible, as if the speaker were pacing, or ill, or both. Betty Howard's voice was low, but clear,
and I caught more of her speech.

She called the man in the room "Hugh," and I nearly spoke

aloud in surprise. Not Stone, surely? Cavanaugh had given me an address in London for him. What would bring two of my conspirators to the outskirts of Manchester at once? For I was certain that whatever Johnson was involved in, Betty Howard was connected to as well.

He offered her a drink, as best I could make out. She thanked him and said, "Don't get up, I can help myself. Will you keep me company, dear?" Several exchanges, then his voice saying, ". . . don't mean to do any . . . done now, isn't it?"

"Soon," she answered. "We'll be done soon, and then you needn't have anything more to . . ."

". . . his. Why should I . . ."

"You'll understand soon," she said, and perhaps he heard what I did in her voice. There was a bang, as of a piece of furniture falling over, and his voice raised suddenly, incoherently, saying something about wine. If I could have moved from my place, I would have stopped listening, but fear had frozen me stiff. So I heard the sound I dreaded, something partway between wheezing and gagging, and a hoarse cry suddenly muffled. Eventually all the noises dropped away. I heard someone moving around the room, and at last the door opened and shut, and footsteps passed down the stairs.

I didn't dare lose my quarry, but I couldn't leave whatever was in that room, not without being sure. So I went to see. I wish I hadn't, but I would do it again.

It was Hugh Stone, according to his pocket-book and a few other scraps of identification around the room. And he was dead of poison. He lay sprawled on his back, one arm flung across the fallen chair, his face unspeakably twisted and his eyes staring. Perhaps there are poisons that lead the drinker gently into Death. Hugh Stone had not been given one of them. There was a note on the table, incoherently phrased and untidily written, declaring that he could no longer outrun his miseries, and that he prayed those who had brought him to this pass would, if they still could, feel some shame for their actions. There was also a single glass on the table, tipped over and lying in its dregs, and an empty glass vial of the sort that chemists use. There was no second glass—except on the sideboard, where the carafe stood, and it seemed clean and dry.

But I leaned close and sniffed, and the sharp smell of claret was in it still.

I dashed down the stairs and out of the inn, still not meeting any of the staff—was the wretched place deserted? Betty Howard was no longer in sight. But she'd gone to such trouble to walk to Fairfield, that I doubted she'd risk being remembered by a waggon-driver now. I set off on foot for Droylsden.

She was at the railway station; she must not have gone back to the lodging-house at all. She was on the westbound platform. I bought my ticket.

I don't know why she got down at Phillips Park. I saw her out the carriage window and *flew* out onto the platform, and she must have seen me but for the bustle of the porters and hand-carts and passengers, all of which I shouldered through after her.

The account in the *Guardian* is quite accurate, except for one thing: she crossed the line at the bidding of a man on the other side of the turnstile, a tall, broad-shouldered man with a tanned, harsh face and a ginger moustache, dressed in a dark blue frock coat. He gestured impatiently, and never looked right or left, but only at her, his eyes angry and bright, and his lips moved as if he spoke to her, though nothing would have penetrated the station noise from so far away. I think she never looked elsewhere, either, or heard the whistle of the luggage train screaming.

When it was over, and I thought to look, he was no longer at the turnstile, and no-one I asked had seen him. I don't believe I was meant to see him, but I did, over her shoulder as she hurried toward the crossing. Now I have to ask: did he see me?

There was no blood at all, only the dreadful dark swelling over her left temple. Somehow in the bustle I was identified as "Miss Howard's friend," I suppose because I was the only one there who could answer the questions put by the constable, the surgeon, and the railway officials. So she was under my care on the way back to Droylsden, in the empty carriage commandeered as an ambulance.

Alone in an empty carriage with a murderess unconscious and dying. Mr. Poe, I suppose, couldn't have known the potential for horror of an empty railway carriage in daylight. She

lay on a pallet improvised between two of the benches and I
sat near, wondering what I was supposed to do if she suffered
convulsions, or even if she regained her senses.

Then her eyes opened and she began to speak. She was still
not conscious, not truly; she didn't seem to see anything before
her. By the time I realized that her first words might be rote-
learned Latin, she had changed to English, and I missed them.
They were followed by, "Of the four elements, water shall be
sovereign. Water shall drown air. Water shall wash away earth.
Water shall quench fire. I don't have to do this. I'm leaving,
I tell you, I don't care! No, darling. Never anyone else. Put
that down, you ignorant strumpet, and get out! Oh, she won't
make trouble, she's loyal to me. We can still stop. There's still
time. I don't mean to do any more dirty work for them. God,
he's dead, Bet, they got what they wanted, it's done now, isn't
it?"

In those last sentences I recognized the echo of Stone's
words in the inn at Fairfield, and realized that at least part of
the rest of the strange, droning speech was also Betty Howard
parroting back the words of others. It was as if the damage to
her brain had broken down a door that had locked her memories in, and they were stealing out in random order. No others,
however, reached her lips. She fell silent and her eyes closed
again. I had leaned close to catch her words, and so I saw now
that she had begun to bleed at last, not from the lump on her
forehead, but from her ear on that side, a slow dark trickle that
dripped into her brown hair. I am not so phlegmatic that the
sight did not horrify me, as much because it meant she would
not live as because of the blood itself.

I did not think to search her reticule until we had returned
to Droylsden, and I sat beside her in her room at the lodging-
house. The first thing that struck my eye was a letter, unmailed,
addressed in her hand to a J. Cobb at a posting-house in Langstone, in Hampshire. I opened it, of course. It was quite short:

> *This may reach you before the journals. Hugh is dead. If
> you would know more come to the West to the place you
> know of. If you come quick you will be safe.*
>
> B. H.

There was nothing else useful in her reticule, except the keys to her luggage. But in her luggage I found an enormous amount of money in bank notes, something over five thousand pounds. I think she hadn't meant to return to London. Was it an orderly retreat—would I find, when I went back, her two properties shut up and offered for sale, the staff scattered? Or would I find her households in confusion and the bailiffs at the door? One would suggest that this was part of the action of the conspiracy; the other, that she was fleeing her fellow conspirators.

I left after giving the landlady enough of the money to keep Betty Howard for longer than she was likely to need it, and to pay for a surgeon, which she was also not likely to need, and to bury her, if necessary, though I left the direction of both her residences in London, and the names of the most responsible of her servants.

Then I came back to London, and to Kitty's letter, which at least allowed me the space of a day jaunt to Tonbridge to look into the land records for Melrose Hall before I had to take up my pen in service of the most furious bout of lying by omission I can recall. Not, of course, before I investigated the state of the house in Waltham Forest and the elegant little townhouse in Chelsea. Betty Howard's residences are, indeed, in disorder. Both of them caught fire and burned to the ground on the night of the 26th. Several servants died at the larger house, including Miss Howard's French dresser. The deed to the house near Waltham Forest was in the name of Andrew Cobham.

I am a coward—I admit it. I can't bring myself to speculate based on that fact, or to investigate those speculations if I could. Not now. Nor can I bring myself to get closer to Alan Tournier. He seems to be part of this vile hornet's nest, and I'm not brave enough to face any more congress with murderers and plotters. So I shall retreat into the recent past, and make a wholehearted attempt to trace James's movements in '39 and after.

RICHARD COBHAM'S JOURNAL

NOVEMBER 1

Yesterday was All Hallows' Eve and did not even realize it, yet no ghosts appeared, no doors to Faerie opened. Almost disappointed. No one will answer questions. Emphatically disappointed.

NOVEMBER 2

Went to stable to visit J's murderous stallion, and no stallion, but found the bloody-damn volume of Hegel, along with a bloody-damn note for me! If I find J, I shall embrace him and then beat him senseless.

Richard,

I hereby return Hegel to your keeping. Though he is dear to me for his own sake and yours, he is a devil in one's luggage, and I'm afraid I must travel light. To that end, however, I've taken Aubrey's *Lives*, in the fervent hope that fate will allow me time for reading.

   I hope you didn't founder my horses on the way down. If so, you've cut off your own nose; I officially bequeath them to you.

                                                                James

P.S. There is a very good hostler's job going begging here. Have you considered honest work?

RICHARD COBHAM'S JOURNAL

NOVEMBER 3

Kitty has written back with information on Coat of Arms. How deucedly odd! The whole thing is going in a direction I had not expected at all. I would sacrifice half my fortune and throw in an Aunt or two for someone, anyone, who would give direct answers to simple questions. And the rest of my fortune and another Aunt for someone who could lead me to my mad, mysterious cousin! If this comes of reading Hegel, by God I will stick to David Hume.

NOVEMBER 4

Terribly excited. Out of nowhere, I thought of the horse. Will begin in the morning. Can hardly wait.

THE GREY HOUND
SUNDAY

My Dearest, Darling Kitty:

You have known me to do some peculiar things now and then, so you will not, perhaps, be surprised to learn that today I, entirely on a whim, purchased a dog. It is a hound, brown in colour, and I was assured its nose is excellent; it cost a mere £6, and looked at me with eyes as friendly as a kitten's; yet when you learn that my intention is to set out across the country allowing it to lead me wherever it may wish, you will conclude that I have gone utterly mad.

And, my love, it may be that I have. But I am searching for something, for a thing not easily found, and I will tell you, for you are not of the swooning disposition, that there may even be a touch of danger or intrigue in the search, which is why, even now, I will not tell you more details. But to reassure you that I have not begun hallucinating about the danger, nor about the peculiarity of the situation, I will tell that, not an hour ago, a woman came up to my room—a young woman, and not unattractive, yet with the coldest eyes I have ever seen. I opened the door, and, before I could say a word, she said, "Search if you wish, but if you fail you will be accursed, and if you succeed you will die horribly." Then she turned away, leaving me stunned and unable to move for several long seconds, after which I bolted out of my room down the stairs, and out the door, but she was gone as if she had never been there—which, you will say, she was not. But, my dearest Kitty, I had had a good night's sleep and tasted neither wine nor spirits, and felt in full possession of my faculties. Yet no one had seen her enter or leave, nor was there sound of any conveyance. Kitty, my sweet, this was in full daylight on the Sabbath, which ought to preclude any evil spirits, do you not think? But if I have enemies, and the enemies are flesh and blood, then I am craven if I let them hold me back from a task I have accepted.

On the other hand, should you fail to hear from me by the end of the month, go to the library, and there find the volume we read to each other our First Night, between the Shelley and the Ashbless, and behind it there will be a box. Open that box—it is not locked—and in it you will find certain letters that will answer your remaining questions while leaving a good deal more unanswered.

Ah, my sweet Kitty! Thinking of that volume, I think of you and of that night, and I believe it is the best single night of my life, and the only greater joy has been the succession of days spent in your company. Do I sound flowery and romantic, my love? Forgive me, I know it is neither your style nor my own, but something about these odd experiences has brought out an Irishman or a Magyar I had not known was in me—can you hear the fiddles laughing and crying as you read?

And now I must ask you to forgive my irony as a moment ago I asked you to forgive my sentimentality. It is all one, and I have something to do, and I confess to you, who know all the secrets of my soul save this latest, that I am frightened. I have a good sword by my side, but I do not believe this will be a matter of giving a pretty scar to a young man who pushes his way to a table I had claimed. I have my pistols, but I wonder how much good two small pellets will do against whatever awaits up the road. I have a sprig of mistletoe, and a silver mirror, and other items you will recognize, but I doubt their usefulness even as I fear to be without them.

I cannot help but think of poor, dear James, my love: he tried so hard to come to a *system*, when it was ever a question of *method*. I know this well, but what of my own method? What of dancing down an unknown road like a half-mad fool? What sort of method is it for a gentleman to write a letter to his beloved in which he fills her with fear he is not man enough to face alone? To ask you to share this fear, when you can do nothing to help, is basest sort of cowardice; I cannot justify it; I can only plead, as excuse, that all of my thoughts are of you, and, should the worst happen, it is you I shall regret losing, above any and all other pleasures in life. I hope this thought will go some way toward encouraging you to excuse your cowardly, but loving and devoted,

Richard

RICHARD COBHAM'S JOURNAL

NOVEMBER 5

Resting for the evening, one day of travel complete. Of every possibility that entered my mind last night as I slept and prepared for this, the one that did not occur to me was exactly what happened: after I gave the dog the scent from the blankets, it set off as if it knew its business, and I spent the day following it at an easy pace; it never occurred to me that the biggest problem I would have is that I would feel the complete idiot, following a leashed dog, subject to the stares of all passersby.

We have been heading west, toward Southampton, and have gone a good distance today. The dog made no objection when I wished to stop at an inn near Fareham, so that is where we rest for tonight, at the posting-house of the Willow, a place as like the Grey Hound as makes no difference. If our destination is, indeed, Southampton, the long journey I had prepared for will be rather short; we ought to be there well before noon tomorrow.

SUSAN VOIGHT'S JOURNAL
(WRITTEN IN CIPHER)

NOV 6

Forgotten my record-keeping here. A very cold trail, and one that has been much swept over with disfiguring brush, by James, mostly. I know him too well now, I think, to be unable to find some of what I mean to record here. Too well too late. One piece of my evidence from the most unexpected source imaginable. Or unimaginable—I certainly would never have. I will include it with these pages.

'39, beginning in February and intermittently thereafter, in London, living in a garret in Shoe Lane (as much for the principle, I think, as for any disguise of his origins or the convenience of the location) near Fleet Street, which he shared with an Irishman named Palmer. Remembered by some of the locals as "the two young Irishmen" (?). Others remember the smaller man (James from the descriptions) as English.

Mid-May to early July, '39, in Birmingham, several addresses, with gaps between. Landlady at one house hostile—referred to the "two Irish ruffians," said they were violent men, and that the police had taken up the smaller man on charges, but had later released him. Two? Was Palmer there as well? On further inquiry, the assertion of violence based largely on a very late-night arrival, the larger man bruised and cut and half-carrying the slighter one who was nearly insensible, his clothing blood-soaked, a large rough bandage around one forearm. Couldn't get a clear picture of the date of the incident, but riots and uprisings occurred regularly in Birmingham all summer. No record of his arrest as James Cobham (not surprising). Too many arrests, again because of constant unrest, to sort out a likely one under an alias.

Mid-July in London again. Movements after the end of the month uncertain, though he definitely returned to Shoe Lane several times between then and November. At that point decamped without notice. Landlord sold both men's possessions remaining on the premises, but from the description, nothing significant.

Acting on irresistible speculation based on the foregoing, I went to Newport, on the Welsh border. Some evidence, very uncertain, of the presence of the two men there on, of all things, All Hallows', at a public bonfire, where an old local dame seems to have made some sort of Three Witches-like fuss over one or the other.

If all of these dates and places are correct, and connected by anything more than coincidence, then I believe there was more than enough in 1839 to break a heart like his, and to extinguish the skyrocket.

I believe he was in Manchester in 1842; I know, because of my piece of evidence, that he was in '43. I might find out for certain if I could bring myself to go back there.

The trip to Blackpool in '47, I already knew, was a feint covering a journey to Ireland, where I believe he spent several months. I have not found any evidence of the man Palmer since '39.

Were the issues at hand purely political, he wouldn't have needed subterfuge and sleight of hand and this thorough professional obscuring of the trail. But Newport changes everything. Newport, and whatever he did after that. But what connexion, if any, does this matter have to Tournier, Johnson, and poor Hugh Stone?

LONDON
NOVEMBER 3ʳᵈ· 1849

Dear Miss Voight,

I write not to continue the discussions that have given me such pleasure, in person and through the medium of the post, but to offer you my most sincere condolences on the sad loss of your cousin James Cobham.

As I am sure you know already, my concerns in Germany did not prosper, and for the forseeable future I shall be resident in England. But the turmoil of my affairs prevented me from hearing your sad news before today. I know you must feel strongly what happened. To your grief as one of his family must be added that of a reformer. Those of us who are concerned in the desperate struggle of the working classes and the transformation of the social order know how little we can afford to lose such a man, so brilliant, so dedicated, so resourceful.

He and I met many times in Manchester in 1843, indeed before I made your acquaintance, dear lady. He did not speak out often in large gatherings, but when he did spoke well and with great effect. He could gather men to him, command their admiration and respect, and lead them under the most trying circumstances. At our last meeting he was deeply dispirited by events which even his skills could not direct and by a sad outcome which no effort of his could have averted, but for which he blamed himself very much. I said what I could to give balm to his suffering, though in light of the grim years which have followed that one, I gave but false hope. I give you now what I believe to be a true one: He will be remembered for his efforts, and by our actions and words in his name. This great suffering of the working people of England cannot continue unabated.

I have brought my friend Marx with me—he has come for the same reason as I!—and this time you shall meet him. I have told him of you. I look forward so much to hearing the two of you discuss matters dear to all our hearts, and I hope that you will do me the kindness to make him laugh with your excellent English common sense. As you will guess, we are not over-joyous now.

> Ever your good friend,
> Friedrich Engels

SUSAN VOIGHT'S JOURNAL
(WRITTEN IN CIPHER)

NOV 7

Part of my answer, possibly: Stone was in Birmingham in June of '39, if not before. The speculation that sent me to Newport means that there are several new people I can ask questions of, if they'll talk, if I can find them, if they aren't in Australia. News of Stone's death has appeared in the newspapers, and a few of his old cronies are in an elegiac frame of mind. So, they talk. Stone was in Birmingham.

I cannot stomach this any more. I feel nearly as bitter, as tired, as James must have in '39, in '42, in '48 perhaps. Was he bitter then? I am trying to remember. I think by then he was so good at hiding what he felt that even he might not have been sure. I fled to history to escape plots and bloodshed and found them waiting for me there. I will go to Melrose and tell all this to Kitty. Then perhaps I will go abroad. Kitty was right all along. I ought to have put on my black and wept into my handkerchief and gone on with my life.

MELROSE HALL
NOVEMBER 7th

Dear Susan,

Let me imagine you opening this letter while sitting as you do with your back so straight that Miss Purvins could never complain, although she wanted to, and you are sitting in the room of a respectable but simple inn, which is also severe, and you are wearing that adorable little chemise that makes your hair seem so dark and your skin so fair, and everything is very severe and constrained. Now that I have imagined that, I must ask you, Susan, to sit back a little, and let your shoulders droop, and allow your back to rest against the chair, and then you must take a deep breath, for I have news that you must not hear unless you are prepared, so do not, *do not* read any further unless you have at the very least taken a good, long, deep breath and do it right now!

Are you ready? Very well, here it is:

James is alive.

I know it is extraordinary, but there is no room for doubt, because I have read pages and pages of letters written in the last few weeks from James to my own Richard, who has known for these weeks and said nothing, though I knew some-

thing was up from the way he was acting, but I thought it was
a mistress, but now Richard is off after James, trying to rescue
him as if he were the hero of a book, only the book was written
by Malory or Spenser, or more likely Disraeli, while Richard
was written by Cervantes, and love him as I do, he is not cut
out for danger or intrigue, and I am frightened half out of my
wits for him, Susan, so I am going too, to a place called the
Grey Hound in Langstone near Portsmouth, which is where
James was until recently, only he has left for parts unknown
and now Richard is following him, and on top of everything
else, there are things in James's letters that I know Richard
will not have noticed, that, well, do you know, I greatly fear
that James cannot be entirely trusted, and once Richard decides
he likes someone he trusts him absolutely and without question. Sometimes I wonder how he reached his majority, Susan,
but you see it cannot be helped, and so I am off this very hour,
as soon as I have seen to the posting of this letter, which I
consider as important as the mission itself, because you must
know what is going on, but that doesn't mean I expect you to
do anything, on the contrary, now that you know, you must
decide what to do, and if you have anything to communicate
to me, the Grey Hound in Langstone should reach me, except
I shall be using the name Claire Donahue, because I look as
if I could be Irish, and then I can pretend to have a nice fit of
temper if I should get into a situation that requires me to escape suddenly.

After such news, I cannot imagine you want me to take time
to answer the rest of your letter, yet I cannot leave unanswered
such matters as your reference to my "shape," which I do
believe you are indulging in imagining on, because, as one
who must look at herself in the glass every day, the fact remains that there isn't quite enough of me *here* while there is
in fact a bit too much of me *there* and even, if you'll pardon
me, *there*, and the only thing that reconciles me to the disappointment of it all is that Richard has made it abundantly clear
on countless occasions that my shape is eminently suitable to
his tastes, most likely because he is seeing the shape he desires
in me, and if that isn't love, what is? but in any case he has
even proved that he means what he says by the excellent way
he demonstrates that if he ever shared the illusions you un-

earthed at the taverns of Oxford, he has thoroughly lost them, which statement must prove that I, at least, am entirely the sensualist, even if you deny it, except that if you were not at least somewhat a sensualist, my duck, you would not trouble yourself about the opinions of the Oxford taverns, would you then?

Sir James is, I think, Sir James Pearse, and I admit it is funny to imagine him and Old Woodworth summoning succubi as you put it, but as I recall my history everyone else was, around that time, so why not they? and as to the transfer from the Callendars to the Cobhams, why, it is odd, but I hardly think it important, with everything else going on, and yes, now I remember dear old Tom Cavanaugh, and I hope he recovers, for he is a nice fellow, far too nice to talk about my vanity, unlike some I could name, and by the way, I adore your remark about pulling out the "vivacious" and "delightful" stops, because it makes me imagine an organ with stops labeled "haughty," "gloomy," "cheerful," "moody," and everything else imaginable, and, thinking of it, I know ladies who do seem to play their own emotions as if they were playing just such an instrument, which must get awfully tiring, don't you think?

As for such matters as the dormouse, which was, indeed, an irritating dog, and Madame Blanche, I can only say that these matters somehow don't seem as important as they did yesterday, and with that I must stop and post this letter and be on my way.

In Haste, Your Affectionate
Kit

Darling, just as I was about to set off, the most remarkable letter arrived, delaying me considerably, because, having opened and read it, I find I must copy it and send it to you, because you ought to read it, and I cannot send you the letter itself because it was not addressed to me, but it came in an envelope, addressed to Richard, and the envelope also said who had sent it, so I couldn't resist, and now I don't know what to make of it, but maybe you will, so here it is, and now truly, I must set off or it will be night before I even leave the Manor.

Kit

Her Majesty's Frigate *Cormorant*
Southampton
The 6th Day of November, 1849

To Richard Cobham, Esq.

Sir:

Allow me to hope this letter finds you in good health, and permit me to offer my condolences on the loss, some few months ago, of your cousin, James. I say this in all sincerity because, although I will freely admit I was never kindly disposed toward your cousin, no trace of this enmity extends to his family, and the loss of a relative is, as I know well, a blow to the heart. And lest you think it unfeeling of me, Sir, to mention that James Cobham and I were not on the best of terms, allow me to explain at once that it is this circumstance which compels me to write.

Someone, Sir, has been asking questions about the past of the late Mr Cobham, and these questions have been directed, in part, toward me. Whether it is a question of foul play in his death, or of his activities while alive, or some combination of these, I cannot say; nor do I know who is asking these questions, save that there is no reason to believe it is Her Majesty's Government, with which, I assure you, I should cooperate instantly and fully to the best of my powers.

But I address you, Sir, to inform you of what is taking place, so that you may take whatever action you feel appropriate, and to assure you that, to the best of my knowledge, I have no information that would be of any use regarding any subject concerning your late cousin's life or death. I have no wish to involve the legal profession, much less the Royal Navy, in personal matters that could have consequences which cannot fail to annoy the family of the deceased; yet, should these

questions and intrusions continue, it may be that I will have
no choice; which is why it seems to me only right to inform
you of these activities, in the expectation that you will take
whatever action you consider appropriate.

> I remain, My Dear Sir, I assure you,
> Your most humble servant
> Lt. Gideon Johnson, RN

SUSAN VOIGHT'S JOURNAL
(WRITTEN IN CIPHER)

NOV 8

He is alive.

I've tried to write more, but Kitty's letter, laid on the writing
desk by my paper and pen, draws my eye each time I try and
I leap up again to pace the room. There, I have written that
much.

I've come back to the desk after an unregarded half hour
standing at the window, looking out at the dark and seeing
nothing. I should weep, I suppose. I don't know what I feel.

But my brain still serves me, at least. Kitty will not find
James at Langstone. The news of Stone's death is public, and
James must know it. If I leave immediately, I may catch up
with him before he moves again.

From *The Times*
November 8, 1849

SOUTHAMPTON, Wednesday, Nov. 7.—The Peninsular and
Oriental Steam Navigation Company's ship *Jupiter* sailed this
afternoon with the usual mails for Vigo, Oporto, Lisbon,
Cadiz, and Gibraltar. She had only a few passengers, a full
cargo, 30 bottles of quicksilver, but no specie. The next home-
ward mails from the same ports will be due on the 14th inst.
by the steamer *Montrose*. The *Pacha* will take out the next

Spanish and Portuguese mails of the 17th inst. The *Indus*, Captain J. Soy, is appointed to leave on the 20th inst. with the East India, China, and Mediterranean mails. The Royal Mail steamer *Severn* is to leave on the 17th with the usual West India and Pacific mails. The packet brig *Brilliant*, Captain Newton, arrived here on Monday from Madeira, having left Funchal on the 25th ult. On the evening of that day the *Brilliant* passed the outward bound West India steamer *Medway*, steering for Funchal-roads. The steamer was firing rockets. She left Southampton on the 17th of October. The brigs *Bart* and *Comet* arrived out on the 21st of October, both with passengers from Southampton. The yacht *Ocean Queen* also passed through the roads, bound to Africa. The *Brutus* arrived from Newport on the 21st. His Imperial Highness the Grand Duke of Leuchtenberg, with several gentlemen of his suite, visited the *Brilliant* on the 22nd, and was much pleased with this beautiful vessel, supposed to be the fastest merchant brig in the world. His Imperial Highness appeared to be in tolerable health. The Russian frigate *Pallis* had not arrived from Lisbon. She was hourly expected.

ROYAL SOUTHANTS INFIRMARY
(SENT FORWARD BY WYE)
THURSDAY

My Adored Kitty:

I have had a slight mishap, and am laid up at the moment, but I have been assured by Mr Browne, the surgeon, that I am in no danger, so there is no need to fear, nor any need to open that box of which I spoke in my last letter. I will, I think, be up and about within a few days, though my left collarbone is broken, which will be an annoyance to me.

I hope Mother isn't driving you to Bedlam, and that all is well. I saw a peculiar pendant a few days ago. It was silver, and took the form of a five-pointed star with a crescent moon to Dexter and a snake below, and I have been trying to remember where I have seen such a thing before. I remember little else about the fellow who wore it, though he seemed of the meaner sort and I did not care for him, but it has made me curious.

My mission appears to have failed, thanks to the mishap, so I believe I will be returning home soon, although I intend to stop for an evening in Langstone in case there is a chance to pick up the trail once more, but, failing that, as I expect, within the week you shall have once more in your arms your loving, devoted,

Richard

RICHARD COBHAM'S JOURNAL

NOVEMBER 8

Hospital. Fortunately, right arm is uninjured, so able to write to Kitty and reassure her, and will write this as well, as it may be important; surgeon still will not swear that I will live, and I ought to leave some record in case of the worst. Still feel weak and head seems to swim, room still fuzzy, could not say what surgeon looks like, although am sure I was not hit in head, and no bandages on head. Surgeon seems worried about how much water I am drinking. Funny that I am not nearly as frightened now, when I may die, as I was when setting out and feared attack; and not at all frightened when attack came, much too busy. The poor dog! Had only known him for two days, yet he defended me, and, perhaps, saved my life.

Memory seems good, so should write down what happened. Have already told police, who won't tell me if they believe me, or if they harbour suspicions, or who was the b———d who attacked me, but telling them has helped me to remember more clearly. I wonder why that should be.

The dog led me to Southampton, to the naval yards themselves, where I found myself looking out at a neat little frigate, while the dog turned about in circles, and I remember being a little excited to think that James had, no doubt, been standing in the very spot I was now only hours before, when I felt a pull on the leash and heard the dog growl. Now I should say it was full daylight, with a bright morning sun blocked by the building I stood against, but the shadows were not deep, and the notion that I could be attacked at such a time in such a place was the farthest thing from my mind; I am sorry to admit that my instinctive reaction was annoyance that the beast had allowed himself to be distracted, and I began to turn to upbraid the dog when I felt a horrible blow on my left shoulder, and then I was on the ground. I don't remember releasing the dog, so no doubt it was simply a case of the leash slipping from my right hand. I can remember telling myself, over and over, to draw my pistol, which I had been carrying in the pocket of my coat, but I could not make myself move for the longest time, and all I could hear was the growls of the dog. I started to get up, but at that moment I was hit again, square in the back, and I do not believe I have ever felt such a thing: pain, and a sudden loss of breath, indeed the feeling that I should never be able to breathe again, and red spots before my eyes. Yet somehow the panic propelled me to turn and this time I got to my feet, and found, to my surprise, that I was holding my pistol.

I got no clear look at my attacker, only the feeling that he was a squat man, poorly dressed, with large, unkempt whiskers growing in front of his ears and well down his cheeks, and that there was curly brown hair peeking out from some sort of grey cap. He had a cudgel in his hand, and I can remember staring at that hand, so that, though I might miss the man seeing him in a crowd, I nearly think I would recognize that hand, which gripped the cudgel as if it knew what it was doing, as he raised his arm to strike the dog again. The poor dog! He was still game, and snarling, but it was clear he was injured, for his hind legs would not work, but were rather dragged behind him even as he kept moving toward my attacker snapping his jaws. I thought to cock my pistol, which I had been carrying loaded and primed and to hell with safety, but I could not make my left arm move.

Ah, that is a moment I shall never forget! The realization, which seemed to take a horribly long time, that my arm would not obey the command of my brain was a terrible feeling, almost worse than the pain and the feeling of suffocation and the weakness of my knees, and I felt a terrible anger, not at my attacker, but at my arm, for betraying me! I was obviously not entirely rational at that moment, but who can blame me?

The man struck at the dog again, this time hitting him in the head, and that made me even angrier, so that if it were possible to kill a man merely through rage, why, he should have dropped down dead on the spot. In fact he did not, but rather began to turn, and I remember how surprised he was to see me on my feet and holding a pistol, perhaps two yards away from him; yet even now I cannot conjure a memory of the man's face, but somehow only of his chest, where his clothing had been ripped open, probably by the claws of the hound as it went for his throat. It was as if I were unable to raise my head, which I suppose is possible, but then, how am I able to remember that he seemed surprised, but still have no recollection of his features? I do remember that when he saw me he froze for an instant, and, I don't know how, but I was able to cock the pistol using my one good hand and my hip. My attacker took a step toward me, and I remember thinking, "I have fired, now my pistol is empty, and I shall never be able to reach the one in my other pocket," and then I thought, "I have missed him, damn it," and then he fell down on his back with blood blossoming from his chest—a horrible sight, yet it seemed positively beautiful to me at the time, which gives me a better understanding of the self-disgust James felt after his fight at the inn.

And then I was down on my knees, though I don't remember falling, and it was only then I recall hearing the discharge of my own shot, which proves that my mind was in a sorry state indeed! The noble dog was still snarling and, moreover, crawling toward the man as if to verily rip his throat out, but I cannot say if he did, because the next thing I remember was waking up in hospital.

The police will not tell me what became of my attacker, though I should be surprised to learn that he had lived, but the dog, they tell me, had to be put down, which saddens me, because it is the first time a living being has made such a sacrifice for me, and, though it was only a dog, I would wish to be worthy of such a gift.

That is all I can remember of the attack, and now that I have written it down, which has taken me three hours, I believe I must rest again.

NOVEMBER 9

Who attacked me? And why? And why will the police tell me nothing? If they are suspicious of me, why am I not arrested, and if they are not, why not tell me about my attacker?

THE SPINNING MAID, OPENSHAW
9 NOV 1849

Dear Cousin,

I expect you'll bolt upon receiving this, but on reflection, I can't bring myself to behave as if I'm snaring a rabbit. I have no desire to trap you, or to make you feel trapped. Bolt if you like. It will tell me more clearly than any words that I am to leave you alone henceforth.

Nor do I mean to threaten you with exposure *in absentia*. I will tell you that I know something of how you spent your year's leave from Oxford, only to make clear what I refer to when I say that that, too, need not weigh with you.

But I should like to speak to you, if only to be able to assure Richard and Kitty that you're well and don't need any of us. They have both gone haring off after you. Since you know very well that neither of them are any more fit to be involved in this than a pair of nursing lambs, I trust that for the sake of their safety at least, you'll consent to see me.

I won't keep you long. I shall come to Fairfield tomorrow morning at half-past ten. If you're there, then I shall see you, and we can each speak our piece and part. And if you're not, that will spike my guns, since I'm afraid I can't guess at your next destination even if I were determined to follow you to it.

I think your present location is moderately safe, by the way. Your enemies would not have expected you to concern yourself with the passing of one of their number. And Miss Howard meant to send you westward, for her purposes or theirs.

Perhaps I will see you tomorrow morning. If not, know that my thoughts go with you, and that they are kind ones, meant to sustain and not to weaken you.

With good will,
Susan Voight

9 NOV.

You may come.

J.

RICHARD COBHAM'S JOURNAL

NOVEMBER 10

Surgeon has pronounced me out of danger, for which I ought to be grateful, yet somehow now I am frightened. Odd that I should become more frightened when told I am not about to die, but I told Kitty I was in no danger, so at least I will not be made a liar and a corpse at the same time.

I managed to reach my overcoat, and was pleased to find my other pistol, still loaded and charged, in the pocket. I have placed it under my pillow, where I can feel it even now as a reassuring yet annoying lump.

THE POSTING HOUSE OF THE GREY HOUND
LANGSTONE, NEAR PORTSMOUTH
NOVEMBER 10th

Dear Susan,

I do not know why I am troubling to write to you, when I know very well that you are nowhere to be found, because while I cannot imagine what you might do after receiving my last letter, I know that the one thing you will not do is stay where you are, so you will be off in some direction and perhaps this letter will chase you all over the world, but I am writing anyway, because I have no one else to talk to, because one thing I had not expected about having these sorts of adventures is how lonely one feels, perhaps because one is making one's self even more alone by using an alias, perhaps just because one is surrounded by strangers, which I am not used to, although I know that you are by now. I have spent three days here, and I do not know if there is anything more to be gained, but at least I know that James was here, and I know that Dick was here, and the poor dear, Dick I mean, shone like a lantern at midnight and made everyone suspicious so that they are still talking about him, and there is a great deal of speculation that he works for Navy Intelligence, and some that he is a French spy.

The landlord's wife is named Eileen, and she is an absolute dear, a short plump woman who is always snapping at some-one but she does not mean it at all, and last night we sat down with some sherry and talked about nothing at all important and I learned nothing, but it was so entirely pleasant that I abso-lutely fell in love with her, she is so kind and good-natured that it makes me yearn to have a little inn of my own, just because it must be good for one's soul, don't you think? Eileen has been married for eleven years, and always talks about her Jack and how he saved her from spinsterhood when she was eight-and-twenty but she says it with a sort of cynical lilt, as if she is laughing at him, but she is really laughing with him, do you know what I mean? and she has her three boys, or "beasts" as she calls them and threatens to do the most terrible things to them, but they just laugh, even the littlest one, An-thony, who is an absolute angel, and if I could be sure of having one like him I might change my mind about children, but I can't so I won't and that's that.

I am rambling, my dear, because I'm lonely and I want to be talking to you, but of course you are out and about so this letter will not reach you, and you probably do not have time to write because you are too busy having adventures, which I suppose I am too, but it doesn't feel like an adventure, or even an intrigue, it just feels like staying at a pleasant country inn.

Do you know, Susan, sometimes I envy you your ability to just go out and do things. Although I am doing things too, I feel as helpless as, well, as Richard was, though I do not sup-pose he felt that way, but then I think what you have given up, and I do not know if I would care to make that trade, because, Susan, you are independent, but you have sacrificed something for it, and that is the family, at least the family the way I know them, though of course this family is not the easiest to be part of or associated with, and we all have problems from time to time, but by isolating yourself as you do you deprive yourself of part of your identity, and more than that you deprive yourself of support in times of trouble. Whatever annoyance we feel toward the Legion of Aunts, as we have called them more than once, I know that if I am ever in need I can call on them, and I wonder if you can say the same, and if not, are you certain you will never be in need, for all of your independence?

There, I'm lecturing you again, and I know this is a horrid time to lecture you, and with what I have been doing here I am the last one to be lecturing, so I suppose I should close now and get some rest, and maybe tomorrow I will learn something. I will write again, even though you may never see this. Until then, my dear, I remain your devoted friend, cousin, and almost sister,

Kit

A letter has reached me. Dick has been in an accident and I fear for his life, and I hope somehow this letter reaches you, and if it does, please come at once to the hospital in Southampton, I have no one else to turn to. And beware of David, he is involved in this somehow!

Kit

10 Nov 1849

Dearest Kitty,

I have found James. He is well, bodily. No, that sounds as if his reason is less so. I don't mean that. But he is so changed that, however similar his person may be to what it was when I saw him last, his mind is a stranger's. Or it may be that I mistook the set-dressings, flies, and stage curtain for the architecture of the stage itself, and am only shocked by the sight of the proscenium arch undraped and the boards laid bare at last. I don't know what I am watching in progress, what play I should expect to see mounted there. And he is not, now, a man one can ask such a question of.

Please, Kitty, please go home to Melrose Hall, and make Richard do the same. I know you can keep him there, and you must. "Danger" has a fine, exciting ring, and seems a synonym for "adventure", but the true words in the case are very different. The story was not written by Malory or Byron or Scott but by the implacable hand of history, which doesn't care about single lives or single fates.

I am not so stupid as to think you will do it only because I've told you to. So I will pay you to oblige me in the most valuable currency I can offer you: the secret James has kept for ten years, that has led at last to this scoured precipice. I don't have his consent to this. To commit what I have learned and he has revealed to paper and then to the mails would be the worst sort of foolhardiness, if I didn't think that his transportation and slavery in Australia, should it come to that, would be better than his death in England.

James was active in the Chartist movement from 1839 until last year. I know that you find these things less than engrossing, and may only have the mistiest notion of what that entails, so I shall tell you that he supported the adoption of the People's Charter, which would give Britain something akin to a true representative Commons. That at least is the political aspect of the business; there is a great deal of social reform proposed as well, which with the genuine reform of Parliament could be got on with.

Proclaiming yourself a Chartist is not, in itself, a dangerous thing, though you will find people who will tell you that the Chartists as a body mean to abolish the monarchy and behead everyone in the House of Lords and are all guilty of treason for the mere mention of the Six Points. But James was rather closely involved in several of the uprisings for which the leaders were arrested and transported, and was one of the faction that endorsed the use of physical force. Not to put too fine a point on it, Her Majesty's government would still be interested to an uncomfortable degree if someone were to come forward and tell them where James Cobham had been, intermittently, during the last ten years, and whom he'd been with, and what he'd put his hand to.

Two of the people who could do that are Gideon Johnson and Alan Tournier. Hugh Stone was another.

And if you ask me what all this has to do with James's almost-drowning and disappearance, I shall scream. I don't know. Possibly nothing. The only way I know to find out is to stake James out, figuratively, like a goat and see what comes to eat him, and I don't think he would care for it. I can't tell you where he is right now, and there's no point, anyway. He will undoubtedly disappear overnight, the damned nuisance. I shall go back to London and propose marriage to Thomas Cavanaugh. I shall fling myself at Friedrich Engels's head—I got a very nice letter from him recently, with a clue in it. No, on second thought, I wouldn't have Engels, it turns out that he knows James. I shall find a nice Peruvian peasant who has never heard of James Bloody Cobham and live with him in sin. I shall take the veil, ideally in China.

I would love to know which of your talents urged you to suggest that this unlovely plot was the construction of Mr. Disraeli. Reread *Sibyl*, darling, with an eye on the politics. And for you to bring yourself to say that perhaps James cannot be entirely trusted—well, from a woman who won't speak ill of my brother, it says a great deal. I believe you are right. I'm also afraid that at this point, the observation makes very little difference to any of us.

As for letters from Lt. Gideon Johnson, R.N.—good God! He makes no mention of Betty Howard nor of poor Stone, but only complains of people asking questions. Of course, he wouldn't expect Richard to know anything of Howard or Stone, and he'd be on the money there. Is this a bluff? Might he be frightened? Why warn Richard off at all? In light of what I know now, the suggestion that he would answer any questions put to him by the government about James is a nice counter-threat—but Richard wouldn't have recognized it as one. Or would he? In those letters from James to Richard, is there any suggestion that Richard already knows about James' more extreme forms of political commitment? You will suggest I ask James, but as I mentioned, I don't count on finding him in the neighbourhood come morning. Besides, I don't think I could. You haven't met the new James.

I'm sorry, dear, but my brain has simply given me up as a bad job. I have to *try* to sleep, though I have no expectation of more success in that quarter than I had last night or the night before. I am living on bread and cheese, apples, coffee, and the invigourating outrage and bafflement that is the lot of anyone in the vaguest proximity to James Cobham.

If I can convince him to flee promptly to the Americas, I will. I'm not sure what will happen if I can't. Go home to Melrose, Kitty darling, and light all your candles and think of me. I have no idea what I'm doing, but I know I must do it well.

All my love,
Susan

SUSAN VOIGHT'S JOURNAL
(WRITTEN IN CIPHER)

10 Nov 1849

Such comfort in the recitation of simple facts. How I wish I knew some! The ones I know aren't simple, and the rest— well, who's to say?

I should go back to London. How I wish I could just go back to London.

There's a half-ruined barn across the lane from the inn at Fairfield where Hugh Stone died. I took up my vigil there, in the window of the loft, and waited. I knew he would be there already; it was only a question of, was he *still* there? I sat for a long, cold, cramped afternoon and was finally rewarded. My perch was a little farther from the inn than I would have liked, and somewhat screened by the half-bare branches of trees, but when the figure rode up on the dark chestnut horse, I knew it was James. I thought of my letter from Delilah Talbot, of her recognizing him, unknowingly, on the street in Dublin from his carriage and movements even in an ill-fitting disreputable jacket. The disreputable garment was a coat this time, a great dark thing like the plumage of a moulting raven. He was hatless; his hair was an unrelieved black in the apocalyptic light of sunset, with none of the subtle warmth I was used to in its color. But the easy economy with which he swung from saddle to ground and the straight line of his shoulders stopped all my scurrying thoughts for an instant. It was true. Kitty might have been mistaken, or the letters to Richard might have been forgeries, but she wasn't, they weren't. It was James, alive.

My heart and my brain spend too much time in each other's company. I should have walked in on him then, and taken advantage of as much vulnerability as he would ever be prey to. But I let sentiment interfere with reason. Or I didn't follow reason to its conclusion: that the man whose past I had just recently disinterred would greet the sight of me in a way that my treasured, maddening, ornamental, wayward cousin James would not. A lesson, I suppose, worth learning.

And so I had a note delivered yesterday evening, with instructions to the boy who carried it to give it into the hands of the man who fit his description, who rode the dark chestnut horse. It took an hour and several drafts to write that note. When his answer came, I still wasn't warned. But it was as if I were standing in thick fog, only barely beginning to distinguish the first outlines of a land completely strange to me in place of the familiar landscape I'd expected. I didn't sleep particularly well last night.

The frost was heavy this morning, like a thin fall of grey snow. I wrapped my cloak on over my habit, mounted my hired mare, and trotted down the road to Fairfield, back straight, hands low, heels down, and my heart flinging itself against my ribs like a caged ape. When I looked back over my shoulder, the mare's prints were visible in the frozen grass, impermanent as the bread-crumbs in a German fairy-tale.

I'd entered that inn before at mid-morning, behind Betty Howard who carried murder in a little vial in her reticule. I had a sudden dread that I might be bound for the room Hugh Stone had died in. But a slatternly woman looked into the dim, shabby passageway from the common room as I came in the door, frowned, and said, "If you've come to talk to the lodger, he's there," with a jerk of her head at a door farther along. Then she ducked back in, and I didn't see her again.

The door she'd indicated opened on a private parlour, also shabby but weakly lit with morning sun through one dusty little window, and with a fire that did not, thank heaven, smoke. I thought for a moment that she was mistaken and that the room was empty. The only warning I had was a slight movement that drew my eye to the arm of a high-backed chair drawn up before the fire. I had barely an instant to see the hand that lay there, fingers arched on the scarred wood, before the man attached to it stood and turned to me.

"Good morning," he said. "I trust the ride over was uneventful."

The voice belonged to James, but the words and the tone were a stranger's, civil, cool, and relentlessly empty of anything but the bare meaning of the words. The face was James's, if he had been starved or sick or passed through some other ordeal. There were shadows under his eyes, and hollows as if the bones of his face were arched bridges spanning only empty air, and a healing scar pale against the weather-darkened skin that disappeared beneath the edge of his open collar. His hair was longer than I'd ever seen it, and damp, and spectacularly untidy, as if he'd given up combing it with anything but his fingers. He wore neither coat nor waistcoat; indeed, the room was too warm for either, but once it would never have occurred to him to be in the presence of a lady without both, or without a neckcloth. I wondered if he meant it for an insult, or if he was simply past caring about anything beyond utility.

None of the things I had planned to open the conversation with could be said to that face. I scrabbled together some of my scattered self-possession and replied, "I didn't fall off, if that's what you mean."

Shockingly, the colour went out of his face for an instant. I nearly leaped forward to catch hold of him. But it was only an instant. Then he smiled politely and nodded toward another chair, less worn than his own. "Sit down if you like."

"If I like?"

"It's up to you."

I moved to the hearth, where I unfastened my cloak and laid it on the sideboard. "Your manners," I said brightly, "are always perfectly suited to the occasion." I was closer to him now, and could smell soap, faintly. He was freshly shaved, and the shirt looked meticulously clean. That much of the familiar James was still there: clean as a cat, whatever else.

"They are," he said. "I gathered from your note that I can dispense with a certain amount of pretense in your company. As it happens, I'd prefer to dispense with it all. That way I don't have to keep track."

"Welcoming me, then, would be a pretense."

The mantel was shoulder-high on him. He rested one arm along it and leaned there, regarding me, his eyes half-closed and wholly impersonal. "I don't recall inviting you to share all my secrets and turn over all the sod of my history. I would think, in fact, that the difficulty of digging it out would suggest to you that I wanted it left alone. Yes, I think welcoming you would be bloody hypocritical."

Said that way, without heat, it had the force of a blow. I found the offered chair behind me and dropped into it. "You didn't have to respond to my note," I said finally.

And that, to my amazement, cracked his reserve. "Oh, of course not. I could leave a delicately-brought-up young woman to ride unaccompanied—unaccompanied? Of course—two miles on a public road in a strange place with absolutely no certainty of meeting anyone at the end of it, thus requiring her to turn around and repeat the performance to no purpose whatsoever. I do it every day."

I closed my mouth, and had it opened for me again by a crack of rather mirthless laughter. "My God, James. After the things I've done in the last month? My God!"

"What have you done?" His eyes were no longer half-closed.

I sat in the full force of that look and tried to steady my nerves enough to speak, tried to decide what he most wanted to know, to be economical and sensible and cold because that, obviously, was how he wanted to conduct this interview. At last I said, "Hugh Stone was poisoned. Betty Howard did it, upstairs. I was in the next room. She had a note that she meant to send to you—here, here it is, I took it out of her reticule. She didn't send it because she died, too, a few hours later."

I stopped then, because I was holding out Betty Howard's note and he wasn't reaching for it. His eyes were on me, and his face was completely still, as still as the room had become.

Then he turned his back on me and propped one foot on the fender, his head bent as if to watch the fire. His hands hovered, as if seeking the pockets of a coat he wasn't wearing; after a moment he laid them both flat on the mantelpiece.

I realized at last that he wasn't going to move or speak, and I could give up waiting for it. There had to be something to guide me through this wasteland of a conversation. If I couldn't find it in James himself, perhaps I could find it elsewhere in the room.

The disreputable coat he'd had on yesterday lay on a bench beside the fire, a heap of rusty black. There was no sign of a hat. Beside the chair he'd risen from when I entered was a little round table that held a candlestick with an unlit candle, a dusty brown bottle, and a thick glass filmed at the bottom with dark amber.

"You've been drinking," I said, and immediately wished I could unsay it.

He raised his head. "I hadn't expected this to be an easy meeting. How lovely it is to find one's expectations fulfilled. Yes, I have been drinking. It wasn't wise, but neither was the alternative. To be honest, this whole passage is unwise, and I begin to suspect the onset of senility on my part. *You* may supply your own excuses; I refuse to take responsibility for those, too."

Some change in his voice at the end of that speech caught my notice. "You aren't responsible for anything of mine."

"Nothing at all?" he asked, sounding nearly cheerful, and turned at last back to me, his elbows on the mantel. It was meant to look relaxed, but it reminded me of a crucifixion. "Then you visit inns that aren't fit to house purse-snatchers because you fancy them, and consort with murderers and scoundrels because you enjoy their company? You put yourself in danger because you have a taste for it? You would do just as you have done, had I never been born?" This time his movements were not casual; he twisted away as if out of the grip of some strong hand and strode to the little grimy window. He didn't lean on anything there. He simply stopped, and his shoulders rose and fell with the force of his breathing.

"Which scoundrels did you have in mind?"

"In the absence of any others, my dear, I'll do." The voice

light with lack of air. Nothing to judge him by but the voice.

I knotted my hands together, pressed them securely down on my knees, and said, "Why did you agree to meet me this morning?"

A fragment of silence. "I don't remember."

I was exhausted, and I hadn't done anything. I tried to gather my thoughts together, to assemble the facts that I had that he might need to know, because as soon as I had given them to him, I could leave. He wanted that. I was close to wanting it. But tension and frustration made my memories spin and fall like dust motes, random and unrelated. I would have to simply tell him everything, in order, and I didn't think I could share the room with him for that long.

Then he said, "And what in hell did you do to your hair?"

Caught off guard, enmeshed in my mental struggles, I answered. "I cut it off. When I went to Oxford to ask about you, I dressed as a man."

His shoulders quaked, once, twice. Then he stalked back to his chair and fell into it. His hands loose on the arms, his head against the high back, his eyes closed—he was laughing.

"I suppose you think you're responsible for that, too."

"No. Oh, no. That's beyond what I can take credit for. Dear grinning Protestant God. Would you like a drink? I think there's another glass around somewhere."

Everything I had tried to judge the conversation by—his behaviour, his voice, the strength of my emotions—had thus far failed me. I found his laughter almost reassuring, because I could make nothing of it, good or bad. "Yes, thank you," I replied at last, "I think I'd better."

It was brandy. I took a gulp, and coughed.

"If you sip it, that doesn't happen."

"I know. I'm only drinking it for the shock."

His mouth curved up. "You've not had enough yet this morning? You must be the devil of a girl for a shock, *mo chridh*."

I had no idea how to answer that.

"All right," he continued, "I'll try to recover my reputation for good manners. You're the guest, so you may decide where we ought to start."

"Start?"

"Our various recitations. Would you prefer to ask me questions, or to relate the series of events that brought you here?"

It was going to be easier than it had promised to be at first; but he was still all steel underneath, however considerately sheathed. "I haven't many questions. May we start with those?"

"Certainly."

"In '39, you took leave from Oxford. You were in London until May, when you went to Birmingham for several months—" (I thought of the story of the two young men coming home late, one of them blood-soaked and half-conscious. I closed my teeth over the emotional digression, because it wasn't what he wanted.) "—and then back to London. In the last days of October, you went to Wales."

"I went to the city of Newport, as I think you know." The steel shone out again. I should not have begun with '39, but it was too late. "Your list of dates and places is admirably accurate. Should I accustom myself to the idea that the list is generally known?"

"No. Your trail was hard to follow, and I had a few advantages that others might not. You were in Manchester in '43, Ireland in '47, among other places."

"Very good." He applauded soundlessly. "And your conclusion?"

There was not enough air in the room to fill my lungs. "You were a Chartist agitator."

His expression frightened me, for all the things that weren't in it. "*Brava.* Right down to the past tense. Because, of course, my cause is dead."

"Is it?"

"Third time's the charm, my dear. The petition in support of the People's Charter was submitted to the Commons three times. Three times it was ignored. Not voted down, *ignored.* They did everything but take it to the top of the clock tower and drop it in the Thames wrapped 'round a brick. In '42 it came accompanied by over three million signatures. Half the adult male population of this green and pleasant land. And still the Commons refused to consider it. My sympathies are all with Guy Fawkes, though I'm sure we'd regret the loss of the Palace of Westminster."

"Were you surprised? You meant to unseat them."

"No, we didn't. They were welcome to keep their bloody seats, if they could convince the adult male population of Britain to re-elect them on a yearly basis. I confess, with most of them, that would have been a job equal to plowing the whole of Sussex with a spoon. Am I supposed to be content to see my nation the last one in Europe with the mummified corpse of feudalism tied to its back?"

"You don't speak," I said slowly, "like someone whose cause is dead."

"I speak like a man who has outlived his cause. At least Guy Fawkes was hanged."

"I . . . would prefer you weren't."

"Well, you'll notice that in the final accounting, I prefer it, too. There were several times when martyrdom was available to me for no more than the price of standing still."

"In Birmingham?"

"What about it?" he said, each word precise.

"There was an incident I heard of. You were brought home hurt by—another man."

"Seamus Palmer. They took to calling us the Two Jimmys, early on. We worked together well."

"Was that one of the times you didn't stand still?"

For answer he rolled up his left sleeve and held out his forearm, elbow and palm out. The scar was glossy and perhaps eight inches long, nearly from wrist to elbow. "Sabre cut," he said. "It laid bare a good bit of the bone. I thought it was a better idea than letting it come down on my head, though. They use the infantry against rioters, but the officers prefer to be mounted, and being gentlemen, carry swords as well as firearms. It all reinforced my prejudices against a career army."

"And Palmer?"

"Saved my life. It got to be a habit with him, I think."

"What happened to him?"

"Unfortunately, I'd never developed the habit of saving his. Newport was supposed to be one of several simultaneous disturbances, widely scattered. We were sent to Wales at the end of October to warn Frost that there had been an informer, that the plans and leaders in Wales and in the North were known.

Frost, the inflexible bastard, simply went ahead. Twenty people died on November 4th. Jimmy Palmer was shot twice in the gut, and died three hours later in my arms.''

"I'm sorry," I said, thinking of bombazine and black-bordered handkerchiefs.

"Yes, well, so was I. You'd have liked Jimmy Palmer. He'd have been reduced to absolute stammering incoherence by you, which to do him justice very rarely happened. Hold on—you've read Flora Tristan, haven't you? Her *Promenades dans Londres*?"

The apparent change of subject caught me out. "What? Yes."

"Then you've nearly met Jimmy. Call up the contents of that prodigious memory of yours, and remember her account of the Chartist meetings she attended. Who did she meet?"

I recalled the pages he referred to. "O'Brien and O'Connor—"

"The young ones. The promising fellows."

"This is beginning to feel like a recitation of capitals in a geography lesson. . . . Stephens?"

"Now there was a fire-eater. If they were all like him, I might have turned Methodist. And?"

"My God," I said, for I did remember. *A man from the ranks of the people whose towering height proclaims his strength. . . . He is the typical handsome Irishman—regular features, a mass of black hair, dark skin, flashing deep blue eyes, a mouth and chin expressing the depths of his passions, and an air so resolute and martial that just to look upon him evokes the sight and sound of battle.* "Palmer."

"Flora Tristan was one of his few moments of stammering incoherence, by the way. She was ten years older than he was, but she had very fine eyes. Do you, by chance, remember her third promising young fellow from those pages?"

I resigned myself to the effort. "Another Irishman. 'A thin, pale young man with a delicate constitution, one of those frail beings for whom existence is perpetual suffering. One of those poetic souls who think only of human progress and are happy only in the happiness of others.' "

He was smiling, a sardonic half-expression. "And I quote. 'The poor boy believes in God, in Woman, in self-sacrifice.

He is twenty years old, his great love embraces all humanity, hope shines on his brow, his trust is boundless.' The Saint of French Socialism was perhaps a little overheated, but not entirely inaccurate. He was nineteen, actually, and already had his doubts about God. Otherwise she was more or less on the mark.''

I stared at him, and he raised his eyebrows at me. "An Irishman?" I blurted out, all the time thinking of the mixed reports of the nationality of the two men in London and Birmingham.

"Five minutes in Jimmy Palmer's company and I talked like the world's own son of Erin for an hour after. Couldn't help it. Oh, and the delicate constitution was a common and sometimes useful misconception, except that living in that damned draughty attic made me cough."

I rubbed my eyes fiercely, because for no very good reason the tears had sprung to them. He would not, I could tell, stand for tears. "I'm sorry. I'm all on end, I'm afraid. I can't seem to think properly. I didn't sleep very much last night."

"Neither did I," he said, almost gently. "Tell me how you found me, and what else you've learned. What is this note from Betty Howard?"

Such comfort in the recitation of simple facts. I believe he knew that, and knew that I needed the refuge of intellect. I told him all of it from the beginning, leaving out only the untidy trappings of my emotions. He reacted strongly only once: when I told him whose name was on the deed to Betty Howard's house. Then he turned pale, and I stopped, until he told me, in a level voice, to continue.

"Kitty was indiscreet," I finished, "but only out of fear for Richard, and only to me, and she knew I could be trusted. Richard never gave you away."

"Do you know, I never thought he had."

"Was Stone involved with the Chartists, too? And Johnson, and Tournier? And does this have anything to do with Stone being sent down from Oxford?"

He granted me, after a moment, one of his half-smiles. "Yes, yes, and yes, each in his own way and to his chosen degree. And yes. You seem to have shown a shocking amount of natural talent for intelligence work in all this."

"Thomas Cavanaugh said something similar. He wasn't being complimentary."

"I'm not sure *I* am. I'd offer you lunch, but the food here is abominable, and the wine is worse."

I smiled at that. "I know. My landlady went on at great length. If you'll let me fetch in my saddle-bags, I can supply the remedy."

"Resourceful beyond expectation. Even my expectation, and I ought to know better. You've been corresponding with Friedrich Engels?"

"Yes," I said, and fled to the stables for the food.

When I'd put out the cold chicken, cheese, bread, salad, fruit, and a bottle of wine on a deal table at the other side of the room and drawn two chairs up to it, he asked, "Why didn't you bring this with you when you first came in?"

"If you were going to be beastly to me, I wasn't going to feed you."

"You mean to tell me I was not the very definition of beastly?"

"Not all the time."

"I am not irredeemable. Thus, I may eat. I'm glad of it. The food here really is awful. What in the name of propriety moved you to exchange letters with Friedrich Engels?"

"What if I told you that, like Flora Tristan, he has very fine eyes?"

"I wouldn't believe a word of it. You should have got him to marry you in '44; the German revolution might have succeeded. What sort of things does he say in his letters?"

"Among other things, he gave you a splendid eulogy. What did you do in Manchester that impressed him so?"

"Stuck my neck out. Nothing more than a few hundred brick-makers did. I don't know. He's a bloody romantic. The Rhineland is full of them."

"Is that why he's in England now?"

"Ah." He busied himself with cutting slivers off the corners of the cheese. "Poor bastard. Huckstering again, unless a miracle happens in Germany."

"I didn't bring that so you could play with it. He'll get by."

"Yes, he will."

"And you?"

"Me? I also intend to get by. Unless you have another sug-gestion?"

"You might consider leaving the country."

He took a long breath and let it out, and set the knife down. "I might. But I'm rather fond of this one, which is why I've risked my life on a regular basis for the last ten years to repair its deficiencies. It's not an easy investment to walk away from."

"You could be hanged."

"If Her Majesty's government didn't hang Frost, Williams, and Jones, they won't hang me. I'd get a cruise to Australia. Or possibly die of fever in the hulks, but I really am more durable than I look."

"Then tell me why Gideon Johnson is making polite and delicate threats to anyone who asks about you. Tell me why Thomas Cavanaugh was beaten because, he says, he talked about you in the wrong places. Tell me why Stone and Betty Howard died, and why you're *here*, for God's sake. If the issue of the Charter is dead, then that's not the reason. What is?"

He folded his hands before him on the table. "Is your heart really so set on my being beastly?"

"You don't mean to tell me."

"No. And if you continue to press for it, I will eventually hit back." He shifted again, resting his elbows on the table and propping his forehead on his knuckles. His sleeve was still rolled up, and the scar shone. "I forgot, for a little while this morning, what I meant to do and what is at stake. I can't afford that. You've told me what you've learned, and where things stand, and I'm grateful. It is an enormous help. Now the most useful, the most helpful thing you can do is to leave me to my own devices. And get Richard and Kitty to go home, for the love of sanity."

"They're in danger?"

"They're in more danger than I am, because they don't know it. If they wash their hands of me, I think I can venture to say they'll be safe."

"But my safety you can't guarantee so easily."

He raised his head.

"It would be possible to find out how much I've learned,

Even if I wash my hands of it, as you say, aren't I a threat to the people who threaten you?''

He closed his eyes, pressed his steepled fingers lightly against his mouth, and said, ''If I have to hurt you to make you go away, I will.''

''What really happened,'' I demanded, ''when we thought you'd drowned?''

''I don't remember.'' His eyes were open now, his face cold. ''And that, sweetheart, is the sad, sad truth. Go home and ask Richard to show you my letters. Or ask Kitty, who is so free with her *cher ami*'s correspondence. Kitty may even know why my father makes it his business to house another man's mistress, or to support and advance your brother when your grandmother would have nothing to do with him. But whatever else you do, go home and leave me alone.''

''I will go to Melrose Hall and guard Richard and Kitty for you. *As soon as you tell me what I am guarding them against.*''

He stood up, a slow, smooth movement. His delicacy *is* an illusion, one he can shed when necessary. He chose to shed it then. ''I forgot about self-willed girls with progressive notions. About their tiresome certainty that they can face down anything, have everything their way, control everyone around them, and still expect reverence and delicate treatment, as if they hadn't just disproved every idiotic generality about womankind. Reverence and delicate treatment are not an absolute right but a courtesy, my cousin, my flower, which I extend to you. And can withdraw. Shall I remind you how my fellow men see self-willed girls?''

He had come toward me as he spoke, and I'd risen to my feet out of sheer instinct. Also on instinct, I reached for the cheese knife. But his hand on my wrist stopped me, painfully, and as painfully drew me closer to him. He forced my arm behind my back and with his other hand held my head so that I couldn't pull away. The length of my body was pressed against his for a long moment, and he looked down into my face with the chilly, distant expression that I had learned, in the course of the morning, to hate and fear. Just before he kissed me I saw a flash there of something else, the involuntary spasm of revulsion. Then he was too close to see, and he bruised my mouth with his.

There was no passion in it; there wasn't supposed to be. There was only a poisonous river of anger in full spate, too strong to fight against. So I simply endured. Then he stepped back and let me go.

He may have expected me to swoon, or to run from the room. He certainly didn't expect me to stand and look him in the eye, and say, "If I were the girl you called me, I'm sure that would have done just what you wanted it to do. Unfortunately for you, I'm an adult." My lips hurt. It was difficult to get the whole speech out clearly.

He turned and walked to the window. This time he leaned. His back was to me.

"It must take a lot of practise to lie not just with words but with your entire body. I hope you learned it in the service of a good cause. The People's Charter was one. I hope whatever you're lying in the service of now is another."

"I think it is," he said, his voice muffled.

I picked up my bags, and my cloak. The food could stay on the table, and I hoped it reminded him of me. "I meant my offer. If you'd told me what you feared and what was at stake, I'd have tried to keep out of your way, and keep Richard and Kitty likewise. My offer is withdrawn. I mean to pursue you like the hounds of Hell, not out of curiosity, but because it's the thing I think will hurt you most. Good day, Cousin."

When I shut the door behind me, I saw him still at the window, with his forehead pressed to the frame. By the time I stepped outside, the curtains had been drawn.

Tonight he will move again, of course. Tomorrow I will do what I can to find and follow him, though I meant what I said in my note to him, that I had no idea where he would go next. I ought to lie in wait for him tonight and follow him, but I'm sure he would know, and would manage to elude me. It is his trade, after all. I think that was the hardest thing I learned at Fairfield—that he is not a high-hearted idealistic amateur, though he may have begun as that. He is a conspirator by trade and by habit. Ten years of it have made him the kind of man that every cause needs, but few will acknowledge, and during those years when I watched him in drawing rooms and dinner parties I was watching a feral creature passing, for survival's sake, as tame.

And the other reason I won't follow him tonight is that I can't. Not tonight. I can't set aside my pain and sorrow to do the work that must be done. He could. If he feels those things, he will have put them away for later, or for ever, and begun to arrange his next escape, sweeping the trail neatly behind him.

I have written to Kitty. At some point I suppose I'll have to pass through London again, to see if she's written to me. And if all my other resources fail, I will have to ask to see James's letters to Richard, though he was careful to associate that, in my mind, with the betrayal of his confidence. Were our positions reversed, a mere betrayal of confidence surely wouldn't weigh with James for a moment. Well, I shall take him as my model. Then, if I find him again, he'll have himself to blame.

ROYAL SOUTHANTS INFIRMARY
NOVEMBER 12th

Dear Susan,

So very much has happened since I last wrote to you that I have no idea how to begin, and less of what you will think of me when, or if, these letters ever find you, as you gallop through the downs on a horse called Lightning, or commission a special to Dover to arrive before the evil Carpathian baron, or rescue our dear James from the clutches of the warlords of Nippon using only the Piece of the True Cross sent by the head of the Papist Church, or whatever else it is I imagine you doing, and although my own activities are tame and even dull by comparison, yet, in looking back upon the mere two score hours that have elapsed since I last wrote to you, I cannot believe it has all really happened, or that I am the same girl who wrote those letters, but perhaps, thinking on it, I am not after all. Ought I to begin with the most significant of events, or ought I simply to tell you of these last days as they came to me? Knowing as I do that you know me so well, you no doubt know most of what I have to tell you, but nevertheless I believe I shall choose the latter, as it will give you, I think, a clearer idea of why my head seems to spin whenever I find myself thinking, which happens each time I stop writing even to dip my quill.

I took the train to Portsmouth, and from there was fortunate to find one leaving right away which, after only a few minutes, brought me to Fareham, where I got a fast train that brought me to Southampton in rather less than half an hour, for which I was grateful, because I was so worried about Dick, as we passed Hook, Chitsfield, Swanwick, Netley, and all the other small stations, that I knew that I should have died of impatience if we had stopped at each one. From the station, carrying only my handbag, and, no doubt, looking like a mother whose child has fallen ill, I hired a cabriolet, which brought me past the cricket grounds and to the hospital, which is on St. Mary's Road near Onslow, should you need to find it, just as dark was falling, so that I was asking after Dick less than two hours after posting my last letter to you, making me grateful for the modern age, whatever annoyances and even suffering it has caused in some ways. I was directed to Dick at once, and found him alone in a tiny room where he was writing on some tablets. When I entered he looked up and, after an instant's expression of astonishment, there was such a look of happiness on his face at seeing me that I thought my heart should break on the spot, and I had made up my mind that I must not touch him upon seeing him, at least until I knew enough of his injuries not to accidentally press upon some wounded part, yet all such good ideas vanished at that moment, and in an instant I was holding him, and covering his face with kisses and using such endearments as "incompetent booby," and "silly fool," and making him promise never to set about such an ill-considered adventure again, while all he could say was, "My own sweet Kit, my own sweet Kit," over and over again, and at least there was no sign that I was causing him pain by holding him and having him hold me, and we were both crying, if you can believe it, as if we were the heroes of some awful drama, such as either of us would have walked out on in an instant.

After the drama came the farce, when he demanded of me

how and why I had come there when he had said there was
no need, and I demanded of him how he had come to be
injured and what were the extent of the injuries, with both of
us talking at once, until at last he told me he had been struck
by a club, and the surgeon had at last confessed a fear that he
was bleeding inside and perhaps he had been, but it had
stopped now, and although he was not, under any circumstances, to move more than strictly necessary, there was no
reason to believe that he should not make a full and complete
recovery. I felt that awful feeling of terror and relief that I am
sure you know, too, but he would not tell me anything about
the attack or what had provoked it until I said, "You were
following James, weren't you?" and then his mouth dropped
open and he said, "How could you know?" and I said, "The
letters in the box, of course," and he said, "You opened the
box?" and I said, "Of course I opened the box, you ninny,"
and he looked as if he were going to become angry with me,
but I added, "Wouldn't you have?" and that caught him up
short, as if he had never for a moment considered it that way,
and his mouth opened and closed once or twice, and it seemed
as if he were going to say, "It isn't the same thing," but, bless
his heart, he does figure things out if you give him enough
time, so in the end he just said, "Yes, I suppose I should have
at that."

Then, after embracing me once more, he said, "Well, I
should still rather not tell you of the attack, but it is evident
that someone would rather I not find James," to which I said,
"Maybe, but if David is involved somehow—" and he cried,
"David!" and got that look he always gets when your
brother's name is mentioned, as if he wished to transform himself into a rabid dog for just long enough to get his jaws around
David's throat, and he said, "How is David involved," so I
explained, and I will tell you now why I think so, it is because
Richard asked about a peculiar token, and the token is one that
I saw on a pendant around David's neck one very hot day
when he had loosened his clothing and was dipping his feet
in the pond, and though he covered it up as soon as he realized
he was not alone, I remembered the device upon it, and so
what else am I to think, all of which I explained to Dick, and
he nodded and said, "Yes, I've seen it too," and I asked him

if his attacker had worn something like it, and he said yes, he had seen it when his attacker's clothing had been disarranged, and then he shook his head and said he must sleep for a while, and he took my hand and fell asleep almost at once, but just as he was nodding off he said, "Why do the police tell me nothing?"

I sat with him for most of an hour, before there arrived the surgeon, who was tiny fat man with pudgy hands and stringy hair, and a look that inspired in me no confidence at all, but he told me I must leave so that he could examine the patient, and this evidently woke Dick up because he said, "I wish her to stay," and the surgeon said, "That is quite impossible, I am afraid. Your sister must wait outside," and Dick said, "She is not my sister, she is my betrothed," and I must say that my first reaction, upon hearing that, was to think Dick was rather more clever than I had thought him, to stretch the truth that way to get what he wanted, but then I realized that Dick would not do that, would not even think of doing that, and, Susan, my heart began to pound and I had to turn away so that the surgeon would not see that I was crying, and I hardly heard him send me out of the room, and it was only much later that it came to me I ought to have been outraged at being taken for granted, not to mention annoyed at getting such a careless proposal, not to mention a proposal at all, after everything Dick and I had told each other on the subject, but after all I was neither, and he really does know my heart, so there it is, he had announced that we were to be married, and when the surgeon left the room, saying something to me about Dick coming along nicely, I rushed back in and veritably threw myself on the bed and he told me over and over that he loved me and I told him the same thing, and we each said more things that I cannot even remember. But, Susan, the shocks were not over, because later, hours later I think, we started talking, and I asked him when we should be married, and he took my hand very earnestly, and he said that he would write to Donovan, his solicitor, and to the vicar, to make the arrangements with the Archbishop of Canterbury and to meet us here and, if I were willing, we would be married at once, and when he said that I started to cry again, and I did not ask him what the hurry was, or what about our family and everything else, because I felt that I understood, though now I do not know if I can explain it, but I told him yes I was willing, and so he wrote the letters, and Mr Donovan came down yesterday and wrote out the agreements, and today at about 4 o'clock the vicar came, muttering about how irregular it all was, and I think he suspected that Dick and I had a family started, but it did not matter, because he had the licence all prepared, and the surgeon cooperated by swearing that Dick was at death's door and could not be moved, and the vicar performed the service with the surgeon and a cheery nurse named Armstrong as witnesses, and there is little to say about the service itself, except that he read all the words, and we said what he told us to, and Dick put on my finger a ring that Donovan had brought up from Melrose and that Dick said had belonged to his Great-Grandmother Arabella, which is, by the way, a very beautiful ring, just a band of gold with a lovely tracery along it, and when it fit my finger as if made for it, Dick gave me a look that said, as clear as words, "It is an omen for us," and I felt the same way.

I know this is very sudden, Susan, and I fear you may be hurt by not having been here, and in fact you are the only one who Dick and I wish had been present, but somehow Dick felt the whole thing was urgent, as if he wanted it to be done with, and indeed, he confessed to me just a few hours ago that he feels a great sense of relief, as if some danger has been averted, and I feel the same way, although I am sure you will consider it nonsense of the worst sort, but I want you to know that we both missed you.

I am sitting by Dick's side now as he sleeps, and the surgeon has once more informed us that, as long as Dick is allowed to rest he should make a full recovery, and the candle the hospital was gracious enough to let me have is now almost burnt down, so I should end this letter now with the promise that I will write you as soon as may be, and hereafter I will sign my letters "Kit" as I always have, and as I always want you to think of me, but this one time I will break custom, because I want you to have the very first letter to be signed by your breathlessly happy friend,

Mrs Richard Cobham

ROYAL SOUTHANTS INFIRMARY
NOVEMBER 14ᵗʰ

Dear Susan,

Your letter of the 10ᵗʰ has reached me here at the infirmary,
and I hardly know how to respond, because this removes any
lingering doubts I may have had that James is, indeed, alive,
but now I fear for you as well as James in entirely different
ways, and if Her Majesty's Government is involved, well, perhaps now I know why the police will tell Dick nothing of the
attack on him, so I am torn between joy and fresh worries, and
though I do not despise your politics, in fact I am happy to
see you and James in your own way busying yourselves with
trying to make our world better, I cannot help but be frightened
for you as well, because I know you far better than I know
the people you want to help, who are strangers with whom I
may sympathize, but to whom I cannot feel so closely bound.
Of course we will return to Melrose when Dick can travel, if
for no other reason than that I cannot think of where else we
might go, because you do not tell me where you are writing
from, so no doubt by the time you receive this you will either
be back home or in gaol awaiting transportation.

I tell you, Susan, that while I am ready to aid you in any
way, should you request it, I will not on my own set out to
right the wrongs of the world, nor do I think Dick will want
to do so. He was angry, I think, when I showed him your
letter, and realized that James had been, while asking for his
help, concealing so many things from him, and as for me, well,
I do not like to think that being an old married woman for all
of eight-and-forty hours has changed me, still, I want nothing
more than to return to Melrose, where I will set about shocking
the family with my new state, after which I will reread *Sybil*
as you suggest. I would also read something of that Engels of
yours, except that Dick says the only work of his of any length
only exists in German, which I cannot read without a great
deal of effort, although Dick has and says it is well worth the
trouble.

Speaking of shocking the family, I have already been able to give such a shock to a complete stranger, and I took a certain naughty pride in it, because someone came to the infirmary with a package for Dick, and, as he came while the surgeon was there, I happened to greet him while waiting outside the room. He seemed to be a gentleman to judge by his carriage, but I would have taken him for a servant from his clothing, but he carried a wrapped parcel, about the size of a jewel-case, and said it was for Richard Cobham, and when I told him I was Mrs Richard Cobham, the saying of which still gives me a thrill, he seemed astonished, and drew back, and when I offered to deliver the parcel, he said no, he must return at another time when Mr Cobham was available, and when he was gone I sat there for some minutes glowing about what is, in fact, an utterly trivial matter, that being the name by which one is called, but then perhaps I have a more trivial mind than I had thought.

But be that as it may, you must not for a moment think that I am not worried about you and concerned about James, and that I do not anxiously await hearing what has befallen the two of you, and I hope you will somehow receive this, and will write to me soon, at Melrose Hall where we hope to be within the week, if the surgeon's prophecy is accurate, and until then please have a care for yourself, and know that you are in the thoughts of your good friend,

Kit

RICHARD COBHAM'S JOURNAL

NOVEMBER 13

First full day as a married man. My Kit is asleep in a cot the hospital provided. Feel good, should go home soon. Feel wonderful. Why didn't we think of this years ago? Her hand is outside the blanket, so I can see the ring on her finger. Woken up by letter arriving for Kit from Susan, but will leave it for her to open, though very curious. Has Susan found James?

Longing to be home, to set up house, to laugh in Mother's face!

NOVEMBER 14

Mr Browne says I can go home on Friday, if there is no change for the worse! Very unhappy to be sleeping apart from Kitty, but we both fear a relapse and wish to take no chances. Saw Susan's letter, she has seen James, and was very disturbed, poor girl. I hope things will work out between them, somehow. I mentioned this to Kitty, and she just shook her head. She is better able to read between the lines of Susan's letters than I am, so I'm afraid she saw something that I did not.

NOVEMBER 15

Very disturbed. Almost the first thing Kitty said this morning was, ''The wedding must have turned my brain to mush.'' I asked her what she meant, and she said, ''A man came to give you something yesterday, and would not leave it with me, and he left abruptly when he found that we were married.'' I asked her for a description, but he did not sound like anyone I know. And what could the package be? I fear the Trotter's Club. But why should the fact that we are married make a difference, unless he leapt to the same conclusion as the vicar? Or unless he noticed the ring and recognised its significance. Could that be? It must be. When a girl tells me she is married, I often glance at the ring, and the Trotter's Club could know well what the ring is. We did not move any too soon; I do not care to think about what would have happened if we had not had the protection from dear old Great-Grandmother Arabella. Now if only she could protect us from the police as well! But we have done nothing wrong, so what harm can their suspicions do? Answer: A great deal.

NOVEMBER 16

Home at last, too tired to write more. To bed, to bed, at last to bed!

NOVEMBER 17

A letter from James has arrived. Showed it to Kitty. She said we should show it to Susan. I agreed, and said we could show all of James's letters to Susan for all I cared. He said I could do as much, though I now suspect he said that thinking I would not do so. But that is his lookout.

Feeling more and more like myself. Over and above marrying K for her protection, I find I quite like the state. This damned mess with J is a nuisance, and it will be good to be done with it.

12th NOVEMBER, 1849
(DELIVERED TO MELROSE HALL ON THE 17th)

Dear Richard,

John Aubrey, herewith, comes home at last to roost, and with him my thanks. Inside these covers is the most unexpected store of history (Lord Fairfax defending the Bodleian Library from barbarians and Cavaliers—scholarship is its own reward, but surely some pagan god of learning took it into account when choosing to preserve his skin well into the Restoration— William Harvey, who "wrote a very bad hand," thus becoming perhaps the first in a long line of physicians to be unintelligible on paper). I know that some doubt his accuracy, or even his veracity, but I'm convinced that our widely-acquainted author has told the truth, as closely as he can recall it. Why do we have such reverence for history when it must be based, too often, on faithless memory?

If you have not spoken to Susan herself, I'm sure you have a good portion of what she knows of me from the Aeolian harp that is Kitty. If you do, I know that you are hurt by what you will regard as my unwillingness to trust you. The truth is that I trust you more than any other person alive. But the confiding nature has been schooled out of me by the last ten years, and as I told you in one of my letters, I am careful with the belongings of others. For so very long, my secrets have

not been wholly my own, and though you might have shared
them and welcome for my part, I had no such brief from all
the other brave men and women who could have faced a noose
had I spoken once unwisely. I cannot tell yet if all the things
I keep from you now could hurt some innocent party if I failed
to keep them. Until I know, I will continue silent, even in the
knowledge that I am causing you pain.

In order not to cause you death, I will also not tell you where
I am. I am sure you went to the Grey Hound; since I could
think of no way on earth to stop you, I prepared for it as best
I could. If you are reading this I assume you did not surpass
yourself and get as far as Southampton. Stop packing, Diccon,
there is no use in going now; you would be perfectly safe and
find nothing whatsoever. If you had gone then, I think you
would have been a dead man. I am trying to preserve you from
that, and if you would remember it whenever you take a huff
over one or another of my newly-uncovered secrets you will
perhaps be more inclined to forgive your infuriating cousin

James

I have got to stop writing to you. I only meant to enclose a
few lines to keep the book company.

J.

Please tell Susan I am sorry. Though she is not likely to believe
it.

BRIGHT'S HOTEL, KENSINGTON
19 NOV 1849

Dearest Mrs Richard Cobham,

Forgive the schoolgirl blot that began this line—from one
thing and another my hands are far from steady. I don't know
where to begin either, dear—I understand your dilemma entirely. Reverse chronological order, perhaps?

No, congratulations first, and didn't I tell you your pretense
of a rake would turn all proper on you soon? Just as well you

did it when I was out of reach, or I would have insisted on reviewing the settlements. No, I'm teasing you, Kit. Richard of all men would never impose on you, or in any way put your future at risk. And if (I know you don't want to hear this now, but it must be said, and then we can forget it) something should happen to him, or if you are in any difficulties, you know you may rely on me for a roof and anything else. I laugh to think of you and Richard behaving like the *dénouement* of a sentimental novel, making the Southampton Infirmary smell of April and May instead of chloroform. I expect the staff was overjoyed.

I'm also overjoyed, at the evidence of your happiness in these pages you've sent, and at the things you can't put into words, the unwritten happiness that I can read because I know you so well. I hope you can read the unwritten as well, because I can't find the perfect words, and you should have them from me. There is too much distance between you and me in a letter, I suppose. And I'm distracted. I shall wish you both well properly, when I see you next.

I hope that Richard is much improved and that the two of you are comfortably settled at Melrose even now. It was courageous of him to put himself at risk for his cousin James, but his cousin James would be furious if he knew about it. And James in a fury is capable of doing and saying things that Richard would never forgive him for. The wisest action that you or he can take with regard to James at present is to avoid him altogether, and to pray to whatever powers you acknowledge that James avoids you.

And on the subject of saying unforgivable things, Kitty, my pet, you are a dunce. Married happiness has turned your pretty head. Do you know of anyone besides me (and at the time you wrote, I didn't yet) who knew that Richard was in hospital at Southampton? Then who the devil would have been sending unidentified parcels to him there—*except the people responsible for harming him?* Just as well, I think, the parcel wasn't delivered, but my God, was there no one, no servant nor groom nor bloody crossing-sweeper, you could have paid to follow the man and report back to you? Give me as good a description of the fellow as you can, and I will try to make up the deficiency in my formerly clever partner in intrigue.

I'm sorry, dear, I seem to be able to find perfectly good words to heap scorn on you and only insufficient ones to wish you happy. But I'm alarmed for you and Richard, and upset at the chance missed. It wasn't your fault, and a perfectly reasonable oversight. It's only that I seem to have more difficulty of late understanding blinding happiness than clear-sighted, premeditated malice, and begin to expect the latter. Well, in the hope of distracting you from my unpleasant behaviour, I'll tell you what I've been up to.

I returned here this afternoon, collected my letters from the concierge (three from you! I believe I scented crisis by sheer frequency, whereas my crises dry up correspondence), ascended to my apartments, and opened the door on what looked like the leavings of a typhoon. My rooms had, with some ferocity, been ransacked. For a moment I stood witless on the threshold. Then I began to laugh and, sitting down on the carpet in a welter of skirts, went on laughing well after I'd run out of breath. One of the maids had come to see what was wrong with me; she let out a shriek, and ran for the concierge. If I'd been asked (if I could have drawn breath to talk!), I would have forbidden the police, but in very short order a uniformed man and a Divisional Detective were at my door with the concierge, who was white and trembling as a pudding. It comes of being rich, I suppose. Had I been in a poor woman's lodgings, I think I might have bellowed until I was hoarse and not gotten such attention.

I was at least standing by then. The constable was distressed by my alternating bouts of perfect calm and half-smothered hilarity, thinking no doubt that my reason was overthrown, and seemed to want to concern himself with whether I was sitting down or if I needed sal volatile or my wrists chafed. The Detective was another matter. He was a rather rough man with apparently no sympathy in him at all, and I took to him at once. We had a fine conversation in which he asked a great many pointed and devious questions and got from me no information of any earthly use to anyone. I was not quite sharp enough to convince him of my absolute virginal brainlessness in the matter, however; he knew that I was aware that we were crossing swords. I commend the Metropolitan Police on their employment of the fellow. He'll go far.

It never once occurred to me to believe that I'd been the victim of simple robbery. I expected to find my obvious valuables gone, to cover the real purpose of the crime, but I knew that the object of the search had been pearls of wisdom, or at least information.

And that was why I was laughing. Our unknown adversary has no acquaintance with Seminaries for Young Ladies, the finest training-ground for espionage in the civilised world. If he had, he would know that no graduate of Miss Trevelyan's would commit a secret to paper if she could help it, or if she couldn't, would leave it anywhere it could be found in her absence. My God, between the Booth sisters and the extortion schemes of the third-floor housemaid, how would I have survived? None of the correspondence relating to James, or my journals ditto were even on the premises. I think *you* could find them—indeed, I'm trusting you to find them if anything happens to me.

I lost nothing I can't do without, though I regret my turquoise and silver parure, which I'd worn to Mrs Overshot's musicale (until I wrote that, I hadn't realized how long ago it seems, and it *is* nearly a month. How long a month can be!) and, from one thing and another, never returned to the hotel safe. A few other frippery pieces, coral and garnet and carnelian. Oh, and they took the black jasperware cameo you gave me for my birthday, the devils. I'd hoped to have it a *trifle* longer than two months! Well, a small price to pay for being able to convince the Metropolitan Police that robbery was the only crime at issue.

No, dear, no evil Carpathian barons, nor specials commissioned, nor piece of the True Cross nor agents of Nippon nor fabulous rewards from the Tsar. Adventure, at least in my part of the island, involves having one's petticoats and stockings flung about one's room, one's every gown pulled from the clothespress and left crumpled in corners, one's mattress hauled off the bed and cut apart, one's pillows ripped open so that feathers drift like dry snow around one's feet wherever one walks, and every drawer in every piece of furniture yanked out, overturned, and dropped anywhere. I'm glad I sent the faithful Alice off on a visit to her family while I was chasing about—if she had been here, she might have tried to defend my territory and belongings and got hurt. As it is, I must put things to rights before she returns, or she'll go off into hysterics.

There *is* a horse, but his name is not Lightning but (prepare yourself) Girasol. Not even a Spanish horse, so I can't imagine what flight of fancy yielded up his name—it's no responsibility of mine. He is Hanoverian, enormous, good-natured, liver-coloured, versatile, and on occasion diabolically inventive. He's fond of challenges and appears to thrive on a handful of nettles a day, contrary to any reasonable expectation. (Though he'll eat his head off when he can get the wherewithal; he's busy making up for lost supper-time now that he's in London.) I have never seen a more perfect heavy hunter type. I bought him at a horse-market in Whaley Bridge last Monday from an aged Romany who, toward the end of the bargaining, cursed me passionately and suggested that my mother stole dogs off the street and ate them. Once the money changed hands, however, he seemed to think highly of me, showing me off to all his relatives, of which there were dozens. He also insisted on filling my water flask with a really extraordinary pear brandy. He said if I wished to make the horse exclusively mine, that once a day I should take a sip of the brandy and breathe into his nostrils. After five days he would obey no one but me, and would come to me as another horse might turn toward his stall. You'll be amused to hear that I did it faithfully, and it's at least done neither of us any harm.

I acquired Girasol because it seems that to hunt James I need a mount of outstanding character. James' is nothing extraordinary (if you don't count his personality; one groom in his wake called him a man-eater, and a devil with a mane, except with that gent who'd brought him—meaning James). But the fellow riding James' horse is so brutally clever and so heedless of reasonable caution that I need a few advantages. Girasol has endurance, surefootedness, speed, and a commendable equine brain, and I have called upon them all in the short time I've had him. If I'd been riding my otherwise adequate hired hack when, for instance, James took off over an ill-marked pass straight across the heel-end of the Pennines *in the dark*, both the horse and I would probably still be there, preserved dead under a fine coating of sleet or else be found years from now at the bottom of a tarn. I shall remember that ride in nightmares for as long as I live.

James knows I'm behind him, you see. No great feat of detection, since I told him I would be. But I believe there is also some party or parties behind *me*, and the need to throw them off while not letting James do the same to me is exhausting and infuriating. So I've come to London to search out information that will let me get ahead of him.

The irony is that I really don't want to confront him again, and will avoid it if possible. But he is already, willingly or no, staked out like the goat I invoked in my last letter, and the tiger (or tigers) appears to have the scent of him, and if I don't become involved in the process of the hunt I will miss the opportunity to bag myself a nice striped rug. I find myself steadily less interested in what happens to the goat, which seems determined to take care of itself.

In the service of my rug, I need some help from you. James said some things at our last meeting that were meant to hurt and distract me, but I think in the heat of the moment he revealed more than he meant to. You say to beware of my brother. James mentioned David, as well; he said to ask you if you knew why James's father has concerned himself so much with David's welfare when my grandmother wouldn't do anything for him. I remember my grandmama's last quarrel with David, or at least as much of it as I could overhear. She'd called him a self-righteous, self-serving hypocritical prig before; this time she called him a villainous, bloody-handed cur. "No innocence so complete, no bond so sacred, that you let it stand between you and your ambition," she said. Afterward, she told me that he was forbidden to cross any threshold of hers in her lifetime, and for the two years until her death held to it absolutely, though she could be nearly civil to him in public, if forced to it. What do you know about David, Kit, and what has it got to do with James's father? Describe this pendant that's worn by clergymen and ruffians alike, and tell me what you think it means. You've seen more of David in the last year than I have—tell me about him.

Also—here I have to go back a little. I told you in a previous letter that Hugh Stone was dead. He did not commit suicide. He was poisoned by a woman named Betty Howard, who seems to have been Gideon Johnson's mistress. She was later killed in a railway accident. But she lived in a house near Waltham Forest *owned by James's father*. Another of the things James suggested I ask you was why his father had housed another man's mistress. Was he only aiming at random, or can you lay hands on some piece of information about Uncle Andrew that you perhaps didn't know you had? You and James were the ones raised at the Abbey, in his household, and you were there more often, more recently, than James. If there is anything you can tell me that strikes you as the least bit out of the common way, I'd dearly love to have it.

The last thing James recommended, in such a way as to give me the strongest distaste for it, was that I read his letters to Richard. I expect that Richard's distaste will be at least as strong as mine, but I had better do it, if it can be managed, if Richard can be talked 'round. Don't send them; I shall come to you. In the meantime make certain they are kept where the Booth sisters would never have found them out. And if Richard proves intractable, I will have to ask you to tell me everything that you remember from your illicit reading of James's letters, with particular emphasis on those parts you think Richard didn't notice.

One of the tigers after our tethered goat seems to be a blonde lady travelling in a dark green crested coach with four horses. She arrived at the place of my last meeting with James shortly before midnight on the 10th. The lady enquired after him, which was when it was discovered that he was packed and gone. She seemed dismayed by the news; she got back in the coach and was driven away, though what moon there was was mostly hidden by cloud and it was patently unsafe, if not impossible, to drive. I learned all this the next morning when I asked after him.

As I pursue this business, memories spring nearly at random to the front of my brain. Useless, all of them, but sometimes strangely affecting. I remember a dinner party I attended perhaps a year ago, to which James was also invited. After dinner, over tea in the drawing room, Hannah Bellamy, who gives vivacity a bad name, started up a game in which we were all to find one word that best described ourselves. It produced, as you might guess, a certain amount of hectic enthusiasm, followed rapidly by witty unkindness and bad feeling. But when the furor had died down, I realized that James had managed to avoid taking any part at all, and I carried my tea over to where he sat a little apart from the others. So, I asked, had he thought of a single word to describe himself?

He was in the act of raising his cup to his lips. He paused, looking at me over the rim, his eyes wide and unreadable, and said at last, softly, "Agile."

Yes, very. I thought of that as I rode through a freezing black rain outside of Peterborough, and realized that one of the weapons James Cobham has under his hand, and will not hesitate to use against his enemies or his friends, is a relentless, selective kind of self-knowledge. He will define himself as whatever will best survive the moment, perfectly flexible, entirely unstable; he will be rigorously amoral out of fear that anything else will make him too firm, too tangible, to slip through the net. He is becoming something he hates because he believes that nothing else can preserve the things he loves. I would rather see him dead.

I have matters to pursue in London which will keep me here for two, perhaps three days. After that, I hope, I will see you at Melrose. Keep well until then.

Your loving
Susan

P.S.—You may share the contents of this with Richard, of course. It seems to be past time that we pooled our knowledge.

FROM THE OFFICES OF JOHNATHAN ADDAMS,
SOLICITOR
NOVEMBER 19TH, 1849

Dear Miss Voight,

Our client, Mr Andrew Cobham, has asked us to put in train certain revisions to the deed of settlement on the property identified as Cauldhurst Abbey, and to such instruments as will assign his personal and family property in the unfortunate event of his death.

In pursuance of these revisions, and to forestall any claims against the estate, we require to inform you that, should these revised instruments be legally executed and carried out, you would not stand to benefit in any way from the alteration in the disposition of the above-named property. Such claims as you presently have upon your brother David Voight or upon his existing property *post mortem* would not be altered by these instruments, but would not be considered to exercise any legal precedent over the subsequent inheritance of Cauldhurst Abbey or the personal and family property of Andrew Cobham.

Any questions you may have on this matter may be directed to me, or to my superior, Mr Addams.

Sincerely,
Lucian Frame
clerk to Mr Addams

MELROSE
NOVEMBER 20th

Dear Susan,

It is very odd, but do you know it seemed all well and good to sign myself Mrs Richard Cobham when all in the flush of marriage, a great deal of which flush, by the way, lingers still and brightens up this horrid November weather, but to see you address me that way in a letter adds twenty years to my age, which is shocking when it happens all of a sudden, not that I am blaming you, I asked for it, and I suspect you did it with affection and with only the smallest degree of evil cackle creeping into your pen.

As you can see we are quite home, having survived a bumpy but not horrible train ride, and Dick is feeling better every day, and, perhaps best of all, we have thoroughly shocked Aunt Louisa, who has taken to her room as if to withstand a siege, broken only by the servants she graciously permits to bring her food, and I find it all rather a delight, only wishing you were here to enjoy it with me, but then, perhaps you will soon be here and we will accidentally wander past her fortress speaking in loud voices about the bliss of marriage and the settlement of the estate, and then we will quietly sneak back to listen at the door and discover if we hear her dying of apoplexy.

Do you know, you were right about making the room smell of April and May for the wedding, because I went and found essence of juniper and apple-blossom, but the staff went on as if it were all very ordinary and they could not be bothered, except for one nurse who became all teary over it, so we made her a witness, and then she got even more teary, except I must stop talking about the wedding because it is no good at all in a letter, and we will see you soon, I think, at least we want to, and I think you will want to as well, because Dick wants to show you all of James's letters, every one, including the one he got on Tuesday in which James says to pass on his apologies to you, which piques my curiosity so much I quite nearly cannot stand it, but Dick does want to tell you everything he knows, and I will let you berate me properly for being a perfect fool when that man tried to deliver his package and I let him walk away, and I still wonder what it was, and I told Dick about it and he got a puzzled look on his face, then his eyes got narrow as I have never seen them. I had the feeling that I was looking at the man who had survived an attack on his life, and it was only then, if you can believe it, that it really came home to me that someone had tried to kill Dick, and I felt the deepest sense of outrage, and then I realized, from things James has said in his letters, that he could have prevented it, that he knew Dick would walk into a trap if he were clever enough, and I do believe that if James had been there at that moment I should have killed him with the pistol I found under Dick's pillow at the hospital, which I know is a horrid thing to feel, and I do still like James, but I was so angry that Dick asked me what was the matter, and I said it was nothing and then he said, "It's this business with James, isn't it? Well, we shall have done with it one way or another. You just get Susan here, and we'll figure it all out, and do whatever we have to, because I am bloody damn tired of it, my love."

As am I, Susan, I am tired of it, and angry, and worried, and frightened, all at once, and most of these things for you, because I just do not like the way you sound any more, and I cannot help thinking about what you are doing to yourself, though I know I can never in a hundred years convince you to give it all up, I wish that you would. When you speak of James as a goat ready to be sacrificed, and then speak of him as becoming what he hates because he believes that nothing else can preserve what he loves, well, I wonder if you know how much you are talking about yourself? But I know I cannot convince you, or stop you, and so I will help you, and only hope that it all ends soon and for the best, so I will tell you all that you ask, including the nature of that mysterious device, which Dick is drawing out as best he can and which we will show you when you arrive to look at all the letters, and I am afraid I can remember nothing at all of the man who tried to deliver the package, because I had become giddy and my eyes saw Dick everywhere, but Dick knows something of the matter of James's father and he says he will tell me about it when he returns, because he has gone off on an errand of some sort, which I write casually but I do not feel casual about it at all, because after he read your letter the first thing he said was, "I will be damned. That slimy bastard," and then would not say anything, but an hour or so later he said he was going out, and he did, and his pistols were not in their accustomed place, so I am writing this letter to keep from worrying myself sick, because he took an awful knock in Southampton and he still is not recovered, you know.

Please forgive me, Susan, for taking that tone with you, it's just that I have turned into a Nervous Nelly, which comes of having to wait, I am much more suited to doing than to waiting, but perhaps—he has returned, more later.

Dick is entirely well, though he seems flushed and angry, but he has a packet of papers he has asked me to send to you with this letter and a note of his own, and he is commissioning two servants to deliver them to you because he does not trust the mails, and is giving each of the servants one of his pistols, so whatever this packet is, I trust it is important, and he wants it sent right away, so I must close this now being not so worried but still and always your friend,

Kit

MELROSE HALL
TUESDAY

Dear Miss Voight:

We expect you for dinner tomorrow, Wednesday, the 21st.
Here are some papers that may be of interest to you. I hope
you appreciate them, as they were not acquired without difficulty. I remain, madam, your servant,

Richard Cobham

RICHARD COBHAM'S JOURNAL

NOVEMBER 20

Kit sleeps in the next room, but no sleep for me, so I may as
well write, and endeavour to get all of this down in exact detail
in hopes that it will relax me and enable me to sleep. Of
course, as soon as I saw S's letter, I knew who was behind it,
and all the murder and kidnapping and bloodletting at midnight
beneath the new moon and who-knows-what had nothing more
behind them than petty schemes for pelf and property. I was
so outraged that for some time I did not dare speak, and then
I became consumed with the need to prove what I knew,
which, now that I think of it, is what happened to poor James.
I am now no longer as angry with him, as I have been driven
myself to certain deeds for no other reason than to have in my
hand the proof of what I already knew, that I had been betrayed, and played for a fool, and for nothing but another
man's advantage in station and privilege. Pah! It is enough to
make me believe in the devil, if I ever doubted his infernal
existence, for thus he must fill the souls of men and drive them
to perdition beneath the cover of the cassock!

When I could stand it no more I armed myself and set off
for the Abbey. It is odd that the dreary length of the ride to
the Abbey did nothing to alter my feelings, or change my

disposition, so when I came to the great yard before Cauld-hurst—and this only strikes me now as I think about it—I stopped and checked the charges on my pistols, an act that seemed normal and natural at the time, but was actually full of significance; I was not carrying the pistols for protection against some unlikely attack, rather I was fully expecting to use them. I put one in each pocket of my coat, gave my horse into the care of the groom, wondering, I now recall, just how good a groom James was compared to this man whose name I did not even know, yet I had seen him a hundred times over the years. No, wait. His name is Valoise, or something Norman like that. I rang the bell, and was greeted politely enough by Clayborough, though he seemed surprised to see me at such an hour. I asked if David were by chance available. Clayborough would see. I nodded. Clayborough went back through the residence toward David, I waited a count of ten, then followed. I remember wishing it were still daytime, because I have always loved the way the sun strikes the stained glass in the "small hall" of the Abbey; the rich blues especially stand out in my mind, though the pagan gods alone will know why such thoughts came to me then. I heard Clayborough speaking to someone, and I heard David's sniveling little voice say, "I am indisposed," and I stepped up behind Clayborough and said, "Then I shall wait."

Clayborough opened his mouth to say something, but could think of no words, so he glanced back at his master, and I took off my hat, handed it and my stick to Clayborough, and said, "I'll collect them on my way out." He looked again to David, but before my dear cousin could say a word I had stepped into his study, with its rows of books on theology, philosophy, and, I am quite sure, hypocrisy in its thousand variations, and its long oak table covered with foolscap, and its long candles, and its two narrow windows shut and shuttered.

I looked hard at Clayborough, and he, clearly upset, at last turned and left us alone in the absence of clear orders to the contrary. I will try to remember the conversation. I cannot be quite accurate or precise, but I recall the gist of it very well.

I closed the door after Clayborough, and I remember doing

it slowly. I had felt many things toward David over the years, none of them Christian; this time I felt a power over him, and I intended to use it. That, I know, is also un-Christian, but so is David. When the door is closed I turned back to him, and I remember his face as if it were an etching before me even now: he stared at me, trying to keep signs of fear from his expression, and failing.

I said, "I have come for the pages torn from James's notebook the day you attempted to drown him."

"What?" he cried, springing to his feet, and looking so sincerely baffled that for an instant I was afraid that all of my careful deductions had been off the mark.

But I let none of it show, and said, "You heard me, David. I want those pages."

"I don't know what—"

"Are you denying that you attempted to kill James?"

"I certainly am! How dare you—"

"I know the truth, David."

"Rubbish. Had I wanted James dead, I would—" He stopped cold, and, even in the light of three candles, I could see him flushing. How would he have finished that thought? He would probably have said that he could have killed him during those two months he was missing, which had not occurred to me, frankly, so now David stood at once innocent and guilty, by his own unfinished sentence.

I laughed. "Very well," I told him. "You are acquitted of attempting to drown my cousin. Now, let me have those papers."

I could see that I had struck fair to the heart, and this sent a thrill through me that neither shooting nor stalking can match. I saw a denial form on his lips, and, with great slow movements, I pulled the pistol from my coat and made a great show of cocking it. He could have jumped at me then, and, as he is not a small man and I am still weak, he could almost certainly have wrested it from me; he could have called for help—and I learned what Clayborough was capable of on New Year's Eve of '44 and have never forgotten it. Yet he did none of those things, but simply watched me. It is odd, thinking back on it, that I took no notice of my injury, though I am now paying for my exertions with soreness in the joint of my left shoulder.

When the pistol was cocked, I put it straight to his forehead and I said, and this I remember word for word, "This pistol is very heavy, David, and I cannot hold it in this position for long. Before I lower my arm, if I don't have those papers, I will put a ball into your hypocritical, evil, bloody-minded brain."

He just stared at me, his mouth open and his breathing laboured. If there is a power in the world that grants forgiveness, I should ask forgiveness for how I felt at that moment, but I will not do so, even in the privacy of my heart. Especially in the privacy of my heart.

I said, "The laws of our country are odd, cousin, but they do not permit dead men to inherit. Nor those who murder innocent children, by the way—"

"I had no choice!" he cried suddenly. "She . . ." He choked off his words then and bit his lip.

"No choice?" I said. Ha! I had no idea who "she" was, but this was hardly the time to say so. "She did not make you take whatever oaths the Trotter's Club requires of its initiates. But my arm is becoming quite tired. Do you see it trembling? I am in a weakened state after the attempt your friends have made on my life, and I cannot be responsible—"

"All right!"

For an instant I couldn't believe I had won. He went back to one of his shelves of books. I watched him carefully, determined to pull the trigger if he emerged with anything but paper in his hand, or even moved suddenly, and I would have done it, too; I know because I remember arguing with myself about whether I should kill him regardless, thinking about Roderick, and how his death had affected James.

David set a box down before me, and sat down. "Open it," I said, still holding the pistol and fearing a trick. But there was no trick; the box held papers, and a quick glance was sufficient to recognize them as from the same note-book as James's letters to me, and to recognize James's handwriting. Even, in that quick glance, I recall remarking on the fact that these papers had never been in the water, and that was significant.

David had nothing more to say. I uncocked carefully, replaced the pistol in my pocket, and said, "You have just saved your life, David. It would have been better for the world had you not. But it may not be too late. I am leaving now, and if you do anything foolish, it will be your last action on this earth."

I turned my back on him and walked out. It was only by chance that I noticed Clayborough, or I should have forgotten my hat and my stick, but I took them, retrieved my horse from the groom, and returned to Melrose. About halfway there I noticed I was shaking from head to foot, and I remember thinking that was funny.

NOVEMBER 21

Met with Susan. Must remember never to underestimate my darling Kitty, nor the amazing Miss Voight who tears apart books with such enthusiasm. The discovery of James's document has changed everything. There is so very much I have been wrong about!

12TH NOVEMBER 1849
(found on the 21ST)

My dear relation:

I no longer have any clear idea which of you is most likely to discover these pages—if, indeed, this survives to reach Melrose Hall, if it isn't intercepted and my notes discovered. My money is on Susan, by a nose. And after lying to her about this two days ago. But I forget, sometimes, that anyone else is clever at the skills I've practiced. It's a dangerous oversight.

I would wager on Kitty, who combines the curiosity of her nick-namesake with a ferret's or terrier's willingness to dig into any promising dark opening, but I cannot think she would take John Aubrey's work seriously enough to linger over it, at least not long enough to find this under her thumb. And Richard—he would never imagine that I would treat a book the way I mean to treat this one. I hope he's not present when Susan, probably, rips the endpapers off the boards of a volume that has, until now, passed through a great deal unscathed.

What follows is an account of what happened during my missing two months, or as much of it as the circumstances allowed me to grasp. When I told Richard I didn't remember what had occurred, I was not, for a miracle, lying—I remembered none of this until sometime on the afternoon of the 26th of October, when my mind began to clear like an overcast sky. The past came back in isolated spots, then streaks of connected events, then whole ribbons of them that accounted for several hours together, until finally, late on the 28th, the earliest parts returned to me in an unpleasant rush and I fell out of the saddle from sheer distraction.

Distraction, indeed. Tell the story, Jamie.

I was damnably drunk by the time I pushed off in the boat— too drunk to be allowed on a body of water, but since it's always difficult to tell how much I have had by what I do, I'm not surprised that no one prevented me. And one person present, at least, would have—*must* have—done everything possible to see that I was not prevented. I wish I could remember if the boat was my idea or someone else's. The drinking was my idea; I'd had two letters that morning, one full of bad news from Rome and Buda-Pest, the other from my father in his usual style. David, I recall, pressed me to read from it at the breakfast-table until I shut him up. But even the drinking might have been augmented; it would have been easy enough to put something in my glass in addition to the wine.

There was a movement at the side of the boat away from the shore; I turned to look, squinting, dazzled by the sun on the water. I had an instant in which to see the grapple caught over the gunwale before the line on it went tight and the boat heeled over, and in my loose-limbed condition I went head-first over the side with barely a splash. Seeing the two figures that immediately laid hands on me and pulled me further down, I almost believed in Richard's fairy-folk, until I recognized what must have served as both breathing apparatus and disguise. The design was grotesque and has appeared regularly in my dreams since.

They clapped a mask with a rubberized cloth bag attached over my nose and mouth and wrenched my arm up behind my

back. I knew I shouldn't draw breath, but that made me do it.
I smelled ether.

I broke free somehow, operating on pure panic, and headed
for the surface, trying to remember which side of the boat
would be visible from shore. I don't know if I picked the right
one; I had only enough time to break the surface and take one
water-blind lungful of air before they pulled me back down
again and got the mask on me. They were rougher the second
time, since they knew in a minute I would be missed, and
Richard or Henry or both would come in after me.

The next thing I had that passed for a conscious moment,
was lying on a hard surface, listening to several angry voices
near at hand. One of them at least seemed familiar, but I
couldn't think clearly about that or anything else. With an
effort I recognized the effects of opium in some form. I will
spare you as much of the dreams and fancies I had, then and
later, as I can, without leaving out things that might make more
sense to a sober, unbiased mind.'

I had also a vague conviction that I had been dog-sick in
the recent past, what with the wine and the ether. I was absurdly pleased at the thought that whoever my captors were,
they hadn't let me suffocate.

Then the voices came nearer, and three new nightmare-faces
leaned over me. They must have been masks, but in my
drugged state they were demons and gargoyles, and so they
have remained in my memory. "Where are the pages?" asked
one. I thought of court pages, tabarded, Mediæval, and turned
my head from side to side. "Where are the pages from your
note-book?" the same one, or another, asked. Visions of children in silk and gold issuing from my note-book—no, they
meant sheets of paper, of course. And that made no sense,
because if they already knew they were looking for pages from
my note-book, why hadn't they simply looked there? Questioning someone who has taken opium must surely be one of
the most fruitless endeavours known to Man. But I began to
struggle in earnest against the effects of the drug then, because
I remembered what I'd recorded, enciphered, in that note-book.

It was only a list of dates and places and encoded names,
only the most damning thing I'd ever set to paper in the whole
of my career as a revolutionist. I was reconstructing the move-

ments of the members of the Chartist underground who seemed most likely to have repeatedly informed on their fellows. Some of my early possibles, it was clear from my notes, had not informed—but if the government were to lay hands on that note-book and decipher the entries, they could convict those people of treason on the strength of my evidence.

From what I had learned and recorded, there were only a handful of my fellows who *could* have informed on Newport, on the meetings in the North, on the hiding-places of so many of the leaders of the uprisings. I still had no certain proof. But if any of the informers knew what I'd been at, they'd know the danger they were in from those people whose movement they destroyed. And more important, if my notes reached sympathetic hands, *the informers would be unable to work clandestinely against another cause*. They would be useless to the government; they might, indeed, be a liability to it. They would stop at nothing to get my notes, once they knew they existed. They could not afford to do otherwise.

It seemed they knew. So I was trying hard not to be completely out of my mind, and not having much success.

I'm not sure why the act of writing on those pages, which I had been doing over the course of several months *before* the accident, should have been wiped from my memory along with the accident and the period that followed it. I believe I even told Richard that I'd bought the thing a week before going down to Melrose, which wasn't true, but I thought it was. I might have believed that my amnesia was a product of drugs and stress—but why forget my notes as well? I think because the failure of my memory was entirely artificial, the things to be forgotten selected carefully by someone else—I understand that selective memory loss is one of Mesmerism's most common tricks.

My hard surface seemed to be swaying gently. One of the gargoyles pushed forward and struck me across the face, and asked for the notes again, and struck me again, apparently forgetting that since I was full of poppy I couldn't feel much of anything. That made me laugh when I understood it, but the way the blows rocked my head was making me sick. They broke off to quarrel with one another. Before I sank back into unconsciousness I noticed that one of the voices was female.

So began a period of near-insensibility punctuated by troubled, unnatural near-awareness. During one of the punctuation marks, I was being moved, I think; at least I recall being carried out of a coach, through a blessed interval of night air—I seemed to be starved for fresh air—across a wet cobbled pavement, and then down a stairwell that echoed and smelled, improbably, of cat urine and frankincense. I can recall that, but not any of the smells or sounds between the coach and the stairs, though I am convinced there were some.

And dreams—impossible to tell which parts of them were prompted by reality. Some of the talking was, I think: wanting to know who I was working for, and with, who else knew what I was doing, where were the pages torn out of my notebook? Without opium, I'm good at this; I can convince myself, during questioning, that I've forgotten everything about the subject at hand, can actually move the answers out of the immediately accessible part of my mind. Drugged, I could not do it. Each question filled my brain with the answer and I couldn't be sure I had not spoken it aloud, except that if I had, they wouldn't ask again. But they asked again, and the whole tormenting process started over.

I believe my periods of near-insensibility were meant to be complete, and I tried, as well as I could, to convince my captors that they were. But after so many years of regular physical damage in the service of the cause and the requisite patching-up afterward, I have a fairly high threshold for opium. So I heard things I believe I was not meant to hear. Some of them I even managed to hold on to. A ship in Bristol-roads on the 20th (of what month, and whether arrived or departing, I could not tell); another at Southampton on the 5th of November; at least two references to "the Prussian gold," and one about something arriving from Paris soon.

My first escape could be staged as either drama or farce, depending on which details one chose to dwell on, and what point of view one told it from. I cannot recommend my point of view for either. I woke bound to a chair in a room lit only by a fire. My chair was drawn up quite close to the hearth, and I remember feeling the heat of it strongly, and being surprised; I knew from the sensation that I had less opium in me than I'd had for a while.

A figure moved between me and the firelight, a skirted figure. I could see the contours of the mask, with its long cruel-looking bird beak and the carved brows ornamented with recurved spines like the thorns of a giant rose. She called me by name in a clear, soft voice I remembered from the most Byzantine of my dreams. Then she said, "Your friends call you Jimmy, I think? Mine call me Helen, sometimes. Would you like to be my friend?"

She put out her hand and moved the hair out of my eyes. Her fingertips seemed too cool for the heat of the room. Perhaps I said something about it; she apologized for them, at any rate, and said they had been wet, and would be warmer presently. Then she turned and busied herself at the hearth.

It was the first time my brain had been clear enough to take note of the fact that I had not seen an unmasked face since my abduction. It suggested that they meant to let me live; or that they were very careful indeed, thinking that I might escape, or be rescued, before they could kill me. Escape or rescue must be possible, then. Why keep me alive? Of course— my notes. They would be looking for them, but if I could be induced to tell their location, that would be easiest. Except that I didn't know their location. I'd thought they were in my notebook. Obviously it was in my best interests not to tell them so.

Then a bar of red light hovered before my eyes and the radiating heat made me close them. For all the good my eyelids would be. "Can you feel that?" the clear voice asked. "Yes, you can. Good."

Dead, I would be able to keep all my secrets. But nothing need stop them from blinding me.

The heat receded and I opened my eyes. I could see the poker against her dark silhouette like a hole punched through it to the firelight. It rose and fell, stopping just above my right forearm, exposed and bound to the arm of the chair. She asked again if I could feel it.

I managed to marshall two words in a broken whisper. "A cliché."

Even without the mask I could not have seen her face, but there was a smile in her voice when she said, "Then perhaps it won't hurt," and brought the poker down.

I still had a little of the poppy in me, just a little. It would hurt more, and soon.

She turned back, unhurried, to the fire and set the poker in it while I caught my breath, sweat and tears creeping down my face. "There," she said. "You can be my friend and call me Helen, or you can have a little more of that." To be her friend, she explained, required only that I answer truthfully her few questions: the catechism I knew well by now. "Will you answer?" she asked, her thumb pressing the burned skin. I shook my head.

I was still waiting for the eyes, for the resumption of that threat. But she tapped my wrist with a fingernail and said, "Look at your bindings."

We were near enough to the fire that I could see them. I had thought they were cord, but I saw now that they were thin strips of leather.

"I make my masks out of it," she said, lifting a hand to her contoured, fantastical face. "I wet it and shape it, and when it dries it keeps the shape. But smaller. I had to learn, at first, how much bigger to cut the pieces, because it shrinks so much when it dries."

I didn't need her to tell me my bonds were wet. I could feel them slightly cooler around my wrists, as her fingers had been cooler. In the warm room, by the fire, the leather couldn't take long to dry.

She said, "I know you were called the Ice-cliff, and that the police questioned you several times. Did they ever threaten to amputate your hands?"

The leather wouldn't do that, of course, but the gangrene that would come after the circulation stopped would make it necessary. "Bronterre O'Brien called me the Ice-cliff because he didn't like me." I found I could keep my voice fairly steady if I could be satisfied with something barely above a whisper. "People who liked me called me the Tomb."

She laughed at that. Still laughing, she asked, "And will you lose your hands for your dead cause?"

"Do I have to decide now?"

She touched the leather at my wrists. "Not yet. Soon." Then she picked up the poker again.

"If I'm to lose my hands anyway, why the poker?" I was trying to forestall the inevitable.

She shrugged against the firelight. "Because the leather wouldn't make you scream." And as I realized that she, too, had been delaying, waiting for the opium to desert me, she laid the poker-end on the already burned skin. I have never believed that there was anything especially manly in enduring pain in silence; I had no objection to gratifying her in this.

We went through the business twice more, at a leisurely pace, though with a good deal less conversation from me. My voice had hardly died away after the last passage when the door to the room, somewhere behind me, opened with a crash. There was a flurry of movement between me and the fire; a man, from the silhouette, and the weight of the blow he struck across the woman's face, and his voice when he said, "You bloodthirsty whore! I told you to keep away from him!"

"You want him to talk? Do you think you can beat him a little and make him whimper? *Je croyais que tu le connu!*"

The French seemed to make him angrier. He raised his hand again, but she thrust the poker between them and continued, "I have not spilled blood, I have not killed him, and I swear he will speak. Can your pretty gentlemen claim as much? And keep your own mouth shut. He's not drugged now."

No, he wasn't, but pain is as effective as opium in overthrowing the finer workings of the senses. I wished the new arrival had gotten out another sentence before she warned him.

He grabbed her wrist and wrenched the poker out of her grip with the other hand. Then he pulled her with him, past me, and I heard the door slam behind them and a key turn in the lock.

She had misjudged me, though only a little. If she had stopped at the leather bindings, left me alone in that room before the fire, my imagination would have been her best ally. I think she would have broken me. But the poker had betrayed her; the poker kept me tied to the present and gave me no leisure to think of the next hour, or the hour after that. And laid repeatedly on my forearm, it had charred the cord around my right wrist.

It took a while, even so; once I had gotten the leather to part, I discovered that the knots on my other wrist and my ankles were too tight to pick apart with my fingers, and I had to work the chair across the floor (maintaining as much of both awareness and silence as I could) until the poker was in reach of my freed arm. I still had the feeling in my hands, at least. I burned through my remaining bonds; there was nothing in the room to cut them with. I tried to stand, and fell, and wondered how for the love of reason I was going to defend my freedom if anyone came in. I tried again with the same result. But this time the section of floor I came down on, near the wall, gave back a rattling sound when I hit it. The wide boards were only laid across the joists there. I lifted one and looked into a black space with no bottom I could reach.

I have no idea what it was meant for—possibly an easy way to dump the ashes from the fire into the cellar in bad weather, instead of carrying them in a bucket out of doors. Whatever it was, it would get me out of that room, which was my only aspiration. I dropped a piece of kindling into the dark hole and heard it land, which seemed reassuring. I would have to be able to set the board back into position after me, though.

If I *can* remember anything harder than climbing into that hole and hanging there, positioning the loose floorboard so that it would drop into place when I was out of the way, I would rather not be reminded of it. But at last I could let go and fall. It was a little farther than I'd expected, and after I landed I believe I lost consciousness for a while.

The boom of footsteps overhead roused me, and several raised voices. The cracks between the floorboards leaked light, which grew stronger as I watched; someone had brought a lamp. I thought about moving away from under my trapdoor and gave it up as pointless. I wished I could make out what was being said above me.

Sound died away above, but a few minutes later I heard commotion near at hand, in the direction my feet were pointing. There was light in that direction, too, now, tracing the outline of a rough plank door in a wall I hadn't known was there. The voices came closer, and in a desperate childish impulse I rolled over and hid my face against the wall. It was all the movement I could make.

The door-latch rattled and the hinges creaked. I couldn't tell if light had fallen on me or not. "Empty," said a voice I didn't know.

"How can you tell? He might be behind the door."

"Christ, you damned fool, look at the floor. There'd be tracks in the ash. Unless you think he can fly?"

"Well, close it then, for God's sake. There may be rats," said the other voice, the one I recognized. It was Hugh Stone.

The first man laughed, the door thumped shut, and the latch dropped.

I doubted there were rats, since they don't live on air and cinders. Neither do I, particularly. I would need water soon, but what I needed most was to lie flat for a while, because I couldn't cross that stretch of unseen floor without a little rest. Exhaustion won out over pain, and I slept.

When I woke I was surrounded by silence and darkness. I hoped it was the silence of a sleeping or deserted house. I found the door across the room and the latch on my side of it and passed through into more darkness, close and airless and with a sickroom smell. And with furniture, which I fumbled over until I found a candle and a tin of lucifers.

It was obviously the room I'd been confined in, before I'd been moved upstairs to the parlour for questioning. I salvaged my boots and what was left of my coat (in the pocket I found my notebook, half the pages torn out, which answered one nagging question at least), and drank the whole of a carafe of water by the cot, after determining that it hadn't yet been dosed with laudanum. I found the laudanum, too, and pocketed it in the conviction it would prove useful. Then, candle and lucifers in hand, I found the stairs.

I wanted to search the rest of the house, but I knew I was not strong enough to do anything but get out and go to ground. The most important thing was to find my notes before someone else did. I wished passionately that I'd had a memory like Susan's and hadn't needed to put anything to paper at all.

I don't think I could find that house again, though I discovered soon enough that I was in London, near St. Giles. I discovered also that it had been less than a fortnight since I'd gone over the side of the boat. After a few days of desperate measures (I had nothing I could afford to pawn, but I had to be sure of food and sleep and dressings for my arm, and some assurance of privacy and security, none of which can be got for free in the rookeries of London—I was not forced to kill anyone to get them, and I'm grateful for that), I was in good enough order to sleep in a doss-house and not wake to find my boots stolen off my feet. Also, and rather sooner, I found out why I'd taken the laudanum with me. Instinct is still a useful force in the human animal.

I was not seen by anyone Richard knows to be an acquaintance of mine (I remember asking him to find out) because I couldn't afford to be. Well, I was seen for a moment by George Wilson, but it was quite dark, and he has a glass jaw. The idiot was on foot in Bethnal Green with ten pounds and a revolver in his pocket. I assume he has a mistress nearby. If I live, I shall pay him back.

I *was* seen by a few people Richard does *not* know: a man who ran cockfights near the West India docks; a German lighterman in St. George's; a red-haired Italian prostitute in Bloomsbury Square; and a big blond man who has a coffee-stall beside the Blue Lion tavern near St. Paul's whom I know only as Lee. It was the latter who got me out of London (hidden in a dustman's cart) when the man who ran the cockfights was killed in a squabble over my whereabouts. From there I worked my way cautiously across the countryside, living on stolen produce, poached rabbits, and carefully-rationed doses of laudanum, toward Dunston.

The time in London was spent trying to lay hands on Hugh Stone; or failing that, to give some kind of warning about him, in quarters that might be vulnerable to information laid by him. I was also trying to find out if my notes had surfaced, or at least caused some turbulence, since my disappearance. They hadn't. It was the last fact I required to convince me that it was David, the Reverend Saint Bloody David, who had taken them. I couldn't tell how well in with my abductors he might be. He might only have taken the pages because he recognized that they could be damaging, and meant to threaten me, or my father, with them later. Or he might have been paid by my enemies to do it, and even to help, in a moderate way, with my capture—but if that was so, why hadn't he turned over the notes? Whatever his involvement, I thought it unlikely that David would be immediately sure of how to dispose of the pages to best advantage, and with David, advantage was the whole point. Principle would not enter in. So I went to Dunston.

Where I was re-taken. I wonder how David justified his fear of my descending on him, to the point of insisting on a body-guard, without explaining what I would come in search of? The study at the parsonage in Dunston may never be the same. I put up an excellent fight against three good-sized fellows, much assisted by the strengthening effects of weeks of hard physical exercise and plentiful stolen food, and by my rather limited ability to feel pain. I shot one of them in the head (sad damage to the plaster behind) before one of his mates disarmed me with a well-flung and heavy chair, which also broke the window. David did not take any actual part, but he was in the passageway; I heard him object when one of the large fellows came down hard on his satinwood desk and collapsed it. If only he had come in to defend it! I would have broken his neck.

One of my opponents was finally driven to pull out a knife, which made David spring from his hiding place squeaking that there was to be no blood—which seemed a little late, given the man I'd shot. I was distracted, and tired, and missed seeing the swing taken at me with one of the fire-dogs, which sent me to the floor. Then the man who'd swung grabbed me by the throat, found the artery there, and squeezed, and I assume I fainted, that being the point of the exercise.

I don't know where I was held the second time, or even why I was held; they should have cut their losses and killed me. They meant to, I believe, but I had a very vague notion they were waiting for something. Very vague. I was now getting enough opium to keep me unconscious nearly 'round the clock—to kill me if it had gone on much longer. But I was roused at last with light in my eyes and cold water in my face, and a woman's voice saying, "Jimmy Cobham! James! Can you hear me?"

It was not the Byzantine voice, but I recognized it. I couldn't think from where. More cold water. "Open your eyes. Open them, or I can't help you. Wake up, Jimmy, you idiot." I wanted to tell her I was trying. I did manage to open my eyes.

There was bright, focused light, and something spinning,

shining, almost filling my vision, and blurry behind it, a woman's face, not masked. I decided the voice belonged to Betty Howard. I didn't wonder why Gideon's mistress should be there calling me an idiot. Her voice droned, and my eyes closed again, and this time she must not have minded, because the next thing I knew I was wrapped in some stiff cloth, with cloth over my face, and Betty Howard saying in a fierce, low tone, ". . . get rid of it. If they learn he was on our hands when he died, there'll be the devil to pay and no pitch hot."

The next voice was Hugh Stone's: "My God. What do we do? Bury him?"

"Don't be a fool. There's not time, and it couldn't be hid. Take him out on the river and roll him over the side. He'll sink quick enough, and if he ever comes up again, we'll be long gone from here."

And Hugh Stone, bless him, did as he was told, as far as I was able to tell. I certainly got wet again. But I was also fished out almost immediately, and flung into a cart, and after a ride of uncertain duration, was tossed out again. The fisher might only have been a hired waggoner. Whoever it was, from the treatment I think he had been told I was dead.

The cold kept me awake enough to saw my way out of the canvas I'd been sewn loosely into, with the pen-knife I found on a cord around my neck. That must have been Miss Howard's work, and my retrieval from the water as well, likely enough. As with so many other participants in this drama, she deserved better than she received. I cut my hand hacking through the canvas; I remember quite clearly thinking the pain was unreasonable.

The dreams were very bad. I managed to stagger out of the ditch I'd been tossed in and across a span of marshland. The wind through the reeds sounded like a hundred raucous conversations in an overheated ballroom, and things, people, animals, seemed to move all around me. I thought, over and over, that I was walking through fresh blood. Once I fell face-first in the shallow water, and might have lain where I was and drowned except that a fat, fantastically wrinkled dowager in a creased satin gown and plumes of sober brownish-grey hauled me up by my armpits, dusted me off forcefully, and offered me her elbow until I could stand by myself. Then I blinked and found myself clinging to an outcrop of twisted branch on the broken stump of an old dead tree. Another time I was attacked by long black jointed insects, a cloud of them, that settled on my shoulders and tore at my skin and hair. That, when I pulled free and looked back, became a hawthorn bush, leafless and skeletal against the night sky. Light streamed by me in greenish scarves, and I smelled marsh-gas at times, and at other times roses and jasmine.

Then a bank lay before me, and I struggled up it, feeling as if weights were tied to my legs and arms and back. At the top was a hedgerow, and a road, and then after a time I couldn't measure, another mass of high hedge, this time of roses. (Real roses; I got a handful of thorns when I caught at them.) That was where I gave up at last, and where the youngest of the Coslick children found me at dawn, my past rudely quarried and my future nearly mined out.

Yes, I lied to Richard when I told him I was well. I was, as Mrs. Coslick sourly put it, "like to die" for a week after my arrival, what with the physical abuse, the exposure to cold and wet, and the withdrawal of the laudanum. After the first week I was aware enough to only *want* to die. I should not have been strong enough to manage horses, certainly. But perhaps some animal sense told them that I was incapable of being anything but gentle to them then, and they responded in kind. Whatever it was, I found that a touch or a word from me was enough to accomplish what took the farrier or a local carter a great deal more effort. And so I found myself employed, though at the time I had still to sit and gather my strength four or five times in every hour.

If I had not been so damnably weak, and so far from everything and everyone I knew, perhaps I wouldn't have been so frightened by the hole in my life. But I was frightened, more than I had ever been save once. And so I committed the indefensible folly of writing to Richard, because I was afraid. Failure of nerve is one of the few real sins in my craft.

I said, at the start of this, that the relative I most expected to effect the discovery of these pages is Susan. Having said so, I assume that Richard, and possibly Kitty, having also read them, will be shocked at the explicitly revolting nature of the contents, at my lack of scruples in laying this kind of narrative before a well-bred and properly-reared young woman. I have been explicit because I wanted, in a sense, to give evidence, to deliver up a kind of testimony to whatever court of concerned persons may someday be required to deal with all this. And I have recounted the revolting matters as accurately as I can because two days ago I saw Susan and was afraid for her, and by extension I am afraid for Richard and Kitty, too. If I can administer a stiff dose of revulsion to all three of you, if I can convince you of the cruelty and consciencelessness and sheer *alien-ness* of the people I have crossed, then perhaps you will stand as far back from this matter as you can until it is over. If you also begin to see that I partake of some of the qualities of my enemies, I will only acknowledge the justice of the observation.

J.

MELROSE HALL
NOVEMBER 22nd

Dear Susan,

Only a short note this time, as we must look into the legal matters of which we spoke and whose urgency you insisted on so eloquently, but I do want to write and thank you for the visit for your own sake, as well as for the sake of intrigue, and to say that if you still take pleasure, as you used, in setting everything around you topsy-turvy while remaining yourself utterly unruffled, well, my dear, you've done it again, because we still have not recovered, and I am myself torn between the joy of seeing you again, delight in the havoc that returned to Melrose along with your pretty eyes, and utter confusion over all that you told us, although it is some consolation to me that, I think, you were startled once or twice too, especially about the whole matter of James's father, but all of this is overshadowed by the news about David, at whom I think I will never be able to look again.

But, Susan, even with all of those Greek swords, it was wonderful to see you, I cannot say how wonderful, and if I seemed teary from time to time, it was from happiness, because I had forgotten how much I missed you, and all of our scheming and playing and laughing of past years, and if the stakes are so much higher this time, and the setting grimmer, let us not, let us never forget how we felt when we first discovered each other, and all that we have meant to each other, because that is what came back to me more strongly than anything else.

Dick slept poorly last night, I think because he was still upset by our conversation, and especially by that document of James's you found in the book, although he had already calculated and proved David's villainy but he is trying not to show it, I suppose out of some sort of need to put on a brave face for me, which is the only time he irritates me, and I hope he learns better soon or I shall kick him. However, while he was sleeping fitfully, he said something about Betty Howard, and wondering just how many people she was the mistress of, and that made me realize that, if Betty Howard helped James escape, then perhaps we had misunderstood her, and that meant that maybe her note to him was not a trap after all. And while I was thinking about that, I suddenly realized something about those pages from James's note-book, and I am sure you have already thought of this, but in case you have not, it seems to me that those pages may be keeping James alive and if they were to suddenly appear, he might not be of any use to them any more, and I told Dick that and he said, "My God! You must tell Susan," so I am doing so, though, as I said, you have probably already thought of it.

I hope we can sleep tonight, but so very much has happened that it will probably be days before it all makes sense, if it ever does, or it may not make sense until everything is over, especially the part about David having stolen those pages the very day, nearly the very hour, when James was taken, because if it was by the same people, why didn't they know, and it being different people is just too much weight to put on co-incidence, so the only thing that makes sense is if David is both working with and against the people who kidnapped James, and that means cousin David has probably come a cropper, and frankly I think it serves him right, and if he escapes with his position, and if he escapes with his *life*, well, right now I think it more than he deserves, but he probably will, because he has the Trotter's Club on his side, and whether you believe in the Dark Forces or not, do not take them lightly, because you heard what Richard said they did to Roderick. I should have said all this yesterday, and in fact I was just about to, when you burst out with your statement that James is always careful with his language and proceeded to cut open the book, but so very much happened that by the end my brain was quite in a spin, and I'm sure that there will be more things that will occur to me as the next few days go by, so you will just have to be patient, even though I know you are not patient, and for all I know have already figured out where James is and are off after him once more.

When you pressed my hand as we were leaving, you asked if I were still worried, and I tried to say no, but I could see that you knew that yes, I am still worried, and it is for you above all, because if I am becoming like Dick, and I know very well what you meant by that pointed remark about those with a foot on each side of the battle-line, then I am afraid you will take too much after James, who I confess I now see as lost to us, whatever may happen to him, and I hope that I am wrong about him, and I hope still more that I am wrong about you, but I saw the look on your face when Dick spoke about going to meet the unknowable where it lives, and I cannot help but wonder if part of what happened to James is result of his too-rational rationality, and if you are not walking on the same precipice.

Do not become angry with me, dearest Susan, only recall that I worry for you because I love you, and I will still love you whatever you have to do, and I know that nothing can stop you from setting out after James, especially after all we learned yesterday, so know that Dick and I, though no longer in the chase, are ready to back your play, whatever it is, the instant we learn what you want, and that, above intrigue and horror, most of all I was overjoyed just to see you and embrace you once again, and along with whatever warnings I may give you, I will always remain your good and loyal friend,

                                                            Kit

THE LIME-TREE, MINT LANE, LONDON
23 NOV 1849

Kitty,

I am an idiot, and that was a very near escape—I'm still
shaken over what I almost did. I was about to set off to see a
friend, and put into his care James's notes and the deciphered
transcript you supplied, when your letter arrived. If this is the
best I can do, it's no wonder that James tried to turn me away
from him. That's right, I didn't tell you that; it was at the inn
at Fairfield. He said some horrible, calculating things in the
hope that I'd run away. Instead I said some horrible things
back. He made me angry as much by thinking I'd scamper off
as by anything he did. It doesn't bear dwelling on, and it did
me a bit of good; a little cold water poured over the head
makes an excellent regular physic for anyone dealing with
James. But to have missed the deadly potential of those notes!
James owes you much for that warning, if for nothing else,
and I've dealt with the problem, I think, satisfactorily.

It's interesting to imagine what must be happening in the
minds of the conspirators now. David has been relieved of
notes that no one knew he had, and he can't tell his cohorts
where the notes have got to without telling where they've
been, thus revealing that David has been a less than ideal co-
conspirator. Heavens, *I* could have told them that, poor creatures. James has (I hope) disappeared like a conjuror's pigeon,
so if they intended to let him lead them to anything, they must
be a little bereft.

I don't think Betty Howard would have thought that James
could lead them to the notes. From James's recollections, it
must have been she who tampered with his memory and made
him forget the wretched things. Well, Miss Howard was already keeping a lot from her friends, obviously. Interesting,
though, that although she freed James, she also tried to gut the
threat he posed to her fellow schemers.

Who, do you suppose, had the deciding of the fates of Hugh
Stone and Betty Howard? It's not something one puts up for

a vote. Have two deaths in close proximity shaken the lower ranks at all? Or are they used to that sort of thing? I'd love to know if Stone's murder was Betty Howard's idea, or if it was done on someone else's order. I've been assuming the latter, because she had that letter from Johnson that upset her so just before she went to Manchester. But the letter might have told her something that made her decide, on her own, to eliminate Hugh Stone from the ranks of people who could talk about her. And I hope you won't tell me you thought Betty Howard's death was an accident. Aren't accidents, by definition, *in*convenient?

Another reflection: from what I overheard in Manchester, Stone still believed that James was dead. Betty Howard knew otherwise, having saved his life; but if she'd done it for her own reasons (and what were they? Not a shared belief in his project to uncover the informers; she'd done her best to wreck that. His pretty face?), she wouldn't tell anyone else. But James left the Grey Hound convinced he was being watched, and I know it wasn't by Howard, because at the time *I* was watching *her*. If James' being alive and free was known to the conspirators in general, why didn't Stone know?

Is the pretty lady in the large coach James's Byzantine poker-wielder? If so, how did she find him again, and having found him, why did she only sit and survey him like a cat watching a bird through a window? He was weak, and alone. Judging by their previous two successes, his enemies could have taken him with no trouble at all. And where did the mysterious lady perch, while she kept her eye on him? Was she so confident he'd stay where he was put that she merely trotted down once a week from Town to have a look? Not likely. Unless she and her entire coach and four had mastered spirit travel, she must have been somewhere within a few miles of the Grey Hound. Portsmouth? Then why did James always see her driving *toward* it? (Why did James only see her going in one direction at all, whichever one it was?)

Did *la jolie blonde* have anything to do with the attack on Richard in Southampton? There has got to be a way to get access to the police records—was the attacker identified? Was the man even found dead? And where *did* the delectable and so-convenient (wouldn't you think someone who makes as much fuss about his own deviousness as James would have *noticed*?) Irish housemaid who visited the Grey Hound disappear to?

Why has David taken up residence at Cauldhurst Abbey? Even David—*surely* even David—wouldn't be so crass as to step obviously, publicly, into the heir's shoes when as far as the county, the family, and everyone but Uncle Andrew's solicitor knew, *Richard* was the heir, after James?

My God, I hate questions.

It's spelled "Damocles," dear, and thank you for the decent, honest laugh I got when I realized that your ever-so-casual reference to Greek swords meant that you were too lazy to look it up. I dismiss as unworthy my next thought: that you'd done it on purpose to make me laugh. I'm sorry; I'll stop second-guessing everyone's motives as soon as this blasted piece of detective work is done.

Why am I doing this? Do you remember asking me that, so many weeks ago, before either of us knew what was really at issue? Or at least, I knew you wanted to ask it, and I answered as if you had. Why are *you* doing this? It's no small thing to assure your friend and cousin that you will support her in what she does, even though it may mean outraging every convention, circumventing every law, and running the risk of being implicated in a charge of high treason.

Richard's motive, I think, is that he wants to see Justice done and Right triumph, and that frightens me; he's already run up against the reality, that in the strange and hostile landscape James travels through, justice is sometimes done by breaking laws, and right triumphs by abandoning virtue and morality and every honest impulse. If Richard tried to live in that country for long, the very air would poison him.

May I guess at your motives, Kit, to see if I'm still at least half the Susan you want me to be? You do it out of love. You make from your quick mind and sharp senses and adamant will a haven for the people you treasure, a suit of armour for them to fight in, a net to catch them as they fall. You weave strength around us—yes, I know I'm one of the ones you love and will protect, and I don't take it lightly. That you've withdrawn your approval from David warns me to let him go; I can't imagine him continuing to stand for long without the invisible bulwarks that you build so prodigally for those you favour. You involve yourself in this because I care about the outcome, and Richard cares, and you love us both.

It seems odd, though, that I don't know if the circle is any wider than that. Is James dear to you still? You were all but brother and sister once; he was your defender and companion long before you met me. You told me once—you were seven, I think, and were in disgrace for being wayward and bad-tempered over some French irregular verb. James was home from school, or wherever he'd been most recently sent to keep him out from underfoot; he got your governess to chat with him in French—to practise, he said, though at fourteen James must have been able very nearly to *dream* in French—and used your verb correctly, and argued it with her until she realized that you'd been right all along. Do you want to save his life? Because that's what's ultimately at stake—not my happiness, or Richard's. James is trying to carry through a hopeless and quixotic project, alone, against the desires of a group of powerful, dangerous, ruthless people who want to kill him. It's not just the notes, of course, not any more. If they were all that was at stake, I could deliver them, James could fly the country, and it would be over. He must need to know who did this to him. He needs to eliminate the danger they pose to him, to us, to his friends. But you say you think of him as lost to us, whatever happens—that may be the answer to my question. Your protection is withdrawn; the cloak of your love doesn't cover him, because strong and stubborn though you are, you won't spend yourself on lost causes.

Why am I doing this? I said that the tethered goat engaged less of my interest, which is still true, though I'd like, against all the odds, to see him succeed. I'd rather he wasn't killed. But I don't want to expend a lot of energy on lost causes, either. Besides, haven't I mourned him once already? It's really awfully James-like to require two separate wakes.

I'm telling you what my reasons *aren't*. I'm stalling off, I suppose. Don't cry, Kitty—this is the last thing you want to hear, but don't cry over it until the game's played out and we know the results. I'm doing this mostly because it's opened wide a door to a room inside me that before I could only guess at by the light along the sill and through the keyhole. It's a room in which all those things in me that, living the normal life of a well-bred woman, I could never use—strength and speed and hardiness; command over my mind and body; respect for the language of my senses; a certain ferocity of the spirit—are not only useful but essential. In that place life is lived as if in mid-air over an obstacle, between leap and landing, with everything committed and nothing certain. *Everything happens fast enough.* Does that make sense? But it seems that I can't open up that part of me without closing the one you want, that makes me merry and confiding and willing to open my hands and heart and let life come to me. I'll try, I'll keep trying, but it's hard not to feel that this cold, pure place and the clean wind that whips through it is *my* birthright, and that I should embrace it.

You always judged me, a little, by yourself: if you loved James you would do this, so I must love James. What drives me is nothing so reasonable and sensible as your absolute allegiance, or even your unconditional passion. One of the things allowed me in this inner place I've found and opened is desire, without sentimentality or shame. I desire James. He is a beautiful male animal of my species. I can take pleasure in looking at him, and can wonder, to my new cool and shameless self, what it would be like to take pleasure in other things with him, things I've read about and never done. But love is something else, isn't it? There's no basis for love between us. I know him only a little, and from the missteps he's made in dealing with me, I think he knows me even less. There's animal desire in it, and the passion the lioness brings to a hunt—but you know what love is, Kitty, and it isn't here.

I've been doing the things I meant to do before coming to Melrose—making calls, in a style that the Legion of Aunts would decry if they knew about it. Visiting young men at their lodgings, for instance. Thomas Cavanaugh has amazed me. I descended upon him, big with irony and news, and failed to surprise him. He, I decided, was one of the people who ought to be included in the widening of the circle of those who know James is alive. He didn't swoon, or clutch the furniture, or even exclaim. He paused for an instant in the act of pouring me a glass of sherry (a retaliatory gesture, I think; there's a nice bit of steel in the boy, under all those manners) and said,

"I'd thought that he might be." And handed me the glass with a steady hand. It seems that Tom Cavanaugh spotted James's emerald ring at a pawnbroker's in the City not very long after the report of his drowning made the rounds. That started him asking the questions that eventually got him pummelled. He also, it seems, shared in the acquaintance of the late gentleman who ran cockfights near the West India docks.

"What are your political sympathies?" I asked him.

He looked startled (finally! I'd thought I'd lost the gift for it), and then shook his head. "No, it's not that. I know something of James's, though."

I was affronted, until he told me that he hadn't had any of it confided to him by James, and had only determined that James was emphatically Socialist and was probably doing something about it. It's a clever fellow, and observant—I suppose it comes of being a painter. And a good-looking fellow, too; my new self is not always under my absolute control, you understand, and I found myself thinking that he had nice long legs, and well-shaped hands, big but graceful. A good-looking fellow but not, you understand, a beautiful male animal. I left his virtue intact.

Oh, the emerald! This is more your speciality than it is mine, so I pass it on for what you can make of it. I don't know how well you remember that ring. I'd noticed once that it was a signet, with a motif carved in the face of the stone, but I hadn't paid much attention to the design. James told me once that it had been his great-grandfather's, Fitzhugh Callendar's. Well, Thomas Cavanaugh described the design, which he'd noticed long ago (painters!) and recognized again in the pawnbroker's case. A crescent opening toward, and partly enclosing, a five-pointed star. No snake. Cavanaugh said it reminded him of a device used by some very minor and obscure order of knighthood in the Middle Ages. There, I have no idea if that's useful, but now you know it.

The man with the coffee-stall proved to be a friend of the ex-deceased, rather than a co-conspirator. When he understood what information I was nibbling for, he didn't frown, but managed to give the impression of scowling anyway—it's something to do with the eyebrows, a wonderfully daunting expression—and made it *very* clear that it was no business of his or of mine, either, where the fellow was or who with, and having sold him his damned cup now and then didn't mean he lived in the bastard's pocket. I sipped my coffee and smiled my absolute clearest and most guileless smile, and said, "You cut it with chicory. I know it's not well thought of, usually, but I like it this way. Have you seen him since the dustman's cart?"

That stopped him, though he struggled not to show it. I gave him my direction and told him to use it if anything needed seeing to.

It seems to me that there's some pattern to the things we know about Andrew Cobham, but I can't make it come clear. The ownership of Betty Howard's house suggests that he's one of the conspirators, but why would he be? His politics march firmly with Lord Brougham's. If you'd ever heard him animadvert on Peel's betrayal over the Corn Laws, you wouldn't doubt it. Not to mention Richard's recollection of James's estrangement from his father the year he went up to Oxford. Were you in the room for that? No, that was after you'd collapsed on the library chaise and ordered us to wake you in no more than fifteen minutes. I knew our betrayal would come back to haunt us. It would have been '37, anyway; James and his father had an appalling fight about the slaves on the West Indian holdings, they called each other some choice names (Richard didn't tell me which ones), and James's father knocked him down. That was the last night James spent under the roof of Cauldhurst Abbey for years. They patched it up, somewhat, in '43, just before Roderick was born.

And if David and Uncle Andrew were partners in conspiracy, why did David kill Roderick? (That's still a little difficult actually to put into words.) And how in the name of sanity did Uncle Andrew come to make a pet of the man who killed his second son? To go through the appalling legal complexities of leaving English property in anything other than the direct line of descent, in order to make David his heir? He can't have known. Can he?

It's been obvious for years that Uncle Andrew had his heart set on a match between you and James, and bitterly objected to the arrangement between you and Richard—but it was also obvious that he didn't like his son, avoided his company, and much preferred Richard, arrangement or no. This all ought to come together in something like a pattern, oughtn't it? But if it does, I certainly can't see it.

I need to visit another young man at his lodgings, a German friend of mine who ought also to be told that James is alive, and who might have access to useful information. He's the one I meant to give the notes to, in fact. I shall tell you what I learn, and also whether my new self approves of *his* legs.

You'll have noticed the new address; Bright's was too far from everything, and after the turning-over of all my belongings, seemed too exposed. The new name is Susan Palmer; the surname popped into my head and I used it before I remembered why it was so near the top. If it bothers James, he can come and tell me so. Stephen Vaughan has also re-emerged, a time or two; he needs his hair cut.

I hope the legal matters are going well. We need to have a net woven and ready to drop on our tigers, whoever they may prove to be, when the time comes. Once we know all the details of what we're hunting it will be too late to engineer the trap, and either they'll get away, or eat us, or both. If we can manage to get James clear before we spring it, it'll be a miracle—if he lives to be got clear, that is.

You're still having David watched, I trust. I know you'd rather he disappeared—but if he does, we need to know it, and quickly. I doubt my brother is as good at throwing off pursuit as, for instance, my cousin is.

It's nine o'clock in the morning, which is my new bedtime. Another advantage of the Lime-Tree is that nobody seems to mind if you live like a bat, and the place is quiet as a ruin during the day. At least, I think it is, though after a good night's exercise in what passes for fresh air in London at this season, I may only be especially receptive to the lure of my pillow. It's calling me now, certainly, so I'll close with the best wishes for you and Richard from your

                                                              Susan

MELROSE HALL
NOVEMBER 24th

Dear Susan,

I was already in tears when I reached your injunction not to
cry, so you were too late that time, because it was not until
you said it that I realized I have given James up either for dead
or, worse still, for better off that way, because do not believe
I cannot read between your lines, or listen between your words,
and when you said that James had done some horrible things
I already knew it from what you said or what you did not say
in your letters and when you and Dick and I spoke, and now
that I have actually said on paper that James may be better off
dead rather than becoming what he has become, I find I do
not really mean it, so I no longer know what I think and I am
still sniveling like a schoolgirl.

My dear Susan, I understand so well when you say you are
doing this because, to break your explanation down to a simpler form, you are good at it. We enjoy doing things we are
good at, which I understand because I have learned that there
are things I enjoy doing for their own sake, and it should be
no surprise, after all we went through at school together, that
they complement yours, and include putting pieces of puzzles
together, especially puzzles of people's character and motives,
and supplying missing links in chains of people's mysterious
actions, and until you made me realize it, I did not understand
that I was enjoying this for just that reason, and now that I do
I do not know if I like it, because this is not a matter of a
Chinese dog, or an Indian lantern, or a stuffed fish, or a stain
on someone's new gown, but of the life of my step-brother,
someone I once cared about deeply, and I suppose I still do.

You tear me up dreadfully when you make me think you
cannot do what you love doing and still be the Susan I have
loved and admired so much, and I will not, I will *not* believe
it, because we are not entities made of good and bad portions,
some of which can be removed to perfect the character, but
rather entire people, certainly made up of contradictory ele-

ments, but each still a complete being. I insist on believing that there will always remain in you the easy laughter, the quick wit, and readiness to say at once and without thinking of consequences whatever was on your mind, all of which filled the innocent young Katherine with such admiration that it was all she could do to keep from swelling with pride when you first bestowed on her the nickname Kitty that she has always used and treasured since. But, Susan, even if I am wrong in all of this, I will take a certain satisfaction in being right in some other directions, especially since you now, at last, admit to being the sensualist I always thought you were, because otherwise you would not speak of men's legs in the same tone I use, although mostly to myself, when speaking of their shoulders, and now you know at last why I married Dick, who I believe must have the finest shoulders in England, and if that is not sufficient reason for a sensualist to marry, it is at least enough to decide to spend enough time around a man to learn his other qualities. If you can look me in the eye and tell me you are not even a little afraid that if you become better acquainted with James's legs you would find his other characteristics even more fascinating, well, then I will perforce admit my mistake, but I will be astonished as well.

Ah, Susan, there is nothing like a good chat about the attributes of the male animal, especially in particular instances, to cheer one right up, and I no longer feel at all teary, but rather my natural, hopeful good cheer has returned in all its vigour, so that I can go on to tell you that I am very proud of Susan Palmer or Stephen Voight or whoever it was who got such a good description of the emerald out of Cavanaugh, because I recognized the device at once as the emblem on a set of books at the very top of a back shelf in the library, which led me to the books, one of which proved to be hollow, which filled me with a sudden desire to open every book in the library to see how many of the rest of them are hollow or hide secret compartments or contain letters within the pages or inside the covers. In any case this book, called *Arka Kahn's Secrets of the Ages*, contains an emerald that is the exact twin of the one you describe, and, even better, a sealed letter, a *sealed* letter, mind, whose seal I promptly broke, read, and have made a copy of to send to you, and if you cannot see how it neatly

solves the mystery of James's father, then I'm afraid I shall
have to withdraw the application to Scotland Yard I have submitted in your name. As for the remainder of your interminable
list of questions, I will nod sagaciously and say that I agree
that those are, indeed, questions, and then I will wait for you
or Stephen Voight or Susan Palmer to unearth more secrets
that will direct me, I am certain, to yet another old tome which
will contain a key that will open a door to Fairyland where
the Queen will answer every question and grant us eternal
youth as well.

I am also enclosing a letter from Dick that he would like
you to deliver to James, if you see him. Dick said *when* you
see him, and I say I am unreasonably hopeful! But perhaps I
am after all, in that I am keeping some hope that you *will not*
see him, because, Susan, if James is to be lost to us, it would
be more than I could bear to lose you, too, although I do not
know why I am saying this, because I know very well that
once you have decided upon a course you are as stubborn as
Dick, about whom you are right, only I think his ideas of right
and wrong are not as intractable as you believe, or he and I
should never have spent the last year and a half as we did, or,
if we had, he would not have married me afterwards, and now
I am crying again, and this time I cannot blame you, because
I did it to myself, so I will end this now, only cautioning you
again to be careful, because your life is precious to many people, not the least of which is your loyal friend and cousin,

Kit

MELROSE HALL
THE 19ᵗʰ DAY OF JUNE
IN THE YEAR 1815

My Dear Andrew:

I read with interest and appreciation your remarks concerning
Bonaparte, and I declare that should you somehow take up a
seat in Parliament you would nowhere find a man more loyal
to your cause than your brother; you have a clear and accurate

idea, I think, of where the Emperor lies within the frame of history, and whence comes the motion, indeed, the *requirement* to expel him from this frame; indeed, you come near to reconciling me to the taxes that threaten Melrose itself, which is no easy task when every day the burden increases. But, Andrew, how is it you are able to present such a clear picture of the forces behind Bonaparte—historical, political, and economic—and then, in the next breath, as it were, to deny and even express contempt for the very rationalism that allowed you such insight?

Ah, Andrew, you still treat me as you did when we were children, believing you could make those clever remarks that pass over everyone's head invisible as a hawk on a cloudy day, forgetting that your brother hears the tone of your voice, and knows something of the mind behind it. When you tell me that you are unavailable on Midsummer, I know what that means, and what it means is that you still hold to your beliefs that not only fly in the face of the Church's teachings—which teachings I know would benefit with a bit of air—but in the face of all that is rational as well.

In my opinion, Andrew, and remember that I say this as a brother, in your heart you long ago gave up believing in spirits, faeries, and powers invoked at midnight with alembic and altar, and you now only hold to them because of your perceived duty as one of the founders, and because of ties of friendship. Let me ask you, then, two questions: What is the value of a friendship that cannot survive the re-consideration of one's beliefs, as one is bound to do over time? And what is the value of a leader who no longer believes in his cause?

I will be blunt, Andrew. I do not trust those friends of yours who gather at midsummer and midwinter to practice those Arts we flirted with long ago. If my belief (and, I believe, your own) in Man's ability to create a world guided by rational thought is true, then their practices have no place in it; and if it is wrong, then consider what sort of world will be created by a Blackman, by a Henderson, by a Thomas. Moreover, Andrew, whether such powers as they invoke truly exist or not—and I, for one, am convinced they do not—what will become of your Club when it becomes filled, as it surely must, with those who desire such power? The quest for knowledge is all to the good, but it is not knowledge they seek, as you know as well as I, but rather power for its own sake. Should you, as you once told me you would, turn the Club into a group seeking only knowledge, my opinion would change, but I tell you frankly that this is not possible; too many of the other sort fill its ranks already, and their numbers are bound to increase.

I beg you, Andrew, to consider what I have said, and reconsider my invitation. You know that Louisa would love to see you and Diana, so please give it careful thought. If you decide to pursue your other interests, we will be disappointed, but we will understand, and hope you know that to you Melrose Hall will always be another home, and I hope that, in any case, you will forgive the blunt language and pedantic tones of your affectionate brother,

William

Melrose Hall
Saturday
[Not received until November 27th]

James,

I am entrusting this to the care of Susan Voight, whom I expect to find you eventually, though I cannot say when. Today is the 24th of November, and a few days ago Miss Voight, Kitty, and I had a talk in which we put together sufficient of your story for my peace of mind. I write this because, as of your last letter, there remain a few issues of epistemology that have not been settled, and I thought it worthwhile to clarify my stand on these matters.

Your error in interpreting Hegel, James, is to pay too much attention to his system and too little to his method. His system, with its rational to real to irrational to unreal, and its becoming and being and not-being, is all fascinating, and were I half the mathematician you are, or used to be, I would, no doubt, delight in the intricacies and completeness of the logic for its own sake. But what is important in Hegel is the way he approaches the world, which, though to him merely (merely?!) the reflection of ideas, is nevertheless driven by internal conflict. Thus, to understand a thing, we must understand the opposing sides whose conflict determines the direction of its movement. To take an example, if we have a man who, on the one hand, wishes to improve the world, and, on the other, refuses to trust even those who are closest to and care most for him, we can see, by using the Hegelian method, that this man will find himself driven to the most appalling acts out of kindness or duty, and in the end will find himself alone, isolated, and bereft even of compassion from those he has used, all with the highest of motives.

I have read your Engels, at least as well as my German will allow, and I have read his friend Marx who has written a great deal in the English papers, and, whatever I think of their goals, I do not believe their methods conflict with them. That is, both of these reformers or revolutionaries or what-have-you seem determined to find the truth and to disseminate it, and then to take the actions that these truths call for. And if they err, then the errors are honest ones. You, on the other hand, have taken actions that conflict with your goals. Some, I know, preach that the ends justify the means. Others say they do not. I say the question is nonsense, because we do not use different means to the same end. Oh, yes, I know all about how a hundred roads lead to the same destination, but that is because we start from different places. If you, James, find yourself required to lie, to kill, and to deceive those who love you, then I would say that either your methods will not lead to the goal you profess, or your goal is not what you have been claiming it is.

I say all of this, you understand, only to further our most interesting discussion of philosophy, and I am curious indeed as to how you might choose to respond to your distant but still cordial cousin,

Richard

LONDON
25th NOVEMBER, 1849

My dear Miss Voight,

I was miserable to learn I had missed your visit. Then, to open your note and find, discreetly phrased, such astonishing news! I have not mistaken your meaning, have I? That the subject of my last letter to you is not a closed one after all? When I understood I gave a shout that must have been heard to the end of the street.

I shall not expect to hear from you soon on this matter, however anxious I become. Meanwhile I hope you will take the best possible care of yourself; your friends cannot spare you!

Now tell me: when you find that object you are looking for, may I be permitted to see it? I think you know you may trust me to give you an honest appraisal.

Yours,
F. Engels

LONDON
25th NOVEMBER, 1849

Dear Cobham:

My sincere congratulations to you on your timely resurrection; as the Christians know well, there is nothing like a return from death to inspire confidence. I have been able to pick up pieces and inferences of your recent activities, and while I cannot in all cases support them, the League will repudiate neither them nor you. I suggest that you consider your actions in light of historical movement: to be sure, the skilled, dedicated farmer can grow more corn than one with less skill or commitment, but no one can grow corn on water, or on soil to which it is not suited. The grand forces of history, driven by the class struggle, provide the soil; we are the farmers. I think you misunderstand this relationship, and thus try to substitute your own heroism (and I do not use the word accidentally) for movements of the masses. If you need to see where this can lead, consider Proudhon and Blanqi!

I would like to send you some of the work I have been doing on the social history of England, because I think you may find it interesting. In exchange, you could, perhaps, send me some of the material you have gathered. The bearer of this note will, I am quite certain, be willing to act as go-between.

Once more, my dear Cobham, permit me to say that I am delighted to find you among the living once more, or rather, still, and I am certain your old friends, so many of whom are now in the Communist League, will feel the same way when the time comes that it is safe to tell them. Until then, please take the utmost care of yourself, and present my warmest compliments to the charming Miss Voight.

Regards,
F. Engels

THE LIME-TREE, LONDON
26 NOV 1849

Kitty dear,

Is this the second letter in a row I've sent to you that begins, I'm an idiot? James went to some trouble to overhear and remember what he could when he was held captive in St. Giles. He then, for a wonder, had the decency to pass what he heard on to us. (I make no claims that he passed on *everything* he heard, as this is not an age of miracles.) Do you remember the text? A ship in Bristol-roads on the 20th of some month, and another in Southampton on the 5th of November? Southampton was swarming with ships on the 5th, of course; Southampton is always swarming with ships. But Gideon Johnson's ship, the *Cormorant*, was at Southampton on that date. It left for the Adriatic Sea on the 8th (no one connected with the Admiralty was forthcoming about her ports of call), and returned to Bristol-roads on the 20th.

James has to confront Johnson at some point, and I'll wager this is the point. Or was—in the life of a steam-ship, a week is a long time to be idle and the *Cormorant* may already be góne. So I must fly. Still no commanding of specials, but I discovered in my last set of peregrinations that there are sometimes accomodations for horses on the major lines, and Girasol likes riding in them; the railway-men make a fuss over him. On the Cambridge-to-London leg, the conductor fed him gingerbread.

So I can't properly answer your letter, except for a few hasty points. Don't make fun of my questions, you beast. It's a form of outlining. Besides, if I don't ask them out loud (well, on paper), I can't tell if you thought to ask them as well, and I don't dare assume we're thinking along the same lines. Too dangerous.

Other than that, I can only say: *Andrew Cobham is a member of the Trotter's Club*? Not to mention (what must be) Blackman, i.e., Lord Growe, who sits in Lord Russell's *and* Palmerston's pockets? *Does* that answer all my questions about James's father? Well, I don't know. But I'll have plenty of time to mull it over in my compartment.

Au revoir, my dear!

Susan

SUSAN VOIGHT'S JOURNAL
(WRITTEN IN CIPHER)

27 Nov 1849

In my compartment, bound for Bristol. I shall probably send these pages to Kitty as soon as I've written them, but it's easiest to scribble this all down anyhow as if talking to myself. No, to pick up from my letter to Kitty, the letter from William Cobham does *not* answer all my questions about Andrew. Perhaps it does for Kitty. Being in the Trotter's Club does not automatically allow one to disinherit one's first-born male child without significant proof of something fairly horrible.

Certainly not proof of treason, or the Abbey would likely be forfeit to the Crown, and the devil of a good trick for brother David to wrench it away from the Exchequer after that. No, the last thing David would want is a charge of treason against J. Unless he could be thoroughly disinherited *first*.

My assumption has been that Andrew has taken this step at David's urging, but am I justified in that assumption? I can't think why Andrew would cut James out otherwise.

Nor can I think why Andrew would pursue any attempt to disinherit James after August, unless Andrew knew that James had not drowned. If Kitty and Richard can uncover the details of this legal action, perhaps we'll know when it was initiated, at least.

Yet another maddening speculation: might this action be meant to harm Richard? After all, if James is the problem, why not merely pass him over for Richard, who is a much closer connexion than David? Richard would never stand for it, of course, but I doubt that would weigh with Andrew.

I'm getting old and slow, I think; obvious why David wanted J.'s notes. He meant to hold them over the heads of the other conspirators if he felt threatened. Imagine his present terror! No ace in his hand to protect him just when his fellows are beginning to fall out and kill each other—*and* the charming possibility that they will find out that he had the notes all along. I'd lay in a wardrobe of black immediately, except that I can't imagine mourning David.

Does the murder of little Roderick have to do with the Trotter's Club? Kitty seems to think they're the very definition of vile and unsavoury, but a six-month-old child? Why, for goodness' sake? What rubbishing mystical nonsense could prompt a group of grown men to such an act? The other possibility is that David took the long view even in '44, and saw the child as a threat to his ultimate possession of the Abbey. But would he, while James was alive, in good health, only 24 years old, and (as far as his family then knew) unlikely to die on the gallows? And more than likely to marry and produce an heir of his own? The inheritance has got to be some odd-coloured fish (as Kitty used to say back at Miss Trevelyan's), or we're missing an important bit about it, because it simply won't stand up by itself.

(Digression: David is in the succession through the female line—that is, as the grandson of Augusta Callendar Voight, sister of Mellisande Callendar Cobham, who is J.'s and Richard's grandmother. Tenuous, no? His right is through the Callendars, not the Cobhams. Why aren't there any Cobham connexions in line for the Abbey? In our branch of the family, there are Voights and Wisharts, and countless resultant Peterses and Hopworths and Craigs and Fentons, sticking out all over like hairs on an unclipped spaniel. Where the devil is the rest of the Cobham family? Even if they're all deceased, there should be a churchyard full of them somewhere.)

My mind rattles from topic to topic, and I mean to let it, in the hope that something will bump into something else and be useful. Fitzhugh Callendar's ring bears a similar device to what seems to be the sigil of the Trotter's Club. All right, the letter Kitty unearthed suggests that old Fitzhugh's grandson is one of the founders, so he might reasonably have adapted an obscure family crest for the use of his new club. But was it an idle choice, or is there something about old Fitz, or that design, or both, that has special significance for a nest of would-be sorcerers? I'm not above using their nonsense against them, if it could be done.

So, politics be damned: Andrew's name on the deed to Betty Howard's house may have to do with the Trotter's Club, not with a Chartist underground. What were Betty Howard's ties to the Trotter's Club? Would the Trotter's Club allow women to join? Silly question. Probably the usual arrangement: no, but they need females for something and so end up with *de facto* female members or satellites or auxiliaries or whatever. The nature of Betty Howard's ties to Andrew Cobham is also interesting. Was she his mistress? Possibly. Gideon Johnson might not be an exclusive sort. Or she kept it from him. Or Tom Cavanaugh's information was out of date—except that Johnson was still corresponding with Howard the week before her death.

Andrew's place in the mystery makes me wonder about James's. Politics seems sufficient to explain it. James himself seems to find it sufficient—

But James is not only an impassioned rationalist, *he is a practised liar.*

I have a sudden awful sinking feeling. We have no account of what happened to James after his accident except his own. We have very little more than that to tell us whether anything that James recounts in his letters from the Grey Hound actually occurred. *We have no proof.* The man at the coffee-stall knew him, and seemed affected by the mention of the dustman's cart, but that could mean anything.

Too agitated to write. I have to lean back and just think, and will put this in the post to Kitty as soon as I reach the station.

THE DUCK, KINGS WESTON
27 NOV.

Dear Kitty,

Pardon me, it's the 28th now, by two hours. Susan is well, unharmed, and with me. Or more accurately, I am with her. She will write, I know, and probably as soon as tomorrow— later today, pardon me again. But this—I was going to write that this has nothing to do with her, but that's nonsense: it has everything to do with her, and with Richard, and you. I'll say, But this is my letter, the one I have to send to you, that I owe you.

Well, that was inarticulate. But I have had a shock or two, which you will understand, knowing that Susan will have told me a great deal since she found me. I am writing to apologise to you for the things I have done to the people you love. If this, or what follows it, sounds a little self-contained, it's because I am trying to be. I am trying not to say anything that rouses your sympathy, or might be interpreted as playing on it. And I'm left with a rather cold-sounding set of phrases.

I never meant for Susan to become a witness to murder, or to see and hear of evil, cruelty, and cold-blooded calculation and be changed by it. It's no use saying I did not ask her to seek out my past. It was there to be found, and the fault for that is mine. The effects will fade with time and with distance from the stimulus—me, and whatever else—but it is a sort of blight, and I am the source of it, and I'm sorry for it.

I apologize for what happened to Richard in Southampton (that is so inadequate it sounds obscene, but I have ruled out fervor). I don't entirely understand it yet, but I apologize for it, because what I do understand is that he would never have been there if I had not forgotten that he would be capable of following me. And if I had not drawn him in in the first place, and even encouraged him to pursue my affairs when I knew they could be dangerous.

But the worst hurt I did to them and to you was to hang a curtain of lies and secrets between us. I am sorriest of all for that—it's another blight, on the past and the future both. I suppose I thought none of you would ever know, but even if that had been true—if all of us had gone to our graves with my career and associations undiscovered—the blight would still be present. The change that has appeared in Susan happened in me, too, years ago, and the pressures that provoked it were never countered or relieved. I brought you less of me than you thought—than you deserved. The poison in the cup will do its work, whether you taste it or not. I still believe in my cause. I'm no longer sure I did right in the service of it.

I mean to stay with Susan for as long as she wants or needs me to. If she still thinks I should leave the country, as she once suggested, I will. If she wants to pursue my quarrel, and I can be of help, I will stay until the business is done, and then I shall remove myself, once I have sent her back to you to be healed. It's a curable malady, Kitty, if one hasn't had it long, and Susan hasn't. You'll get your old friend back.

I'm glad you married Richard. Whatever I've said in the past to tease you both, I know you make each other happy, and you deserve happiness.

Sincerely,
James

Dear Susan:

You have only yourself to blame for this one, because if you had not sent along your little journal, in which you manage to point out that we can believe nothing that James has said, and that our whole network of supposition may be based upon nothing but what James wants us to believe, I would not have screamed so loudly I nearly caused Aunt Louisa to die of the stroke, though no such luck I am afraid, and then Dick would not have come bounding down the stairs with such a pale, grim face, not to mention a sturdy walking stick held in his hand as if he by God meant to use it, that I felt horribly ashamed, and then we would not have had that long talk and he would not have shown me the letter and I would not have made the discovery, and, for all I know, we all would have been better off, because I do not know if this helps us, but I know that now Dick feels like the worst sort of cad because of a letter he wrote James that I never read but can certainly imagine. It began simply enough, with my reassuring Dick that I had only been startled, and he demanded I read him your letter and the other pages at once, and when I reached the part that made me scream he looked up at me and said, "My God in Heaven," and you know how rarely he uses profanity, but it did seem called for, and then he became extremely agitated, and began saying the most horrid things about James, and all I could do was stand there and listen until he started talking about James's father, making some remark about "bad seed," and at that point I had to say something, because you know how I feel about that sort of nonsense, and, really, Dick does not believe it himself, but he was angry, and, more than angry, I think, frustrated about this whole, awful business.

Well, one thing led to another, and I found myself defending Andrew, and Dick got a terrible look in his eye and said, "Do you want to know what sort of monster dear old Uncle Andrew was? Do you want to know about James's father?" and without waiting for an answer, he dashed up the stairs, and in five minutes had returned, waving a piece of paper and saying, "You have never looked through my father's correspondence, have you? Well, it is part of the estate, so you may as well see it, and here's a good place to start." What could I do, Susan? I read it, of course, and then I read it a second time, and then a third, because, although I was horrified, as Dick knew I would be, I saw in the letter what he did not see, and of course you will see it too, and then all I could do was cry and say, "Oh, Richard, Oh, Richard," over and over like a schoolgirl, and he held me and said he was sorry for shocking me like that, and more nonsense that he supposed would soothe me, but eventually he realized that there was something about the letter he had not at first understood, so of course I had to point it out to him, and I shall remember as long as I live the look of anguish that came over his face, and I can hardly forgive myself, except that I always think it is best to know these things than to have them around and not know them, do you not?

And if that were not enough, a letter from James arrived by the afternoon post, and Dick, who was already very disturbed, actually broke down and cried when he read it, and I have never seen Dick in such a state, but then he apologized to me, as if he had offended me! and straightaway went back up to his desk and wrote a note to James. As for me, I should write to James myself, but I honestly cannot think of what to say, and so if you would be so kind to tell him, for me, that I still care for him, and I accept all of his apologies the more readily because I can see what they have cost him, and what it has cost him to follow his dream. You have noticed, I am sure, that I have not spoken of any of my researches of late, and that is because I have, at least for now, entirely given them up, not because I no longer believe that the gate to the other world is there, but because, put simply, Susan, I am afraid now to follow my own dream, seeing what it has done to dear James to follow his. But whatever he has done, and for whatever reason, he is our own, and we cannot forsake him, and you knew this before I did, for which I applaud you and love you more than ever.

Well, in any case, I have copied out the letter from Diana,

which Dick says is in the '27 stack if you want to date it
precisely, and I will not insult your intelligence by spelling
out what it implies, and I'm also including a sealed letter, and
that is to James from Dick, and Dick asks if you at all can to
see that he gets it, please, and I hope James responds, because
I do not know what to think now, except that everywhere I
turn, matters become stranger and darker, and if it is not the
past waiting to devour us, then it is the future that holds threats
that fill me with the feeling that sorrow is waiting beneath the
seal of the next letter.

But this is only a mood, darling Susan, and will soon pass,
and we will be with you once more, to see this through to the
end, and Dick and I will both work harder than ever now, and
maintain our faith, and until all is over and we can again sit
in peace and comfort as the family we truly are, be of good
cheer and write soon to your trusting and affectionate,

                                                    – Kit

CAULDHURST ABBEY
21ST OCTOBER

Beloved,

Please, please tell me that all is arranged and that we may go,
now, to-night! I cannot stay another fortnight under this roof,
with this man. I know you still love him, and hope that inside
that devil's shell there is a decent man still, but I have no such
hope. I think he is mad or nearly so. He spends the night in
his study and emerges at dawn in a rage. Then he seeks me
out and berates me, and often strikes me, and the things I
understand out of his tirades terrify me because they suggest
he suspects the worst part of our secret. The *best* part of our
secret, love, if only we were free! I do not know when he
sleeps, or even if he does; he eats sometimes enormous meals,
sometimes almost nothing; he is one day slovenly in his dress,
refusing to let his valet come near him, and the next he strikes
the man for some fancied speck or stain on his coat or boots.

Today he came home early from the cubbing, and on foot,

and cheerful. Spartan had refused at some obstacle, and he had dismounted, pulled out his pistol, and shot the horse dead. And after killing the best hunter in his stables, he walked home in his riding boots, merry as a grig! But Jamie had ridden part of the way with the hunt on his pony and witnessed it, and though he said very little he was perfectly white, and his governess said he had not eaten his dinner and so was not permitted to come to the drawing room after to see me.

That threw Andrew into a rage, and he said the boy would never learn self-discipline surrounded by women. Miss Soames was to send him down to be taught manners immediately, though it had been Andrew's order that he not be allowed to come to the drawing room if he misbehaved. Thank God for Miss Soames: though she is too harsh, she saved Jamie from who knows what harm to-night. She said that she could not govern the boy if there was no consistency in his punishment. Andrew raved at her and she gave her notice. He replied, "Notice be damned, you sour-faced harlot, you may leave my house to-night and whistle for a reference!" He was so angry he forgot about Jamie's punishment. I arranged for the governess to spend to-night at the lodge-keeper's house.

I am afraid for my life, and not only because I will pine and die if I cannot live as I ought, as your wife. I am afraid for Jamie even now, as things stand, because he is my child and Andrew would hurt him if only to hurt me. If all were known, what ghastly thing might he do? But whatever may come, I will not leave the boy with him. I would rather he killed Jamie, and me, too, than see the dear child left in his hands without his mother to protect him. As best she can— oh, my love, I feel so helpless and frightened! Free me soon, soon from this nightmare, and make me forever your only and adoring

Diana

MELROSE HALL
WEDNESDAY

My Dear James,

If I am fortunate, indeed, more fortunate than I deserve, then you have not yet received the letter for you that I entrusted to Miss Voight; if so, please do not read it, for it contains sulphurous fumes in the form of words that you neither need nor deserve. But I doubt that Providence has been so kind, so I can only hope that you will somehow find it in your heart to forgive the cruel words I but lately sent you; words themselves so unforgiving that to ask you to pardon them feels like hypocrisy worthy of David. I begin to wonder if there is not a little too much similarity between me and David, and this is no easy thing to say, because if I am capable of his sort of hypocrisy, then of what else would I be capable if circumstances conspired against me? And it is only now, looking at it in this light, that I can see how circumstances conspired against you, James, leading you into a madrigal of deception, lies, and half-truths to accompany the concerto of violence, torture, and fear that you had fallen into. To be then cruelly rejected by me must have been a crushing blow on top of all of that, and it is as if I am now feeling that very blow on my own shoulders as I think of it.

We are never so much ourselves as we are in time of crisis; and in your crisis you showed that you could be determined and courageous, whereas my Kitty has shown that no matter what is going on around her she can think as well as any man and better than most. And I? What have I shown? Excuse me, but now I fear I am falling as deeply into self-pity as I lately fell into righteous indignation; I shall take as an example your recent letter to Kitty, and restrain the impulse to ask for pity. What is it, do you think, about this family that flies to such extremes? Self-righteous indignation, repentance, sorrow, triumph: we can do nothing by halves. I believe you asked me that yourself a long, long time ago—a month, I suppose—and

I answered glibly. So much for that wisdom you called upon in early October!

I suppose by now Susan has told you the startling news that Kitty learned from a letter I showed her, or, rather, attempted to batter her with as part of a silly argument. Why it should make such a difference, I cannot say, but it does. To my mind—or, rather, to my heart—it makes all the difference; it was only when Kitty pointed out the obvious to me that I began to see what I had done to you, which is all to the good, but it is still entirely an emotional rather than a logical change of heart, and that should put paid to your belief in that cold rationality you called upon at the same time you asked for my wisdom.

I am rambling, James, I suppose because I have little to say except two things, and they are too briefly and simply stated for the occasion, but let me try anyway. First, I am truly sorry to have attacked you so, and wish I could undo it. Second, I stand ready, now more than ever, to help you in any way I can; you need but call, and, whatever the circumstances, you will find at your side your affectionate brother,

Richard

SUSAN VOIGHT'S JOURNAL
(WRITTEN IN CIPHER)

28 Nov 1849

At Portishead—we've been in one place for over four hours, and it feels positively unnatural, not to mention dangerous. But another storm blew up at sunset. Not weather for riding, certainly not for riding all the way up the coast to meet the Chepstow ferry even if it were wise to take it. It's not, of course; we can't risk being seen and identified. One of the many drawbacks of skulking is that it's so very much slower than the way the righteous travel.

No, we're waiting for a boat, ideally a small one, ideally one whose owner has a sufficient number of things to hide that he won't be surprised if we do, too. James (who doesn't seem

nervous at all, in addition to the other things he doesn't seem)
says the weather is still too bad for anyone to take anything
across the Severn. If we're to be stuck here for a while, I
suppose I'll have to record the events of today and yesterday
for Kitty. I'd rather not. But regular reports are one of the
duties of the job, aren't they? And I still set great store by
duty.

I began my inquiries in Bristol after Gideon Johnson, knowing that an officer of the Royal Navy is harder to hide than J.
on the run. Rather, Stephen Vaughan made the inquiries, with
his angelic face and guileless smile and freshly-barbered hair
(barbers, by the way, are an observant lot; I haven't yet met
with one who believed I was male after five minutes under the
scissors. Fortunately they all seem to have a sense of humour
as well). Mr Vaughan disarmed his auditors with the shame-
faced admission that he owed Mr Johnson a sum of money—
no, not a paltry one, or at least not paltry to Mr Vaughan, and
debts of honour, you know . . . Henry would have expired with
embarrassment at what I think was a fairly accurate piece of
mimicry.

It was late afternoon by the time I learned that Johnson had
gone on some piece of ship's business to Redland and was not
expected back until the next day. Convenient, thought I, since
neither James nor I can have free access to him on shipboard.
I proceeded to shake the fidgets out of Girasol in a nice trot
to Redland.

Except that Gideon Johnson wasn't where he was supposed
to be, and I was left to plod stubbornly along looking for his
next likely landing place through an increasingly blustery
thickening darkness. He'd sent ahead to bespeak a room in
Redland, but hadn't arrived. Another gentleman had, however,
and had asked about Lieutenant Johnson, and said he was
meant to meet him there. Was the gentleman still there, I
asked? Oh, no, he hadn't taken a room, but only asked if the
lieutenant had arrived.

Well, that would be James, or someone else entirely, and if
the latter, with my luck, probably someone intending to kill
Gideon Johnson. Also with my luck, probably better at finding
him than I was. Had they any idea where the second gentleman
was headed when he left? No, of course not. Well, I'd already

covered the ground between Bristol and Redland, if not quite as attentively as I would have if I'd known there was no Johnson at Redland. Nothing for it but to continue on toward the Severn until I found Johnson or James or got my feet wet.

The sky had begun to spit rain in my face when I came upon the farmhouse. It was a ruin, its roofless broken walls rising like the upthrust jaws of some giant reptilian skull against the clouds. The high stone wall around the kitchen-yard was in better repair, but the wattle-and-daub barn behind was transparent as lace. The wood that must once have grown a proper distance from the steading had crept nearly to the walls on either side in the form of coppices and elm-scrub. Girasol's ears swivelled forward before I heard it: the dry rattle of flames, and the sound, half-cough and half-grunt, of someone receiving a blow. Then there was a shout and a scuffling racket. It came from the walled kitchen-yard. Once I knew where to look I could see the light from the fire brushed faint and irregular across the lattice of the barn wall.

The ground was soft and Girasol's hooves made no sound, but I thought if I rode closer whoever it was might hear the clinking of the bit. They were too busy, as it turned out. From my perch in the saddle, I could see over the wall to where the flames, finished with the dry brush of the yard's waste ground, were starting in on the barn wall. The fire threw fitful light on the three figures in the kitchen-yard. One, rather largish, lay on the ground as if he'd just arrived there; as I watched he rolled slowly onto his face. One stood beside the fallen man, clutching an elm-log like a club, all his attention on the third person in the yard. That person was James, a strange and threatening figure in his loose black coat, empty-handed and still.

There was something terrible about his expression in the uncertain light. There was no fear in it, or anger, or any human emotion at all. It was the fixed, acute gaze of the hunting hawk or the stalking cat, precise and passionless. That expression, shaped by those pure gem-cut features, seemed prepared to view all the business of the fire-lit yard as an exercise in cold mathematics.

Then the man with the club shouted again, and glanced toward the flank of the roofless house, and saw me. He gaped, and James moved. I twisted in the saddle to peer into the darkness beyond the farmhouse, because I knew, as James must have known, what the shout meant. Reinforcements. I saw the blaze of a pair of torches across the road.

I wheeled Girasol away from the kitchen-yard wall, a dozen, two dozen feet; then I turned him hard 'round and gave him his head. The wall was a featureless darkness before me, high as my mount's shoulder, made visible only by the light of the fire that showed on its other side. I had admired this horse; I don't think I'd loved him before that, before I felt the thrust of his hindquarters and the stretch of his neck like a starving man reaching for bread, and saw the light fill my vision as the wall seemed to drop away. We landed abruptly, fire-dazzled, in the kitchen-yard, only a handful of feet from two men lying motionless in the burnt grass and another on his knees, cradling one arm with the other. The pale oval of face that turned upward to look at me, bemused, was James's.

"Get on," I said.

He shook his head. "He'd never get both of us over."

There was no need, I noticed, to explain the situation to him. He knew pursuit was closing in. The only two exits from the walled yard were the gaping dark door of the farmhouse, through which men's voices already echoed, and the narrow door to the barn, set in the wall that was now sheeted over with fire. The yard was perhaps wide enough for Girasol to get in one full galloping stride before he reached the opposite wall. "Yes, he will. Up."

James scrambled up behind me with less than his usual grace, which caused Girasol to sidle and lay his ears back. Then I urged the horse around, to circle past the wall he'd cleared already in order to get up something like speed. *Yes, he will*, I'd said. It was easier to say than to believe. James's right arm was hard around my waist; his left joined it almost reluctantly, and I heard air hiss past his teeth as it did. Then the wall was in front of me.

He will, I thought—no, I made a prayer of it, to the horse-goddess of the Celts. I matched it to the beat of Girasol's two front hooves as they came down for the last time, one, two— *He will*—and then curled beneath him like a cat's. An explosion of power from those great hindquarters and we were hanging in the air, committed. I was out of the saddle and over Girasol's neck, his mane cutting at my face. James's weight had come forward at the same time to lean against my back—consummate horseman that he was, he would also feel it at the base of his spine, the moment to shift. I heard his coat flap, and a shout behind us, and a rushing crackle from the fire as part of the barn wall collapsed. Much too late it occurred to me to think that if there was a ditch on the other side of the wall, Girasol would break his legs.

It wasn't a graceful landing; strictly speaking James was right—combined we were too much weight for a horse to get over a wall that high, with an approach that short. But Girasol didn't stumble, or go down, and neither of us fell off. And we were free to plunge on down the westward road in a cold slanting rain that would wash our trail away as soon as we'd made it.

James was first to remember to breathe, a gasp of inhaled air that was nearly a sob. He used it to say, "I promise never to doubt your taste in horses."

"I didn't really think he could," I admitted.

"I know. It doesn't matter." I could feel him after that taking long measured breaths, his chest rising and falling against my back. Finally he said, "What's his name?"

"You'll laugh. I didn't give it to him. It's Girasol."

An unguarded splutter from over my shoulder. "No. *Sunflower?*"

"I told you, I had nothing to do with it."

"Sunny for short? On the basis of the evidence, I'm surprised it's not Pegasus. What in hell is he?"

"Hanoverian."

"Um. You could call him Friedrich."

I told him I didn't think so. My hair was channelling the rain straight over my forehead and into my eyes. The discomfort was almost welcome—it was the only thing that rescued the conversation from perfect unreality. I let Girasol drop back to a canter. "How about Albert? Very patriotic."

"That's not Hanover. I think you're stuck with William or George."

"You'd object to James?" I asked sweetly.

"No, that's the Stuarts. I'm sorry," he said after a moment. "Could we stop?"

"Now? Here?"

"Yes, please."

He slid as if boneless down Girasol's wet flank, took four quick strides off the road, and was briskly and unspectacularly sick.

He didn't expect me, I think, to hand him my handkerchief, white in the darkness as a rabbit-scut. When he didn't take it immediately, I said, "A lady always carries one, you know."

"Not usually for times like these. Nor in her trouser-pocket." His voice was the light, rather breathless one I'd heard him use once or twice in the inn parlour at Fairfield.

"For when it's needed. And I never heard a lady defined by the width of her skirt. Take it."

He did. After that I handed him the flask from my saddle-bag, the one with the Romany brandy in it. "I hope you aren't obliged to object to this, too. It will make you feel better, especially in this weather."

The hand that took the flask from mine was wet and cold and shaking. "You need to get indoors," I added.

He handed the flask back; it wasn't noticeably lighter. "No, it's all right. This always happens."

Then I remembered. "That's right, you told Richard so, didn't you?"

In front of me there was a moment of startled stillness. "I did. You read them, I take it."

"All of them. We all did." I felt suddenly, unreasonably, guilty about it.

"We?"

"Richard, Kitty, and I. We thought it was time for a family conference."

"Not David?"

"No. He was *persona non grata* even before we found your essay in Richard's copy of Aubrey. You were right, by the way: I was the one who deciphered your clues. In the letter you sent with the book you didn't say, 'Between these covers'. You said, 'Inside'. Odd, for someone so careful in his choice of prepositions. And of course, you needn't have included a letter in the first place, so I knew it must be a piece of cleverness on your part. After all, you wouldn't simply write to Richard out of kindness, would you?"

Silence—not the startled silence of a moment before, but only a steady-breathing pause, an interval perhaps for a tired mind to gather itself.

"We should be going on," I said mercilessly. "Where is your horse?"

"Dead. They ambushed me in the barn and shot the horse by mistake instead of me. I bought the poor devil an entire month more of life."

"You were waiting for Gideon Johnson?"

"No. No, he was to meet me at Redland, and seems to have left me to kick my heels. I was going on to . . . another place where I thought I could arrange a meeting."

"Newport." I heard him draw a long breath, and let it all out. "I can't see you," I told him.

Another breath, then, "Yes."

"Who ambushed you?"

He laughed, an airy, helpless sound. "I thought, actually, that it might be Government men. Will you be required to stay away from embassy parties, do you think?"

"I don't go to those in trousers. Come on."

Once I was back in the saddle, I offered him the stirrup to help him mount. He used it, and his right arm across the cantle, and still failed to regain his seat. "Ah. Damn. I don't suppose there are any fences nearby."

I asked sharply, "What's wrong with your other arm?"

"He cracked me with that blasted log."

I slid down again. Girasol swung his nose around, as if he wanted to know if there was something he ought to be doing. "I'll give you a leg up and get on after."

He was impressed, I thought, at Girasol's patience and my agility, but he only said, "Do you have to travel with two saddles, or do you always ride astride?"

"My habits all have divided skirts. And I wouldn't be shocked if I were you—do you think we'd have made it over that wall on a sidesaddle?"

"If I'd ever ridden sidesaddle," he said, for the first time in something almost like his usual tone, "I could tell you."

What I found, after a little more riding and hardly any conversation, wouldn't usually be dignified with the term "inn". It was a little tavern with a scrap of yard before it and a shabby sign over the door that with much squinting could be made out to display a grossly fat white duck. There was a dry shed behind with two stalls, only one large enough for Girasol to lie down in, and a room upstairs that could be let to travellers on the rare occasion that a humble one might stop between Redland and Portishead. The bill of fare at that hour, offered from the landlord's own larder, was bread and butter, brown ale, and rum. I had everything but the latter sent up.

James seemed to have got himself a bit more in hand by the time I'd arranged for food and a fire and hot water and a poultice for his arm. Not perfectly in hand; he didn't laugh at the poultice. But he sat on the hearth, his knees drawn up to cradle his left arm and his ale mug in his other hand, and said at last, "Why are you here?"

I weighed the possibilities. "Because I have information for you. And I'm afraid you forgot to have anyone forward your mail."

"Not . . . because of what you said, at Fairfield, when you left?"

The fire was to his back, but it lit *my* face reasonably well, I was sure. "What, to apologise? Oh, do you mean am I doing it to hound you? No, on reflection I found I begrudged the energy it would take. But for efficiency's sake let's not simply start up where we left off. What's most pertinent? Ah, of course. Richard has retrieved your notes."

"Richard has . . . How?"

"At gun-point, from David, in the study at Cauldhurst. Did you know that your father, or David acting for him, or David pretending to act for him, has set matters in motion to disinherit you?"

I couldn't tell if he had heard that and set it aside to deal with later, or if he was too tired to keep up entirely. "Where are they now?"

"The notes? Safe. It was Kitty who realized that they couldn't be delivered without announcing that there was no longer any reason to keep you alive."

His fingers were rigid around his mug. *"Where are they?"*

"Kitty deciphered them. Then I memorized them and burned the pages."

Ale slopped over the rim and shone on his hand and the floor. "I knew it. I *knew* it. You bloody mad—"

"I know that I did it. Kitty does, too, but I asked her not to tell Richard, and she won't. Now you know. Are you going to have me killed to silence me?"

He banged his mug down on the hearth and stood abruptly, which must have brought his forgotten left arm to his notice; I heard him grunt.

"Should you have a sling?" I asked.

He paced the short space before the fire. "All right," he said eventually. "All right. I suppose I can understand. . . . Who would you give them to, if you could?"

"Friedrich Engels."

He stopped and gave me what even in the half-light was obviously a speculative look. "You're aware, then, of what he's doing?"

"Of the League? Yes. It's what you were afraid the informers would turn their attention to next, isn't it?"

He nodded. Then he leaned on the mantel and looked down into the fire. I buttered another slice of bread as an excuse to move, and settled into a chair where I could see his face in profile.

"How many of them," I asked, "are in the Trotter's Club?"

He looked at me, his head a little tilted. "I don't know. Is it significant?"

"David is a member. Your father is one of the founders. And the man who attacked Richard in Southampton was a member as well."

For the second time that night I felt the pressure of his surprise in his stillness. I didn't mean it to be the last. "Richard went to Southampton?" James said.

"Following a scent-hound who was following your horse."

"Oh, Christ."

"He was set upon on the dock, in daylight. The man broke his collarbone with a cudgel before Richard shot him—dead, he thinks, but he never received confirmation of it. But Richard saw a pendant around the man's neck that Kitty says David also wears, and that she identifies with the Trotter's Club." I described it as I fished the packet of letters out of my saddle-bag, and held out to him the one written by William Cobham to his brother Andrew.

James left off rubbing the space between his eyebrows to take and read it. When he was finished, he said, "My father wears a pendant like that. But is it significant? Secret brotherhoods go in and out of fashion. The Trotter's Club may only have become the latest fad. How is Richard?"

"Well enough to hold David at gun-point. He was in hospital in Southampton for a while, however. He and Kitty were married there."

I'd made sure he was turned toward me, and that the light fell well on his face. He *was* tired; the reaction was visible, and the change from blank surprise to pain was slow. "I see," he said. The wind picked up suddenly; rain dashed and streamed on the windowpanes, rattling. Then he asked, "Were you there?"

I couldn't help feeling a little disappointed that he'd thought to ask. "No," I admitted. Inspiration prompted me to add, "I was at Fairfield at the time, meeting you."

"Ah. Of course." His voice was harsh when he continued, "I would hate to have you think I wasn't taking note of your aim. It's excellent."

"I don't have to aim, my dear. It's only a list of facts."

"I see. Do you have any more?"

I thought, or seemed to. "It may have to do with the Trotter's Club, or with the inheritance, or something else we don't know about yet. But Richard combined some things he knew with an inspired guess and confronted David with it, and surprised a confession out of him. Did you have any suspicion that David killed your brother Roderick?"

His right hand caught at the corner of the mantelpiece, then slid slowly down the stone of the fireplace, and he followed it until he was sitting on the hearth again. His eyes were wide and unfocused, and every structure in his face showed where the cords of his self-command had snapped. Then he dropped his head to his knees. Eventually he said, "Well, if you wanted to see me off my guard, that certainly did the trick."

I had, of course. But once it had happened I was sick with it, sick up to the throat with my facts and the bludgeoning I'd done with them. I had my revenge for whatever he'd done, whatever called for revenge, and could now try to clean the blood off the sand and get on with matters. I remembered suddenly another in the packet of letters, the one that Kitty had sent along to deliver to James from Richard. "I'm sorry," I said, meaning more than I seemed to, "I have a letter for you. I should have given it to you right away. It's from Richard."

He looked up at that, with no clear expression but with a sense of collecting his strength, of putting his nerves back in almost their proper arrangement. I found the letter and handed it to him.

Common decency, which I used to have a certain quantity of, would have prompted me to find something to do on the other side of the room. But watching his face had become an irresistible act of trespass. So I saw the flicker of surprise in his brows and mouth as his gaze moved across the first paragraph, and then to nearly the end of the second when his eyes closed tight. "Do you know what's in this?" he asked.

"I don't read other people's letters," I said sharply, forgetting for the moment that of course I did—I'd read his to Richard, after all. But there was some awful thing here that wasn't of my making, and I wanted to snatch the letter back and throw it in the fire. I wouldn't have been able to; his fingers were white on the sheets.

He finished the letter, motionless except for his eyes and the hand that shifted the pages. Then he folded it gently, in half, in half again and again until it was small enough to fit in his palm. He leaned back against the stones and began, softly, to laugh.

"What?" I said.

"Nothing. I'm being disinherited. It's all right. Just facts. Christ, basic decency is its own God-damned defense. I must never have—" The laughter caught on itself and fell silent. He stood up quickly and was at the door to the room in two long strides, and had it open before I could speak.

"Where are you going?"

He stood in the doorway, his back to me. "I'll be back. I promise. Please, I have—" His words stopped as if a knife had come down on them.

"Go," I said, and he did.

I'm not going to ask him what was in that letter. I don't think I want to be told. Perhaps I ought to have gone out after him, but I didn't have the courage. I hung up a blanket—we could each have the illusion of privacy, anyway—and went to bed. I lay awake for a long time, but I didn't hear him come in before I lost the battle with exhaustion at some unmarked hour.

I meant to continue this entry, to describe today, but writing this has been almost as dreadful as living through it. I'm not cold-blooded enough to go on, not yet. Perhaps I'll send this as is. More later.

James just tapped at the door and said that it might be clearing westward. He glanced at my heap of scribbled-on paper, but only glanced; he didn't say anything, or even seem curious. Of a piece with the rest of the day, and I wonder how long it will go on—how long it *can* go on, before I scream at him, or he comes apart at the seams. To be fair, I'm ever so much closer to the former than he appears to be to the latter. That, in fact, is the problem. I'll tell it in order.

This morning I woke up in bed behind my blanket to a collection of unfamiliar smells and small homely noises. My man's clothes, which I'd draped over a chair in the vain hope that they'd be dry by morning, were gone, and my saddle-bags had appeared in their place. I'd packed a waist and a divided skirt in one; I shook the creases out as best I could and dressed. That was as long as I could delay, and as well-fortified as I could make myself. Time to face James again.

There's a painter—or maybe there are several, at any rate I can't remember a name or names—who has made his name painting idealized scenes of the Life of the Common People. Whoever he is, he would have been proud to take credit for the tableau on the other side of my makeshift curtain.

It was hard to tell what time it was; the sky outside the window was grey with morning or rain. The room was lit mostly by the fire, as it had been last night. My coat, trousers, and waistcoat were draped over the back of the settle to dry, and the settle had been drawn close to the hearth to speed the process. My hat, I realized for the first time, must have come

off in last night's excitement. It had nothing about it that would
identify me, and I hadn't liked it, anyway.

James sat on a three-legged stool before the fire, all his
attention on something in an iron pan on a salamander. Beside
him was a toasting-fork with two pieces of bread, ingeniously
braced at an angle to the flames between one of the fire-irons
and his foot. He wore shirt, breeches, waistcoat, and boots,
and his sleeves were rolled up. His left forearm was bandaged,
but he seemed to be able to use it. His hair was damp from
rain or washing, except in front where the fire had dried it and
it fell forward in an unattended tangle over his forehead. He
hadn't shaved—of course, he'd arrived with nothing but the
clothes he stood up in. He didn't look tired, but the warm light
from below that the fire cast would have filled in all the shadows.

Then he turned and caught sight of me, and smiled a little.
"Breakfast in a few minutes," he said. "There's hot water in
the kettle there, if you want a wash." A little more of the
smile. "I have to choose between good manners and food. If
I stand up, the bread will fall in the fire."

"You're absolved," I said, my voice rusty, and left to do
homage to necessity. Downstairs, even the kitchen was quiet,
and I wondered what time it was, and where James had got
whatever was in the pan. When I came back I poured some of
his hot water into the basin (he was busy turning a piece of
cheese into even smaller pieces of cheese, and didn't look up)
and took it behind the curtain to wash with. Then I stiffened
my spine and went back out to see if normal hostilities were
scheduled to resume. After the night before, I thought he deserved the first shot, and I was prepared to let him take it.

"Just in time. Would you like it at the table, or will pic-
nicking around the hearth do? Oh, and I am sorry there's no
coffee. None to be had nearer than Portishead. I did try,
though."

Nothing but mild amiability in both text and tone. Perhaps
part of the retaliation was in making me wait for it. He turned
out what looked remarkably like an omelette onto two treen
plates, added a piece of evenly-toasted bread to each, and
handed me one. "There's butter on the cupboard there, out of
reach of the heat. And the tea should be ready."

"Where did this come from?" I asked, in lieu of all the other things I wanted to say.

"Well, not from downstairs. There seems to be no provision—literally—for feeding anyone in this place. The locals must only come here for the bad beer. I bought the ingredients from a cottage down the road. A farmer's widow. I hope you don't mind," he said, faintly anxious, "but I traded her one of your cuff-links."

"There's money in my saddle-bag. Didn't you look?"

"I was trying not to do that." He was sitting with his knees drawn up and his plate on them. His eyes were on the food. "You should eat it before it gets cold."

At close range, it was obviously an omelette, a highly successful one. "How did you learn to cook?"

He swallowed a bite and smiled. "Nomadic life. If you don't cook, you don't eat. And the more you know about food, the easier it is to tell someone else what you want for dinner. Don't you know how?"

"No. I suppose I don't think much about what I get for dinner. As long as there is something, I mean. I don't think much about food."

He stopped with his fork in mid-air and stared at me. "Are you really a relative of mine? How can you not think much about food?"

"I think about coffee."

"Ouch. I *did* try."

"I didn't mean that. What's in this?"

"Eggs. Aged cheese. Butter. Some thyme. I didn't know if you liked onions, so I didn't look for any."

I took another bite, and swallowed it, and said, "How do we try to arrange another meeting with Johnson?"

He stopped chewing, started again, swallowed in his turn, and said, "Actually, since we've begun, there are a few topics to get out of the way before that."

"Yes, I know. I'm to let you go first and do precisely as I'm told. Within limits. I don't think it would be wise to send me back to London, or Melrose, because I doubt I'd be a jot safer there than I would be here."

"I wasn't going to say any of that." I'd expected him to frown. He seemed to have forgotten how. "I'm prepared . . .

I'm afraid I don't trust my judgment anymore. Well, about food, maybe, but not about . . . about my affairs.'' He took a breath and let it out sharply. ''Whatever you think should be done, I'm prepared to do. If you still think I ought to leave the country, I will. Or I could turn myself in. I'd get transportation, but that's an improvement over being drowned or shot, and it would end the danger to you and Kitty and Richard. Or if you still want to solve the . . . this wretched business, I'll help. I don't know if it's important anymore. I can't tell.''

Last night he'd spent most of the conversation looking into the fire. This morning he looked at me, with an effort, and also with an effort kept his voice even and calm. There was more light in the room by then. I wondered if he'd slept at all.

''And you think I can?'' My voice was under noticeably less control.

''It's not personal for you, the way it is for me. And I think there's nothing left of this quarrel but the private bits. Is that true? You can deliver the contents of my notes to Engels, and that will protect the Communist League and draw the informers' teeth. You shouldn't be in danger after that; they'll have no power to defend, no reason to make a warning of you. And Richard was only at risk because I'd involved him in this. The whole web collapses if you take me out of it, I think. Doesn't it? It all only matters to me. Or is there something I'm missing?'' He set his empty plate on the hearth and paused to rub the space between his eyebrows, as I'd seen him do last night. ''I feel as if I'm missing something. As if I've left an entire parenthetical statement out of the middle of the equation. I can't . . . trust myself with it, anymore.''

And he looked at me, waiting.

I hadn't known until then how much faith I'd placed in James's thinking. Not in his judgment, or his morals—just the pure detached process of his thoughts. Now here he was suggesting, regretfully, that his thoughts were no longer up to it. He was prepared to lay his future—his life—in my hands.

My face may have reflected some of that. He stood abruptly and turned to the settle, where he laid a hand on the shoulder of my drying coat. ''I'm sorry,'' he said. ''I'm making it sound as if you have to pick up the responsibility for my actions. You don't. I only meant to tell you that if you have a clear picture of what's happening, and what should be done, I'm willing to act on it. That's all. And if you don't—'' He shrugged.

I broke the resulting silence with, "And if I don't, what? You'll sit here on your backside waiting for whoever walks in next, friend or foe?"

Perhaps I felt I'd waited long enough for him to take the first shot. But he only lifted his head a little and said, "I don't know. I suppose I'll think of something."

I sat cradling my tea mug and being angry. This was not the same person I'd snatched out of the kitchen-yard however many miles down the road last night. What the devil had happened?

Then of course I remembered. I had. And had arrived bearing a full accounting of the wreckage in his wake and the kindnesses he had cut himself off from, possibly forever. And a letter from Richard, which had broken him like fine china dropped on tile. I felt a burning tightness in my throat and a brimming in my eyes and grabbed up my tea, knowing that I could control both with a swallow or two of liquid. But the mug was empty, and a tear spilled over.

He was kneeling beside my chair in an instant, one hand on the arm of it. He didn't touch me, or even move to touch me. His instincts, I observed, could be trusted even if his brain couldn't. He opened his mouth to say something and then shut it again.

"Could I have some more tea, do you think?" I asked, when I knew I could do it steadily.

Still without a word, he brought the pot and poured.

I didn't actually scald my tongue. "All right," I said. "We don't know enough, is all. It *feels* as if we know entirely too much, and none of it connected to any of the rest, but that's nonsense, it's only that we're missing the ligaments. So it's still worthwhile to find Gideon Johnson if we can—I'd love to know what was in the letter Betty Howard got before she left London. And after that, I think we should go to Manchester."

"Manchester?" he repeated, but not as if he were preparing to object.

"If your quarrel is still public, Friedrich Engels is the only person I can think of who would be able to tell us so. He wants to see you anyway. Oh, blast, I forgot!'' I darted back to my saddle-bag and rummaged. ''He gave me a letter for you.''

''Oh, good,'' said James, in his airless voice. But his face was calm by the time I looked up, and he was pouring himself more tea. He opened Engels's letter briskly and read it likewise. ''Well, that's nice,'' he muttered partway through. When he finished he sighed and folded it again.

''Bad news?'' I asked.

''No, a show of support, actually. More or less. Very well, we'll head for Newport, then, and try for a meeting with Johnson. Or at least Portishead. Bristol won't be safe now, and Johnson will know it. Would you like me to try to get a cryptic note carried to him?''

''Yes. That's the next thing, I think. A meeting in Portishead if possible, nowhere specific: ideally *we* find *him*. If not Portishead this evening, then Newport tomorrow or the next day, with the same arrangements. Is there any advantage to crossing the Severn tonight? Would we find anyone to take us after dark? My God. Now, why should Johnson go to the trouble? What can we offer him to induce him to meet us?''

''Promise never to bother him again?''

''Well, it's a start,'' I said. My head was inclined to spin. ''You don't think he's one of the ones who kidnapped you, do you?''

James stood still, holding the plates he'd gathered. He hadn't forgotten how to frown, after all. After a moment he answered, ''No. He might want to kill me for other reasons entirely. And he might have been involved with the ones who did it. But it didn't quite seem like one of his. Don't be any less careful, though.''

''Where are you going?''

He stopped at the door and raised his eyebrows. ''Downstairs. To do the washing-up, if I can't find someone in the kitchen to bribe to do it for me. Can you spare another cufflink?''

''You do the washing-up and I'll give it to you for your very own.''

His lips pressed together. "You'd only see it on the card-table next week."

"Why wait until next week?" I asked, and his smile finally broke out.

We found another horse to hire. James rode peacefully beside or slightly behind me all the way to Portishead, stopping when I decreed it, taking whatever route I chose (though there weren't many choices to be made), doing anything I asked him to, advising where necessary—but only advising. I felt as if I'd acquired an unpaid footman, and told him so.

He smiled and shook his head. "You'd make me shave. You could claim me as your groom, though."

In the old James, *either* of the old Jameses, there would have been a spirit of malice in the performance, a determination to put me to a great deal of inconvenience in the name of letting me have my own way. There was no malice in him today, only easy, nearly passive acquiescence, and he made every effort to keep that from being inconvenient. He was like a good-natured and thoughtful invalid, and by the time we reached Portishead in the afternoon and found a room to stay in I wanted to knock him off his horse just to see if I could make him angry.

We spent the last few hours combing the town for signs that Gideon Johnson is here, or is on his way here. If he received the note sent from the inn, he could have reached Portishead before us, and so we felt obliged to look for him. But neither of us really expects him until Newport. If then.

So I shall close here and put this in the post to Kitty. If all goes well, mail sent to us care of Friedrich Engels in Manchester will catch up with us by no later than the 3rd of December.

I feel as if I've been travelling for weeks, in a strange country, out of all contact with the rest of the world. Is there still a rest of the world? Or will we go east again to find London gone, and Melrose, and nothing left but miles of empty land and the sea? What a strange feeling.

NOVEMBER 29th

Dear Susan,

I do not know how you can do those things you do, and I do not know how you can write them down after you have done them, and I do not know how you can send them to me when you have written them, but you ought to know that my admiration for you has risen yet again, if that is possible, and Dick just shakes his head in amazement, although he does not know everything, because I only read it aloud to him translating your ciphers and I skipped over the part where James read Dick's letter, because it would make him feel just awful, and he feels bad enough already, as do I, but never mind that. If I were as cold and calculating as you try to be, and Dick pretends to be, and James really is at least sometimes, I would announce that it is good that James now knows where we stand, so we can all work together as a family should, which makes me giggle, imagining Aunt Louisa nodding and saying, "Yes, dears, we should work as a family to foil the conspiracies and frustrate the power of the State," but the fact is, all I can think of is what you and James have been through, but I know that sort of thing does not help at all, so I

Susan, I am sorry. David has been killed. The police came 'round just now, shortly after noon when I was in the middle of writing, and said that he had been found just outside the stable of the Abbey, apparently strangled some time during the night, and I do not know why this should hit me so hard because we had been more than half expecting it, but somehow it makes everything so real, and so very, very frightening that I want to beg you to drop everything and come home so I can look at you and know that you are safe, and I want you to bring James home, too, but I know all of that is impossible. Why is it that all of David's faults seem so unimportant now that he is gone, and why does my heart keep insisting on virtues for him I know he never possessed, and why does the idea that he brought it on himself seem somehow disloyal? Dick took the news hard, he has hardly spoken a word since the policeman came, Aunt Louisa had some sort of fit and screamed about devil-worshippers and Chartists, if you can believe it, until Winter, the chemist, came by and gave her something to calm her down, but I still cannot get her ravings out of my mind, and I keep wondering if it was hysteria or if she somehow knows something, and if you can assure me that it was only hysteria, you will go a long way toward keeping my own hysteria at arm's length. Anyway, it is almost evening now, and I wrote the first part of this letter late in the morning, so I should finish it so that you can at least hear from me if you happen to be some place where letters will reach you.

I had spent the morning going through William's letters, and, while none are as obvious as the one I sent you, there are others that bear out the conclusion we reached, and maybe the most horrid part of hearing about David was that I had just reached the conclusion that, with what we now know about James, he is out of the line of succession for Cauldhurst, or maybe in it even more strongly, I must ask Brian, but this could mean that, if David were to eliminate Dick, he might get the Abbey and Melrose, and it may be that was his idea all along, but it means nothing now, does it?

Dick has just left for the Abbey to see to arrangements there, and it frightens me to think of what he might find when he goes through David's things, and I think it frightens him too, so I shall set this aside until he returns, and maybe I shall play Patience like some Mediæval princess whose husband is off in Barbary on Crusade, which image is nearly enough to make me smile in spite of everything.

It is now quite late, and I really should send this off to you. I will let you know what Dick has discovered as soon as possible, until then, please keep me informed as you have been, and know that I remain your affectionate

Kitty

SUSAN VOIGHT'S JOURNAL
(WRITTEN IN CIPHER)

29 Nov 1849

Waiting must be the most exhausting activity known to Man. Waiting for some unspecifiable, unpredictable sequence of events that James assures me I will understand and know how to act on when it occurs is, not to put too fine a point on it, Hell. I have begun to wonder if even mere survival is an unwarrantedly lofty goal, let alone survival unscathed. But some of this gloom is due, I think, to an entire day without any real action. I understand now what James meant when he said he could be defeated by his own imagination.

We crossed the Severn in the dark, threading between the Portishead and Newport lights like a bead on a long, twisted string. It was a hard crossing and a mad thing to do, but it ensured that, however expected our presence in Newport might be, the timing of it would be beyond anyone's prediction. And we thought we might be expected. After all, Betty Howard's note asked James to come "to the West to the place you know of". It also suggested that the sooner he came, the safer he would be. Our only hope was that we were so late in coming they'd given up on him arriving at all.

There was no passing James off as my groom, since the horses had been left in Portishead. Instead we took a room in a working-class lodging house, claiming to be husband and wife, and there, if anyone cares, goes my reputation. I really didn't think of it at the time. I suspect James did; he resisted the idea until I forced him to see facts: Anything else would have prevented public contact between us, unless he wanted the landlord to accuse me of loose conduct and toss me out.

The fact of my reputation, as opposed to the theory of it, was never in danger. After a day's riding and spending most of the night on the river, I was so tired I could hardly speak. James was in no better case, though he tried to disguise it; he'd not only been awake as long as I had, but had helped with the sailing as well. Once he'd fed the fire in the grate, he stretched out on the floor in front of it and sighed.

"There's no need for that," I said sharply, from my bench. I'd chosen to sit on something without a back, to keep from dozing off instantly.

"For what?" he asked. It turned into a yawn.

"Sleeping on the floor. Take the bed. I'll have the settle."

"You take the bed. I'm not going to fall asleep here. I'm only resting. Ask me questions and I'll stay awake."

"All right. Newport isn't Portishead. It's a city. How will we know if Johnson arrives?"

He lay on his back with his arms folded under his head. It wasn't a position one could rise from, or even change very much, casually. The light from the fire and from the lamp on the table next to me fell full on his face. I recalled him sitting on the hearth or standing before it, in the tavern room the night I'd snatched him out of the kitchen-yard. Now here he was, making no effort to secure for himself even the least of physical defences against me. I didn't think he had many mental ones in reserve. Then, of course, I wondered if I was supposed to think that.

His eyes had closed. He opened them and said, "We're conspirators. What's one of the few advantages of conspiracy?"

I was too tired to keep more than one thing at a time in my head, and I was already busy being irritated. "I thought I was supposed to ask *you* questions."

He yawned again. "Excuse me. Co-conspirators. At least, usually they're an advantage. I've been here before."

I extracted all the available sense from that, and said, "But what are you going to do?"

He didn't answer. And his name, twice, didn't make him open his eyes.

I waited for a bit to see if he'd wake. His chest rose and fell steadily. As I watched, tension went out of his face as if melted out by the heat, and left it, under the thickening beard and the scars and hollow places and lines from wear and weather, nearly the one I'd known from my girlhood. Nearly. Humans, like metals, are malleable, and you can deform a sheet of metal with hammer-blows and then tap it out flat again. But any metallurgist will assure you that the whole sheet has changed, and only melting it down and rolling it again will undo it.

I contemplated self-sacrifice, rejected it, and slept in the bed.

When I woke the sun was strong through the open curtains, and James was sitting backwards in a ladder-back chair, his boot-heels hooked on the leg rungs. His chin was propped on the back, and he was staring into the fire. He had a cup cradled in both hands. I might have moved or made a noise; he turned his head a little toward me and said, "You are not hallucinating. You *do* smell coffee."

I tried to speak, failed, and cleared my throat. "What time is it?"

"Eleven. It's a lovely day. Have some coffee." He removed himself from the chair as if he always sat in them backwards, and in fact as if it were the only normal way to sit in a chair and everyone ought to do it. The pot was on the hearth to keep warm; he poured a cupful and brought it to the bedside with a flourish.

I dragged myself nearly upright and rubbed my eyes. "What *is* wrong with you?"

"Nothing, at the moment, and I'm treasuring every instant of it. You take it black? Of course you do." He smiled, moderately, and continued to hold out the cup.

I took it, sipped, and felt a little better. "What do you mean, 'of course'?"

"Don't you take it black?"

"Yes, but—"

He nodded. "There you are, then."

"And how do you take *yours*?" I asked, trying not to growl.

"However it arrives. You see? Indicative of character."

"Oh, God. Go away. I'm getting up."

"You're badgerish in the morning. I shall remember that. I'll be downstairs if you need me." He went out, trying, obviously, not to smile.

It wasn't until I sat up and prodded my fingers through my shorn curls that I wondered what I looked like. And wondering seemed to open a floodgate of difficult thoughts, because hard on its heels was a sudden consciousness, deeper than my intellectual assessment of the matter the night before, that I'd spent the night alone in a room with a man. A man, furthermore, whose reputation was such that no one would believe I'd put my feet on the floor this morning *virgo intacta*. Heavens, it ought not to have been worth an instant's thought by this time. I'd spent the previous night alone with the same man; at least, he'd been there in the morning. I had no idea where he'd spent the night. The emotional storm that had broken in its earlier hours might have washed him up anywhere. And that morning he hadn't been leaning over me where I lay, with a peace-making smile and a thoughtful and distressingly domestic cup of coffee. My face burned as if I'd scrubbed it with sand. "Idiotic, artificial, bourgeois morality," I said aloud, with conviction. I'd even been fully clothed. Horizontality does not equal immorality in the arithmetic of sensible persons. By that measure, how many sensible people am I acquainted with? Perhaps four?

Defending one's honour by sleeping in one's clothes is hard on the clothes, and requires a deal of effort to repair the ravages. I had, in the end, all but a bath in front of the fire, and washed my hair—an impossibility with three feet of hair, so I thanked Providence for my crop—and with hot water and the heat of the grate took the worst of the creases out of my woolen skirt.

James, with the disturbing accuracy I was beginning to expect of him, stayed away for long enough to encompass bathing, hair-washing, and dressing. When he knocked at last, I was sufficiently recovered to be apologetic about my bad mood. He waved my apologies aside. His manner was pleasant and comradely, and I was pleased to forget I'd been such a fool as to blush over his actions or mine only an hour before. He swept me out of doors (somehow—I felt like a kite on a strong gust of wind, but am not sure what he said or did to produce the effect), where he bought two baked potatoes from a woman with a warming-can at the end of the street. A fine, straightforward set of actions; to anyone watching from a few yards away, I'm sure that's how it looked. From my vantage point at James's elbow, it was not quite that.

"Don't look shocked, Annie," he said, when we were still a step away and she was not really looking at us. "Though I'd never stop you looking pleased." There was a faint, unfamiliar lilt in his voice. He was smiling a little, a social expression fit for street use.

The woman turned. She was, I thought, perhaps ten years older than James—though James had had money and leisure, however he'd chosen to employ them, and the lack of them can hasten age just as possession of them can sometimes hold it back. In spite of his warning her eyes widened and her lips parted. Then her mouth closed briskly. She did not look pleased.

"The clack was that you'd died," she said. Her voice was rough with calling.

"Almost. I may yet. Would you be sorry?"

"Nah. There's sixteen whores in a house up the road'd be broken-hearted, though."

He was still smiling; I realized at last that it was for anyone else who might be watching. Now he raised one eyebrow a fraction and said, "She's my cousin."

"Well. Shall I beg her pardon?"

I said, "No," quickly, mostly to keep from hearing how James would answer.

"Two, please," said James with a nod at the can, handing her twopence.

"They're ha'penny."

"I know."

She opened the can lid, and as the steam cloud enclosed her, James asked, "Do you remember Johnson? Tall, red hair, hands like two sides of bacon? The lad that Pomeroy said to his face didn't give a damn about the working man?"

"Didn't give a damn about one thing but himself, was the comment." She handed him two potatoes. "Your man knocked him down. I do."

"Well, he may come to town. If he does, I'd like to hear of it. Where's Pomeroy nowadays?" He'd passed me a potato and was busy buttering and salting his, not looking at the woman. She was prodding potatoes in the can.

"Churchyard."

His hands kept moving, but not, it seemed to me, with his attention on them. "I'm sorry," he said after a moment. "What happened?"

"Crane let go. He always said it would. Said if it happened

on his shift they'd blame him just to get rid of him. Well, it did, and they blamed him, but he didn't care in the end, did he?''

"He would have, if they stopped widow's pay on account of it."

She straightened up and looked him in the face. "You got to marry before you can have a widow."

They had both forgotten me, I suspected. I didn't mind. Whatever this was, it was intensely private.

"Well," she said at last, wiping her hands on a cloth pinned at her waist. "You'll want to see Davis. You know where?"

"Number two shed?"

She nodded. "He's made foreman."

"I'll remember to congratulate him." His attention, again, was just slightly elsewhere, and his accent was entirely his own.

"Where do I send to you if I see your man?"

"Showell still keep the place by the old church?"

"I suppose you think he'll be glad to have you under foot. Man's got a business to run."

"And so do you." James smiled at her suddenly, the genuine smile that wasn't for street use. "Thank you, Annie. I'll remember you in my prayers."

"If you pray to something, I don't want to be brought to its notice. Jimmy. Watch yourself, boy."

He nodded and, me in his train, went down the street; downward, toward the harbour.

We crossed two streets before he shook off that uncanny mixture of abstraction and alertness and looked at me as if he saw me. "What is it?" I asked.

He rubbed the space between his eyebrows. It was almost a familiar gesture now. "Nothing, exactly. Or . . . you develop—one develops a sort of sense about these things. As if information were a solid thing, that you could see moving around you. I've got a feeling that we're on a collision course with a great deal of it."

I was alarmed. Having feelings was not what I expected of James. "Is that good, or bad?"

"Good."

"No matter the information?"

"It's always better to know than not to know." He looked down at my potato, which I'd half-finished. "No butter *or* salt?"

I shook my head irritably.

"Readings of character are all very well, but that seems excessive."

I hadn't the faintest idea what he was talking about. "If I put butter on it, it tastes like butter. I like the taste of the potato."

James stared, arrested out of all proportion to the subject. "Readings of character, indeed. I stand corrected. And warned."

"*Will* you stop talking nonsense and tell me where we're going?"

He went back to walking, this time with me beside him. "To meet Evan Davis. Pomeroy used to know everyone and everything in this town. Davis knew almost that. I assume, since Pomeroy's dead, that Davis will have inherited the mantle. I haven't seen him in a long time. He used to be sound."

"Sound?"

"Not the sort to hand one to the constables." His face was calm. "I don't know if he's the sort to hand one to one's former allies."

"But we're about to find out."

"I think it's a fair risk. And if he helps us, we're very likely indeed to find Johnson before he finds us. And *that* may be unnecessary, but it would be comforting not to have to test the point. Do you agree?"

It wasn't an idle question; further, I saw that the facts that had preceded it hadn't been a matter of courtesy. I was being asked for an informed decision. "We should meet with Davis. But if you have any sense that he's untrustworthy, then I say to hell with Johnson. We get back across the Severn if we have to swim."

James, I found, was watching me, wearing a curious intermittent expression that was partly a smile. "Who taught you to swear?" he asked.

I returned the smile and ignored whatever else was in his face. "Are you shocked?"

"That depends," he replied, "on who taught you to swear."

Even in the cold air I could feel the heat in my cheeks. "Grandmama did, actually. By example."

I found I was waiting for his response, though I couldn't imagine what anyone would have to say to that. But all he said, after a few moments more, was, "Here we are."

We stood before a dockside warehouse, a great barn of a place only a little the worse for age and weather, that bore a sign above the double doors identifying it as Meager & Son Ltd., Shed No. 2.

The man we'd come to meet was small and broad and brown-haired, with a carrying deep voice that made me think he was a treasure for some choir come Sunday morning. He was directing, and sometimes leaping in to help with, the movement of half a dozen bales as tall as he was. James, with a hand on my arm, signalled that we would wait in the shadow by the door. I watched James with the edge of my vision. His gaze moved from Davis, around the warehouse to the other men, and back to Davis; I thought he was listening, too, for the voices and footsteps of people out of sight.

Things seemed at last to be put right, and Davis called for a break and came slowly toward the door, head down. James stayed where he was and watched him come. When Davis raised his eyes from the sawdust, alerted by what, I couldn't tell, there were only a dozen feet between him and us. He stared, his eyes narrowed, his hands fanned and tense at his sides.

"It's the beard," James said, unsmiling. "I knew you'd like it."

Davis opened his mouth and uttered an obscenity I'd only heard once before in my life. "I figured you for dead or halfway to China."

"Why?" All of James's features had sharpened suddenly; Davis had said something he hadn't expected.

Davis shook his head like a dog coming out of water. "We can't talk here. Come on."

"Out in the yard."

"You'll freeze your arse off. Pardon," he added to me.

"And I won't be overheard, and I'll get a good long look at anyone before he gets too close. Unless you have another suggestion?"

He did. We ended up in another warehouse, smaller, empty, and falling down, open for most of its length to the pale blue wintry sky. It got us out of the wind, at least.

James levered himself up onto an empty crate and sat, his feet dangling. I found a more sedate perch on a nail-keg. Davis remained on his feet. "Evan Davis," James said, "Miss Vaughan. A friend of mine." Another alias, I noticed. Stephen Vaughan's sister, perhaps? But I couldn't use Palmer here. "Now, what have you heard?"

"Well, back in August, that you were dead."

"No, let's start nearer to home. That's old news even here."

To my surprise, Evan Davis smiled, a short, fierce expression. "Christ Jesus, it's nice to have you back."

It wasn't irony. Something had caught fire here that was unfamiliar to me, but that I thought I might recognize if I knew fighting men. It reminded me a little of meetings I'd attended, of intelligent men and women in the presence of someone they trusted to lead them. I'd seen people look at Friedrich Engels that way.

Davis clasped his hands behind him and said, "The old man, Broeder, in London, sent word you wasn't dead, but that somebody had tried to peel you for what you knew. Then you went again, and the rumour was all 'round after a month that anyone asking after you could look by the Devil's right hand, and that this time there was someone said he'd seen you laid out and cold."

"Which proved to be Hugh Stone?"

"It did. Damned fool, but I thought he might know a corpse if he saw one. Seems not."

"Personal experience may have taught him better," James said mildly.

"Aye, I'd heard he took poison."

"Was given poison," James corrected.

Davis's surprise seemed genuine. James turned to me. "This part's yours. Do you want to tell it?"

Startled, I studied his face. His preference, I thought, was that I should speak; but I also thought that the choice was genuinely mine. I began with the barest facts about the murder, but at James's urging, the tale expanded to include the whole of my surveillance of Betty Howard.

Davis's face was determinedly blank by halfway through. When I finished he shook his head and looked at James. "Where did you find her?"

"There aren't any others. And you can't have this one," said James.

"Well, Miss Vaughan," Davis sighed, "you get tired of the Devil's right hand, here, come see me."

I'd thought myself reasonably experienced in matters of flirtation, but that exchange left me without a thing to say. I folded my hands in my lap and tried to look composed.

James let a breath out in a hiss and said, "All right. I know why you thought I might be dead. In spite of having heard, as I knew you must have, that I was seen in London in late August. Why halfway to China?"

"Because the latest story is that the swine who tried to peel you, and lost you, is still on your track. And that he's laid an information with the Queen's own dear lads against you, and they'll believe him and shoot you on sight because, isn't it the damnedest thing, he's one of their own."

"When did you hear this?" James snapped.

"Mercer heard it when he went up to London, early last week."

"Was it old news, or fresh?"

"I don't know. I could ask. But I wasn't finished."

"I've guessed it," James said, absent and alert once again. "The fellow behind it all turns out to be Gideon Johnson."

"If it's your arse he wants, I suppose you'd know," Davis said, with the resigned air of a man used to having his best stories spoiled. "I remember him. He made your friend the Devil look like a nice quiet partner for whist."

"That's Johnson, all right." James settled his elbows on his knees and propped his chin on his thumbs. "Did Mercer say who'd told him?"

"Jessie Bates, in Covent Garden. Didn't say where she'd got it. But she don't rattle."

"No. Not bad, for being done in haste," James said, as if to himself. "Evan, Johnson may be on his way here. In fact, given what you've just told me, I'm nearly sure he is. I need to know when he arrives, and where he goes when he does. Can you put the word out?"

Davis watched James for several long moments, his jaw working. "It might be easier . . . just to stop him, Jimmy."

"*No*. Anybody who lays a hand on Gideon Johnson, I eat his God-damned heart on toast. I mean it, Evan. Double for you."

He shrugged. "Only got one heart."

"I'd throw in your liver, but I don't know that there's any left. No, whatever may happen to him after, Johnson has to leave Newport alive."

It was like sitting in someone's drawing room in my usual style, taking in everything, secure in the knowledge that no one knew I was doing it. Except that I was going to say something. "Because you're here?"

James's eyes met mine, and the sudden, uncontrolled smile flashed on his face. "There aren't any others," he said obscurely. "Exactly."

"What?" Davis said.

"If Gideon Johnson dies in Newport while I'm here, expect incontrovertible evidence to appear that proves beyond doubt or pardon that I killed him. Suspected revolutionist murders naval officer. Gallows business. So let's go further yet: while you're keeping a watch for Johnson, keep one over him as well. Just in case."

"Christ," said Davis, in a tone of polite disgust. "Well, it'll be easy enough to get word out. The place is a damned beehive as it is."

"I thought there was something. What?"

"Nothing's certain yet. But rumours are thick as fleas on a tinker. Something's to be called: anything from a general strike to a rising. And probably before Christmas Day."

James stared. "Bloody hell. Who by?"

Davis thrust his hands in his coat pockets and studied James in return. "We'll see, won't we?" he answered finally. "You've not heard any of this?"

"No. But I've been hard to reach."

"Well, it won't hurt you to stay that way for once. Go rack up and let me see to this for you."

The name of Showell was mentioned again, and James hopped down off his crate. Davis put out his hand to help me up. "Remember, if he puts your back up, come see me."

"Thank you, Mr. Davis," I replied.

"*No*," said James. "I'm a violent man."

"That you are," Davis responded happily, and let us out into the wind again.

Showell ran a little dark public-house nearly in the shadow of a Nonconformist church. I didn't mind the dark, and liked the warmth a great deal. I made straight for the stool I spotted beside the fire. I'd have sat in the grate if I could.

James followed me with two mugs. "This will warm your hands even if you don't want to drink it," he said, handing me one.

"What's in it?"

"The only thing you might object to is rum, and there ought not to be much of it. Food is on its way."

It did warm my hands, and the inside of me, too, when I tasted it. "Thank God," I sighed as the fumes went up behind my eyes. "I may decide to live after all."

"I forgot," said James, leaning against the table, grinning, "that you wouldn't object to the rum."

"That depends on how much rum. And the source, I suppose." I had another sustaining swallow. The knots in my muscles had begun to untie themselves in the heat of the fire, and I felt them yield further to the persuasion of warm spirits. "If your friend Evan Davis offered me this, I'd suspect him of wanting to take advantage of me."

James ducked his head; then he began to laugh anyway, making the effort pointless. "You kept your countenance like a duchess. I had no idea you'd had so much experience with importunate fellows."

It was foolish of me, but that rankled, a little. "Well, now you know."

"Why haven't you married, Susan? You must have had offers."

His tone had changed, in a way that made me half-throttle my mug and think, quite distinctly, *Damn him.* "Would you like the list?" I regarded him with at least the countenance of a duchess, and some hope that he could be shamed into changing the subject.

Silly me. This was, after all, James. "Not if it would be indiscreet. Anyone I know?"

"I was officially out, what? Six years ago? Seven? Whenever it was, I had four offers that year, and three the next. I've had three more since then, though none of them in the last year, which may mean that I can finally stop worrying about them."

He was now sitting on the table, swinging one foot and watching me, head tilted, as if I were a demonstration of mechanical toys. "Were they awful?"

"Heavens, no. The earl was a little long in the tooth, but the marquis's heir was a lovely thing. A face like a Greek statue, and half the flowers in Covent Garden Market every blasted morning in the front hall. And the banker's son, who was also nice to look at, and behaved as if London pavement would not be worthy to receive my slipper-tread until it had been gold-plated, if then."

James was trying very hard not to laugh again. "Did you frighten them off by offering each a *précis* of his desirable characteristics?"

"No, unlike some people in my family, I have excellent manners. I was very kind to them all, but told them that I had no intention of marrying."

"Ever?"

We had reached, at last, ground that I knew was solid under my feet; or at least, we could reach it with a step on my part. "You've concerned yourself in the cause of freedom in this country. You hate slavery. Do you know the laws regarding marriage in England?"

His foot had stopped swinging. "I do. I won't insult your intelligence by saying that coupling them with the word 'slavery' is putting it too strongly. But surely a man who loved and respected his wife wouldn't employ those laws against her?"

"Some of them are not in the husband's power to ignore." I spoke calmly, though it was an effort; I didn't think that the effort showed. "And in a world where unmarried men and women are kept as separate as if they had an infectious disease, tell me, how can I know before marrying him if a man can be trusted to grant me my rights?"

"And the . . . comforts of marriage don't outweigh the risks?"

There was no reading his voice or face; I knew, at least,

that there was no pity in either, or amusement. "I think I am not a cold woman. I think . . . I would like physical love. But I won't sell myself into slavery for it."

"Other women have taken lovers."

Yes, this was, after all, James, who would simply say it, who would know that if I could be shocked by the suggestion, I had no business holding forth on the subject. "Someday, perhaps, I might take a lover," I answered, and was grateful not to sound breathless, which, to my annoyance, I was. "But never a husband."

Then the bread and butter and ham arrived, and cider, carried by a stout boy in an apron. We ate in silence. I have no idea what James busied himself with; I reviewed, determinedly, the conversation in the warehouse, trying to fit its parts in order into the things I already knew. When I'd finished my share of the food, I felt strong enough to discuss some of what I'd been busy thinking. And, to be fair, the rum may have had a part.

"Davis said things that match with your account of what happened while you were missing."

His eyes, just then, were on his mug; I think for an instant he didn't understand what I'd said. Then he looked up. "You thought it was a lie."

"We thought it could be a lie."

The battle he fought could be judged by the perfect emptiness of his face. "I see. Fair enough. It's even a lesson I'd want you to have learned. I think." He set the mug carefully on the table.

"If Johnson intends to do you harm," I said, "and if someone else means to implicate you if Johnson is harmed, wouldn't it be better to leave now? What use is there in trying to interview a man who means to kill you? He'd tell you nothing that would benefit you."

James came and sat on the raised stones of the hearth, his knees drawn up and his forearms laid on them. It occurred to me that my being a head taller than he once he did so was no accident. "Imagine, as an exercise, that Gideon Johnson *doesn't* intend to do me harm."

"But Davis—" Then I closed my mouth and considered again the conversation in the warehouse. "If you're meant to think he's your enemy, so that you'll strike first to protect yourself—''

"Thus removing Johnson from the board, *and* preventing me from finding out anything he knows, *and* putting me in an untenable, not to say ugly, position with the law. It would be elegant.''

"Davis meant to mislead you?''

"I don't think so. I'm prepared to trust him. Which doesn't mean that he couldn't have been misled. Now, if Johnson's ill-wishing of me is a fabrication to make me protect myself, what corresponding story has Johnson heard? And from whom?''

My hands closed on each other painfully. "That's why you have to talk to him.''

James nodded. "That's why. If you can gather in enough lies and see where they fall, sometimes there is a clear space in the middle of them. And that's where the truth is.''

He stood and took up my mug. Then he added, "Two warnings: first, the rumour may be genuine, and Johnson may dearly want to kill me, in which case it would be silly not to be prepared for the possibility.''

"How?''

He made a noise that might have been laughter, in some other place or time. "I wish I had some more comforting answer. Enter into the confrontation expecting the worst, and maintaining an inventive frame of mind. You'll understand, I think, when it happens. I hope.''

"Lovely.'' My stomach was suddenly full of moths. "And your second warning?''

"If the rumour isn't genuine and Johnson isn't the author of all my miseries, then when he comes, *if* he comes, he won't be alone. He may believe he is. But if there's a third party with a stake in clearing the board of Johnson or me or both of us, he'll want to have an agent or agents present to keep events on course and to tidy up after. Johnson is dangerous. But don't forget to watch over his shoulder, too.''

He walked to the table and leaned on it with both hands, his back to me. "Do you have any idea,'' he said, his voice suddenly rough, "how much I wish you weren't here?''

The days are so short now; the comfort of daylight is in

limited supply. We waited for word until midnight. James
waits very well, like some camouflaged predator who knows
that perfect stillness will eventually be rewarded. I find that I
don't wait well at all. James dealt patiently with that, also.
Then we returned to the lodging-house, or I did, and James
escorted me. After seeing me settled, he went out again. I
didn't mention the difficulty I'd be in if he failed to return; I
was sure he had thought of it. I should have tried to sleep.
Instead, I've written this. Now, perhaps, sleep won't be unimaginable.

James returned. His face told me immediately—calm, but
honed and intense, like the face of an athlete who understands
the contest and is prepared. "He's arrived," he said. Then he
went to the settle, stretched out on it, and as far as I could tell,
fell asleep. I am going to lie down on the bed and try to do
likewise.

NOVEMBER 30th

Dear Susan,

It is a cold morning, the kind where you expect to see hints
of frost lying across the hedges, and where the sun, struggling
up to her zenith, seems weary and uninterested in warming
anything, and when you step out of doors you taste the wind
and think that there may be snow soon. But I have only been
out of doors once and now I am in the bedroom, at the lovely
mahogany writing desk with its funny little drawers everywhere that we had such fun with on a similar morning many
many long years ago, before we seriously thought of marriage
or love, or imagined the joys and worries the future might
bring.

I stayed up all night waiting for Dick to return from Cáuld-
hurst, and all night I found myself staring out over the mul-
berries and beyond them to the wall, where there is a little rise
in the road and you can just make out the head of a rider
should one be approaching from the north, and you thus have
a little warning of a visitor, even if you do not always know

who the visitor is, and I do not know when exactly, but I gradually became aware that something was wrong, and I broke the nail of my left forefinger from pressing it against the chair. Eventually I fell asleep, I suppose at about three o'clock, and awoke stiff and feeling, well, the way you always feel when you fall asleep in your clothing sitting up in a chair. What woke me was the sound of a carriage out in the court-yard, and you can imagine how my heart pounded upon hear-ing it, and then I recognized Wixon, who is the constable, and I stood up, straightened my gown, and made myself walk slowly and carefully down the stairs, and I managed to reach the door just as Wixon pulled the bell, so I let him in, and I can still remember how my hand looked as I reached out for the door, and I stopped it there, resting on the polished brass knob, thinking that in another moment my happiness might be gone forever, but then I took a breath and pulled the door open, and as Wixon reached up to take his hat off I said, "Is Richard alive?" and he did not even seem startled by the question, but just said, "Yes, ma'am," and my knees nearly buckled at that moment, but I managed to say, "Won't you come in?" but he did not want to.

I said, "What is it, then? Has he been hurt?"

"No, ma'am, but I spoke with him, and, well," and he paused there, and seemed very uncomfortable, and looked around a little, and said, "We spoke of the idea of him paying a visit to the Continent." "To the Continent?" I cried. "What-ever for?" He said, "Well, it is difficult to say, ma'am. We just spoke of it, you know." And I protested that I did not understand, and he cleared his throat and said, "Well, ma'am, I cannot say exactly." And then I realized that he was trying to tell me something that he couldn't say directly, but that Dick was alive and uninjured, except for his poor shoulder which still gives him pain, but I could think again, so I said, "You spoke to Mister Cobham at Cauldhurst, did you?" and he said, "Yes, ma'am," and I said, "You were looking into the death of my cousin?" and he said, "That I was, ma'am," and I said, "Did you learn anything?" and he said, "Well, we found a note, ma'am," and I asked what the note said, and Wixon said that in it, David, writing to some friend of his, said he feared for his life, and spoke of Dick as wanting to kill him, and I said, "Not Richard!" and Wixon said, yes, ma'am, and no doubt orders would come to hold him for investigation, but the orders had not arrived as of yet, and then I realized what Wixon had done, and so I kissed him and said, "Bless you, Constable Wixon," and he turned red as a beet and cleared his throat, and then I even had the presence of mind to ask to whom the note was written, which earned me a funny look from Wixon, but he said, "A . . . uh . . . person named Tournier," which made my knees go weak again, but I did not let Wixon see it, so he just tipped his hat to me and left.

Well, the post arrived just an hour later, and it contained a note from Richard that I will copy and pass on to you, and I do hope Wixon does not get into any hot water over this, and I suppose this does not change anything except that the stakes are higher now, because Richard's liberty is at issue, so we must solve this, but I am not entirely certain how to proceed, and I am very tired, and I am feeling almost as if I had taken opium, only I have not, but still there is that odd feeling that everything is happening at a distance, which I attribute to lack of sleep, so I shall rest for a time, and then eat something, and then consider the matter again, but I thought I should at least write to you as soon as possible, so that you would be informed of the latest developments.

It is difficult to avoid jumping to conclusions, Susan, but it is more difficult to imagine that David wasn't killed by whomever kidnapped James, probably when they found out he had taken James's notes but had not turned them over. It is probable they caught him, questioned him, learned what had happened, made him write the note incriminating Richard, and then killed him, although, if it were that simple, why would they have left his body near the stables, so it is likely there is much that I am missing. Being in such a state, Susan, seems almost to free my mind, and my imagination, set free, roams to the oddest places, none of which provide solid footing, but all of which must be looked at to see if perhaps paths lead out of them that are worth following, and of all of these, the one that will not go away is the idea that, if the government are interested in these Chartists, which seems entirely reasonable, and thus interested in the traitors who can supply them with information against those who conspired against the government, which also seems reasonable, then that leaves us with Her Majesty's government working hand in glove with the Trotter's Club, which I simply cannot imagine, even in the odd state of mind that possesses me at this moment. But if the Trotter's Club have no such support, then tell me where are they getting the resources to follow people all over the country, to kidnap them, to hold them in houses against their will, to have people killed at their whim, and to hire bully-boys to attack James? Tournier has never been all that rich, you know, and I can think of no one else in the Trotter's Club who holds great wealth, which makes it very tempting to believe Her Majesty's government are involved, but that is too far-fetched, I cannot accept it, and so must seek some other explanation, although I am at a loss as to what, because tempting as it may be to look for some foreign power financing the Trotter's Club I cannot imagine to what end, although this brings to mind the Prussian gold of which James wrote, and it is even possible that some of it was delivered to the Grey Hound, if you remember the heavy box James unloaded for the mysterious Fair-haired Woman, about whom I am still puzzled, but that would be too nice and neat, so perhaps we should look for someone with the means, which must be considerable, and the motive, which is unfathomable, to provide money to a group of sorcerers who involve themselves, or at least some part of whom involve themselves, in conspiracies against conspiracies against the Crown, all of which makes me dizzy, so I hope you can shed some light on this, which I confess I am only thinking about because the alternative is worrying about Dick, and I cannot do that any longer or I believe I shall go mad, and then I will be of no use to Dick, or to you, or to James, or even to myself, although I should not be at all surprised if Aunt Louisa preferred me in that condition, but now it seems that I really am rambling aimlessly, so I shall dispatch this and then sleep, and no doubt matters will seem a bit more clear when I awaken, so until you next hear from me, believe that I remain your faithful friend,

Kitty

FRIDAY

My Darling Kitty,

As our friend has no doubt informed you, I have been called away to the Continent for a time. I will write you when I know where I will be staying, but at the moment, as you can imagine, everything is in great confusion. Please give my warm regards to Susan and her friend, if you are in touch with them, and assure Susan that I will at least make certain that I stay somewhere with decent coffee. Until I see you again, my love, please guard your health with all of your energy, and think loving thoughts of your affectionate,

Richard

SUSAN VOIGHT'S JOURNAL
(WRITTEN IN CIPHER)

30 NOV 1849

I was right. Everything around us is being slowly wiped away, like chalk off a slate. The cloth will reach us soon, or we will run into it without warning, and we will be gone also. So easily. Next I shall hear that London is burned to the ground, Calais swept flat by storms, Brussels consumed by the very ground it sits on. I want to exact a promise from somewhere, that I won't be left to face the end of the world alone, but I can't think where to turn for it.

RICHARD COBHAM'S JOURNAL

30 NOVEMBER

By God this London town is a dreary place! All I can see from my window is a street where walk people bundled against the cold, and a barber's, which makes me think of blood. Lee is a friendly fellow, though, and recognized me before I had said a word and when I told him I was in trouble, he just nodded and took me home, gave me a room, and said we would talk later. He returned in two minutes to give me a glass of the best coffee I have ever had, took my note for Kitty, and vanished. Riding through the night looking over my shoulder probably made the coffee better. I wish I at least had a pistol, though in fact I doubt that it would make me any safer.

LATER

Have had a pleasant chat with Lee, whom I believe I like very much. He is friendly, and has a very straightforward demeanour, yet he knows who I am, and apparently has heard of my father's father. He said that London is not safe and suggested an inn "near Portsmouth" where he had friends. "Oh," I said with contrived carelessness, "is Coslick one of you?" "Both Coslicks," he said with his easy smile, as if it were a matter of no great moment. Then he handed me a piece of silvered glass, a sprig of mistletoe, a knife, and a pair of pistols. I thanked him, still trying to make it seem natural, and, just on a wild guess, said, "But the Trotter's Club still have the edge." He shrugged and said, "They think they do, because they think Leuchtenberg will protect them forever even without seeing results. That's their illusion." At this point my mind was racing like mad as I tried to think of a way to keep the information flowing in hopes that I could sort it out later. I said, "Perhaps I'm just a pessimist." ·

He said, "Don't be." He had a cup of something, and here he passed his hand over it in what seemed an automatic gesture and drank. Then he said, "We know that you have the power, and your wife has more. You will be hard to stop." I said, "I'm worried about James, though." "Your cousin," said Lee, "is trying to put himself beyond the reach of the Trotter's Club, and in so doing, has put himself beyond our help. But be of good hope. The Old King has never repudiated us, though the Queen knows nothing and will not aid us. But the power remains, and all may yet be very well. You should leave for Portsmouth. I'll return for you in an hour."

I expect the hour is nearly up. I will attempt to find out more when I arrive, as I expect to, at the Grey Hound.

DECEMBER 1ˢᵗ, VERY LATE

At the Grey Hound, spoke with Coslick at some length, but learned nothing; he seems more close than Lee was. I asked him if he would have told James more than he was telling me, and he smiled and said, "Him, I knew." But I am exhausted from the multiple conveyances I used to get here, many of which were not comfortable. I think these people may be somewhat mad, but then perhaps they are not; the police are, after all, almost certainly looking for me. I worry about Kitty. I wonder what James is doing.

SUSAN VOIGHT'S JOURNAL
(WRITTEN IN CIPHER)

1 DEC 1849

It's better tonight—*I* am better. The events of the 30ᵗʰ are twenty-four hours and eighty miles, by rail, behind me. We are stopped for the night in Birmingham. Tomorrow we will continue on to Manchester. I am aware that this has turned into a particularly distasteful tour of James's past geography, but he seems to be bearing it well. Indeed, the only thing he seems to have difficulty bearing is me, though I'm doing all I can. Things are only made more of a trial by confrontations like tonight's. He must know that. Why does he persist? But for his sake, as well as for the sake of accomplishing what we have to do, I can command myself.

David is dead—one day it will be possible to weep for him, to say, "My brother is dead," and feel tears spring to my eyes—and Richard is accused of killing him. I don't believe that. Certainly not because I think there is any bar in the family temperament to killing. Had David been shot, I would be less inclined to doubt.

The events of the 30ᵗʰ, now, without further delay. James, freshly shaved (I pointed out that I was nearly used to it; he said he wasn't. He said he frightened himself every time he rubbed his chin), took me out that morning to have a look at Gideon Johnson, who had lit for the moment at a bookseller's stall, where he turned over pages and scowled. "He knows my habits, you see," James murmured into my ear, half-laughing. We were in a printer's shop across the road, watching through a window. James, of course, knew the printer.

Johnson was a large man, ruddy-faced and red-haired, and his civilian clothes were neat, but without ostentation. From across the road, there was nothing else I could tell.

"Now," James continued, "tell me: Is he being followed?"

I studied the street and the storefronts. It was a busy place. Alongside the bookseller's were a greengrocer's and a poulterer's, and a draper's beyond that. People hurried and lingered everywhere I looked; waggons and carts rattled past, or stopped to unload. "I don't see anyone, but how could you, in this?"

"It will be easier when he moves again. In fact—" James turned suddenly to the printer. "Lowell, may we run up to your parlour? Just to get a look from higher up?"

Lowell agreed to it, and James led me up the stairs and into a little, tidy room with a pair of windows overlooking the street. I could see Johnson, still hovering over his table of books. Then with a last quick look 'round, he stepped out into the street and began to saunter down it.

"Good," said James. "Now look."

I saw a great many people, and waggons, and carts, but from higher up. "No, nothing."

"Don't look at any one thing. Fix your eyes in one place, but don't focus on it. You see Johnson walking?"

"Yes—"

"Don't focus on him, either. Just take note of his motion. Now, somewhere in the crowd behind him there is something moving at the same speed, in the same direction."

"I see him." A low-crowned grey hat with a black band, over a charcoal-coloured coat; pearl-grey gloves, a cane with a tarnished silver top. "There."

"You very nearly frighten me, sometimes," said James, satisfaction in his voice. "He may be a confederate of Johnson's, but I don't think so. And don't ask me why, because I couldn't tell you. Now, I want to talk to Johnson for possibly two minutes. But I would much rather that the gentleman behind him doesn't see me do it.''

''Then you'll need to distract him, won't you?''

''I will. Why do you ask?''

I took a deep breath and said, ''Whoever he is, he must be someone who would recognize you. There's no reason he would recognize me. I'll distract him.''

''How?''

There wasn't much time; Johnson was moving slowly, but he would be out of sight soon. ''I'll make a disturbance in the street.''

''He'll slip by.''

''So he'll have to be in the middle of it from the start.''

''Good.'' James was already at the parlour door, and I was close behind. ''If he looks like offering you violence, let him go instantly. This is not the moment for heroics.''

Once we left the printer's doorway James melted into the crowd like butter. I began to push my way through, until I remembered the way motion eddied when you knew how to watch for it, in the busy street. If I could learn to see, I could also learn to melt.

On another subject, he had once said, ''You'll understand, I think, when it happens.'' Now my thoughts ran too quickly to be quite linear, and my skin seemed to sting with the blood rushing under it. Everything I saw was as sharp as if it had been cut from paper. As I moved, I thought—I wouldn't call it planning, exactly; it was more a review of the circumstances, the assets to hand, the difficulties that might be present. My clothes no longer looked like a rich woman's, and instead of a bonnet and pelisse I had a kerchief and a shawl. The poulterer's lay ahead of me. Eggs? No, too quickly done with. But chickens—There were four hens, live, crated, and quarrelsome, at the poulterer's door. I handed the man in the bloody apron who was bending to lift them a five-pound note and grabbed up two crates in each arm. Ungainly business, easy to loose my grip on the lot; but not, I hoped, before time. I stopped long enough to spring the catches on the lids, then restacked my burden: bottom crate with the lid up, top one with the lid down. Melting, at speed, carrying four crated hens, is not a task for a beginner. For the first time in Newport I was glad it was cold.

I saw him ahead of me, grey hat, dark grey coat, cane, gloves. He was tall and broad-shouldered. There was a carriage coming toward us on the left that would require him to step to one side. I was beside him, on his right, when he did. If the collision with the crates bruised him as much as it did me, it justified what I heard him say. I was busy letting go of half my livestock.

The two hens, flung out of their crates, transformed into an explosion of feathers and squawking between us, and my out-raged scream must have sounded quite authentic, since it was as much startled out of me as planned. Then he looked full at me, and I almost forgot to drop the other two hens.

He was deeply tanned and harsh-featured, the lines those of a man who frowned often. He had a ginger moustache. He was the man who had stood on the other side of the turnstile when Betty Howard, crossing the line at Phillips Park station, died. Then the second pair of hens went off like avian bombs in our faces, and I let go another shriek and stumbled forward and fell onto his chest. There had been no recognition in his eyes.

He could have got away from me if he'd taken his coat off, but nothing else would have prevailed against my death-grip on my lapels. I screamed, in the meantime, for him to look what he'd done, and what did he mean to do about it, *et cetera.* The voice and manner were gratifyingly like my model, namely the woman in Birmingham who'd complained about her two violent Irish lodgers. Several people in the street had seen the collision. Some agreed with my view, and said so vigourously; others disagreed, likewise. Since I had no interest in winning the argument but only in prolonging it, I was de-lighted with both factions. My only frustration was that I seemed to have no sense of time. Had enough of it passed?

The hens, of course, were gone, their necks probably already wrung and their corpses hidden under coats or bundles. The man with the ginger moustache finally produced his pocket-book, snatched a note from it, and flung it at me, and pushed past in the direction Johnson would have gone. It was, I was delighted to see, a five-pound one.

Staying in character, I walked back down the street, past the printer's (making sure to catch the proprietor's eye through the window), and went in at a public-house two doors down. There I sat down on a bench and trembled like an under-boiled pudding for perhaps ten minutes, at which time James came in and sat down across from me. His expression was a bit strange.

"Tell me you do this sort of thing all the time, and I've only happened to miss all the other occurrences."

"What?"

He folded his arms on the table and buried his face in them. "Nothing," he said, muffled. "Nothing. I need a drink. If you tell me you don't, I shall kill you."

I called, in a ladylike fashion, for two pints of porter. "Did it work?" I asked, managing not to squeak.

He raised his head, took a long shuddering breath, and opened his eyes. He still looked a little wild. "Yes. Perfect. We have a meeting place. And Johnson now knows he's being followed. Which, given Gideon Johnson, may mean he's not being followed anymore. I may not get on with the man, but I have to acknowledge that he's awfully good."

"The man who was following him was at Phillips Park station, on the other side of the crossing, when Betty Howard was struck." I said it all on one exhalation.

James stared. "Jesus," he said finally, with some of that accent that is not quite his own. I don't think he would have noticed that under stress he had resorted to what must have been a blasphemy of Seamus Palmer's. "Well, I wish I knew what that meant. I suppose we may find out. Did he recognize you?"

"No." Now that I wasn't shaking, I could feel in myself a certain exhilaration under what I'd thought was simple lightheadedness. I had done what I meant to do. I had even done it with a modicum of style, and in the face of what might have been a deadly change in the nature of the task. I had to struggle to contain a burst of giggling.

The porter arrived, and James drank a third of his straight off. "All right. We have a meeting place, and time. Johnson is a filthy-minded rat-eating bastard, but he offered a meeting place."

"When? And why is he a—"

"Four o'clock. It will be twilight, unless the weather comes down again, in which case it'll be night. I wanted it earlier, to give him less time to prepare something unpleasant for us, but he won't meet me in the open in broad daylight, or anywhere too near the town. He points out, and rightly so, I admit, that there are too many Navy men at and around Newport."

"And why—"

"The meeting place is south of here, near Nash, in the Severn marshes. There's a hut—there was a hut, anyway. If the weather stays clear, then I hope there isn't a hut anymore."

"I don't understand you," I had to say finally.

He smiled a little, wearily. "It's the place where Jimmy Palmer died."

There was still a hut. In the plate-flat, colourless landscape of the marshes, you could see it, squat as it was, for half a mile. We were on a pair of hired horses, which would have been foolish if James hadn't known where to find the solid footing in the hummocks of salt grasses and the threads of water like capillaries of mercury between them, gleaming under the last light of the sky. When we were what I later recognized as just out of easy rifle-shot of the hut, James motioned for a halt and slid out of the saddle. "Stay here. If I come out and wave, bring the horses in. If I don't come out, or if I come out and whistle, ride like the devil back to town and try to find Davis. He'll help get you away."

"Unless he makes me a better offer," I said, which made him smile. I couldn't tell if it was the twilight that made him seem a little pale. "Did you expect me to memorize the route we took to get here?"

"No. Did you?"

"If there were landmarks, I'm afraid I missed them all."

"It's all right. It's like gambling; you weigh the risks. If I don't come out and wave, assume the risk of drowning is smaller than the risk of getting killed in there." He sounded bizarrely cheerful.

I stayed mounted and watched him walk toward the hut. There was no point in trying to creep up on it; whoever was there could see the horses. I had donned my man's clothing again, and was glad of it; it would be better for wading, or fighting, or fleeing. Once more, my time sense had deserted me, and I had no idea how long it was before James appeared at the low door of the hut and waved.

It must have been a dreadful place to die, or to watch someone die. The ground around the hut was nearly dry, in comparison with its surroundings, but the place had been wet, and was in a suspended state of collapse. The piled slates of the walls were black and green with lichen or moss or some similar growth, and the board roof, its planks perhaps salvaged from some wreck, looked slick with rot. There was no opening save the door. Even from outside, it smelled of decay and the sea.

James was standing outside an arm's length from the wall, and Gideon Johnson was crouched in the door-frame, smoking a modest cigar. He looked me up and down in a way I thought was meant to be insulting, taking in my trousers and my cropped hair. I studied him in much the same way. He had looked large from across the road, but this close he was enormous, even crouching. When he straightened up, I thought, it would be like watching a monument lifted into place. His coat was buttoned against the cold, but his collar lay open and his neckcloth was gone. One of his hands dangled between his knees, and I remembered James's description of them: like sides of bacon. "What the hell is this?" Johnson said, still staring at me.

"The only other person I expect to arrive here tonight," James said with great precision. "She produced the commotion in the street this morning."

"If she dressed like this, I wager she did." He stubbed his cigar on the ground and stood. I was right. "Is she armed?"

"I have no idea." James seemed mildly startled by the idea. "Are you?"

"No," I answered. "I do bite, however." Johnson snorted. "Mr Johnson, I'm sorry my cousin is so reluctant to introduce us. I have no idea why. I am Miss Voight. I can't think of a single reason why you shouldn't be told that, since I assume you're perfectly capable of finding it out."

"I am. Cousin, you say? God, I thought he'd taken to carrying his comforts around with him. But then, the whole family's big on comforts. And killing. Which are you good for?"

"Careful," James said gently.

"You be careful, you little bastard. Especially with your cousins. I hear you're short one already. Maybe two, by now."

It was my voice that asked, "What do you mean?" I hadn't known I was going to speak. James was on my left, and I was afraid to look at him.

"You haven't heard? One of our Jimmy's cousins has murdered another, and bolted."

I'd felt a mounting, half-controlled force on my left, in a way I couldn't explain. James was suddenly in reach of Gideon Johnson but he hadn't touched him, or threatened him. There was only that gathered naked power, all in the soft voice in which he said, *"Which one?"*

Then I realized what Johnson had said, and what James had asked, and I clutched my hands to my mouth.

Johnson stared down at James, no contempt in his face now. "The parson. He was the one who got his neck wrung. They're saying Richard Cobham did the wringing."

"The parson is her brother," said James, unchanged.

"Then her brother's in hell," Johnson said deliberately, through his teeth. "When you're like this, you'd pass for your damned father."

"And where have you met my father?" James spoke so quietly that I had to strain to hear him. His hand flashed out and I muffled another cry; the motion ended with James's little finger hooked through a fine chain, drawn from under Johnson's collar and pulled taut. A silver medallion suspended from the chain winked between them in the twilight. "Or do all the officers in Her Majesty's Navy wear one of these now?"

A crescent, a star, and a serpent. Johnson winced as James tugged a little, and said, "Your papa has one like it."

"I know. So did the parson. I had some hope that we could answer each other's questions, about that and whatever else, like civilized men. But if you prefer to caper about disguised as a half-witted brute, I'll just kill you and ask my questions elsewhere."

Gideon Johnson's chest swelled. Then he let all the air out of his lungs at once. "You would, wouldn't you, you bastard?"

"I would."

"Let go of me."

The little finger straightened, and the chain dropped back against Johnson's shirt. He was most of a head taller than James, and half again as broad, and the chain caught around James's smallest finger had been very thin. Perhaps, I thought, it was only that I was still stunned by the news, and so couldn't understand what James had done.

I *was* stunned. I wanted to sit down, but there was no place but my saddle that wasn't wet. It might not be true, about David, about Richard. James would find out. I realized that the pressure against my lips was my own fingers, and let my hands drop to my sides.

Johnson stepped out of the doorway. He swept James a mocking bow and gestured for him to pass inside—or that was the start of the motion. It transformed itself partway into something swift, with one of his great fists on the end of it. The sound of the impact was sickening.

It knocked James into the doorway. He caught one of the door-posts (the roof made a grinding, rustling protest) and kept himself from falling flat immediately; then he dropped unsteadily to sit cross-legged on the sill. My hand was in my pocket. I couldn't remember putting it there on purpose. But Johnson stood where he was, his hands curved loose at his thighs, breathing loudly.

James shook his head once and seemed to regret it. There was blood at the corner of his mouth. He touched his jaw gingerly and said, "You must be a dab hand with a belaying pin."

"It's a steam-ship, you idiot."

"Shocking waste of natural talent. Are we even now?"

Johnson replied with a dazzling obscenity and helped James to his feet. I didn't understand this any more than I had the previous threatening passage between the two men, but I suspected this one was because I didn't understand Johnson, or anyone like him. But James, I thought, did. I was certain, as Johnson was not, that James had known what Johnson would do, and had waited, cold-blooded, for the blow. A shiver went through me that had nothing to do with the wind.

There was a little shuttered lantern in the hut, on a moss-eaten wooden shelf halfway up the wall. Lying beside it were a Colt revolver and a large pistol I thought might be of French or German make. Johnson opened the lantern partway, and the shuddering weak light showed that someone, not too long ago, had brought two sections of tree trunk to the hut to serve as seating or tables. I accepted one, and looked forward to seeing which of them would take the other. Johnson, of course. And once he sat, he would notice that James could look down on him. I felt, unreasonably, a little sorry for Johnson.

"Where did you hear about my cousins?" James asked.

"A telegram. From a friend."

James's eyebrows rose. "My. One of my cousins dies, and a friend of yours thinks the matter is of enough moment to warrant a telegram. To you." One corner of his lips—the side that Johnson hadn't hit—tugged upward. "May I guess at the friend?"

"Alan Tournier. He bloody well wouldn't have sent one to you."

"No," said James. He was smiling on both sides now. "He sent a very different set of messages to me."

"What do you mean?"

"Let me tell you how I've spent the last few months." And James proceeded, in concise form, to tell him about the notes, the abduction, his eventual escape, and the widely separated adventures of himself and his relatives since then. Partway through I noticed that the words were not quite as cleanly-made as I was used to hearing from James. His face must have begun to swell.

Johnson interrupted sometimes. The first was to ask, "Was I in your bloody note-book?"

"Yes," said James.

"And what did it tell you about me?"

"Inconclusive."

"But you don't think I'm in your nest of informers?"

"Isn't that," James said gently, "one of the things I'm finding out now?"

Johnson, curiously, pinched his lips together and was silent.

The second interruption was at the end of my story about Betty Howard. "I didn't send Betty a letter," he said. "I haven't—hadn't written to Betty for a year. I told her in April it was over with us." He looked down at his big hands and scowled. "She wouldn't get out of it, you see."

"Of what?" asked James.

"Of the dung-heap she was in with the Trotter's Club, and Stone, and your father. When I found out what she was doing—"

"It's a very old business."

"Christ, I don't mean honest whoring! It is—"

"I don't, either. I meant spying. Seducing, luring, blackmailing, and whatnot with the power of sex predates the Old Testament, I expect. Is that what you were talking about?"

Johnson rubbed his fingers over his face. "Yes."

"It's no worse than anything I've done. Or you. And she believed in what she was doing, at least until September."

"But then who wrote her that letter?" I broke in.

"Somebody who wanted Hugh Stone dead," Johnson replied.

"Not you?"

Johnson turned on me, his expression fierce. "Would you like to know what I want? I want to be left alone. I want to get the hell out of all this. I've got a good berth on a good ship and a chance to put all you plotting, scheming, lying bastards behind me. I was wet behind the ears when I got in with the Chartists."

"So was I," James said peacefully.

"You were born dry," Johnson snapped. "The Devil breathed on you, you son of a bitch. The Charter looked to be not a bad business, not as bad as some of the shite the Lords and Commons were shovelling. And I thought it would make a stir, and I liked being in the middle of a stir. I liked trouble. But the Charter's done now, isn't it? And I'm tired of looking over my shoulder."

"And the Trotter's Club?" asked James.

"I'd like out of that, too."

"But you still wear their jewelry."

"You can't just walk out."

"Why not?"

"Jesus, Jimmy. What's the matter with you? It's not just the hocus-pocus, though if you had the brains everyone says you do, you'd be afraid of them just for that. If you'd seen . . . But the other stuff is just as bad. They've got a crew of strongarm boys would scare the piss out of you, and they're up to their elbows in meddling with the government. You know about power, Jimmy. You know the sort of people who want it, and use it, and don't care where it comes from.''

''What are they meddling with in the government?'' James asked, before I could.

''I don't know. No, honestly I don't! I've done my damnedest not to know. I thought they might let me go without a fuss.''

The third time Johnson broke into James's recitation was at the end, when I remembered and mentioned the letter that had come for Richard from Southampton. ''That one, I wrote,'' he said.

''Richard never got it,'' I told him. ''He was already at Langstone, trying to trace James. He followed him to Southampton, where he was set upon and nearly killed.''

Johnson at first seemed unmoved. Then his eyes narrowed. ''After I wrote the letter.''

''It was a threatening sort of letter.''

''It was supposed to be. It sounded to me as if someone was trying to blame me for whatever had happened to Jimmy.''

''And who told you what was being said?'' James asked.

''Tournier.''

James sighed, forcefully. ''May I ask an impolite question? May I enquire why in the name of sanity you have trusted Alan Tournier?''

''You're the only person who never did, God damn you. And we all thought it was only because you resented him, for being able to give you a run for anything when nobody else could. What did your bloody note-book say about him?''

''A very good possibility.''

''Well, it would, wouldn't it?''

There was an odd, stretched pause. ''Gideon,'' James said, ''the hand-carried rumour that met me in Newport, which was designed to reach me as quickly as possible, was that you had turned your coat and were serving the government in something more than your capacity as naval officer. If I hadn't insisted that nobody was to touch you, any one of a dozen people might have taken a crack at you on the strength of rumour alone. It also suggested that you had informed on me, and meant to see me killed on sight. That followed hard on the heels of an ambush outside Redland that would have done for me if Miss Voight hadn't happened by, which in its turn followed your failure to meet me in Redland. On the evidence of that list, don't you think it's possible that you were being set up?''

Johnson, breathing hard, was silent.

James asked, ''Why didn't you meet me in Redland?''

''I was waylaid,'' Johnson replied bitterly.

''You were what?''

''Two men tried to rob me outside of Bristol. They shot my horse.''

''And got away.''

''Yes, they got away! I suppose you wish I'd blown their heads off!''

''No. I wish we knew who they worked for.''

''It's not Alan.''

''Why shouldn't it be?''

''Because Alan doesn't want me dead!'' Johnson shouted. Then he fell silent, his jaws working.

''Maybe not. Maybe he is trying to help you out of the Trotter's Club, which is the next thing you're going to tell me. But you know a lot about them, and about him. And someone seems to have wanted to prevent us from talking, to the point of trying to convince me to kill you. You haven't asked why I went to Southampton.''

''To talk to me. Why didn't you?''

''Because, symmetrically enough, I was waylaid. They made a mistake, and I got out of it. I think I was to be imprisoned again. But I was certainly not going to be allowed to confront you, at least not at Southampton. By the time I'd realized that, I'd heard about Hugh Stone's alleged suicide, and I thought I ought to go to Fairfield to see if someone had been untidy enough to leave any clues there.''

Richard, I thought, had also not been meant to speak to Gideon Johnson. But Richard would have been deemed expendable.

Johnson wound his fingers together, over and over. ''Why the hell should it be Tournier? Why not your father?''

''Because he's not in the country.''

"Yes, he is."

James's moment of silence had the force of running into a solid object at full tilt. "Since when?"

"A month, I think. Or maybe a little less. I don't know what ship he was on, or I could tell you."

James stood where the lantern light couldn't reach his face. But I knew a little of what the sides would be in his internal battle: the cold intellect, trying to weigh the meaning of this one fact among many; and the emotions in full spate. Anger, certainly. Pain, perhaps, and grief, and fear. James had not replied, and showed no sign of ever replying, to Johnson's question by saying, *Because he wouldn't want to do me harm.* "How do you know? Have you seen him?"

"Never again in my life, if I can manage it. Alan told me, but why in hell would he lie about that?"

"He wouldn't, I suppose," James said. He swept the hair back from his face with both hands and muttered, in what I thought might be Gaelic. "What I don't understand, what I cannot figure out from any point of view, is why haven't they simply hired a sharpshooter with a good rifle and picked me off at a hundred yards' range? Why do they go to the trouble, over and over, of keeping me alive?"

Johnson stared. Then he began to laugh. "Hell, boy, that's one you could ask your papa."

"Why? What do you mean?"

"The old king proves his fitness to rule. Holly king and oak king—except the point is to keep the crown on the old one."

"Keep trying. I'm not getting any sense out of this yet."

"Let's just say you owe it to the Trotter's Club. You're safe as houses, Jimmy-boy, until Midwinter."

"You're joking. They'd never go to that much trouble for one of their idiot—You're joking."

"Christ, no, not about that lot. And when the Club do take a swat at you, you'll recognize them by the method. No knives, no guns. No drawing of blood, you see, by anyone who hasn't the right."

James stared and shook his head. But I was remembering James's own account of his questioning, when the masked woman defended herself by saying that she had not drawn blood, and when David had insisted, as three men struggled with James in his study, that there was to be no blood.

"Don't look at me," Johnson said. "I'm getting out of it. I won't tell you they're not ready for Bedlam."

It had, I thought, been a merciful distraction in its way. James paced the short space available, and I saw when the light moved across his face that intellect had the upper hand again, if imperfectly. "Your invitation to a party at winter solstice was not in this telegram, I take it."

Johnson shook his head.

"Then what was? Tournier can't have sent you a telegram for the sake of telling you that David Voight was dead. What else was in it?"

"What business is it of yours?"

"Gideon."

Johnson raised his head, chin jutting, at the whiplash of James's voice. But he answered nonetheless. "It was about his sister Eleanor."

"Tournier has a sister?"

"She's had to go to the family place on the coast—something sudden, a death in the family, it sounds like—and Alan wanted me to meet her in Bristol and escort her on to Swansea."

"And why you?"

"None of your damned business."

"I see. Your sentiments do you credit, but a man isn't washed clean of sin just because you plan to make him your brother-in-law."

For an instant I thought James was going to get himself struck again. I clamped my hands over my knees to keep from moving. But Johnson settled for saying, "Christ, I forgot. The Ice-cliff. You can smile and laugh and slap a bloke on the back, but there's nothing behind it. Is there a man on earth you'd turn a hair for, or he for you?"

James's face was in shadow when he spoke. "Probably not."

"What's the matter?" Johnson asked.

"Nothing. I'm tired. Odd how it can hit you all at once."

Johnson shook his head and stood up. "Well, I know what's hit me. If you'll pardon me a minute." And he walked out the door.

"What—" I began.

"It's indelicate," James explained. "Or I'm sure he'd have told you."

Johnson's voice wafted back in out of the night. "It's high time we were out of here."

"What time is it?" James asked me.

I fumbled for my pocket-watch. "Half-past six."

He whistled softly. "He's right. Susan . . . I'm sorry about David."

I expect in his odd way he was. "Thank you. You believe it, then?"

"Don't you?"

"I think so. I knew if they found out—well."

From outside, Gideon Johnson shouted, "Jimmy!" Then we heard a gun-shot.

I was nearer the doorway, but James was through it before me. Johnson was backed against the outside wall of the hut, his mouth agape, his big hands loose. He was staring at a figure silhouetted against the sky. The lantern had cast so little light that my eyes adjusted quickly to the dark, and as they did, the figure acquired sharp features, narrowed eyes, a moustache of a familiar shape. In better light it would have been ginger-coloured.

He fired again, as James knocked me aside and sparks leaped off the slate of the wall. I was on my hands and knees in a puddle, and I saw James reach for the pocket of his huge black coat; I heard him curse, passionately. I thought of the two pistols on the shelf in the hut. Moonlight shone on the barrel of the gun in the other man's hand.

And I reached into my coat pocket, cocked the pistol there, drew it out, and fired, then cocked and fired again. Someone cried out as it went off. I don't think it was the man I shot at.

I thought later of Richard's account of the man he killed in Southampton. I never believed I had missed. Dark as it was, I could tell. I could see his face stiffen, his mouth open under the moustache. He fell in stages: first the gun, which made a little splash when it hit the ground. Then his knees buckled, which left us kneeling across from each other. I don't know if he could see me, or anything else. He didn't fall slowly because he was trying not to fall; he was beyond trying things.

This was only the process by which gravity claimed control of his remains. Then he fell forward from the waist, face-first into the water, and onto his side.

James's voice was in my ear, his breath moving my hair, and his hands were painful on my shoulders. "Susan. Let go. Do you hear me?"

It occurred to me for the first time that the shots had been very loud. James was on his knees behind me, close enough that I felt a tremour run through his body, and another. His hands slid from my shoulders down my arms, pressing them toward the ground. I noticed at last that my arms were still outstretched with the pistol clasped before me, in firing position. I let them drop slowly, until I was held hard between his hands, as if I was cracked down the middle and he meant to hold the pieces together. Then he closed his fingers around mine, and I released the pistol into his grasp.

This is all very clear. Nothing is uncertain, nothing is blurred by the speed with which things happened, or the unfamiliarity of the actions, or the faintness of the light. I remember exactly what occurred with perfect clarity.

James put his arm around my waist and helped me to stand. Then he turned back to the hut and knelt beside Gideon Johnson, who sat leaning against the wall. From that direction I heard an irregular bubbling sound, as if the marsh around us was breathing.

"Too damned dark," James muttered. "Where is it?"

"Never mind," whispered Johnson.

After a moment I heard James say, "Jesus."

"Eh. You've got to go."

"Shut up while I close it with something."

"No. Use your brain. They're—out there now. That's why he—Take the boat."

"You've got . . . of course. Where is it?"

I heard the smile in Johnson's voice as he said, "Rope tied around back. You can—can pull it right in now."

"You're a clever beggar, Gideon Johnson," James murmured.

From far out in the dark, a strange voice shouted. "You there! You're surrounded. Give yourself up, man!"

"Run for it, Jimmy," I heard Johnson say.

Bitterly, James answered, "That seems to be the plan."

"Your girl's witness. Their mistake."

From the marsh, again: "You there! Do you hear?"

James flung up his head. "Susan!" he hissed. "Untie the horses and drive them off."

I could still move. I was glad. I did what he'd told me, splashing my way to the horses, who were half-mad with the smell of blood and gunpowder, and the noise. They hardly needed driving. But I couldn't think where the water was coming from. Hadn't the ground been dry when we'd arrived?

"Now get the pistols from the shelf and put out the lantern." I did that, too. I couldn't hear the sound of the marsh bubbling anymore. Somewhere outside, at a distance, there was a shot, then two more; someone must have thought the horses carried riders. When I came out again I found James on the other side of the hut, dragging on a rope. In the darkness ahead there was the rustle of something brushing through the tall grasses, and a bump.

"There," he said. "Let's go."

"Johnson?" I was reminded by the half-clogged feeling in my throat that it was the only thing I'd said since we'd heard the first shot.

"He's dead."

"They said we're surrounded."

"We are." He spoke quickly. "But only half by men. The Severn is a tidal river. You're standing in seawater." And he pushed me over the gunwale of a skiff that seemed to have appeared from thin air, and shoved it off the grassy hummock it had run up on.

He used one oar as a pole for as long as the grass could be seen above the water. Eventually he fitted both in the oarlocks and began to row, following the tide up the river channel. At that point, he must have decided that we were far enough from pursuit that it was safe to talk. "Johnson came in this. He ran it up onto what was then solid ground, and tied a line between it and the hut, so he could pull it in when the water rose. I thought you said you weren't armed?"

"I was lying. Who do you think that was, out in the marsh?"

"I don't know. It might have been the constables."

"Johnson was killed so that you would be found with his body."

He rowed a stroke, and said, "That's what was supposed to happen. Yes. As Johnson pointed out, they made an error. They neglected to account for you. You can testify that I didn't kill Johnson. And now it's their man who'll be found with the body, and with a discharged pistol."

"And dead." I sounded horrible even to myself. "Are they going to think he shot himself?"

"Susan . . ."

I didn't answer him, and he never seemed to find the rest of the sentence.

We spent the night in the loft of a cow-byre, which seemed discreet. That was where I tried to write my journal entry, and failed. I'm not quite sure why I thought it made sense to try. I didn't have trouble falling asleep, because I seemed to be in a state between waking and sleeping anyway, and was no more committed to one condition than the other. I don't think James slept.

I have no idea how he got us to a train station. I wasn't paying attention. If anyone stared at our saltwater-marked clothing and James's bruised face, I didn't notice. It wasn't until we reached the outskirts of Birmingham that I began, unwillingly, to think. "Where are we?" I asked.

James told me. "Why in heaven's name are we in Birmingham?"

"Because it's halfway to Manchester," he explained patiently. "Which is where we're going."

"I'm sorry. Of course it is." To Manchester, to see Engels. I would have to see someone else. I would have to talk to another person. James hadn't expected me to talk to him all day, so the matter hadn't arisen before. Well, if it had to happen, then the sooner, the better. I sat quiet, beginning to rebuild the outer walls of the rooms of my mind, that would allow me to be a social creature again. A little higher this time and thicker, because the things they protected were a little more volatile than they once had been.

I was interrupted by James's grasp of my upper arm, which was too tight. "Susan, stop it," he said in a fierce, low voice.

"Stop what?"

"If you fell to bits right now I could take care of it. Of you. Let go the bloody death-grip and let me handle it."

I frowned at him. "That hurts," I said, looking down at his hand.

He let me go. "All right. I suppose I *would* rather you were able to travel on your own feet, at least, for another hour. But that's all I need." The accent with which tension sometimes coloured his speech was in it now. "Do you believe that I'd think the less of you?"

Birmingham has all the untidy character of a city taken by surprise by its own success. It's noisy, too, and busy, but that's nothing to a Londoner. The bustle of the platform, seen from the carriage window, held only a normal unreality. The steam gave its giant's hiss, and we stopped, and I stood up. "I could grow used to travelling without baggage," I said.

Behind me I heard him say, furiously, inexplicably, "*Dhia*. Kitty is going to kill me."

James found rooms for us, two of them, under the eaves of what must once have been a rich man's house near the railway station. They were tiny chambers, plain and warm, and had a door connecting them that James immediately picked the lock of.

"Your step-sister does that very well, too."

He blinked up at me from where he still crouched, his hand on the knob. "You think I wouldn't know a thing like that? I was just thinking about having dinner brought in."

"I'd rather go out for it. Unless we ought not to be seen."

"We're not fit to be seen. I also mean to try to finesse a change of clothes. Will you be all right by yourself for half an hour?"

"You can organize dinner *and* a change of clothes in half an hour?" I asked in mild astonishment.

He stood, his eyes downcast. "Yes, probably." He sounded tired. "Susan, I understand if my presence is a little inhibiting. But at least while I'm out, could you try, for both our sakes, to have a good raging fit of hysterics?"

What rose up in me was a spark of polite anger. "I don't understand what you want. What in God's name would be served by my turning into a watering-pot at this juncture?"

"You," he answered harshly. "And ultimately, me. Do you

seriously believe you can . . . go through what you did last night, and then simply not think about it again? Do you believe *anybody* can? You are required at this point to bloody well go to pieces.''

''What makes you the judge of what I'm required to do? You and Kitty, demanding a parade of emotional display for your personal edification. She, at least, responds in kind. Very well, here's an emotion. I'm angry. Will that do?''

Against his pallor the bruise on his face was stark. ''It's a start.'' He left the room; a moment later I heard him clatter down the stairs.

I had to sit on the bed, because my legs trembled too much to hold me. I gripped the bed-post and concentrated my whole attention on my breathing, and had my muscles back under conscious control in a gratifyingly short time.

James returned with a raised pie and woman's clothes for me, a dark blue worsted travelling suit and a good cotton chemise, both second-hand but clean and smelling faintly of lavender. There was also a black woolen shawl. I thought, with longing, of my heavy cloak, still in my luggage in Bristol. That, in turn, reminded me of something else. ''Girasol!'' I said.

''I sent a letter from the station this morning. They'll take him to London. Will that do, or do you want him in Manchester?''

''No, that's just right. We ought not to need him, as long as you're content to travel by rail.''

That was the sort of conversation that prevailed through dinner. I think now that James was willing to let me have my way for that long simply to make sure I ate. When we were done, he sat back in his chair, drew a long, warning breath, and asked, ''Are you still angry?''

''No.''

''Why not?''

''Oh, James. What on earth would be the point?''

''I already told you. If I weren't afraid to leave it that long, I'd wait until Manchester. Are you just shy of behaving like a human being in front of me? I may even have earned it. Is Engels as daunting? Or would you cry if *he* told you it was all right?''

"I don't deserve this," I told him.

"My God, I don't think I do, either," he said roughly. "But I admit it's a damned biased view. Listen to me."

He was, unexpectedly, kneeling in front of my chair; I would have had to kick him to get past. He took my hands before I could see what he meant to do and snatch them out of reach. "Here, in this city, ten years ago—about that many blocks away, as a matter of fact—I killed for the first time. It was the night before I got the sword-cut on my arm. I thought, then, that I'd be waging a soldierly fight for the cause, even though Palmer and I were already in Feargus O'Connor's piece of it and doing things that weren't very soldierly at all, even on the surface. I was prepared to kill in hot blood, in battle. I ended up killing a night-watchman who was about to give away the presence of three men and a dozen rifles. I cut his throat. He looked so surprised. Even dead, he still looked surprised. And he bled—have you ever seen a hog butchered? Except that the hog had a man's face. He wasn't a soldier. He was a middle-aged man with a job. Seamus Palmer practically had to drag me away because I couldn't move, and I couldn't think because I knew if I could think I would be looking into the mouth of Hell and I wasn't sure I could survive the experience. When we were five streets away I was sick as a cat, but I still didn't think. When we were outside of town I began to cry. I didn't know I was doing it until I found I couldn't see to walk. Then I lay down in a ditch and cried like an infant with the colic, until I couldn't breathe, until I was sick again. Seamus Palmer stayed with me the whole time, and said after, that there was no shame in it, that if I couldn't mourn a man I'd killed, then I should not be left to live, but shot down like a mad dog."

By the end I don't think he quite saw me; his vision was turned inward, and his shallow breathing disordered his words.

"You were nineteen years old," I said. The words brought his eyes back to me, wide. "And young for your age in some ways. You could be excused."

His hands clenched on mine for a moment so hard I could almost feel the bones grind. Then he let go. "And what are you?" he whispered.

"Older." I pulled my chair back from him and crossed the

little room to stand by the bed-foot. ''When you were twenty-four, did you still weep?''

He had stayed where he was, except that his empty hands had closed over each other at the edge of the chair, and he'd turned his face away. In a voice made oddly deep and rough, he replied, ''No. But I'm the Devil's right hand. You're not.'' For a moment longer he stayed where he was; then he lifted his head and stood. ''If you need me, I'll be within call.'' He passed through the door into the next room and closed it precisely behind him.

I found myself strangling the bed-post again. I tried on the clothes he'd brought and found that they'd do. Then I warmed water over the coal-grate and washed. I put on the chemise and wrapped the shawl around my shoulders for a dressing-gown, since I doubted I'd be called upon to leave the room again. Then, to prove I could do it, I sat down with pen and ink and a great deal of paper and wrote this. As I can barely keep my eyes open after all that, I will go to bed.

Of course I can't sleep any more. I find I can laugh, if a little damply, over that; he meant to rob me of my peace of mind, and he did. And it was right that he did. But I think it would be a very good joke on both of us if there was a kind of symmetry to this: While I lay slumbering in my airless coffin of the emotions, he went sleepless. Now that I'm returned to the hurtful, wakeful world, is he on the other side of the wall enjoying the dreamless rest of honest men?

I dreamed of his night-watchman, but with a ginger moustache, and woke with a cry. I was not weeping, but I felt as I had the first time I fell hard from a horse, as if my lungs were compressed beyond remedy and that I would die, unhurt, for lack of air.

I heard the sound of the door at once, and found that his candle was on the stand near my pillow, and he, dressed but for coat and waistcoat, sat on the bed beside me. The tears began to fall down my face, burning like hot wax.

''Thank you,'' James said softly, and put out one hand to brush a curl of my hair out the path of the tears. ''Kitty really would have killed me.''

Something in my chest broke like a bubble of glass, and I

was blinded. After a moment I felt him stand, and I flung out my hand. "Don't leave me," I begged him.

He said nothing more; he only lay down beside me on the narrow bed and took me in his arms, making a shield for my back with his body. He stroked my hair, and sometimes kissed it, and stayed, and said nothing just as I needed him to, during that long, nearly unendurable passage of pain. But I did endure it, and my reward was that it grew less at last, until I drifted, drained, in a featureless mental landscape that was not the poisoned one I'd washed away with weeping.

Then he said, whispering slowly against my hair, "In our memories, there is a graveyard where we bury our dead. They all lie there together, the loved ones and the ones we hated, friends and foes and kin, with no distinction among them. We have to mourn every one of them, because our memories have made them as much a part of us as our bones or our skin. If we don't, we've no right to remember anything at all."

He slipped away sometime after that. I had fallen lightly asleep, perhaps, and woke at the sound of the door closing. The coverlet was drawn up over my shoulders. From sheer exhaustion I slept, but woke again, and dozed off again, and woke, until at last I knew that my mind had returned to rule my body, and wasn't going to let it rest immediately. I gathered my shawl around me and resorted to the ink-bottle and the pen, my own dose of laudanum.

The little table at which I write sits in the dormer-window—and thank goodness there is a dormer, or there'd be no room in this chamber for any table at all. It faces east, where the sky is no longer black, but indigo. I can count on my nerves now—and so, for that matter, can James—but it would be even better if I could count on the rest of me as well, and I can't sleep in railway carriages. I am going back to bed.

DECEMBER THE 2nd, 1849
LINCOLN'S INN, LONDON

My Lord:

It having come to my attention that my cousin, Richard Cobham, Esq., is being investigated on the charge of the wilful

murder of Mr David Voight, and being further aware that Mr
Cobham is currently abroad, attending to certain business interests on the Continent, and is thus unaware of these proceedings, I thought it only right and proper to take it upon
myself to look into some of the facts surrounding the death of
Mr Voight and the potential charges related to it. In this regard,
I should hope your Lordship would be gracious enough to
provide me with the answers to certain questions which will
allow me to proceed with my investigation and aid in con-
structing Mr Cobham's defence, which the Right Honourable
Lord Charles Bingham, Q.C., has agreed to present, should
this prove necessary.

In the first place, would your Lordship be good enough to
tell me if it is true that the entire suspicion against Mr Cobham
rests on a single letter, allegedly written by the deceased, and
that this letter does no more than indicate a certain fear by the
deceased of Mr Cobham? In the second place, is it true that
there is not the merest scrap of physical evidence against my
cousin? (I do not say "my client" because, my cousin having
no information that he is under suspicion, nor, indeed, any
reason to imagine he would be, he has not retained me.) In the
third place, is your Lordship aware that Mr Cobham has a
cousin, James, who stands to inherit Cauldhurst Abbey, and
that James, contrary to what some persons may have informed
your Lordship, is not only very much alive, but Mr Cobham
knew he was alive, as may be proven through various pieces
of correspondence that can be presented to your Lordship at
any moment? Finally, is your Lordship aware that Mr Cobham
sustained a broken collarbone on November the 8th, and would
certainly have been unable to strangle a man as large as the
deceased nor would he have been able to drag him to the back
of the stables, as the Inspector's report claims was done? Of
course, should your Lordship request it, the surgeon who attended Mr Cobham, a Mr Browne of the Royal Southants.
Infirmary, is available for questions at any time.

I hope to hear from your Lordship when convenient, and if,
as I expect, this is merely a matter of the police being careful
as well as thorough, and Mr Cobham is, in fact, not under
suspicion, I should hope to be informed of this, so that any

unpleasantness he might encounter upon his return can be avoided.

I remain
Your Lordship's Humble Servant,
Brian MacCormack Solicitor

MANCHESTER
2 DEC 1849

Dearest Kitty,

Oh, we are so complex, such a tangle of adamant convictions and needs, so many of which can't live side by side. On one hand, I think that I hate letters, and shall never open another, from you or anyone. On another (not "*the* other", for why assume only two? Perhaps in our souls' selves we have as many hands as the six-armed Indian goddess Kali, and for as many purposes), I'm casting aside the mask of journal-writing, the subterfuge that allowed me to pretend that there was no receiver of my thoughts but me, and steeling myself to speak to you openly. Not without veils, for the medium of paper is itself a veil, and words, in the hands of such as we, who beat words into swords or teardrops or rings of scented smoke as if by instinct, are only the finest weave of another. But it's dishonest, and cowardly, not to begin the page with "Dear Kitty" and confront from the outset whose heart my words have flown to, and sometimes pierced.

I have your letters, the ones from the 28th, the 29th, and the 30th, all here by me. I wish I *could* be with you, and not only to be of what comfort I could. If I were with you, it would mean that I'd lived another past, and might, from the present shelter of your company, look ahead to a future very different from any I envision now. I'm forbidden, you see, to shut any of my inner doors, and not only by you. It seems as if it must be beyond my strength to hold them open. But if you both believe that I'm as strong as that, then perhaps it's I who am mistaken. And if holding them open results in the occasional tear during the writing of letters, well, a lady always carries a handkerchief.

How strange that the news you must have expected to strike hardest is now only confirmation, and part of it even a relief: David is dead; and Richard, though at risk, is still free. (I confess, even knowing the raw facts, I read the first page of your letter of the 30th in mounting terror—dearest, when you dwell on trivial detail, my blood runs cold and my flesh creeps. All I could think of was that this might be fresher news than poor Johnson had had. When you wrote that your knees buckled, I more than sympathized.)

Some of the refinements, however, still have the power to shock. Good God, I have no idea what business Aunt Louisa has raising the subject of Chartists. It makes my hair stand on end. If you can get her to tell you, do. I recommend, if all else fails, the device of making her so angry she tells you out of spite. For that matter, what can she know of the Trotter's Club (I assume those are her devil-worshippers) and why would *she* think they would kill David?

And this oh-so-convenient letter found on David's body— bah, as Engels would say. But I do wish we could lay hands on a copy. What might it tell our rather better-informed eyes? For one thing, I can't help but wonder, influenced by the last few days, if it really does implicate Richard. That is, *Richard* Cobham in so many words. Wixon, after all, believes James to be dead. On another of Kali's hands, our adversary—adversaries—seem to mean everyone to think James is dead, so they wouldn't try to blame him for this. Then again, that wool has been pulled from a lot of eyes of late. Then yet again, there is a witness (Hullo! Remember me?) who could tell anyone exactly where James was when David died. Then again and again and again, David's murderer might not know that. My God, I sound as if my brains have fallen out.

The questions of who is financing the Trotter's Club and why, and whether there's an unholy overt alliance between them and the government (as opposed to the unpleasant *de facto* one that may be in place simply because some of its members hold seats in Parliament or appointments to office) are not going to yield to my speculations now. I'd forgotten about the Prussian gold, however. I'll bring it up with James and Engels tomorrow. Not tonight; nothing short of the house burning down will get me to disturb James tonight.

Richard's letter, as you've copied it, gave me a desperately needed laugh. You can get very good coffee in Vienna. You can get it closer to home than that, too, if you like it cut with chicory. I wonder if I was supposed to tell you that?

You had a letter from James? That must be what he does when he ought to be sleeping. I had no idea. I'm not amazed that it should make Richard weep, having seen James in a state that would make Nelson's Column crack open and *bleed*. Richard seems to have had his revenge in the letter he gave you to deliver through me, however. If what he intended wasn't revenge, I'm afraid something may have gone a little amiss.

As for that other news, the matter of Diana Cobham's letter, I know that you, at least, understood some of the character of the blow the information would deal. Richard, it seems, did not, or only partly did. I will not attempt to meddle in what lies between James and Richard now, and if you'll pay the least heed to my advice, neither will you. It's not susceptible to outside influence, at least not in any beneficial way. And I don't say this because I object to meddling—you of all people know otherwise.

One thing that my journal-writing allowed was the relatively detailed accounting of events in order, and I think I must keep that. I feel the need of your eye on matters, your way with the subtlest of puzzles, and I think if only I can tell you everything I witness, I can have you nearly present. That theory is only as good as the witness, of course, but we will work with what we can get.

James and I spent the journey to Manchester (in a first-class compartment; the intermittent privacy it offered seemed worth the price, under the circumstances) reviewing our assumptions before receiving the next wave of information, which we meant to get from Friedrich Engels.

"At least we know who to blame for it all, now," I said.

"Do we?" asked James.

"You cannot tell me that Alan Tournier is another feint. Can you?"

"No, I don't think I can." He sighed and rubbed his forehead. "Since Oxford, Alan Tournier and I have been clocked and measured and pitted against one another—I felt, sometimes, like one of the principals in a cockfight. It would have been a miracle if we hadn't seen each other as rivals. I feel a little foolish at having missed the point when it became a blood feud, but I suppose I was busy.''

"What do you think he's trying to do? Ultimately, I mean. Besides putting you out of his misery."

That surprised a smile out of him. Then he replied, ''I expect he'd like to see me discredited before I tell anyone either that he was a member of the Chartist underground, or that he helped betray it. I think we can now be moderately certain of the latter, by the way. I'm not sure how far he's prepared to go to discredit me, however.''

"Short of murdering you?"

''Ah, but that *doesn't* discredit me. Unless he does it in such a way that there's clear posthumous evidence that I wittingly and maliciously committed acts of mayhem and treason.'' Another smile, this time one-sided and ironic. I wondered if the phrase was a quotation. ''He may eventually give up the effort to establish my guilt, cut his losses, and do away with me. But the fact that he hasn't yet suggests that he wants something more than just safety from discovery. It would be a lot easier simply to fly the country. Especially for a man with kin in Brittany.''

"But you do believe Tournier is the person behind it all?" I asked, coming back to my original, inadequately-answered point.

"Do I?"

"*James.*"

"Better question: Do I believe he's the only person behind it all? And how many versions of 'all' did you have in mind?"

"My heavens, how many do *you*?"

He dropped his head back against the bench cushion and regarded the compartment ceiling. He looked distressingly composed. ''To pick one at random: I think I remember you telling me that I was to be disinherited, possibly at David's instigation. How could that benefit Tournier? And if it did, why, then, kill David and undo whatever had been done?''

I said, my heart sunk to the vicinity of my ankles, ''You're saying that there's more than one plot in motion.''

"There is more than one person involved. So, more than one set of interests. So, invariably, somewhat more than one plot. How much more, we have yet to learn."

"Many," I suggested. " 'How *many* more.' "

"I tend to think of plotting as an infinitely expandable miasma, rather than a group of discrete objects. But I don't feel strongly enough about it to defend the grammar. To pick another example at random: My father has been in the country for approximately a month, but neither Kitty nor Richard knew of it, which suggests almost beyond contradiction that Richard's mother also knew nothing of it. My father has returned unexpectedly from a long sea voyage. Why do I not feel like Telemachus?"

"It can't be relevant. Your father is *not* a Chartist."

"No," he said, and he brought his gaze down from the ceiling at last and smiled at me. "He isn't, is he?"

"Oh."

"And that, I find, bothers me a great deal. Forget Odysseus—all the available parallels are with the House of Atreus. Fond as I am of Greek tragedy, I'd rather not take part in any."

"You're to be sacrificed for good winds?"

"Or eaten. Which reminds me," he said, rummaging in a pocket of the black coat. "Care for an apple?"

We arrived late this afternoon, still strikingly baggage-less but rather better dressed than we'd been on arrival in Birmingham. I continued to dread facing Engels, or indeed anyone who hadn't been a part of the heightened, deadly life I'd lived since leaving Bristol.

I've only just realized—this is how James came to be parted from us, Kitty. Not by ideology; not by guilt or shame; not even, really, by the need to keep other people's secrets. It's that, once such things happen to you, the world you had before them becomes a stranger's country, with a language you know only imperfectly and customs you only partly share. And those who *didn't* travel with you to that new, frightening place are its inhabitants. We weren't there, in Birmingham in '39; and a space must have opened up between us and him, a space I'm sure he regretted but didn't know how to close. In Manchester, it would have opened further; and when Seamus Palmer died in his arms, every bit of that old life that had us in it must

have been so far away that the only way to reach back to us
would have been to leave the banks of the new life entirely
and sail for days out of sight of either landfall. Now I, too,
have become for a while an emotional *émigrée*. I will do my
best, Kitty, not to be stranded on this shore, far from you.

I was startled at first by the house, until I recalled that Engels in Manchester was not the bird of passage I had become
accustomed to in London and Brussels, but a man of business,
a clerk in the family firm, in his own irritable words, a huck-
ster. I, at least, blessed the condition this afternoon, as I looked
up at the fresh-painted door with its polished knocker and
thought of a proper bath.

Engels opened the door himself, to my surprise. For an instant I saw us through his eyes, by the wiped-blank expression
of shock he wore. My shorn hair, which would have been new
to him, my unfitted clothing and working-woman's shawl, and
the pallor and shadows of sleeplessness and weeping. And
James, of course. He would not have seen James for a very
long time.

It was James who spoke first. "It's awful, really, the people
who'll show up on the doorstep at dinner-time."

Engels flung his head back and laughed, in an unrestrained
German-student-fashion that one finds either alarming or endearing, depending on one's prejudices. You, Kit, would be
delighted with him.

I must stop and describe Engels, if only so that you will
understand why he was able to say the things I will tell you
he said. He is part chivalrous German Romantic, part hard-
headed revolutionary theorist, and any number of things besides, and when he comes bounding into a room full of his
friends ("bounding" used advisedly), they all behave as if
someone has just opened a window. He is tall, though neither
gangly nor burly, with brown hair and sharp dark eyes with
eyebrows like a Spanish *tilde* marked with a chisel-pointed
brush. He rides like a cavalry officer, usually one in mid-
charge. I have no idea how many languages he speaks, and
speaks impeccably; I have certainly never stumped him. He
loves a fight as much as he loves knowledge (which is saying
a great deal), and sometimes more, sad to say, than he values
the perfect comprehension of his fellows. That's his great

weakness, I think: that he'd rather quarrel than correct a mis-apprehension. His age is James's; Engels is the younger by fifteen days, which he claims James wasted, thus allowing Engels to get a head-start on him that James has never managed to overcome. James choked on his wine and called him, in German, a lying unshaven dumpling-eater.

Did I say that my journal entries regulate the chronology of events somewhat? Shall I return to the form, Kit, as a mercy to you? I haven't even got us in the front door, and already I have sat us down to dinner! Perhaps it's an instinct to dwell on pleasant things, as one tries to do in letters.

"Come in, come in, come in!" our host demanded, recovering from the sight of us. "You look like a pair of ghosts in an Italian opera. You're late, I'm sure you are. Mary, they've come!"

Mary Burns was already halfway down the stairs when he said it, and she came straight to me and took my hands. She is Engels's companion of many years, an Irishwoman from Manchester, and better described as striking than beautiful. She has a fine cool self-possession entirely in contrast with Engels's demeanour, and is sometimes a little reserved and proud. She is a woman of the working class, and Irish, and has chosen (as you did, my brave Kit!) to live openly with a man outside of marriage. If being proud serves as a bastion against her critics, then I would wish her twice as much pride.

As I say, she took my hands and surveyed me top to toe, and shook her head. "We'd thought to feed you straightaway, but you look as if it's the world's own miracle you can stand on your two feet. If you'd rather keep to your room this evening, you shall, whatever Fred says."

I assured her that the best restorative I could imagine would be conversation and food. It wasn't, of course; I longed to shut myself in somewhere private and be empty-headed, if not asleep. But I feared withdrawal as much as I dreaded company.

Mary, still clasping my hands, turned her eyes almost warily to my left where James stood. Whatever she'd made of me, it seemed to be multiplied at the sight of James. But she said nothing to him, only suggesting, "They'll want a sight of their rooms before dinner, Fred."

"Yes, of course. Cobham, I'll show you to yours. Mary, has Miss Voight's bag gone upstairs?"

I must have radiated puzzlement. James gave me a swift look and said, "I wired Bristol yesterday morning, too, and had it sent by rail."

I thought of my cloak, my own clothes, my hairbrush. The suddenness of it, the unexpected thought for my comfort when I had been thinking of nothing at all, made my eyes swim. I was spared trying to speak to thank him; he was already on his way up the stairs behind Engels. Mary Burns looked from me to him and back to me. "Ah, now," she said, but that was all she said, and I couldn't tell what she meant by it.

Mary left me at the door of the room allotted to me, with the warning that dinner would be in an hour. "It's simple," she assured me. "And you can eat and talk only just long enough to keep Fred from being wild with curiosity, and then you can come back and sleep for a fortnight if you please. Though if you wake and want supper, it'll be there, too. If your cousin's the boy he was, he keeps a soldier's habits—he eats what he can get when he can get it, against the times when there's no food or pause to eat it."

"I've noticed that," I said. "Do you know him very well, Mary?"

Her face impassive, she said, "Nobody knows him well. His foes'd come closest."

"Would they?" My bag was there; the tub was set before the fire, and the maid was already emptying cans of hot water into it. "And yet he's still here." But Mary had already shut the door behind her.

I was downstairs again, quite clean, delicately scented, glossily brushed, very faintly rouged, and dressed in garnet merino with a white lace bertha, in forty-five minutes. Really, cutting all one's hair off changes one's life. Engels was in the parlour when I entered, but no one else. He sprang up as soon as I came in and led me to a chair, but didn't sit again himself. I think he is constitutionally unable to talk and sit still at the same time, unless he has food in front of him.

"I've come down before James?" I asked.

"I'm afraid I kept him talking just a little."

"Unfair," I said, and smiled at him. "I was hoping I might

be a fly on the wall during that first conversation. I've wondered nearly all the way here what the two of you would say to each other."

"Do you think we're done?" said Engels on a crack of laughter. "No, no. I'm going to wring your cousin dry, I'm going to dissect him and read his entrails. You'll have plenty of time to listen to us."

"What was in the letter you gave me for him, before I left London?"

"Didn't he show it to you? Poor old *Spinne*! What did he say about it?"

"Nothing. He sighed. Oh, and early on he said, 'Well, that's nice.'"

"Bah! Scoundrel. I'll have to harangue him, then. I might even get him to argue with me; he's in a weakened state."

"Is he?"

The italic eyebrows rose vigorously. "You must know he is, surely?"

"Tired, perhaps."

Engels shook his head, impatient. "Are you tired? Is that all? Or are you a little more than that?"

I examined my inner disarray and, in a few matters, outright dilapidation. "A little more," I admitted.

"And you've been in motion and in peril since only, what? Wednesday?"

Less than a week. It had seemed longer.

Engels continued, "Your cousin has been constantly in danger and away from any secure and friendly place for four months. This house, tonight, is as nearly a place of safety as any he has come to in that time. His self-control is formidable; but it takes some of its strength from the pressure placed on it. That pressure is, for a little while, removed. If he does not come down to dinner, it will not surprise me."

I felt ashamed that I hadn't seen that, and even a little resentful that Engels had. But Engels fought in Baden in '48. I'm a neophyte in the business of living with danger.

Engels half-sat on the arm of a chair, the most stationary position he'd had since I'd entered. He closed his square hands on his lapels and said, "May I be impertinent? Very impertinent?"

"Since I don't think I've ever seen you do it before, I can't resist. Yes."

He asked briskly, "Are you lovers?"

For a second I couldn't speak. "No," I said, more sharply than I'd meant to.

"There, I told you it was impertinent. I apologize. I ask because it is sometimes a relief. But it is not the only one."

My face was scalding hot. "No," I said again, "we're—" It stopped me, the search for the word. It was the first time I'd sought to describe James with any term except cousin. Engels, for an uncharacteristic wonder, didn't interrupt. "Friends," I said finally, the word unstable on my tongue. I wasn't sure it was true.

"Good. Then he is quite surrounded. And so are you, *Spinne*, and you aren't to forget it. If you sit making webs in the corner at dinner instead of being your good sharp-tongued self, I shall make you eat in the kitchen. No, better yet! I shall send 'round to Wolff, to come and make bad riddles in German, and you will laugh until you squeak."

"I did not squeak," I protested. "Never." Actually, Kit, I may have done, on the occasion Engels referred to, because I was laughing so hard I couldn't draw breath. And so would you have, if your German were as good as your French, and you heard Willy Wolff making up riddles on the spot, the answers to which were, I remember, white-pudding, glove buttons, the tail of the landlord's terrier, and my right shoe. I added, "Is Wolff in Manchester?"

"He is. If I could convince you to stay, we'd have enough people to staff the newspaper."

"Well, you can't," said James from the doorway, smiling moderately and leaning with every evidence of perfect relaxation. I believe Engels and I between us jumped six inches and must have looked guilty as confessing pickpockets. "And Engels, I forbid you to seduce my cousin. Editing a revolutionary newspaper is just the sort of trouble she'd like."

"I'm surprised she hasn't done it already, then," Engels said. He turned to me. "Harney has a new paper. Shall I put in a word for you?"

"Not at the moment, thank you," I said. "I'm in the midst of a project."

James dropped down on the settee. "Don't use me as an excuse. History would damn me if I deprived you of a wider audience."

"*Spinne* says she gave you my letter," Engels said brightly, looking as if he meant to fall, hawk-like, on any undefended word.

James's eyes flickered between us at the nickname. He said, "She did. And I'd like to know what you heard about my activities to make you think I was trying to advance the revolution single-handed."

"Ah. What *were* you trying to do?" Engels had begun pacing in earnest, a neat, measured gait that was clearly not at all consciously maintained.

"Protect the movement, and a few of the people in it."

"It can't protect itself, then."

"Don't you think it deserves a little help on occasion?"

"I do. I believe you deserve it, as well. Why did you set about this as if you were a knight on a quest?"

"Pardon me?" James asked, his composure somewhat jostled.

"Why didn't you take anyone into your confidence? Or ask for help in collecting your information?"

James stretched one arm across the back of the settee. "Confidence was the issue, wasn't it? I didn't know whom to trust."

"At first. You must have cleared a few people almost immediately of the suspicion of informing."

James nodded. "The dead ones were fairly easy."

It was true: he was in a weakened state, or he'd never have tried to escape through irony. Engels, of course, pounced. "Harney. Ernest Jones might have helped, even from prison. Webber. O'Brien, certainly, of all men."

"*Not* O'Brien," James said abruptly, in a momentary thinning of his sardonic mask. "Of all men. I know you've thought . . . well of him. I'm sorry."

It gave Engels pause, which ought to have provided James with a bit of satisfaction. If it did, none of it was visible. "My point," said Engels on recovering, "is still valid. If I can think of three men in one minute, you must have been able to settle on a—a dozen in an hour. You didn't try."

"I didn't? Foolish of me. Why didn't I?"

"Because you had—had forgotten that the fight of the Chartists was the fight of the masses. Out of devotion, you thought of it as yours alone. And when it fell mortally wounded, you b-believed that bringing its enemies to justice was a duty that fell only on you."

James, breathing deeply and audibly, closed his eyes and frowned. "That sounds like a remarkably stupid thing to do, Engels."

"It does, doesn't it?" Engels said, smiling beatifically.

James slid down the cushion until his spine curved like an open parenthesis and his head was propped on the back of the settee. "You don't suppose there might have been just the least little quantity of intellectual curiosity mixed in with the chivalry?"

"Possibly. In that case, what made you think you were the only one concerned in the matter with sufficient intellectual curiosity?"

"Ah." James said, "And what if I told you that I thought I was the only trustworthy person with the unsavoury skills necessary to unearth the facts?"

Engels, alarmingly, sat down. I saw Mary come to the door of the parlour and stop, watching. I don't know if Engels saw her. "That is quite a different matter. One I would like to take up with you tomorrow, if you'll let me. For now, where are these notes of yours?"

James inhaled, exhaled, and opened his eyes. "In the spider-web. Susan memorized them."

Engels stared at me. "Did she?" he said at last. "I think it's time you let them go, don't you?"

"You would have had them two weeks ago," I told him, "except that we thought the informers might be reluctant to kill James as long as they didn't know where his notes were."

"Has that changed?"

"We don't know," James replied for me. "Possibly. Once you're done flaying the inadequate hide off me, I'll ask you a few questions in return, and we'll see if we can't eliminate a variable or two from the problem."

"And if you don't mean to flay him this very moment, you can come get your dinner," Mary said, resigned.

Engels jumped to his feet and flung an arm around her.

"Now I'm in trouble. I've let the meat get cold, eh?"

Mary smiled up at him. She almost never smiled at anyone else. "And would I be expecting anything else, and me living with you and your great celebrated mouth this many a year? It's a wonder you can keep your tongue between your teeth long enough to eat at all."

It was at dinner (roast veal and assorted vegetables, all very good and not, after all, cold) that we discussed relative ages, led into it by an extremely silly theory that national characters could be identified with signs of the zodiac. We passed Ireland by, out of respect for Mary's feelings, but Engels took on Germany himself, and was both appallingly accurate and ridiculous. Then he wanted to know what the English were.

"Scorpio, of course," I said immediately. "Very good dancers, reticent to a fault, and always scheming for an advantage."

"I beg your pardon," James said.

I was puzzled for only a moment. Then I pressed my fingers to my lips. "I forgot. Oh, heavens, I *did* forget. But you *are* a very good dancer. November what?"

"The thirteenth. Vixen. I doubt you forgot for a minute."

I really had forgotten. I tried to remember, without seeming distracted, where I'd been on the thirteenth, and where *he'd* been, and recalled crossing the near end of the Pennines on horseback in the dark. I returned my attention to the table and found James watching me, looking penitent.

The topic set us to comparing birthdays, of course, and resulted in Engels's comment about James. You'll be able to tell from the above that we were very informal. After all, if you sit down to dinner with only three other people, you feel foolish talking to only two of them.

After the apple tart, Mary and I stood to leave, and James and Engels did likewise. "No port?" I asked.

"Of course," replied James, "if you think I *ought* to fall asleep face down on the table, it would be just the thing. Should I?"

"Oh, my God, your letters!" Mary said suddenly. "Susan, I'm that sorry I didn't remember sooner. But the first sight of you—well, it wasn't letters I was thinking of."

I assured her that if she'd given them to me immediately I

might not have got down to dinner, which would have been a shame. She returned while James and I were standing at the bottom of the stairs, bidding Engels what we all agreed would probably be good. night, and handed me three envelopes from you.

"Not," I suggested, "a good sign."

"Not?" asked James. Engels and Mary had tactfully disappeared. I proceeded up the stairs and James trailed after.

"Or possibly she only forgot all her postscripts." I noticed about one envelope the signs that there was a sealed enclosure inside, and opened that. I stiffened my mental spine and said, "There's a letter to you from Richard."

We were standing at the head of the stairs by then; his room was in one direction, mine in the other. After a paralysing silence, James said, "Dear me."

"Yes, well, no one will make you read it. And if you do read it and you need to abuse him to someone, you can count on me."

"I thought you liked Richard."

"I do. And contrary to reason, instinct, or expectation, I like you as well."

He took the letter from me, carefully, with a little wry smile. "Thank goodness for the bonds of family." I was in the act of turning toward my room when he added, "Susan?"

I looked back at him. The letter from Richard was unregarded in his hand. "I wasn't . . . sure that you knew about Mary," he said in an odd voice.

The tension went out of my shoulders. "Yes, of course I knew about Mary. We're good friends. Do you think Engels hides her, for heaven's sake? What are you—" Then I thought of what he might be getting at, and stopped. "No," I said through the constriction in my throat. "I have *not* got a *tendre* for our host. You're very busy about my romantic life, aren't you?"

"I'm sorry. I had the best of intentions, really. Why does he call you *Spider*?" he said abruptly, as if he hadn't meant to do it.

I tried hard not to smile, but there was no help for it. "It's a little out of date, actually. When I first met Engels—when I first fell in with that whole lot, in fact—I would sit in a corner with a book in my lap, or something else that I wasn't really paying attention to, so that I could pretend to be doing something else while I listened to the arguments. One evening someone said something particularly indefensible. And I'd got so comfortable, and so carried away with the reasoning of it, that I objected out loud."

James was smiling, too, his head a little to one side as if he were watching the past as I described it.

"In the awful silence that followed—no, don't laugh, it really was awful at the time—Engels said, 'I believe our spider has finished her web. Think before you speak, my friends. Fools are her lawful prey.' "

"Sitting in corners, observing everything, catching everything, and never letting it get away." James shook his head, still smiling. "You must be the only woman on the face of the earth who understands that that's a compliment."

"Oh, surely not the only one. May I ask you something now?"

He lifted his chin a fraction. "Yes."

"Engels knew to expect us. Didn't he?"

"Of course he did. I wired from Birmingham. What if they'd been out of coffee?"

"Good night," I announced, and went to my room.

There I lit a lamp or two, kicked off my shoes, started in on your earliest letter, and was promptly caught in one of a pair of epistolary explosions.

I was not as quick as you, in the matter of Diana Cobham's letter, but hearing the things no one is saying is your forté, after all. When I did realize what I had just read—beyond, of course, the first foundation-rocking implication of what I had read, which was that this was a quite grim and desperate love-letter from James's mother to Richard's father—I had to read it again to be sure, and your covering letter as well.

And one sentence leaped off the page at me: "I always think it is best to know these things than to have them around and not know them, don't you?" James, on a quite different subject, said nearly the same thing, only a few days ago. I wondered if, when he learned this, he would be of the same mind.

That was when I remembered the letter from Richard.

I opened my bedroom door. It occurred to me, just before I

did it, that it might be possible to leave the room by the window, and that, depending on what was going to happen in the next ten minutes, it might be easier, taken altogether, to do so. But I opened the door.

He leaned against the wall in the passageway, just opposite my room. His hands were in his pockets, and his eyes were half-lidded: the picture of ease and unconcern. The corridor crackled with the tensile, imperfectly-leashed, unbearable energy he'd shown to Gideon Johnson in the Severn marshes.

"I understand," he said softly, "that you have startling news from Kitty."

Your letter and its enclosure were still in my hand, somewhat the worse for the sudden closing of my fist. I tried to speak, failed, swallowed, tried again, and finally nodded.

"Will you tell me, or would you rather I read it?"

I separated the copy of Diana Cobham's letter from yours and held it out. He took it and bent his head to read.

I said, as if the words were ripped out of me with a hook, "Not in the corridor!"

He looked up. "Am I wrong? Is this the sort of news that is improved by its surroundings?"

The most hideous thing in the whole hideous confrontation was that I knew, suddenly, that he wasn't really seeing me. It wasn't me he spoke to. It was some hateful part of himself that stood real as flesh before him: his demon, the author of his pain as well as the voice he called on to react to it. A perfect circle of torment.

He read the letter. He only read it once. Perhaps Richard's letter had told him the gist of it; or perhaps he shares your ear for things not said. I didn't stay to watch, this time, because I wanted to. I stayed because he might need something, and I might determine, in time to be useful, what it was.

He looked up and asked, "Did Kitty seem to think that this news was more than startling?"

"I don't . . . know what you mean."

"Did she, for instance, think it might be unwelcome?"

I was now, I recognized frantically, quite out of my depth. "Yes. She did. She says she cried."

"Kitty cries at a great many things. How would *you* describe it? Unwelcome? Bad?"

With the last of the air in my lungs, I said, "A desecration."

James nodded. "That's close. And was there anything in Kitty's letter to suggest that she had been unsure, before she resolved to send this, whether I would want you to share this desecrating piece of information?"

I thought again of that sentence—*it is best to know these things*—and summoned the courage to say, "If I could have chosen, I wouldn't have wanted to share it. I couldn't choose, and Kitty couldn't choose, because I had to be told. It is relevant to the danger we're all facing. This must have been the basis for disinheriting you. David must have known of it."

His face told me I had chosen a particularly unwelcome response. "I hope it made him happy. The House of Atreus as staged at a penny-gaff. I'm a bastard. All right, I'll get used to it eventually. It's survivable. Richard, apparently, thinks it's damned-near laudable. That it expunges all my sins." For the first time, his voice was not quite steady as he said, "Why is it that no one but me has counted the number of actors on stage? It's not just the three in the centre, two wronged lovers and a brutal husband. No. There's an innocent married lady off to stage right, and her son, aged eight, named Richard. And do you know *why* no one has thought about them?"

I shook my head.

He held out the copy of Diana Cobham's letter and said, "Because the woman who wrote this letter never did. *That*, I may not get used to." He said it like a man spitting out vinegar.

"You've forgotten an actor," I said, in defiance of good sense and self-preservation. "You've forgotten Jamie."

He stared at me—at *me*, I think, this time. "No. In this play, Jamie is only one of the properties." Then he let go of the letter, which rocked erratically down the air between us to land half-tilted against my skirts. "I'll see you in the morning," he said, went down the passage to his room, and closed the door behind him.

For a wild moment I thought he ought not to be left alone. Then I realized the intent of his parting words. They were a characteristically Jamesian promise. They were a payment to ensure his privacy. So I picked up Diana Cobham's letter and went back to my fireside.

Through it all, I'd had no urge to cry. And just as well; if he'd thought it was out of pity, he'd have killed me. Kitty, I have re-read this, and I see that I *can't* describe for you what it was like. It was like standing within range of an exploding volcano—or inside a burning house, with the heat and flames moving all around you and cutting you off from the outside, and you think the only thing you can do is stand still; maybe the fire won't reach you; maybe the ceiling won't fall quite where you are. I do think he could have killed me; I think he could kill nearly anything in that state, possibly just by raising his voice. I ought to be afraid of him, oughtn't I?

He spoke the perfect truth, about his bastardy. It's survivable, he'll get used to it. But it's not simple illegitimacy that touches his pride, I think. It's partly that David knew it, and would have gloated; Richard knows it, and seems to have misused it somehow. I don't believe he cares what the world at large would make of it. But people who are close to him can hurt him with it.

He'll get used to the new, unflattering picture of his mother, too. Though not, I think, quickly. Yes, he's agile, but my God, there are limits.

What preys on my mind, Kit—this is a horrible thing to admit to, I don't think it would have occurred to me to wonder about this six months ago—is that I can't remember how Aunt Diana died. She died at Cauldhurst, I think, and she died in '27 or '28. If I feel brave, I shall ask James tomorrow. Heavens, I've changed. I remember writing to you after my confrontation with him at Fairfield, saying I couldn't ask him anything. Now I'm contemplating, if grimly, jabbing him in an emotionally tender spot in the hope that he'll roar.

Why *am* I not weeping over this? Is it that James has so damnably many problems that one more seems only to be expected? This one, at least, will not kill him, so when weighed against the others, it becomes almost paltry, at least until the deadly ones are resolved. Even so, tonight I won't knock at his door if I can help it. Not, this time, because I'm afraid of him. Because tonight, for him, this must seem anything but paltry.

Oh, bother, I think I'm weeping after all. Never mind. Good night, Kit dearest. I am going to go and fall apart one nerve at a time. I think we'll be here for a day or maybe two, and I'll see to it that anything after that can be forwarded.

All my best love,
Susan

MANCHESTER
2ND DECEMBER, 1849

Richard,

There are two possibilities: either you are a knave, or a fool. The first would be less insulting, and if you know me as well as I had thought, then you know me well enough to have written this letter intending to wound. But perhaps I was wrong, and your knowledge is faulty in one or two places. Perhaps you are only a fool after all.

Unless, of course, you can explain to me how my being your father's bastard somehow excuses all the wrongs I have done you to date, and requires you to forgive me. Your last letter to me was honest, and accurate. This one is poisonous sentimentality masquerading as true feeling. This is pious artificial middle-class morality. It comes dangerously close to suggesting that you are called upon to forgive my trespasses because I would not have been capable of anything else *but* trespass. You held me accountable for them a week ago. Nothing has changed in that week, except this revelation, that Andrew Cobham was cuckolded by his wife and his brother, and I am the result. Do you believe, perhaps, that base birth will tell, ultimately, in one's character? Why else would the discovery have called down these fulsome regrets?

You will say it is because we are half-brothers. We were half-brothers on the twenty-fifth of November, when you wrote previously. Nothing has changed, except that you know it now. What fantastical characteristic of shared blood turns backward in time and makes you a liar on the twenty-fifth?

After that letter, I would have crawled to you like a whipped dog for your forgiveness. There was nothing in it that was not true, or deserved, and the effect of it on me, I think, might have satisfied the most exacting standards of what was due you in recompense. Now you assure me that my affectionate brother stands at my side. Pardon me; I cannot find him. He seems to have been displaced by a patronizing hypocrite.

The truth is that you have been my brother in all but blood for all my life. And more than a brother, in the love I felt for you, the trust I placed in you, the fast friendship and understanding I thought I received from you. The withdrawal of those, by the agency of your last letter, was a terrible wound. It also seemed a final proof of all the things withdrawn: you knew me very well indeed, I thought. You denied me your friendship, which I held most precious, when I failed you in all you most valued in me. This new loss is worse than the old one. This new letter tells me that I was never understood; that the brother I loved was not real. If you were the friend I always thought you, and as wise as I always believed you, you would never have written these things to me, and sealed them up with that letter from my mother.

I will do you one last favour, in the name and memory of the figment you have replaced. I will clarify a misapprehension of yours. Circumstances did not conspire against me. I was not led into anything, nor did I fall. I chose my life and my course. I chose to do wrong in the hope that right might come of it. I regret it. I would choose differently now. *But the choice was mine.* Deny that, falsify it, tinsel it over with pious, pitying justification, and you deny everything I am and every scrap of what little good I have been able to do in my life. Good or bad, *give me credit for what I have done.* I would rather go honestly to Hell, admitting that I leaped knowingly into error and folly, than enter into the sweetest Heaven men can dream of by whining that I had been pushed.

Very sincerely indeed,
James Cobham

RICHARD COBHAM'S JOURNAL

DECEMBER 2nd

Hang me if I don't begin to see why Susan Voight takes such pleasure in spying and intrigue; I believe one could become habituated to it. But part of the job must be to write it down, as Susan does, neat and precise, with every possible detail, so I shall attempt that too, and see how well I can do it.

Spent the morning playing cat-and-mouse with Coslick, and, though I am certain he had the better of me, I took pleasure in realizing what the game was, and knowing I was playing it. After some hours of trying to figure out why he was so unwilling to talk to me, when he had clearly been willing to talk to James (and I'll swear Coslick told James a great deal that James never set down on paper!), I finally cornered him just after the noon hour while he was reading *The Times* and said, "Well, aren't you going to try to get me drunk?" which took him aback, and then he laughed and said, "Damn me, you *are* a Cobham, aren't you?" which pleased me, though I could not say why. But I reminded myself that people more used to these games of deceit and subterfuge than I am could very well play the flatterer for a reason. So I said, "I am, that. And I am a Cobham who wants to find what's missing." "There's a great deal that's missing," said he. "Well," said I, "let us begin with the lovely fair-haired girl, eh?" "Who?" "*La belle dame sans*—" "Oh, her." "Well, where can I find her?" And he said, "If I'd known, I'd have told your cousin, wouldn't I?" "Would you?" and we went on like that, with me getting nowhere at all, until at last Coslick said he had wasted enough time and got up and walked out the door, tossing his journal onto a table. It popped into my head that Susan or James, or even Kitty, would likely pick up the newspaper, figure out which article he had been reading, and put together all sorts of marvelous conclusions from this. I admit I felt more like a child playing than a grown man with a mission as I walked over to pick up *The Times*, and I even remember feeling a smile on my face, a smile which must have vanished as soon as I saw that it was dated November 8ᵗʰ, the day I was attacked in Southampton.

Then there was a sudden, brief, but furious artillery exchange in my head, consisting of, on the one side, the notion that only brain fever could account for imagining significance in the date of a journal someone is reading, and, on the other, my inability to come up with one rational reason for Coslick to have been sitting there reading a copy of *The Times* from three weeks ago, unless he expected me to pick it up and look at it. Eventually, that side won, and I skimmed it, stopping, naturally enough, when I saw the word "Southampton" in large, bold letters. I read the entry twice, finding just what Coslick had expected me to find, after which I set the journal down where I had found it, only opened to that page, after which I returned to my room to write it all down. I must be careful not to gloat overmuch. I have learned something, and perhaps passed some sort of test, but I am surrounded by people who are very good at this kind of thing, and, pleased with myself though I am, I must face the fact that I am a rank beginner. If I can keep reminding myself of this, it may prevent me from falling into at least an obvious trap. Because I must not forget that there is torture and death at the end of this game, and among the facts I am searching for there is one that I already know: I could not survive what James survived. It is also difficult to remember that I am in hiding, that the police are looking for me, and that I must be careful with whom I speak, and even who I allow to get a good look at me.

LATER

Very frustrating. I have the feeling that I have learned something important, but I do not know what it is or how to interpret it. Must write to Kitty, who will be able to ask Susan, who might know, or might know who will know. Wasn't that hard to get, either: just took train to Southampton, wearing big floppy hat to hide features somewhat, and walked to pier, asked around a bit, found Henderson, mate on the *Brilliant*, pretended to be from *The Times* and intending to write about his ship, got him drunk and talking, and that was that. Spent most of time asking about things I didn't care about while thinking of a way to ease into what I wanted to know; when I finally did answers came easy and simple, though incomplete. Still, must go ahead and write to Kitty and see if this leads anywhere.

LATE NIGHT

Middle of the night, woke up with heart pounding, and memory of conversation ringing in my ears. Already wrote to Kitty, and put letter in post care of Coslick, then went to sleep, but felt as if I had missed something, then just now woke up with a face in mind, and remembering piece of conversation with Lee. I haven't Susan's skill with conversations, but must do my best. We were talking about Trotter's Club, and I tried to find out who was in it, and brought up Tournier, and Lee said something like, "I never liked him. He and his sister would come by and he was never polite. When I found out he was in the Trotter's Club, I wasn't surprised," and that was the whole of it, but somewhere in my dreams, I suppose, I put together an image of what a sister of Tournier's might look like, and I'll be damned if I didn't come up with the woman who visited me the last time I was here, and who must be the woman in the carriage James saw, with the peculiar arms on the coach. Am I imagining this? I shall consider the matter and dash off a note to Kitty before I sleep; I hope I will be able to sleep.

SUNDAY

My Darling Kitty,

I am still missing you desperately while taking care of my business interests here, which are going very smoothly, and I believe we shall be part-owners of a steam-transport company before too much longer. I had a jolly time, during the negotiations, speaking with the sailors, who speak the oddest lingo, and love to talk about overheard conversations among dignitaries as if it were the greatest joke in the world; which I suppose it is, for their ships are small, and landlubbers (like me, in fact) often forget how easy it is to overhear things, so they scandalized and entertained me for quite some time with these tales. I will not shock you, my dear, by telling you some of the tawdry things they overheard from the mouths of those in high places in this strange country of Leuchtenberg, but can you imagine, or could our old friend Stephen Vaughan imagine, why a highly placed figure might speak of bills submitted to Parliament, and why this requires a provocation? It nearly makes me happy of my ignorance, my dear, because it sounds quite threatening, although the sailors thought nothing of it; yet why should this grand fellow swear he could arrange the provocation, if only the others would promise to submit the bill? Curious, isn't it?

But all of this is unimportant. What matters, my love, is that I miss you, and that I hope my business will be finished soon. Please give my respectful greetings to our friends, and tell them to be of good cheer, until the return of your affectionate husband and love,

Richard

PART THREE

ACTUALITY

From *The Times*, December 4, 1849
THE CHARTISTS IN NEWGATE

Mr Alderman and Sheriff LAWRENCE and Mr NICOLL, the other sheriff, presented the reports from the several prisons of the city. The health of the inmates was represented as very good, and the condition of the prisons was stated to be extremely clean and well ventilated.

Mr Alderman LAWRENCE presented petitions from Bezor and Shaw, the Chartists, who had been sentenced at a period of great public excitement to imprisonment in Newgate for Chartism. It appeared that the two Chartists had, upon their introduction to Newgate, misconducted themselves in the most extravagant manner, and so abused the very great privileges to which they were admitted that it became necessary to limit these privileges, and to place them on the system prescribed for the regulation of persons convicted of crimes under ordinary circumstances. A great change had, however, been wrought in the conduct of the refractory Chartists. For some time they had both acted with remarkable propriety, and the language of their petitions now presented to the Court exhibited the improvement unequivocally. Bezor, who it appeared had a poetical turn, wished to have opportunities, not of translating the Psalms of David, but of turning them into verse. The two prisoners prayed, too, for an increase of light and fire, and the use of paper and pen and ink, not for the purpose of inculcating and disseminating dangerous doctrines, but for that of a more frequent and agreeable communication with their families. The petitioners also prayed for some alteration in diet, and as there was good reason for believing that their conduct had undergone a very advantageous change, it was to be hoped that the Court would listen favourably to the application. (Hear, hear.)

Mr Alderman COPELAND said he happened to be one of the visiting magistrates when the refractory conduct of the Chartists was complained of in the prison, and certainly during his experience he had never witnessed behaviour more incompatible with the discipline necessary to be observed in a place appointed for the confinement of criminals. If, however, the Court were of opinion that faith could be placed in the sincerity of the change stated to have taken place, he would not oppose the relaxation of the restrictions to which they had been subjected.

Mr Alderman WILSON said he had brought the subject of the refractory conduct of the petitioners before the Court several months ago. The Chartists had certainly been allowed very remarkable privileges, which they had abused, not only by writing to and receiving from Chartists outside letters imbued with their dangerous politics, but by other conduct at variance with the spirit of prison subordination and control. Irritated by the course pursued by the magistracy for the preservation of order, they had petitioned the Parliament, the Secretary of State, and the Queen, but they so grossly abused the indulgence extended to them that it had been found necessary to continue the restrictions. It appeared that now they were penitent, and that they solicited as favours what before they considered to be their right. He wished the petitions to be referred to the Gaol Committee to inquire and report . . .

. . . Sir P. LAURIE thought it would be prudent to refer the petitions to the sheriffs and visiting magistrates of the prisons, with orders to inquire into and regulate the indulgences of the petitioners. It was notorious that the abuses they had committed on the occasion referred to extended to attempts to excite political sympathies of the most dangerous kind, and the magistracy of London had resorted to the most judicious expedients to remedy an evil of such magnitude.

Mr Alderman HUMPHREY deprecated any course likely to occasion delay. If the petitioners had shown symptoms of contrition such as had been described, it would be only fair to give them the benefit of the change. (Hear, hear.)

Mr Alderman CARDEN said it appeared to him to be a difficult matter for the visiting magistrates to act if they happened to differ in opinion as to the treatment of the prisoners. (Hear, hear.) It was all very well to talk of discipline and the exercise of its rigours in some cases, and its mild application in others; but what was really the character of the men of whom they had been speaking? Were they not the very persons who were ready to join in the tumultuous scenes so well calculated to lead to the destruction of property and life? He believed they had connexion with the Chartist journals by which so much mischief had been propagated, and that they co-operated to generalize the venóm of the doctrines to which they were known to be favourable. (Hear, hear.) When, some time ago, he asked some of his friends to accompany him to Newgate to view the prison system, he was answered with the objection that the severity would no doubt be a revolting spectacle, but when he overcame their scruples and they visited the places of confinement, they saw that a gaol was much more comfortable than a workhouse. He hoped to see the workhouses superior in point of living to prisons, and the poor treated with more tenderness than the criminal. (Hear, hear.)

Mr Alderman SIDNEY said the magistracy had no right to treat with extraordinary rigour men convicted of the offences with which the petitioners had been charged. The petitioners had been sentenced to imprisonment for two years without labour. Some of the members of the Court seemed to think that they had met with extreme indulgence. At all events, whatever mode of treatment they might have formerly experienced, they were at the present moment confined in the condemned cells of Newgate. (Cries of, ''No, no.'')

Sir P. LAURIE said it was true there were fifteen cells, but they were not what were called condemned cells. Newgate had no cells of that description at present.

Mr Alderman SIDNEY said the fifteen old cells and the five new cells in Newgate were dismal and solitary in every sense of the word, and he did not see why they should not be called ''condemned,'' for they were as bad as the cells so called at more early periods of prison experiment. He could see no reason for refusing to grant the indulgences sought for, and he was sure the magistracy were bound to carry out the law without aggravating the punishment beyond the intention of the Judge, or the views of those who made it. He could not help saying that prejudices had been strongly exercised against the petitioners, and that in their case the laws of humanity had been violated.

Mr Alderman CHALLIS said the statement of Mr Alderman Sidney contained gross misrepresentations. The treatment of prisoners in Newgate was marked with kindness and in no instance had there occurred the least infringement of the laws of humanity, however chargeable the authorities might be with the exercise of remarkable lenity.

Mr Alderman LAWRENCE and other aldermen denied the statement of Alderman Sidney as to the existence of condemned cells.

Mr Cope (the governor of Newgate), in answer to questions from the Court, stated that the conduct of the petitioner Bezor had much improved within the last three or four months.

Alderman THOMPSON said the governor's representation satisfied him that the discipline might undergo relaxation in the case of the petitioners. He deprecated the irregularity which had crept into the discussion, and hoped the matter would be referred to the Gaol Committee, who would act according to their judgment as to the merits of the case.

The petitions were accordingly referred to the Gaol Committee.

MANCHESTER
4 DEC 1849

Dear Kitty,

Well, I promised you I'd bring all the thorny questions before James and Engels yesterday, which is an implied promise to pass on the results, isn't it? It didn't go anything like the way I would have predicted, had I tried to imagine it when I wrote to you. But Engels certainly kept his word, dear; whatever I may have missed when he took James up to his room couldn't have been nearly the conversation I was witness to last night. I almost wish I'd gone up to bed immediately after dinner. It did have a certain bizarre value as spectacle, however. Not unlike an exchange of rocket fire at sea, in which someone seems likely to be burned down to the water-line when all's said and done, but my God, the reflection of the fire on the water! I feel *burdened*, Kitty, positively burdened, with something that's not my business and that I can hardly do anything about—in fact, that I'm not sure I completely comprehend. Bah. Frustration is bad for my handwriting.

I made my "report" to Engels yesterday morning quite

early, before he left for the mill. I sat in his study and recited, now that I think of it, the way we did for Mlle Duchamp, when we'd been set to memorize some piece of French verse we hardly understood. (Feet together on the carpet, back straight, hands folded, and the chin level, Mademoiselle, *level*, not so, with the nose to the *ciel, oui, très drôle, mes perroquets.* Horrid old inquisitor.) Engels's job was to write furiously while I did so. When I finished, he surveyed the list of names, dates, and places, and so did I, over his shoulder.

"O'Brien," Engels said, his voice, for once, empty of expression. "This is what he meant, last night. Harney will be distressed."

I had heard, a little, of Bronterre O'Brien, who was one of the Chartist leaders, but not enough to follow the emotional undercurrents of the matter either the night before last or this time. "Damning?"

"It seems so. And several others as well. Taylor? Ah, sad, sad. That is old news now, but still—" He *was* upset, I thought; he sounded distinctly more German suddenly. I thought of James and his unconscious—possibly unconscious—lapses into piecemeal Gaelic. Engels shook his head. "On the basis of this, I have to believe some damage has already been done. But there is no hemorrhage, not yet. We are in time. Certainly damage in another quarter, but there, too, we are in time, I think. Stubborn fool. Easier, surely, to beat himself over the head with a brick."

He leafed through the pages again. "O'Connor. Do you know, *Spinne*, I could almost be frightened of your cousin, sometimes?"

"No, you couldn't," I said promptly. "Why do you say so?"

He leaned back in his chair and drummed his fingers on the arms. "Feargus O'Connor is the great Moses of the Charter. William Lovett may be its founder, but O'Connor is its battering-prow and general and crusader. Your cousin reveres him. And yet, look." He leaned forward, snatched the top sheet off the pile, and handed it to me. "O'Connor is on his list. Cleared; but I know of no other man among the Chartists who would have dared to inquire into Feargus O'Connor's loyalty."

The names that meant the most to me were on the list as well. Stone, Johnson. It reminded me of all those months ago, when they had been only names to us, and then levers to pry information free, and then threats. All those months ago, when they had been alive.

And Alan Tournier, of course, who still is. I tapped his name where it appeared on the sheet and asked, "Do you know this one?"

Engels leaned forward to look. "Not in person. He has been mentioned to me, in letters. Not, I see, a connexion to be encouraged?"

"No. He seems to be behind the plot against James." I reminded myself of the conversation on the train, on the way here, and added, "One of them, at the very least. Engels, haven't you another desk to sit behind?"

He yanked out his pocket-watch and consulted it, with a vigorous French syllable. "Tonight, after dinner. The three of us will talk." He dropped the list into a drawer and locked it. "If your cousin can bring himself to wake up and come downstairs, that is."

"It's still awfully early."

"How do you think I made up my fifteen days?" he asked, beaming, and swept out of the study calling for Mary.

I spent a pleasant, quiet day, helping Mary with household things and talking about mutual friends, and reading the journals, which are delivered in breathtaking quantity and variety to any house that has Engels in it. Finding David's murder noted in one of them took me aback. Oh, what a horrid thought: I will go back to Bright's and find an avalanche of sympathy notes from friends. I must remember in my next life to choose my acquaintance solely on the basis of their contempt for all the polite forms.

Kitty, I hope I'm not heartless. I do sometimes remember that I no longer have a brother, and it *does* bring me up short with a sort of mental stoppage of breath. I even discover tears in my eyes, sometimes—but more for the possibility of what I might have found in a brother than what I found in fact. David and I didn't know each other well, and what we did know, we either didn't understand or didn't like. Someone, I'm sure, would say that he did not deserve to die, and if all he'd done was make me dislike him, that would be true. But when my eyes start to fill with tears, it is at least in part because I feel sorry for myself: why, of all the people in the world I might have been related to, did I have to get a bad egg like David?

I also found mention that the murder of a naval officer outside of Newport was still being investigated. Interesting, I thought, after the obligatory shiver. James had thought that if Johnson died, he would be implicated. Had he been, and it hadn't stuck? Or had we managed to throw off the sequence of events sufficiently that the evidence doesn't point strongly enough to James after all? Or—nasty thought—is Tournier, or whoever, holding that card for later? The *Times* seemed not to have considered the matter worth mentioning.

James almost made me doubt his promise of the night before. By noon he had still not come downstairs. I finally went, barefoot, to his door and put my ear to it, which required first overcoming my terror of what seemed to me to be the inevitable consequences of such an act (that he would open the door and catch me at it, of course). I was not caught; and there were small noises, none of them identifiable, which proved that the wretch hadn't simply locked the door and gone out the window. If you don't believe James could go out an upper-storey window in broad daylight without anyone being the wiser, you aren't sufficiently familiar with your step-brother. At about three o'clock he appeared in the parlour, neat as the proverbial pin, flawlessly composed—in other words, nearly indistinguishable from a well-embalmed corpse except that he was upright, mobile, and articulate. Ought it to be comforting to know that one's cousin could probably tie his cravat elegantly on his death-bed? He made fluent small-talk, which, after a while, caused Mary to regard him gravely for five freezing seconds and leave the room. He watched her go and asked me for the *Guardian*.

Dinner was better because Engels was there; but even he directed occasional curious looks at James when the object's attention was elsewhere. The object's attention, truth to tell, was mostly elsewhere throughout the meal, though it wasn't always obvious. I realized at last that he was simply avoiding thinking at all, at least until there was something sufficiently difficult and distracting to concentrate on. Given the events of the previous night, if I had been James, I am not sure I would have done it differently.

He had his distraction after dinner, when he, Engels, and I scattered ourselves around Engels's study and began to compare notes. I shan't subject you to the whole recitation. James was accurate and concise; I was belatedly taken aback at what had happened and the relatively short time it had occupied, and so was not always the cool reporter of events I might have wished to be; Engels paced, his eyebrows climbing his forehead or threatening the bridge of his nose depending on what he heard. What James did couldn't be described as pacing. It was a nearly-aimless course of motion, in which he sat, or wandered to a shelf or table and examined what was there without really seeing it, or leaned on things. It looked like the work of someone trying to stay awake, but I think it wasn't quite what it looked. It was more tiring to watch than Engels. I, as you might imagine, picked a chair and stayed in it.

I described to them your suppositions about the gold. When I made the connexion between it and the box that James had taken off the coach, he shut his eyes and sighed. "The devil fly away with it. Yes, that would be right. That was why she wanted me to bring it down for her, wasn't it? So that later I would realize what it was, and that I'd had my hands on it."

Engels insisted that we back up at that, and James described the fair-haired woman.

Engels said, "I met her. In Brussels," and we both stared. I have never seen Engels like that before, that cold, inward-looking face. "Her name is Eleanor Turner. She did not seem interested in politics so much as in power, and in men who had it. The trail she left behind her was studded with broken lives and careers. She is enough to make one believe in succubi."

"A taste for damage. That sounds right." James's left hand settled over his right forearm, an almost unconscious gesture.

Your other suggestion, that the gold was meant to fund the Trotter's Club in some unspecified activity possibly connected with the government, was taken seriously, but failed to produce the immediate acclamation of the first. "My prejudices are showing, I know," James said. "But if I were a foreign power, I wouldn't give money to a social club of ruling-class play-acting madmen for any purpose, substantive or not. The Trotter's Club couldn't destabilize a card-house. And as for Her Majesty's Own, the Home Office have enough money and agents already, surely, without having to resort to would-be spell-mumblers? Or funds from Prussia?''

''Might this Trotter's Club be a front for something else?'' Engels asked.

James crossed his arms over the top of a chair-back. ''Possibly. Most of the people I know are in it would be utterly incapable, but a few—are capable of both resourcefulness and unpleasantness. Not, however, in the official guise of the organization. I suspect they sacrifice pigeons.'' Suddenly he drew breath and turned his face away. ''No. That's not quite fair,'' he amended roughly. ''However resourceful they may or may not be. They may have sponsored the death of a six-month-old child.''

Engels met my eyes. I don't know what they told him, but it must at least have included a warning not to ask. As James resumed his wandering, I said in as firm a voice as I could muster, ''The membership includes one or two people with seats in Parliament. Lord Growe for one, which, if I recall, already gives us a connexion to the Home Secretary.''

Engels looked thoughtful. ''James's, and I confess, my prejudices aside, they should be watched. Other names?''

''Most of the dead people in the foregoing narrative, I'm afraid.'' James had braced himself against the mantelpiece and was prodding the coals with the shovel. ''Alan Tournier is on the list, however. And Andrew Cobham.''

Not ''my father''. I waited, teeth sunk into my lip, for Engels to say it, wondering what the response would be. But he only asked, after a moment, ''Any others?''

James and I between us named a few others; the sort of people who belong semi-publicly to a secret society, and thus not likely to be a danger. James listed a few I didn't know, explaining they'd been frequent visitors to Cauldhurst Abbey at significant times, or under unusual circumstances. Engels wrote them all down.

It was James who asked about the rumour of a rising, the one that Evan Davis had passed along.

"This was in Newport?" Engels asked sharply. James nodded. "I have heard the rumour also. Or more accurately, the rumour of a rumour. I have not been able to learn where it originates. It is not yours?"

James stopped torturing the fire. "What do you mean?"

"When I heard it, I wondered if it was your work."

"That's not work," James said slowly. "That's bloody irresponsible mischief. You can't have thought I would do that."

"Not as mischief."

"No," he said. "It is not my work. Or anyone else's that I know of. And if it's not anyone's that *you* know of, then there's a strong possibility that it's counterfeit business."

Engels raised his eyebrows at James. "And an equally strong possibility that it is a piece of adventurism on someone's part. Perhaps even on the part of a Chartist faction; you would not necessarily have heard. There is a delegate's conference called for this month, you know. Why should it not be a manufactured show of popular support for that?"

For just a moment, I could see James drawing himself together, hardening himself against something. Then the outward manifestation was gone, but I thought the internal armour had been set in place. "It would certainly have to be manufactured. There *is* no popular support for it. You couldn't get six adults to march with a green flag tomorrow if you combed all of Lancashire."

"I believe you know that is not true."

"Figuratively, it's true. There is no significant popular support left for the Charter. It burnt itself clean away last year. Though God knows no one's told the government or the newspapers. You can still shout the word on a crowded street corner and frighten the editor of *The Times*. Nobody will turn out to cheer for a delegates' conference."

"What would they turn out for?"

James folded his arms. "Do you mean, if there was a genuine rising, or only another Anti-Corn Law League Sunday picnic and speeches?"

"You sound bitter."

"About '42. I am bitter. We talked about that in '42."

"That was seven years ago."

"I'm good at grudges. Do you want me to answer your question?"

Engels watched James for a moment in silence. Then he said, "Yes."

"All right. I'm not even sure, any more, that you could get people to turn out if you promised them O'Connor, what with the Land Plan coming apart at the seams. You can usually get up a local fracas against some mill or shop if you don't care that your crowd won't stand long, or under any pressure. But if you've heard rumours in Manchester, and Davis has heard them in Newport, then it may be a shot at national trouble. And if that's the intention, whoever means it to happen will have to manufacture both the rising and the reason for it. I'm not aware of any Chartist faction with both the moral bankruptcy and the available talent to do that. On the talent side, for instance, I *might* be able to engineer such a thing. Given time and resources. But no one has asked me to."

I recognized at last the tone and cadence of James's voice, flattened and inflexible. He'd used it on me in the inn at Fairfield, when he'd meant to drive me away. I found my hands were clenched in my lap.

"Would you do it, if you were asked to?" Engels said, very calm.

"No. I haven't quite declared moral bankruptcy."

"It would require that?"

"Engels." James paused, for no reason I could identify. Then he rubbed the space between his eyebrows and began again briskly, "Setting aside momentarily the arguments for and against adventurism. If you cannot think of a quick and exceedingly dirty way to get the bonfires lit, up and down this island, then I commend the absolute purity of your principles. Give me O'Connor, O'Brien, Harney, and a dozen innocent men and women in one room, plus a judicious quantity of explosives, and I will give you a rising. If I could arrange for Ernest Jones with his throat cut in prison as well, you could have an absolute bloodbath."

I wanted to swallow when he finished, a reflex against nausea; but my mouth was too dry. Engels stood on the other side of the fire from James, unmoved, I thought at first, by the things he'd said. Then something in the set of his jaw changed my mind. "That would get you a bloodbath," said Engels harshly. "Would it get you the Charter?"

"No," James replied. "I know that. But when I wake up out of a sound sleep in the middle of the night I have to wonder if everyone else knows it, too. It's safer now—I'm not sure you *could* get O'Connor, O'Brien, and Harney into the same room at once. But until last year it was my *bête noire*."

Engels walked to the window and back. "If it would get you the Charter, would you do it?" he asked. It was a horrid question, made worse by Engels's conversational tone.

"Nothing, now, will get the Charter adopted."

"If it would—"

"No. I wouldn't do it."

"Why not?"

James's hands were knotted together, and his lips were white where the steepled forefingers pressed against them. He stared across his hands, across the fire, at Engels. Then he released the pressure against his mouth enough to say quickly, "Hurrah for the Socratic method. Do you ever wonder why none of his students simply hauled off and hit the old bastard? *What are we talking about?*"

I saw, more than heard, Engels give a great sigh. He turned away to the window once more, and seemed to find the tassel on the drapery cord interesting. "Method, I think." His tone continued commonplace, though it must have been reflex. He would not have expected either of us to believe it. He went back to his pacing. "Have you ever met Louis Blanqi? I think you'd get along."

James dropped into the wing chair furthest from Engels's desk. I had seen the posture well enough to read it a little by now, the indolent curve of the spine that said he wouldn't be roused to anything but mild irritation, and hadn't the energy to express even that. The armour was back in place. "I might—yes, I have. A year ago, over dinner at someone's house. He was waiting for me to tell him he was clever, but I got drunk and forgot."

"Clever? Yes, he is clever." The implied "but" at the end of that sentence hung in the air like smoke from one of Uncle Matthew's cigars. James and I both waited for it. Engels flashed us one of his smiles and said, "Marx has coined the

term 'Blanqism' for the belief that one can bring about the
revolution without the working class, if only one is clever
enough to organize the proper *coup d'état.*"

James propped his elbows on the chair arms and clasped his
hands. After a moment, he sighed and said, "I thought we had
established that I was not, for the past year, engaged in single-
handedly bringing about the revolution. No, pardon me. Perhaps we hadn't established it. I did *say* so, I believe."

"Yes, you did, didn't you? Well then, how *do* you propose
to bring about the revolution? We have a group, now, you
know: the Communist League. What programme would you
propose?"

"Education. Recognition and support of the natural leaders
among the workers in all parts of the country." James stopped
and looked at Engels. "Pardon me, the world. I still think like
a Chartist, you see. Supporting workers' demonstrations and
risings. I could probably give you a few more if you wanted
to wait for them, but I'm out of practice."

"Education?" said Engels. "Yes. Education is good. The
more the working class knows—about everything—the better
it will be able to take command of its own destiny. But what
is a 'natural leader' of workers? And do you really propose to
support them before knowing their programme? Because
someone is thrust into a position of leadership of the class,
does that mean he will lead them well, intelligently? And will
you support a rising that is doomed, or will you try to con-
convince them to wait until it is possible for a rising to *succeed*? And how will you know the d-difference?" His voice,
though no louder, had increased in intensity, and he had
stopped pacing. His gaze, too, was intense, and fixed on James.

"Which of those," said James, precise and cautionary,
"would you like me to answer? You mentioned Webber last
night, yourself. Friedrich Lessner is another man I'd call a
natural leader of the workers. I had a friend in '39 who was
another. And what in hell constitutes support but making sure
that they *will* lead intelligently and well?"

Engels laughed suddenly. "You would have made a fine
Jesuit. No, no," he added, holding up his hand. "Don't lash
me with your scorpion's tail, at least not yet." He began pacing once more, an odd look on his face. "As for Lessner, he

is one of ours, by which I mean he is a Communist." He spoke slowly. "I would not call Lessner a natural leader. I am not certain the term has any meaning. Lessner earned his position of trust. And that is what it means to be a leader."

"Right." James' elbows were on his knees now, and the tips of his fingers were pressed lightly together before him. "I should have known you wouldn't let the word 'natural' stand. But he's a leader by virtue of having become the sort of man whom his fellow workers look to and say, 'Well, Friedrich, what should we do about it?' He was that before he ever came to Cologne. It's why he came. And when he came, you grabbed him up and said, 'Here, read this. Do this. Talk to that fellow.' You supported the things in him that already made him a leader, and you directed and refined the thrust of his leadership. You can't create leaders, is all I meant by 'natural'."

"I think, you know, that you *can* create leaders, and I even think we in the Communist League are trying to do so." He waved his hand. "But that is another matter. What I want to make clear now is that your workers, especially your British workers, have to be convinced, and you convince them neither by telling them what a fine man you are, nor by valiantly allowing yourself to be executed for acting in their place. When the time comes to allow yourself to be executed, you will know. In the meantime, the task is much harder: You must tell them the truth. You cannot lie to the working class, James, not even once. They will know, and they will never trust you again. Lie to the bourgeoisie all you want, because they will only hear what they wish, and to the aristocracy, because they will not hear at all, and certainly to the government, the organ of the other two. But *never* to the working class."

"Well, thank you at least for the assurance that I'll be able to spot my martyrdom in advance of the fact. What are we talking about here, Engels? Proper management of a revolution? Or are we working our way around to an unfortunate exchange of personalities, in which case, must we?"

"We are talking about the future of mankind."

James gave a furious, hissing sigh and left his chair. "Lovely," he said, reclaiming his position against the mantelpiece. "I *could* point out that we're always bloody well talking about the future of mankind. I can do it, when I've got the leisure—and the mental resiliency, which I don't swear to right now—all night. But just now I am easily distracted by what's not being said. You object, I think, to my methods.''

"So, then," said Engels. "You will not rise to my bait about truth? You are a clever English trout, and must be coaxed into the net. Well, I am a spear-fisherman, so I will simply say it: James, you could become an invaluable revolutionist; you could make great, even vital contributions to the movement; you—no, I will not list your virtues, you don't like it; you know what they are. But you are *lazy*.''

I have no idea if Engels knows James well enough to read his face, or knows faces in general well enough to read all of them. James, perpetually difficult to read, was quite still against the mantel, and only a shadow along his jaw suggested that, for an instant, he'd clenched his teeth. "Dear me," he said at last. "How is it, do you suppose, that I get so tired?''

Engels made a sound I couldn't interpret: it may have been derision, or honest laughter. He said, "By running around exercising your legs so that you are not required to exercise your brain.''

"Well, of course not. I thought brains were the contribution of people like O'Brien and Stephens and Julian Harney. And you. I am the very quintessence of the leg-man. Every movement needs one or two.''

At that point, I thought, *Careful. Careful.* But I'm not sure even now which of the two men I wished could hear me.

Engels stopped pacing again, which made me curious about the significance of the pacing and the suspension of it. Watching James, he lifted those expressive eyebrows just a little, and said, "Should we stop?''

Hard-voiced, James replied, "No. Not now. I appear to have been an inadequately effective revolutionary. What ought I to have done, instead of what I did? It's a little late; there are men, good, bad, and indifferent, who are dead and buried because of what I've done, and I hate to think they might have died only because I was lazy. What ought I to have done?''

"And still you evade the issue. No, do not interrupt. I am not your father con-confessor, to give you absolution for your sins. If you have made mistakes—and who has not?—and if people have suffered from your mistakes—and how else would you know them for mistakes?—you must nevertheless go on and, and learn, and not repeat them. I am interested—the *movement* is interested in what you will do in the future. How c-can I know if you are interested in learning from those mistakes? All you have done for this entire conversation is wiggle-waggle like a, like a Jesuitical trout.''

"Dear, great, grinning—" It was said very quietly, and I thought had the clenching of teeth in it. "I ask a direct question, and *I'm* the one accused of being slippery."

"James, this is a harsh life, and no one can command another. Sometimes those who pass through the fire of the movement leave nothing of themselves behind but ashes. Some become so exhausted they cannot continue. I give you my word that if you are in such a state, I will not press you, either with guilt or with the force of words, and I will still consider you a comrade and a close friend. But you must choose. Take some time to rest, if you wish, and to think. But if you wish to continue, I mean, if you wish to continue now, then stop playing middle-class intellectual games like a, like a Proudhon. Do you understand?''

James's right hand was curled around the edge of the mantel, and the fingers were white. The coals hissing in the grate hid the sound of his breathing. "What do you want? Abject submission? You can have it for a price."

Engel's pacing had taken him to the other side of his desk. James took the one swift stride necessary to place him across its tidy surface from Engels and said, "Tell me. Why did we fail? Last year, last summer, you wrote in the *Neue Rheinische Zeitung* about the situation here, claiming it was the very Platonic ideal of a revolutionary powder-keg. You say there is no use in encouraging a doomed rising, that the requirements for a revolt of the people have to be in place before that revolt can succeed. They were there. The people were ready to stand for their cause—for the *third time*, for the love of reason. And the Charter failed. Why? Why did we fail?" On the last word, James's fist came down on the desk with a sound like a distant cannon. Then he stood still, his hand pressed to the wood, his eyes fixed on it and blind.

Engels leaned over the desk. I hadn't properly recognized

the difference in height between them; Engels is over six feet tall, so he had to bend, trying to meet James's eyes. He spoke quietly, but very distinctly. "Because the leaders of the Chartist movement were brave, dedicated, self-sacrificing men and women who thought that all it took was to be brave, dedicated, and self-sacrificing." He straightened up. "They lacked political vision. They did not tell the truth because they did not *know* the truth. You can no longer be that way. You must either grow beyond that, or leave the movement, or you will destroy yourself. I look at you and I see how close you have come to destroying yourself already. If you choose that, I will be saddened, and so will many others." For the first time in what seemed like hours he glanced at me. Then, with an almost embarrassed wince, he began to pace again.

There was silence in the room, marred only by the sound of the fire, and of Engels's foot-falls. James broke it at last with, "So. It's: Bequeath my ashes to the movement; or learn to walk through fire." I wondered if Engels noticed, as I did, that he had ignored the second option he had been given. "I thought, after the last ten years, that I knew how."

"The Romantics represent a certain step forward in literature," said Engels, "insofar as they encourage individual thought, individual responsibility, and breaking the hold of King and Priest on individual conscience. Besides, many of them are revolutionists. But they become wearying after a while, don't they?"

James raised his head at last and met Engels's steady, evaluating gaze. One corner of his mouth twitched. "Bugger that, Engels. If you think that was a Byronic fit, you should see me on one of my *bad* days." He straightened up and thrust his hands through his hair. "If I'm hard to spear, you're at least as hard to net, you know. Very well: If I were to stand bravely before you and say, comrade Engels, I am a soldier in your army, place me where you will, what *would* you do with me?"

Engels blinked, then stepped around his chair to a bookshelf and pulled down a thick volume without, it seemed, having to look for it. He set it on the desk in front of James and said, "To begin with, I would have you read that."

Dazed, James said, "Everyone concerned with my improvement seems to want me to read large books." He opened the front board, and the initial leaves, and said, in a changed voice, "Oh." He stood with his hand arched lightly over the title page and slowly, softly, began to laugh. "Oh, my. Would you like to lecture me on the consequences and inevitability of choice? No—no, I'm sorry. That was unworthy. Not to mention unintelligible. Engels, I'm sorry. I'm going to go upstairs now and put the pillow over my head. Do you mind? I shall do my best to think about this, but not now."

Engels looked at me, his eyebrows eloquent, then said to James, "Mind? No, Dr Engels considers it an excellent tonic. Go with blessings, my son. I will see you tomorrow."

" 'My son.' I've got fifteen days on you, remember?"

"I told you: you wasted them."

"All right, you can adopt me. Just think what Mary will say. Good night, all." James walked from the study well-commanded and in no particular hurry. He didn't turn as he closed the door.

I waited until his steps on the stairs, quick and light, faded away. Then I said, "What he was asking was, if God loves us, why does he allow evil in the world?"

"Pardon?" said our host. Fits of abstraction are rare in Engels.

"When he asked why the Charter failed. When his cause was broken, I think he had a sort of crisis of faith. And it may be that he's . . . not used to doing without faith."

"And so he has trapped himself in the ruins? And is starving, no, *poisoning* himself on a d-diet of other men's failure? There is a type of blindness that can result from fever or a blow to the head. This is no crisis of faith; it is that blindness. But until he can see, he cannot—cannot choose what to do next. And he must choose."

"I expect he's distracted by the possibility of imminent death," I muttered.

"Do you think so? I disagree." He began to pace once more. I wondered if Engels's household went through an unusual amount of carpet. "Distracted, yes, but not by that."

"Well, he *ought* to be," I said, with rather more asperity than I'd meant to show. The view from my spider-in-the-corner position had been excellent, but there had still not been enough of the discussion to tell me what the choice was that

Engels was concerned—agitated, in fact—that James should make. "It will all be irrelevant, Engels, if the people who abducted him get their hands on him again."

"Are you saying he should live as if he is sure he will *not* live?"

"No! Of course not. But this may not be the ideal moment to ask him to take the long view of his future." Chartists and devil-worshippers, I thought. And his father, and of course the letter last night. But if James hadn't felt like mentioning the last two, I certainly didn't mean to bring them up.

Engels frowned at me. He'd picked up a turned, pearl-shafted pen from his desk, and was rolling it, absently, fiercely, between his fingers. "What makes you—or him—think th-that reflection will wait on the perfect moment? The future will not sit hat in hand in the entry waiting for him to c-call it in." He slapped the pen down on the desktop with a click. "I beg your pardon. I am not angry with you."

"With James?"

"No, not with him, either. I was right. He is in a weakened state, and not in any good way. Perhaps he will not—no. I said it was not too late, and I am *not* wrong."

"Engels? You're talking to yourself."

Engels flung himself into the chair that James had been driven, finally, to leave. "Until tonight I have never had a conversation with your cousin that I didn't enjoy. He held nothing of himself back in serious talk; he brought all of his mind, temper, wit, and heart to it, unfettered, unclouded. You could warm your hands at him when he was like that."

"My goodness. Was this *very* long ago?" Everyone else who'd said anything to me about James had agreed that his single most distinctive characteristic for the last ten years was an impenetrable reserve. Then I wondered if Richard had been privy once to the bright, uncontained person Engels was describing. If he had seen that, and had it withdrawn, it might account for his bitterness now.

"We last talked like that two—no, almost three years ago. In those days he needed honing still—well, and so did I. Then came the events of last year."

"In which you were honed, and he was not?" I was feeling absurdly defensive on James's behalf.

"In which he had already been placed in the wrong position, doing the wrong things for the wrong reasons."

" 'Had been placed?' " I asked.

"There is something amiss with my grammar? What idiocy on his part caused him to remain there, I could not be-begin to guess."

"You *are* angry with him."

Engels stared at me, eyes narrowed. "Tell me, Susan: if you knew that someone thought of James Cobham as nothing more than a piece of artillery to be aimed and fired, would you be angry? And if you learned that he knew it as well, and allowed it, would you not be angry with him? And if you learned that, worst of all, he believed it to be true—?"

The coals still burned in the grate; I heard the wind rising outside, and a few drops of rain against the window. Engels rarely called me by my first name. "But this has nothing to do with me, does it?" I said at last, and couldn't keep the catch of despair from my voice.

"Nor with me. Except for the waste, the abominable waste, which hurts us all."

I rose and went to Engels's desk, where the book he'd offered James still lay open. What I felt, on looking at it, must have been a little like what James felt: amusement, anger, sorrow; even, perhaps, a bit of fear. It was Hegel's *Science of Logic*, Kitty, and I wondered why I hadn't guessed that.

"Well, Engels," I said unsteadily, "our waste and hurt may have to wait in line behind everyone else's. And at the present rate, *none* of us may live long enough."

"Now it is you who are talking to yourself."

"Enter it on the waste side of the ledger," I told him, and went upstairs to contemplate the relative benefits of emigration, nunneries, and being locked in a garret room at Melrose.

I did not go to bed. I sat by the window of my room, which looks out over the back garden of the house, and watched the bare branches of the apple tree thrash in the wind and intermittent rain. Which was why I had an excellent view, shortly after midnight, of the person who came in through the gate at the bottom of the garden, rusty black coat lifting on the air like a sail, dark head hatless and tangled and obviously unencumbered by the pillow its owner had declared he meant to put over it. Whatever he'd been doing, it didn't make him either stagger or limp, which I found reassuring. If I hadn't been listening for it I would never have heard his tread on the stairs, even with my door open, which it was by then. When James reached the passageway and saw what must have been the underlit spectre of my face (I was holding my candle) poked past the door-frame, he gave a perfectly satisfactory start.

"You should wear a hat. You'll catch cold," I said.

It shocked a splutter of laughter out of him. The shadows under his eyes were like the prints of a sooty thumb on his colourless skin. But the corners of his mouth remained unrepentantly, wickedly, bent, and the hand that raked his hair back was steady.

"Thank you, ma'am," he replied softly. "Next time, I will." With a nod that was close kin to a full Court bow, he turned and disappeared down the dark corridor toward his room.

The devil's in that man, I swear, Kitty. The next time he goes out he'll have more with him than a hat, if I can manage it. If I am going to lose my sleep anyway, I want a little exercise to go with it. Oh, stop laughing, you know that's not what I meant.

In spite of being awake entirely too late last night, I was up this morning in time to see Engels again before he left. I decided not to tell him about the peregrinatory nature of one of his house-guests. I did suggest to him that, however much we liked his hospitality, we were probably due to leave it very soon.

"Why?" he asked. "Where do you need to go?"

I opened my mouth, and shut it, and felt like a fool.

"I tell you again: you are safe here. And who knows? That may make more of a difference than anything you or I can think of to do."

He was speaking, of course, of James. I find I am getting bloody tired of speaking of James, but I can't seem to talk about anything else. Horrible man. I'm quite sure that Engels, at least, has better things to spend his time on.

So I'll finish by saying that I have not the faintest idea how long we'll be here. Send letters with whatever passes for perfect confidence in this family nowadays.

In loving and poorly-rested exasperation,
Susan

DECEMBER 4th
MELROSE HALL

Dear Susan,

I have considered carefully, and I have decided that too much is happening too fast, and, if it cannot simply stop, as common courtesy demands, then it might at least slow down and give us a chance to catch our breaths and maybe put a few of the pieces, if not together, then at least on the right board, because attempting to solve seven or eight different puzzles at the same time and all without so much as a candle to see them by, while someone is shaking all the tables and someone else is mixing the pieces together, is rather unfair, and I shall certainly speak sharply to whoever is in charge as soon as the opportunity presents itself.

Poor James! I am amazed, Susan, that the poor dear is able to put one foot in front of another, much less actually think, and yet he is still asking all of the right questions, as are you, and if between what the two of you have gone through and what Dick has found out, which I am forwarding to you along with these letters, I cannot make some sense of all this, well, then I will feel as if I am letting the side down, to use a phrase that the boys have never used, bless their hearts, because if they had I believe I should have kicked them, because this is not a game, and if I speak lightly, you know very well that I do not mean it lightly, and that hearing your voice, as I do, through your letters and journals, and thus knowing of, and almost being at, the Severn marshes, makes me feel cold and trembly in a way that I have not felt since you forced me to read of Mr Poe's Tattle-tale Heart, or whatever it was called, that made me vow never to read such things again, but now they are real, and happening to those I love. Even James, the

most rational of all you rationalists, invokes the powers beyond
when in a moment of crisis, and you are too much the rationalist to see it, and will not, I am certain, admit it even now,
but it fills me with terror and pity, and, I am sorry to say, with
the craven wish to be spared the direct experience, but also
with the determination somehow or other to see it through, and
do what I can to help us all reach the other side alive in body
and well in spirit, all of which is, I fear, too much to ask a
Providence in which none of us believes, unless, perhaps, we
shall begin worshipping your Kali of the many hands, who at
least seems more nearly to correspond to the situation, but that
is a dangerous way to look at the world, because taken to its
conclusion, it would have us all worshipping some monstrous
spider, or *Spinne*, if you prefer, because it seems we will never
be able to see the entire web whilst caught up in it, nor to
escape it until we can see it, so perhaps we must count on
your Engels, who specializes, I believe, in understanding spiders, but he is too caught up in preparing his own webs to
take the time to more than glance at ours, except where they
happen to intersect.

I am going to confess, Susan, that I was actually disappointed that your reputation has been secure in fact, and I
maintain a certain hope that by the time this letter finds you
you will be a fallen woman, which I hope for many reasons,
the least important being that there are things we could then
talk about which as of now we cannot, but there are other
reasons as well, having to do with James, and with you, and
now I trespass into areas that are certainly none of my business
and your lips are looking quite thin and angry, and I believe
you want me to leave this matter alone, and so I will, perhaps,
for a while, but I cannot help thinking. Oh, Susan, I keep
skirting around what really matters, because my poor heart
does not want to dwell on it. You have pointed a pistol, and
pulled the trigger, and a man is dead, and bless James for doing
what he did after, but I hurt for you so, proving that I am not
a Christian at all, because a Christian would be concerned with
the life of the man you killed and your soul for killing him,
but I only worry about you, and of course James and Dick,
and I realize now that I have not thanked you for telling me
how to get in touch with Dick, which route it took me all of

this morning to establish, but I'm assured we can at least communicate, though it will mean an extra day or two between
posts, and I have already passed on to him copies of your
material, as well as the letter from James, and if you can swear
off opening letters, then I can swear off copying them, because
do you know my hand actually *cramped* from all the copying
I did, and I kept trying to find things that Dick did not have
to know about, or that you did not have to know about, but I
couldn't, so I just kept at it, becoming ever less precise as I
went, as I am certain you noticed, and in the process learning
not to wear anything I care about, because after a few hours
of copying one gets sloppy with the ink, and my green tea
gown is ruined beyond hope, which is sad because it was the
one I was wearing when Dick starting making bawdy remarks
about ''green sleeves'' that ended with a demonstration on
why ladies used to wear them, and you know how that ended,
and of course it is small of me to even mention such a trivial
matter when you are risking life and limb, but I do so anyway,
and make no excuses.

But, dare I say it? it was worthwhile, Susan, by which I
mean the information from Johnson was worth the trouble it
took to get it, because when that is combined with what Dick
has said, and your conversation with James, it, well, it solves
nothing, but it puts so many pieces of the puzzle on the same
table, and I can see that they are arranging themselves in some
order, even if I cannot yet make out the picture, but I can see
the big, empty shape in the middle of it, and ask a few sensible,
straight-forward questions, the answering of which will go a
long way toward getting us to the other end of this tunnel, and
those questions are, first, what is Leuchtenburg trying to accomplish in Parliament, and, second, why is Tournier hiding
his sister, that is, what is her rôle in all of this, which I ask
because of a note I got from Dick, which I suppose I shall
have to copy and send along too.

I did, I think, make some progress, just an hour ago, after
penning the above, because I went and did just what you said,
Susan, and made Aunt Louisa angry by engaging her in a
conversation about Dick's future, and what we would do, and
where we would go, and I kept calling him Dick because I
know Aunt Louisa hates that, and then I dropped James's name

into the pot, and Aunt Louisa stormed off into her room, shouting at me that Dick and I would have no future if the devil-worshippers had their way, and serve us both right for letting that little bastard run about, which shocked me more than anything else, because how can she have known James is alive, and why choose this moment to reveal his bastardy? So I went to her door, and, as if I were furious in turn, cried out that James had never been in the Trotter's Club, and she screamed back that James was dead. Do you see what this means, Susan? There is another bastard on the loose somewhere, and this bastard has some connexion with the Trotter's Club, and to the family, and it has all passed beyond confusing, and if I were given to headaches, I believe that I should have one now, but in any case I am going to stop for a little and nap.

I am back again, Susan, and several hours have passed, six or seven, I think, at any rate it is nearly midnight, and I really do not want to talk about it although I know I must, so I suppose I should begin by telling you that after my nap I went over to Cauldhurst, and I have emerged triumphant, although it was terribly frightening, between one thing and another, to be going through the effects of a man who died by violence, but, really, I have had such an easy time of it compared to you and James and even Richard, that it is laughable of me to complain about it, but, fright aside, it was difficult, because he had boxes and boxes of letters and notes and memoranda, and it will take months to study them all, and I should have despaired if I had not managed, almost by accident, really, to solve the riddle of his system, which was quite simple and based on dates and then I pretty quickly found what I wanted to know and more besides, and I'm afraid I may shock you a bit, if you are not beyond being shocked by now.

You see, I was thinking as I was writing, which is silly, I suppose, because how else do you think, really, except by writing or talking or something of that nature, but you know what I mean, and I was thinking about what Aunt Louisa could have meant about another bastard on the loose, and I know very well that you would be wondering how Aunt Louisa knows all of this, and that is a good question, but I wondered who it was, and whether it was someone we know but do not know is illegitimate, or if it was someone we had never heard of,

and then I took my nap, and as I was lying there, I wondered
if anyone had even told Aunt Louisa that David was dead, and
then I sat bolt upright, and in a flash like a stroke from the
heavens I added up all the columns and got the wrong answer,
although I did not know it then, because, you see, I just could
not help but think how neat and tidy it would make everything
to discover that David was illegitimate. Oh, I am certain you
are laughing now, but it was a terribly pretty idea, and in any
case you will stop laughing soon enough. I jumped up and
tried to engage Aunt Louisa in a conversation so I could pick
her brains just a bit, but she was having none of it, and I could
not stop wondering about David, so I bundled myself up,
called Wye, and had him bring me straight away to Cauldhurst,
where I started trying to find out, only at first I did not know
how to, but then I remembered Roderick, and I thought he
might have written something around the time Roderick was
born that would give me a clue, but he didn't, however I found
something else instead, and it had to do with the Trotter's
Club, and it was an awful packet of notes, all about vivisection
and horrible things, but right in the middle of it was something
about how no one should shed blood that was not his own,
and there were other things around it, and I kept reading, and
eventually I realized that when they said his own they did not
mean his own, but they meant his father's, or his sister's, or
his brother's, or his son's, and it was all about what sort of
knives to use, and what time of year to do it, and what time
of day, and, well, I know you could bear to hear all of the
details, but I do not want to write them, and I don't have to.

There was, however, a man at Cauldhurst, a policeman of
some sort, who was at first quite severe with me, and asked
me questions about what I was doing there, and, well, in the
course of the matter I learned the answer to the question that
had sent me to Cauldhurst in the first place, although the exact
way I learned it from him is not terribly important except to
say that I was not as clever as you, but perhaps I was luckier,
so I will just tell you what I learned, which is that David has
a son. That's right, sanctimonious David fathered a bastard on
Alan Tournier's sister, and unless I miss my guess, Tournier
wants the bastard to inherit, and how Aunt Louisa knows about
it, I have no clue, but Aunt Louisa knows everything, as you

recall, and my head is still spinning with the implications of all this, so that I cannot put it together, but at least you know, and believe me, it is true, because I was able to confirm it from David's own hand later, once I knew what I was looking for, and I really cannot think more now, but I will send that much along to Dick, to see what he can make of it, and I send it to you for the same reason, although I suppose the best way is simply to copy this letter and send it off to Dick, so he will know how I have replied to you, and it will give me another excuse to write a short but sentimental note to my beloved, but I wish I knew how the Prussian gold fit in, because I think that is the biggest piece of the puzzle we are still missing.

I should tell you that I have received word from Brian that he has taken steps already to have Dick's name cleared, and I am hopeful that we shall soon have good news on that score, but there is nothing left, and so we are splintered, and I feel a terrible sense of incompleteness, because it is bitter waking up alone each morning, though it never used to be, which may be a better argument for preserving your reputation than your remarks to James, not that they did not have some sense to them too, but I can hardly speak on the subject, having got myself married, and even having the effrontery to feel pleased about it, but there is more to this than I can make sense of, Susan, because while everything you say is true, and the laws of marriage are nothing short of barbaric, nevertheless there is something reassuring about the promise of the life-long companionship of one whom you love and who loves you, and while it seems silly to think that love ought to require such a promise, still it is a consolation to me, perhaps only showing my own weakness, but then there are enough sides to this question to invoke once more the goddess with whom we began our meditations, if not the spider, and I do not believe I have the energy for a serious consideration of them, and on top of that my hand is cramping, and I really ought to make a copy of this letter as well, to send to Dick, although this time I really shall engage in some judicious editing, because there are things we can talk about that Dick doesn't need to know, but it still means more dreadful copying, so, for now, that will be all you hear from your faithful friend,

Kitty

DECEMBER 4th
MELROSE HALL

Dearest Beloved Richard,

I am enclosing a copy of a letter I am posting to Susan along
with this one in which I describe some things I have learned,
but I did not tell her exactly how I learned them because she
has enough on her mind with what she is doing and has done
and with poor James, and I know you, too, are having to hide,
but I need to tell this to someone because I am still frightened
even though it is all over. Following up my idea, Richard, I
went to Cauldhurst, as you will see from my letter to Susan,
and I knocked, but all the servants were gone, so I admitted
myself with your key, and it was not until the door shut that
I realized I had neglected to bring any light with me. I could
see a little from the daylight through those high, thin windows
in the main corridor, but it was quite frightening, and all I
could think about was that David had been killed, not just that
he was dead, but that someone had killed him. I came to David's study, and thank all the spirits there was an open window
and I found a lamp and lucifers very quickly, because it was
afternoon and getting dark, but I felt better once there was
light, so I started opening doors and I found some boxes, and
then I went into a little room that connects to the study, and
may have been a priest-hole once, though it is not hidden now,
and it was full of boxes too, as if David had spent his whole
life collecting paper, and I am certain they will make an interesting study someday, but this was not the time, so I started
searching them and I must have spent an hour or more, and
was just finding things out when the door was flung open and
I screamed like an old woman! It turned out to be a tall, dark
man of middle years with an enormous moustache, and he
demanded to know what I was doing there, while I could do
nothing except stand there like a complete idiot taking deep
breaths with my hand over my heart, until he asked again, and
then I took an even deeper breath and asked him what *he* was

doing there, and he said he worked for the government and they were investigating a murder, and if I was tampering with evidence they could hang me, which made me so angry that the next thing I knew I was screaming at him that I was Mrs Richard Cobham, and if anyone was entitled to go through David's papers I was, and then he just stepped forward until he was nearly on top of me and grabbed me by the arm as if I were a child and he shook me and said that I had no more right to be here than, and I can quote this, I think, because it is etched into my memory as if by acid, "The dead man's whore or her whelp, and all you red bastards can rot," and then he dragged me out of the room and threw me to the ground, and then I looked at him, but he was staring down the hall, so I turned to see what he was looking at, and it was Wye, who was holding the biggest pistol I have ever seen, it looked like a duelling pistol from a hundred years ago, and I almost screamed again, but Wye just said, "Shall I kill him, Mrs Cobham?" and I think I squeaked once or twice, but then I shook my head and managed to say, "Let us go home," and that is what we did, and I hope you do not think it forward of me, or of Wye, that I sat up next to him the entire way home and held the arm he didn't need for driving, but he was very respectful of me, and helped me down, and said not a word about it, and it was not until I'd had a glass of tea and caught my breath that I realized what the bully had told me, so I wrote to Susan as much as I thought I should tell her, but I am telling you more.

And that is my adventure, my love, and I miss you terribly, but writing about it has helped me, only I hope you can come home soon, and that when you do you will at once hold and kiss your shaken but adoring & loving,

Kitty

... As there are four Elements, so are there four Deaths of Sacrifice, by which Prophecy shall be given, and the Goodwill of all Spirits purchased. These are the Death of Air, which is hanging or strangling; the Death of Water, which is made by Drowning; the Death of Fire, which is to be burnt alive; and the Death of Earth, which is done beneath the Ground or in a Tomb of stones.

These Deaths only shall yield true Prophecy, when that the Sacrifice shall be brought forth after them and Examined by the Judges, and by the King's Wisdom, and by the King Himself. No Death by the Sword, or by the Knife, or by any Thing that draws forth Blood shall yield true Prophecy.

Nor shall it call down Power upon the one who Slays by it, unless he be Engaged upon the Hunt of the white Stag. The Hunting of the white Stag is the King's Hunt, for it confers the Rule upon the Prince, and confirms in his Kingship the old King.

At the Dark of the year do the King and his Wisdom and all his Ministers and Judges go forth to seek the Stag, for he is Father, Brother, and Son to the King, and of his own Blood. He shall be pursued in all Honour, for his is the Royal line; and with much Cunning, for his is the wisdom of the Salmon, given in his Eating; and with many great Feats of Strength, so that he who shall slay the Stag may be called Greatest among Great men, Worthiest in all that Worthy Companie.

They shall not hunt the Stag with Hounds of sight or scent, or any Dog of the common coursing, but only by their own skill and fleetness take the white Stag of Kingship. They shall not hunt Him with hackbuts or any Gun, but only the Weapons that take their Power from the strength of the Hunter.

Then shall he who has the Right bring the Stag to bay, and Slay him, so that his Blood is fed to the Earth and his Power falls upon the King, his Hunter. And the King's Wisdom shall confirm him in his Rule with the Blood of the Stag and dedicate him to the Throne of Earth, that the Companie of the King may be strong in Craft, and Mighty. Then all shall honor the Name of the Stag, and receive thankfully the Power he has vouchsafed to them.

But if he who has not the Right sheds the Blood of the Stag, or of any Quarry of which he is not rightful Huntsman, which is that Quarry that is to him Father, Brother, and Son, that Blood shall be to him Poison, and accursed. His Fellows shall not rest until he is Dead, and left to lie Unburied and

Unmourned; and none among them shall speak his Name again, or do aught but dishonour to his memory.

From *La trône terrestre* (probably 18th century, but written in an antique style)

MANCHESTER
5 DEC 1849

Dearest Kit,

Well, barely the 5th. I'm exhausted. I remember how casually I swore to pursue James in his next nocturnal outing—never again! Or at least, I'll think longer next time. One might as well try the same thing with a cat. And he, the devil, had the temerity to laugh at me.

But he *can* laugh, intermittently. That's a good sign, and a great advance. Toward what, I cannot begin to say, but it must be better than the person I've been travelling with for a week. (Only a week?) That person was a collection of fragments held into man-shape by an outer shell that, depending on the moment, might be unmarked and brittle as glass or itself in a state of suspended collapse. A creature like that fears laughter; it will break if it laughs. James seems to an equal degree better and worse than he was. Does that make sense? No, I expect not, but I assure you, it's encouraging and horrifying at once. The more I know *of* James, the less I know him. I wish I could tell what, exactly, he's doing. Other than wearing me out, that is.

But, Kitty—only a week? Dear heaven, how can I have had what seems to me an entire life—joy and suffering, terror, laughter, anger, exhilaration, melancholy, and more of any of them than I ever had before this—in one week? How could I survive such a life for an entire month; and having tasted it, how can I survive in the old one? Do you remember, we used to long to cut our hair, dress in boy's clothes, and run off to the gipsies? Irresponsible, we were told, and dangerous. No, the real danger is that running away to the gipsies is fairy food. Had we done it, neither of us would have thought of coming back.

I don't know what time James came downstairs yesterday,
but after luncheon I passed the door of Engels's study and
found it half-open. Inside, at the desk, was James. There were
several newspapers open before him, and a few more scattered
on the floor around his chair. Both his elbows were on the
desk; one hand cupped his forehead as if holding his head up
was too much work for his neck alone. The other held a pen,
the dry end of which was between his teeth. Immediately in
front of him lay a sheet of foolscap half-covered with what I
could recognize even from the door as his handwriting, close-
spaced and black and leaning like a hound on a leash. As I
watched, he dipped the pen and made more notes, and with a
muttered word, snatched another journal from the bottom of
the drift of paper on the desk. To do it, he had to use the hand
his head had rested on. As soon as he took it away, his hair
fell in his eyes, and I realized that that was what the hand had
really been doing.

I think he genuinely did not know I was there. The corridor
was in shadow, it's true, and the door was only half-open. But
the eyes in the back of his head are the least of James's defences against prying cousins. And oh, Kitty, it was prying. I
knew, as I watched, that I would be unwelcome; whatever he
was doing had nothing to do with me, with my obsessions, my
demands on him. But I have so rarely had the chance to observe him and not be observed in turn. After many minutes
(my left foot was going numb), he set down his pen and laid
both hands over his face as if it ached; as if it threatened to
come loose from the bones beneath and needed to be pressed
back in place. In that relatively safe moment, I fled to the
kitchen and helped the cook peel oranges until the sympathetic
chaos in my mind and stomach had receded, leaving behind a
dull headache and a persistent melancholy.

How long has it been since you have seen your step-brother?
Four months? One-third of a year? I wonder if you would
recognize him on your doorstep at this moment. I told you a
month ago that he was changed. It's true, inside and out, it's
true. I have called him beautiful, and he is; but it is a harsh
beauty now, battered away to the underlying stone—all that's
left behind by the blaze inside him. Engels is right in saying
that he has come close to destroying himself. To say that he

hasn't been using his brain is not quite accurate. I began to understand that as I watched, and as I thought back over the past week. The mind works: driving, desperate. It works because the heart cries out for it, for help, for solace, for release. The energy gathers, lit white as phosphorus burning—and something fails. There is no solace, no solution, no answer, and the energy turns inward and consumes. He is a sealed chamber, in which the process of combustion can continue only for so long as there is oxygen and fuel. And so he turns to action—not to heal himself, but only to stop it, to silence the mind and the heart, in the hope that the oxygen will last a little longer.

I've become unintelligible, I'm afraid. I do think I almost understand it, but I really can't put it into words that don't sound like a spiritualist talking about ectoplasm. Is there some absolute balance of mind, heart, body, and spirit that the organism longs for, and will tear itself apart for lack of? You accused me, once, of neglecting my soul. If I have been doing to myself what James has done, I see why you felt you had to speak.

Later, of course, I slipped into the study to see if there was anything to be learned from the journals James had strewn about. They were gone, along with the sheet of foolscap. The study was as inhumanly tidy as Engels always leaves it.

Dinner was pleasant and civil and wildly frustrating to both Engels and me. James was clearly making conversation with an effort, and would slide out of any serious discussion with the desperate graceless speed of a man ducking a sword-thrust. We had the discussions anyway in the end, by unspoken agreement, hoping that he might rise to one in spite of himself, but it was a vain hope.

Oh, but just before dinner, the strangest thing, and of a sort I never thought to hear in this house! I had dressed for dinner and was in the upstairs passageway at the head of the stairs when I noticed James's door was open. No, that's not precisely what happened. Since fleeing the corridor outside Engels's study earlier in the day, I had been fishing for James, as if to make up for whatever opportunity I might have missed by turning chicken-hearted then. I had made any number of apparently casual passes near his door; if there was no one in sight I'd even put my ear to the panels, hoping for any sound at all. Yes, it has been a shocking day for listening at doors. I'd given it up at last and changed for dinner, and come out to find the silent, frustrating door partly open. I very nearly flew down the hall to it, limited only by the need for silence.

When I peeped around the doorframe I was so startled I nearly made a noise, for only a few steps inside the door was Mary Burns, her back to me. She was watching James, who sat in a chair before the fire, his hands over his face, his shoulders racked with his breathing, as if he'd been running.

"You were dreaming," Mary said, her voice flat and ungentle. "Tell me what it was."

His head came up with a snap, but he looked into the fire, not at her. "Why?" he said at last.

"Tell me your dream. It can't hurt you."

"I don't remember it."

"Yes, you do. Tell me."

After a long pause, during which he didn't move at all, he said slowly, as if he were waiting for words and phrases to form in his mouth, "I was . . . sinking face-first in mud. And I sank down until it seemed that I was under the earth. My head was off my shoulders, and I was carrying it in my hands before me, face down. It got steadily less heavy as I went down and down through the earth, until it might have been made of paper, it was so light."

His voice was roughened, I thought, with sleep, and with reluctance to tell what he remembered. I wondered why he told it; heaven knows he's perfectly capable of refusing. Mary made no comment.

He continued, "After I'd gone down for a long time, I was . . . I came into a little stone room, where there were perhaps half-a-dozen women. Their faces were painted with mud, and streaked with black mud or paint, with black around their eyes. They turned to look at me when I entered, as if to ask why I was there, and what did I want? They seemed impatient, and I was . . . I wanted to apologise." He laughed a little at that, a burst of air without voice. "I didn't know why I was there, or what I wanted, or why I was carrying my head instead of wearing it. Then they were gone, and I saw an eggshell, that had been cracked opened and emptied and filled with water. And there was a bit of milkweed, of fluff.''

"Floating in the water, in the shell?" asked Mary.

"No . . . not floating, or . . . having anything to do with the eggshell, it was just there. And then I was coming back to . . . to above the earth, and my head was heavier and heavier in my hands until I woke and my head was back on my neck and all the weight of it hung on my spine like a stone.''

Mary walked to the fire and stood in front of it, which forced James to look at her. Then, hard-faced, she said, ''The egg means life, and rebirth. Healing, sometimes. The water's a journey. The milkweed's journeying, too, but between this and the other world.''

"Am I going to lose my head at the end of it?" he asked. He was smiling a little, but it was an insubstantial thing.

"Your head weighed the less, the less worth it had. On this journey, it may be that your brains and your cleverness are no good to you.''

"Christ, don't let Engels hear you say that," he laughed, brittle as ice. Then he added in a very different voice, "They're all I have.''

"Then I suppose you'll make do. It was only a dream, after all.'' She turned away from the fire, and I drew back into the passage out of sight. But I heard her say to him at the door, "Or it may be that your grand wits won't be the burden to you they are now.''

If there was any answer forthcoming to *that* comment, I didn't hear it, being halfway down the stairs. But she came to me in the parlour shortly after I entered it, and took me aside to the little bay window. Neither Engels nor James had come downstairs yet. "How much did you hear of that?" she asked.

I think I blushed. "I'm sorry. From when you asked him to tell you what he'd dreamt. I shouldn't have stayed.''

"I think it's a very good thing that you did. Whatever it does to him, the knowledge will do you no harm.''

I laced my fingers together and stared at them. "You don't like him, do you?"

She was silent for a moment. "It's not so easy as that. I like him very well, most times. We disagree on a thing or two, and we've fought over those, honest quarrels in the free air.

But I've seen him like this once before, though not so bad as he is now. When he's like this, I think I've let a barrel of gunpowder into the house, and I'm afraid. Do you wonder that I'd want to know what's happening in that black head?''

"So you ask him about his dreams?''

This time Mary was quiet for long enough that I looked up at her, and met her eyes, because she was busy studying me. "You think, may be, there's nothing to them?'' Then she frowned. "You didn't know that he has them.''

"Everyone dreams.''

"When they sleep.'' ·

I wanted to say, Yes, of course when they sleep, until I realized, nearly, what she was trying to tell me. "But James was—''

"'Your cousin was not asleep. It's why I went in.''

That, of course, was when Engels came into the parlour and brought the conversation to a close. Engels, you will be sorry to hear, my dear, is not the sort of person who will countenance even the idea of visions, outside of the sort one might have during a high fever. And I confess, neither am I. James, as you're probably aware, would find the whole notion revolting. So what was he doing, however reluctantly, providing Mary with a detailed recounting of one? Mary must have been mistaken; he must have been asleep. For however worn down he is, he is not feverish. If it was not sleep or fever, I would have to fear for his reason, and that, on top of everything else, is more fear than I can give house-room to now.

After dinner, as I said—or nearly said—when I began this letter, I lay in wait for James to leave the house, and followed him when he did. I could tell you the names of all the streets and lanes, which I memorized, terrified of losing my unwitting Virgil and finding myself astray in the back quarters of Manchester with no idea how to get home. I could tell you, but you wouldn't know them. I couldn't tell you the names of the passageways less than lanes, all of which James seemed to know like the fingers of his hand, dark or lit. He had no compunction about slipping through unfastened gates, or even vaulting the occasional fence (it was after the second that I realized I was, for all practical purposes, following a cat, and had only myself to blame if it was a trying experience). I was sorry I hadn't found myself a new suit of man's clothes.

It was a tour, not all-inclusive, but a fair sampling, of brick-yards, mill-sheds, streets of labourers' lodgings, and places where men go who have no lodging, the waste places where, if one keeps to oneself, there's room for a bit of a fire built from stolen coal and salvaged wood, and the constables turn a blind eye. Now I was able to add frustration to the list of grievances I had against James, right after exhaustion, because none of the places where he stopped offered a spot for me to hide within earshot.

Kitty, this is a difficult business to describe in order. I was much too busy, while following him from Engels's house, to notice any change in James, but I think now there must have been one, gradual or sudden. Because when he stepped into the light of the fire the men had built on the brickyard's edge, he was no longer the constrained, contained, leashed, and driven animal I'd had dinner with. Shoulders straight and free, cap rakish on the rumpled hair, the half-grin on his face that of a man who knew a very good joke and was prepared to share it—and the inner fire turned to light at last, so that the brickyard seemed perceptibly brighter where he was. It made my spine prickle. Something, for a little while, had freed the James Cobham that Engels had described to me. You could warm your hands at him. The three men around the fire were on their feet, in alarm at first, I think. Then I saw their faces change. Two of them recognized the newcomer; one didn't. James sat on his heels at the fire for probably half an hour—well, he began on his heels.

He always began on his heels, at each stop. Always that sensitivity to the dominance of height, embodied in the immediate rejection of dominance. After that, I suppose it depended on the course of the conversation. Sometimes he knelt, or sprang to his feet, or bent, hands on knees, and sometimes crouched in a tripod of left foot, right knee, and the toe of his right boot. Once, laughing, he fell over backward, and was good-naturedly pulled upright and dusted off by the nearest of the company. His hands flew as he talked, drawing punctuation, emphasis, counterpoint in the cold night air. Once the drawing was actual; a stick scratching throught the cinders in the lane behind a woolen-mill, ending with a gesture and a wry face that made the men gathered around him laugh. The mobility of his face—I watched in a kind of wonder, Kitty. I'd never seen this man in a drawing-room, and had seen only his shadow in the last week, barely visible through suffering and endurance and fear.

And he listened as well, leaning forward, the whole of that invisible light focused on the men who spoke to him. I could see them expanding under it, unfolding before him their own best and strongest selves. Can you imagine how wild it made me, to be able to see all this and not hear a word?

Sometimes a flask would go around the circle. James never refused it the first time, but often passed it by on the second. Sometimes food would appear from somewhere, and that, too, James took sparingly. I was startled at first, thinking how close some of these men must live to poverty; but one does honour to hospitality, however easy or hard it may be to provide. Which reminds me: did you have any idea your step-brother can crack walnuts between his thumb and forefinger? Either hand, dear.

There's no light without heat, of course. I was witness to three quarrels in the course of the night, two of them strictly verbal (one set James to pacing the rough ground furiously, like Engels; the other made him grab the cap off his head and hurl it to the pavement), and one that required my delicate-seeming cousin to physically subdue a hostile man at least half again his weight, in a company that for the most part seemed not to have decided if it were hostile or not. That one may have been precipitated by James not drinking when the flask came by a second time. A voice was raised; then the big man stood and reached for James, who had not moved from his accordion-folded crouch. In a move too quick and unexpected for me to follow, James swept the big man's legs out from under him. By the time he rose again and charged, James was on his feet; he side-stepped the lunge and brought his elbow down hard at the base of his opponent's skull. Two more such passes and the man stayed down, though I think James took one blow at least in the course of the fight. (I saw bullfights in Barcelona, when Grandmama and I were there. This lacked the cape and the blood, but was otherwise very like.) Then James was blazingly angry at the whole gathering, white-faced with fury. When James is blazingly angry, his voice is quite soft, as I've already observed. I couldn't catch a word of the tirade.

The third quarrel, the verbal one with the cap, took place at the back door of a weaving-shed. It ended, from what I could tell, in a draw and wary politeness, and James strode away up the dark lane, coat-hem swinging. I slipped from my hiding place and followed, and found, at the end of the lane, that I had lost my Virgil. I stood consumed with a sinking panic. Then the voice I'd been unable to hear all night said behind me, "I hope you're finding this entertaining."

He was leaning in a doorway in the dark. I could barely see him, shadow on shadow, until he stepped out where the lamps could touch him.

The breath had been frightened out of me. When I could, I said, "How long have you known I was there?"

"For about five minutes. How did you get there?"

"I followed you from the house."

I watched him run the course, in memory, between there and where we stood. "God damn it," he said precisely. There was a phantom scent of alcohol on the air, but he was not visibly the worse for drink. "Does most of your acquaintance underestimate you on a regular basis, or am I the only bloody fool you know?"

He was angry—at the man he'd just left, at me, at himself. And he was still that brilliant, glorious, lit-from-within James. It was all I could do to keep from staring in open-mouthed admiration. "Oh, most of them do it," I replied, trying not to squeak. "Do you think this is wise?"

"Are you sure you want to bring up wisdom, given your present circumstances? Do I think *what* is wise?"

"Wandering the streets at night when there are people who want to do you harm who might know where to find you."

"No, it's not. That's why, when I'm alone, I try to keep moving, and when I stop I do it in public." He caught my face between his two cold hands and glared into my eyes. "And why I *didn't bring you.*"

"Hah," I said, paralysed. "It never occurred to you."

"Why in hell would it?"

"So that I could keep watch at your back. Which I have done all night." I had, too.

He stood with his hands bracketing my face, his own blank at first. Then he seemed to see me again. "No," he said at last. "I don't want you to do that."

"Someone ought to."

"Probably. But not you." He dropped his hands suddenly. "I have one more stop I meant to make. I can't think of anything to do but bring you along."

"I can behave in company." I could feel the wind on my cheek now. "Lead on, Virgil."

His lips twitched and pulled into a smile. "Remember, you asked for it. All right, Cousin." He stepped back and shook his hair off his forehead and laughed. "Follow if you dare, and turn it all into verse later. We've been standing still much too long."

If James Cobham requires a personal motto—how does one say "Never stand still" in Latin?

Clambering over walls and slipping through unfastened gates was at first only a different kind of trying when done with James's knowledge and support. I am convinced we didn't need to do it, or didn't need to to the extent that we did. He may have minded not having been a witness to my efforts earlier in the evening, and wanted to make it up to himself. But after a very little while, it was as if I had caught a spark from the fire in him. After that, I was out of breath as much from laughter as from exertion.

If anyone spotted us that night, besides the man we went to visit, it was only for seconds at a time. The rules of the game, I discovered, were to see as much as possible without ever being seen ourselves. And strictly within those rules, the series of challenges and obstacles became a guided tour: the fifteenth-century Cathedral, Chetham's Hospital, the shining dark river with its soldierly rank of bridges. He displayed them with a grin, with proprietary satisfaction, and without a single word. Equally silent, I took them all in with delight.

At last the game finished, as it had begun, without discussion or the crossing of boundaries. We had come past the new railway terminal, into a street of squat, crowded row-houses, a few of which still showed a light. With a curious half-smile,

James tucked my arm through his and drew breath as if to speak. He must have changed his mind; he only stood looking at me. We are not so different in height. The heat of him penetrated his coat and my sleeve. My heart-beat was quick with the last half-hour's progress, and now didn't seem as if it would ever slow down. He shivered, and laughed suddenly, and laid his hand over mine where it rested on his arm.

"Thank you, Miss Voight, for the dance. It was lovely."

"Thank *you*, Mr Cobham." I was laughing, too. "It's considered unfashionable to dance with your relatives, you know."

"Is it?"

"It makes you look as if you can't get any other partners."

"What if I don't want any?"

My overactive heart was lodged in my throat. I managed to say past it, "Then I hope you don't mind being thought dreadfully out of fashion." It sounded too solemn in my ears.

We crossed the street and entered a narrow space between buildings that led to an even narrower space behind the rowhouses. There was a wooden stair there that gave access to the whole second floor. James took the steps two at a time; he had been here before.

The door he knocked at was opened, slightly, by a boy of perhaps ten, who regarded us both with grave suspicion.

James blinked at him. "Heaven and earth, but you've got to be Harry. You won't remember me, but I knew you when you had the biggest black eye of any creature in Manchester."

The pale young face screwed itself up over that, then cleared. "Jimmy?" the boy breathed.

"You do remember! Harry Holland, I'd like to make you known to my cousin, Miss Voight."

I put my hand out promptly, and he shook it, as if such a thing had never come his way before. "Pleased to make your acquaintance," I told him.

"Is your da to home?" James asked. As he did, a man's voice was raised warily on the other side of the door.

"Harry! Who is it?"

The boy disappeared behind the door. "Dad, it's Jimmy!"

The silence was profound. We heard three heavy steps in the hall, and the door was flung open. Framed in it was a man who might have been built on an armature of wire, and given flesh by an ungenerous hand. The bones of his face were massive and unpadded; his neck and hands seemed made of twists of cable, and his shoulders and arms were beams and knobs of muscle and bone under his shirt. He stared at us—at James.

"Hullo, George. Did I wake you?" said James, his voice ludicrously normal on the cold air.

For answer, George Holland reached out, grabbed James by a twist of his lapel, and dragged him inside. I would have been alarmed, except that Harry was smiling hugely as he shut the door behind me. And somewhere down the dark passage before me, I heard James laugh.

By the time I'd followed Harry to the kitchen, James had been thrust into the only chair with a back. The kitchen was grindingly bare and scrupulously clean, and lit with a pair of tallow candles on the table. A slate lay beside the candles, with what looked like a lesson half-done on it. Holland snatched the cap off James's head and flung it on a peg at the door. Then he dropped onto a bench and stared at James. "By God," he said. "By God."

"George Holland," James said cautiously, "my cousin, Miss Voight."

Holland leaped to his feet in alarm. "Sorry! Sorry. I saw you there, but I didn't see you, if you take my—I'm that amazed, is all—pleased to meet you, miss."

"It's all right," I said, and perched on a stool. "He has this effect on everyone, you know."

"I do not," James muttered.

"Harry, fetch Jimmy and his cousin a glass of beer."

James gave a quick shake of his head. "Actually, I don't need a—"

"I do," I interrupted. "Thank you, Mr Holland, Harry, I'd love a glass of beer." Young Harry beamed at me and scurried off.

In the moment of silence that followed, James said, "I heard about Mag. I'm sorry."

Holland looked at his hands. "She didn't linger. And the Association got her up a grand funeral."

"I heard that, too. I was in Ireland. By the time word reached me, it was over."

"You wouldn't have come?"

"Of course I would have. Why not?"

"The town was a little hot for you just then, boy."

James shrugged.

"Well, it's a fact, you're here now, aren't you?" said Holland with satisfaction. Harry reappeared with beer, handed me mine reverently, and retired to the corner of the hearth, where he watched James and me as if we were dinner and he meant to eat with his eyes.

James tilted his head to one side. "Should I not be?"

Holland frowned. "You don't know? You're a wanted man."

"Am I? What charge?"

"For questioning, in the matter of the death of a naval officer in Newport."

"Ah."

"Were you put up?"

"More or less. I didn't do it, if that's what you're asking. But I was there, which makes someone awfully damned happy." He swallowed some of his beer. "Good lot. George, what's behind these rumours of a dust-up to come off later this month?"

"I don't know. I'd think you would."

"If you don't? Why would you think that?"

"How many times have I gotten the word from you, by God? And if I have it from you, it's square right enough, and I'm not the only man in this town knows it."

"Well, thank you. But no, this one comes up blank. I don't like it. I don't know who's behind it, or what it's to be, or why. Nobody raises a row just because someone tells him to."

Holland looked thoughtful. "There's the business about the bank."

"Rochdale? Ugly mess and no mistake. But that's not riot-fodder, only a hard lesson. My God, as well lay the chicken in the fox's mouth and say, 'Take care of this for me,' as trust a rich man with your money. Besides, the rumour's gone round in Newport, as well."

"Who do you give your money to, then?" Holland asked.

"The working men need their own banks. Organized by the

trade unions, maybe." James smiled suddenly. "You've heard me say this before."

"Aye, I have: the workers won't get a fair living out of the mill until they own the mill."

"That would be it," James agreed, the smile wider.

"So your advice is, if there's a holiday called, or a meeting, or whatever it is, don't do it."

"Who am I to tell you what to do? Just be careful about it, that's all. Know who's calling it at least, and even then think long and hard." James's glass was empty. Harry darted forward for it, and James laid his palm over the top and smiled, and shook his head. "No, thank you, young Holland. I have to go."

"Have you got a place to put up? You and your cousin are welcome to set down here."

"We're fixed. But thank you."

"How do I get a word to you, if I need to?"

I emptied my glass and handed it to Harry with a smile. He looked ready to expire with joy.

James shook his head. "If the blue-bottles want to ask me hard questions, it's better you not know. But why would you need to?"

George Holland's scowl was a wonderful thing; it should have been frightening. Instead it gave his heavy face a kind of grace and dignity that would have moved Thomas Cavanaugh to grab for his charcoal. "Jimmy, we're all still here. Sometimes it seems as if the old men have forgotten that, that there's men and women on the spinning-floor and at the brick-moulds who want their work and their wage, and something for their kids better than picking lint and starving. It's come apart here, but it's not fallen. We could use you, Jimmy."

James sat still at the table, his hands laid one over the other on its surface. His eyes were on Holland. "No, George." Holland opened his mouth to speak, and James repeated, "No. You can't give the chicken to the fox to tend. I was born in a house with its own bloody *name*. I'm a member of that class that gives their last year's clothes to their servants and thinks they've fulfilled their duty to their fellow man. I grew up eating food bought with the labour of men and women my father—'' It was a momentary stop, but I heard it, ''—claimed to own.''

Holland picked up the empty glass from in front of James and looked into it. ''We're not good enough for you?'' he asked, his eyebrows halfway up his massive forehead.

James, alarmingly, burst into constricted laughter. ''Well, you damned well couldn't fit into my cast-off coats, man. Try again.''

''No, I won't,'' said Holland mildly. ''I can't see the use of it. You'll get out of this way of thinking or not, and I'm not the man to help you do it. I'll tell you, though. A rich man can see waste and not hate it like a poor man does. I hate waste like the devil, Jimmy.''

James took a great straining breath and let it out. ''I have to go.'' He stood, and Holland did likewise.

''Come back when you can. You're always welcome here. Miss Voight, I hope we'll meet again.'' He thrust out one of his knotted-wire hands, and I shook it.

''I hope so, too,'' I said.

The trip back to Engels's house was not a game, and James, though pleasant, was the sealed and secret person I'd grown used to, then had had driven out of my head, and now passionately resent. We now had to avoid the constables—the ''blue-bottles''—in earnest. That did not explain the extinguishing of the light. The conversation with George Holland did. At least, it must have explained it to James. We had reached the bottom of Engels' garden when I got up my nerve. I caught up with James by the apple tree and grabbed his arm.

No use for a preamble. ''You're being ridiculous.''

He stopped dead in the dark. ''I am?''

''All right, not ridiculous, perhaps. But unreasonable. Illogical.''

''Why?''

''Do you believe that one's station matters?''

He was silent for a moment, because he knew now what I was talking about. ''I believe it shouldn't.''

''In other words, you believe that the class you were born into makes you different from Holland. Or Engels, who's been in the middle class all his life.''

''Susan . . . Engels thought I'd fall in with the lot who think you can engineer a nice revolution and fit the working class into it like cattle into a pen. *Au contraire*, as it happens. I have no desire to become another Bronterre O'Brien, sitting in London coffeehouses fulminating over who's plotting to do him the next bit of personal damage, telling anyone who'll listen how if *he'd* only been given the running of the thing, the working man would be living in paradise now, and never so much as *seeing* a working man from one week to the next if he can help it. He'll sell the workers out to the middle class every chance he gets, because he honestly thinks the only thing that will better a man is aspiring to the next class up. With an example like that before them, what sensible poor man is going to trust me if I stand up and offer to lead him out of slavery? How long before somebody says, 'And tell us, Mr Cobham, by what means *did* you grow rich?' "

In the silence that fell after that, I could hear the wind hissing in the branches over us, and down the street, the sudden surprised bark of a dog. "You've been wanting to say that to someone for a long time, haven't you?"

James made a disgusted noise and started toward the house.

"It's not true anymore!" I called after him.

He continued to walk, unhurried.

"It never made any sense, you idiot, but now it's not even true. You haven't got a penny of your own. You've got less than George Holland does. You're an impostor. You're *not Andrew Cobham's son.*"

He'd reached the French doors into the dining room by then, the ones first he, then I, had left unlocked behind us when we'd slipped out. He stopped on the step.

"Christ Jesus!" he said furiously, in Seamus Palmer's accent.

When I reached the doors, he was gone; when I reached the foot of the stairs he wasn't in sight there, either. I could not even tell if he was in the house. I went upstairs in a venom-spitting rage, with absolutely nothing to vent it on except letter-writing.

Enough. Good morning. I *hate* your step-brother.

All my love,
Susan

MANCHESTER
5 DEC 1849

Kitty Dearest,

Gracious, your special messenger stopped three beating hearts in Manchester this evening, and the only reason there weren't four was because Engels had an appointment that kept him out until after dinner. But there we were, arrested in mid-thought, and each one of us for entirely different reasons, I'll wager. Well, we all thought *someone* had died, but I expect it was three different someones.

On the contrary: it would seem I am an aunt. I don't know what to make of the idea of—what did Gideon Johnson say her blasted name was?—Eleanor Tournier as my good-sister. No, I do, actually. I think it's revolting. Helen, you realize, is one of the canonical diminutives for Eleanor. Helen, of the masks and poker. I was going to ask what could David have been thinking, but of course, he wasn't. Gracious again, how did *Aunt Louisa* get hold of this piece of news?

I am perfectly willing to subscribe to the notion that Tournier wants his sister's child to have Cauldhurst. But he would have to do it, quite literally, over Richard's dead body. I, at least, am delighted that Richard is playing least in sight, however much you may complain of cold bed-sheets.

Talking of Richard, what a trump! I would never have thought it of him. Whatever became of my indolent, detached, conventionally rakish cousin? I don't miss him at all, if he has been replaced by this fellow who winkles secrets out of steamship crews. The boys at this end and I will worry Leuchtenberg and see what comes of it. Bavaria, dear! This has to be our hinge-pin.

So I don't object to your alarming special messenger; I see entirely why you thought all this should reach us quickly. In fact, I may see more than you thought I would, but if you believe it's better not to tell me, I shall respect your decision. (But if you were confronted with David's ghastly spectre in the gloom of the study, pointing a bony, threatening finger and letting forth an uncanny shriek, and aren't saying so, I'm giving you up entirely. If you'll remember, I *adored* "The Tell-Tale Heart". On the other hand, I doubt even a spectral David could manage to have bony fingers. So perhaps I've read too much into your special messenger after all, and am only judging your fright by the one you gave me.)

How can you say that James is asking all the right questions, or that I am? We can't know until all the answers have been given, to the questions we ask, and the ones we never think of. I have heard so many questions in the last week that I have quite lost track, and toss and turn in my bed wondering which ones I've overlooked, and which will be the one that, could I have elicited the answer, would have averted disaster. By day I know we'll all get out of this scrape unharmed, if somewhat changed. By night, when my spirits are at low ebb, the future seems like a forest on fire beyond a range of hills, the air threaded with smoke, brightness rimming the horizon and reflecting off the clouds. No, I'm not having visions as well. Only doubts and reservations of a thoroughly earthly kind.

As my previous reference to visions cannot have reached you by the time you wrote this letter, I have to admit that I'm not sure what you mean about invoking things. I haven't noticed James invoking anything, unless you're saying that, in times of stress, he forgets his atheistic principles and swears like a Christian. That, I had noticed. I think it's amusing. For blasphemy, there is nothing like one's childhood gods. It occurs to me to wonder: do I believe in any god, or even positively *not* believe, as James does? I believe in systems and methods. I believe in the beauties of philosophy and poetry. I believe that the work we do and leave behind us is our afterlife; and I believe that history lies, but sometimes so well that I can't bring myself to resent it. I believe that truth is beauty, but not, I'm afraid, the reverse. It doesn't seem sufficient to sustain one in life's rigourous moments, does it? Perhaps I shall embrace Islam. Its standards for poetry seem very high.

Do you suppose I have already changed more than I had noticed? *Would* I have objected, once, to you urging me to indulge in a therapeutic act of physical intercourse? Well, I *have* resented being asked to hang my emotional linen in public, I recall, and if that's what you're talking about when you envision me thin-lipped and angry, then I suppose I'm the same old badgerish Susan you remember and love. But do you really think losing my virtue to James would do anything but complicate matters? I know it would addle my brains for weeks or even months, and heaven knows how it would affect my subsequent dealings with James. And can you imagine your step-brother deflowering his cousin without a certain quantity of complex and conflicting aftermath of feeling? I would be shocked if he didn't. Were I already an experienced woman, we might bring each other some measure of comfort; but virginity has such a dreadful load of emotional baggage attached! It's why Engels asked if we were *already* lovers, I think. .

Heavens, what a paragraph. For a virgin, I am very well read. And I look forward to learning, one day, what things you've felt you *couldn't* discuss with me yet, given the inclusive nature of what you felt you *could*. I have never, never understood why the purity of womanhood should have to be defended by sending a girl ignorant, superstitious, and terrified to her marriage-bed. I thought they *wanted* us to procreate; shouldn't they be fostering desire, instead of stamping it out?

I am very sorry about your gown, dear. I realize that sentiment is irreplaceable, but I am sure that if your dressmaker will copy the old gown, Richard, when he comes home, will help you christen the new one.

James was also impressed with Richard's news from shipboard; I let him read the copy of Richard's letter, while busily passing yours along in summary as I read it. "Impressed" may be the wrong word. He was moved in some way, as evidenced by the immobility of his face while he read, and the time he took over it. I wonder if James will ever completely abandon that impulse toward secrecy—if the time will ever come when he will no longer need it. His face was quite mobile over your mention of a constable "of some sort" at Cauldhurst, however; I had to read that part to him verbatim, and still he looked dissatisfied. "I'd have you tell her to keep away from Cauldhurst," he said at last, "if I weren't sure she knows she ought to. And knew she ought to when she went." The All-Wise has spoken, dear. *Did* you know? Perhaps it's his not-very-flattering way of saying that you were aware of the risks and judged them acceptable. I'm sure that brotherhood, when done properly, is a taxing set of duties.

Your letter arrived in the evening, when we were about to go in to dinner. By that time James and I were on an amicable footing again, and had been since breakfast. (And have been through the present moment; I didn't mean you to think that we've quarrelled again since.) The only reason I was downstairs in time for a meal that could be called breakfast was because I woke at nine o'clock and couldn't fall asleep again. I was somewhat stiff from running and climbing, I'm sorry to admit. So imagine my groggy amazement (not yet alleviated by coffee) when your step-brother sat down across from me at the breakfast table. Very nicely dressed, of course, and precisely shaved, and looking as if he'd slept a bit less than I had.

"I want to apologise for last night," he said gravely.

Sometimes the brain rallies, in spite of a shortage of sleep and coffee. "Which part?" I asked.

He stared, then gave me the smile that's not for casual use. "Well, not any of the good ones."

"I suppose you're thinking of the argument in the garden. You needn't apologize for that. You got the last word only on a technicality, you know."

"You don't mind them, as long as you win?"

"Of course not. Do you?"

"I'm more broad-minded. I don't even mind if I lose. Or I don't always mind, anyway. I was responsible for starting this conversation, wasn't I? Should I ring for more coffee?"

"No, I've barely started on this pot. I can probably spare you as much as half a cup."

"Please?" he said humbly, and I laughed and poured.

"Actually," he continued after drinking a little (black, of course, as I hadn't asked for cream), "you were ahead on points, but I stopped the discussion part-way. Surely that requires an apology?"

"If you want anything more substantial for breakfast, you had better ring for it. Does this mean you want to take up where we left off?"

"No," he said slowly. "Do I get the choice?"

"Yes, of course. I don't *think* I've sunk to forcing you to do things for your own good."

He met my eyes, unsmiling and curiously intent. Something scampered across the pit of my stomach and up my spine. But he only stole one of the currant buns off my plate and said, "Has the mouthpiece of reaction entered the house yet today? Probably carried in gingerly with the fire tongs?"

"*The Times*? I'm using it for a chair-cushion." I wasn't; it was on the seat of the chair next to me. I handed it across the table. "Do you read it?"

"Faithfully. On the principle of knowing the enemy. Besides, there have been days when one out of twenty of the advertisements were in code."

I stared, my cup halfway between the saucer and my lips. "Not really."

"Well, not one in twenty. But you can't imagine the satisfaction of announcing the arrival of a crate of rifles on the front page of *The Times*, particularly if you can disguise it as an offering of railway shares."

"And here I always assumed the secret messages were hidden in the letters."

"No, no. The letters to *The Times* are sacred. The patient's pulse is a useful diagnostic and ought not to be tampered with."

As he spoke, he was, in fact, scanning the mosaic of the first page with a practiced eye. I turned my attention to buttering another roll and reading the Salford paper desultorily. I wanted to watch him, but I knew he wouldn't let me do it, or wouldn't provide me with anything to see if he *did* let me. A noise made me look up.

It was the sound of James choking on his coffee. "My God," I said, half out of my chair, "are you all right?"

He couldn't quite speak, but he nodded; and when he shifted his napkin from his nose and mouth to his streaming eyes I could see that the cause of the mishap had been laughter. I dealt with my curiosity by snatching *The Times* away from him. The article head caught my eye immediately, since it was THE CHARTISTS IN NEWGATE. So I read it.

"The Psalms of David in verse," James gasped, still hidden behind his napkin. "I am trumped. They ought to hang the canting bastard. They would, if they had the least idea."

"I believe I've missed the context," I said, laying the paper down.

"No, you've got the whole thing. Almost." He emerged recovered and grinning. "If you're reading with your proper *Times* filter in place, anyway. Mind Alderman Sidney's comments, since even though he won't stand up to anyone for long, he's in the right of it here."

"Why, inherent absurdity aside, does the mention of turning the Psalms of David into verse prevent you from swallowing?"

"When I wrote to Shaw and Bezor and said as a last resort, bludgeon the bastards with religion, I had no idea that Bezor had a turn for shameless mummery. Ernest Jones will hurt himself laughing when he hears this."

I looked again at the article. "They weren't allowed letters."

"A thousand material blessings on the Church of England, *mo chridh*. They're allowed tracts, and three-quarters of the printers in Britain are Chartists."

"You wrote a coded letter in the form of a C. of E. religious tract?"

"It was very Low Church."

I opened my mouth twice before I said, "I would commit murder for a copy." Then I heard what I'd said, and added, "No. But I really do wish I could lay hands on it."

"There were only two copies. I'll do my best to see that they both get burned."

"Spoil-sport."

"I'd have to emigrate. I couldn't face you."

"And you're complaining about someone else's facility for shameless mummery?"

"*I* have the grace to be ashamed. *Vide* my unwillingness to let you see the results. Is that really all you're having for breakfast?"

I sighed and folded the Salford paper. "Yes. I *meant* to have another currant bun, but I was forestalled."

"It wouldn't have made a difference. You can't hunt the darkened streets of Manchester like a lioness on the diet of a finch. Come down to the kitchen with me, and you can eat anything I leave behind."

"If you ring like a civilized human being, they'll bring you whatever you want, just to keep you out of their way down-stairs."

He stood up. "I hate keeping out of the way." He turned at the door and raised his eyebrows at me when he saw I hadn't got up. "Oh, I see. Well, bring the coffee-pot with you, if it means that much to you."

I did, too. I had a lovely morning sitting at the scrubbed table in the kitchen with my coffee-pot in front of me, pre-tending to guard it jealously (I growled whenever he reached for it, and made him invent a new diversion I could pretend to be distracted by whenever he wanted a cup). He sat on a stool and teased the cook, who turned red and laughed until she wept, and made him an alarming amount of food. I was induced to take an egg and a slice of ham, after all, and given a currant bun to replace the one I'd been robbed of.

The rest of the day I spent writing letters to all the people I have been neglecting while writing to you. Most of them were masterworks of hypocrisy, of course, but there was one to Thomas Cavanaugh that was candid, if not exhaustive. I felt he ought to be told, at least, that I had not yet come to any lasting harm, and that I had taken his elusive friend James in hand. Remembering the beating he'd got once over his interest in that very friend, I didn't tell him where I was, or for how long, or any of the other details it might have put him at risk to know.

I would have loved to have gone out, to have seen some of this city by day, but I would have risked being seen in return. If I was already associated with James in the minds of either the constables or Tournier's friends, I would have been risking Engels's and Mary's well-being, in addition to James's and my own. So I settled for letters, reading, and a nap. I am not sure how James spent the afternoon, but when he came down-stairs for dinner he seemed subdued and even a little sad.

Hello, I'm back—I wrote all that after dinner and before Engels came home, as you may have guessed by all the dashy endings of words and the squiggly articles. Worst handwriting in the family at the best of times. I broke off then because I knew that, unless someone had an excellent reason for putting it off, we needed to pore over Richard's and your intelligence about Leuchtenberg. So I swept down the stairs not long after

I heard Engels come in the front door (I waited long enough, that is, for Mary to greet him properly; he is hardly ever away from home for dinner, and I could tell that it had weighed on her spirits) and told him that I had news that merited a conference in the study.

"With sherry, I hope," he suggested, smiling.

While I was agreeing to that, James came into the hall. Engels raised his head and ceased to smile; he regarded James over my shoulder, a long, oddly piercing, considering look. James, by the time I'd turned to him, was considering nothing at all away in the middle distances, quite thoroughly distracted.

"In ten minutes, in the study?" Engels said to me, and I agreed.

And so the Manchester branch of the conspiracy gathered again in Friedrich Engels's study to deal with the myriad shining facets of the problem that are proper and particular to it. As it turned out, it was the sort of conversation in which one puts down one's sherry glass and forgets to pick it up again. You say in this latest letter that Engels is mindful of our webs only where they intersect with his, which is quite true; but tonight I learned how many of his knots and crossings are ours as well. This is a very large pattern indeed, Kitty dear, large enough that I wonder how I penetrated so close to the centre of it without quite noticing it was there. I feel as if my veins are full of snow when I think of the individual hopes and happinesses at stake, even, perhaps, a whole slice of the future, hanging in part on what we do now.

Enough dire language. The only way I can think to explain it to you is to recount the debates in the study tonight, and let you live it as I did.

I could not very well show Engels your letter, dear, any more than I could show it to James, and for the same reason. If you don't stop enquiring about the legs of gentlemen you haven't even been *introduced* to, I will have to consider you a bad influence. The Legion of Aunts would concur. (Never mind the encouragement to get myself relieved of my virginity at the earliest available opportunity. You would have made an excellent bacchante, you know. Twine grape leaves through your hair for your next ball.)

So I gave as thorough an accounting as I could of Richard's

gleanings from shipboard in Southampton, the mysterious fair-haired woman's connexion with Alan Tournier, and—most devastating, and oddly difficult to confess to someone outside the family (he was my brother, after all, however reprehensible I may have thought him alive or dead)—her connexion with David. Engels began pacing, as far as I could tell, at the same spot he had two days before.

I finished, "Leuchtenberg is a Bavarian duchy, which means Prussia, which means, throwing coincidence in the dustbin where it belongs, our Prussian gold connexion. But, Engels," I said at last, in a state of high frustration, "what the *devil* would they want out of Parliament?"

"It is difficult," Engels said after several lengths across the carpet, "and also dangerous, to attempt to guess at the precise details of international diplomacy. But we must look at the recent events in Prussia, and consider what Prussia could want of England that England could supply. Prussia was frightened to her old aristocratic bones by the risings last year, and I do not think she has stopped trembling yet." He stopped and looked sharply at James. "Well? What would you think?"

James, sitting straight-backed in the wing chair, lifted his gaze from his hands. "Me?"

"You. If you have not forgotten how it is done. Or would you rather find some more comfortable lodging in which to hide?"

All of my conscious processes and half the unconscious ones, I swear, must have stopped then. My friend Engels, who never trotted when he could gallop, who never mediated when he could confront, had just given James his ultimatum. I wanted to say, *Not now*, and then wondered, If not now, when?

James, to my surprise, did not raise his hackles. "It's all right," he said. "I'll do what I can. Just . . . ask the question again, do you mind? I'm thinking of six things at once and not doing any of them justice."

Engels nodded vigourously. He was pacing again. "Consider what you know of the Prussian ruling class. What do they most fear? What would they most wish from the English Parliament?"

James surprised me again by leaving the wing chair and dropping down cross-legged on the hearth rug. Engels didn't seem surprised at all. Engels, in fact, abruptly changed direction, so that his face was turned from the fire.

"Mm. The Prussian aristocracy don't want their bubble burst. They've assured the world that they've pacified Germany, dominated Italy, bloody well crushed Hungary, and all that's left is a little mopping-up after. You know and I know that the working classes in all three countries see it rather differently. And I think Prussia knows better. They crushed the nationalist movements, but one or two clever boys in Wilhelmstrasse have to have noticed that they've only removed the middle class's device to distract the working class from the matter at hand. They've got the Roman candle put out, temporarily at least. Now Prussia's got to be scared out of their well-polished boots that someone will notice the match sticking out from under the arsenal door. Yes?"

"I see it differently," said Engels, "but yes, you are, I believe, describing what elements in the Prussian ruling class think. In fact, we are now in a period of reaction; the working class is in retreat, and we are forced to regroup and to take the opportunity to catch our breath, prepare ourselves, and educate the working class. I don't think there is a powder keg anywhere that is ready for its train to be set, but Prussia is not without fear, just as you describe. Also, there are strong elements pushing for a liberal constitution, which would be of immense benefit to the middle class and useful to the working class as well."

"You think that might happen?" James said, his attention suddenly acute.

"As with many such things, it might happen, unless it is stopped. I think your clever fellows in Wilhelmstrasse would like to stop it. What, then, is the best way for them to allay their fear? What can they do to allow themselves to breathe easier in the face of what is still a very powerful, if demoralized, working class?"

James smiled wryly. "I'm perpetually hopeful, if unrealistic. Thank you, I suppose I have to admit you're right about the condition of the powder keg. At any rate, the actual question is, how might Prussia reduce that power and increase the demoralization? Or at least, prevent anyone from doing anything to fix it. Censorship's failed them for—well, for as long as they've done it. They've arrested every known revolutionist they could lay their hands on, and exiled most of the rest. Which also hasn't worked, because *they've* all—'' James stopped, wide-eyed, as if shot.

Engels nodded. "Yes. What we might call the 'active' element in history. Or the 'conscious' element. The element that Hegel thought primary, and that Feuerbach dismissed entirely. We put it in its proper place, and find that it is decisive. I suspect Wilhelmstrasse agrees.''

"*Engels.*'' James had, in some flexible fashion, managed to go from sitting cross-legged to kneeling in one motion. "Engels, they couldn't . . . couldn't possibly. Could they? God damn it, if you've already thought of this, why are you so *calm*?''

"Pardon me,'' I said. "I'm sorry to have to admit it, but I'm lost. If one of you would . . .'' I couldn't decide if what I was asking for was that they should go back, or go on, so I let the sentence dissipate.

Engels nodded to me. "England is full of *émigrés* just now—revolutionists exiled from Germany, from France, from Hungary. And many of them, including your host, are busy writing home from her shores. The Prussians are not known for patience. The English capitalists needed the theories of Reverend Malthus before they could justify their Poor Laws, but the Prussians intend to solve their problem with a bit of gold scattered here and there, in order to create some sort of rising among the English working class, or perhaps the Irish, or the Welsh, or all of them. After that, with a few words in the right ears, Parliament can be convinced to pass an act, after which we will all be invited to leave the country, or perhaps allowed to stay if we p-promise not to write or speak to anyone about anything, which I, for one, would find inconvenient.'' He frowned. "America might provide a refuge.''

I was too horrified to speak. Engels and Mary; his friend Marx, and his wife and children; the rest of the lively, argumentative community of German, Italian, French exiles and their families who had made me welcome, let me contribute my mite to the future they meant to build. It was not merely Cobhams and Voights who were to be swept away by the plotting of our enemies.

"It had already occurred to you, hadn't it, that this might happen?" James stood abruptly and stopped Engels's pacing by the simple expedient of standing in front of him. "Hadn't it? Why didn't you *say* something about it?"

Engels looked kindly down at James. "Go sit on the floor. I want your brain, not your legs."

James made a furious noise, turned back to the hearth, and, not content with sitting, dropped down and lay on his back, his knees bent, his hands folded on his stomach, and his gaze on the ceiling. I regarded the whole proceeding and posture with amazement, which was only enlarged when I looked back at Engels and found him beaming upon your incomprehensible step-brother.

"Not Ireland," James said. "You'd have to spend all the money on feeding ten thousand of them until they were strong enough to lift a pike. Mary," he injected, sending a sharpish glance at Engels, "is even more of an unwarranted optimist than I am. And not the Welsh. England hasn't been really afraid of Wales, as a body, for five hundred years. With reason, Newport aside. It has to be England proper, and it has to be this persistent rumour of trouble, doesn't it? Which means they've spent their money, and will have already softened up key members of the Lords and Commons, or will have begun to. If we could trace the gold, we could find the starting-points for the rising, but I don't know that we can do it in time. *Damn* it," he said, pressing his hands over his face, "it literally slipped through my fingers."

Engels gave me a quick look that I might translate as "I told you so", but it might just as well have been childish glee. Then, still pacing, he said, "Yes to all of that, but you are still thinking like a Chartist. You want to find the solution to this problem, and I, too, want to find the solution. But the solution to any problem emerges from our goals. We will parry this thrust—quite legally, by the way—and simultaneously advance our aims. How? And this is not a k-kind of test, by the way; I do, not know the answer myself."

James stared. "*Kirschen*," he said. "You cheated. Advance your own bloody aims." (For all the good it will do you, Kit, I remind you that it means "cherries" in German.) "You're distracting me, you hound. Yes, of course I think like a Chartist; I've been one for ten years. If I knew quite what I was now, I suppose I could think like whatever that is. You're a Communist. What goals do your solutions emerge from?''

"Making the working class conscious of its historic mission. And—as you told me a long time ago, and now I agree—it must re-rely on no one but itself." He shook his head. "But let us go back, just a little. This underlines what I have been saying about the importance of leadership; do you now understand what I am asking you to do? Or, rather, to become?''

James regarded the ceiling as if he meant to reproduce the mouldings. "Yes," he said.

"And will you?"

"Who says the Germans are hard on verbs? What a nice choice of tense that was.''

I found that I had risen from my chair. "I think I should go. You'll both be more comfortable.''

"I have nothing to hide from you," James said in a curious, breathless rush, turning his face to me. It was expressive of mild shock, as if he were disturbed by his own words. Then in a more measured voice, he added, "But—if you'd rather go, it's all right.''

I clasped my hands to keep them still and sat back down. I hadn't the courage to look up for Engels's response to it all.

For some reason, whatever came next seemed to require James to meet Engels's eyes, at least in James's estimation. I saw him try. It's hard, however, to maintain eye contact with someone who is pacing. He said, "I'll ask you a question that *I* don't know the answer to: I'm afraid of the job you're asking me to do. If I think about it, the future starts to look like the sea looks to a man afraid of drowning. There aren't a lot of things that frighten me. Why is this one of them?''

"Because it is frightening.''

"What a comfort you are.''

"I am not a priest, and I thank you for noticing. But the dialectic works here as everywhere else. That which can bring us the greatest joy can also b-bring us the greatest sorrow. That which most exhausts us can fill us with the most vitality.'' Engels came to a sudden halt before the fire and looked down at James, who was nearly at his feet. "And when we take upon ourselves the most profound task of history, we feel g-great exhilaration, and a great fear that we will not, in the end, be sufficient to our task. But that ought not to stop you. That the runner does not know if he will prove the fastest does not keep him from the race; rather, it is exactly why he runs.''

Kitty, nothing in this conversation was predictable, up to this point or after. I should stop telling you I was surprised, and let you assume that I have scrawled invisible question and exclamation marks in the margins. But it would never, never have occurred to me that James at this point would roll over, bury his face in his arms, and laugh himself breathless.

"God *damn* you, Engels," he said at last. "There's only one other man in the world who could do that to me, and I don't think he's on speaking terms with me at the moment."

"Oh, *what*?" I burst out. "What are you talking about?"

"Herr Engels," James said, raising his rather flushed face to me, "has just replied to my confession of weakness with a direct appeal to my strengths. Or to another set of weaknesses, it may be. Very dialectical. You should ask him for a copy of *The Science of Logic*. I imagine he has buckets of them."

"Herr Engels," said Herr Engels, "is, in any case, still waiting for an answer."

"So am I," I said, with heat.

James, his chin propped on his knuckles like a schoolboy, said to me, "I have a sad passion for living on my nerves. For hanging over precipices. I adore it. I have, I think, a submerged dread of being robbed of the opportunity to do it. I have just been promised a lifetime's supply of it. Thank you, Engels. Your answer is yes, may Hegel have mercy on my manifestation of the absolute idea." And he dissolved once again into a fit of stifled, painful laughter, and hid his face.

"Good." Engels set off across the carpet again. "Then we shall begin at the beginning. Our first duty is to our class, yes?"

"No," said James, still hidden. "Bugger our class, our nation, and the horses they rode in on."

Engels stopped in mid-pace and stared down at James. "I beg your pardon?" he said.

James rolled over. "*Is* my first duty to the aristocracy? I hope not. Am I missing something?"

"The aristocracy? M-m-my word. Your class is the working

class, James. Am I imagining things, or have you not committed yourself to it? And did you not just do so again? What difference does it make where you were born? Am I to feel less of an obligation to the proletariat because I came from a middle-class family that allowed me sufficient education to arrive at the conclusion that the future lies with the proletariat? You are not making sense.''

There was a long silence in front of the hearth. ''Oh, dear,'' said James at last. ''I'd wager . . . in fact, if I had to wager, I'd put five pounds on the possibility that you've had to explain that to an Englishman before. You'll notice I deny nationalism and bow, reluctantly, to the possibility of a rough outline of national character. In fact, I'd put *ten* pounds on the possibility that no English *aristocrat* would have thought of the matter differently, thus putting paid to my sweeping statements on *both* class and nation. I owe you one cherry. Now, do I accept the idea that one chooses one's class?''

Engels laughed a little. ''Once more to ontology? Man answered the question about the relationship of his thoughts to Nature well before it occurred to him to ask. Since you made the choice ten years ago, it is probably time for you to accept that one can so choose.''

''Mm. I've spent the last ten years surrounded by people I admire who've done just that.'' James's words were chosen, seemingly, out of a store of reason and a custom of easy debate. But his voice was the one I had heard before, that sounded as if it were underfed by breath. Under the surface of the subject a thing I couldn't glimpse was swimming. ''I know we differ on O'Connor and probably always will, but he did it. Ernest Jones did it, even if his detractors do point out that he lost his fortune first. I think he made his commitment before he lost the money, but that's . . . No, it is relevant. So did I, didn't I? Two cherries. I hope they're out of season. All right, I'm a member of the working class. I can get used to that, too.''

''Good. Then, as I said, our first duty is to our class, correct?''

James's concentration appeared to be on the ceiling again, and wasn't. ''All right. I have just played out several possible scenarios in which my first duty is *not* to my class, and they all end badly. I venture to agree, pending further testing.''

Engels muttered something I didn't catch, in German. Then he said, ''We are in a period of reaction, as I said before. Let us begin by recognizing that. What the working class requires now is time to regroup and prepare for the next round of struggles—and I can safely predict that these will begin in not less than a month nor more than fifty years. As you English say, Nostradamus ain't in it.''

''I, at least, would say nothing of the kind. Facetiousness. I claim forfeit of a cherry.''

''Interruption without advance of discourse. I win it back. So, for now, agitation must wait, and education is vital, as is protecting ourselves. We cannot expect the working class to protect us; if we could, we would not be in a period of reaction, and would need no protection.'' He paced some more. ''But this does not mean there are not important elements of the working class available to us, as I am certain you discovered last night and the night before when you were exercising your legs and, no doubt, your lungs.''

''My ears, I see, get no mention. You know very well what I was doing last night and the night before. Stop trying to undermine my credit with my cousin.''

James did not appear at all surprised, but I was. ''You knew he—that he'd gone out?'' I asked. No one had mentioned that *I* had been out as well, so I thought it best not to bring it up.

''Spiders ought to be able to recognize their own kind, *mo chridh*,'' James said to me. I suspected him of spotting my omission, and being amused by it.

''But,'' said Engels, ''your ears failed, at least to gather the source of this manufactured incident, or you would have mentioned it already. So we have certain limited forces. What do we do with them? Can we learn where the gold went? Well, in part, no doubt, it has gone to lubricate certain gears in the machine of Parliament, and that portion we cannot find, nor do we care about it. So I fear we come back, after all of this, to what you said some time ago: can we find out how they intend to contrive the provocation with the forces at hand, and can we do so in time?''

''My ears did not fail, thank you. I was taking a pulse or two. Why do you think I was so willing to admit that the workers were not, in the natural way of things, prepared to rise at the moment? They're not angry, they're anxious. That, too, can be exploited, by those who know enough about the working people, as long as they don't *care* about them.''

"But where will they attempt it? Here in Manchester? How can we find out?''

"Not where, who. Not geography," James murmured. "People. We're looking for anyone who . . .''

As his voice trailed away, I said unsteadily, "The notes.''

"You're very quick," said James, still looking as if someone had hit him unexpectedly across the face. "Does this mean they *are* something other than an exercise in pouring salt into wounds?''

Engels cleared his throat. "Would you mind letting the German in on your exchange of English ciphers?''

"James's notes," I more-or-less repeated. "The list of possible informers. That's exactly the set of people with the knowledge and lack of scruples to manufacture an incident. There will be a large overlap between the informers and the people who've taken the Prussian gold.''

Engels stopped his pacing. "Oh," he said. Then he added, to James, "*Now* you may reclaim a cherry," and began pacing once more.

"*One* of you had better explain what all these blasted cherries are about," I exploded.

"Gracious, no," James said kindly.

Engels shook his head at me. "It would be irresponsible." Then he turned to James and said, "I suppose now you will want permission to use your legs.''

"Well, here's the irony of the world," James replied, rolling over again and leaning on his elbows. "Now you've got me just where you wanted me. I *can't*. Alan Tournier has set the machine in motion. I'm now wanted for questioning in the murder of Gideon Johnson. Every constable in Britain will shortly have my name, description, and perhaps even my likeness. Which doesn't necessarily stop me, but it slows me down significantly, and time seems to be of the essence.''

"We have to be careful," said Engels. "If we simply denounce everyone on the list, a certain number of them will be victims of vengeance by their fellow workers. Others will be considered liabilities by the government and perhaps killed, with the blame attached to the workers.''

"And an internal blood-bath could set the workers' cause in England back for your whole fifty years. It's one of the reasons I was so close-mouthed about gathering the information.''

Engels looked down at James and sighed. "This Tournier is a pest.''

James made a noise that could have come from out of the coals. "I'll have it put on his gravestone. Where the evidence is very strong that someone on the list informed against the Chartists, we *have* to expose him in some measure. We just can't do it publicly. In other words, we have to *discredit* the informers, rather than denounce them. You say the League has been engaged in the creation of leaders. Then you must know where those leaders are and how to get information to them. I know a few others, scattered around the country, whom I think could trust to do the job right. As few as twenty people with the ear of the working class and the authority to be believed by them, armed with the information we have, might do it. Though I'd rather have a hundred. All we have to do is undermine the influence of our targets. We don't even have to stop all of them. A brush-fire or two won't mobilize public opinion.''

"And so the leg-man is threatened by cramp in his writing hand," Engels said wryly. "I shall be composing a great many letters, and you will be also, I think.''

"I've written a letter or two in my day," James replied, pretending offense. His eyes slid, quickly, to mine, and a smile pulled at his lips for a moment. I thought, as he must have known I would, of the tract.

Engels's pacing brought him back toward the hearth. "I would very much like to do something about this Tournier, however.''

"For now, we do what we do about anyone else high on the list. For the rest of it—do you mind having to stand in line?''

"What do you have in mind?" Engels asked.

James rubbed his hands over his face again. "Nothing, yet.'' He looked at Engels over his fingertips and added, "Don't look so damned surprised. He's had me so thoroughly on the defensive since the end of July that for most of it I didn't even know it was him. I haven't had the opportunity for much more than evading the latest pitfall.''

"But you are not content with that."

Even in the kind light from the grate, James's face, eyes now closed, was harsh as a carving in ice. "He has hounded me. He has harassed and harmed and caused the death of members of my family. And he has betrayed my cause. I am also not a priest.''

Engels stood once again with James at his feet, and seemed about to speak. In the end, he didn't. Instead I rose, and said, "Gentlemen, if you'll excuse me, I've a letter to finish myself.''

"Give her my love," said James from the hearth rug, then stopped, startled perhaps by the ease with which the thought arose and the words formed.

Ridiculous tears sprang in my eyes. "I will," I said, and left as quickly as I could.

James sends you his love, Kit. Oh, my dear, my dear, I wondered if I would ever have the chance to write those words. I think we will get him back after all.

The morning of the 6ᵗʰ now. The ink wasn't dry on the sentence above when I heard the tap at my door, as if discussing James's emotional life were enough to summon him. I wiped my eyes, thrust these pages in the secretary drawer (that's the crease in all the upper right corners) and called, "Come in!"

"It might have been anyone," James scolded, slipping through and closing the door after him.

"Of all the people presently in this house, accepted wisdom makes you the last one I ought to let into my bedchamber. As worst possible case, I don't think you ought to talk.''

"The alternatives to talk—never mind. I brought the rest of the sherry.''

The decanter was pinned under his arm, and the glasses were fanned between his fingers like a card trick. "More reprehensible yet.''

"There's not enough left to get either of us drunk, let alone both of us. You don't have to have any.''

"Reprehensible and clutch-fisted, too. Put those down and pour before you drop something." I wiped my pen and made room on the secretary for the decanter.

"I'm sorry—I'm interrupting, aren't I?"

"It was all done but the signature. Do you know, of all of us, it seems to me she's had it hardest?"

"Kitty?" He handed me my glass. "I'm not sure. It may only seem that way because neither you nor I could play the part she has done."

I looked up. "That was very wise. Are you practising for your new job?"

"No," he said, with an irritable twist of his mouth. "I'm trying to remember how to use my brain. One would think I'd get a little encouragement." He sipped at his sherry and carried it to the hearth, where he sat on the rug.

"Pardon. Consider yourself encouraged." I stayed in the straight-backed mahogany chair that I had drawn up to the secretary. "Why do you sit on the floor so much?"

"I retain an alarming number of schoolboy habits. One of them is that I think best lying on the rug. Sitting on the floor is the next best thing, I suppose."

"And Engels knows it," I murmured, amused.

"What?"

"Never mind. If you want to lie on the rug, don't feel you have to deny yourself on my account. *Did* you come here to get me drunk?" His description of the quantity of sherry left had been less than accurate.

"No," he said slowly. He raised his eyes, large, dark, and direct, to mine. "I may have come to get *me* drunk. I have an unaccountable desire to talk about my family, and I don't know if I should encourage it or scotch it."

"Dear me. Which members of it?"

"The good ones. *Is* Kitty holding up?"

"If she isn't just putting an encouraging face on it for my benefit. It would be unlike her to do so."

"It would, wouldn't it?" He had another swallow of sherry. "You've known her for a long time."

"Donkey's years. We met at school. I was . . . oh, ten, I think, and she was nine."

"She was too young for it," he said, watching the fire

gnawing on the coal. "I thought so then. But she'd run through her governesses, rather."

"Well, it was the saving of me. I was too young as well, and desperately lonely. And it may have been the saving of her. She was wild as bracken; it took the concerted lure of thirty other pupils, a half-dozen mistresses, and a strange setting to divide her attention sufficiently to slip a little learning past her guard. After that she remembered that she liked it for its own sake, and the rest of her school career could proceed in a more normally hellish fashion."

A smile played around his lips; he tilted his glass and studied the slow-moving film the liquid left behind. "And why were you there too young? I expect you could have run through a few suffering governesses yourself."

"Oh, no, not in those days. Not before Kitty rescued me. I was an orphan, recall, and Grandmama was somewhere in the Southern Hemisphere, and all Papa's relatives could think of to do with me was send me to school. Not their fault that none of them had a household able to take in a perfectly helpless girl-child in straitened circumstances. They couldn't even have done it if I'd been pretty and charming, which I wasn't."

He stared. "Weren't you?"

"Not a bit. Mousey and inarticulate, except when suddenly uttering exactly the wrong thing, however acute, at the worst possible moment. And given to bursting into tears for no apparent reason. No talents to speak of. I was rather horrid in my own way."

"Is this your revenge for my tract?"

"Pardon?"

"You're describing a book I'll never have a chance to read in the original." He shook his head, finished his sherry, and asked, "But you say Kitty rescued you?"

"Valiantly, if unawares. Which is not the way she remembers it, by the way. According to her I was cool and capable and self-possessed, natural idol and cynosure of all my peers. I was actually stiff and shy and frightened. When I discovered that this little incendiary half-wild child-demon thought I was the equal of anything in school for brains and courage—I suppose I felt I should try to live up to her aspirations for me."

You will have to excuse the foregoing, Kit; it's what we

talked about, and what I said. I would never presume to argue with you over your recollections and interpretations of our childhood, but I trust you would never expect me to falsify mine. Whether I had any business discussing our shared past with your step-brother is another matter, but it seemed called for.

I leaned over with the decanter and refilled his glass.

"I hadn't decided yet," he said.

"To get drunk? Then don't drink it."

He sipped absently. "When I—when I determined that I would step back from the family," he began, and paused. It was not an invitation to interrupt, and I didn't. "I thought that drawing away was all I was doing to widen the distance. Seeing less of all of you, communicating less, taking less interest in the family's business. But that wasn't . . ." He pulled the fingers of one hand down his face as if smearing them through paint. Then he laid that hand on his upraised knee, and pillowed his chin on it.

"Distances can be traversed," I said mildly, to my glass.

"I suppose that's why I didn't settle for distance. I made a set of masks. I don't think I knew I was doing it. I had a nice blank one for myself, so that no one I loved would know what was happening underneath and be frightened, or hurt, or sorry for me. But I made masks for all of them, as well. All of you. The further away I got, the more I needed to see my family as simpler than they were, easier to assign a type and a rôle. Cartoon masks, caricatures, without contradictions. You read my letters to Richard."

It seemed, for a moment, like a change of subject. Then I understood. "Kitty as temperamental and self-indulgent. And me, an *houri* in stout footgear and Serviceable Stays."

He winced. "The memory on the girl. I acknowledge the inaccuracy and retract it."

"I don't know. I rather liked it—if I can keep the spangles and kohl, too."

The quick upward glance he sent me had something in it of gratitude. "An unlimited supply of spangles and kohl. And I like your footgear."

I poked the toe of one foot out from under my skirts. "Tooled Spanish kid slippers the precise colour of burnt sugar.

You had better like them. I think they're *angelic*."

"Mm. Now you know how I feel about food."

"The way I feel about my shoes? I hope not. *Do* you stand at your open cupboards and gloat over your store of cheese?"

James laughed, and in an abrupt gesture drank off his sherry. It warned me, a little. "Then, of course, there's Richard."

"You didn't include Richard in your list of extremes."

"No, I didn't. I characterized him on every page, instead."

That made me drink off *my* glass. I refilled it, because it seemed to me that we had come, suddenly, to a difficult place in the road. "How so?" I nerved myself to ask.

"May I have some more sherry, please?" He held up his glass.

"Decided, have we?"

"I'm keeping the possibility open." The little space of quiet, in which the coals hissed, and crystal sang against crystal, and liquid ran clucking, was genuinely peaceful. No decisions hung balanced. When James stops weighing what he will and will not say to you, the suspense of all the past conversations becomes overwhelming by its absence.

He drank and sighed. His mouth flattened in a wry grimace before he said, "To put it as dramatically as possible, I was betrayed by my own mask-making. I built Richard quite a nice one. Not any more complex than the others, mind, but very highly polished. So highly polished, in fact, that what it showed me was myself reflected back."

I clutched my glass and mentally floundered, which I hope did not show. I had read James's letters to Richard, and thought only that James knew aspects of Richard that I didn't. But they weren't aspects of Richard at all. James had been writing to himself.

James continued, "One of the problems with falsifying people's characters for your own purposes is that they're always breaking out of the mould and behaving as themselves. And since you didn't expect it, you call it an aberration. If you've done a really thorough job of lying to yourself over it, you'll even call it a betrayal. Then you decide it's their fault that you can't understand them, and the whole thing descends into farce. Painful, but a farce." He sighed again.

"How wonderfully general and detached you make it

sound," I said sharply. "Are you talking about Richard?"

"About . . . my misreading of you, and Kitty, and Richard most of all, yes."

I sipped my sherry. I hadn't realized until I failed that I had wanted to see if I could make him angry. I suppose it was a last, ignoble test for honesty. "How long have you and Richard been friends?" I asked at last.

"The easy answer is, all my life. Practically speaking, since I was old enough to ride a pony from Cauldhurst to Melrose Hall and back without dependably getting in trouble for it. Which would have been . . . I don't know. I might have been six. I know it wasn't much more than a year before my mother died, and that was when I was seven. My—Andrew remarried when I was nine, and for Margaret's sake I was sent to school. Subsequently, a year with not one surviving memory that isn't awful, until Richard arrived at the same school at the much more reasonable age of eleven. But he was my salvation well before that."

"As Kitty was mine?" I asked.

"Different." He smiled down at the wine and, after a moment, shook his head. "Oh, Lord. I'm about to tell you something I hadn't planned ever to tell to anyone. Do you mind?"

I managed to turn my unladylike snort into laughter halfway through, and resolved not to finish the contents of my glass. "Until I hear it, I can't tell you if I object to the contents; and if you're asking about the principle of breaking faith with yourself, yes, of course I mind."

"It wasn't a promise. I just hadn't planned to. All right. We had a sort of ritual, Richard and I; I can't remember when it began, or how. I would ride over to Melrose in the afternoon, drop down at full length on the nursery hearth-rug, and say, 'Well, here's the worst thing that happened today.' Then I would tell him whatever it was. It must have started after my mother died and before I was sent to school, because before that I don't think I would have needed to do it.

"And Richard would say, 'At least it wasn't any worse.' At which I would ask, What's worse than that? and he would begin to suggest things that would have been worse. Each more ridiculous than the last, until I'd be laughing and joining in, trying to top him. He did it for me, on and off, until we both went to Oxford. Then I suppose I found other ways to deal with the worst things. But I don't know that any of them were as effective as Richard's." He drained his glass again, folded his forearms around his upraised knee, and met my gaze reluctantly. "I have always needed Richard a great deal more than Richard ever needed me."

"I don't know how you can tell at this remove."

"You mean that Richard might have grown up someone else without the influence of me. I think he would have. But it would have been a perfectly fine someone else. I don't *think* it's excessively Byronic to say that without him, I might not have grown up at all. I certainly wouldn't have been perfectly fine."

"Children are notoriously resilient."

He opened his mouth; then he shut it and shook his head. "No, I can't argue with that. Besides, I might be lured into talking about the less-than-good members of the family."

"Why talk about any of them? What's changed?"

James smiled, surprisingly. "Besides all of us?"

That made me bite down on my tongue. I sipped a little sherry across it to blunt the pain. "And everything. Yes."

"I've felt . . . haunted by Richard today. No, don't be alarmed, I haven't taken up premonitions. But I keep being reminded of him. Until tonight—well, I can't hear Hegel mentioned but I think Richard's looking over my shoulder."

"You thought Kitty's message this evening was about him."

For a moment his eyes closed. He nodded.

"Write to him."

"I did." The face he raised to me was stark. "After his last letter to me."

Finally I understood your reference to a letter from James. Written after James had stood in the corridor outside this room and read Diana Cobham's letter to her lover, and let it fall. "That night?"

It was the tone of my voice, I think, that made him smile, a crooked expression of self-satire. "Immediately. It was unforgivable from beginning to end."

We who beat words into swords or teardrops. Then I remembered: James had been writing to himself. Did Richard know, does he know, who James was writing to?

"You wouldn't have forgiven it," I said.

He set his glass on the hearth, empty. "It's been an illuminating day," he said. His expression was still satirical, but gentler. "Today I learned that kinship isn't inevitable. That class and nation and blood are fluid unless one chooses to fix them for oneself. Engels declared me free to choose my class, without regard to birth. If birth doesn't fix one's class—what else might it fail to influence?"

"Almost everything, I suppose, hypothetically," I said, exasperated. "It hasn't failed to influence you for thirty years."

"No, it hasn't. But like everything else in the past . . . week? the idea takes a bit of getting used to." He picked up his glass and unfolded himself from the hearth rug. "I should let you finish your signature."

Obscurely disappointed, I said, "I'll do it in the morning. I imagine it's that already. You're not leaving the decanter here, are you? The maid will think I'm a tippler." It was nearly empty.

"Whereas, in fact, you are a hardened elbow-bender. Finish yours and I'll take the glass. Never mind, you *have* finished yours. Can you stand up?"

"If I can't, you know where the door is." I did, in fact, stand up, and didn't sway. "Wait, let me check the hall. There are worse things for the maid to think of me."

"You are a grown-up lady. The maid won't care."

I ignored him while I opened the door and determined that the corridor was, in fact, empty and quiet. "My principles agree. My nerves tell me this way is much easier."

"Your nerves are made of oak and spring steel. With a lace doily thrown over top like a bird-cage cover." He leaned on the door-frame and said in a changed voice, "Thank you, Cousin. When I'm renegotiating kinship, can I put you down for any particular post? Or, granted the opportunity, would you rather devolve into nodding acquaintance?"

"With a man who now knows I was homely and inarticulate in childhood? I counted on the ties of family to keep my secret safe." I was uncomfortably breathless, possibly from the wine.

"I'm good at secrets," he said softly, smiling. With the hand that wasn't tending the decanter and glasses, he took mine, and raised it, for an instant, to his lips. "Good night." And he was gone, silent, graceful, and dead sober after three glasses of sherry, into the dark passageway.

I was just tipsy enough to be unable to sleep. So I wrote all this down.

It's snowing, enormous clotted flakes of it sticking when they land. The garden already looks like a sheep-shearing yard. I hope it doesn't slow the mail. Good night, Kit. Mere conversation and a kiss on the knuckles is more than enough to addle my brains already. Physical love would certainly reduce me to imbecility, and I hope you won't wish it on me.

With love and spirituous fumes,
Susan

WHITEHALL
DEC. 6th

Dear Louisa,

I'm sorry to impose on an old friendship for such a cause, but it appears that your son Richard is involved in a matter that concerns my office. To be blunt, my dear, there is a question of murder, and, more than that, a question of the security of the Crown. I am required on the one hand to press the matter, and on the other to drop it. In light of whose son he is I should much prefer to drop it, and I will do so if you can but assure me he isn't involved with the veritable viper's nest of Chartists and Atheists and red republicans presently infesting England. At the moment, he is quite safe at his inn near Portsmouth, thinking we think him on the Continent, but he cannot remain safe there for ever, and I really must know what to do. Feel free to call on me if you are able to travel. If you are not, a note will do, or, if you prefer, I will send my personal secretary to you.

I hope this causes you no inconvenience, and I further hope you realize that you remain ever in the thoughts and affections of your good friend,

Sir George Bankston

THURSDAY
THE GREY HOUND

My Dear Brother:

Let us begin with important matters; those that are merely life and death or involve the future of humanity can wait their turn.

Ah, me. You have seen death up close, James; you have taken human life; you have thrown yourself into a struggle for the future of mankind; you have been tortured for doing so and nearly killed. Don't you think it is time for you, perhaps, to grow up a little?

It may be that I wrong you again, as I did before (and I'll thank you not to contradict me on that subject), and that what you have been through has robbed you, temporarily or permanently, of the ability to hear what another says beneath the words he uses. But I think not. I think you have received a shock, and are lashing out in the only direction available to you, the way an unjustly punished child smashes a favourite toy because he cannot smash his father. In fact, I ought to have predicted it. But, just on the chance that you actually failed to understand, let me try it all again.

My good, dear James, I was hurt—horribly, badly hurt— that you had failed to take me into your confidence; that you had instead used me as an ignorant tool, when, as you ought to have known, I'd happily have been a knowing tool. In fact, it was exactly because I considered you a brother that you hurt me so. The hurt turned to anger, and in a moment of weakness I dashed off a letter—one that, in point of fact, I had doubts about before I sent it on its way. But I had had some rather severe shocks, and taken a bit of a physical, as well as a spiritual, buffeting, and so I lashed out at you, rather as an unfairly punished child &c.

I have not a copy of my most recent letter to you, but I remember the gist of it, and I remember telling you that the discovery that we were brothers made all the difference. Poor James. Have you still got that letter, or have you burned it? If you have it, kindly read it again, and this time read it as carefully as you read my remarks about David Hume, and recall exactly who was writing those words. As Professor Brindle used to say, "Perform the transformation yourself."

But then, of course, after he would say that, I would always turn to you for help, because the equation always appeared cloaked in mystical symbols that very nearly made sense but didn't quite. I'll take pity on you, as you did on me, and lay out the missing pieces. The discovery that we were in fact brothers was not, as my words implied, the *reason* for my change of attitude, rather it was the catalyst; and this is a thing, my dear brother, that you would know had you read my letter with a clear head, or, rather, had you permitted yourself to know. The discovery brought back to me, first, all our history, all those arguments with God and each other, our helping each other home when neither of us was quite in a condition to walk, the feeling that you remember as well as I that we were alone in a world that was determined to beat us into its image and our only defence was laughter. I then remembered when you began to drift away. I can nearly put a date to it: it was on a Sunday afternoon, and you set down Wollstonecraft's *Vindication of the Rights of Woman*, and I asked you about it, and you started to speak, gave me an odd look, and then just shook your head. That was the moment, James, when the course of your life took a turn that left me behind, though I did not quite realize it then, and you probably never saw it in those terms.

The next station for my train of thought—for it was not a fast train, and insisted on stopping everywhere—was the realization that, with what you'd undergone, you *could not* take anyone, even a cousin, even a brother, into your confidence, because they were not your own secrets you were protecting. Of course, you had said as much, but that could hardly apply to me, said I to myself. In condemning you, I had put you in an impossible position: choose between duty to those who trusted you, and duty to one who loved you. And it was here that I realized that what I had taken as a personal affront was the act of someone in an impossible situation making the best of it he could. Typical for our family, don't you think? My

God, James, when I think of this family I can only laugh or go mad, and so I laugh.

I then took a detour to consider your politics, and came to the conclusion that I had no right to judge you, nor you me (which, I hasten to add, I know you have never done). To be sure, we are both members of the class you propose to topple; but you have never berated me for my loyalty to that class, nor have I any right to condemn you because your ideals lead you to betray it. Well and good so far, but James, what is this working class that has won your loyalty? Of them, you never write. I do not know them; I never see them except when in London, and you know how rarely I go into the city. But in all of your letters, in which the cause you serve is an invisible presence, the working class is a visible absence; that is, the only figures who parade through your life, it seems, are those who are in some way directly concerned with your cause, but never those whom this cause is supposed to benefit. Can you then blame me if the cause appeared, from my perspective, to be as abstract as the Absolute Idea that Hegel puts at the top of his entire system and then promptly forgets? And with the cause having no real life, as I saw it through your pen, it took on no more real importance than an adventure, a game, a distraction.

And this thought was no sooner formulated than exploded: the fault may have been yours, insofar as you ought to have tried to communicate something of those people to me, but the error was mine. These are real people, and their suffering is real, and the distance I feel from it, the abstract quality it assumes from my vantage—quite as aristocratic, or perhaps even *petit bourgeois* as you might say—says a great deal about my vantage but nothing at all about the condition of that class of which your friend Engels writes so convincingly. I began, in other words, to realize that your feelings about the working class were rather like mine toward slavery after reading Mr Darwin's account of his voyage: that I had never actually seen a slave made no difference, nor should it have. This tiny leap of logic and feeling put the train into motion once more.

My next stop, and the last, was the sudden understanding that I had no choice but to attempt to undo, in some measure, the damage that I had done. You will, I know, protest that I ought have said all of this before; my reply is that I did; if you failed to see it, I think it was because you chose not to. But then, you have been through a few different kinds of Hell lately, and are perhaps not seeing things the way you would have before; I ought to learn to suspend my judgment on such matters.

As for bastardy itself, I know you too well, I think, to believe you will care much for the matter. Susan has suggested that you are disturbed by the suffering that lay behind the bastardy, and this I can believe, but when I consider who has suffered from Andrew's deeds, I only think of little Roderick, whom I saw only once, and such an anger builds up in me that it interferes with clear thought; but at least the man I hold most responsible is taking his well-deserved place in Hell, or an even more well-deserved place in Oblivion. I sometimes see this entire family of Cobhams, Callendars, and Pearses, as accumulating debts to the world over generations, and periodically attempting to pay them off. I hope history will remember me as one of the ones who made a payment; I know history will so record you.

I doubt very much, by the way, that this letter will change your feelings; I do not, that is, expect you to whistle merrily, saying, "Well, yes, old Diccon is right, and off we go." But in a certain way, it scarcely matters. You may cut yourself off from me, but I will not cut myself off from you, and you are quite unable to bring me to do so, so you may as well save yourself the effort of trying.

That said, let us move on to matters of less moment but more importance: to wit, this peculiar situation in which we find ourselves. As you are probably aware, I am just now in hiding from the authorities, who believe I killed David, which, by the way, I did not, though I have come close to doing so on more than one occasion, as you well know. I have been learning a few things, and of those I will provide a quick summary by doing what the inestimable Miss Voight has been doing, to wit, by providing you with a copy of the significant entries in my journal and trusting that Kitty will pass or has passed on the news from my letters to her.

The thing about hiding and skulking is, when it isn't fascinating, it's *tedious*. I had learned and done nothing for several days, until yesterday when I received Kitty's package of letters, which set me on the track of Tournier's sister. I borrowed a horse, a chestnut mare with a wonderful gait, by the bye, and set off in the direction from which you saw that mysterious coach arrive. Several hours of riding produced no result whatsoever, except for giving me time to compose the reply to your letter that appears above. This country, James, is too big. When I returned, I spoke to Coslick about the woman, but he either has no idea who she is or is feigning ignorance.

Do you know, it would be quite remarkable if you were able to return to Melrose whilst I hid here at the Grey Hound, and we had to correspond that way. I could perhaps argue with you, trying to convince you of the ultimate rationality and knowability of it all, and give us a nice sense of closing a metaphorical circle. Any sense of closure would be a relief. On the other hand, we must be careful what we wish for, so I suppose I should be content with my lot, as you must be, whether you like it or not, to know that I remain your affectionate brother,

Richard

RICHARD COBHAM'S JOURNAL

DECEMBER 7th

Wrote to James. Tried to be cheerful, optimistic, and truthful, but I wonder if he'll ever read it, and, if he does, *how* he'll read it. He has become unpredictable. I have always had the feeling that unpredictability in a person is a virtue, at least insofar as it ensures that the individual isn't boring, but now I wonder if the reverse is not true, if predictability isn't a necessary ingredient in goodness, whatever that is. But such speculation is silly, and I should not even indulge in it if I weren't so infernally restless. I cannot shake the feeling that events are passing me by, that the centre of action has moved away from here, that while I hide from the authorities, matters continue to unfold elsewhere, and that I shall be called back once all is settled.

Coslick, at any rate, is pleasant company, if no more communicative than he was before giving me the *Times*. Twice today I asked him if anything interesting has happened, and twice he has nodded vigorously and gone on to tell me how Mrs Coslick's favourite kettle has been burned, or so-and-so's oldest broke his arm, and I pretended the greatest interest and pressed him for details. Both times I made him laugh before I did, which certainly counts as a victory, but is little consolation for the lack of news.

David's funeral is today, and is no doubt going on even as I write these lines: Cauldhurst will be filled with near and distant relations who will wonder where I am, and who will have heard (at least by the end of the service) that I have married Kitty and will be wanting to have a look at me, and it affords me great satisfaction not to be there, but it is horribly unfair that Kitty must go it alone.

I miss Kitty so. I know that each letter I write her increases the risk to both of us, and to Susan and James by extension, and so I will not do so without good reason, but it is difficult.

DECEMBER 7TH
LONDON

My dear Miss Voight,

I find I am torn between thanking you for the gift of your confidence, and wishing with all my heart that you had withheld it, rare though I know it must be, only because the news you have conveyed is so alarming. I fear for your safety; and I am more distressed still by the knowledge that I can do nothing without reducing it substantially.

Should that change—should it be possible for me to perform any service to your benefit—I beg of you, never hesitate to ask it of me. I suspect it will not come as a surprise, and I hope it will not be perceived as an impertinence, if I tell you my feelings for you are a little warmer than those of simple friendship. I know they are not returned. But if, as a friend, you require to call upon me, do so in the knowledge that it cannot place you under an obligation to me, and that I will respond unstintingly.

Sincerely,
Thomas Cavanaugh

DECEMBER 7th
MELROSE HALL

Dear Susan,

Well, I have such a number of things to tell you, and no idea at all in what order to tell them, that I very nearly decided not to write at all, and it has been a good thirty minutes since I first wrote "Dear Susan" and all the intervening time has been spent in standing up, pacing back and forth, wandering to the window, looking out, and then sitting down again, so that by myself I have been engaging in all the movements of all the people in those remarkable conversations with Mr Engels which you report so well, with the exception of lying down on the carpet, which I might have done just to be complete if said carpet were a little thicker and a great deal cleaner. Had I your memory, my dear, then I should, well, then I should remember things better, I suppose, but I only have my memory to work with, and it is right now stuck inside a head that is buzzing away and has no idea where to set itself down. Perhaps the carpet would serve, after all.

You conclude your letter of the 5th by saying that you hope I wouldn't wish imbecility on you, and perhaps I do not, but then at least you could share my state, because I must say, Susan, that I have never thought of myself as stupid, yet most of what James and Engels spoke about seems to be either in another language, or about something that has nothing to do with the world I inhabit, yet it seems so important, and it leaves me with the annoying feeling that I am one of those ladies who sit in the parlour and drink tea and gossip while the men speak of the issues of the world and smoke cigars, to which they are welcome, and incidentally keep all the good port to themselves, and that last by itself is enough to make me resent the feeling, although I can't blame you for it, so I shall either have to learn a great deal about this politics of yours or teach you how to summon spirits from the other world, which may sound flippant, but that world has seemed very close these last few days, and I almost feel as if I could step through to it if I just had a few hours to prepare myself and the leisure to concentrate, but instead I am forced to think of this world which, I am sure you will say, ought to satisfy me, and, really, it does, or it would if Dick were here, but I still feel as if I had been listening to a conversation in Basque.

But that is only one piece of our tapestry, really, and there is so much more, there are so many different parts, and they all bounce off each other, so that it makes me remember when we sneaked into the billiard room and you tried to teach me the game, but I was not interested in learning, because as soon as I realized that hitting this ball with that one made it careen into that one and that one, which in turn hits that one again, I became absolutely fascinated with watching the process, and cared not a bit how to go about using those rules to accumulate a score. It is as if you have your ball, and I have mine, and James has his, and so on, and we strike each other's in odd directions and at unusual angles, and so the billiard balls go bouncing off the cushions unpredictably. But it is not quite like that either, now that I think of it, because we are not just little balls that stand still until another strikes us, but we are full of our own energy, and go in our own direction, and being struck by another ball does not make us move, it just changes how we move, and I should be extremely curious about how you would be moving had James remained in your room another five minutes! Ah, are you getting thin-lipped, Susan? Don't, because, you see, that is really my secret and entirely selfish reason for wishing you to experience the pleasures and pains that I have in being intimate with a man, it is nothing more than there being things we could giggle about together that, as yet, we cannot, because you would not giggle, and beyond that I will not talk about it, because I'll just have to say something like "You will understand some day", and then you'll be absolutely right to be angry with me.

Good heavens, Susan! I have used all of this paper, and not even begun to tell you all the things I have to tell, but then you can only blame yourself, because if you were not so interesting you would not provide such competition, but no, you write and I must respond to what you say, or I should find myself in the room I threatened you with, and that would never do because it would give the Mysterious Missing Aunt Louisa, of whom more later, too much satisfaction.

I am absurdly pleased, Susan, at how your report was received, because it is approval somehow of us, I mean of you and me and what we have been and, somewhere in my heart, still are to one another, and no doubt this is a terrible feeling to have, but it is mine and I propose to keep it. But I do not know what to think of what you are feeling, or not feeling, about David, because it seems wrong that you shouldn't cry for him, and I have chilling memories of what you said about the conversation in the train carriage after you killed that man and what James did, but this is somehow different, and, well, the sad fact is I must have not liked David very much myself, only I never let myself know it, because I find that I do not much care either, except that sometimes I remember what you said about how I cast a net of protection over those I love, and how I had removed it from David, and he died so soon after, and that makes me feel afraid, but I know you didn't mean anything [one line crossed out] like that, but it is odd, only don't worry about me, because I am really fine, or would be if you and James and Dick were all here. I am still envious of you for having all those adventures, only now I *know* that I could not keep up with them, so I will be content with my part, and sit here safe in Melrose, except for attending the family functions that you and James and even Richard are able to escape, and be horrified at the thought of what has happened to James, only, well, he does seem to be getting better, doesn't he? I do not feel nearly so distressed about him after your letter of the 5th as I had up until then, but I am absurdly pleased to be of assistance even to those billiard balls I do not understand, especially through your good offices, and so here is gratuitous mention of gentlemen's legs, just to prevent you from reading this aloud, because I would much rather you summed up my letters than have my private thoughts used as fodder by social reformers, thank you very much. Of them all, though, I believe I could get along with Mary, who seems to have more common sense than the lot of you, who are very clever about Earth and Fire and wholly ignorant about Air and Water, and no, do not ask me what I mean, because I think I could no more explain it than you could explain to me half of what James and Engels were talking about, but you have my permission to ask Mary, to whom my regards in any case.

But, do you know, you never fail to startle me, by which I mean that it would have been a million years before it entered my head to think of you being an aunt, though it is certainly true, but goodness me, now I do wish David were alive, because suddenly there are any number of things I wish I could tell him, which you can mark down as another of my thoughts to put in the safe-hole, which reminds that I have very few thoughts left in the safe-hole, while you still have a good number, I think, and when this is all over we shall have to requisition a bottle of Dick's best port and take them all out. But, you know, when I read where you asked how I knew you were asking all the right questions, I became quite cross, and it might have lasted until I came to the end of your epistle, in which I was proved right on all counts, and, while I certainly have no idea what all this business between James and Engels about cherries refers to, I am fully convinced that you owe me one, so there, but I did not remain cross long in any case, because your remark about becoming a convert to Islam because of its poetry made me laugh like a heathen, and then your remark about the gown! But you do not tell me how you responded when the All-Wise explained what risks I should and should not take, which is a pity, because I suspect I should have enjoyed it, but you are no doubt right in not gratifying me in this, so I shan't press you.

And I have nothing to say about the second remarkable conversation you and James had with Engels, except for two things, one of which is, "So there," as I mentioned above, and the other is that I send James my love, too, and I am delighted to welcome him back to humanity, and I am not I am not I am *not* going to say anything about what you two talked about, because I feel as if I shouldn't even have been told, except that I'm *so* glad it happened, and so glad you told me about it, even though it made me cry, that I've started underlining words again, so I will say no more about it, and

instead tell you about the funeral, which you have been kind
enough not to mention, or else which you were hoping I would
be kind enough not to describe, but I fear I must, so take a
deep breath, while I take one here, and we shall both begin.

Brian and Henry were two of the pallbearers, and I didn't
recognize the others except they were certainly churchmen,
which means that the Trotter's Club weren't officially in attendance, though I hadn't expected them to be, but in any case
the service began at a church in Tonbridge I'd never been to,
a rather gaudy place, to tell the truth, with enough gold fixtures
to make one think it Papist, and the prayers were pure High
Church, and given by an archdeacon, which means that David
was important enough for the Archbishop to send his representative, which would have pleased David. I arrived just in
time, because I was waiting for Aunt Louisa, assuming we
would be going together, and I discovered too late that she
had already left, but Wye drove me there and I was not actually
late, so you can imagine how surprised I was to find out that
Aunt Louisa wasn't there at all, and I still have no idea where
she is, but her brougham is gone too, and the coachman, so I
expect she was not stolen by gipsies, more's the pity.

Even more surprising was who was there, in several instances, but the top of the list has to be Andrew, whom I did
not notice until we were at the graveside, where he stood off
to one side wrapped up in a black greatcoat and wearing a top-
hat, his moustaches all stiff and waxed, and his face, though
thin, still the same, with all its hard planes and big eyebrows
and sunken cheeks. When the service ended and we were preparing to leave, in a hurry, I might add, because there was a
bitter wind, and I wonder what it must have been like trying
to dig the grave in such ground, I made it a point to try to find
him to talk to him, but he was gone as if he'd been a spirit,
so I have no idea what he was doing or why he was there,
certainly I never saw him talking to anyone, and I really can't
imagine that he felt he should pay his "respects" to David,
but I should at least have liked to find out how Mother is, and
ask why I have not heard from her and how to reach her, and
he ought to have told me that much, whatever else he is involved in, and even if he did not see me he must have known
I would be there, and I have decided that I simply do not like

him. Now I am beginning to be worried about Mother, though there is probably no good reason for it, but, Susan, she does not even know that I am married, and it all just makes me want to kick someone, probably Uncle Andrew, no, let me be honest with you and say I could almost kill him, I am so frightened for Mother, and there, now I can put in a claim to having the worst hand in the family, so just give me a moment and I shall try again.

All right, I am better now, and I can tell you that most of the Throng of Distant Cousins failed to recognize me, and many of the rest, along with those auxiliaries of the Legion of Aunts who were present, pretended not to, which proves that word has gone out both that I am now married and that it was all a very hasty and irregular business, and watching them look past me while simultaneously attempting to glance covertly at my waistline was almost enough to make me burst out into giggles, which would have confirmed all their worst fears about me, but I refrained anyway. Looking at all the Voights and those related somehow to the Voights, of which there were an entirely respectable number, I wonder how you could have emerged from among them, because they are all so, well, ordinary, by which you know I mean no offence, but how did you turn out so different, and do not go blaming it on me! But I did enjoy walking among them all and pretending to be enough of an idiot not to realize I was being snubbed and I took a horrid pleasure in secretly laughing at them all. Almost the only one who acknowledged me was a child of eight or nine whom I couldn't even place, but she approached me when no one was looking and pressed my hand in a most adult manner, which I found very touching, and I wondered whose she was but didn't want to ask, and I didn't notice her during the rest of the service.

I spoke briefly with Henry, who made a point of walking right up to me as if deliberately to spite the Legion and the Throng, which proves his heart is in the right place, and I told him I knew about the events of last October, and that you were worried about him and what had happened, but he just laughed and said it had cost him all ten quid he had borrowed from you to get out of it, and I am sure you said it was five, and perhaps it was, but Henry remembers it as ten, but in any case he apparently escaped unscathed thanks to corruption in high places. We were joined then by Brian, who embraced me right in front of everyone, for which I was more grateful than I can describe, and Henry pumped his hand enthusiastically for the success of his examination, and I chimed in as well, on your behalf and Dick's, and Brian then asked how Richard's business on the Continent was getting along, and Henry said, "Ah, is that where he is?" and I felt bad for deceiving him, but what could I do? Brian said he felt certain Richard would be home soon, and I gave him an inquiring look, and he smiled. We spoke of other things, and at last Henry wandered off, and I said, "Truly, Brian?" and he said he hoped so, at any rate, but he had written a letter that he believed would help, and we would just have to wait, but it was involved in something larger, and I asked what he meant, and he pointed to some men in bowler hats who were standing by the cemetery gate and explained that they were from Sir George Bankston's office at Whitehall, and I asked him who *that* was and he said if I didn't know that was for the best, and I almost started arguing with him, but I remembered in time where we were, and instead just swallowed and tried to smile. He asked me then where Aunt Louisa was, and I said I didn't know, and asked where his mother was and he said she was still in Asia and was not expected to return for some time yet, and then we strolled a little without speaking, and then he walked me back to my carriage, handed me up to Wye, and said, "Please give my warmest regards to James, will you?" and he winked at me and was gone before I could get a word out, and you may make of that what you will.

I see that I have said nothing about the procession, nor the service, nor, really, anything, but Susan, I cannot, because if I do it will sound as if I am complaining, and I have so little to complain about compared to you, and the only thing wrong with it was that it was tedious, except for what I have told you, so please be content with that and do not require me to relive the hypocrisy of that archdeacon speaking of some unknown prelate with your brother's name and strange men and women named Craig and Fenton and Voight pretending to be sad, all of which was enough to make me renounce the world and live in a cave with my limbs in some horribly uncomfortable position, but then I probably would get no letters, and letters from you and Richard are now what I look forward to more than anything else in the world, so I shall simply have to stay at Melrose and muddle along as best I can, anxiously awaiting the next time you write to your friend and cousin,

Kitty

MANCHESTER
8 DEC. 1849

Dearest Kit,

I've let the ink dry on the pen four times since the salutation. Things have changed, things are different; one of them I think you expected, and the other was so far from expected that had you set the best of your imagination on the trail of such quarry, you would *never* have caught it up.

For the first, expected news, language and law offer me a range of bald statements, all unsatisfactory. I thought I understood when, after your first night with Richard, you insisted on making a whole tale of it, the events in order and garnished with apparent irrelevancies like grace notes and ornaments to a musical score. I thought, in fact, that it was an impulse exclusive to you, and I delighted in the form of the recitation as another part of the nature of my dear Kitty, newly revealed to me. Either I misunderstood, or we have one more thing in common. We certainly have another experience in common, at least approximately. I could tell James, if I chose, some of the ways in which he is like his brother, and different. I think I won't. But you and I will know.

Do you see why I understand? If I go on in this fashion, trying *not* to make a fine story of it, I'll never manage to get anything said at all. I have taken a lover, and it has addled my brains just as I warned you it would. Between one thing and another I'm thrown entirely off my stride. Perhaps if I continue to put words on paper I'll get my voice back, so to speak. But these paragraphs, so far, look to me as if they'd been written by someone else. I was quite right about virginity's emotional baggage. One ought *not* to assume an entirely new personality simply because one has had carnal knowledge of someone else. Do *men* go through this much rubbish over their first experience? Or do they wake up the next day, say to themselves, "There, that's done with," and get on with whatever they were doing? I suppose I could ask.

Stop, stop, stop! This is idiotic. I'm going to have to nerve myself to tell it, and tell it properly. But I resent the domination of my emotions and the unyielding rule of my flesh. How do I balance mind and body when body demands everything, and if denied, simply wrenches itself and all my resources away from my mind's support? But I will try to imagine your look of gentle reprimand whenever I am tempted to skid off into the intellectual distances. Begone, all safety lines and nets. Simulated boldness, if sufficiently well simulated, may become fact, as I learned long ago.

The day before yesterday James got to the breakfast table before me, and so I found coffee, rolls, eggs, and smoked salmon waiting, along with a wickedly sympathetic-seeming cousin. There was cream for the coffee, I noticed.

"Aha!" I said, pointing. "You *do* have a preference."

"I thought you might want it this morning. Softens the impact of the coffee on one's stomach, you see. In cases of overindulgence in drink. Would you like some?"

"No," I growled. "Would you?"

"Yes," he replied, beaming at me. "But only because I like cream in my coffee."

I gathered the tatters of my dignity to me and told him, "Mr Cobham, the salmon stands at your elbow."

"Touché." He conveyed some to my plate, and poured my coffee. "Eating like a lioness this morning?"

"Yes, and you're looking more like an antelope with every word that leaves your mouth."

"You'd have to catch me first. Keep up your strength with the fish in the meantime."

I won't subject you to the entire array of nonsense with which we studded the meal. Neither of us thought to seek out the newspaper. We did digress once into matters of substance.

"Do you find it changes the complexion of things, a little," I asked, "to learn about Alan Tournier's sister?"

His hands circled his cup and were still. The shape of them is most noticeable when they curve around something: the palms and fingers all tapering, the middle finger somewhat longer than average even when flexed. "A little," he said at last. "I still don't see what Richard saw, that gave away the relationship. But if he saw it, I believe it."

"And you think she's the woman who called herself Helen?"

Another fragment of silence. "Yes."

"Poor Gideon Johnson. Not the best object for one's affections. Especially since while he was being chastely admiring, *she* was having my brother's child. Has it occurred to you that something will have to be done about that child?"

He sighed. "I'm glad it's occurred to you, too. But she *is* its mother."

"Hmph. Something I don't understand about what Johnson said at Newport. Why was Tournier recruiting Johnson as his sister's escort to Swansea at the same time he was planning to get Johnson killed? Ideally, by you?"

"Insurance," said James. "I might have missed."

I think I gaped. "If you failed to kill him, *she* would have?"

"And found a way to implicate me, though I were on the other side of England at the time. You haven't met her. But no, I think—I prefer to think—that she would only have been the mechanism for preparing another attempt."

One of us changed the subject then, fairly smoothly, and we went back to fencing until Mary joined us. She seemed happier than she'd been since we'd arrived. I wondered if that meant she considered James somewhat less volatile. Or it may have had nothing to do with James. Just because I take regular readings from the barometer of his face and carriage doesn't mean that anyone else gives a rap about the weather in that quarter. Engels, it seemed, had produced a blizzard of letters for the morning post the night before, while James had been making inroads on the sherry and my peace of mind.

"My turn, then," James said, and rose from the table. "If I don't come down to dinner, throw me in a bit of antelope, would you, Athena?" he said to me.

"Cannibalism," I said. Mary looked at us both in confusion. "Grass, if I can find any under the snow."

"Ugh," he replied cheerfully, and swept out of the room.

I sat contemplating the significance of Athena. Mary stared at me and shook her head. "No," she said, in response to nothing I could identify. "Leave me to my breakfast in peace. Then I'm going to the shops. Are you wanting anything?"

A ridiculous list crossed my mind: cherries, traets, *The Science of Logic*. "No, I don't—yes, actually. Mittens, if there's a pair to be had. I didn't come prepared for snow."

She shook her head again, as if I'd asked for carob pods or myrrh. "You're an unnatural creature," she said, but she smiled as she did it.

James produced his own heap of envelopes in time for the afternoon post and came down to dinner. There was a smudge of ink on his right middle finger. His eyes were clear, his smile easy and genuine, his mind and tongue quick enough to make him formidable, delightful company. We were still on the soup when Engels nodded to him and said, "Hello. Welcome back."

James returned his look for a moment, before he replied, "I don't know that I am, entirely. But I've sent my luggage ahead as earnest of my intentions."

"That's enough, for the present."

It was one of the most pleasant meals I've had in months.

Afterward we moved to the parlour for tea. Mary and Engels went in first; James stopped me outside the door. "I have to go out," he said softly. "Only for an hour or so, but I ought to do it now."

"What is it?"

"I want to tell George Holland the names to be wary of. He's one of the ones I trust to spike the necessary guns."

"You can't send a note?"

"He can't read. Harry can, a bit, but not anything so complex as this."

"I'll go with you."

James shook his head. "I'd rather you stayed. Someone should know where I've gone and what time I left. And—" He grimaced. "It's the oddest thing, but I find it does make a difference, knowing the police are after me." I must have looked mutinous; he added, "*Do* be sensible. If I'm taken up, won't it be ever so much more fun to engineer a daring rescue than to be taken up with me?''

I tried hard not to smile and failed. "I like your definition of 'sensible'. All right. An hour, and then I panic?''

"Perfect. I ought to be back inside of it.''

So I drank a cup of tea with Engels and Mary, pretending with some success not to be thinking about the French doors in the dining room, the gate at the bottom of the garden, the lanes, alleys, and streets past the new railway terminal; managing not to look at the clock on the mantelpiece above four times. After three-quarters of an hour I excused myself and went to sit in the dining room in the dark, which allowed me to open the doors for him five minutes later.

Cold air rushed in with him, and a dusting of snow. There was more on the shoulders of his coat, and sparkling on his cap.

"Harry asked me to give you his best,'' James said, his voice breathless and happy. I couldn't see his expression. "I think he's in love with you. My feet are frozen.''

"Don't drip on the rug. It went all right, then?''

"Like winking. Well, except for one or two patches. But no one saw me.''

"Then I'm desperately jealous. I haven't been out for two days.''

He laughed softly. "Next time you can go, Athena, and *I'll* stay here. The wind's nasty.''

"When and why did we settle on Athena?'' I asked tartly.

"Goddess of war and wisdom. Don't you think so? And who says I've *settled* on anything? Except that I really can't bring myself to think of you as a spider.''

"You're a loose cannon, James Cobham,'' I sighed.

"Yes, but I'm just the thing if you need a deck cleared in a hurry. I'd better go before I drip on the rug. Good night.'' With a flick of the disreputable black coat, he was gone.

In a vengeful fit, I asked Engels for the loan of his copy of the Hegel, and took it upstairs to read. I tossed my secondhand black shawl around my shoulders and settled down with it, prepared to wade through philosopher's German, which I can do when I'm concentrating. But I found that, like James, I was reminded of sundry family members by any reference to dialectic.

From pondering the possible state of affairs between Richard and James, I proceeded to wondering how things were at home. I recalled, for the first time, that there ought to have been a funeral for David at some point. And here was his one close relative sitting in Manchester. I would have hated going, but I ought to have, for the sake of a bit of involuntary weeping and a sense of brushing the grit off one's hands at the graveside. A feeling that there, that was done, and we could get on with it—not mourning in the conventional sense, I realize. Was a sufficient honour guard of Peterses, Hopworths, Craigs, and Fentons got up such that no one felt the lack of the deceased's sister?

That reminded me of something I had asked you once: about the curious dearth of Cobham connexions. Since I now had one of the rare creatures just down the hall, I resolved to go and enquire. With my brain still mistily full of German syntax, I tossed off my shawl, left my room, and strode down the carpeted passageway, noticing vaguely that it was early by the standards I'd been holding to of late; the lamp at the head of the stairs was still lit. I tapped at James's door.

"Jamie? May I come in?"

I have no idea what moved me to use the old household nickname. I felt, foolishly, as if I ought to offer an apology through the door panels.

His voice was rough-edged as if with disuse. "Not if you object to men who haven't got their shirts on."

"I've been to Rome. I've seen a lot of very nice statues that haven't got *anything* on."

"There's a difference or two between statuary and a living person, as it happens." His words were measured and level, as if he were discussing a minor philosophic point.

I was still thinking half in German. "Hmph," I said, and slipped through into the room.

I hadn't seen that room before. It was the same size as mine, and was similarly laid out and equipped, except that its window looked out over the street. The illumination came from the fire in the grate and the lamps at the table and on a chest by the bed, where it shone on the coverlet turned back and the white of the sheets. The paper and hangings were wine-coloured; in the rich, low light, it was like standing in the heart of a garnet. It was a tidy room, except for the black coat spread over a chair before the fire to dry, and a pair of stockings dropped on the hearth.

James was sitting sideways in a scroll-back chair drawn up to the table. His left elbow was propped on the chair back. His right hand, and his gaze, were on a book opened on the table. It looked as if he'd meant to be there for only a moment, and got absorbed enough to forget he wasn't comfortable.

"There's the colour, of course," he said, not looking up. "Poetry aside, nobody's skin is the colour of marble." His feet were bare, and the right one was propped up on a chair-rung. His back was bare, too, of course. The skin of it was not, indeed, at all like the white of marble; it was a burnished light-oak colour, and it shone in the fire- and lamplight with its own smoothness.

"And motion," he went on. "Breathing. Little shifts of muscle. No one's ever really motionless."

I thought, rather wildly, of the dialectic. I'd disturbed the lamp flames when I'd come in the door, and they still shuddered in the last of the draught. The moving light hid whatever motion might be happening in it. And if he was breathing enough to move the down on a chick, I couldn't see it. The symmetry and structures of his back were like the ones that Donatello and Michelangelo had taken such care over. His voice, something else that statues didn't have, was light and cool, but the space after his words was full of the charged pressure that comes before a bolt of lightning.

He finished, "So if you're uncomfortable after all, it's no reflection on your liberal upbringing. You needn't feel as if pride ought to make you stay."

It was not a very large room, and I found that I had taken two or maybe three steps into it, and was significantly closer to him than I had been. He still did not look up; I don't know if he heard me. No, that's not true. I know.

I did feel uncomfortable. There seemed to be a hard little sphere of India rubber rebounding furiously off the inside of my stomach. I drew breath, when I remembered to, in bursts.

I have felt desire; I know what it is. I have read books not intended for virginal females, and heard stories, and seen pictures—seen, at times, the inexplicit embrace of some pair of lovers that spoke to that part of my imagination that I am not supposed to have. To all those things, I have responded, and I know how it feels. You and I have talked about it, Kitty, giggling and blushing sometimes, sometimes without a thought of a smile. But the ache of desire that had sprung up in me, that came and went in time with the hammering of my heart, was beyond anything in my experience. Desire and fear—or if not fear, then some other powerful agitation. What a strange response, to want something with your whole self, mind and body and spirit, to the exclusion of everything else, and know that you will be granted it, and still feel such anxiety, such ambivalence.

I took another step and stretched out my right hand, very slowly, so that I had time to notice that his skin radiated a little warmth into the cooler air before I actually laid my hand on his shoulder.

He flinched, and drew in the breath that all the room had been waiting for, and the muscles that had been held so still knotted and slid under my gaze and my hand. I froze, my palm against his skin, afraid to leave it or draw it back. Under my fingers I saw a white webbing of scars—the claw marks of the thorn tree that had torn his back during the half-dream journey to the Grey Hound. "Does it hurt still?" I said witlessly, my voice all to bits.

He lifted his bent head at last, so that the firelight fell along the side of his face and showed his closed eyes and the brush-stroke of his lashes and the fine texture of the skin over his bones; and his left hand closed strongly over my fingers and held them where they lay. "No," he said. The word was neither light nor cool.

We were caught and still like that for what seemed a long time. He would not move again, I realised, until I did. His hand, though strong, would not prevent me from withdrawing mine from his clasp. I was light-headed for lack of air. There was such heat in me, such a ringing bodily craving, that at first I couldn't understand why he did nothing, nor what I was supposed to do. Then it occurred to me that there might be heat in him, too, and the only way that he could give me the whole choice, for both of us, alone in that room where time had ceased to pass, was not to move at all.

I leaned down, and at the place where the column of his neck met the top of his shoulder, I pressed my lips.

The turn of his head was so quick that I couldn't say precisely how his mouth came to be under mine. His right hand freed the page it had pressed upon, and caged the back of my head. His lips moved, and brushed, and I wondered what would happen when I collapsed, because I didn't think I had the strength to stand much longer.

Then as quickly as it began, the kiss was done. James released me and rose and went to the window, where he stood gripping the frame on either side. His shoulders rose and fell as if he, too, had been starved for air. His head was bent, his face hidden. I clutched the back of the chair he'd left, because now I was certain I was going to fall without it.

"Consider—" he said, and paused. "Consider leaving. If you don't leave now, I promise you—" He turned his face to me, and I saw him struggle to smile, to control the tone of his words, to cleanse the warning of any hint of threat. "You're not likely to leave with your maidenhead."

The quaint word made me smile, and brought me a portion of my strength back. I was light-headed still, but I knew I would not fall. "I've considered," I whispered. I held out my hand. "Come here."

He released the window frame and stayed where he was, looking into my eyes as if searching for confirmation. His breathing, deep and quickened, shifted the patterns of shadow across the planes of his breast, the arch of his rib cage, the cobbled muscles of his stomach. Finally he walked back to me and without hesitation took me in his arms and set his mouth to mine. All the perfect joinery of his back was under my hands, as clear as it had been to my eyes. His lips were changeable as weather, as his own expressive face. They strayed across my cheek and jaw and found my ear, as if to whisper in it; but the message was all delivered by touch. I felt, for a moment, as if every nerve I had was centred in the curl of my ear.

I pressed my face to his chest and inhaled the faint odour of sandalwood and the heated scent of his skin. It was like being very drunk, when you can only command one sense at a time, and that only by an effort. I let my mouth travel, exploring, across his chest, and heard the pull of his breath. I heard, too, a throb almost below sound, the beating of his heart. I was fascinated by the softness of his skin. No one admits that men are soft, too, dressed over hard bone and muscle in that close-fitting warm silk they so admire in women. James's skin is as close-grained as mine.

He held me away from him for a moment, studying my face again. I studied him in turn. I have so rarely been able to watch him openly, to stare, to gather the information of his features at leisure. I had never been able to do it with him aware of it and allowing it. It was another kind of drunkenness. His pulse fluttered in his throat, just a little below the hard-cut line of his jaw bone.

Then he moved behind me. His hands smoothed the hair back from my temples, stroked flat over my ears; his fingers trailed down the back of my neck to my shoulders, then slid down my arms and circled my wrists, and carried my hands up with them to my shoulders, where he bent his head to kiss my fingers, his breath warm. He kissed the back of my neck, just above the collar of my gown, and began to unfasten the hooks. I felt like wax in the heat of the friction between hunger and fear. I thought I would melt into the carpet before he could finish.

In the same caressing motion he pushed the gown off my shoulders and down my arms, off my wrists. My arms were bare under his hands; within the broad, low neck of my chemise, my shoulders were bare, and he touched his lips there, as if they could mark me. He untied the petticoats at my waist, and I stood in a pool of cloth, vividly aware that between my body and the air there was nothing but a layer or two of cotton lawn.

And my stockings and shoes, which seemed in my half-delirious state to be a problem of moment. I stepped out of the slippers as gracefully, as unobtrusively as I could, and then stood in the middle of my skirts, feeling foolish. But James knelt before me and looked up, a fugitive smile hovering at his mouth and eyes, and took my stockings off with great ceremony. I felt like an Indian maharani, who would not ex-

pect to lift a finger in her own toilette. I balanced on each foot
in turn and laughed softly down at him.

Then we both ceased to laugh. Reflecting back, I recognize
the instant for what it was: one of the last decision points for
both of us (his ultimatum at the window was only one of the
first). He knelt before me, his eyes on mine, waiting for an
answer I must, eventually, have given him, though neither of
us spoke. Then he raised his hands, and they passed under the
lace at the hem of my chemise, over the thin cotton of my
drawers, over my thighs and hips to my waist.

They faltered there, and I closed my own hands over them
and over the lawn of the chemise, moving them right and left
to the little flat button at each side that fastened the drawers.
His fingers trembled slightly. It moved me as much as the
brush of them against the bare skin at my waist. The drawers
dropped lightly, billowing like a handkerchief around my ankles.

One layer of cloth between me and the air. None between
me and his hands. His fingers traced lightly down the outsides
of my legs. I was frantic with self-consciousness and longing.
He was hindered, or need be hindered, by nothing at all now;
he had all the advantage; my God, my God, I thought desperately, did he not mean to use it?

He meant to. He caught the fabric of my chemise against
my bare legs and began to slide it slowly upward, and as he
did, he kissed the flesh exposed by its passage. At the sensation
of his lips on the skin of my thighs, the breath sobbed out of
me and I grabbed at his shoulders, because my knees would
no longer hold me. His hands were at my hips, steadying me,
slowing my collapse until we were both kneeling, face to face,
in the scattered debris of my clothing.

The chemise joined it on the floor. Nothing between me and
the air; but he became my clothes, the heat of his bare arms
and chest against my skin, the heat of his clad lower body
against my bare one. My arms were locked around him as if
I'd been shipwrecked, and he were a spar I'd found floating.
I was terrified by the heat, by the knowledge that I could not
control or predict this, by the pure contact of his hands on my
body where no man's hands had been. And I was terrified of
what I might do that would cause him to stop and move away,

because I couldn't imagine, couldn't bear the thought of being in my room and alone, and what was happening left unfinished. It's the conflict, I believe, that leads to swooning: two absolute and opposing demands of the instincts that require to be met immediately. The brain, asked the impossible, ceases to work. I did not swoon, but I know I hovered near it more than once.

He lifted me suddenly from my knees, from the floor, and brought me the three necessary strides to the bed. I had forgotten the available comfort of a bed; I was beyond thinking of place or convenience or custom. I made, I think, a little protesting noise when he let me go. He stepped away and dropped his fingers and his gaze to his trouser buttons. That was his hurdle of self-consciousness, during which he didn't meet my eyes. But he didn't turn away, or veil himself in a dressing-gown. He unfastened his trousers and his drawers, and slipped them off as I had cast my shoes off, as gracefully as it could be done, and let me watch, and see.

I saw the long, clearly-defined muscles of his thighs, and the shorter swelling of the calf muscles. I saw the narrow, hollowed haunches defined by the smooth muscular curve of his buttocks. I saw the way the scatter of curling dark hair on his breast, that thinned to a line bisecting his torso, continued and widened and thickened below his stomach and surrounded what the statues had also not had: an erect phallus. The Romans and the Celts had had statues of crossroads gods so equipped, until conquerors or thinner-blooded descendants had vandalized them. Michelangelo had sculpted for patrons who served a god that did not celebrate the sensuality of Man.

He was aroused, and by me. I hadn't thought I had room for another measure of feeling. I was right to think of pagan deities. This was not a Christian act. He was beautiful and frightening as some young god. But I was beautiful and frightening, too: his body told me that. My body told me. I was the goddess of the land, and he was the young king who came with worship and passion to celebrate us both. For the second time that night I stretched out my hand, and he came to me.

With his hands and mouth and all the length of his naked body he set himself to drive out ambivalence, to leave me with nothing but desire, and he succeeded. It wasn't until I had only one of my five senses left, and nearly all of that focused in one place in my flesh; it wasn't until I gave a great shuddering cry that I couldn't contain, and held onto him with all my strength that he broke my hymen, swiftly, when the pain could be surrounded and swept aside by the annihilating force of pleasure. Like his skin, his cry, when I heard it, was not unlike mine.

My senses, my thoughts, returned one by one like a flock of startled birds. For a little while I wondered if I would ever catch my breath again, but that, too, was restored to me, as it was to James. He had one elbow beneath him, but he hadn't drawn away. He was smoothing damp hair off my face, watching. Even in the cool air we were wet with sweat like spent racehorses. I caught his caressing hand suddenly and pressed a kiss into the palm. He closed his eyes for a little longer than a blink and smiled.

"I'm sorry; I know it hurt," he said, half-whispering.

"I knew it would." I smiled, and laughed, which was pleasant and disturbing with him pressed against me, and added, "I'm very well-read. Even so, I wasn't quite prepared for the rest of it."

"The rest?"

"The part that didn't hurt."

"Oh."

After a moment, he said, "I have been misled.'

"Hm?"

"You don't wear stays. Serviceable or otherwise."

I smiled sleepily and pillowed my head in the hollow of his shoulder. "I can't be correcting your every misapprehension. I'd never get anything done."

I woke to find him in my arms, asleep. His hair was a dark tangle on the pillow and in his eyes, and the shadow of his beard showed on his cheek and chin. It was, obviously, not an angle I'd seen him from before. Eventually his eyelids moved and opened, and I watched as the distance of sleep faded out of them, as comprehension replaced it. He moved one hand, a little, and touched my lower lip.

"I just won a wager with myself," he said.

"If you wager with yourself, how can you *not* win?"

"I could have not won this one. I wagered that you wouldn't have gone away by the time I woke up."

Past the interesting constriction in my throat, I replied, "It's too cold. I don't know about you, but I'm not coming out from under these covers until spring."

Unsmiling, he asked, "How will we pass the time?"

This was my turn, my exploration, and the pace mine to set. I had intended it to be slow, but I lost track of my intentions part-way, overcome by my senses. Once he laughed, a short, airless gasp, and said, "You *are* well-read." Then he stopped, because we had robbed each other of the ability to think.

Eventually, he said, "We can't really stay here forever. D'you want the housemaid to come in to poke up the fire and find your bed not slept in?"

"She can find me in this one," I said, drowsy again.

"No, she can't. She doesn't come in this room until I'm out of it and have left the door ajar. Mary will think you've been kidnapped."

"I doubt it," I told him, recalling various glances and comments from Mary. "Oh, all right, you can have your bed to yourself."

He caught me by the waist as I sat up and said, "Do you really think I want that?"

I smiled and shook my head.

"Don't look at me like that. You're not helping. Oh, mercy, is that really the sky turning light? All right, I'm getting up."

He wrapped me in his dressing-gown, pulled on his trousers, and divided my clothes between us to carry.

"I can find my room by myself, you know."

He looked rueful. "I know. But it would be so damned unchivalrous, if someone happened on you sneaking down the hall, to leave you to bear the whole of the censure. If there is any."

"Instead you'll make quite sure that the household knows which room I came from."

"Censure or credit, I want my share." He stuck his head out the door. "All clear. Come along, Temptation. Do you know you look very nice in my dressing-gown?"

We were nearly to the door of my room when we heard a tread on the back stairs, and the voice of the maid calling softly down to someone else. I hadn't really been alarmed at being seen before that, but there's something instinctive that responds, in spite of reason, to the thrill of skulking, and makes the blood race at the possibility of discovery. I grabbed James's elbow with one hand and the door-knob with the other, while keeping my bundle of clothes pinned under one arm, and whisked us both inside. We leaned against the door and each other as footsteps passed in the corridor outside. I laid my hand over James's mouth, because he was laughing.

I'd put out the lamps before I'd gone to his room; the only light was the glow from the subsiding fire in the grate. James kissed my palm, and I fastened the bolt on the door. So much for the housemaid finding *anything* in my room.

"Aren't you sore?" he asked, breathing irregularly, after his hands had found their way beneath the dressing-gown and I was struggling with his trouser buttons.

"Yes, but it keeps getting superseded by something else," I admitted. "Oh, *bother* these."

This time he picked me up and carried me over his shoulder, head down, to the bed, where it was a little while before I stopped giggling.

It was a long while—several hours—before I woke up and rolled over, and said gravely to him, "I think you've missed a meal."

He blinked, and asked, "Would you forgo a pair of shoes for me?"

I had to think for a moment before I understood. Then I said, "It would depend upon the shoes."

He covered his face with both hands and laughed. "You'll be angry, but I'm going to ask anyway. Will you marry me?" The unsupported voice, the one that happened when he couldn't breathe, but had to speak.

I nudged his hands apart to see his face, and found it faintly overcast by tension. I kissed his closed lips. "No," I said gently.

He blinked again and asked, his voice unaltered, "May I ask you once a year, every 7th of December? In case the answer changes?"

"Yes. I don't think it will."

"Oh. I only ask because I hate the thought of not having breakfast with you for the rest of my life."

"My dear," I said. "Jamie. That's a different question."

"Oh." He closed his eyes. I watched his throat move as he swallowed. "Will you have breakfast with me for the rest of my life?"

"Probably," I admitted, as the inexplicable tears welled in my eyes. I thought at first I was only seeing the sparkle from them, until the moisture clotting his lashes pooled enough to send a single shining trail down the side of his face.

"It's a pity," I said, "but no one can bring us coffee with the door bolted."

His eyes flew open. "I'll bring you coffee."

"Wearing nothing but your trousers and a dressing-gown? Barefoot?"

"Trust me," he said. And, wearing nothing but his trousers and a dressing-gown, and barefoot, he was back with the coffee-pot in fifteen minutes.

We did our best to be normal and sensible, once we separated and dressed and came downstairs. (I contemplated the pleasures of having him help me dress, and abandoned the notion immediately as impractical, if either of us were to appear in public before dinner.) We were not entirely successful. Mary watched the pair of us read the newspapers for perhaps twenty minutes—during which I would have *sworn* that we neither said anything much, nor looked at each other, particularly, and sat across the table from each other and didn't so much as touch *hands*—and finally said, "Oh, give over, will you not, and it's a great blessed relief to the whole of your acquaintance. Jimmy Cobham, sit up and behave like a civilized man."

This last because James had pitched forward face-first onto the table and pulled *The Times* over his head. "I'll have to emigrate after all," he sighed, emerging. He looked at me, his eyes bright. "Are *you* prepared to receive the congratulations of our friends and relations? You're blushing."

"Nonsense," I said, aware that he was right. I nerved myself to meet Mary's eyes, and found such a kind look waiting for me that I more than understood the impulse to hide one's face under something. I suppose I'm sadly naïve, Kitty, but unless the housemaid carried the tale, I don't know what gave it away to Mary.

Later in the afternoon, just before Engels came home, Mary

found an excuse to take me aside (since James and I did not, of our own volition, part yesterday for much more than five minutes at a time; I remember you and Richard, early on, and know you'll understand). "Your choice is your own," she said to me, "and you're a grown woman. You'll know best what makes you happy. But I'd have wished you a more comfortable man."

I set my fingers over hers where they rested on the window sill. "I'm not a very comfortable woman," I told her. "Think how guilty I would have felt, turning some nice, quiet man's life topsy-turvy. This one nearly deserves me."

"Nearly," she said, and smiled, and went back to managing her household.

Engels's response was just as characteristic. We were all gathered in the parlour when dinner was announced; James stood and put out his hand to me. I laid mine in it and rose, and we exchanged an unsmiling look of a sort I'm beginning to realize will be part of the vocabulary that he and I share. Engels, witness to the entire exchange, twitched his eyebrows and made a thoroughly Germanic sound in his throat. I suppose in anyone else it would have suggested scoffing. I think he felt rather smug, actually.

It was during dinner that the unimaginable thing happened. We were in the midst of a discussion, brought on by the snow, about the Christmas holiday, and how it was celebrated in Germany. "It's all quite grand and complicated," Engels said. "I believe it is a lure. Once a year, one splendid party to make the hardened atheists wish they believed in the divinity of Jesus."

I laughed. "So why not believe in an astronomical occurrence and a desire to spit in the eye of winter, and dedicate your gilded gingerbread to that?"

Then we heard the front door bell, and the quick passage of the maid to answer it. A moment later she stepped into the dining room and said, "Beg your pardon, but there's a caller asking for Mr Cobham."

James's head came up, of course, his face honed and cautious; but it was Engels who asked, "What manner of caller?"

"A lady, sir. An . . . older lady."

Well, that ruled out every possible candidate in all our

minds. "I'll be right there," James said, half out of his chair.

"Show her into the study," Engels directed the maid, "and offer her refreshment." His hand, unexpectedly, had come down flat on James's where it lay on the table. The maid nodded and left the room.

"What?" James asked, arrested half-standing.

Engels said, "Who do you think this is?"

"I've no idea," he replied lightly. "I didn't think I had any flirts in Manchester." That with a fleeting smile at me.

"Think," Engels told him.

"I am. I have been. I believe I'm ready for almost anything that could happen in your study."

Engels asked calmly, "Are you armed?"

"No. But a God-awful nuisance to subdue, even so." James cast an apologetic glance toward Mary. "I know—mind the porcelain. I'll do my best. Engels, you'll feel a right idiot if it *is* an elderly lady."

"Fine. Bring her to the parlour for tea." Engels lifted his hand. "Call if you need anything," he said, and picked up his fork.

I had risen, too, of course. James looked thoughtful, I looked inflexible (I tried to, anyway, and must have succeeded in some measure), and in the end I followed him out of the dining room.

The study door stood open, spilling quantities of warm light. James stopped on the threshold. Past his shoulder I glimpsed the woman before the fire, the back of a little plump figure in travel-creased black silk, the shape of her black bonnet distorted by the tossed-back veiling. James was absolutely motionless.

Then he stepped forward and said, "Good evening, Aunt Louisa." And stopped, as if all of the usual next things to say were inadequate, which they were.

She turned quickly. It *was* Aunt Louisa. Her face made James cross the rest of the room and hand her to the chair nearest the fire. "You knew I was alive," he said, as if dismissing the point. "What's wrong?"

I had seen her less than a month ago, when I came to Melrose so that you and I and Richard could put our heads together. I could see only her profile from where I stood, but even that much of her looked years older, and exhausted, and frightened. Gloved hands folded tightly in her lap, little pink mouth pinched tight, she peered up at James as if for a sign from the heavens. "My son is in danger. Will you help him?"

The shortest and most straightforward speech I had ever heard out of Aunt Louisa.

James said, with no sign of surprise, "Would he want me to?"

Aunt Louisa said, "He is your brother."

Motionless again, and the perfect blankness of shock on his face. Then he dropped neatly to crouch beside her chair, back to the fire, and looked up into her face. "How long have you known?"

"Always."

I think James had forgotten I was there—no, I don't. But he was prepared to let me deal with the overhearing of this conversation in whatever way suited me. Aunt Louisa, I thought, might not have noticed me at all. She opened her reticule with shaking fingers, drew out a folded paper, and handed it to James. She took off her bonnet while he opened it and read. When he finished, he asked, "And have you taken any action?" The question was calm, steady, the voice I imagine (absurdly) of a general accepting the battlefield report of a frightened subaltern.

"I have just come from London. I saw George there—not at Whitehall, it did not seem wise. We met privately. He said what he says there."

"You know, of course, what he wants."

Her lower lip trembled. "I do. He . . . mentioned your name. I told him . . . I told him you had drowned in July."

"And he said—?"

"That he was sensible of the grief your family must feel." She was angry. Under the fright and weariness, there was a flash of stronger metal than I had ever seen in her before. "He didn't believe me, of course."

"No. Then that's not where you learned I was alive."

Aunt Louisa raised her head and looked, suddenly, to me. So much for not having noticed I was there. "Katherine—" Her face pinched, as if she had a pain somewhere. "—My daughter-in-law is not the only one who can pry and snoop when she wants to.''

Oh, Kitty, I swear I had forgotten how the second raid on Aunt Louisa's jewel-case ended. Of *course* she has it in her to be devious.

James looked down at the paper in his hand. ''Do you mean to give him what he wants?''

Aunt Louisa opened her mouth, distressed. Then she stopped herself, and sniffed. At last she said, ''If it is the only way to protect Richard.''

Their eyes met, James's and his aunt's. My aunt's. I refuse to try to work out the relationship between Aunt Louisa and James. ''Correct answer,'' James said, his smile one-cornered. ''You may not be able to protect us both. For once. I'll try to keep you from having to choose.''

''There's a letter,'' she said, reaching again in her reticule. ''From him. I suppose Katherine was to pass it on. It is for you.''

Aunt Louisa cannot have understood his expression, if she noticed it. The terrible instinct for self-control deadened his face, but not before his eyes had widened, saying, Here. Here is a vulnerable place. She held out the letter, sealed in its envelope, and he took it without looking at it, held it, unexamined, with the other sheet she had given him.

''Thank you. Yes, she would have passed it on. But of course, it wouldn't have arrived so quickly.'' His eyes dropped for an instant, then returned to hers. ''You knew all this time?''

I thought at first that she didn't understand him, or did not mean to respond. Then she drew breath and said, ''William was always kind to me. Always. And a good father. I knew he didn't marry me for love, but he made me happy. And I tried to make him happy in return.'' In her lap, her hands twisted and closed and twisted. In one of them, I noticed, was a handkerchief. ''When we left India and came back to England, he met his brother's wife—'' That stopped her, temporarily.

''Your mother was . . . very beautiful. And clever, and lively. She made him laugh, and argued with him. She could sing, in Italian and Irish. Everyone admired her. I suspected, when you were born, that—But I watched William, and your mother, at your christening. Then I was sure.''

Her voice dwindled as she talked. I don't mean that it became softer, but that its presence grew less. It sounded like the voice of a pretty, timid girl who came from India to her husband's family home and found a rock waiting that would wreck the ship of her marriage and her hopes.

''She knew I did not like her. I do not know if she realized that I knew about her and my husband. I wanted not to like *you*. But there are ways in which you remind me of him. I loved you at first for his sake. And then she died, and William became so distant. I never told anyone about Diana and William. And he *was* kind to me, James.''

Tears were cutting down her cheeks now, zig-zagging from crease to crease. Her eyes were red and swollen. ''He gave me your brother. He gave me Richard. I am a stupid old woman, but I can do this much. I can protect my son. I can be proud of that.''

James took her clenched hands between both of his. ''*I'm* proud of you,'' he said.

She rose, blind with tears, and he stood and took her into his arms. When I left and closed the door behind me, she was sobbing into his lapel, and he was stroking her hair, staring over her head at a distance that wasn't there.

I went back to the dining room and explained that it was James's . . . that it was my Aunt Louisa, come to tell James about some family problem, and that she had learned where we were from my cousin Kitty. I must have looked unaccountably stunned, because Engels said merely, ''Oh?'' and made a satirical essay of it. Mary laid her hand on his arm and served dessert.

In half an hour, James brought a much recovered Aunt Louisa into the parlour to meet her host and hostess and have a cup of tea. She was offered food and a bed for the night as well, but in something like her usual style, she refused both. ''I have a room at an hotel. No, I have no intention of putting perfect strangers to the trouble of lodging me. Though I am terribly grateful for the offer, of course. And delighted to have met you. Mr Engels, what did you say your line of work was?''

"Manufacturing," he said kindly, while I looked at the ceiling.

"It will be the lifeblood of England, they say. My papa was in the East India Company. Which is trade, I am not ashamed to admit it. The Company made England wealthy, and an empire. A nation of shopkeepers. Though it is not as if the East India Company is the same as a shop. So good of you to have my nephew and niece to visit. Susan, they buried your brother today."

She said it that way because she knew it would give me a shock. "Ma'am?" I said.

"You heard me, miss. David's funeral. You ought to have been there."

I took a deep and strengthening breath and said, "A shame you had to miss it, too."

It bounced off. "You should at least have put on your blacks by now. I suppose you haven't so much as a pair of black gloves about you."

"I'll see to it right away, Aunt."

Mary, behind the teapot, looked as if she might fly into bits, moved to sympathy, outrage, and amusement at the undeniable grim humour of the dialogue. James was only smiling, faintly, at his knees, which gave me the fortitude to remember that Louisa had been good to him in spite of the worst provocation, and that I could be the same to her in the face of considerably less.

After ten minutes more, she left in a hackney, and I collapsed on the settee. James came back from seeing her out and said, "If there *is* an afterlife, your credit is unassailable."

I bounced up at the sound of his voice. Engels and Mary had left the room, and I couldn't remember hearing them do it. Perhaps I was stricken unconscious from release of tension, and they had gone then. "Do you realize I'm going mad with curiosity? What trouble is Richard in? What's all this about 'George' and Whitehall?"

For answer, he handed me a letter from Sir George Bankston to Aunt Louisa. And you have a fragment, a mere scent, of your revenge, dear, because I suppose I shall have to copy it out for you and include it. Since, as James has Aunt Louisa's original, I cannot simply recommend you rifle her papers and steal it.

After I had read it, James said, "You understand what's behind it, I think."

I looked up from the page in horror. "He wants an exchange. Richard's safety, for you."

"Brava." He didn't seem horrified. A little preoccupied, perhaps, but not upset. Or not outwardly.

"What will you do?"

He smiled. "First rule—one of them, anyway—in this sort of game: Don't let your opponent make the rules. Sir George says the options are Richard, or me. I propose we think of a few others and offer them instead."

"What did Richard say in his letter?"

James stood before me as if he wanted not to be still. "I haven't read it yet."

"Don't you think you ought to?"

"Yes. Do you think you ought to have gone to David's funeral?"

"No. Yes." I let the contents of my lungs out in a little explosion. "Just go and read it. You'll survive it." Then I caught his face between my hands and kissed him. He returned the kiss rather desperately. Then he walked out of the parlour. He would walk to the gallows like that, I think, brisk and businesslike and with unconsidered grace.

I gave him roughly half an hour before I went looking for him. I found him in the dining room, with a candle lit on the sideboard, leaning on the glass of the French doors with one arm raised and his forehead braced on it. My insides gave an awful leap of distress.

He heard me, and turned his head. His face was blank and pale and marked with tears. "It must be the Celt in me," he said, his voice falling unsteady as feathers. "I've been given everything I most want. My brother's forgiveness. Your love. And it only makes me afraid of what will be taken away, to pay for them."

I put my hands up to his face and wiped away the tears. "Possibly the Celt. It's a profoundly stupid thing to think."

He closed his arms around me and kissed me, and I tasted

the salt on his mouth. "Profound and stupid. Yes, that's how I feel."

"What did he *say*?"

"He suggested I ought, perhaps, to grow up. What's your opinion on the matter?"

"Oh, I won't endorse that. He can't be thinking clearly. What else did he say?"

"He led me by the hand in the most insulting fashion through the reasoning behind his last letter. Or it would have been insulting if it hadn't been justified." James played with my hair while he spoke, which made me wonder if I now knew why cats stretch and purr when stroked. "He . . . reminded me of some things we share. And he made me laugh. I'll have to get him out of this scrape so that I can tell him so. Do you know, the worst thing about not being a rich man anymore is that I won't be able to drape you in diamonds. You'd suit diamonds."

He had made James laugh. I wouldn't have thought that anything was likely to make James laugh between the time he'd left the parlour and my finding him in the dining room. There was a genuine mastery of understatement at work here. I wrinkled my nose. "Diamonds are vulgar. It doesn't matter anyway—I'm a rich woman. I mean to keep you in shameful luxury inappropriate to your working-class allegiance and finance the publication of your seditious pamphlets."

"I suppose I'd better write one, then." He was smiling into my eyes in a fine disturbing way.

"And besides, I'd rather be draped in you. Or vice versa."

"Figuratively? We could try to work it out. Your room," he asked, placing kisses at regular intervals along my jaw, "or mine?"

"Whichever's closer."

He led me to the dining room door, but halted with his hand on the knob. In the candlelight, his face took on the stopped-short look that means he's been surprised by his own mind. "Oh, blast. Don't murder me, my goddess. I've just thought of a riposte so worthy, I'm willing to pay for it with a few minutes away from you."

"Good for you," I said, keeping my grip on his hand. "What's my consolation? What if I raise the price of your riposte?"

"Raise it," he said, pulling me close. "I'll pay. Is Engels still up?"

"He may be in his study."

"I wonder if he'd lend me a book?"

I stared. James's gaze was fixed on nothing, and he was biting back a smile. "All right," I said, "I can see I'll get no good out of you until you're done. In the meantime, my room in five minutes. Or I come down and fetch you." I kissed him with great concentration, in order to make sure he wouldn't forget, and half-ran up the stairs.

He didn't forget, dear. He is lying asleep in my bed as I write this, and the mere writing of it causes such a stir in me that my hand trembles. The intensity abates somewhat with time, I trust, or I will either kill myself with exhaustion or go mad trying to think of love and anything else simultaneously. I will close here, since I should wake him and ask what he'd like for breakfast. Recently become my favourite meal of the day. *Appalling* sentimental nonsense.

Mindlessly yours,
Susan

Postscript, barely in time: I had to rip open the envelope to include this. I really am addled, Kit. Don't, don't, *don't* stir a step from Melrose. I know: your definition of sensible is very like The Wretch's, and you think your next act ought to be the daring rescue of Richard. It would be, if you were not, almost certainly, being watched as closely as he is. Once again you have the hardest part of any of us—you must stay where you are and appear perfectly unruffled. Anything else is likely to alarm, or at least alert, the opposition. If—I'm sorry, that's silly, *when*—you write to Richard, tell him the same thing. Sit like a rock and pretend complacency. As long as he doesn't move, everything balances where it is. When he moves, things will start to fall down, and it would be so much nicer if they could all fall in the direction we push them. I know it's hard, but think of the favour I am doing you, dear. You know how you hate going about in the snow.

S.

8 DEC 1849

Dear Henry,

I do hope that dousing this in violet scent was enough to cause you to open it in private, because this is a matter for the utmost secrecy, and one that involves the safety of rather a lot of people. I am about to ask a favour that will put you in danger, as well. I know you will say you're not hen-hearted and don't mind that sort of thing, but I doubt you've taken part in a venture of quite this class before. I can only assure you that it is quite a good part, and that I have absolute confidence in your ability to carry it off. And Cousin, I require this of you so desperately that I can't even ask if you will do it; I can only tell you what it is, and trust that you won't fail me.

I suspect that you've been roped into staying a few days at Melrose Hall to provide manly support to the ladies after the funeral (or at least, to keep Brian company while he does so). I want you to invent some innocent pretext (or not so innocent; if anyone else noticed that you received fragrant correspondence, this letter will perhaps help you misdirect suspicion) to leave Melrose for at least several days. I believe James's black gelding is lodged in the stables there; bring him. In fact, you may ride him. I promise you that you have the permission of everyone most concerned in the question. Meet me at the Lion in Hounslow at dinner-time on Monday the 10th. I will explain all the rest of it there.

We emerged equal in obligation, I think, after our meeting in Oxford, since you didn't tell anyone you had met me there in disguise and I didn't tattle on your gambling in the Locket. But if you will do me this favour, I will be so deeply in your debt that I don't know what would square matters. I'm sure you'll be able to think of something.

I am counting on you, Henry, and pray you will respond bravely to the summons of

Your loving cousin,
Susan Voight

DECEMBER 9th
MELROSE HALL

Dearest,

I've just received an extraordinary letter from Susan, so full of unexpected events that I do not know how to begin telling you about it, yet I can't simply copy it, for it is full of the sorts of things ladies cannot tell even, or perhaps especially, to their husbands, but I can make a summary by saying that Susan and James are lovers, and, as far as I can discern, they are both horribly self-satisfied about it, when in fact it is we who ought to be self-satisfied, but I bless them both, as I know you do, and that would be the whole of it except that the important matter is that you are in danger where you are, and not only that but, as you will see from the portion of Susan's letter I *am* copying, especially the postscript, you are not to leave, which frightens me horribly, but I do not know what to do except to trust to James and Susan, which I could do without a second's hesitation if it were only my life, but it is yours, and I am terrified, and the worst of it is that I have to write back to Susan and be nice and chatty about all the news she has told me, which is, really, terribly important, because I think the effects of their love will last far beyond the present, to the time when we are all able to laugh about the danger we are now in, but it is so difficult, and I miss you, but at least, with this letter, and the part of Susan's I am copying, and the other from an acquaintance of your mother's in Whitehall, you will know to be alert.

But I will send this off, my love, and trusting that it will all work out well, I will keep my spirits up and write to Susan while thinking only of you, and anxiously awaiting the moment when you will again hold in your arms your adoring,

Kitty

RICHARD COBHAM'S JOURNAL

DECEMBER 10ᵗʰ

Got a present from James today, a copy of *Science of Logic*.
I was in my room when Coslick came in, holding a parcel,
saying it had arrived for me by "the route you know". I said
that, in fact, I didn't know the route, and I had no idea how
letters were getting back and forth, only that I gave them to
him and they seemed somehow to arrive, and he said that's
what he meant. Looking a bit leery, he held out the parcel, but
I couldn't imagine what could be dangerous about a parcel,
unless it contained an asp or something of that order. I opened
it and the Hegel emerged, and I laughed so hard tears came.
Coslick said, "What does it mean, for the love of Christ?"
and I said, "Not Christ specifically, I'd say rather the Absolute
Idea," and he looked at me as if I had brain fever, so, for his
peace of mind, I said, "It really only means that James is a
wicked, wicked man," and he said, "Yes, well, I knew that,"
and left me, shaking his head. One of his children, Anthony,
came running into my room at about that time and asked what
had happened that I was laughing so, and I said, "This book
is very amusing, you ought to read it when you get older,"
and that made me laugh more.

I must never let James know that, later, I tore open the front
and back covers to see if he had concealed another secret message, but there was none. Then, with nothing better to do, I
began reading the thing, which I had not done since university
(another thing I ought never to let on to James) and got oddly
caught up in it. Perhaps it is the difference between reading
when you have to, as I did at university, and reading for its
own sake; on the other hand, perhaps it is simply that I have
lived more; but I kept finding meaningful passages, which I
had never used to do. When he speaks of, to translate loosely,
"holding (grabbing? grasping?) the opposites in their unity",
it almost seems as if I have walked that road without knowing
it. And, still in the introduction, he talks about how dry and
empty are the forms of grammar when studied by themselves,

but how full of meaning they are to one who has studied languages; I cannot help but feel this, too, has echoes in my experience: understanding of the general is so much deeper when one has wrestled with the particular.

In his discussion of the relationship of appearance to essence, I could not help but think of Kitty, especially now when all my contact with her is through letters, in which, thanks to her refusal to end a sentence—or, indeed, to break one up by any means other than a comma—one would think her foolish and scatterbrained, yet how far from the truth this is! And yet, in another way, both the form and content of her letters provide a key to unlocking her personality.

What would James make of this use of the dialectic? Susan would understand it.

It is peculiar that, when first I studied this book, what moved me most was Hegel's concept of pure thought as the centre of all, and I kept trying to make sense of that, along with Kant's *Ding an sich*, to find and master the unknowable; now all of that seems beside the point, and what matters is the method, or how one might seek to achieve an understanding of the world. It is ironic that I used such similar words to James when I wished to hurt him, and now they are coming back to me as though my arrogance is to be punished by my own phrases and thoughts. The most abstract of the philosophers and yet the most pertinent and practical!

I still wish it were safe to write to Kitty, but, failing that, I think I will return to old Hegel and see what else he can tell me. Perhaps I will keep reading until I am stumped, and then I will write the problem to James in German and let him puzzle it out as best he may.

DECEMBER 10ᵗʰ

Dear Susan,

I have it all now I see it and it is all so clear about you and James and me and Dick and everything and there isn't any need to worry because I have it I understand wait until you hear and here it is *cherries* are *crickets* don't you see how that makes it all make sense about Aunt Louisa and all those people who think they can frighten us and make us do what they want and fit us into their plans but we won't let them because now we know the secret and it all makes sense so I'm going to have Wye post this right away and go lie down goodbye

Kitty.

RICHARD COBHAM'S JOURNAL

DECEMBER 11th

It appears I am in danger. Perhaps reading Hegel is not the best way to prepare for a life-and-death struggle. On the other hand, perhaps it is! Alerted Coslick, who sighed but did not appear surprised. Told him we were to do nothing but wait, which he accepted with a scowl I understood perfectly. Still, what wonderful news about James and Susan.

My poor mother. My poor Kitty!

DECEMBER 11th
MELROSE HALL

Poor, Long-Suffering Susan,

This morning, or, really, this afternoon when I arose I asked Wye if I had given him a letter to bring to the post and if he had done so and he said he had, and what he thinks of me after asking such a question and after the look that, no doubt, appeared on my face at his answer I will never know, but it is probably what I deserve, though it is hardly what you deserve and so I apologize not so much for my consumption of prodigious amounts of opium but for suddenly concluding, in the middle of my debauch, that I ought to write to you and actually doing it and producing a letter the contents of which I have not the least notion of and would rather never know, so if I have frightened you and you feel the need for revenge you can get it simply by returning me that letter. I am extremely tired today as a result, and feel rather as if I am walking about shod with iron but otherwise none the worse for it except for the pinpricks of my conscience, and though I did have one moment when I thought the Shimmering Gate had opened for me, I had consumed so much opium that I cannot pretend to reliable perceptions, but it was odd because I thought I saw Great-Grandpapa Woodworth and he was holding several small somethings in his hand and dropping them one at a time toward a form prostrate at his feet while giving me the kindest smile you could imagine, none of which makes sense now, though perhaps it did four-and-twenty hours ago.

Aunt Louisa returned yesterday, just before I began my debauch, and went straight up to her room, so that I was spared whatever glance she might have given me and also of deciding whether to speak to her, which I think I really should do, and perhaps I will tomorrow, because she is Dick's mother, after all, and with all of this I really ought to make some effort to understand her, don't you think?

But Susan, my dear, all of this is quite beside the point, and I cannot tell you how delighted I am for you and James, for you most of all, because I think you know the worlds of happiness that I wish for you, and even with all of the trouble and confusion that surrounds us now, and how frightened I am, especially for Richard, the realization that you and James have become lovers, and, for all I can tell, in the best way, is a consolation to me, and seems almost to be by itself a beacon of future happiness that I can hold to now when it is so dim and murky ahead, and even your befuddlement is a joy to me because it means that now, without question or doubt, an emotion has, ah, I must stop here, because the next word was about to be penetrated, and before your letter I should just have written the word and gone on, but now I must catch your eye as I write the word and watch as you make that expression you made when Mrs Wallinger asked the room why there was a pile of straw in the corner and we knew that if we burst out in laughter we should be accusing ourselves, and so you see now, don't you, but laughing aside I rejoice that emotion has *got through* so strongly that you must work to be able to write rationally about it, and when you have settled down and are your perfectly composed self once more, we will still have that much more understanding of each other, and you will, by-the-bye, settle down and be your perfectly composed self once more, but not too soon, I hope, and to answer the question you almost asked, the feeling does abate with time, or rather it changes, in that it becomes something warm and friendly and normal and *right*, and if the intensity is diminished, then in some ways what replaces it is even better, as I suspect you will be telling me before too many years have passed, and I know very well that just at this moment the idea of the flames burning lower is both unthinkable and horrid, but trust me, you will have plenty of time to bake yourself good and brown first, and it will all work out very well.

But it was the least bit cruel of you to write about it so well, and in such detail, and with such passion, when Dick is so far away, but maybe it is just as well that he was not here, or it would have taken several days to finish reading it, not that I would have begrudged the time, though you are lucky, by the way, if you fall asleep right away, because I find that I am usually wide awake afterward, and filled with energy, and Dick does the best he can but soon he drifts off to sleep with this odd little smile on his lips that is as far as can be from the way his face looks at the moment of crisis, which is all twisted up and almost angry and he snarls as if he were a jungle animal, which makes me feel like one too, only he tells me that when my own crisis comes my eyes become wide and I gasp for breath like a fish, about which I should be embarrassed, but Dick tells me I am never more beautiful, all of which is to say that you must tell me what James's face is like, because no two men are the same that way, or in most other ways, now that I think of it. The only thing that puzzled me was when you report that he left for coffee and you said he was gone for ten minutes, which makes me wonder how you could stand it, because from my memory of the first time Dick and I got out of bed, I would have had hysterics if he had been gone that long, well, maybe not hysterics, but it seems like an age and I will bet you would not have let him go if you had known he would be gone that long!

And I am not surprised you did not remember how the second raid on the jewel-case went, because it was not your room that was uninhabitable for days and days, but I remember it afresh every time I hear a cricket, so I have no excuse for not having thought of it, but you could have pushed me over with a breath when I read that Aunt Louisa showed up there, and I just no longer know what to think, of her or of anything else, I only wish we knew a *few* people who could be understood in a nice simple phrase or two, which makes me glad I have never had the chance to know Tournier at all, because I should probably discover that he ran an orphanage and I would not be able to hate him with a clear conscience, so I will remain ignorant of him if it's all the same to you, and the same goes for Andrew, because whatever we may think of him we must also remember how he held us all together after Roderick died, and how kind he was, and you know as well as I that there were sides to David that were praiseworthy, which is a silly way to put it because it sounds as if I am suggesting we look at everyone in little slices, but I just mean that everyone is so complicated, and everything would be easier if I could simply dismiss from consideration those I dislike, instead of having to understand and hate them.

But I am rambling now, which means I ought to finish and get this posted after begging you to give my love to James and assure him that I am going nowhere near Cauldhurst, and, though I know I need not say it, pleading with you to be careful of my Richard, and if I do speak with Aunt Louisa, or if anything else of interest should happen, you may be assured you will hear from your anxious but nevertheless overjoyed,

Kitty

LONDON
13th DECEMBER, 1849

Dear Richard,

I remember sitting in my little room above the stables of the Grey Hound, trying to begin a letter to you—that first letter, in which I admitted to having clung to my life against both odds and evidence. This seems nearly as clumsy and hesitant as that, and I haven't the excuses I had then. Now I am in health at least, and at least no more at risk. It is as if truth forms as forbidding a landscape between us as my deceit once did. Forbidding because of its strangeness; crossing, I am wary of its ditches and bogs, and whatever its coppices shelter. You can cross—*have* crossed—that landscape in a single stride; it is your nature. Mine is so timid and mistrustful in the face of kindness and hope that you may expect to see me for a long time to come traversing that ground in suspicious fits and starts, rolled up half the time like a hedgehog convinced he is in danger of being eaten.

What a difficult and unpredictable illness secrecy is to recover from! I suffered a relapse, when I did not tell Susan what I meant to do in London. She, inured in some measure to intrigue-craft and its requirements, did not ask. It was an insult not to tell her, because it might have seemed I thought secrecy necessary. I only thought the knowledge was a burden she need not bear, even as I knew that she would not thank me, now or ever, for choosing her burdens for her. But not telling her seems as well, in some unfathomable way, a blow against myself. (I do not intend to maintain this unreasonable silence; Susan will have the whole tale, both the events I meant to happen and those that happened very much in spite of me. Your mother would disapprove of my revealing all the sordid facts to a lady I hold in esteem. You, I think, would disapprove if I proposed to do anything less.)

I don't understand this, Richard. I have had my heart pleasurably broken half a dozen times; I am not such a fool as to call any of those episodes love. I was in love once, by my perception of it. No one you've met—a young widow in Cologne, beautiful and intelligent and accomplished. She liked me very well, but she didn't love me, and that, as they say, is that. (Which is not what I said to myself at the time, as you may imagine.) But this is as if I had been living incomplete all my life without ever knowing—one arm, one leg, half a brain—until one day with an audible click and not a moment's warning, I am completed. Binocular vision, no need to hop, and an ever-so-much easier time of it climbing ladders.

What nonsense I write! What I mean is that this hardly seems encompassed by any concept of love that I know or have heard tell of. I wake every morning staggered anew by the whole idea. I feel as if I have stumbled sightless into a new world and found a place waiting for me that allows even for my blindness—and at the same time, I know, I *know* that I cannot manage to fill it with this rickety frame and meagre understanding. And yet, I am filling it. I am living in it. Being, nothingness, and becoming; resolution of internal contradiction by synthesis—this isn't love, it is a demonstration of practical application to a doubting Hegelian. More nonsense. I am off-balance, half terrified, wholly bemused, stunned as if I had been clouted with the blow that precedes enlightenment. Whatever I am, I am certainly *not* complacent.

I have no idea what you must think of this liaison with Susan. The world that we inhabit by accident of birth will display a wonderful unanimity of opinion: they will say that I seduced my cousin, and the more imaginative heads among them will mention not only her virtue but her fortune as well. Lust and money, says the high-minded revolutionary in tones of deep disgust. It sounds like self-justification and sentimentality to say that taking Susan into my bed was only an admission that the audible click had happened well before that. Perhaps I ought to have been satisfied with the rarefied air of courtly love—but I was not, and I think in retrospect I am glad I did not try to subject Susan to that particular piece of juvenile idealism. I am *trying* to be an adult, Richard; be patient with me.

I stand by what I have done, and will continue to do so all my life, regardless of how Susan herself may choose to order her future. She may give me up, Richard. She is free to do so. (The thought produces a sensation very like falling from a great height.) I don't believe I am free to do likewise, and I find I am content—no, wrong word, if there is contentment somewhere down this path, I have not reached it yet—that it should be so. Susan did not give herself to me, as the polite expression goes. I gave myself to her, in a much more than physical sense, and I cannot undo it if I would. So I hope that you do not disapprove *very* much, because it won't be any earthly use if you do.

I hadn't meant to devote so much space to writing about Susan. It's not that I don't want to; the reverse, rather. But it makes me feel bereft to be apart from her, even as I am aware that the creature who completes this poor cripple is still in the world, and that no less an authority than my brother can vouch for her existence.

There, that came out almost naturally. It's hard for me still, coming to terms with the idea that anything so right as that we should be brothers should be drawn up out of that well of pain and betrayal and deceit. When it was dug I did not exist and you barely did, so I can only take my measure of its depth by what was there seven years later. What is still there, if truth be told. But I have no wish to be reminded that I've been hunted like a hare in part because Andrew Cobham still resents having been cuckolded. Too demeaning, no romance.

Well, I suppose I shall have to come 'round to accounting for my whereabouts at some point in this letter, and it may as well be here. I find that the past two days' news is interfering with my ability to concentrate on writing. The hare (that's your correspondent) arrived in the thicket of London on the morning of the 11th. I refuse to rehearse my parting with Susan in Manchester here. The parting from Engels was surprisingly affecting; I wish the two of you could meet. Though I am not sure I wouldn't end up the worse for the association. He could tell you several undignified stories about your near relation. He and I fought a duel once, in Cologne—it had to do with the young widow only insofar as I think it was done partly to cheer me up. The most exquisite attention paid to the forms and every gentlemanly observance . . . except at the end. I lost, by the way. At any rate, I bid Engels farewell in Manchester with the depressing conviction that it was for the last time, and can only trust to the future to prove me wrong.

London, with no more back-tracking. What I wanted was to engineer a meeting with Sir George Bankston, ideally without consulting him in the matter. To that end, I trotted 'round the city accumulating scraps of information by means of diligent playacting. (Others might call it "spying" or "intelligence-gathering," but that's only lacquering the low theatrics with an unearned dignity. What would *you* call a handful of costume-changes and as many assumed voices, postures, attitudes, and names? Playacting. I do Wye, for instance, to such perfection that if he caught me at it, he'd beat me senseless.)

You will say, perhaps, that I was careless. Not so; or if it *is* so, then I have been careless for most of a decade and have managed through the grace of whatever force protects a career liar to avoid the consequences. But I was somehow located by Tournier's faction, and the consequences fell largely on another.

I was in Covent Garden Market late the night of the 11th; the theatres had just let out, and the market and the surrounding streets were full of play-goers moving toward their next amusement. They included Sir George among their number. His next amusement, I happened to know, was an illicit boxing-match near Smithfield Market, and I meant to follow him to it and separate him from his companions in the confusion (have you ever attended an illegal match? All the confusion one could ask for, and ideal for my purposes), in order to have a little uninterrupted conversation.

Then I saw a familiar face in the throng, quite close and turned fixedly toward me: a female countenance, rosy even in the irregular light of the market, dark-eyed, surrounded by a wild loose cloud of black hair. My feelings on seeing that face were nothing like the ones with which I first regarded it. It was the little Irish woman from the yard of the Grey Hound, who had claimed to be the rector's housemaid, and who I now suspected to be in the service of Eleanor Tournier. From her expression, before she turned and pushed away from me through the crowd with every evidence of desperation, she had recognized me.

I think now that the recognition was pretense, that she had known I was there, and that I was meant to believe that she had only just then found me out. But it was only subsequent events that suggested it. At the time, it seemed necessary to catch her up and prevent her from revealing my presence to anyone for at least long enough that I could reach Smithfield Market unpursued.

I could move even less freely through the crowd than she. She had only to elbow the press of people aside, and tread on the insteps of occasional drunken bucks; I had to get through knowing that a fashionable after-theatre crowd would contain a certain percentage of people who could recognize James Cobham at close quarters. So she was well into the tangle of lanes that surrounds the market before I was clear and could move quickly.

I may have been less than a minute too late. She lay at the side of a little vest-pocket court, in the light from the lamp over the door of an old-clothes dealer's. Her neck was broken. I had barely time to determine it before I heard a commotion down the lane and knew that her murderer was raising the alarm, and that I was to be found with the body.

As it turned out, I was not, for all the good it did me or the poor girl who had become the body. I know the area and can travel through it quickly, vertically as well as horizontally. I do not believe I was ever seen, however much I may have been speculated upon. And that I was speculated upon, you will soon have confirmed.

My revulsion for this nest of maggots outstrips my ability to describe it, Richard. For the sake of a clear account, I am trying to maintain some small distance from these events I write about. But this one murder, so needless, so casually done, has sickened me more than any other act I have witnessed. Perhaps the sudden imposition of kindness on my life led me to believe that kindness had imposed itself everywhere, and that even my enemies were transformed. I swear, I was nearly lulled into thinking I could let it be—get you out of danger, I thought, and then I could play least in sight, leave the country for a year or two. Tournier is as good as finished as a conspirator, though he may not know it yet. Let the Trotter's Club fall of their own weight, which would have to happen eventually. We might already have drawn the teeth of this manufactured incident intended to destroy the community of radical *émigrés*—or if we hadn't, there were enough people now who knew of it that surely it could be staved off without my help. I could visit India, perhaps, and cut up Aunt Julianna's peace—with Susan, if she would. Then I could come home after a while, with the past paid off and done. In short, I forgot what these creatures will do, with little provocation and no compunction at all. There is no safety or security for you or me or anyone we love as long as they are free to act. So if they—Alan Tournier, his sister, whoever else has committed and sanctioned so much cruelty and death—want me so badly,

I shall let them have as much of me as is necessary to choke them.

If the constables—or anyone else—searched for me that night, it was probably in every doss-house and on every two-penny-rope in London. I slept sound in the embrace of ancient Toryism: namely, the Clarendon. Servants' rooms, as I was passing myself off as someone's footman. Yes, the stout traditionalists who stay at the Clarendon still travel with their whole bloody household.

With the Smithfield plan derailed, I was forced to fall back on my less desirable reserve. Last night Bankston was engaged to attend a rout-party at the home of Sir Hugo Bishop and his Lady. Susan's been there; ask her. More playacting. The rôle: wealthy gentleman of fashion. The costume for the night was evening-dress, and my own, for once. It felt no less like a costume and a rôle than any other. It is a problem I have struggled with before—not that you become someone other than yourself, but that you become no one at all.

It was easy to come in over the garden wall, since in this weather there are no clandestine flirtations going on in the summer-house. (You may tell Susan I said so, and see what she replies, and what colour she turns. Oh, unfair; she wasn't flirting, but the gentleman with her wished she would.) On the way I examined the gardener's shed, also suffering seasonal neglect, for future application. I reached the terrace unseen, and occupied it inconspicuously with the aid of a cigar (I smoke them only when I want to pretend to have stepped out to blow a cloud). From there I flagged down a servant in the dining room and asked to have a message delivered to Sir George Bankston.

If I tell you what the message said, I would be exposing one of the most discreetly conducted extramarital affairs in the history of society London. Just because I know about it does not mean that you ought. But the lady in question summoned Sir George to the study for private colloquy, and if that isn't an excellent footing for an interview in which you mean to have the upper hand, I have never prepared one.

None of the rest of the circumstances were ideal, of course. Sir Hugo is with the Foreign Office; and no party at that house is ever less than half full of Her Majesty's servants of one branch or another. I would have much preferred Smithfield Market. But I drew a high-backed, deep-winged chair nearer the fire, laid the fan and lace-edged handkerchief I'd brought with me on a table nearby (and lit the lamp there as well, to be quite obvious about it), and made myself comfortable.

He didn't keep me waiting long. The fan and handkerchief did their job; he locked the door after himself, assuming that all the necessary cast had arrived. Well, they had, poor fellow. You may imagine his distress when he came to the fire and turned, and found me in the chair with one knee drawn up to steady the pistol I was pointing at him.

One may be fooled, and not *be* a fool, and this must be said of Sir George Bankston. No bluster nor quailing nor, a blessing on the man, any bellow for help, which saved me having to lope, since I had no intention of actually shooting him. No, he transformed on the instant from hopeful lover to . . . I cannot find a noun that means one of that set of people who is accustomed to thinking quickly and clearly when looking down the barrel of a pistol.

I said, by way of explanation, "James Cobham. I believe you wanted to see me."

"Not," he replied quite coolly, "under these circumstances, however."

He tried hard not to be visibly disturbed when I told him he no longer had you to hold over anyone's head. He hoped I didn't mind if he took the liberty of verifying it. Not at all, said I. (My only assurance that it was true was that I had planned your escape, set Susan to execute it, and hadn't heard that she'd failed. I didn't say so, by word or look.)

Then I explained why I was troubling to tell him about it in person: namely, that in exchange for his immediate and continuing lack of interest in my family, I was, figuratively speaking, prepared to deliver to him the heads of four high-ranking Whigs, including a cabinet minister and Bankston's own immediate superior, Lord Growe. Bankston, you see, is a not-so-closet Tory, and has no hope of advancement as long as Growe and his cronies sit where they do now.

"Why stop there?" Bankston said deliberately. "You could bring down Russell, too, and the government with him." I assured him that precipitating general elections was not, at the moment, in my power nor any of my bread and butter.

He wanted to know how I proposed to give him his Whigs. Not an unreasonable question, I told him, but not one I intended to answer. All I would say was that, inside of a fortnight, I would provide him with a scandal of such magnitude that anyone involved in it would be barred for life from public office, and one or two might even end by seeing the sunrise through a rope window. Did he doubt I could manage it?

"You must think I'm as mad as you are," he answered, which wasn't one of the several things I had expected him to say. He knew, he said, that I was among the instigators of a plot they'd got wind of—that I and a cabal of Red foreigners meant to strike a blow in Britain that could destabilize the whole political structure of Europe.

I told him not to believe everything he heard. "But me, specifically?" I asked.

Oh, yes. My name, or my description, had cropped up often in the last few weeks, and not only in the matter of the Navy man who'd been killed at Newport. (Has anyone passed that piece of news on to you? I hope so. I haven't the strength just now.) It seemed they had found a girl murdered in Covent Garden the night before, who had had connexions to the Irish and European rebels, who carried documents connecting me to the plot. And two witnesses said they had seen me with her only minutes before she was found dead.

I have no idea if I managed to hide everything I felt and thought in that moment. Probably I did, but for an instant I lost conscious track of what my face was doing. It was the first I knew that I had not escaped a clumsy (and brutal) attempt to implicate me in a murder, but fallen part-way into a rather more clever (but equally brutal) entrapment for treason. Then my vision cleared, and I found Bankston watching me closely.

"Every word of it a lie," I said. "Even you aren't convinced it's true." We are in similar trades, he and I. We both know about the laying of false evidence, the testimony that sends a man up the stairs in the morning because someone, somewhere, finds it better that he should be silent.

"I will have to be convinced it's true, unless I am given an alternative," he replied. "You will have to give me some evidence to outweigh this story. And to outweigh what I *know* to be true: that you have been closely involved, at various times in the past, with Red Republicans, that you have taken part in treasonous meetings and acts with full knowledge of their nature . . . and that you have, at least once, held a gentleman in Her Majesty's service at gun-point in a house which you entered by stealth. I assume you weren't invited?''

I had to admit the justice of the last accusation. I admitted nothing about the ones before it; not because my admission would change anything, but because it wouldn't. I was involved in this, after all, because of a list of informers. Bankston could not have found me out without information being laid, but once he had it, he could verify it all. And that, as they say in so many circumstances, is that.

"You see," he added after a little space, "that you are asking for a bit more than you might at first have thought. Does it change your offer to me?''

I have rarely felt less like laughing, but I did, quite involuntarily, surprising both of us. "Yes, it does," I said. "As well as your Whigs, I'll give you the people behind your Covent Garden murder. Will you object to getting them cold? They aren't what you want, but I'm not going to give you what you want, and I think you know you can't pry it out of me, so you'll have to settle.'' What I *had* offered him, I told him, would solve a great many of his problems, including several he didn't yet know he had.

"Will it, indeed?'' he asked me, with a hard look and more query in his voice than the question might seem to merit. The above conversation, Richard, you will understand to be as accurate as my memory can supply; I haven't Susan's gifts. But that last speech from Bankston I know perfectly. And my answer, which was, "Yes, it will. Now it will have to, won't it?''

He felt it necessary to point out that whatever I was about to do would have to be done with no help from him or his office. I assured him that if he would simply refrain from actively hindering me, it would be enough. That, and to pull back his vultures—pardon, agents—from my family. He reminded me that I was a wanted man, and that he could do nothing about that. Then I wouldn't ask it, I told him. How was he to communicate with me, he wanted to know? I laughed and told him that when I sent him a message, he would know it.

"And if you pike?" Bankston asked.

"Then you may hang Richard Cobham," I told him. "And if you think that means nothing to me, ask yourself what other reason I have for walking into Hugo Bishop's house like a partridge into a poulterer's."

And after that, I walked him out the terrace doors and locked him in the gardener's shed. It was a matter of form, and we both knew it; it can't have taken him above fifteen minutes to get himself out. I had made sure of it before I went up to the house, after all. But assurances of non-interference aside, I saw no reason to deny myself the quarter-hour that would keep Bankston from having me followed, if nothing else. One ought to make it as easy as possible for a man to keep his bargains.

Besides, when one has the weary conviction that, by winning the present battle, one has made the loss of the much larger war inevitable, one likes to revel in the small temporary advantage. My shelter in Manchester was even more secure than Susan or I thought it was; I was safe from physical harm and unpleasant realization both. You may have noticed, Richard, what the result of my present course will be. Bankston did, and forced me to both see it and admit it, if not in so many words. I cannot, after this, remain in England. I am marked out as a revolutionist and suspected traitor in too many places; my name has been on too many tongues; if I stay I will be arrested and brought to trial eventually. Engels told me recently that dying for my cause was not at present the best service I could give it. For me to be hanged, or transported, or even imprisoned now would do no good to anyone, and possibly much harm.

You may wonder—others have, even to the pages of *The Times*—what feeling a man has for the land of his birth, when he has committed treason against it. The answer is, often, much love. Treason is defined by other men, and not by any law of nature. Nature itself has made humans seek to improve and perfect their state—an impulse which in due course humans extend to the State. For ten years I have, in my perverse way, tried to serve Britain and its people. Exile will be hard to face.

Bankston wanted to hear the details of my scheme, and I

wouldn't tell him. To you I will freely confess that at the time it hardly deserved the dignity of the name; it was more a determination than an actual plan. And no, I did not promise Bankston he could hang you on the strength of a determination. It would be difficult for him to bring any real charges against you now, and in a fortnight, unless you do something very rash indeed, it will be virtually impossible. Hanging you would solve none of his present problems, and would create several new ones.

I thought of almost nothing else on the journey from Manchester to London—well, the parts of my thinking that were coherent were almost entirely about the problem of bringing down the opposition. About half my thoughts of Susan were coherent, and they made up the rest of the measure. The incoherent parts of my mental processes, about Susan or otherwise, are by their nature difficult to recount, and you very likely wouldn't care for them anyway. I didn't, particularly. Being connected again to the world of feeling, I have to pay the price of it in perfectly reasonable anxiety.

But I laid facts and near-facts out for my review, such as: my turncoat conspirators, probably headed by Alan Tournier, have been making a dead set, not at killing me, but at associating me with proof of acts of treason and murder. I was to be disinherited as well, with David to replace me as heir—to benefit Tournier's nephew? But if so, why kill David? (This seems to me the least plausible part of our conjectures, but I can't, as yet, replace it with anything more likely.) Gideon Johnson seemed to think that if I *was* to be killed, that under the would-be Druidical aegis of the Trotter's Club it would be at winter solstice. We have a confession (undocumented, sadly) of murder from David, and circumstantial evidence suggests that it was somehow connected to the Trotter's Club. Kitty discovered unsavoury documents relating to the group among David's papers, suggesting that Roderick's murder might not have been an isolated event. And Andrew Cobham has returned, unannounced, to England.

It is too late to connect the Trotter's Club with Roderick's murder—but if ritual murder was part of the club's repertoire, it seemed to me that we ought to be able to get other evidence of it, incontrovertible evidence. My recollection of Andrew's

seasonal house parties at Cauldhurst, particularly during the
years surrounding Roderick's death, is that they included not
only Growe, but Samuelson, Wilson Lewis, and Geoffrey
Parks-Gifford, all men of substance with their party. I know
that all four are still cronies of his (the effort required to stop
myself from writing "my father's"!), which I doubt they
would be if they had parted from the Trotter's Club bearing
such secrets. These are the men I was prepared to promise to
Sir George Bankston, and I believed I, or we, could deliver
them. I am more sure of it now than I was when I promised
it.

By the time I had locked Sir George in, an icy rain had
begun, and I felt miserable, unjustly persecuted, as only a man
can who has had the luxury of choosing his own miseries. I
pulled what Susan calls the Dreadful Coat close around me
and my cap down over my nose (hoping that no one would
look closely enough at me to notice the splendour of my evening clothes beneath), and set out to find sanctuary for at least
a few hours.

Do you remember, from the document I mauled your copy
of Aubrey to send to you, the list of my helpful contacts in
London? Disturbing coincidences: the red-haired Italian girl in
Bloomsbury had been attacked by a customer and was in the
charity hospital; the German lighterman had had an accident
on the river and was drowned, alas. All in the last fortnight.
If I'd had many more such, I might have gone the whole night
and never felt the cold, such are the heating properties of anger
and horror mixed, and the sudden need to keep moving
quickly. I had no great hope of my friend with the coffee-stall;
he would have packed his cart and gone home, and I had no
idea where home was. When I reached his usual pitch and
found him lighting his pipe in the shelter of a counting-house
doorway, I was more disturbed than otherwise. In cases like
this, innocence is not usually proclaimed by deviation from
one's routine.

But he saw me watching from my shadowy spot, and
crossed the street, and stopped on the pavement near me, pretending to fuss with his pipe and never looking up. He'd heard
about the Covent Garden murder, he muttered out the corner

of his mouth, and that I was in the city, and he'd waited to see if I'd come.

"And who else is waiting?" I asked him.

He shook his head, frowning ferociously at his pipe in lieu of me. "If anybody thinks it's worth standing in a pissing rain to lay you by the heels, he can have you. I'm for home. If you're coming, do it round about, but quick-like." And he spat out a Blackfriars address and walked on.

Which is how I ended up thawing myself at the hearth where you had a restorative cup of coffee not so long ago, because, of course, Lee was on the square. I apologized to him for doubting it, and he called me a shocking name (I will not add it to your vocabulary) and refilled my cup.

"Your mate Stone's gear went under the hammer last month," Lee told me.

"No mate of mine," I assured him.

Lee grunted. "Thought you'd want summat to remember him by, anyway." He took a little parcel off a table in the corner. It was wrapped in what seemed to be several layers of silk handkerchief, and I wondered, but didn't ask, where Lee had got them. I unfolded them to reveal a little book bound in tan leather.

I found myself oddly unwilling to open the cover. "What is this?" I asked instead.

"Maybe it's the Bible from his night-stand," Lee growled. "In the old times there must have been coves didn't believe in guns, but they got killed right enough anyway."

It wasn't a Bible—or at least, it wasn't a Christian one. It might have been printed a hundred years ago, or eighty, or sixty; it purported to be full of wisdom from centuries before that. The age and worth of the wisdom are both more than suspect. Its title was *La trône terrestre*, and I think—I very much fear—that it is one of the things Kitty may have found among David's papers. I wish I hadn't seen it; I can't imagine it helps Kitty sleep nights. Though for all I know Kitty is better fortified than I am against this sort of abomination.

I don't mean to sound so very overwrought, and after all, why should I be? I had been speculating for days on the probability that the Trotter's Club practiced ritual murder—as good as hoping that they did, so that I might catch them at it. But to find it laid out and celebrated in print, in poetic metaphor of mixed quality, in the company of equal parts contemptible Christian parody, childish superstition, and repellent self-serving philosophy, made me damned near quaking-sick.

"Page hundred sixty-seven," Lee said in a hard voice.

"Why?"

"Read it," he insisted, and so I did.

When I was done, I was at once baffled and disturbed. "Stag-hunting?" I asked him.

He said something under his breath, angrily. "And you a University man, and bookish. Try again, and pretend, may be, that it's in French or suchlike."

And he was so like a professor disgusted with a slow pupil that I found myself reading the passage as I might have read *Le roman de la rose*, and understood that I was not reading about a king and his court hunting a stag. I remembered a disjointed comment of Gideon Johnson's, about the old king proving his right to rule.

I have sat over the last paragraph for an unreasonably long time, Richard, because I think I cannot bear to tell you what I read. I cannot bear either the sense of it, or the near-legitimacy that interpreting it to you will give it. But I was made to read it because in our hands the knowledge may be weapon and armour both, and if I can't share it I have weakened it, or even thrown it away.

La trône terrestre offers an outline for a sacred (word mine and used satirically) hunt, in which a man may prove his superiority, or his fitness to hold his position, or his worthiness to receive some honour, by, at winter solstice, hunting down and killing one of his near relatives. Father, brother, or son, specifically, as Kitty mentioned in her observations among David's papers. One is, happily for the relative, barred from using guns or dogs. Do you suppose they've done this often? What a lot of hunting accidents among our best families are suddenly cast in an unsavoury light! In talking to Susan not so long ago, I compared my immediate family to the house of Atreus. That seems to have been spot-on.

I burned the book. I did it after Lee observed bitterly that there was no telling what sort of leather the binding was made of. Probably calf or kidskin, but I think he said it to complete the dismantling of my intellectual defences, which it succeeded in doing. Then he relented and pointed out, partly in a spirit of apology, that the knowledge is, as I said above, useful. And it is, isn't it? If what he showed me is relevant, we may be able to catch the Trotter's Club red-handed in as heinous an act as we could wish. Lee also suggested I get a few hours of sleep. I laughed. That was when he told me that my second cup of coffee had had something in it that would make sleep not only possible, but inevitable, and that I might as well lie down before I fell down.

To state the obvious, I hate losing control of events. So you will understand the condition I had been reduced to when I tell you that I didn't offer a word of objection, but only put my head down on my knees and waited for oblivion to gain on me. I didn't have the heart, quite, to thank Lee, but I ought to have done. When I woke, he said, he would be gone, off to the neighbourhood of St. Paul's. He strongly suggested that I not remain in London for much longer than it took me to get to my feet.

I have taken his advice. I am writing this from a tavern at Gravesend, where I'm sure my attire and face mark me as a dissipated town buck much the worse for whatever he did the night before. Well, the last is certainly true. Since I am sending this to the Grey Hound, you may know that I trust you and Susan and even Henry to have brought your liberation off without a hitch; by the time this reaches you, if you have not been taken up again or heard any dreadful news of me, you will know that you are free to return openly to Melrose Hall and your Kitty.

I may reach the Grey Hound before you leave it. I would reach it tonight, except that I intend to make a detour. I am going to Cauldhurst. It should be safe enough; David is dead, after all, and Andrew, I learned when I came to town, is in London meeting with his solicitor. About what, do you suppose?

I'm sorry, Richard. I want not to talk about any of what follows, not only because of what it is, but because I have no way to get at it that doesn't produce, in my inner ear, the sound of your voice recommending I grow up. Perhaps that's the right thing to do, to not talk about it. How much do you know of chemistry? Can one combine poisonous elements and produce a compound that does no harm? That's our kinship, if so: created out of poisonous things, but not itself a toxin. I know that, and it should be enough. But the man who is writing to you has never, never been able to leave well enough alone; when confronted by the Devil, he will try to measure his horns.

I believe Andrew Cobham is capable of hunting me down and killing me for the sake of his pride and his position alone. My death would, in his eyes, both avenge his dishonour and make it forever secret. It would also preserve another fine old secret that he must be afraid we share.

Mesmerism is not the only device for suppressing memory; time, an imperfect understanding, and a hail of other seemingly more significant events will push a fact or set of facts into some unexplored mental cave, and one is lucky if there is so much as a trail of crumbs left to find it by. You'll be wondering by now what I am working my way toward, in my usual circuitous fashion. Did I tell you—yes, again in the document hidden in your copy of Aubrey—that the loss of my two months and my subsequent helplessness frightened me more than I had ever been save once? You observed, in that first letter I received from you when I was hidden at the Grey Hound, that the child was father to the man, that I was not likely to drown. You referred, I think, to me at the age of seven, when I managed to not-quite-drown myself in the ornamental water at Cauldhurst.

I had not only inhaled a quart or so of the pond, but had done it on a particularly raw day in late October as well, and had the reputation of being weak in the lungs. So I was moved temporarily from the nursery to one of the guest bedrooms in my parents' wing, for the convenience of the doctor and the housekeeper on whom the job of nursing me had fallen. If I hadn't been, I would never have been able to hear the row between my mother and—well, at the time I thought of him as my father, so we may as well leave it at that for this purpose.

That much, I have always remembered: that my parents fought on the afternoon of the accident, though I hadn't at the time understood what they were fighting about, and so the text of it was mostly pushed into the far reaches of my memory. I recalled, too, that my mother died soon after, of a fall from which she never recovered, a fall suffered during an attack of fever brought on by fear for my health.

I didn't hear the whole of the quarrel, only that he blamed her for the accident, that she was a bad mother; where, he would like to know, had she been when I'd gone in? And who had she been with? She said that if he hadn't turned my governess off *she* would have been with me. Their voices grew at once louder and harder to understand, or perhaps I was drifting in and out of feverish sleep. I remember that he called her a God-damned Irish whore, and I felt a childish outrage, a determination to drag myself out of the big strange bed and defend my mother's character. Then her voice dropped, resonant and full of poisonous hatred, but unintelligible. I heard a blow, and a cry from her. The door of her chamber banged open, and her running steps passed in the hall; an instant after, I heard his as well. I had struggled to the door of my room when I heard the second blow and her scream, and the sound of her fall. I opened the door and saw, at the top of the stairs, my father, looking down. I didn't see her. Then he turned and met my eyes. There was no rage in his face, or fear, or anything but a blanched white emptiness. Frightened and uncomprehending, I retreated again behind the closed door, beneath the bedclothes.

I heard the subsequent commotion, and the return of the doctor. I now know that he must have been told what was always told to me: distracted with fear for me, she had fallen. Cauldhurst was never the brisk, noisy establishment that Melrose Hall was, but that evening it was silent as a ruin drifted over with sand.

What happened next I have always remembered, even though I didn't understand it at the time. I have tried, now and again, to tell myself I dreamt it, but I have never been able to believe that. It is the fearful thing that no other fear has equalled.

Very late that night, as my mother lay unconscious in her chamber, my father came into the room where I slept. I woke when I heard the door shut. He sat on the edge of the bed and struck a match, and held it up close to my face, studying me for as long as the light lasted. The match burnt his fingers and went out. He struck another and let it burn itself out in its turn, again holding it near my face and staring intently at me. A third match, and the same treatment, and each time he never spoke, nor made a sound, even when the flame burnt down to his fingertips. Then for a very long time, it seemed, he sat in the dark, and I could almost feel his gaze searching blindly for my face. At last he rose from the bed and left the room. I swept the spent matches off the coverlet and lay awake until morning, when the housekeeper came to tell me my mother was dead.

Andrew Cobham killed his wife, by accident or by intent, and covered it up; and he did it because she had been unfaithful, and because she had finally been driven to admit what he had suspected before: that his son was not his at all. He would have killed me that night, if he could have disguised the act. He might have done it anyway, if I had spoken, or flinched, or behaved, somehow, differently. I never knew that that was what I had been afraid of until I read the letter from Diana to William and remembered it all, and understood it. Now I may be able to find some better proof of it than a sick child's memories, and I am going to Cauldhurst to try. I won't be long about it, whatever I do or do not find. I will arrive in Langstone on the 15th if not before.

Your latest letter was nicely judged for dry wit and steadfast reason, leavened with a pinch of sentiment. I wish I could have returned that kindness. I wish I could have returned to the discussion of Hegel. I wish, I hope with all my heart, that soon you and I will be able to meet, on paper or in person, freed of secrets and tragedies and the dreary scuttling burden of my plottings. If they were like a house, with a front and a back door, we might be passed through them and out the other side by now. But they are like a pit; we have got to the bottom, and can get out only by traversing the whole weary depth again, it seems. Perhaps it's just that I've sent all my courage and hope away with Susan. When I reclaim them, I can believe in and write of happier things.

It's precious little satisfaction you've got out of having a brother, so far. As soon as I am able, I will do everything in my power to remedy that. You have shown me more kindness all my life than I can recall having warranted, and I would like you to know that the debt is at least acknowledged, however long it may take me to accumulate the capital to pay it.

It gives me comfort to be able to sign myself

Your affectionate brother,
James

WHITEHALL
THURSDAY, 13 DECEMBER, 1849

Dear Mr MacCormack,

I am directed to inform you that the matter to which you referred in your letter of the 2nd is of no further interest to Her Majesty's government or judiciary. I am further directed to apologise for any inconvenience this unpleasantness may have caused your principal, and to suggest that it would be of benefit to all concerned for this matter to go no further than you, your principal, and your humble servant, ·

Wm Dowling
Sectry to Sir Geo. Bankston

THURSDAY, LATE NIGHT
THE GREEN WIFE

My Love:

As you can see from the address, I am no longer at the Grey Hound, but have progressed from ashen dog to verdant woman, and whether my safety is worth the loss of Coslick's brandywine and Mrs Coslick's fritters, I will have to let you know in a few days. I have as yet no opinion concerning potables or comestibles here because the one meal we have eaten—and a large one it was!—we sent out for, but I have been assured as to my safety, and I even feel rather safer than I did; for testimony there is a certain knot of muscle in the back of my neck of which I had been unaware until I relaxed. In the meantime, I do not know for certain how long I will be here, or where I will be next, but it has been suggested to me—alas!—that I ask you not to write to me here except in case of some dire emergency, and that in that case to use the name Victor Friehoff. When will I see you again? I do not know. Soon, I hope.

In the meantime, if you will allow me a little complaint, I must say that my room is cramped and draughty, the bed is too small, the outhouse is too far away, and my neighbours are too loud, with the exception of Susan, who is off in her room writing to you after ordering me to do likewise, wherefore I am obeying her, because she has become a woman one does not easily disobey, though, to be sure, I do not mean to imply that she has become less feminine, or that I expect James to be henpecked; but rather she has a certain confidence about her, as if she knows what those around her ought to be doing, and there is a look about her as her eyes flick from one side to the other as if she is constantly making calculations. Travelling with her was odd, because sometimes I would be just another calculation, and I think one that often annoyed her, but then something—usually following a mention of you or James—would change and the old Susan would appear for a time, the intensity softened by human concerns, until the next moment for action approached. An odd woman, your friend Susan!

She arrived late on Tuesday afternoon while Coslick and I were verbally fencing; I was trying to worm some information from him on the background of his group, and he was being coy, but I had about come to the conclusion that he is a member of two different societies, and somehow James is an overlapping concern. I asked him point-blank if this were true, and he gave me a smile that was not unkind and shook his head, and at that point Mrs Coslick called out, "Coach, Charlie!" and the groom got up from his spot near the fire to attend to it. Coslick also rose to see to the new arrivals, which he often does, but not always, and on this occasion I believed it was an excuse to avoid answering my question, so I followed him and nearly ran into his back when he stopped suddenly, so I went around him and nearly bowled over the amazing Miss

Voight, who was just in the process of raising her veil. I have no idea what sort of expression I gave her; amazement would probably not go 'round it without tearing, although I had known from your letter that something was up. But she seemed utterly in possession of herself, Coslick, and me, and she informed me in a very few words that I should take myself off and shave.

I started to protest, but it began to penetrate that she would have a reason for wanting me to, and no doubt everything would be explained later, so I contented myself with muttering under my breath and went off to remove my new beard as quickly as I could, staring into the glass and watching myself emerge from the soap and wondering where fate and Miss Voight would have me off to now, and if I would survive it, and feeling not in the least heroic. But then, I suppose, the one being rescued is not expected to feel heroic, only grateful; which is why everyone would prefer to do the rescuing. She had made an opaque remark about cousin Henry, so it should not have surprised me when he suddenly appeared in the mirror, but it did. I spun around and stared at him. He was dressed in a greatcoat that would have looked proletarian on anyone and looked absurd on him. He made a pirouette and said, "How do you like it?"

I said, "I bloody like it, or I like it bloody, as you prefer."

"Eh?" he said. Then, "Oh, I see. Sorry. I ought not to have startled you."

I said something like, "Why by the Christ Jesus are you here, Henry?"

"Can't you guess?" he asked me.

I noticed he was looking over my shoulder at the mirror, so I looked too, from his features to my own, and said, "Are we supposed to bloody change clothes as well, then?"

"Or change bloody clothes, my dear Richard," he said, bouncing like a puppy. "Calm down. Don't you *like* being rescued?"

"Would you?" I said. But by then it was beginning to be funny, so I finished shaving and put on his clothes, which, really, fit me rather well, but I did not dare let myself look at the picture I made or I should probably have dissolved into laughter, which wouldn't have impressed Miss Voight at all.

So I came down the stairs, finished becoming Henry pretending to be a coachman, which by rights ought to have fooled no one, and somehow managed to climb up to the cab, which isn't as easy as it looks: the damned things are built oddly. But the team was good, and driving a pair is, thank God, still driving a pair no matter what the vehicle is, so I believe I made a passable coachman. I must remember to tell James so; he will be pleased. I was in sufficiently good spirits, in fact, that two or three times during that part of the journey I leaned down and yelled, "Will madame be requiring anything?" until Miss Voight suggested that this was not, perhaps, as funny as I thought it was.

And, as luck would have it, it was about three minutes after the last of these exchanges that the authorities stopped us—at least, they looked like the authorities, and they had pistols. I had one, too, which I had almost given to Henry until I realized that he might use it, but I never even thought of pulling it out; I just sat there while Susan exchanged a few words with them, and then we were off again. I have no idea if we were in any danger, but it frightened me a bit at the time. No, in fact, I confess, it frightened me a great deal; I find that I am ashamed to admit how much, in the face of how cool Susan's nerve was, whereas after our encounter with the armed men I was so shaken I managed to get us lost three times while pursuing a large stable that was really quite stationary, and was even where it was supposed to be. Susan made no remark about it, however, and we were quickly out of the coach and onto horses, mine being good old Cavalier, which made me feel much better about everything.

Susan and I talked a great deal as we rode, mostly about her and James, and it was really very pleasant, because it is obvious that she is very much in love with him, and at the same time, I think, she is not quite certain that love fits in with her principles, though it certainly does with her disposition, and in all of this she and James are even a better match than we had supposed, and you are quite correct, my love, I do feel horribly smug about the whole thing, and so should you. We also spoke of you, and no doubt you felt your ears burning, but there is little to say except what you already know, which is that we both care about you a great deal. At one point—

this was much later, after we'd arrived at the Green Wife—Susan expressed worry about you. I don't remember how she put it, exactly, but she seemed very guarded, as if she were uncertain whether she ought to mention it. I told her that I was worried too, but that I did not know what to do about it, and then I began to whine a bit, and she told me rather sharply to stop it, all of which I mention only to make certain you understand that you are in our thoughts.

But to return, we rode at an easy pace through the night until we reached the inn while it was still dark, and I took care of the horses while Susan arranged the rooms, or perhaps she'd had them arranged already: I don't know and didn't ask. Once settled in, she had some sherry delivered to her room and invited me to join her; it isn't until this moment I realized that it could be seen as odd: my being in her room alone with her at that time; perhaps these intrigues are robbing me of sensibilities I should have denied that I had. But in any case, I certainly needed the drink, and I suspect she did too. The first thing I said was, "How safe are we?" She said, "Fairly, I suspect," and I had to be content with that, so we talked a little more, and that was where she said that she was going to write to you as soon as she had word we were safe, with a look that said that if I didn't do the same she'd have me cast into the nether darkness, not that I needed the order! But I did feel the need for some sleep, so after a bit of a glass I left to get some, and got a great deal indeed—I believe I slept for twelve hours, in spite of the horrid bed, and it was dark again when I awoke; it is a peculiar feeling to miss an entire day.

After awakening, I knocked Susan up nearly at once, and found her already awake and drinking coffee. She had some sheets of paper on the desk in front of her. I decided not to ask, but she volunteered the information. "This is an article Engels is writing for the English version of the *Neue Rheinische Zeitung.* Unfortunately, I managed to leave without the first page, and it isn't complete anyway; it took him longer than he'd thought it would. James thought that was funny." She added that he probably wouldn't mind if I read what there was of it, and I said I'd love to do so over a meal, and she looked startled, as if the thought of food hadn't occurred to her. We decided on a whole roasted chicken and some potatoes, and bread, and pudding, and she decided that she'd go get it from another inn, so I waited in her room and drank coffee and read what there was of Engels's article. I can't tell you much about it, because it made little sense, even though I read it several times while waiting. But eventually she returned and we occupied ourselves with eating every crumb—I don't remember when I have been so hungry!—and, later, with talking about you, and then about this peculiar situation in which we have landed, and thus used a good deal of the night. We neither of us wanted to write to you until the word came that everything was all right, which word did not in fact arrive until a few hours ago, it now being Friday. We had much conversation during this time, but I haven't the memory to report it word for word, so I can only repeat what I said earlier about my high degree of respect for her, and about her curious changes of demeanour. I should also add that it is clear from every word she says that she thinks very highly of your intelligence, and often repeated that we would be far less clear had you not been able to piece together a great deal of the puzzle from the tiniest scraps of information; I need hardly add how proud I felt to hear her speak so!

Eventually she received a message, by what means I do not know, and announced that we appeared to be safe, and that, furthermore, it was time to move again. I told her that I would write to you at once, and I left her alone so she could do the same, although I have the feeling she jumped the gun a little and had been scraping away while I slept. And now that I have written this much I see that dawn is approaching, and with it, fatigue. This nocturnal existence is very odd, but I expect that within a day or so I will be on a more normal schedule, because Susan, though she will not tell me the details, does say that we will be moving again soon.

Kitty, my love, I do not know what to do. I know that you need me to be there, and I need to be there with you. Today is, or soon will be, Friday. On Saturday, at the moment the sun is setting, do you go into the back garden, and stand there facing the gate, and I will reach toward you, and we will give each other what comfort we may. I do not know what result this will produce, if any, but it is all I can think of, and I am desperate to do something. I do not know what the next step of the plan is, but I fear we will again find it unsafe to exchange letters. If this gives us each only a small comfort, still, that will be something to treasure, as I treasure you, and I hope and know that you still treasure your loving and adoring,

Richard

(Fragment of unpublished article by F. Engels)

What offends the intellectual above all is the suggestion that ideas, especially *his* ideas, are also part of the material world; that is, that his ideas emerge from society at a definite stage. We can understand why the intellectual detests this notion, and we even sympathize with him, but our sympathy does not alter the case. The current theories explaining the natural world could not exist before the invention of the microscope allowed us to examine nature in the minutest detail, thus explaining enough about Nature to permit God to take a well-earned hiatus; but they similarly could not exist before the domination of industrial capital reached a point where free-trade became an issue, and with it, the need to see the individual man as capable of rising to great heights on his own, regardless of birth: the God who directs everything is acceptable to an aristocracy that wants to rule on its own authority, but capitalism needs a God who only sets the machines in motion and allows the individual capitalist to reach whatever heights he is capable of. And it was this very industrial capital that allowed the microscope to be perfected!

I am no exception: my own ideas about capitalism could not exist before capitalism, and are the product of the very class struggle they explain. The bourgeois intellectual desperately wants to exist apart from society, especially apart from the class struggle, and to believe that his ideas have emerged only from his own brain.

It is important to understand this relationship. The Reverend Malthus required an industrial capitalism that would make human beings into pieces of a machine before he could formulate his theories of population, and Parliament required Malthusianism to justify its Poor Laws. The next advance in the productive forces will put paid to the theories of Malthus, but it will take the action of the working class to overturn the Poor Laws and the system that created them.

THE GREEN WIFE
BISHOP'S WALTHAM
13 DEC 1849

Dear Kit,

I believe all is well; Richard is fine, at any rate, as am I. Henry is probably fine—if he has done as I told him to, he is certainly fine. If he's done something rash, he is still probably all right. And if he's drunk on Coslick's brandy, it's his own look-out. I haven't heard anything from London yet, but I'm not worried—this is the earliest I ought to have received word, and I am forbidden to fidget for another twenty-four hours.

I have not been out of the company of other people for the last three days, and I have never felt so alone. It's not simply because my lover has not numbered among that company, either. I have always been comfortable travelling by myself, adventuring, even doing perilous things. This is something quite different. However alarming it may be to know that your life depends on your actions, it is nothing to knowing that at least two other people's depend on them as well. And with no hope of aid from anywhere else, should something go wrong—!

But nothing did go wrong, and we have only to wait for word from London; after that, two gentlemen will have themselves a long and not disagreeable ride on horseback, at the end of which they will be called upon to wait—that abominable word again!—for the commencement of our final campaign. I look forward to trousers after so long.

I was sorry to have to rob you of Henry so soon after the funeral. Brian would have been a better match for Richard, in colouring and stature, but what in Henry would have seemed only another ill-considered undergraduate prank would have been the ruin of Brian's career. And Henry was delighted with it, of course, as soon as he had it all explained (or at least, as much of it as I would explain: that Richard was not on the Continent, but in hiding a few miles from Portsmouth; that he was in danger from government agents because of things James had been involved in; that James was not dead, but himself in danger from all sides, some of them brutal and unprincipled; and that by involving himself in this scheme, he also placed himself in some of the same danger. That last, of course, was his favourite part. Where in the name of heaven does this family's lack of basic caution come from?)

I'm sorry. I could go on like this for pages, and do you every possible disservice thereby. I have been living with stark, dull, unrelenting fear for days, a kind of fear that is nothing like what I felt on the banks of the Severn, or in the ruined farmyard outside of Redland, or even in the inn at Fairfield. There was no time, then, for anything but fear mixed with the tumultuous thrill of action. This has been—do you remember what hide and seek was like, with an insecure hiding place and a clever seeker, and how, with nothing more than a game at stake, one's heart would pound fit to burst, and one's lungs work like a punctured bellows, until it seemed as if the hunter must hear them both? And nothing to be done about it, nothing, except to stay still and try to believe in the unbelievable: one's own safety and ultimate success? I am not fitted out for this, the cold-blooded, iron-nerved part of intriguing. Last night I lost my temper, and my nerve as well, which the temper I think was meant to camouflage, and flashed out at Richard in an odious, odious way. He was prepared, on the instant, to respond as I deserved, but only for the instant; then his face grew grave and sad, and he said, "I know. I won't lie to you and say that I am sure it will all come right. But I think it will. After so much—" We sat together in silence then, and both, I think, journeyed back in our minds through these last months, and even through the years before, when it seemed that what we had of happiness and self-knowledge was all we would ever have. We have, all of us, so much more now, and so much promise of more to come—I understand what Richard means. That we should be robbed of our hopes now would be worse than a cruel joke, foul treason from a Fate that has not seemed, of late, to hate us so much as that.

I am sorrier still, to have pressed all my fears and doubts on your shoulders. If I were a good Christian, I would lay my future in the hands of a God who, I have been assured, is the embodiment of love and forgiveness. But if I were a good Christian, I would not be hiding in a hedge-tavern with a male cousin, praying to pagan gods and abstract principles to speed and prosper the intricate plots of an unrepentant atheist. I would be wearing my black bombazine and sitting in a drawing room with my eyes modestly on my embroidery. I was used to embroider quite well, Kit—do you recall? I expect you can't remember the last time you saw me do any. I last set an embroidery stitch when I was at Miss Trevelyan's, and I was a well-mannered young lady of fifteen. The sampler read—or would have, when finished—"When I was young and in my prime, here you may see how I spent my time." Each chain-stitch began to seem to me as if it tightened like a noose; each cross-stitch as if it marked away another hope, another possibility. Horrible, horrible promise: that I might grow old and die leaving such a thing behind me, such an indictment in rhyme of what I'd seen fit to make of my life! I had finished the "w" of "how" when I took the linen out of the frame, walked to the fire, and dropped it onto the flames. I could not know, when I watched the cloth brown and blacken, that the course that began so would encompass murder, treason, and this unspeakable patient terror. Merciful goddesses and principles, send me word from London!

I shall crow, perhaps, one day, about the ease with which we extracted your Richard from the Grey Hound. There is a livery stable in Queen's Gate Mews where I stable my horses; the man who has charge of the day-to-day conduct of the business is capable, discreet, and formerly in Grandmama's employ. Mr Thompson brought a closed carriage and pair, with Girasol tied behind, to the Lion in Hounslow a little before sunset on the 10th. Then he took Girasol and James's horse ahead into Hampshire. How did Cavalier come to be at the Lion? He arrived under Henry, who rode from Melrose to the Lion and discovered that, for the next twenty-four hours, he was to play the coachman, and after that, as much of the fool as he saw fit. We made a few miles that night, in order to be as difficult to track as possible; but the bulk of the distance was covered on Tuesday. I sat in the carriage with the blinds drawn, mumbling the plan over as if it were my devotions on a string of beads, trying to foresee trouble, trying to remain alert to the changing nature of possibility, as the author of the plan put it. It had been made so quickly, it didn't seem as if it could be sound; it didn't seem as if two people who had never seen the ground and had no experience in such work could bring it off. I had worked myself into a fever of anxiety by the time we turned into the yard of the Grey Hound on the evening of the 11th.

At such times, one cannot imagine what natural behaviour is; stepping naturally from a carriage and entering an inn is as great a challenge as mimicking after a glance the steps of some Polynesian dance. But I crossed the yard, rustling respectably in my shabby-genteel black gown and pelisse, to the inn. I cannot remember a single feature of that yard; between absorption in my Devotions and the dense veiling of my bonnet, I might as well have crossed Dartmoor in the fog. Behind me Henry was stepping down from the box and handing the reins over to a groom, keeping his hat-brim sunk and his collar raised. He would enter behind me, ostensibly making for the common-room.

Immediately inside the door I encountered an immense florid-faced man in a very clean apron whom I now know to be Coslick. In a low voice, I asked, "Where is Mr Cobham?"

The cast of suspicion in Coslick's face was immediate and pronounced. But behind him, stepping quickly from a parlour, was Richard, brought out by the sound of my voice.

I flung back my veil and commanded, horrified, "Shave. Now. As quickly as you can."

His hand flew to his chin, and all the space above it was occupied with a look of polite inquiry. "Serve you right if I cut my throat in the rush. I suppose you couldn't have warned me."

"No, I couldn't have. The alternative is for Henry to grow his, and since he can't do it in a quarter of an hour, you'll have to make the sacrifice. But hurry. If sunset catches us here, we're all in the basket."

It was quite nearly a respectable beard and moustache, Kit dear, the nice treacle colour of his hair, and I felt like an infanticide making him scrape it off. But had anyone noticed the general attributes of my coachman on the way in, the sudden appearance of a beard must have ruined everything!

He did it with only three nicks and no further protest. You must have prepared him for something like this, for he never stopped for questions or bafflement. When he came downstairs again, he had already changed clothes with Henry. The greatcoat largely hid the difference in their respective builds, and Henry's coachmanly beaver, when Richard put it on, would do the rest, I decided. Without preamble I described to Richard the route he was to drive, and Henry kindly (and without too much digression) enumerated the quirks of the carriage horses. Then Richard went out to take his place on the box while I reviewed with Henry what his job was: stay indoors until descended upon by Her Majesty's Own, when he was to protest vigourously and offer no resistance. If, by the 14th, he had not been descended upon (which would mean that things had gone dangerously wrong, a fact I saw no reason to impart to Henry), he was to make his way back to Oxford with every appearance of casual innocence. Coslick blandly assured me that these young sprigs could be lured into some pretty shocking escapades when they got free of the book-cracking, and that he was sure this particular sprig had had no idea of the gravity of the situation, and that he, Coslick, would say so to anyone. Rather overcome by such prompt comprehension, I pressed his hand and fled to my seat in the carriage.

The one bad moment was when we were hailed outside of Langstone. I couldn't hear the command, but it *was* a command by the tone. I doubted it would prove to be robbers. How would an innocent maiden lady of obvious but impoverished gentility in an unfashionable carriage respond to a challenge in mid-highway by unknown mounted men? I raised the blind and dropped the window, and called out, "Thompson! What is it? Why have we stopped?" Then I pretended to see the two men, one of them with a pistol drawn, for the first time, and gave out with a fairly satisfactory wail. All the time, I could think of nothing except what James had said in one of his letters to Richard, about almost never looking coachmen in the face. The man without the pistol flung open the carriage door and peered inside.

"Travelling alone?" he asked peremptorily. I nodded. "I must ask you to raise your veil."

My face must have been convincingly white; it certainly wasn't male. He looked deeply disappointed. After a grudging circuit of the carriage, we were ordered to move along. The only difficulty was in not actually taking to our heels.

Richard located the old barn on the outskirts of Waterlooville with a little difficulty in the then-failing light; but the real Thompson was there, with Girasol and Cavalier baited and saddled. The saddle-bags were in the boxes strapped behind the carriage; thank heaven we weren't searched. Thompson drove the carriage north, back to London, while Richard and I set out by the lanes and sometimes across country toward Bishop's Waltham. Girasol seemed to be pleased to be returned to the duty roster, if such things can be presumed about horses.

We talked very little at first, and what we did say was about the present moment: mind this muddy stretch, do we take this turning, et cetera. A little more moon, we were agreed, would be a great help. (It is a measure of the desperate nature of the case that we would risk laming two such horses by riding at night.) But after an hour or so, we rode in a world in which the only pressure was the immediate one of getting safely from one place to another. It freed us to speak about the things that had temporarily receded.

"Kitty has passed on news from your letters," Richard said, a little constraint in his voice. "I think . . . well, it's not my place to think anything, I suppose. Are you happy?"

"I won't pretend to believe you mean at this very instant." I contemplated the question, riding disembodied through the darkness. "I haven't had time to be happy yet. I think, given the eventual leisure for it, that I have as good a chance as anyone."

Cavalier tossed his head under a little pressure from the reins, and sidled closer. I doubt it gave Richard any better sight of my face. "That's awfully equivocal."

"I'm superstitious, is all. So many Greek myths in which the gods hear people bragging about how well things are going. Are *you* happy?"

It was a moment before he said, "Not for weeks. No, it

hasn't been that long, has it? I miss Kit. And you'd think it would get easier, with time, but it's actually gotten worse." He sounded mournful, and rather young. He, too, may have been feeling our disembodiment and the freedom it gave us.

I smiled. "I told her months ago that you'd offer her marriage, you know."

"Did you tell her to accept?"

"Gracious, no. I told her the advantages were all on her side as long as she didn't."

He made a little sound that I'm used to hearing paired with a smile. I was startled when I recalled where I'd got used to it. "I hope you weren't too disappointed in her," he said.

"I try not to insist on my principles as the universal order. And if I had, Kitty would have put me in my place pretty smartly."

"Then I take it you don't mean to marry James?"

"No."

"Does . . . he know that?"

"Yes, he does. Richard, I feel like a suitor being asked if his intentions are honourable."

He laughed. "If James ever hears of this conversation, he'll skin me with a look."

"Perhaps not. He's—" Then I remembered that I hadn't meant to talk about him, and stopped.

"Different," Richard finished for me. "Not so determined to order the world before it presents itself. I'm speaking of myself now, you understand. In the interest of not ordering the world before consulting it, I'll let James define his own difference. Was it very bad?"

"I beg your pardon?"

"I'm sorry. My brain's running on, and my tongue is left to catch it up as best it can. I was thinking of how matters stood before I had to scarper, as of the last letter Kitty had from you then."

"That was a long time ago. Wasn't it? Where was I writing from?"

"Portishead, I think."

It was Girasol's turn to jib at the bit; I gave him an apologetic pat for the unwarranted pressure on his mouth. "My, that was a *very* long time ago." I thought about whether, even in the dark, I wanted to tell Richard that in slightly over a week I had killed one man and lain with another. Richard would find it disturbing. Put that way, *I* found it disturbing. "What was your question?"

"I think you've answered it, one way or another. Except, was James horrible? He's capable of it, under stress."

"So am I, I've discovered. No, James was bloody decent, actually. If we were riding all the way to John o' Groats, I could probably explain it to you. You're right, let him define the difference. You'll see him soon. I hope. Oh, blast it, did that thing read 'Meonstoke?' We'll have to back-track."

And by this method, we managed to reach Bishop's Waltham shortly after dawn without eliciting any undue expressions of distress from each other. As I say, it wasn't until last night that I called him names—and no, I won't tell you which ones, because he didn't deserve them. You may now bristle in his defence. But you can't stay cross with me for long, because I was the one who pointed out to your dearie that, since we had shaken our pursuit for the moment, it was safe to send you a nice long letter. Though I'll wager it won't be as long as the usual run of mine.

Gracious, I'd nearly forgotten—I haven't answered your last letter, the one dated the 7th. Well, by now you know where Aunt Louisa was during the funeral, and I can't believe she was any sorrier to miss it than I was. But Andrew was there? The cheek of the man! Could he *not* know that his family is busy unearthing his sordid past? That his Trotter's Club protégé Tournier is making a dead set at doing his putative offspring in? Did he *not* have a part in the plan to expose and disinherit his heir? Rubbish, says I. I haven't your ability to balance and forgive, dear Kit. And as for his general decency during the black days after Roderick's death, I can't help but think we don't know the whole story. Well, we certainly don't know the whole story; and some of it may have to do with Andrew. (Confess, Susan—some of your lingering resentment stems from recalling that he was kind to all of us then *except* James, with whom he was only somewhat less cold.)

Kitty, my dear, when did your mother go missing? I'm sorry, I don't mean to sound as if I'm making light of this. Far from it. You didn't mention that you hadn't had a letter from Aunt Margaret recently. When *did* you hear from her last? I can't think what sort of difficulty she might be in, or why; but then, I would never have thought to see Aunt Louisa in Manchester.

Your billiard-ball analogy is—I almost said striking, but of course, now that I've stopped myself I wouldn't think of saying it—not only apropos, but further-ranging than you may have thought. It disturbs me to think that some portion of the spin on all of us was imparted by previous generations, especially by long-dead Callendars. I resent them. (I exempt only Grandmama, even while I acknowledge how very much of my motion is attributable to her.)

Are you really all right, dear? You say you are fine, or would be if Richard and James and I were there. But of course, we aren't, and aren't likely to be for some time yet. None of us would be willing to pay for our safety with yours, or your well-being. If you can't bear it, give a yelp, and I shall come instantly and . . . do something. What, exactly, I couldn't tell you at this remove, but I'm a clever girl most days. Only just now I am rather worn down and scuffed with worry. My feelings are being turned into a sort of emotional pemmican—stripped, pounded, smoked, and dried over a low fire. How much would you like to wager that rehydrating them is just as exhausting as the drying-out?

You will have to explain to me someday—today, if you like, I'm not particular—why you say we have a grasp of Earth and Fire and not of Water and Air. First, I suppose, you'll have to tell me what they signify, besides dirt, flames, rivers, and oxygen. No, I'm sorry, I should cross that last bit out. I don't mean to seem scoffing; I'm not such a lump as to deny the power of symbolism or insist on the barefaced meaning of everything around me. But I think you mean a very particular set of symbols when you capitalize those four words, and I don't know them. You see, you needn't feel stupid about politics, any more than you should be embarrassed at not having been born knowing Turkish. I know nothing about your disciplines, after all. You said once that they were your way of carrying a pistol. Do you still find them so? If it's true, don't let your scoffing rationalist relations discourage you from whatever you require to keep your chosen weapon ready. Security never called upon is security nonetheless, and I would not deny you any comfort or support.

I haven't the faintest idea why you would want to live in a cave, no matter what condition of extremity your relatives drove you to. They're damp, pitch-dark, and a uniform fifty degrees Fahrenheit. And unless the roof were very low, I can't think what sort of contortion of the limbs would be required to live in one. So don't do it. Go up to London and order poor Thomas Cavanaugh to squire you to the opera. Tell him I suggested it. Really, much better than spelunking.

I ought to have written more here about Richard, oughtn't I? He is very well, dear, quite fit, though terribly restless away from you. Though he does not quite thrive on a diet of intrigue, he is rather like a newly-sharpened knife, very bright and precise at the edges. Or it may be that I have only learned to see him properly. I've always liked Richard—he's thoroughly likable, after all—but I don't know that I appreciated him as he deserves until now.

Oh, I am going really thoroughly mad with *waiting*. Much more of this and I mean to go get drunk.

Barely the morning of the 14th; word at last from London. We move again. I feel as if I haven't had any sleep since before the ride to Bishop's Waltham; I am going to try to trap a few hours of it before we set out. I'm not sure what my itinerary is, beyond the next twenty-four hours; you might try writing to me in care of Richard and sending it through the usual channels.

Doggedly yours,
Susan

TO: S. VOIGHT, THE GREEN WIFE, BISHOP'S WALTHAM 13/12/49

LIFE IN THE OLD DOG YET. HOLD OUT FOR OUR TWO DOZEN.

I LOVE YOU.

J.

RICHARD COBHAM'S JOURNAL

DECEMBER 15ᵗʰ

It is about eleven o'clock, and I am at the Laughing Cup, near Andover on the Test. An odd sort of inn, it is only one storey, but extends back from the road almost to the river. A cheery place—I can hear music from down the hall—but I take no pleasure in it. All cheerfulness seems false, happiness a deceit, and the knowledge that someday I will feel differently has no breath of reality to it. It has taken me some few hours to become calm enough to write, and I would sleep instead if I thought I could.

James, who has neither belief in nor patience for prophecy, has a habit of saying things that feel prophetic after the fact. When he spoke in his last letter of the evil, which word he carefully avoided, of our enemies, I accepted it and agreed, but did not feel it as I do now.

I ought to have recorded what happened while everything was still fresh in my mind, but I could not for some few hours, and now certain details are already unclear. No, that is wrong, because some of it will, I think, remain vivid all my life, but there are other parts that I cannot sort out in my mind and I doubt I ever shall.

I remember waking up in the late morning at the Grey Hound with the sun shining directly into my eyes through a slat in the shutter. I had as well an ache in my head and a queasy feeling in my stomach, both of which were products of the prodigious amount of sherry I had consumed the night before, and I remember being furious at the sun for daring to be in my eyes. I lay there wondering how long I would have to wait before the sun moved enough to let me sleep again, but the concentration required for such a calculation was beyond me. Moreover, now that I was awake, certain requirements of my body drove me from bed, although it was miserably cold thanks to my failure to light the fire. I stumbled into some clothes, and off to the necessary room. Someone was hitting something metal with a hammer not far enough away, and I entertained wicked thoughts toward him, though not as wicked as those I entertained toward James, whom I ran into as I was returning to my room and who gave me such a cheerful greeting that I nearly throttled him. What is it about escaping the aftereffects of a debauch that makes one wish to behave badly toward those who suffer them? I cannot claim innocence of this crime myself, though this knowledge did nothing to assuage my irritation at James. I do not remember what I said to him, but it was certainly not brotherly. I remember him laughing, and I remember him opening his mouth for a rejoinder, and I remember smelling smoke at that instant and being annoyed that some fool could not manage his grate properly, and, from downstairs, someone yelled, "Fire!"

There was an instant, then, when James and I looked at each other, just the briefest instant, yet it seemed to last for a long time, and then he coolly turned into his and Susan's room while I went into mine. That part I remember clearly, for I was very calm; I never came close to panicking, and in that time I may have gained some understanding of why James takes pleasure in, as he puts it, hanging over precipices— breath seemed to flow easily through me, and I saw everything with a startling clarity; more than that, though, I felt my mind function smoothly, like a machine, laying out the steps I must take logically and in order. And, now that I think of it, my hangover was gone, which may perhaps justify anything for those disposed to get them.

I walked into the room, knowing somehow that this fire was no small affair, and knowing also that it was more important to do everything efficiently than at breakneck speed. I picked up my chair and broke first three panes of glass, and then the muntins. Then I threw a few handy items, including this notebook, into my valise, and flung the valise out the window. I know that I turned away before they hit the ground, and I remember looking around the room to make certain I had left nothing vital, then I put my coat on and stepped out into the hall. James and Susan had been faster, because they were already passing my room returning from downstairs. They both appeared quite calm. James had on his greatcoat, and Susan was also prepared for the weather, with her hands in the pockets of a gentlemanly riding-coat; it seemed for all the world as if we were about to take an afternoon stroll.

They turned back as I emerged, and James said coolly, "The front door won't open. We probably ought to jump."

"All right," I said. "Let us—" and we were interrupted by a scream, which I think came from one of the children. It is horrible to say it, but that was a fine moment, because we all of us understood the significance of the scream, and the only question was the precise action to take.

James said, "Could you hear where it came from?"

"Downstairs," said Susan, already moving. "I suspect from the kitchen."

She was the first one down the stairs; James was second, until he took the lead by vaulting over the banister. Oddly, what I remember most is how slowly he seemed to be moving, how slowly we all seemed to moving. The awareness, the certainty that this fire had been deliberately set, was there all the time so that I do not remember ever coming to the realization, but it was in the background, as it were, of my thoughts.

James ran into the kitchen, closely pursued by Susan; I was a couple of steps behind them. There was smoke all around me but it was thin, and in the condition of my brain it seemed to me to be a mere annoyance with no connexion whatsoever to the fire that was driving us to this action. Much of what happened, it now seems to me, was disconnected in this way. I remember James yelling at me to put a handkerchief over my nose, and calling me an idiot in the process, and I remember doing so, but these two memories do not feel connected with each other, nor can I place them in the sequence of events that I do recall. In fact, going down those stairs is the last action I can place precisely in my mind for some few minutes.

I remember rolling on the ground outside, taking a deep breath of clean air, and looking back at the remains of the window I had broken through, and I even had an absurd moment of regret for the cost of the glass; I do not know if there was a glass window in the kitchen or if I had contrived to be in an entirely different portion of the inn by that time. I think I was handed a child through the window, but I am not certain if that was actually me, or which child it was, or who did the handing. I do not even remember for certain if I was inside or outside when I first saw the actual flames. Outside, I think.

No, it was in the kitchen, because I can now recall a beam of wood over my head with a thin line of flame on it, connected to nothing and appearing almost innocent in all the confusion. I remember the burning ceiling collapsing at least three times and in three different places, which means my memory is playing tricks—I suspect I just remember pieces of ceiling falling onto the floor in front of me; but whatever fell was certainly on fire. By that time there was a great deal more smoke in the air.

At one time I came across Coslick lying stretched out on the floor, I think of the kitchen, and it was obvious that he was dead because his skull was caved in; there were beams of burning wood around me, and I was carrying something heavy, perhaps a child, and trying to keep my handkerchief over my nose at the same time. This must have been just before I went through the glass, though I remember it the other way around. Did I carry a child through the window? Or something else? Or give the child to someone else to hand to me? I cannot be certain.

My next lucid moment was after I had somehow made my way to the front of the inn. I think I was looking for my valise (my room faced the front) and about the time I found it I also found Mrs Coslick, who was holding her children (all of them, I think) and screaming that her husband was still in there, and there were a few faceless people who had been in the inn standing about the yard. By this time flames were visible, not so much in tongues as one hears about, or even sheets, but almost as creeping vines of yellow and red as if the fire were growing in random flaws about the structure. Over the screaming was the very loud cracking and popping sound of the wood.

James and Susan appeared from around the corner, and I jogged to them, saying something about Coslick, when Susan spun around and fell, which was closely followed by a sound that could not be mistaken for the crackling of the wood, which was unquestionably a pistol shot.

I do not remember covering the ground between us; it seemed as if I was suddenly beside them, madly attempting to look around for the assailant while also looking at Susan and not doing a good job of either. James had placed himself between Susan and the hedge. He had knelt down next to her, and was holding a Colt's, and it seemed the pupils of his eyes had shrunk to tiny pinpoints while his face seemed blank as uncut ivory. Susan was holding a pistol, a small one, though it seemed large in her hands, and she was saying, "I'm all right, I'm all right, I'm all right," though there was a large blood spot on her left side—a blood spot that grew even as I stood there. I remember my feet going numb. Someone put a handkerchief over the wound, but I cannot now remember whether it was me, or James, or Susan herself. We were in the yard in front of the inn, the road was about thirty feet away, and just across it was a thick hedge. Whoever had fired the shot had to be there.

"Take care of Susan," I repeated.

"I'm all right," said Susan again. Her voice sounded strong.

"You aren't armed," said James, his voice as cold as ice and distant as China.

I stared stupidly at my valise for a moment, then managed to find my pistol, all the time aware that the assassin could be drawing a bead on any of us. As I found it, James said, "It can't be the Trotter's Club. They won't draw blood."

My pistol was unloaded, so I wasted more time loading and charging it; all the time I heard the crackling behind me of the Grey Hound burning while I strained my ears to hear the sound of another shot, as if hearing it would have done any good!

"Take care of Susan," I said once more, needlessly.

"I'm all right," said Susan.

"I will. Take care of yourself," said James, and I charged across the road and through the hedge like a boar. A movement caught my eye some distance away, on my side of the hedge, and I set out after it. A breathless, hazy time later, I realized it was dark, and that I no longer had any hope of catching the assassin, and it only then occurred to me that he might have circled back and returned to the Grey Hound for another attempt. This thought grew in me as I made the return journey until I had convinced myself that I would find James, Susan, Mrs Coslick and the servants all slaughtered. I knew very well that no such thing was likely, yet it became more real with each step. Had anyone wished to do me harm I should have been an easy target during that journey, even though it was dark, for I paid no attention to my surroundings until at last I stood before the inn, which was marked by some sort of awful red, glowing outline as if to laugh at what it once had been. Susan would have found something poetic to say about it, I'm sure.

I saw James in his characteristic lounge near the stables before he saw me; if he had called to me I fear I would have shot at him from sheer nerves. I said, "Susan—" and he said she was all right, the wound was trifling, which reassured me as well about the phantoms I had conjured. I started babbling about what we should do now, but he cut me off and demanded that I return home and I was so overcome with relief and the desire to see Kit that I made only a token argument, especially when he suggested that I borrow a horse. "Ride slowly," he said, as if I were capable of anything else. "My conscience will be easier if we don't lame Mrs Coslick's horse." Of course, it was only hours later, as I rode, that I realized that James must be suffering the torments of the damned, blaming himself for Coslick's death; at the time I just nodded and saddled the horse, which is a tired old gelding of some greyish color, I mounted and said, "James, I will see you again," and he asked if I were engaging in soothsaying or wishful thinking, and then cut me off with a laugh when I started to answer.

I intended to ride through the night and the day until I reached home, but I am no longer five-and-twenty, and exhaustion at last insisted I stop at the first inn that showed signs of life. It had been dark so long that I was amazed to find it was still before midnight when I stepped inside the Laughing Cup, exhausted, my clothing torn and soiled. What a sight I must have looked entering! I lay down, utterly done in, and found that I could not sleep, and so I write. I am in a tiny room, and the only comfort I can find is that there is no glass in the window. I believe I will always hate glass windows. I should mourn Coslick, but I cannot yet; it is all too fresh and too horrible; but tomorrow I will be home.

DECEMBER 15th
MELROSE HALL

My Beloved Richard and My Dear Susan,

I am writing to you together because you may well be in the same place, and because the information I have is of interest to you both, as well as to James, and above all because I almost feel as if there is now nothing that cannot and should not be shared among us all, because the most private and personal matters seem to touch upon our safety, and the windstorm of politics and intrigue that blows through our lives leaves careless disarray in its wake and forces us to cling to each other for shelter and protection.

It was early yesterday that Brian found me in the upstairs parlour, where I was reading a French romance about which I can tell you not author nor title nor subject, which will, I think, indicate something of how agitated I have been, because you, Dick, at least, know how absorbed I become in romances and how difficult it can be for you to command my attention when I am reading, yet when I heard Brian's footfalls my heart skipped a beat and even before he knocked I was standing, clutching the book to my heart as if it could shield me from a blow, and when he came in and saw me, he smiled as if to say he understood me and wished to give reassurance at once, and we must never forget that there is really so much goodness in this family, and yet when I saw that he held a piece of paper in his hand I began to tremble again, but Brian at once said, "Richard is out of danger. This found me today from Lincoln's Inn. Read it," and he held it out to me, but before I could touch it Aunt Louisa walked directly in without so much as clearing her throat before bursting through the doorway, her hand stretched out for the paper and a look in her eyes of mingled desperation and torment, so that I almost stepped back, but the paper called louder, so I quickly took it from Brian and said, "I shall read it aloud," which Aunt Louisa, after an instant's hesitation, agreed to. My dears, it was as dramatic a moment as you could find in a French romance, I think, with me reading words that I could make no sense of, and Aunt Louisa standing before me, her tiny body leaning forward as she strained to hear every word, while Brian stood between us as if unsure whether to go or to stay, and as I said before, I didn't understand the significance of the letter, a copy of which I will enclose, but Aunt Louisa did because she gave a great sigh and rushed forward, I thought to embrace Brian, but then she and I were embracing and crying into each other's shoulders and I do not know how long we stood there, but at last I looked up, and there was Brian with the most peculiar look on his face, holding a handkerchief in his hand, and moving it slowly back and forth between us, uncertain which would require it first, and it was so comical that I had to laugh, and then Aunt Louisa began to laugh, which I realized I had never heard her do in my life, and she was not even looking at Brian, so I think she was only laughing from release of tension and because I did, but that was in some ways the most remarkable event of this entire adventure. When we had at last stopped laughing, I took the handkerchief from Brian's drifting hand and used it to daub Aunt Louisa's eyes, while she said, "Bless you, Brian, I am proud of you and grateful," at which he blushed bright red and looked at the floor. Then, most remarkable of all, perhaps, Aunt Louisa said, "Let us take some tea," so she and I went down the stairs arm in arm and sat in the west room and drank tea together, while Brian, perhaps as amazed as I, retired, I think, to the library, and Aunt Louisa asked me if I thought you, Dick, were truly safe, and I said I did not think entirely safe, but at least out of danger from Her Majesty's Government, and much safer than you had been, and for the rest we had to trust in you, Susan, and James, and she seemed to consider that carefully and said, "It does no good to tell boys that they shouldn't mix themselves up in such matters. But I wish they had more sense. And that Susan Voight is far too mannish for her own good." I repeated that we would have to trust you, and she said, "But they don't even know what they are up against," and I said I thought we did, and if she noticed the change from *they* to *we* she made no response, but said, "That fool David thought he knew what he was doing, too, and look what happened to him!" and I said that none of us was like David, and she told me not to speak ill of the dead, especially my own cousin, which almost made me angry but I remembered that she was still Aunt Louisa so I apologised and then she got an odd look on her face and said, "He never knew if he was looking for God or for the Devil, you know. That was his problem. I don't think it was really his fault. He was always looking up to find God, but the Devil was under him the entire time and he didn't know what to do about it." And I asked her what she meant, and she seemed to come back to the present and said, "It is certainly nothing for young ladies to concern themselves with. You leave that horrid place alone, do you understand?" and I said I did, although I did not at the time, but it made perfect sense later, if you see what I mean, because Aunt Louisa always talks about practical things as if they were full of significance, and about mystical things as if they were next Tuesday, but I am certain you, Dick, know all about your mother, and I do not mean to imply a criticism, though she is awfully hard to get along with sometimes, but I think this has been very good for us, and I expect to get along with her much better now, even if I did disobey her, but what else would she have expected after telling me so much, so she probably knew what I would do all along.

Pretty soon after she said that, she abruptly decided that she had spoken with me long enough, and with a remark about wasting the day away, and if I didn't have things to do she certainly did, though what those things could be I cannot imagine, she left me there and I went up and found Brian and embraced him and thanked him for all his help, and then I went back to the parlour to think about the remarkable things Aunt Louisa said, because it seemed there was something important there, but I couldn't ferret it out, and I was thinking about it when a telegram arrived for Brian which caused him to dash out at once without a word, and frightened me all over again, but then I realized that if had anything to do with our problem at all, it must be that Henry had to be extricated from the authorities, so I just sat there playing patience and thinking until late that evening when I finally went to sleep, a little reassured but still frightened and lonely, and the next morning your letter, Susan, arrived, and it made me feel better, and I cried a little more, though I do not know what you mean by asking me if I am all right, because of course I am worried, but you and James and even Richard have had all the real scares, while I have had nothing to do but fret, and while it is hardly pleasant, my little problems certainly do not compare to killing someone, or being killed, or facing torture or arrest, for goodness sake, but yes, I have heard nothing from Mother since October, and had assumed she was with Andrew but she has not written, and that is unlike her, but I know it is a long way away so I have tried not to worry about it and I was fine until I saw him at David's funeral, and that brought it home very suddenly, but I am certain she is fine and you are not to worry about it while we have everything else to worry about and neither will I. And then your letter, Dick, arrived in the second post, and I cried some more and felt even better, and it is delightful that you both think so highly of me but I suspect you don't anymore now that you realize how long it took me to understand what Aunt Louisa was talking about when I'm sure you both saw it right away and now think I'm horribly stupid, but you must consider how distracted I was.

It turned out I was right about the telegram, because early this afternoon Brian returned with Henry in tow, and Henry was excited as a puppy about his adventure, and disappointed that I knew so much about it already, but he still insisted on telling me how he was taken up by men at gun-point and held captive by authority of Her Majesty, and all of the "awfully clever, I think" things he had to say to them until Brian retrieved him, and though Brian seemed to think it only a trifling matter Henry wouldn't stop talking about it until he caught sight of Aunt Louisa listening and scowling, this was in the small dining room, by the way, over breakfast, and after he saw her he looked guilty and, if he didn't stop talking, at least spoke in quieter tones thereafter, as if that would help if Aunt Louisa decided to eavesdrop! Dick and Susan, upon reading this back, I realize that I sound as if Henry annoyed me, which isn't right, because I was grateful for his help and glad that he was able to have an adventure from it while taking no real harm, but I was also impatient with him, because it was while he was talking to me that I realized at last what Aunt Louisa had been telling me and I determined to act on it, now that I had reason to believe Cauldhurst would not be watched, and so without further delay I had Wye call for the rig and I set out for the Abbey.

This time I felt different going in, in part because all that has happened has perhaps blunted what the Legion of Aunts would call my "finer sensibilities", and in part because I had been there once before after David's death, but mostly because this time Wye came in with me, and I knew, although I didn't see it, that he had that huge pistol in the pocket of his greatcoat. I lit the lamps as I entered because I didn't know if I would be done before dark, and I walked to the middle of Great Hall and called in as loud a voice as I could, "Clayborough! Are you about?", then waited for what seemed like aeons, and was just about to set off to search the rest of the Abbey for him when I heard great, ponderous footsteps and Clayborough appeared from the door that leads into the kitchen. He approached very slowly and looked at us quizzically, and I could see him study Wye and feel Wye study him back in much the way two dogs who meet on the street will investigate each other while deciding what attitude to take, and I hoped it wouldn't matter because it would not be pleasant to see them have at each other, Wye with his quick detached coldness and Clayborough with his large hands and capability for murderous rage that none of us present can ever forget. I started to speak, but before I could more than open my mouth, Clayborough said, "How did you know I was here?", which caught me up short because in the first place, I wasn't certain how I knew, and in the second, he had entirely lost the servile manner he had had ever since I was a child, as if David's death had freed him and he was no longer anyone's servant, but merely "an Englishman, as good as the next", as they say, which I suppose makes sense and I ought to have expected it, but it caught me off guard. After a moment to think it over, however, I said, "Well, for one thing who let in the man who accosted me the last time I was here, and, for another, where would you go, and for yet a third, why would you go anywhere?" He nodded, and I started to address him as Clayborough, but caught myself, changed my tone, and said, "Mr Clayborough, would you be kind enough to show me the way to the secret rooms in the cellar?" and he scowled and said, "Why would you want to see those?", which was enough of an answer to my question that I suppose I could have left, but I really couldn't have, if you know what mean, and it was a great comfort indeed to have Wye standing so coolly next to me, so I said what was mostly the truth, which was, "I want to see the place where they murdered Roderick," and he winced and, in an instant, he was the servant I had known as a fixture of Cauldhurst since I was a child, saying, "Ma'am, I had no part in that, and no knowledge of it," and I said, "I know that, Mr Clayborough, but I want to see it," and he hesitated, nodded, and taking a lamp from the wall led the way down the stairs and into the basement and then through a passage that was hidden not so much by design as by the placement of the furnishings, but, if you need to find it, the door is quite readily visible if you move the drapery between bookshelf and divan on the west wall of the northernmost room.

The door opened to a short corridor, at the end of which was a wide room with an altar at one end of it and all about it gilt masks, as from some uncivilized tribe of Negroes from the dark parts of the world, hung on the walls, and the ornaments were symbols, some of which I recognized, especially the one behind the altar, which was a larger version of the same one the members of the Trotter's Club wear about their necks. I nearly faltered as I entered, because I knew as I stepped through the door that, indeed, little Roderick had been killed here, but I still looked around the place, and even looked behind the draperies, all of which held evil symbols, and behind one was a small door, which was not locked, so I opened it and found another room quite as large as the one with the altar, but this one was filled with crates and boxes and casks that seemed quite new and recently placed, for there was little dust on them. I asked Clayborough what they were, and he answered me, now seeming torn between his old manner and his new, saying, "I'm sure I, that is, I don't know. They were brought by some men a couple of weeks ago. You were here when they were loading, you know," and I said, "The same day I was here? December the 4th?" and he said, "I don't know the exact date, ma'am, but it was the day your man," here he indicated Wye—"pulled out that pistol he's been fingering since he got here," and I said, "You were watching?" and he said, "To make sure that man didn't hurt you, but you didn't need me because of him." He gestured toward Wye again, and all this time Wye made no motion or reaction, and I shook my head and said, "Did that man, the policeman, bring the boxes?" to which Clayborough said, "Policeman? Him?" to which I answered, "He claimed to be," which brought a snort of derision from Clayborough but then he said, "That's right, he was having them loaded in a few at a time," and I asked what he meant and he said, "It took them three or four days, I mean, and he'd spend all day here waiting for a waggon to pull up in back, and then he'd have some men carry the boxes down, and then the waggon would leave," and I said, "Well, let's see what's in them," and he said, "All right," as if it was a matter of no great importance, and then said, "Hullo!" and held up a trinket, and I took it from him, recognizing it at once as James's pocket-watch! I suppose, Susan, I don't have to tell you what that means, do I?

We all looked at each other for a moment, but then I put the watch into my coat pocket, and told Clayborough to go ahead, and he opened up the box nearest him, a small crate, with a single wrench of his shoulders and arms, and there before me were some number of odd little pieces of brass, looking almost like tiny coins. I asked Clayborough what they were and he shrugged, but Wye answered, "Percussion caps, designed for the Brunswick rifled musket. Current military issue." I accepted this, and then looked at several long crates, then at the round kegs and the various smaller boxes, and then we opened up one of the crates to be sure, and there were, indeed, eight muskets in it, and we calculated that there might be five hundred muskets in that room, as well as caps and supplies for them all, after which I looked at our flaming lantern and at the kegs that almost certainly contained gunpowder, and became very frightened indeed, and so we made our way back out the way we'd come, and I did not stop trembling until we had said good-bye to Clayborough and were on our way back home, which we did at a greater speed than was probably good for the horses, but Wye seemed to know how badly I wanted to be back at Melrose.

You can imagine, I think, how my mind was whirling when I finally arrived, and I thought to take a good drink of sherry, but then I noticed that the sun was nearly setting, and I re-

membered you, Dick, and so I walked directly to the back
garden and stood there and stretched out my hands, and closed
my eyes and thought of you, and for an instant it really seemed
as if you were holding me, and my fright passed, my mind
seemed to clear, and it was as if I was standing on solid ground
for the first time since we've been apart. Dick, my love, I do
not know if the news from Brian means you can come home
now, though I fervently hope it does, but if you must still hide,
I think that now I can stand it for a little longer, and I hope
you and Susan can make some sense of what we found at
Cauldhurst, and I hope, oh, my dears, I hope so many things,
and I fear so many things, but I will try to be strong, so remember always that you are both in thoughts of your own,

Kitty

DECEMBER 16th
LATE
MELROSE HALL

My Dear James and My Poor Susan,

I do not know if or how this letter will find you, but I am
writing anyway, because I know that you, Susan, are all right,
even though Dick and I are still horribly worried, but we have
to trust that your wound was not serious, and I believe that if
the worst happened I should know, so that I am going to write
this in faith that it will find you, and find you healthy. As I
write, my beloved Richard is snoring lightly and the worry
lines have gone from his face, though only, I think, temporarily. He arrived this morning, just minutes after I had returned
from posting my last letter, which letter may, I now know,
never reach you, and he looked more beaten down than I could
have imagined him, it almost broke my heart, but after all he
has been through, and both of you as well, I should add, I can
understand it, but he began to feel better the instant he crossed
the threshold, which makes me long for the day the two of
you can cross it as well, cross it knowing that you can stay
for as long as you want, though I am no longer certain if that

day will ever come, but I must have faith in that, too.

He told me everything that happened, of course, and while he did so I may have begun to understand more of what is behind all of this, because we had a sudden insight which, if it is true, clears away some of the confusion, though certainly I may be wrong, but I will tell it to you and you can decide if I am just being silly. We were lying in bed, all explanations finished, and holding each other, and making small talk the way one does, and I happened to remark that I really must make some effort to read Hegel just so that I could understand Dick's conversations with James, and I wished my German were better, and Dick said he'd be delighted to help me with translation and summaries, though Hegel certainly tested the limits of his German, and I said, "What is it all about, anyway?" and he said, "It is about understanding a thing by understanding its movement, and that the movement is caused by the unity and conflict of opposites within it," and I said I didn't understand and he laughed and said that he didn't either, but then he said, "Everything is made of contradictions, and if you see something that appears to be a single whole, well, it isn't really, because parts of that whole are in conflict with other parts, and that conflict is what makes it what it is, all of which makes sense when talking about Nature, but this Engels of James's wants to apply it to society as well, which I'm not certain I can accept," and I said, "Well, society is just people, and any group of people have conflicts," and he allowed that that was true, but that didn't mean you could always understand those conflicts or simplify them the way Engels wanted to, and I said, "It would help a lot if we could understand the conflicts in our enemies," and he agreed, and then all of a sudden I realized what I'd said and sat bolt upright in bed and said, "What if that's what's been going on all along?" and he asked what I meant, and I said, "Well, what if everything that's been driving our enemies is that they are trying to undercut each other, as David was trying to hoodwink the Trotter's Club, and," and he broke in and said, "And Andrew Cobham is trying to undercut Tournier and his sister," and then I got really excited and said, "Not just that, but how do we know Tournier and his sister are really together, maybe they're after different things," and then he said, "It might be

Eleanor who had Susan shot, because she isn't in the Trotter's Club and so wouldn't mind drawing blood," and I said, "Why shoot Susan, anyway?" and he said, "Trying to shoot James, but it was a long shot for a pistol, and besides, Susan was wearing trousers, and she has dark hair and is almost James's height, so the assassin might have either missed or been confused about which one was James," and I said, "Let me think about this."

We talked some more, and then we got out of bed and put our heads together over the letters we had and we assembled the facts and the pieces and guesses, and I am not certain of any of this, but some of it, at least, may be right, so let me just set it down for you as neatly as possible so you can decide for yourselves.

Alan Tournier wants control of the Trotter's Club, and he is also trying to get control of Cauldhurst, which is probably the traditional center of the Trotter's Club, and might even have been an important place as far back as the time of Sir James, in the 1760s, and he also wants to make sure no one finds out about his activities in the Chartist movement and he can accomplish both, and I should say this is something of a leap, but it does fit the facts, if he can get James disinherited and convicted of treason, because then Cauldhurst will be forfeit to the Crown and he thinks he can convince the Crown to give it to him. Since Richard has a claim on Cauldhurst, that is why he attempted to have Richard blamed for David's death, and it is why he had David killed, and he probably also discovered that David had betrayed him by holding back James's notes, so he got revenge on David at the same time and to this end he has also made a deal with the Prussians, and is using the Trotter's Club and his influence in the government against the *émigrés*, which is how he will earn the gratitude of the Crown so they will give him Cauldhurst. It is probably Tournier who filled the basement of Cauldhurst with weapons so that he can blame it on James. If he does want James convicted of treason and Richard of murder, then the latter part has evidently failed, but he may try again, and even if he doesn't, he will probably continue with the rest of his plan.

Eleanor, his sister, knows of her brother's plan, but isn't content that her livelihood and that of her child should be at

Alan's sufferance, so she is trying to gain control of Cauldhurst herself and she also wants Richard convicted of murder to get him out of the way, but she'd prefer James to be dead so that she can, she hopes, press her child's claim to Cauldhurst, which might not work even if she could prove David was the father, but it might, and we must speak with Brian about this.

Andrew Cobham wants to retain control of the Trotter's Club, to which end he needs to foil Alan Tournier's plans, and he can do both of these by *killing James according to the traditions of the Trotter's Club*. I don't think Andrew cares one way or the other about the *émigrés* or the list of informers.

Sir George Bankston wants to know who the Chartists are, and he wants the *émigrés* out of the country, and although I don't think he cares about the Trotter's Club or any of their machinations, he is willing to work with them to get what he wants, just as he is willing to work with James to get something else he wants.

That is what we have, and, my dear James and Susan, now that I have set it down this way, I am convinced that we are right, because it explains so much that we haven't been able to explain before, but if you think we are mad let us know and we will try again, and now I have run out of things to say and I have to stop writing which is awful because I don't know how to send this, and I wish you could read it because I think it terribly important, but at least now I have my Richard to hold again so I will do that until I hear from you, which I hope will be soon, but when you get this, even if it is all nonsense, at least you will know that Richard is safe, and I'm sure you know, even now, that you are both ever in the thoughts of,

Kitty

LANGSTONE
16 DEC 1849

Dear Kitty,

Richard will have given you a decent summary of the events of the last few days, I'm sure, and the news that, though I'm hurt, I'm not *badly* hurt. I am, in fact, well enough to write this almost certainly *enormous* letter, full of horrible things. What else am I to do, confined to bed? I don't know how to cheat at cards, after all. I'm sorry, that's a reference I'll explain later, I hope, if I remember.

I apologise in advance for what I think will be the journal-like nature of this letter. You see, I do know that you will have heard Richard's account, and that, of the two stories, the view through his eyes will mean the most to you (though I trust I come in only a nose behind!). This really is as much written down for myself as for you. When time turns these events into something like a detailed evil dream, smudging their boundaries and arranging them out of order, I will want to know that this letter exists, to restore the proper proportion of good and bad, human and inhuman, to my memories. If, that is, I still have any use for either memory or proportion by then. The events of the 15th give me a little pause when I'm committing myself to future projects.

Now, where to begin? Where I left off, I suppose: in Bishop's Waltham, delicately wringing my hands.

The ride between Bishop's Waltham and Langstone is much easier in daylight. It was a melancholy landscape, suited to meditating on one's ills and injustices; a sky the colour of two drops of ink in a cup of milk, brown leaves on the oaks rattling in the cold wind, other trees bare and rubbing their branches together as if for warmth. There was ice on the puddles, under the banks where the sun hadn't reached. Girasol pretended to be frightened of the sight of his own breath clouding the air at the end of his nose.

I've got ahead of myself already. We were in the yard of the Green Wife, clutching our meagre baggage and watching the landlady's son bring the horses round, when I told Richard we were on our way back to the Grey Hound. He made no immediate response, but only said after a pause, "I'll be with you in a moment," and ducked back into the common room. He returned in five minutes, and still said nothing particular, but mounted Cavalier and followed me out of the yard and the village.

We'd gone half a mile or so, with Richard looking thoughtfully forward between the horse's ears, before he said, "Did he learn to think like that, do you suppose? Or has he always had a mind like the Hampton Court maze?''

''What?'' I asked, before I understood who we were talking about, and what had prompted it. ''How would I know? And come to think of it, why would I care? Whatever sort of mind he has, it's presently employed in the service of keeping us all from prison or the grave. Don't distract him.''

''Do you think I could?'' he asked. ''I wouldn't have thought it.''

We managed another eighth of a mile, perhaps, in silence before I said, ''If you haven't already decided what you think of him, you'd better do it quick.''

Richard shook his head. ''I decided years ago. I admire him. I'm a little in awe of him. I'm sad for him, sometimes. When it seems called for. And I'm afraid of him. Nothing's changed, particularly.''

''Afraid of him?''

''Aren't you?'' he asked, turning toward me at last.

''No.''

''How strange. Or—are we not using the word in the same way? I'm afraid of pistols, under certain circumstances, but I'm a very good shot.''

''Under certain circumstances?'' I repeated, hopefully.

Cavalier stumbled a little in a frozen rut, and Richard took a moment to collect him again and to apologise to him, out loud. Then he said, ''James suggested, in one of his letters, that I'd never seen him . . . that he hadn't given me cause to fear him. Odd that he should think so. That epic New Year's Eve after Roderick's death seems to loom large in everyone's memory but his—unless he thought there was nothing remarkable in what he did, which is itself a bit frightening.''

''What,'' I said slowly, ''did he do?''

''You were there. Weren't you?''

''I was there for a glimpse of it. After that, I was waving burnt feathers under your mother's nose in the drawing room. By the time I got back, James was sitting on Clayborough at the foot of the staircase, explaining to him, in the most ordinary tone of voice ever heard, that if everyone would be on his best behaviour henceforth, no one would mention the incident to Andrew.''

"He was—" Richard stopped, and gave an abrupt, exasperated sigh. "It was as if there was a sort of—He had a kind of . . . intensity. It was all very efficient. I can't explain."

"Well then, you needn't try." I could remember the unreality of the scene: James with his hair in his eyes, blood on his knuckles, and not suffering from so much as shortness of breath, keeping Clayborough (a head taller and possibly six stone heavier) pinned to the carpet; David halfway up the stairs and pressed against the wall, his knees drawn up as close to his chest as his stomach allowed, clutching the side of his face with one hand and watching the two men below him, his eyes enormous. Had Richard seen the James from the ruined farmyard outside Redding, or the one who had faced down Gideon Johnson in the marsh? Or a combination of them, or some other formidable James? "And if we can't find something other than James to talk about, I am going to ride off without you."

"Pardon?" said Richard, shocked.

"Granted. Do you and Kitty mean to have children? I know she never used to favour the idea, but she's capable of convincing herself to want whatever it seems best that she should, within limits, so I've no way to tell what her real opinions are on the subject."

After a long, tumultuous silence, Richard said, "Susan," and stopped. Then he began again, slowly, "Sometimes I have to be away from Kitty all day, or even several days together—not this time, I mean for perfectly normal reasons. And I hate it, and I think about her all the while I'm gone. I don't think she's initiated a parting between us of more than a few hours since we . . . since we took up with each other."

"I've noticed. Yes?"

"Well—the two of you—I mean, you and . . ."

"James," I filled in, with resignation, since I was the one who'd asked to change the subject.

"Yes. You've . . . it's very new between the two of you. And yet, you're here."

"And he's in London. I see. Gracious, Richard, ought I to be trotting around behind him over the countryside? I'd like to see his face if I tried."

He looked at me as if I were speaking some Hottentot dialect. "Susan, I can't tell if you're trying to be stoical, or if you just don't think it's any business of mine. Or if you're being perfectly candid."

"If I knew what you were getting at, maybe I could tell you," I grumbled. "No, I beg your pardon, I think I know what you're getting at. You want to know if I intend to live in James's pocket henceforth."

He at least didn't look shocked this time. "I . . . don't think I'd have put it that way."

"What do you know about tigers, Richard?"

"I . . . beg your pardon?"

"Wolves, you see, live in packs, and mate for life, and hunt together. Tigers, on the other hand, require—oh, I forget what, exactly, but something on the order of five miles between them and the next tiger to make them perfectly comfortable."

"You're saying," Richard said carefully, "that James is a tiger."

"No, I'm saying *I* am. I really don't know what James is. The question hasn't come up."

Richard gave a little despairing sort of chuckle. "I am, as usual, out of my depth."

"Oh, Richard." He'd managed to make me feel guilty in spite of everything, the beast. "I'm different from Kitty, is all. She set her cap for you, and got you, and was instantly uncomplicatedly happy, assuming that everything else would take care of itself. And for Kitty, everything *does*, bless her. For the rest of us, things are a little more complicated."

Richard rode with his eyes on his hands for a few strides, and said, "She would probably say that they wouldn't be if you didn't insist on making them so."

"Yes, she would, wouldn't she? Think of this as my way of keeping them uncomplicated. I don't know what's going to happen next, and so I try not to think or talk about it, to avoid accidently making assumptions and plans."

"What would you like to have happen next?"

"I would like, and I quote, to remain alert to the changing nature of possibility. And to *stop talking about James*. I would have sworn that before all this started we had perfectly adequate lives and topics for conversation."

"Were they perfectly adequate lives?"

"I never heard you complain."

"I won't argue with that. But we were all living with . . . blindnesses and evasions, that we didn't know about until they were exploded. Who knows what damage they might have done in the end?"

It seemed the moment for one of us to say something brisk, so I stepped into the breach. "Well, independent of anything else, I plan to live to be one hundred, become famous for always saying exactly what I think, and be a constant embarrassment to all my descendants, assuming I have them. What do you want from life?"

Richard studied the road between his horse's ears once more, and said, "More of it?"

That shut me up quite effectively for miles.

We did, finally, find other things to talk about. Books: I thought Mr Thackeray's *Vanity Fair* was wickedly funny; Richard thought it was wicked, and accurate, but not so amusing. Painting: Richard expressed passionate approval of Delacroix; I said that no artist's work moved me as Turner's had on first viewing. Architecture: we agreed that natural forms, and not the remains of Greek temples, were the proper models on which to build Man's structures, and admitted at last that we would both like to live in a Gothic cathedral. In short, we had a much better trip than I'd begun to fear we would.

When we rode into the yard of the Grey Hound, Coslick came to the door, wiping his hands on his apron. He shook his head at the sight of Richard, but waited until we'd dismounted and Richard was within hearing to say, "Bad penny."

"Thank you," Richard replied gravely, without a moment's hesitation.

"Queen's men took the young one off yesterday," said Coslick. "It was as good as a play."

"No doubt," I said, feeling sourish and old in the face of Henry's imagined enthusiasm.

Richard at that point introduced me in form to Coslick. He nodded and shook my hand. Then he said to Richard, "Letter's come for you."

I almost asked if there was anything for me, but controlled the impulse. When I saw the handwriting on the envelope for

Richard, I had to control a great many impulses. I let him take it away to read in private.

My reward was to have a woman come flying into the empty taproom where I was sitting glumly—a little woman whose face and figure must have been exquisite in her youth and were still handsome—saying, "By all the blessed saints, if it isn't Miss Susan Voight I'll eat my own shoe, I will. John told me about the lady who came to fetch Mr Cobham away, and when I heard you described, I said, 'Doesn't that just sound like little Kitty's Susan, John?' And so you are. Well, I'm pleased to meet you. Bless me, you look worn to the nub. And your hand's cold as the latch on the door. Where's that man's wits gone, not to show you upstairs straightway? Come along and have a lie-down and a glass of currant wine before dinner. You know, if anyone told me I'd be welcoming a lady wearing trousers into my house I'd have said St Peter'd have the Devil to supper first. But you look fine as any gentleman in 'em, missy. Don't bring it into fashion, though. Can't you just see me in my old man's drawers? I'd look like two full sacks tied together."

And by this recitation, Kitty, you will have already guessed that I was being met and conducted to my room by Eileen Coslick. She said she remembered you very well and sent her best. I also met, in a noisy and invigourating rush, like a summer rainstorm, the three boys, Jackie, Sam, and little Tony, plunging down the stairs and all talking at once to their mother. Jackie, being at the uncomfortable age as regards the opposite sex, gazed from my face to my britches, turned reddish-purple like a ripe plum, and ceased to be able to speak at all. His brothers seemed delighted to be spared the competition.

Mrs Coslick sorted the argument out in some mysterious mother-fashion, dealt with it, and sent the three off to the kitchen on various errands (Sam was delegated to play butler and bring my currant wine). She led me to a snug little room with a many-paned casement window looking out over the garden, a high bed spread with a pieced coverlet, and two rush-seated chairs and a footstool.

She showed me the amenities, and when Sam arrived, had him build up the fire. "Ma'am, pardon," Sam said to me when he'd finished, "but Da said—*Are* you kin to Mr Jack? Will he be along, too?"

Jack—I was stopped for only a moment. The inn yard had leaped at me when we rode up, in a way it hadn't done when I'd first arrived to spirit Richard away. It was like the stage setting for an often-read play, built and lit, only waiting for the character whose lines had defined it for me. The character's name here had been Jack.

In Sam's round face, shyness was going several rounds with excitement. He's possibly of an age with Henry Holland, in Manchester.

"I hope so," I said. "Is he a friend of yours?"

"Oh, yes, ma'am. He's a right 'un. He taught me to cheat at cards."

I must have looked a little stunned. "Did he?"

"Only so as I could tell if th'other cove was doing it. And he taught us all to swim under water. Are you his sister?"

I only opened and closed my mouth once before I said, "No. I'm his cousin, Miss Voight."

"Pleased to meet you. Then can I tell Jackie and Tony that he'll come?"

"If he can."

Sam would have liked something more precise, but his mother sent him rather sharply off on another errand. When he'd gone, she said, "Since your cousin left here—your cousin James, that is—we've not had much news of him."

That answered the question I couldn't think how to ask, about how many names the Coslicks knew him by. "I last saw him four days ago. He . . . was well."

I could see her shoulders settle, relaxed. "Be glad for it while it lasts, then. He's not the sort to stay that way long, the creature. I'll never forget the morning when Tony came creeping in to wake us, and the last stars not even out of the sky, saying, 'Ma, Da, there's a dead man down under the roses, unless maybe he's a ghost.' And both nearly true then, and not for the last time. Scared me half out of my skin when we got him inside and he opened his eyes. He was so full of fever and what he'd been dosed with, that whatever he was seeing, it wasn't in the room with him, but he spoke out in that heathen language and I thought the hair would creep right off my head.''

"Heathen—was he speaking Gaelic?"

Mrs Coslick propped her knuckles on her hipbones. "Do you think I wouldn't know the sound of decent Irish spoken? He's a travelled lad, seems, and might have been talking anything, I suppose. But the way it rang out went straight into your bones."

"If he was dreaming," I said, feeling uncomfortable, "it might have been nothing but nonsense."

"That's so," she replied, but I didn't think I'd convinced her. She seemed, in fact, disappointed in me. "The joint should be done in an hour. Come down when you're ready."

I drank the wine while standing at my window, looking out through the thick panes down the slope of the ground bleak with winter, to the arching canes and bronze-coloured dead leaves of the overgrown roses at the bottom of the garden.

As I had nothing to read, I was downstairs in the common room first. Richard descended a quarter of an hour later, pale, frowning, and distracted.

"Gracious, what's he done this time?" I asked.

"I thought we'd agreed not to talk about him?" he replied, eyebrows raised. His gaze was, on the surface, mocking. He sat down across the trestle table from me. "What are we drinking?"

"Richard, if you—Nothing, yet. Eating dinner shortly."

"Well, we're drinking something now. Or I am." Richard bobbed back up and went into the taproom, returning with a bottle and two glasses.

"That your brother should drive one to drink," I said, watching him pour and catching the scent of brandy, "is not uncommon. But I'd like to know how he's gone about it this time."

Richard, after all that trouble, only looked at his full glass. "He's not been harmed. The girl—the Irish girl he met here, that . . ."

I took pity on him. "I remember. Go on."

"She was murdered in London, in such a way as to place James under suspicion of murder and treason." He pressed his fingers against his eye sockets for a moment. "James says that several of his allies and contacts are dead or missing, under suspicious circumstances. And Lee—you remember Lee?—showed him a passage in one of Hugh Stone's books that suggests that the Trotter's Club mean to kill James at winter solstice. It's all couched in hunting imagery, apparently, and I can't tell from what James writes if it's figurative or literal. That is, if they intend to, to hunt him, or if this whole abominable half-year has been their metaphoric chase." He jabbed his fingers through his hair in a gesture of frustration very like one of his brother's. "God, Susan, it makes me sick. Really, physically sick."

"What about Bankston's people?" I asked, pretending that it didn't do the same to me.

"Oh, he accomplished the business he went to do. That's James all over, isn't it? I'm a free man. But *his* case is worse than ever, it seems." He finally drank from his glass, half of it at a gulp.

"They believe he committed this murder?"

"No. That is, officially, yes, they do. But if he'll deliver up the Trotter's Club, he'll be allowed to get away."

I couldn't say what it was about that speech that struck me: a hesitation, a tone, a *lack* of hesitation at the wrong moment. I said, "There's a catch, isn't there? What is it?"

"James thinks . . ." Richard pressed at his eyes again, the way one might press a sore muscle. "He thinks he'll have to leave the country. Permanently."

It had got dark in the room while we sat; Eileen came in from the kitchen with a brace of candles. "Will you want dinner in here, or upstairs?" she asked.

"Here, I think," I told her. "Thank you, Mrs Coslick." Then I watched the candlelight move over Richard's fingers and the edges of his tight-closed lips.

He finally dropped his hands and stared at me. "Nothing? You have *nothing* to say to that?"

I can't recall ever feeling so much pity and irritation mixed. "Did you really believe that he would be able to stay?"

"I—" He swallowed, and finished bitterly, "James seems to have believed it, until Bankston suggested otherwise."

"Or wanted not to believe anything else."

"And when did this realization come to *you*?"

"While we were in Manchester. Nothing changes because of it." I sat with my hands folded on the table. He was angry with me because he needed to be angry; I didn't mind. Eventually he would arrive at the understanding I had: that wherever it leads us, we have to go forward. Nothing else offers any chance at all.

Dinner was very good, especially the baked fish and the turnips, during which Richard began speaking to me again. We finished with coffee, which we drank in the common room, in the company of the three other guests: a middle-aged couple, and a smartly-dressed stout man who looked as if he sold the finest and most extensive line available to the public, of something.

I was staring at the slice of darkness I could see between the curtains when Richard asked me, was anything wrong? Coslick appeared with the coffee-pot at the same moment.

"What time is it?" I asked.

"Just gone nine," Coslick replied before Richard could produce his watch.

"Did you ever find another hostler?"

"Yes, ma'am."

"Does he sleep above the stables?"

Richard and Coslick were both, by this time, looking at me as if I'd begun to nod and talk to people who weren't there. "No. No, ma'am. He's a local man, and stops in the village."

"Hah," I said, and asked for pen and paper.

"Can you tell me," Richard said when he'd gone, "or would it not be good for me?"

I realized I was smiling, which made me smile more yet. "Oh, it's just that I take a certain unworthy pleasure in reaching a conclusion even slightly before your brother. It happens so rarely." Coslick brought the pen, ink bottle, and paper, and I scribbled:

> *Mine is the third room from the stairs on the first floor, facing the back. If you don't come to it immediately upon reading this, I will be responsible for the consequences.*

> S.

Richard craned his neck, but my handwriting is (or at least in this case was) too bad to be read at an angle. I rose and told him, "I'll be back."

Then I got a lantern from the kitchen, crossed the yard to the stables, and went up the flight of wooden stairs I found there. The door at the top was latched but not locked; I tapped at it (I might, after all, *not* have reached the conclusion first), but there was no answer, so I opened the door.

No one had occupied the room since James. I remembered his list of its fixtures in one of the letters to Richard; they were all there, picked out in the lantern light. It was at first a small shock, like returning to some childhood haunt and finding it unreasonably like one's memories. I almost expected paper and books on the table, the black coat on the peg.

Then I saw that the fire was laid, and the tinder box was near on the hearth. There was a candle, unburnt, in the stick on the table. The tick was folded at the foot of the bed, but there were a pillow and a comforter laid on top of that, that I thought wouldn't ordinarily have been stored there. I laughed when I saw them. I wasn't the first to have arrived at the conclusion, after all. I folded my note into a tent and set it on top of the bed linens. Then I went back to the common room.

Richard looked up when I came to the table. "You thought he wouldn't—?"

"Well, imagine if it were quite late, and he were tired, and had slipped without thinking into that infuriating self-reliant close-mouthed . . . One or both of the Coslicks entertained the possibility, I think. The room's half made up. I have a very nice chamber upstairs with two chairs in it, and after I get a bath, I want to go and sit in one of them. In an hour, you may have the other, if you haven't anything else to do."

"I suppose I could lame a horse riding through the dark to the nearest place with a railway station, where I would discover that there was no train north until tomorrow, anyway. Thank you, I would be delighted to keep you company."

"Lovely. In an hour then." I went to arrange for a can or two of hot water, and an hour in which I didn't need to think. Of course, not needing to is no guarantee that one won't. You should not believe, because I am more shrub than vine, that I have no feelings at all in the matter. Parting from James, know-

ing that he is still resident on the planet and more or less well,
is not so difficult a burden to bear. Not knowing if he is alive
or dead changes matters, I find. I was labouring not to ask
myself why, if he had finished with the business in London,
he hadn't yet arrived at the Grey Hound. And so I watched
the steam curl up from my wet knees and told myself I was
succeeding as well as could be expected.

I thought about not troubling to dress again. If Richard was
going to be upset by the presence of his brother's lover in an
exceedingly demure wool flannel wrapper, he could go sit in
his own room. But dealing with Richard tongue-tied and not
knowing where to look was too tiring to contemplate. The only
virtue of the shabby black gown I'd come masquerading in
(odd that I don't think of my trousers in that light anymore)
was that it closed down the front, and I could get into it without help. Poor Alice, back at Bright's keeping my unworn
wardrobe in order and wondering who the devil (she would
never, even in the privacy of her own mind, wonder who *the
devil*) was pressing the creases out of my skirts. Answer, Alice:
Nobody. I am a perfect tatterdemallion without you. I dressed
grudgingly, and put on stockings and half boots against the
cold of the floors.

Six months ago—*two* months ago—it would never have occurred to me to consider being alone in my bedchamber in my
dressing-gown with any man in the world. Stranger still that I
might have not done so out of consideration for the gentleman's feelings. From my vantage point inside myself, I don't
seem like an abandoned woman; but the list of things I've done
would certainly qualify me in anyone else's eyes. Is this how
it happens and what it's like, for those women on the fringes
of society that the high sticklers don't invite to their homes?
Do they just do one thing after another that seems right or
necessary, leave off doing, one at a time, the things that seem
every day more like pointless formality or polite hypocrisy or
outright falsehood? As paper and pen are my witness, I swear
never again to snub a dashing widow. After all, I will now be
playing whist at her table, won't I?

Richard was wholly unimpressed by my consideration for
his feelings, probably because I didn't mention it. He was

carrying one of his bags, which he set down on the floor just inside the door.

"Planning a hasty exit?" I asked, watching.

"Potentially useful items. Would it preserve or endanger your reputation if I shut the door?"

"What reputation? Do as you please, I don't think anyone's left awake, anyway."

"I heard someone clanking in the kitchen. An innkeeper's work is never done."

I sat, as I'd promised, in one of the chairs. "Kitty mentioned unwisely, not too long ago, that she'd love to run a nice quiet little inn."

Richard blinked. "There's no such thing."

"I'll tell her you said so. It will be better coming from you." And there, my dear, I have.

He sat in the chair on the other side of the fire. "I'm sorry," he said abruptly. "I've been a damned tiresome parcel to haul around the countryside, haven't I?"

I conquered the resulting inevitable speechlessness and replied, "My God, of course not. You've been a lamb. A brick. Whyever would you—oh."

"Oh?"

"I've been badgerish, as Jamie says, and you thought it was your fault."

"I *have* been pretty slow. And I feel so . . ." He shrugged briskly, frowning. "Useless. I've hated this entire episode, being in hiding. And then you had to come and lead me out of it, like an infant on a pony."

"Gracious. Do you know, I've never seen an infant drive a carriage and pair?"

"Ho, ho. You know what I mean. I'd rather be doing something useful."

I folded my hands tightly in my lap. "It's that sort of attitude, you know, that wins you the opportunity to shoot perfect strangers in the dark."

"Before they shoot you," he answered slowly.

I had forgotten the man on the dock in Southampton. "Or club you to death. On those terms, what's so very awful about hiding?"

"Having your life out of your own hands," Richard said

on a long sigh. "You haven't exactly relished the last few days, have you?"

"No, but not because of you. It's the waiting. I can't bear it. Which brings me back around to, if James finished with Bankston before he wrote to you, *where is he now*?"

"I'm sorry. That's right, I didn't get to that part. He's gone to Cauldhurst, the idiot."

I leaned forward and grabbed the chair arms, and heard all the glued joints crack. "He has *what*?"

"Based on a childhood memory, he believes Andrew was responsible for the death of his mother. He says he's gone to find some further evidence of it. I'm not sure that's the whole of the reason."

"*Damn* him. He tells Kitty to stay away from the place—high-handed, but sensible—and then what does he do but go there himself!"

"Also . . ." Richard looked like a man bearing unwelcome news. I leaned back in the chair again, the better, I suppose, to react to whatever it was. "Also, Kitty told you about the man she found at Cauldhurst, I think."

"The policeman?"

Richard nodded. "Or whatever he is. Because he seems to be somewhat more than a constable. Certainly a great deal more threatening. I think he would have done Kitty harm if Wye and his pistol hadn't appeared at the opportune moment."

Kitty, dear, am I telling you anything you don't already know when I say I was upset with you then? I'd known there was something you weren't telling me. Now here it was, and if I'd known it, James would have known it, too, and been that much more cautious. I have forgiven you, of course. But the next time you wonder if you ought to tell me something like this, please, please, please don't waste time wondering.

I would have bludgeoned Richard about it, but he already looked apprehensive. I clenched my hands on the chair arms and tried to think of something comforting to say.

That was the moment when the familiar voice broke in cheerfully from behind us with, "Got your note. Richard, if you stay unchaperoned in ladies' rooms, your reputation will be in tatters."

James was leaning in the doorway of my room, arms

crossed, ankles crossed, my folded note pinned between two fingers of his right hand as if he'd materialized it. He was white with weariness, thumbprints of shadow under his eyes; and he was grinning impartially at both of us. I was reminded of a retriever who has just brought back a thoroughly unretrievable duck.

"I know," said Richard. "That's why I've made a point of doing so."

I was standing on the hearth rug, though I couldn't remember leaving the chair. For that matter, I couldn't remember Richard leaving his, but he had. For a moment, none of us quite seemed to know what came next. Then Richard pulled his gaze from James to me, and said, "I'm not going to toss you for it, you know."

"What?" I said cleverly.

"I yield to you," Richard said, with the faintest bow and a sweep of his arm toward James.

I am proud to say that I am not *perfectly* thick. I walked to the door, and James uncrossed his legs and stood on them. It must have looked terribly deliberate and restrained. It wasn't, really. Part of me was aware of what my body was doing, and his; but I was looking into his face and he into mine, and I think that if anything had come between our eyes, it would have been smashed to powder. At first, when I reached him, I only rested my forehead against his collarbone, testing the solidity of him and hiding my face from him and Richard both. Then he gathered me into an embrace that might have endangered a more delicate woman's ribs. His lips were still cool from the night air. I found myself, as I held him, feeling for bandages beneath his clothes.

"Unscathed," he said to me under his breath, with a quirk of his mouth, and I could at last smile at him and move away.

James stepped into the room and closed his hands over Richard's shoulders, and such a look passed between them as I may never have sufficient history to interpret, and may never want to have. I don't think it would have broken anything, except possibly a heart or two. Then Richard drew him closer and put his arms around him, as if he were much more than a year older than his brother. I suppose, just at the moment, he might have been.

Then Richard stepped back, curiously diffident. "You should know," he said, "that I wasn't certain if I ought to show Susan your letter to me, so I didn't." He shrugged. "I mean . . . oh, never mind."

"Did you tell her the important bits?" James asked.

After a moment, Richard replied, "Some of them."

"Did you use it as an opportunity to discuss me when I wasn't there?"

At that my eyes flew to his face. But it matched his voice, good-humoured and rueful.

"I know some of the contents are awful," said James, "but at heart, it's just a letter from one of your relations. You should treat it as such. If you didn't promptly turn it into an occasion for gossip, my feelings would be hurt."

"Well, we did, and you knew we did, so stop tormenting Richard," I said brusquely. "Sit down. Do you want anything? Mrs Coslick told me to raid the larder if we liked."

James shook his head and subsided into the chair I'd been in. "I ate on the way, not long ago. I think not long ago. I saw Eileen on the way in, but I should talk to John—to Coslick—before I drop, which may not be long from now. Lee sent him messages."

Richard sat down slowly, almost contemplatively. "I think something liquid is in order. Preferably something that will leave my mouth with a better taste than I have from thinking about—about other things."

"*I* just sat down," said James. "And I don't think I can get up again. And if I have anything stronger than shandy, I'll fall asleep." He really was exhausted; the candles on the table beside him made much of it. I wondered how he'd got himself from Cauldhurst to here.

"I suppose I can give you an opportunity to gossip about me," I sighed. "Richard, is your heart set on anything particular?" I stopped with my hand on the door.

"Sherry seems to be traditional, which is why I took the trouble to procure a bottle from the Green Wife before we left. You'll find it in the bag about two feet from your right foot, next to a larger bottle of something rather stronger, which was reserved for my use in case it turned out that I wasn't able to return to Melrose. Careful, my wine glass is in there, too, wrapped in a handkerchief.''

James made a sound halfway between sighing and laughter. ''Wait 'til I tell Kitty what you consider an adequate substitute for her. Goddess, may I have sherry after all? Then I won't have to watch you go out of sight.''

''The marriage of sentiment and consideration,'' I grumbled, and rummaged for the sherry. It was just where Richard said it would be, in the pack beside his pistol-case. I was reminded again how different my life had become in six months. Had Richard reflected on the same thing, I wondered? Six months since he'd last seen James, and so much in them. I unwrapped Richard's wine glass; it, and the glass from the currant wine that I'd left behind when I went downstairs, and a teacup on the dressing table, left for whatever reason but clean at least, were the only things in the room suitable for drinking from. I thumped down on the hearth and doled out the rations. James got the teacup, and not much in it.

''Well,'' he said, leaning back and folding both hands around the cup, ''are there things we ought *not* to talk about, just to mark off the territory? How well up are you on the events since you went into hiding?''

''You're going too fast,'' said Richard. ''First, you must say kind things to me for having thought to bring the wine. No, excuse me, for having *actually* brought the wine; I've been reading Hegel. But before *that*, I must be allowed to toast the two of you. I want you to know, and I speak on Kitty's behalf, that we are delighted for you both. I know you had some questions about that, James, so let me answer them. As far as Kitty and I are concerned, this is the best thing that has happened in years outside of a Southampton hospital room. So here's to you both, and I'll thank you to blubber appropriately.''

This time James actually laughed.

I was glad my back was to the fire; I felt the rush of blood in my cheeks, but I don't think it was visible. Trust Richard (and you, by extension, I suppose), to make a great ceremonial fuss over two people's extremely private gratifications. I said crisply, ''I blubber when I'm miserable. Why ought I to blubber because someone toasts me for being devilishly lucky?''

"Oh, don't disappoint him. Couldn't you summon up a sniff, at least?" James asked me. I met his eyes and received, unexpectedly, one of those long unsmiling looks that seem to go straight to my spine.

"Stop that," I told him, "or I'll summon up something quite different."

James gazed into his teacup; then he raised it, gravely, to meet Richard's glass. The sound when the two met was sharp and reverberant, arresting as a street-conjurer's bell. "Thank you," James said softly. "I'm glad you approve."

"Especially since it wouldn't make a damned bit of difference?" Richard asked, grinning.

James smiled fractionally. "But it would, you know. Not in what I did, perhaps, but around the edges of how I felt about it. Does Hegel have anything to say about that?"

"I'm still back at the bottle of wine," I said, examining the color of the sherry. "Does that mean that there's the thought of bringing the bottle, and the bottle itself, and the synthesis is that you end up bringing the bottle?"

"She reads German," James said to Richard, who was laughing.

"No, we're talking about the transition from something to nothing. That is, from a full bottle to—what *were* we talking about, anyway? I think it was boundaries for conversation. We were going to talk about what we were going to talk about. Georg Willhelm would have loved that. He'd have probably made a few remarks about how it was as difficult to understand pure conversation as no conversation. Which is true, now that I think of it. No, no boundaries. What's on your mind?"

"After that introduction," said James, shaking his head, "I'm almost afraid to claim to have one. I ought to have got a few hours' sleep in the room over the stables after all."

"But you didn't dare," I told him.

"No, I didn't. All right. You got my letter, you are effectively caught up all the way to Gravesend, or we'll assume you are until I refer to something that doesn't sound familiar, at which point one of you will stop me. Cauldhurst."

At that he sipped his sherry. I thought at first that I was the only one in the room who would recognize the movement, the enforced pause, the barely perceptible change in his face. Then Richard said, ''If you'd rather not, don't.''

''Hmph. Andrew Cobham and my preferences have damned few points in common. D'you know, I hate that place. I can't remember ever not hating it. Isn't that stupid?''

Richard nodded. ''I was about to make the same comment. I've always loved it. Stupid? No. Interesting. But perhaps we had best leave that side of it alone for now. What happened?'' He said nothing about the sudden reference to Andrew Cobham.

''Well, my first surprise was finding that Cauldhurst was still under surveillance. Pardon, the *appearance* of surveillance.'' He smiled at Richard, who did not return it. ''Bankston, you see, had had time enough to pull his man out, but there was what I took to be Kitty's policeman, a harried-looking cove with large black moustaches, coming out the kitchen entrance. This was about . . . it would have been three o'clock or so yesterday.

''There was a closed carriage in the stable yard, with the coachman on the box. No one I recognized. Our man with the moustaches came up to the carriage and spoke, and someone pushed the curtain aside. I was lying flat under the rosemary hedge by that time, and couldn't hear a thing, but the view was all right. And lo, the person in the carriage was Andrew. Done with business in London, it seemed.''

James rested his head against the chair back. ''I had about a minute in which to wonder what I would do if Andrew went into the house and stayed. But he made some lengthy speech with hand gestures that suggested he was rattling off a string of orders. Then the coachman whipped up the horses, and the man with moustaches fetched a horse out of the stables and rode away also. Richard, did you know the place is *empty*? No, I'm sorry, I'm skipping ahead. So Kitty's policeman is either not working for Bankston, or is not *only* working for Bankston, since he's pretty cool about taking direction from Andrew.''

''Or,'' said Richard slowly, ''Andrew is working for Bankston.'' He screwed his eyes shut, opened them, looked at his wine glass as if he'd forgotten what it was, and said, ''Or maybe Bankston is working for Andrew. Or they're both working for Prussia. Or maybe the Mikado of Nippon. Dammit, I wish Kitty were here, and for more reasons than usual. Susan, are you planning to make a record of this conversation for her? Blast.''

I decided that he did, in fact, want that question answered, and told him that yes, of course I was. Richard remembered what his glass was for and used it; then he settled in with an expectant look at James.

James obliged. "I suppose you'd have to have met Sir George. Bankston is capable of employing Andrew, but only in the way it would be safe to do so: indirectly, and without Andrew's knowledge. Devilish sharp, is Sir George. So, Andrew didn't stop the night at Cauldhurst. Why, I wondered?

''That was when I discovered that the stranger had fetched his own horse because there was no one to fetch it for him. Or any other cattle in the stable. And, once I'd got in through the second floor linen-room window—you know the one—no household staff, either. The house isn't formally shut up, mind you, with the furniture under holland covers and the silver locked up downstairs. Just abandoned, for all practical purposes. No Clayborough, no Mrs Denning, no grounds staff, no one at the lodge. Which explains why Andrew didn't stay, but why empty the place?''

James drank off the last of his sherry and sat with the cup in his two hands again, turning it slowly. "According to the receipt book, severance wages were paid by Andrew's bailiff to the whole staff on December 1ˢᵗ, with a week's pay in lieu of notice—damnably clutch-fisted ʾor ˙ set of people who've mostly worked there for over ᵃ decade. Receipt for the sale of the horses dated likewise; they were let go in a lot at Tattersall's at a breakdown price. I couldn't find anything to tell me why. If the bottom had fallen out of sugar, he might need the money to shore up the Jamaican property . . . but it would make more sense to liquidate the Jamaican property, wouldn't it? Then it occurred to me that the why might be self-evident: that the place might have been emptied *so that it would be empty.* But for what?''

''No wonder you and Susan get along so well,'' said Richard. ''You both have this astonishing fondness for lists of questions.''

"Yes," I said sweetly. "I suppose we both hope that, just this once, someone might answer one." I regarded Richard in a way that ought to have made him quail, but I think he's spent too much time in my company.

Richard found the sherry and poured more into James's tea-cup without bothering to ask James if he cared for any. "Though I suppose I've been doing the same."

James replied, "That depends on whether leading statements such as that last one count as questions."

Richard made a shooing gesture and shook his head. "No, let's get the story first and then ask each other questions none of us can answer. I assume, then, that after seeing—Andrew—you simply went away?"

James sat for a moment staring into Richard's face. "He and I were never more than civil to each other all my life, he never took an interest in me unless I seemed liable to embarrass him, and I always wished passionately that he and I could manage somehow not to be related. Richard, does it really bother you that I've given up calling him my father?"

"Christ, no. It's just that I'm so used to thinking of him as your father that I have trouble readjusting, too." He shook his head. "Maybe we should have set some boundaries, just so we could get through one entire episode without wandering a thousand times like—like one of your metaphors."

That got him a wicked, lopsided smile. "My metaphors do not wander. Besides, I am not going to pander to your woefully literal mind. Catch up as best you can. All right, where was I? Oh, with the household records. No, I came to root through Andrew's personal things, remember? Except there weren't any. David's papers and books in the little study, mountains of them—did that man ever throw anything away? But Andrew's desk in the library was empty. The secretary in Andrew's sitting room upstairs had a tailor's bill from three years ago caught at the back of the drawer and not one thing else. Isn't that interesting? So, clever bloke that I am, I looked in the fireplaces. Grates cleaned out in the sitting room, in the library. The kitchen, however, had the remains of a great deal of paper in the stove, too well burnt to recognize, but I'd lay odds it wasn't back numbers of *The Times*. The kitchen, for the love of mercy. Does that sound like Andrew's work to either of you?"

I put my glass down on the hearth and went to sit on the bed, because my back was scorching and my backside was getting sore. "It sounds as if he's getting ready to bolt. But no one's after him. Or at least, I don't know who would be. Besides us, of course. But why suddenly burn papers you've had for years, unless you're afraid of them falling into the wrong hands?"

"Careful. Richard will complain about your interrogation points."

"Well, let him do it, then. In the meantime, you can pull off my boots for me." I thrust out a foot and got a grip on the bed-post.

James took my heel in his hand and, instead of pulling, examined my half boot. "Very nice. I like the fancy-work on the toe." Then he shot me a look.

I returned it, until I remembered how annoying these little passages can be to uninvolved onlookers. And I didn't feel as if I ought to exact my revenge from Richard so long after the offence. "Pull," I ordered.

"Yes, ma'am." He set my abandoned footgear neatly on the hearth rug, and I tucked my feet under me. Richard seemed to be working to restrain a fit of giggling. James tried to glare at him, and only managed to look conscious.

"Never mind," said Richard. "Go on. I mean, with the story," he added.

"Nothing much else. Someone had been cooking in the kitchen, but it might have been the man I saw coming out. By this time it was late by country standards, and I had a powerful itch to be off the premises, anyway. So I tramped across country to where I'd left my horse, and rode to Tunbridge Wells where I put up for the night. Came on here today. You are now caught up, as best I can manage. D'you want to return the favour?"

James may not have fallen asleep after two cups of sherry, but he was affected by them, at least to an informed eye. The lightly-applied tension that seemed to be his natural state had been released; his shoulders had settled into the cushions behind them, and the hand that didn't hold the cup was draped and still over the chair arm. I recalled Richard pouring him more sherry, and wondered suddenly how calculated that had been.

Richard nodded. "Certainly." He drained his glass, hesitated, then took the bottle and poured in some more. "The bottle," he said, "has nearly turned into its opposite. Or maybe it has something to do with *aufheben*."

"Which brings up the point," said James, smiling faintly, eyes closed, "of how you translate *aufheben*."

"I don't," said Richard. "I don't know, really. Cancel? Except it also means maintain. So we cancel and maintain the bottle."

"And while we do, you answer my question," James said. He opened his eyes. "Don't you?"

"Well, yes. Susan announced—when was it?"

"Earlier today," I said, covering a yawn with both hands.

"Yes. She announced that we ought to be going. I asked her where, and she said we were coming back here, where they'd never look for us. That's when I decided we'd need something to drink, for which you haven't yet thanked me, by the way. And then we made our way here, talking about you. And that's pretty much it, I think."

"We did not, in fact, talk about you," I muttered. "Much." Neither of them took any notice.

"It can't have been earlier today than right now. It just turned tomorrow a quarter of an hour ago." James stretched his legs out before him and yawned, too. "I did feel bloody clever when I realized that the one place you might be safe, after you were demonstrably gone from the Grey Hound, was the Grey Hound. Thank you very much for bringing the sherry. If you thought we needed it, you must have gone through the entire contents of Coslick's cellar last week. What did you bring as a substitute for Kitty, by the way? No, don't fetch it. I wouldn't drink it if you tried to pour it down my throat."

"As far as I can tell," said Richard, "it is distilled spirits of Byronic corn and Gaelic humours in marsh-water. I'm frankly afraid to drink it, but you probably wouldn't notice."

I confess, I'm not sure I remember that speech correctly. Or rather, I remember Richard's description of what he'd brought to drink as I transcribe it above, but what I heard might not have been quite what he said. I was leaning against the bed-post to keep my head from dropping forward, but I had nothing to prop my eyelids with.

"What happened to the iron ring?" Richard said.

The question seemed to wake James up nearly as much as it did me. "To the what?" he asked.

"The ring Eleanor Tournier gave you."

"I got rid of it."

The pause was pregnant enough that I looked up at Richard. He was frowning at James.

"What?" James asked.

"*How* did you get rid of it?"

"All right, if you have to have the whole tale. It's not very interesting. What with one thing and another," his lips twitched, like a shrug of the face, "I didn't think of it until I'd bolted off to Southampton. I slipped the trap laid there, but in the course of it I gave someone a bit of a clout with that hand, and it was swollen afterward. You know."

"Ah. I believe that's a compliment. That you're sure I know how one's hand swells up when one hits someone," Richard added when James looked puzzled.

"Oh, get away with you," James replied. "Well, there I was with that ring on, and suddenly I didn't think I could bear it there another minute, but with my hand swollen, it wouldn't come off. It was the middle of the night, but I found a black-smith at last, at Chandler's Ford, and he got it off."

"A blacksmith?" Richard asked, leaning forward. "And at a ford. How did he do it?"

"With a chisel, unfortunately. Do you want to see the scar?" James transfered his cup to his left hand and held up the right.

Richard settled back again, grinning. "No, no, I'll forgo the pleasure. You went to a specialist. You reassure me. What did he do with the ring?"

"Richard, are you drunk?"

"What, don't you remember?"

"Of course I remember. He did what every blacksmith in the world does with unwanted bits of iron—he tossed it on the scrap pile to be turned into something else later on."

"Hmm. It would have been better—well, that ought to do."

James laughed. "Ought to do what? Richard, do you think I've been bewitched on top of everything else?"

"If this were a poem, you would have been. Life isn't so neat as art about cause and effect. Wouldn't you rather be in a poem, all things being equal?"

James seemed about to respond in kind, but Richard suddenly burst out with, "By God, James, it's good to see you again!"

James was neither drowsy nor drunk—at least, not in that instant. He was—oh, I was tired, and I can't trust my perceptions, but he seemed unshelled, somehow, the perfectly vulnerable James that one sees in rare flashes. "I was afraid you never would," he said softly. "I didn't have any faith, really, that I'd get this far. But I had to keep moving forward as if I did. And I kept thinking that it would—no. Never mind. I missed you. *Dhia*, I can't believe I missed your wedding."

"It wasn't that big an event." Richard looked into his glass, twirling it a little by the stem. "I never believed you were dead, you know. I mean, I thought you were, but I never believed it."

"I suppose that's why people make such a fuss about funerals. The human animal's way of saying, 'No, it's over, *really* it is.'" James's expression became rather fixed. "I've missed a lot of funerals in the past ten years. If I'm trying to avoid having my nose rubbed in the finality of it all, it's not working. How do you know you didn't believe I was dead?"

It was only at this last question that Richard looked up from the wine glass. He stared blankly at James for a moment, then suddenly burst out laughing, startling me thoroughly awake again. James waited patiently for the laughter to die down to a chuckle, which took at least a minute, then said, "Well? How *do* you know?"

Richard almost started up again, but said, "Because my idea of you had not yet transformed itself from the finite to the infinite. Does that help?" James didn't answer at once.

I decided I could listen just as well lying flat on the coverlet, and being newly startled, was in no danger of dozing off. Richard looked toward the window as if seeing something else entirely, and wore a faint and thoughtful smile. "In fact, if you want to know the truth, it's because I didn't mourn. I know what I do when I'm mourning. When Father died, I let everything grow dim—I almost *made* everything grow dim, and it was as if I kept the world at a distance. I found I would be sitting, staring off at something, and not even know quite what I was thinking of. And at other times, I would tell myself over and over again, 'He's gone, I'll never see him again,' because it seemed important that I convince myself of it. I still haven't, quite, but I've made progress. When I heard of your death, there was none of that. I remember thinking, 'James is gone,' and there was no response from my emotions. And when the family went into mourning it was just more odd behaviour from my family, having nothing to do with you.'' He looked directly at James. ''There. Is that more of an answer than you wanted?''

"No. It's . . . more of an answer than I knew existed. You know the inside of yourself so much better than I know the inside of me. I . . . if I were doing that, I don't think I would know it.''

''Wollstonecraft,'' said Richard.

James raised his eyebrows.

Richard said, ''You don't know yourself because you spend all of your time looking out. It bothers me when I see something wrong, but I'm not likely to see it unless it parades itself in front of me. When I read that book by your man Engels, I kept relating it to myself, and to what I'd seen, and agreeing, but it was all at a distance. You want to know what's happening around you, not for how it affects you, but just for what it is. And when you see something that's wrong, you want to change it. You're a born social reformer, and I'm an idiot not to have seen it years ago. Wollstonecraft.''

If anyone had said those things to me, I would have been pleased. James didn't look pleased; he looked a bit bleak. ''Is that why I'm given to examining the motives of everyone except myself? Most of the time, I swear, I think of myself as an extremely literate wild animal, acting entirely on instinct. And no wonder there are so many social reformers who are bad company at dinner. What were you born to be?''

''Happy,'' said Richard. ''Flaws and all. I'm a natural dilettante, and I take pleasure in it, if no pride. And as for you, my gloomy brother, I doubt there is much you could learn from me on any score. But Susan could teach you a great deal about being happy, and, to judge from some few things that I probably had no business being told, almost certainly will. I don't know if virtue is its own reward, but for those born to fight, fighting must be. I can't believe I'm saying all this. I believe you two have conspired to debauch me, cleverly tricking me into suggesting it, and even supplying the wherewithal.''

"I intend to make *me* happy," I said, and yawned, my cheek against the coverlet at the foot of the bed. "*He* can fend for himself."

James sent a quick, grave look at me. There is no such thing as communication mind to mind; but the timing of that look, and the context, and Richard's reading (accurate, I think) of James's character combined to suggest James's thoughts to me. His inclination is to look outward; in our union, whatever it's to be, he'll turn first to me, to ensure my happiness before seeking his own. Well, it will be up to me, I suppose, to make sure he remembers that some of my happiness is coloured by his.

"I have never," James said to Richard, "had to trick you into debauchery. I wish I had a guinea for every time you dragged me away from my books at Oxford to bet on a race between two roaches, or climb the chapel roof, or talk Piggy Wilson into seeing if he could get drunk while standing on his head."

"That was not debauchery; that was part of your education. And so is this, I suppose."

"That—Richard, I'll get *sick*."

I couldn't make sense of that because I'd let my eyes close; when I opened them Richard was pouring the last of the sherry into James's cup. Richard stopped with an inquiring look.

"No, all right, I probably won't. What do you mean, your wedding was no great event? When did I become the only romantic in the family? Or were you just trying to get an objection out of me?"

"For heaven's sake, James. I said that *minutes* ago; how am I supposed to know what I meant? I think Susan is falling asleep."

I said, "I am not," but neither of them seemed to hear it;

I may only have thought of saying it. And, I have to admit, Richard's comment may not have actually followed the conversation I thought it did. I don't remember anything after I told them I wasn't falling asleep, which seems unfair.

I did wake up when James said, "Wouldn't you rather have your head on the pillow?"

I felt for it and realized I was still wrong way 'round on the bed. I swapped ends with as much dispatch as one can when one is actually asleep.

"Now that that's taken care of, would you like to be under the bedclothes? And possibly, not even in that dress? Which is rather awful, by the way. Have you got a nightgown?"

I opened my eyes. The fire was banked, and the only light was the candle on the nightstand. James was sitting on the bed wearing his shirt and trousers, but the shirt was unbuttoned, and his neckcloth hung untied around his neck. Richard had gone. "Covers," I stated. "No nightgown." I caught the ends of his neckcloth and tugged, until he had to lean forward with his elbows on the coverlet and kiss me.

"I used to be tired," he said conversationally, as he unbuttoned the rather awful black dress. "I wonder what happened?"

I said suddenly, "You taught Sam Coslick to cheat at cards?" as the fact swam to the surface of my brain.

James's hand stopped, and he winced embarrassed. "I did that. Jackie, too."

"Why?"

"So they could recognize—"

"He told me that one. Why?"

James began again on my buttons, focusing all his attention on them. "I was sick as a horse and weak as a kitten. I could barely sit propped up in bed, I was so weak. And I was afraid that if I didn't do something really interesting, they'd go away."

"Self-reliant, independent, lone adventurer James Cobham. You did it for the sake of the company. Of two boys, ages eleven and thirteen."

"They're quite conversable fellows, once you get to know them," he said.

"Are you done with those yet?"

"Yes, ma'am."

"Thank God for that," I said, because I wasn't tired anymore, either.

I woke up in that infuriating clear-headed state that makes it impossible to drift back off. From what I could see past the curtains, the day promised to be exceptionally fine and bright. When I turned my head, I was reminded why the bed was so warm, and why I felt as if someone had adjusted the counterweights on the universe while I slept. The contours of a bare muscled shoulder and forearm; the slope of one cheek; a longboned hand; and a quantity of dark hair, somewhere between ebony and rosewood in the light strained through the curtains. The rest of him was draped with the coverlet or buried in the pillow.

"Jamie," I said. Not a twitch. I said it louder and prodded the bare shoulder with a fingertip. Down in the pillow something made a noise. "You had a message for Coslick from Lee?"

Another unidentifiable noise; then his head tilted to show one closed eye and his nose. "Gave it. After I helped Diccon down the hall to bed."

"Gracious. Did you have to wake him up? Coslick, I mean."

The visible eyebrow drew itself in toward the bridge of his nose. "Are you awake?"

"Yes, very."

The visible eye opened, balefully. "Does this happen often? I'd like to know now, so that I have time to become resigned to it."

I stared into the eye, which was reassuringly clear. "You don't consider it grounds to throw me over?"

He rolled his face out of the pillow at last and opened both eyes. "I see. You're trying to be rid of me." He smiled. "I thought I was the one who woke up bright and jolly, is all."

"You're just a bit the worse for drink."

"Slander. I have a head like the business end of a hammer. Speak softly to Richard, though. Oh, when this is over, I am going to sleep for a month."

We found we were looking at each other and not saying anything, because all the things that sprang to mind were better left unsaid. Besides, since we'd both had the same unfortunate thoughts, it would have been pointless. Finally I shrugged and asked, "Breakfast?" and we began to move, reluctantly, toward the rest of the day. Little did we know . . .

I put my gentlemanly rig on again, since when I asked for advice and presented the options James suggested that burning was too good for the black bombazine. Because he didn't have to make any similar decisions, he was dressed before me (I took the opportunity to suggest it was due to his slovenly habits; he replied that it was years of practice with trouser-buttons, and would I like the chance to improve my skills?). Then he went off to hunt me a cup of coffee.

I heard his voice in the hall, and Richard's, as I shrugged into my coat. I was smiling faintly to myself in the mirror as I brushed out my hair, wondering if Richard was suffering as much as James had thought he would be. Then I heard the cry of "Fire!" from downstairs. For a moment the word seemed lodged in my brain in two places at once: in one, it froze my every nerve and muscle; in the other, it might have been in Russian for all I could understand what it meant, where it came from, what I was supposed to do about it. The sun was slanting benevolently in through the windowpanes, the room was orderly and solid around me, and someone had shouted "Fire!" somewhere below.

James came in the door, and the universe started up again, turning at a different angle, one that made the peace of the room an illusion and the cry from below the only real world. That was the world in which James moved like this, in which his eyes looked out of his face as if behind them there was a precise and impervious clockwork calibrated, wound, and operating at its peak.

"Coat, money, and weapons, Goddess," he said, his voice level. "Quick as you can. I think we're being smoked out." As he spoke he flung the black coat over his shoulders and checked the pockets. I yanked my gloves and greatcoat on, dropped the pearl-handled revolver in my pocket, tossed a scarf around my neck, and followed him into the hall and down the stairs to the front door.

The latch lifted when James tried it, but the door wouldn't swing inward. "Or we're to be baked, but that seems optimistic on someone's part," he murmured. "Let's fetch Richard and find out which window he wants to go out."

We met him in the upstairs corridor. James told him about the door. "Come down," he finished, "and we'll break a window."

"What about the kitchen door?" Richard asked.

"I'll wager five pounds it won't open."

"Done," Richard said promptly.

It was a very odd conversation; in addition to the words themselves, both James and Richard sounded curiously distant, as if they were thinking and talking about something else entirely. For that matter, I was hearing them in much the same way: everything was quick, but calm, like a pool of unruffled water in the middle of a gale.

Downstairs one of the children shrieked. James looked, and I said, "The kitchen," and ran for the stairs.

He passed me by the simple expedient of going over the stair-railing; the black coat belled in front of me like raven wings. He landed, and landed again at the foot of the stairs, and didn't touch foot to any step between, I'd swear.

The kitchen was full of smoke, but I saw the black coat swing through it, and the white flash that was his shirt. The coat was wrapped around something—someone, and he pushed the resulting bundle to the floor. Between the smoke and my tearing eyes I could hardly see. Then I took my first breath, and thought the air itself was on fire. A lady always carries a handkerchief, I remembered telling him, as I scrabbled for it in my pocket and tied it over my nose and mouth. I wished I had something to wet it with.

The smoke was everywhere, but thickest on my left, and roiling into the room. There was something in the fireplace there, a dark mass traced through with red where it smouldered. Somewhere in the kitchen there was probably a pail of water, but I had no idea where. I pushed the scrubbed oak table in the middle of the room over onto its side and used it as if it were a firescreen, shoving until the top was jammed against the fireplace opening. I looked up to find I'd had help at it; Richard was just doubling over next to me, coughing painfully.

James appeared like Mephistopheles beside us, irregularly

sooty and masked with a dishcloth, and thrust a handkerchief at Richard. Over my head, through the murk, I thought I saw a candle; then the smoke eddied, and I saw it was a little cat's-tongue of flame, licking down a ceiling beam.

I grabbed James's arm and pointed, and he nodded. He spared the air to say, "Out, as quick as we can."

"The Coslicks," I said, and coughed.

"They go first. Come."

With a strange groaning noise, something fell from the ceiling off to my right. No, it *was* part of the ceiling, I realized; plaster falling away from lath that smoked, and glowed, and sagged. We seemed enclosed in a burning box, as if the rest of the inn and all its rooms were gone, leaving only this little oven at its heart, and eight people to be baked in it. Eight. Where were they? James, Richard, me—I tripped over James's coat on the floor, and found Mrs Coslick and Tony wrapped in it, the former half-conscious and Tony crying in the weak, quiet way of children in an extremity of despair. I dragged them both to where I thought the door was, which, of course, wouldn't open.

"Five pounds," Richard croaked behind me. I turned to find him hammering at the catch on the casement window. "Bugger it," he said, twisted the skirts of his coat around his arm, and slammed his elbow through it. For an instant I could smell the cold, clear air from outside. Richard smashed more glass out of the frame; then he rolled backward out the opening. His head and shoulders reappeared in it, and he stuck out his arms. "Little one," he gasped. I passed him Tony, who screamed when I grabbed him away from his mother. Richard and I both ignored him.

I couldn't lift Eileen Coslick to the window frame. It seemed a confusing, insoluble problem, and I had just enough wits left to realize that I'd breathed too much smoke. Suddenly she was snatched out of my arms and bundled out the window, and James was smiling at me, his teeth very white in his blackened face. "You, too," he said, jerking his head toward the window.

"No!" I cried. "Three more."

"Got 'em," he answered, and I saw Sam behind him, his eyes round with terror. I grabbed him by the arm and began stuffing him through to Richard like washing through a mangle.

There was another unearthly groan, larger, above us, and a cracking sound. James spun away and disappeared into the smoke. Richard yanked Sam out through the window, shouted something, and sprang through the opening back into the kitchen. I heard James cry out, a word that a few moments later I heard properly; it was "John". But before that, a long dark shadow dropped through the smoke, and the whole room shook with a noise and concussion like an explosion. Richard had gone in the direction James had disappeared; I did the same.

And ran into Richard's back. Beyond him James knelt on the floor, his arms around someone. Beside them—I couldn't make out at first what it was, because the angle was strange. It was a large man, partway under a fallen beam and very still.

Then James was up and thrusting Jackie into Richard's grasp. Jackie shouted and struggled, until James laid a hand on either side of the boy's tear-stained face, looked into his eyes, and said ferociously, "He's dead. Your mother needs you. Go."

Seven. All accounted for. We could go. And I kept thinking, Eight, it was eight.

Then James was boosting me out the window, and the cold air in my raw throat made me cough and gag all over again. James rolled gracelessly through the opening after me, and half-dragged me away from the building.

We had all taken in too much smoke; none of us was thinking clearly, or we would have remembered what the real danger was. Even when I staggered past the kitchen door and noticed the iron bar thrust through the loop of the door handle and wedged on both sides against the frame, even then I didn't think about what it meant or how it had come there.

James's arm was around me, not so much for comfort as to keep us both on our feet. We came into the inn yard, and saw the other three guests who'd been in the common room the night before, wearing the universal dazed look of people who have participated in disaster. I have no idea how they got out, but I was glad at the time that I hadn't had to take responsibility for it. Richard was there, too, with Mrs Coslick, who had revived enough to be weeping and calling out hoarsely for her John.

Then I fell down. That's what it seemed like, anyway. I didn't feel anything—no pain, not even the force of a blow— but I was lying on the inn yard paving wondering if I had slipped on something. At that point, I noticed that I was holding my pistol, and that it was cocked; then, finally, I remembered hearing a sound over the roar of the fire that I knew had been a gunshot.

I wasn't afraid. I was annoyed, actually. First, because we had escaped the fire, and it had been horrible, but we were supposed to be done now, weren't we? And second, because the lulled and stupefied part of my brain had woken up and was haranguing the rest, asking who the devil did we all think had set the wretched inn on fire in the first place?

James was crouched beside me, his back mostly toward me, Gideon Johnson's first-rate revolver in his hands. He seemed terribly exposed, and I realized I thought that because he wasn't wearing the black coat. I considered pointing out to him that he was probably the one they were shooting at in the first place. Richard appeared in the circle of my vision, his head dark against the blue of the sky. He was also holding a pistol. I wondered what the other people in the yard thought of the three of us. My left side began to ache, just above my waist, and I could feel my shirt sticking wetly to my skin there. "Damn," I said. I was rather proud of the offhand sound of it.

James lifted me off the pavement, carrying me in his arms while he moved, quickly, toward the stables. My midsection felt stiff and squeezed. I looked down and saw my scarf tied around me, with something else folded and bound beneath it over what must be the wound. Over James's shoulder I could see what was left of the Grey Hound, the upper storey fallen mostly in, the sky above it wavering with the heat, the fire itself visible only against the smoke, or where the front of the building lay in shadow. Fires seem strange in daylight. I reflected that the shabby black dress had achieved burning after all, unworthy though it was.

I don't remember the transition from sunlight into the gloom of the stables. I do recall thinking that my eyes would adjust soon, as I picked out the corner posts of the stalls and the stairs up to the room that had once been James's. Then a harsh voice away on my left said, "Stop there, or I blow her brains out."

A sentence like that has a wonderful power to clear one's head, I find. With an unpleasant wrench, my senses were mostly restored to me. I lifted my head from James's shoulder and looked for the source of the voice.

At first I thought I hadn't got my wits back after all, that I was populating the shadows with goblins. But I gathered the apparition's features together and recognized him as real, and more important, as the unimaginably ugly man who had driven Eleanor Tournier's dark green coach. He was every bit as uncanny-looking as James had described him.

He had his arm around Eileen Coslick's neck, and a pistol to her head. She was crying steadily, her eyes shut. I looked for the boys, and found them in an empty stall, blank-faced with terror, except Jackie, who stood with his hands knotted on the partition and his face working. He was trying to think of something to do. I hoped he wouldn't.

"If you've got a barker," said the ugly man to James, "put it down now."

"No," said James, hoarse from the smoke but steady. "Only my friend here." It was true; I could feel his hands. The pistol would be in his pocket, and if he reached for it, the man would shoot him. My pistol, however . . . It was still in my right hand, pressed between my body and James and hidden by the fold of my coat. A wonder I hadn't shot myself with it. Useless in my hand; at that range and in my present state I was as likely to shoot Mrs Coslick. I turned my wrist and nudged James in the ribs with the butt, three times. "Do you mind if I put *her* down?" he asked.

The man's pistol no longer pointed at Mrs Coslick's head; it swung between her and James and me, as if the revelation that we were unarmed gave him more freedom of movement. "Do it slow," he ordered. "Then you can saddle me two horses."

"Two?" James repeated, going slowly to his knees.

"I'll take her with me," the ugly man said, with a jerk of

his head toward Mrs Coslick, "to give you second thoughts about stopping me."

James shot him. I have never seen any sequence of events happen so quickly. I felt the stable floor beneath me; then James had my revolver in both hands and fired three times, faster than I can imagine ever being able to. Eileen Coslick fell to her knees, screaming, the sound of it muffled by the deafening noise of the shots. Jackie dashed out and flung his arms around his mother. James rose and moved to them, looked down for a moment at the woman folded up and sobbing, at the boy's white, frightened face lifted up to him. Then he took three more steps to where Eleanor Tournier's coachman lay. Unhurried, he cocked the pistol and discharged it, one more time. Then he walked back to the Coslicks—the remaining Coslicks.

"Take your mother upstairs," he said to Jackie.

"My John," she gasped, wiping her eyes.

"I'm sorry," James said. "I couldn't save him."

She stared up at him, that worn, pretty face haggard and filthy, her eyes red as coals. "He died because they came for you. It was you they wanted."

I closed my eyes because I didn't want to see her face anymore, because I didn't want to see his now, if he turned it toward me. But I couldn't close out his voice. He only said, "I know that." Everything I didn't want to see was alive and vivid in his voice, and I cringed away from it as if what was in it could poison me, too.

I heard and felt him kneel at my side, close enough that I could tell he was shivering. In retrospect, I would say that perhaps twenty minutes might have passed since I'd been shot. At the time, it seemed like hours. He might have lifted me up then, or I might only have felt as if I were floating, and not for the last time.

I woke in the tack room, where a cast-iron stove warmed the air to near-summer, and a shuttered candle lamp on a shelf cast barely enough light to show me where I was, and that I wasn't alone. Eileen Coslick nodded on a stool beside me. From the buzzing in my ears, the ache in my joints, and the hot soreness that seemed to emanate from my eye sockets, I suspected I was feverish. The soreness in my throat was from the smoke. I may have made a noise, because Mrs Coslick's head came up suddenly.

"I'm all right," I said, and coughed. The muscles in my left side protested when I did. "James?"

She poured water into a cup and held it to my lips. I wondered where the cup came from. They had burnt her house and livelihood to the ground. "He'll do. He's lying down across the way, in the straw."

"He doesn't seem to need much sleep," I said, and recognized it as nearly irrelevant.

"Does he not need any? He wasn't sleeping last I looked."

And I saw that the grief that stood stark in her face had expanded to include him, and me. It was too much, all at once. I had only been shot, and not, I thought, badly hurt. Eileen Coslick's pain encompassed the loss, forever, of her husband, and her home, her future, and her trust in the safety and certainty of her life and her sons' lives. What certainty did life offer, anyway, besides the certainty at its end? What point in labouring on for years, only to have everything stop suddenly and finally in a burning kitchen, all the effort wasted?

I imagined I saw him for a moment, James, lying on his back in the straw, open-eyed and staring into the darkness, fighting that same emptiness and decay of hope, trying to win the ground back an inch at a time. We can only go forward, I thought I said to him. There is no other way open. But by then I must have been half sleeping.

He was with me when I woke again. With the soot washed off, a few burns showed on his face and hands; there were probably more under his shirt, which was clean and borrowed. He laid a hand on my brow, checking for fever.

"If we're short of cash for a doctor," I said, "I think I have another cuff-link somewhere."

"He's been already. For ungrateful, sharp-tongued, temperamental women he says he charges double."

"Then he'll have both wrists matching. How am I?" My personal inventory included a dry mouth, an aching left side, a sore throat, and a nagging queasiness.

"Nearly as well as it's possible to be and still have been shot. In and out, very clean, missed everything vital. The doctor declared that you'll be bedridden for a week. I'm afraid it gave him a mistaken notion of my respect for his profession when I laughed.'' He filled my cup with water as he spoke and steadied it in my hand. ''It was probably a pistol. If the fellow'd had a rifle, you'd likely be undamaged and I'd be stone dead, given his standard of marksmanship with a handgun at that range. Especially since I was such a helpful target, having left my good sense in the kitchen.''

''That was the smoke. James,'' I said, ''you're talking a lot.''

He closed his eyes and pressed his lips together. ''Sorry,'' he said after a moment. ''It comes and goes. Speaking of going, do you feel up to being moved?'' His voice was lowered and roughened, with smoke or lack of sleep, or emotion.

''Ugh. Better now than later, I suppose. The fever will probably come back by evening. It is morning, isn't it?''

''Yes. There's a household in the village that's made room for Eileen and the boys, and another that's offered you houseroom. It will be a more comfortable recovery there than in a tack room.''

''What about you?''

''I'm your luggage.''

''Well, as long as they'll take me *and* my luggage. How is Mrs Coslick?''

I watched his face; he nearly said something terrible in answer, forgetting that he was answering me and not himself. He throttled that and replied, ''The boys—needing to help them helps her. Otherwise, she's in a bad way, of course. In answer to the unspoken question, no, she doesn't still blame me. She never really did. But every time she sees me, she remembers yesterday, and always will, there's no getting 'round that.''

No, she never really blamed him, unlike him. ''When do I move?''

''Whenever you're ready. Church is out, so your new landlords will be at home.''

''Let's find out how fit I am, then. When we're comfortable, you can explain everything.''

''Explain?''

''Yesterday,'' I said firmly, ''I learned that one can be in the middle of events and still not be able to tell what's happening.''

My charitable family's name is Dowd, and they can spare the room; by the standards of village society, they're pretty well inlaid. Two spare rooms, a pair of maidservants, and a cook (female). The son is making his way in the world via an Indian posting; the daughter married a gentleman farmer in Sussex last year. As I observed, *sotto voce*, to James, gentlemen farmers rarely insist on extortionate dowries. He said I was a cynical creature; he preferred to assume it was a love match. In fact, I was moved less by cynicism than by resentment; I am not used to being condescended to by provincial matrons. You would have been shocked, Kit, to see me grit my teeth and bear it in apparent humility. Well, I could hardly make a stately exit in my condition, could I?

The doctor visited; warned in advance, I received the order about the week in bed with a reasonably straight face. He said he would bleed me if the fever returned. I pretended docility at that, too; if the fever returns, I'll make sure he isn't told.

After that, James sat by the bed and answered questions. Really, a perfect round of compliant behaviour from everyone today. I wish I had written the above account before I picked his brain, since until I tried to write it down, I didn't know quite how much I didn't understand. But I did ask about the mechanics of the attack on the Grey Hound. There were two men, one to fire the building and another to wait in ambush with the gun. The one we found in the stable, the coachman, was the burning cove. The doors had been jammed, the fires set, and a sort of smoke bomb put down the kitchen chimney, to drive the inhabitants out that much faster. The smoke bomb landed in the kitchen just as Tony was fetching the kettle from its hook; his shirt caught fire, which was when he screamed. James had entered the kitchen to see, through the pall, Eileen Coslick's sleeves smouldering as she tried to beat out the flames.

"They might have been badly burned," I said cautiously, as he fell silent. "But for you."

He turned an uncomprehending face to me. He had talked throughout in a cool, businesslike style, and I had been grateful for the chance to touch on everything with my mind only. Now the healing distance failed him a little. "I don't have to tell you what I've thought. You know already. So you know, already, that I tried that for balm. And I can't separate it from the recollection that always follows it.''

''You didn't ask anyone to try to kill you.''

''But I knew it was likely.''

''Why?'' I asked, and shifted irritably, trying to find a position in which my side didn't hurt. ''I thought we'd decided that you were safe until the 21st?''

He rubbed the space between his eyebrows, and I realized with a pang that I'd known he was about to do it. The familiar gesture was like a memory, a piece of him recalled years after the fact. ''One ought not to put much faith in druids, obviously,'' he said at last. ''But it's true, if they'd succeeded, their Midwinter party would have been a sad disappointment. At least, if we're correct about their motives and intentions.''

''Might it have been Bankston's people after all?''

James shook his head. ''Not that I think honour would forbid, but as long as there's a chance he'll get what he wants by doing nothing, that's what he'll do. Besides, not the right style, somehow.''

''The Prussians?''

''Why would they step into the middle of an operation they'd contracted out and paid for? And why would either Bankston or the Prussians employ Eleanor Tournier's coachman for the work?''

''Never mind,'' I sighed. ''Why was he in the stable?''

James offered me his best reconstruction; as he pointed out, it was difficult at this remove to ask the principal. The plan must not have allowed for the presence in the inn yard of Richard, armed; me, armed, if a little the worse for wear; and James alive, armed, and particularly dangerous. The partner with the gun had abandoned the coachman when the attempt failed and Richard set off in pursuit. That left the coachman to try to secure his own line of retreat.

He ought, James said, to have shot James when we came into the stable, thus completing his mission and removing the worst threat with one bullet. But he might have been assigned the job of setting fire to the inn because his nerve didn't run to pulling the trigger in cold blood. I thought, but didn't say, that he might not have harmed Eileen Coslick after all. James had been in no mood to gamble on the man's hypothetical better nature.

James told me that Richard returned to the inn later in my day-long swoon, in good time to learn that I wasn't mortally wounded. James had handed him his valise and sent him to Melrose with instructions that he and you were not to let each other out of your respective sights.

"What did he think of the story about the coachman?"

James shrugged one shoulder. "I didn't tell him." In response to what must have been my look of outrage, he said, "It wasn't on purpose. Of course I should have told him. It didn't occur to me; it was done, it was in the past."

I read the long, pinched line of his mouth, and my breath stuck in my throat. "I should have been awake."

"No. You shouldn't have. You would have hated it, and without being able to hit me over the head with something, you wouldn't have been able to fix it."

So Richard had seen another of James's frightening faces: the machine-self, that calculated odds and weighed necessity without allowing for the counterbalance of human hearts. The Ice-cliff.

"He'll forgive you," I said.

James looked at me, his eyes wide open and dark. "Does that make it all right?" he asked, as if he truly had no way to tell.

The conversation wound down after that, and I slept, woke famished and did something about it, and, eventually, wrote most of this. The fever has come back a little tonight, as I expected, but it's moderate, and I know how to deal with it— I'm going back to sleep.

17 DEC 1849

Sitting up, and dressed—James complained bitterly about regularly having to find me something to wear, ". . . and you the great bean-pole that you are, *mo chridh*," was the comment. I was unsympathetic, and he returned at last with a dark green carriage dress that is loose enough not to bind around my poor abused ribs, but not so loose that I look like something set out to scare the crows—while sitting, at least.

He also returned with your letter, which, in the absence of Richard, I claimed and read, and then handed to him without comment. He was cross-legged on the rug beside my couch by then, of course, having watched my face while I read. I had only half the favour returned; he read leaning against the couch, one elbow on the upholstery beside me, and my view was limited to his profile. There were several spots at which his expression became stiffly unreadable, but the grand reaction was to the percussion caps, which not only stopped him but sent him back to the previous page and forward again. "Well," he said, to which I asked, "Well, what?" but he gestured for me to wait until he'd finished the last paragraphs.

"Well, well, well."

"You said that, or part of it. My God, James, are the Trotter's Club planning a raid on the Houses of Parliament?"

He clicked his tongue and frowned at me. "It's set-dressing, sweetheart. You've forgotten. *I'm* the one stirring the rabble to revolution. I must be, mustn't I? All those guns are in *my* cellar."

"Good God."

"Just so. My coffin is to be figuratively nailed shut with musket-balls. If Bankston gets wind of this, it's going to shake his confidence in me."

"I suppose we can trust Wye to recognize percussion caps?" I asked.

"Oh, yes."

I pinned him with the look that always got the youngest girls at Miss Trevelyan's to admit to having hidden Miss Woodroe's parrot in the cellar to frighten the cook. It worked this time, too.

"Goddess, it is impossible for a man to keep a secret of any size from his valet."

"You're saying that, while he was in your employ, you seduced Wye to a life of violence and treason."

"No, I'm saying that there was no use in my employing anyone who couldn't already hold his own in a life of violence and treason."

"Gracious. What sort of past does he have?"

"Appalling. Kitty is in the best possible hands. My original plan was to place Richard in them, and if Richard hadn't displayed such a damned wide independent streak almost from the start of this miserable fracas, it would have worked very well."

"You meant Richard to hire Wye?"

"As it turned out, he'd already done it, but yes, once I washed up half-dead at the Coslicks' feet, I began to fret over the safety of my nearest and dearest. So Clayborough *is* still at Cauldhurst. Where was he when I was prowling the place, I wonder?"

He sat with one knee drawn up and his hands clasped motionless around it. His hair was caught in his collar at the back; I freed and smoothed it as I said, "So the Trotter's Club have a lovely basement armoury they can say belongs to you. Who are they planning to say it to? And when? How are they going to use this?"

"I am a clever bloke, but I haven't quite got the knack of reading minds yet." He sighed forcefully and dropped his head back to rest on my hand. "Four days, love. Whatever they do, they have four days to do it in."

"And we're twiddling our thumbs in a not very satisfactory seaside resort. Oh, how *could* I have done something so stupid as to get shot!"

That startled him enough that I got a kiss out of him, which was what I'd wanted. Then I took another nap. I am living mostly on water and sleep; I can't seem to face food until afternoon, but the regimen is doing well by me, I think. Tomorrow, if I

Your second letter arrived, making whatever it was I meant to say in that sentence completely beside the point. James covered his eyes partway through reading it (your letter) and said something in French sufficiently idiomatic that I couldn't make out a word; then he said something in English that, if I were a properly reared young woman, I would never have heard before.

Since I'd got the first reading of your previous letter, I'd let him have first pass on this one. You may imagine my reaction.

"I have been making a collection of dangerous oversights,

is all," James explained. "And after telling you there were more sides to this quarrel than there seemed. I forgot to keep counting." At that he leaned across from the chair he occupied, handed me the pages of your letter that he'd finished with, and read on, until interrupted by my yelp over the same revelations that had made him swear.

"Eleanor Tournier as a free agent?" I wailed.

"Makes you feel a right blockhead, doesn't it? It's possible that she may all along have been the only one of the conspirators who knew exactly where I was when I was at the Grey Hound."

"And so the only one who might guess to look for us there this time. James—"

He told me that if I wanted the rest of the letter I'd have to let him read it.

"A three-way fight in the Trotter's Club, or its immediate surroundings," he said when he finished, handing me your last page. "It would account for the facts as we know them."

"And everyone wants Cauldhurst."

"Everyone but me. If Alan Tournier wants it forfeit to the Crown as a result of my bad behaviour, ostensibly so that it can be awarded him for services rendered—namely, turning me in—where does he think *Andrew* is going to be all this time?" James closed his mouth suddenly. Then he opened it, and said, "Ah. Of course. I'm supposed to take care of that, one way or another. Either Andrew does me in at winter solstice and Tournier brings evidence against him for it, or I kill Andrew first and Tournier slays me, just too late to save the worthy patriarch. Reality is wonderfully flexible, in the right hands."

I was about to say that I didn't find the subject particularly funny, when I looked at him and realized that he didn't, either. "Tournier's are the right hands?"

"It was his great gift to the cause. Once Alan Tournier had applied his personal touch to an event, a disturbance, an illicit activity of any kind, it was practically impossible to tell truth from fiction from pure mythology. I wondered, sometimes, if even he knew what the truth of the matter was."

"Were you ever . . . afraid that he'd use it against you, this gift? Against the Chartists, or against you, personally. Everyone said—the bad feeling between you was of long standing.''

He slid out of the chair and dropped down on the carpet at my side once more. It allowed him to be close to me, but to keep his face averted. ''Once any movement, or even any nation, has an underground of that sort—covert, high-handed, answerable to very few—the movement has a knife at its throat. We all knew that.'' He leaned his head back, slowly, and I thought from the changed line of his cheek that his eyes were closed. ''As for using his talents against me, I was always fairly sure that he had, several times. I even wondered if he had engineered my betrayal of Hugh Stone, but he took that so hard that I couldn't believe . . . And even *I* suspected my motives for doubting him, after a while; as Gideon Johnson said, maybe I only resented the fact that he was a match for me.''

''Is he?'' I asked.

After a long silence, so long I thought he might not answer, he replied, ''Yes.''

I watched my fingers pleat the stuff of my skirt while I flogged my brain out of its mire and back onto the good dry ground of useful speculation. ''Given Kitty's and Richard's theories, do you suppose Andrew knows that the cellar at Cauldhurst is full of munitions?''

A long breath, in and out, from James. ''I think so,'' he offered slowly. ''He was certainly on easy terms with the man responsible for having them loaded in. And he would have had to order the emptying of the house, which made it so easy to get them there. But I doubt he knows *all* the possibilities inherent in those five hundred guns. If he does, and he thinks he can still swat Alan Tournier down and keep control of the Trotter's Club, after letting Tournier have all the good cards . . . then I was raised by an idiot.''

''Are you safe for four days, then, from everyone except Eleanor Tournier? And Sir George Bankston's potentially shaken confidence?''

''Twisty, isn't it?'' he said, turning his face suddenly to me, with a quick, wry smile. ''I wonder if *la soeur trés jolie* has realized that tipping Bankston off about the guns will bring the whole monumental plan down around everyone's ears. Which she seems to want to do, if she's sending her employees to kill her brother's guest of honour. But all for the possibility that she can prove an unlikely claim to Cauldhurst on behalf of her child? Whose existence I'm beginning to doubt, by the way.''

"That's wishful thinking," I said harshly. It had occurred to me, too, that we would all be relieved of one responsibility at least if there were no child.

"You're right. But still, it seems a little distant and rational for Mlle T.—Christ, of course it does. Yes, she'll try to get the prize for herself, because why not? But most of all, she wants to spoil her brother's game, because he ruined hers.''

"What?"

"He took her strongest piece off the board. David."

"My God." I had a disturbing thought, and spoke it aloud. "You don't suppose she was in love with David?"

James regarded me with one eyebrow lifted. "Perhaps I wrong her," he said.

"What a quantity of venom to bring to bear against one's brother, if you're right."

"Oh, there's a history there, I imagine, that I'm just as well pleased not to know. You remember . . . my account of my missing two months? And the man who came into the room and stopped her when . . .''

"I remember." It's one of my endearing traits, I believe, that I'm willing to spare people the necessity of finishing painful sentences. The man who stopped Eleanor Tournier, with a blow and a foul name, from torturing James.

"It was Alan. The voice and carriage—I couldn't identify them then, but they match his.''

"My," I said, my own voice sounding thin in my ears. "What a horrid family."

James shrugged, his head tilted, his face hidden. "He and I always did have a lot in common.''

I twisted my fingers in his hair and pulled, until he had to turn back to me. For an instant there was a spark of something in his eyes that might have shut a wiser woman's mouth; it was certainly not self-pity. I am not a wiser woman. "And what are Richard and Kitty? And Aunt Louisa, and Brian, and Henry? And me? Tell me which of those has given you anything less than kindness, not to speak of love. You've been hurt unjustly. But if you treasure that hurt more than you regard the kindness, then you have more in common with the Tourniers than you know, and were best left to them.''

I'd let go of his hair, and so he was free to lift his chin a little. It was not pride so much as a slight, involuntary recoil from a blow. There was silence between us for a moment. Then he lifted my hand and laid his cheek against it, and nodded. Head still bent, he said at last, ''It's not happiness you'll teach me, is it?''

''No,'' I replied in a reprehensible croak. ''But it may be more valuable after all.''

''And happiness may come of it.'' He kissed my knuckles, and let his lips rest there as he murmured, ''If it's allowed the time.''

We sat quiet for a little while, and I blinked away an ignoble threat of tears. Suddenly James raised his head from my side and stared startled into my face. ''Hullo,'' he said, more breath than voice. ''Do you suppose any of them, besides Andrew himself, knows that I'm not his son?''

''David knew,'' I said, when my voice came back.

''And so Eleanor may, also. I wonder if she's remembered to mention the fact to her brother? What if he has no idea that . . . Kitty thinks he had David killed and Richard blamed for it because they were both in line for Cauldhurst. But he could as well have killed David because of the notes, and to queer his sister's pitch, and blamed Richard because he knew I'd have to do something about it.'' He raked his hair back from his face with both hands and held it there, as if it might get away. ''Susan, if Kitty and Richard are right about most of this, and I think they are, Alan Tournier *can't* know I'm illegitimate. Because if I have no legal rights to Cauldhurst, then if I'm hanged for treason, Cauldhurst *isn't forfeit*.''

James thinking aloud is always a daunting phenomenon to share a room with. ''Is it important?'' I said cautiously. ''That he doesn't know?''

''It may be. My bastard state is already a wedge between Andrew and the Trotter's Club; if he means to kill me, he's knowingly breaking a taboo. They'll disown him at the very least if they find out. And if Alan Tournier learns that his sister knew this and kept it from him, he'll turn on her.'' He rubbed his eyes roughly. "Slowly, slowly," he said as if to himself. "We may be able to pivot nearly everything on this, but only if we're sure."

"We're not even sure that Andrew Cobham plans to murder you at winter solstice!" I burst out. The bald statement made it sound preposterous. But I reminded myself that the Trotter's Club had sponsored the killing of the infant Roderick.

"No, but that we have only to wait for." Intense, genuinely amused, he grinned up at me, and I recognized, with a bolt of fear, the man who'd responded to Friedrich Engels's promise of challenge and danger. "If he's going to do it, he'll have to get me there, won't he? I think we can safely take any manoeuvring meant to land me in the cellars at Cauldhurst as confirmation. As for Tournier . . . I'll think on it."

Kitty, it was nearly enough to bring my fever on again. He's going to do something awful, I can tell, and how can I stop him when I'm laid up with a pair of holes under my ribs? One way or another, I am going to get to my feet tomorrow and see how long I can stay there. In the meantime I shall post this, and you will finally have proof that I'm alive and well enough to be upset. I'm sorry you had to wait so long for it. My best to Richard; tell him I know it's a pity I'm such a shrew. My best love to you as well, dear, and do stay out of the opium for the present; you see from the above how we all benefit from your clear head!

Take care,
Susan

Postscript, on the morning of the 18th he's going, and will post this when he does. I can't very well keep him from it; he points out quite reasonably that if the Trotter's Club are going to try to lure him into the cellar, he has to be somewhere they can find him. He is going to London. There's no love lost between James and Bronterre O'Brien, but O'Brien's self-esteem can be counted on to keep him from wondering why James would come to see him at all (the foregoing abridged, of course, from James's explanation). I asked, wasn't O'Brien one of the informers? and James kissed me on the lips, smiling, and said, "Exactly."

I ignored, as best I could, the cold that pinched at my heart at that, and said, "And what am I to do in the meantime?"

"That will depend," he said slowly, "on what happens next. Get well, for a start. As soon as you feel equal to travelling by rail, go to Melrose. If you don't hear from me by the evening of the 20th, you'll know I've gotten in over my head."

"At which point, your faithful and conspiring relations should . . . what?"

"We'll think of something. Any road," he offered, with a smile that required only half his mouth, "we know where I'll be on the night of the 21st, don't we?"

I'll close now, and bid him good-bye. I hope to see you and Richard soon.

S.

LONDON
19 DECEMBER 1849

My Goddess,

You will be pleased to know that, though I have been assiduously poking my nose into other people's business, no one has yet tried to cut it off, or the head it's attached to. In other words, I am well; I hope this letter finds you the same.

I have already received my invitation to spend winter solstice at Cauldhurst. I ought not to have been surprised, since there is so little time left, that all parties involved moved so quickly. But it offends my sense of propriety, not to mention my pride. If I didn't already know I was being beckoned into a trap, this haste would enlighten me. Wouldn't you think they'd credit me with a little instinctive wariness, if not actual cunning?

This won't do; my apologies for the foregoing tone. This brittle, heedless cleverness might have sufficed for my early letters to Richard from the Grey Hound—then my concentration was as much on what I had no intention of saying as what I said. Part of every letter was devoted to a sleight of hand that I was only half aware of performing, a series of would-be graceful diversions to keep Richard from realizing how much he hadn't been told. Devious yourself, you know how to watch for the palming of a secret; even if I wanted to try the trick with you, it would be no use.

And I don't want to, though the reflex is hard to curb. The cautionary voice I listen to whispers, "She won't care about that; don't tell it." Then memory supplies your face, sharp-eyed at the end of Engels's dinner-table, watching all that happens, hearing and recording not only what is said but how, and I know you *will* care. Or the whisper comes: "Don't tell her that; she'll be upset." Well, of course you will be. *I* am, after all, and I expect you to show as much, if not more, sense than I do. What I fear you will likely fear, as well. I cannot at once employ such excuses as these and believe that I have treated you with the respect you deserve. The excuses must go.

My companionship with you, my Goddess, seems to be as much a state of ethical house-cleaning as it is an exaltation of the spirit and a carnival of the body. Do you doubt the last two? Never doubt them. You are the fire in my nerves and blood; the heat and smoke of that burning tempers my courage and clears my vision, until I feel almost that I can see *into* this solid world to its theoretical bones, the shape theology calls its soul. This is the first experience of my life that makes me question what I have always believed: that death stops everything that we are, and uncreates us down to the last atom. This one thing, my feeling for you, seems too large and strong to be extinguished by the mere breaking of the box of flesh and bone that holds it. If anything is left of me after the end of my life, it will be this.

There is, I think, an assumption that romantic love is universal, and the entitlement of every human being. If what I feel for you is romantic love, I am inclined to doubt the assumption, or at least, its definitions. Or is love properly defined as the urge to mate, marry, and procreate, and this staggering experience of mine something else, an uncommon frame for those things, bearing some other name? A great many people have, and are perhaps even entitled to, the happiness of finding and living with a suitable mate. If they also enjoy what you have brought me to, none of them has mentioned the fact to me.

Love, say the young bachelors, the wilder debutantes, the dissatisfied married men and women, is leg-irons; even those who seem happy in the state refer to it as being "bound," as if love by its nature is a period of confinement. If that, too, is part of love's proper definition, then I don't love you. What I feel for you has given me freedom on a scale I have never conceived of—I, who have spent my whole adult life in the cause of liberty.

Do you remember—pardon, of course you do; one of your goddess-faces is Mnemosyne, after all—when Engels asked me to agree that my first duty is to my class, and I told him that, having examined some of the options, I would accept that as true? One of the things I weighed against my duty to my class, marvelling at the mingled fear and cold-bloodedness with which I did it, was my duty to you. (I had one, I knew; that I had not yet admitted it to you, or admitted the feelings that had prompted it, and that I might never have the chance to do so, made no difference.) That was my first inkling of this new freedom. Here was no destructive polarity, no exclusive choice between passion and principles. My duty to you required my duty to my class. To deny the latter would have reduced and blasted the thing I offered to you, and tainted the former with a mean and cowardly spirit. How many seeming clever people are there, who would declare that the overthrow of principle in the name of love is romantic? Am I far off the mark in imagining your Dianic scowl (the one the huntress must have worn when siccing her dogs on a trespasser) at the news that I would entertain for a moment such a choice?

I have told you this as part of my house-cleaning. This is at the core of me, the deepest secret knowledge at the centre of my heart and mind, and my old and hardened instincts say to withhold it. Whatever you tell, they say, never tell the truth. But they have also told me, in the hard years behind me, that there is one person I must never lie to: myself. I have broken that rule, to my misfortune; I hope I learned from it. I will not lie to myself again—and so I cannot lie to you.

How can I explain this? You are not an extension of myself; a pen is an extension of myself, having life only because I've picked it up, passive, unmoving unless moved. You are not my mirror; *are* there people who want to look at their lovers and see nothing but themselves? You are not my conscience, my muse, or the sanctifying angel of my hearth—don't laugh, Susan, you've read that kind of nonsense in the penny-press, too. I call you my Goddess, but I think you know the spirit in which that's meant. No, I can't explain it, other than to say that I'm required to deal with you as I would like to deserve to be dealt with.

You will have observed (possibly with some annoyance) that I make no reference to how you feel about this, about me. I don't really know enough about that, you see. I am, frankly, afraid to ask. I have almost unlimited physical courage, but it requires courage of a different order entirely to attempt to breach the privacy of your heart and mind and ask for the answer to so impertinent a question as, "Do you love me?" I would, in fact, prefer that you not answer it any time soon, until I can forget that I have come as close as this paragraph to begging for a kind reply. Otherwise I shall imagine any kindness you show me to be prompted, at least a little, by pity, or even self-sacrifice. (Rubbish. Self-sacrifice is not one of your vices. But I'm speaking of my imagination, not the reality it works upon.)

Another curious assumption of the world around us seems to be that, when one loves, one deserves to have that love returned in precisely the style and measure one offers it in. Whatever you feel toward me, I will accept it, though forgive me for hoping it may prove to be no cooler than friendship. Does this sound strange, from a man who has shared your bed? But physical pleasure is at best an undependable glue to join two hearts.

This is difficult to the point of being painful. I have to tell you, because I can't be sure there is anyone else to do it, that if you don't love me, you must not manufacture the feeling as a kind of excuse for what we have shared. You may find that as the novelty of lovemaking fades, your attraction to me fades as well. Other men can please your body as well as I can, and may better please your mind and heart. If that proves to be the case, you must not settle for me. It is not faithfulness, but a heartless sham, to stay where you don't love. No one who values you properly would wish you to be anything but absolutely true to yourself when faced with such a choice.

Richard would shake his head, appalled, at the foregoing, and call me gloomy again. But dearest heart, I am only trying to look my fears in the eye. Perhaps that will banish them, as the sun burns away mist. If not, I would rather face them now and whatever blow comes with them, than to have both of us suffer for my cowardice at some later date. So bring me anything, even indifference or hatred, and I will survive it—anything but a fiction.

I am, you'll notice, assuming that I will be granted the time and luxury of surviving your indifference. This is a perfectly damnable moment to be pledging undying devotion to you. Winter solstice is Friday night. If the mails are kind, you may receive this as early as Thursday afternoon. I plan to give Death the slip this time, too; but you will have observed that I'm not immune to the occasional stupid mistake. If I make one on Friday, you may be spared the messy duty of trying to reply to these sentiments.

I'm sorry; brittle cleverness again. I don't want to die. I never have wanted to, to my recollection, and have never understood those who claim—or claimed—they welcome Death as a kind friend, or even as their only recourse. Death is not a solution to any problem I have, and I will fight it to the end of my strength. But I have to admit that there will, one day, *be* an end to my strength. Given what hangs on it this time, I prefer that you, and Richard and Kitty, too, recognize the possibility that I may lose this contest, and take steps to protect yourselves in the event. Since I have no possessions of any significance, I haven't got a will. But I leave to you three my love, and my gratitude for all you have been and done throughout my life; and to you, Susan Voight, this letter and the knowledge that you are, late-come as it may be, the central and sustaining power of one man's life.

Enough, more than enough; are you torn, Goddess, between wishing to know what I will find next to say about you, and knowing that we haven't the leisure for it? We *will*, one day, have the leisure. Until then, I shall return to recounting the chase in progress.

I went up to London from Langstone giving much hard

thought to the best way to lead the Trotter's Club to me. I was pleased to find that I was to be saved the trouble; I was to be led to them. Though he tried not to show it, O'Brien was exactly as glad to see me as I had thought he would be, and an order of magnitude less so when I told him I was *persona non grata* with nearly everyone, and could impair his social standing merely by waving to him in the street. I was assuming, I added, that his social standing wouldn't be enhanced by a stay in gaol. Layers and layers, my heart: an honest revolutionist's reputation is never harmed by prison. But that shot went wide, I think. I took to my rooming-house bed (narrow, empty, and cold) last night knowing that if Tournier had not already drawn him in under his shadow, O'Brien would inform on me to the police. There was no heavy knock in the night, and I thanked Alan Tournier for my undisturbed rest.

This morning I went to O'Brien's favourite coffeehouse, intent on battening myself on him for at least long enough to find out what he might say to me next. I was startled when he greeted me almost cordially—though I might have been excused for thinking that his teeth were clenched behind the smile. If he hadn't received an instruction or two from someone since yesterday evening, I shall take holy orders. After a somewhat constrained chat over the bread and butter, he said that he had to meet a friend, and would I care to come along? For the moment it took me to consider this, I wondered, were *any* of us pulling the wool over anyone's eyes? Was I meant to fall blindly into this? Did O'Brien really think I was oblivious to the manoeuvring around me? Did Tournier truly think that O'Brien had the necessary skills to lead me by the nose? I accepted the offer and went with him, of course.

Imagine my surprise when I found myself led into a fencing school. They're an abiding fashion in Europe, but English gentlemen have mostly given up the sport, choosing to prove their acuity of eye and strength of wrist with shooting instead. O'Brien's friend was a self-effacing young Frenchman, not of my acquaintance, and after I was introduced I moved out of earshot.

I wandered the length of the empty *salle* to a rack of blades, and found an *épée de combat*, its points attached and sharp. I was toying with it, feeling its balance, idly shifting through the positions, when a door at the end of the room opened. It led to another, smaller practice room, and the two men who came through it had, from the looks of them, been engaged in a lesson. One of them was the fencing-master. The other was Andrew Cobham.

We might both have been turned to marble, for all we moved; but I was suddenly, acutely aware that I held a length of steel; that he also held a duelling-blade in a grip that whitened his knuckles; and that the distance between us was as nearly the fencing measure as I could have established without testing it. I had ice in the pit of my stomach then, because for a wild instant I feared that this was our confrontation, and I had, in spite of all my cleverness, been delivered to it unprepared.

I saw him with the heightened awareness that fear and incipient violence gives. It had been the better part of a year since we'd met face to face—well, only slightly less time since you did last, since I would imagine your last sight of Andrew was at Christmas. I had seen him lean from the carriage window at Cauldhurst a few days before, but only well enough to recognize him. I suppose he looks older than he did; I don't recall his hair and moustaches as so nearly white, and the lines around his eyes and mouth are probably more marked. His Jamaican tan is fading and sallow. But I saw him then as a stranger, not as someone I could compare to his own past image. This man reminded me of nothing so much as an eagle in captivity, ragged, angry, hunching on his perch hoarding his strength for the strike of beak and talons that will free him.

He stepped back to let the fencing-master pass, and my paralysis was broken. The fencing-master, I saw, had a fresh scratch on his jaw, seeping blood. I changed my grip on the *épée* as Andrew had changed his, ready to return it to its place in the rack. "James," he said, with the breath of a nod.

He had expected me. He had not, perhaps, expected me unannounced at that moment with steel in my hand, but he had intended that I should meet him there, and that it should seem accidental. The ground appeared under my feet again; this *was* the meeting I had thought I was going to, after all.

We had an exchange of near-pleasantries while he dressed, which were some of the most fantastical minutes of my life, I think. (Though he did pause for a moment, towelling his neck, and say, "Or would you care for a match?" I looked into his face, which told me nothing, and declined politely, trying very hard not to laugh out of sheer recoil of emotions.) I must have sounded sufficiently normal to set him at ease, however odd I felt. I glanced into the *salle* at one point and saw that O'Brien, having delivered me as requested, was gone.

He invited me to come with him 'round to his club. That, I told him, wasn't possible; I was, unfortunately, likely to be taken up by the Metropolitan Police if recognized. After a cold and inscrutable look, he said he'd stand me a round at another place he knew, then, "better cut to suit your cloth" was the way he put it. It was a gin shop on the upper floor of a building a few streets from the fencing school, rather rough-looking even in the middle of the afternoon and probably only quasi-legal. I was meant to be insulted, I suppose; I was more curious as to how he knew of the existence of such a place.

There was whisky as well as gin; the barmaid brought the former for me and the latter for him, as we sat at a heavy, unwiped table near the shuttered window. Out of sheer contrariness, I opened the shutter louvres to watch the rain pattern the glass and mar the view of the muddy street below. No one in the place was sufficiently moved to object.

I don't think either of us looked at home in the setting. I wore a decent suit and a driving-coat, and he was stiff and formal in black, with a beaver that must have cost enough to buy the room, and a silver-topped cane worth at least that. He sat rigidly straight with his hands folded over the cane's head and his gin untouched; I was, as usual, tempted to uncommon efforts, but resisted, and so neither slouched nor tilted the chair back on two legs. It was very bad whisky, but I nursed it anyway, thinking wistfully of the bottle Richard had mentioned at the Grey Hound.

Then Andrew said, "There are crates of weapons hidden in the cellars at Cauldhurst. Are they yours?"

I didn't have to feign surprise. Whatever I'd thought would be the conversational gambit, the guns at Cauldhurst had never occurred to me. "No," I said as soon as I thought I could do it firmly.

"I don't believe you," he said.

I smiled for the first time since he had come through the door at the fencing school, and said, "All right."

His hands clenched on the top of his cane. "Why did I expect anything more from you? When have you ever showed any concern for my good name or yours? You've already said you're a wanted man. Who would believe anything but that a cache of weapons hidden in your cellars belong to you?"

"Pardon me," I interrupted. "They're *your* cellars. I'm only the heir apparent."

"Was that how you thought of it when you put them there? Did you *hope* to blacken my name if they were discovered?"

"I repeat, I did not put them there."

"I will believe that . . . if you help me remove them and turn them over to the government."

I thought about reminding him that I didn't really care if he believed me, but I didn't want to put too many hurdles in his way. "That would be difficult. The government and I are not on speaking terms right now."

"You needn't summon up that much courage," he said, with a nicely judged lack of heat. "I will deal with the government. But if you won't assist me, I assure you I will lay an information in Whitehall about you and the guns, as earnest of my innocence in the matter. And when you are caught, you will hang."

I stared out the window, as if pondering the threat. In fact, I was weighing the progress of the conversation, trying to decide if I had seemed sufficiently resistant and could now knuckle under. I was suddenly profoundly sick of the whole thing, and wanted it done with. I turned back to him at last and asked, "What do you want me to do?"

He looked down at his hands. I admired the pose; he might almost have been thinking about the question, instead of waiting to ask for what he'd wanted all along, waiting to tell me the thing that was the sole purpose of this meeting.

"Meet me at Cauldhurst," he ordered at last. "There will be no one there to see you; I turned off the staff as soon as I found the weapons. I couldn't have anyone blundering onto them. Can you come down on Friday?"

I gave myself the luxury of saying, "I don't believe I have any prior engagements."

"Come down in the evening—no, you'll want to travel after dark, won't you?" he offered with a delicate curl of his lip. "Nine o'clock, then. I'll meet you behind the stables."

"Why not at the house?" perversity made me ask.

His face was, for a moment, quite blank. Then he lifted his chin and said, in the politely freezing tone I am so damnably familiar with, "I thought you were skulking?"

Then he rose and laid money on the table, too much for the drinks. I saw it and lifted my eyes to his.

"For your travelling expenses," he told me, and gave me a surveying look. "Or do you, in fact, *have* sixpence to bless yourself with?" Then he smiled (having got something more immediately satisfying from the meeting than even my presence at Cauldhurst on winter solstice), swept me a little bow, and left.

I had another moment of emotional recoil when the door closed behind him, and I sat with my arms folded on the table and my face hidden in them until it passed. Proud words and confident, the ones I spoke to Richard at the Grey Hound about not thinking of Andrew as my father. Many's the fool marked out by his pride and confidence. He did not sire me, but to my reflexes and reactions, to my ungovernable emotions, Andrew Cobham is my father. My father had just heaped upon me his nicely-calculated scorn. My father had just come from honing his duelling skills. My father had just offered me poisoned bait, and meant to kill me at the dark of the year.

After I sat up I drank off the rest of my bad whisky and watched the rain leak in around the window frame while I made my plans. I have no idea if the Trotter's Club care about the precise timing of astronomical events, but on the chance that they do, I looked up an old friend with a hobby in astronomy, and had him calculate the hour of the solstice. Answer: ten minutes to ten on Friday night. My arrival at nine could be meant either to ensure an early start so that the climactic blood-letting may be arrived at before ten, or to give them plenty of time to prepare the ground, and me, for a starting time coinciding with the solstice. Or neither—but surely, if a band of hopeful druids were determining the timing of their sacrifice by sheer artistic whim, they'd never settle for something so prosaic as nine o'clock?

Richard, damn him, would lift an eyebrow at that interrogation point. I shall spend the rest of my life hearing that pleasant, cultured voice commenting drily on my every rhetorical device.

My blessing on the authors of *La trône terrestre*, who declared that one is not permitted to shoot one's sacred victim. It is hard, after all, to dodge a ball, or parry one, or to defend one's self with any found object against a man with a pistol. To every quarry its proper weapon: for boars, a spear; for foxes, the hounds; for men, the sword, I suppose. Andrew may be polishing his swordsmanship, but mine is in quite good order, and though he has the advantage of me in reach, I will back myself for speed and endurance, and for pure foulminded inventiveness. I don't count on a fair fight, since there is no such thing, but I trust my ability to take my own advantage of unfair conditions.

I am come at last, I suppose, to the inevitable: telling you what I think I may have to make happen on Friday night. I have racked my brain to think of some other way of accomplishing it, since I know both you and Richard will greet this as the work of a maniac who takes a certain pleasure in seeing how nearly killed he can get himself. Perhaps the proof of that analysis is that I can't think of anything else to do that will accomplish what I want.

These men (and woman) will not be brought to justice on any charge from me, or even from some better-respected citizen. Their past crimes are deftly buried; their intended ones are too bizarre, too enormous, to be believed on the basis of any simple testimony, without the most overwhelming proof. I have to make them prόvable. I can't think of any way to do it but to arrange for them to be committed before witnesses.

That means that I have to offer them my throat at winter solstice, and let them come close enough to tearing it out that there can be no slightest doubt in the mind of any observer that it is their intention to kill me. If they are stopped too soon, they can claim that whatever sport they engage in is only that: sport, perverse and cruel, perhaps, but not mortal. To break the Trotter's Club and cut Alan Tournier's feet out from under him requires nothing less than charges of intended murder. I am telling you this because you will want to find some way to lessen the risk to me. Risking me is, I'm afraid, essential. Remember, please, that the price of reducing the danger to me is your safety, and Richard's, and Kitty's, and Engels's, and that of a great many friends of mine and yours who deserve our protection.

If you can manage it, please, Goddess, dearest heart, *don't come to Cauldhurst*, and keep Kitty and Richard from it as well. I'm half counting on your wound keeping you immobile at Melrose, and Kitty and Richard in attendance on you, but only half, because, though I'm hopeful, I'm not foolish. Still, don't come. Everything I know or can guess about whatever is to happen on Friday says that it will be a nasty business, enough to sicken a carrion-eater, with its capacity for nastiness only enhanced by the presence of anyone I love.

I've not asked about your health, because I expect to be able to evaluate it in person long before a letter from you could find me. I refuse to entertain any thought, now, but that you're mending quickly. Any other case—there is no other case possible. If I believe otherwise, I will be back in the yard of the Grey Hound with the need for action past and no company but my conscience, which was not, at the time, an easy companion. I will not talk about that. Only, if you feel even friendship for me, don't risk any more hurt in the service of my adventures.

I had hoped to come to Melrose Hall before Friday, but I doubt now that I will manage it. The manufactured incident— or, as it's proved to be, incidents—that the Prussians bought from our cabal of plotters is unexpectedly tenacious. It's a motley array of trouble: one or two assasination attempts, several mill fires, a rising of miners in the west. But they're all meant to happen more or less at once on the 22nd (Clever, no? A diversion from any potential outrage over such parts of the Trotter's Club's business as can't be hushed up, and nicely timed to make the discovery of the guns, shortly after, as inflammatory as possible), and all to be attributed to a group (fictional) with connexions to the trade union movement and the German, Italian, and Hungarian elements among the *émigrés*. (How they could have avoided having any connexion to the French as well, I cannot imagine, but then, I'm not being consulted.)

Still, we've learned this much, and think we can derail most if not all of it. I've thrown in my lot with Engels's League for the next twenty-four hours. His friend Marx is astounding: a good-natured lion with a brain that can take your breath away in even casual conversation. I landed in upon him last night at a damned inconvenient hour, bearing a piece of news I thought important enough to trouble him with. I was treated very kindly by the whole household, for Engels's sake, of course; but I think Marx is not difficult to impose on at most times, and his wife and the family friend who serves as house-keeper are prepared to be his dragons when required. They offered me a bed, but I declined; they are at quite enough risk, just now, as it is. Besides, I was fairly sure I would be turning the rightful occupant out if I accepted. Their quarters are worse than cramped.

Oh, even at the inconvenient hour, the children were still up; I think there had been some earlier distraction, and Lenchen, as the girls told me to call her, was trying to nudge them toward their beds as I arrived. Usually I don't mind serv-ing as an excuse for bad behaviour, but I felt rather guilty this time, especially after the discussion ran to chess and whether it was really anything like planning battles; when I raised the example of Waterloo, the girls wanted to know if it wouldn't be possible to have a chess game with more than two players, and set me to designing it. I think the oldest girl is about six, for the love of mercy. I realized all at once that I had been quite relaxed and happy for the past half-hour, and that it must be *hours* past their bedtime. A strange, unexpected island of peace in this miserable ocean.

There was more; I wish, and rather desperately, too, that you were here, and that I could tell you all of it. Or better still, I wish you had been with me, and we would sit now and compare notes on the Marx family. I console myself with the promise of: Later.

I am best at attack and defence, pursuit, any active venture. I am even good at waiting, I think. What I hate, and I can recall too many such occasions in my past, is the situation that requires me to simply *endure*. But that, too, I can do. I suspect that winter solstice will be mostly of that kind. My plans are as well-laid as they can be, and I expect will be well-executed. I am better prepared for this fight than I ever have been, or expect ever to be again. I hope, you see, that you value me rather highly, and I would never casually risk anything you valued.

I have either too much or not enough to say to you for the inch of candle I have left in the candlestick. You are as dear to me as anything ever seen in this world. When this is done, perhaps you will give me the time and opportunity to show you how much that is.

With all my heart,
James

LONDON
21 DEC 1849

Kitty dear,

I don't know why I bother to write—yes, I do, and I'd better admit it now, to both of us. I won't see you again between now and whatever happens tonight, and I run the risk of never seeing you again. If I am killed, you should know about the things I've done in the last day, because, admit it, it would drive you insane not to know.

My mad dash from Melrose was nearly an exercise in futility. I certainly didn't need quite so much dash, at any rate, since all my hurry got me to Bright's at eight in the evening, and *nobody* in London is in at eight in the evening. I sent out notes, knowing full well that neither of the addressees would answer them until possibly this morning, then sat in my room and let Alice change my dressing and fuss over me. I was horribly under the weather; whether it was the worry or the travel, I couldn't say, but I was queasy in a way I knew boded no good.

But hurrah, hurrah, at half after eleven, the maid knocked with a card. Thomas Cavanaugh was downstairs, and I'm sure he thought I ought to meet him there. I sent down that he was to come up at once. Reputation be blasted. Surely care for my reputation should be outweighed by concern over my having to tromp up and down the stairs?

Besides, he must be much quicker on them than I am. He was at my door in jig time, and I think my greeting must have frightened him, it was so warm. He's fallen a little in love with me, you see, and it was unkind of me not to remember that and try, at least, to be formal, Oh, but I was so glad to see him! I think Alice put him at ease by leaving the connecting door open, and crossing back and forth in front of it in the bedroom at regular intervals, shooting raptorish looks at him at each passing.

James, I told him, was about to do something likely to get himself killed, but if he wasn't, he would have to be got out of the country instantly afterward. Could Cavanaugh arrange it?

Well, if his face hadn't been a study before, it was then. "What is he about to do?" he said, in a harsh voice.

"If you're asking, do I want you to collude in murdering the P.M., the answer is no," I replied. Then I explained as well as I could—as well as anyone can—about the Trotter's Club, and some of the political and familial complications. Not all of them, for lack of time, and because I didn't want the poor devil to swoon clean away.

Cavanaugh laid his lips together rather tightly. Then he said, "Why not have the lot of them arrested, then?"

"There's no proof, at least none that would be useful at law." I was feeling extremely ill, and thought about asking Alice for more tea, but decided the effort would be worse than just sitting still.

"What is he going to do that will require him to leave the country?"

"Oh, he's already done that. But when it's over, it will be worse, won't it? I mean, he'll have irritated one set of powerful people or another, no matter how it turns out. Excuse me."

I bolted with as much decorum as I could for the dressing room, where Alice had already set the basin out. She closed the door behind me, too, which was decent of her. I felt much better when I returned to the sitting room, though the dressing-room mirror told me I was the colour of the white keys on a pianoforte.

Cavanaugh was standing at the window, holding the curtain aside and looking down at the street. I disposed myself on the settee again. "It's snowing," he said, with very little inflection. "Quite hard."

I opened my mouth to recommence haranguing him, when he turned from the window and croaked, "Is it his child?"

I found my hands had folded themselves over my middle in that horrible clichéd way that bad serial novelists describe. My heavens, Kitty, the first sign in my life that I have any maternal instinct at all, and it's banal.

I did finally get my tongue away from the cat and said, "How did you—" I was going to finish with "guess," but it made it all sound like a parlour-game at Christmas.

Cavanaugh produced a bleak-looking smile and said, "It might have been bad oysters at supper. Except I can see you didn't have any." He gestured at the tray Alice had brought up for me earlier, with tea and toast. The teacup was mostly empty, but the toast had exactly, obviously, one bite taken out. These cursed observant artists.

"To answer your earlier question," I said, "yes, it's his."

I saw his hand close very hard around the curtain, before he let go and sat back down.

Kitty, I hereby declare that Thomas Cavanaugh is the world's own brick of a man. He didn't rant, or moralize, or go into poetic agonies about worthiness and purity. I, at least, know a great many otherwise free-thinking young men who would revert to the approved idiocy, as delineated above, under the pressure of such a moment. No, he only said, "Why do you think I can help?"

"Because, unlike mine, your foreign friends aren't likely to be arrested in most of the countries of Europe. Oh, that's an exaggeration. But if you tell me that platoon of French painters you go to the opera with don't know a few lovely rich *bourgeoises* who'll do them favours, I'll eat my gloves. I imagine," I muttered, "they'd go down as well as anything would, just now."

Cavanaugh looked meditatively past my shoulder, and said, "I could do it, I suppose. It would be easier if you could tell me what, exactly, is going to happen that Cobham will need extracting from."

"Wouldn't it just? But I'm not sure. Either they mean to chase him through the woods or cut his throat in the cellar."

"Not at all the same thing," Cavanaugh agreed mildly. "When is this business taking place?"

"Gracious, I didn't say? Tomorrow night at ten o'clock."

He stared. "I can't do it. Not in the space of twenty-four hours. Are you—it's impossible."

"Forgive me if I hope you're wrong. You don't have to stop it, just spirit him away afterward."

"How many fellows are in this Club, anyway? Is Cobham going to knock them all down like the Little bloody Tailor?"

"No," I replied, twisting my hands together in my lap, "I'm counting on Sir George Bankston for that."

"Bankston?" Cavanaugh repeated, much struck.

"What's wrong?"

"Nothing. He's a relation of mine. Some sort of second cousin, I think," he amplified, after seeing that my eyes had practically fallen out of my head.

"Then you can do me another favour. You can go with me to see him at a painfully early hour tomorrow morning, and get him to do what I want."

I must have used my "and that is that" voice on him, because he did what I told him to without any further fuss. I dressed to awe a duke this morning, and Cavanaugh brought a hired carriage around to Bright's, and formed my retinue when I was shown into Bankston's offices in Whitehall. Early as it was, it was later than I'd intended, because the snow had continued through the night and was still falling, if slower; the streets were awful.

We were almost denied; there was an atmosphere of subdued panic in the place, that I guessed had something to do with the disturbances scheduled for the 22nd, which must have begun to leak rumours audible to ears as quick as Bankston's. Not at all a cheerful panic; I would wager that Bankston's people weren't part of the cabal that set them in motion. Well, of course I'm wagering that way. If Bankston wants it all to go smash, he has no stake in taking up the Trotter's Club and saving James's life, does he?

After a long pause to inquire, the secretary let us in. Bankston is a large man—large, not fat—with a striking head of grey hair and hands that look better suited to a mattock than a pen. He stood before the window when we came in, with the light (what there was at that hour) behind him, and a creased sheet of paper in his hand.

I introduced myself and declared that I was James Cobham's cousin, which produced a look on his face quite unlike anything I had been prepared for. But he urged me to go on, and I tried to explain why I was there. Since I had no idea how much he already knew, I'm afraid it was almost incomprehensible.

At last he took pity on me. "Miss Voight," he said, "I believe you have been forestalled."

I think I managed to say something like "I beg your pardon?"

"Your cousin has already engaged my interest in his affairs." And he handed me the sheet of paper he held.

It was dated the 20th and read:

Dear Sir George,

I'd be grateful if you'd send as many men as you may see fit, including a constable or two, to Cauldhurst Abbey by a quarter to ten on the night of the 21st. When you get there, you should be able, with very little effort, to gather proof that Lord Growe, Wilson Lewis, Charles Witt Samuelson, and Geoffrey Parks-Gifford, along with a few other choice and influential fellows, no doubt, are guilty of intent to commit murder. They intend to commit it in a particularly shocking and sensational fashion, too: they are all members of a pseudo-religious society that participates in ritual murder on special occasions, of which this is one.

Now, wouldn't you say that was nearly ideal for your purposes? If you can't ruin the lot of them on the strength of this, I wash my hands of you. I hope I needn't warn you not to move on them until you have sufficient assurance that it's murder they have in mind—though I hope, too, that you won't have to actually let them go through with it, since I am the intended victim. I, for my part, undertake to stay alive until you get there.

I can't say precisely where you'll find them and me, but I think it won't be very far from the house itself. I

*would be willing to wager that part of the exercise is to
conduct the business as much as possible on the grounds
of the original abbey. We are all supposed to be on foot,
so however much ritual coursing my friends are planning,
we can't go terribly far. (If the weather doesn't improve,
they'll be coursing in cold mud to their knees, at best,
and may they have joy of it.)*

*I am counting on your self-interest to make you act in
this matter, and on your reputation to make your actions
stick. I have had this delivered on Friday morning so that
you'll have no time to plan anything more elaborate than
having everyone taken up after the fact. And that, I'll have
you know, is a gesture of respect; I know you're capable
of accomplishing a great deal more with this than I want
you to, if I give you enough time for it.*

> *Sincerely,*
> *James Cobham*

"Do you have anything you'd like to add?" Sir George
asked when I'd read it, with a dry manner and a lift of the
eyebrow that made me wonder if people who engage in covert
activity are all sarcastic by nature.

"Are you going to do it?" I said.

"It was the point of my agreement with your cousin," he
replied.

"Then no. Except—may I come with you?"

Bankston raised both eyebrows. "No," he said politely.

"I don't believe you've thought it out." I sat very straight
in my chair, my hands folded and quiet in my lap, trying to
look every inch the self-possessed, capable, cool-headed creature I didn't feel. "I'm familiar with the grounds at Cauldhurst.
I can direct you quickly to the places where the Trotter's Club
are most likely to be found."

"No, Miss Voight. If your cousin didn't think I would require a guide, then I will assume I don't. I'm sorry, but time
seems to be short, especially in view of the state of the
weather. I hope you're easier in your mind about this business
now. I'll have my secretary show you out."

And he did, for all the good it did him. Because, of course,

I am going down to Cauldhurst with Cavanaugh instead, to help manage James's spiriting-away.

I don't believe in whatever the Trotter's Club are using as an excuse for their abominations. I don't believe in whatever it is you burn candles to, or for, my dear. I'm not even sure I believe in God. But I find I want some more-than-natural insurance just this once, and of course, I have none. Yours, Kit, will have to suffice for both of us. Oh, I *will* see you again, won't I? We will carry this off with a fine, high hand and all our names will be celebrated down through history as escape artists *extraordinaire*. Won't we? I miss you so much already that I feel as if I'm suffering a premonition of exile to purgatory. But now I have to dress, and load my pistol, and gather up anything else I have that seems to be what daring adventurers bring with them to life-or-death meetings. Courage is nothing like romance paints it, is it, Kitty? Adieu, and my love to everyone at Melrose.

Your determined
Susan

SATURDAY, THE 22nd OF DECEMBER

Dear Aunt Julianna:

I know very well the fears that arrive with an unexpected letter from a relative, and I wish to God I did not have to confirm them all, or that there was at least a way to make the news gentler or softer, but there is none. My poor, dear Aunt, I am more than grieved to have to tell you that Henry, your son and my beloved cousin, is lost to us. He passed away in the early hours of this morning in hospital of injuries sustained in a tragic accident last night.

I do not yet know all that led up to the accident, and you will know more when I do; yet I could not delay informing you and take the chance you might first learn of this by rumour or through a less sympathetic hand. The little I know is that there was a stalking party being organized on the grounds of Cauldhurst—a quite illegal party, by the way, it not being the season—and Henry learned of it, though I swear I do not know how. You know better than anyone, my poor Aunt, how head-strong Henry was, and how, when there was something he wanted to do he would simply do it without thought of con-sequences; or when he felt something was wrong he would act to repair it. In this case, I think, upon learning that the grounds of the Abbey were to be violated, he went on his own to correct the, matter, without so much as informing the authori-ties or the family about his intentions, and in doing so received a stray ball that pierced his proud, cheerful heart. He was awake when I reached him a short time after the accident, and he pressed my hand warmly as I held him. He was able to speak a little; he assured me that he felt no animosity toward whoever had fired the shot, and knew that if there was any guilt, those guilty would receive what they deserved without any action on his part, which I think you may take as assurance that he never lost his faith as a good Christian.

A waggon quickly arrived to bring him to hospital, and as he was being assisted onto it, he begged me to assure you of his love, which I now do. Those were nearly his last words, for he lost consciousness during the ride and never regained it. Though it is but cold comfort, you should know that the authorities are pursuing those involved with all vigour and that some arrests have already taken place. I know it would please Henry on your behalf to know, in addition, that steps have been taken to keep his name, and thus yours, out of the news-papers; it was his nature to care little what anyone said of him and yet to remain sensitive to protecting his name on behalf of those who shared it, and in taking these steps we believe we are only fulfilling what would be his wishes.

It goes without saying that I will send you more information as it becomes available, and that if there is anything at all that I or anyone else in the family can do, we stand ready. The services will be held at Melrose on Monday week, and I know that prayers will be spoken, not only for Henry, but for you as well.

Aunt, I know that such a blow cannot be softened, but I hope there can be some consolation in the knowledge he was loved by all who knew him and that the vigour and joy with which he assailed life continue not only in the memories of those of us who were blessed to have known him, but, I have no doubt, in the eternal life that he has begun, and where I believe his laughter, wit, and charm are even now earning him the love in Heaven that he had so well earned here on Earth.

With affection and deepest sorrow, I remain your devoted nephew,

Richard Cobham

RICHARD COBHAM'S JOURNAL

DECEMBER 23rd

It is strange, but the most vivid memory I have of Friday's events is of following a trail of footprints with spots of blood on them, and this is something that never happened. That is, I did follow a trail of footprints in snow, but there was no blood. After that, my memory fades and fragments, and though there are pieces I do remember after that, I'm not even certain they are of real events. If they are, I do not wish to remember them clearly. And yet, can they be worse than what I do remember, which includes an act more cold-blooded than I thought myself capable of? A futile act at that, which makes it worse. Shall I confess here what I have done, knowing that, should this fall into the hands of the authorities, it constitutes a confession? Why not? The act was committed before unimpeachable witnesses.

It was very cold and still snowing when I left Melrose, arrangements complete, a pistol in each pocket of my coat, and my lips warm from a passionate kiss by my brave Kit, who held her fear back behind her eyes with a strength that would have been beyond me. It was late morning when I set out, but the sun was already threatening to set when I reached Cauldhurst; a dismal day.

I gave the horse and some last instructions to Wye, then let myself into Cauldhurst and made my way down into the basement, where I placed myself on a crate of rifles and waited an eternity, give or take an hour.

I put out the lantern and sat in the dark, and entertained

fears of rats and gnawing things, as well as of the Powers that had been invoked for years in the next room. I fingered my silver, and sometimes took out one of my pistols just to hold it in my hand. I played games with myself to keep the darkness out, and I called out to the Powers that might protect me, but they seemed fantastical in that place, even though those that would destroy me seemed real and almost tangible. I am a coward; let me confess that here once for all.

And then I almost cried aloud when I heard footsteps just outside the room, footsteps that were followed by the unmistakable sound of a pistol cocking, even though I had been waiting for just such a sound. But, determined to appear more calm than I was, I cleared my throat and said, "Don't shoot, James. It's me."

There followed a collection of blasphemies that seemed almost like a benediction, succeeded by the opening of a door and the glare of a lantern that hurt my eyes. James said, "Richard, you fool, I thought I told you—"

"Oh stop it," I said, trying to sound lighthearted. "If you really thought I'd stay home and let you have all the fun, you're an idiot."

After a pause, during which my eyes began to adjust, he said, "I'm not really surprised, come to think of it. But I had hoped—why are you down *here*, of all places?"

"Because this is where I knew you would come, and no one else would see me."

"No one else? You're the idiot. What if one of *them* came in?"

For just a moment, I thought he was speaking of those Powers I had made myself so frightened of, but then I realized what he was talking about and said, "Why would they?"

He ignored the question. "Who told you I'd even be on the grounds today?"

"I deduced the dialectical necessity of it."

He glared at me, and made a remark about the dialectic that none of our professors would have thought physiologically possible.

I smiled at him, and he finally smiled too, and shook his head. "As long as you are here," he said at last, "I may as well ask—since this is more your property, strictly speaking, than it is mine—if you have any objections if I redecorate it."

He was carrying a large white bundle over his shoulder. I didn't need to ask what he meant.

"Of course not," I lied. "How long a fuse do you have?"

"Long enough."

"Then let's get to it. You'll have to tell me what to do."

It took about fifteen minutes to do what was necessary, then we scrambled out of the house and took up a position behind the north wall, our backs to the water where James had once almost drowned, and there we waited for quite a while. It was dark by now and the snow had stopped. Eventually I said, "Could the fuse have gone out?"

"I doubt it," said James. He looked up at the sky and cursed.

"What is it?"

"It's clearing. There will be a lovely half-moon for them to see the lovely tracks in the snow. When does it rise tonight?"

"I don't know."

He cursed again. "It snows for them, then clears for them. I swear, Richard, you could almost convince me—"

"Almost," I said.

He chuckled. "Whatever I have to contend with tonight, Diccon, I'll at least have the consolation of knowing it is tangible."

"Really? I'd say that among the things you have working for you, I'm happy that some of them are intangible."

"Very dialectical. I meant—"

"I know what you meant. You meant a lot of things. Above all, you meant that you're actually going through with it."

He looked at me as if I'd spoken in a foreign language. Then I heard a thud followed at once by several others, and I almost asked what it was before I realized, and it was an astonishingly short time later that we saw the flames emerging from all the windows of Cauldhurst.

James had the presence of mind to look around every once in a while to see if anyone was coming; I just watched Cauldhurst burn. "So much," said James, "for evidence of a plot against the State."

I nodded. "Plots are intangible," I told him, hoping to make him laugh again. It didn't work.

He said, "I know that you've always . . ." His voice trailed off and he gestured toward Cauldhurst, where the flames were making certain they had discovered each exit.

I could see through a few of the windows, and all I saw was fire. One of the windows had opened onto a small, family dining room that had held a large, complex buffet-cabinet of Brazilian rosewood. The cabinet had been made up of drawers and cupboards that connected to each other, and had been empty as long as I could remember. James and I used to chase each other through it when we were small. I said, "It doesn't matter."

"Of course it matters," he said impatiently.

"I mean other things matter more. I'm glad that you and Susan—"

"So am I," he said. "I hope we have the chance—oh, bother. Excuse me. I'm not going to start on that."

"I know. I hope so, too."

I wanted the fire to show me the future, or enough to allow me to prevent the worst of it, but even if it had, I would have disbelieved my own sight. Whatever else I believe in, I cannot deny causality. James said, "Of course, don't you?" and I realized I'd said something aloud, but I wasn't certain what it was and didn't want to ask.

We continued to watch the flames. James said, "I know you take no pleasure in—"

"It doesn't matter," I told him.

"It does, though," he said.

I said, "If this is the worst thing that happens today, we'll consider ourselves lucky."

"Yes." He consulted a pocket-watch by the glow from Cauldhurst, holding it up over the wall so the fire reflected in its face. "Almost time for my appointment," he remarked.

I didn't answer.

From our vantage point, we saw them arrive, all within a few minutes of each other, in well-appointed coaches, which then drove off, no doubt to return at a previously arranged hour. The first arrival I didn't recognize, nor the second. The third was Andrew Cobham, which brought a sharp breath from James, followed by another and rather Gaelic-flavoured outburst of blasphemy.

"What is it?" I said. "You must have known—"

"I knew he'd be here."

"Well?"

"Can you see what he's carrying? I'm an idiot."

I looked. "Your eyes are better than mine. I can see he's holding something—"

"A bow," said James. "You hunt a stag with bow and arrow, you don't fence with it. I'm an idiot."

I stared over the wall. "James, you've got to—"

"No," said James.

I knew there was no point in arguing with him, so I didn't. "Give me your Colt's," I said.

He started to ask why, then nodded and handed it over. The metal was very cold. It didn't fit into the pocket of my coat, so I stuck it into my belt, then fiddled with it until I found an angle where it didn't press into my stomach or my leg.

Another coach arrived, left two men I didn't recognize, and departed. The next coach had ducal arms on it, and the one after that deposited Alan Tournier and his sister. I said, "From here, I think I could—"

"But you won't," said James. "Don't interfere. I need this to work."

"I—"

"Don't you dare."

"All right."

Cauldhurst burned, not like the Grey Hound, but in its own way: carefully, with attention to detail, as if it were intelligent and aware and wanted to take its time consuming each morsel of history. A tongue of flame would appear in a window and then vanish, as if it were waving at us; saying hello and asking if it were doing well enough. We watched.

Another coach arrived, leaving off two more men, and then another on its heels with one man. They all stood in the yard and watched Cauldhurst burn and commented on it in words that we couldn't hear, but the fire was obviously unexpected and they were clearly disturbed. I found myself outrageously pleased, and I think James was, too. By the light of the burning building we saw they were all dressed in knee-length robes with hoods. It would have been less peculiar, I think, had the robes reached their ankles, because the ten men and one woman had mundane shoes and boots and trousers and a dress that went not at all with the robes. As we watched, they donned thin masks that did little to hide their features, and as they did so James said, "I think it's time to introduce myself to the Trotter's Club."

"Are you sure they're all here? Eleven is an odd number."

"And prime, as well. Quit trying to delay me, Richard."

"James, I—"

"I'll see you later, Richard. Don't take foolish chances."

"Coming from you, that's—all right. Good luck."

He vanished into the night, and, as I watched, emerged about five minutes later, having contrived to approach them as if from the burning building itself. I sometimes used to wonder what James wouldn't sacrifice for an effect; now I think I know.

Cauldhurst worked itself up to a constant glow. Sometime while we were watching the Trotter's Club arrive, part of the roof of the new kitchen annex had collapsed. I almost think I remember the sound it made, though only as the echo of a memory. The new oven was iron and might not have been destroyed. But no, the heat would deform it. The north wall was sheeted over with flame; I could no longer tell where the windows had been. Would anyone see the glow in the night, deduce its cause and bring out help? Probably not; there were no houses close enough. Against the glow, James confronted our enemies. I saw them speaking, but could hear nothing, except at one point when James threw his head back and I heard his ringing laughter. None of the others seemed amused.

Then they searched him, which we'd expected, and found nothing on him they thought it necessary to remove. I touched his pistol, nestled into my belt. When they were done they continued the conversation. Tournier seemed to do most of the talking, and once he made a wide sweeping gesture that included the wood all around the house. James nodded.

After ten minutes or so, James abruptly turned and walked away from the house, toward the wood. They stood watching him, not moving, and it suddenly seemed as if they were playing a children's game; I could imagine them saying, "Now, we must count to one hundred before we set out after him, and no cheating!" It was grim, ugly, horrible, and absurd.

I ducked behind the wall and set off, paralleling James and trying to keep far enough to his side that none of them were likely to come across my footprints in the snow and realize they were being flanked. There was a soft glow off the snow from the starlight, and in this I could, if I was careful, see to avoid obstacles on the ground; I wasn't certain if it was enough to allow them to track James.

I tried to walk quietly, but I didn't succeed very well. James did, and it was all I could do to stay with him—catching occasional glimpses of movement through the trees, some thirty yards to my right. How long this continued, I don't know. It seemed like hours and hours, but it could not have been.

At one point, I saw James stop and look around, as if calculating which way to go, and at that moment I heard a whispering sound that seemed to be calling my name—it was so clear I turned around, then dismissed it as my imagination. Then it was repeated. I turned again, and saw a dark shape in the trees, and I was scrabbling for my pistol when it stood up and said, "Richard, it's me."

For an instant I had that disorienting feeling one gets when confronted by a familiar voice in an impossible context, then I said, "Henry?"

"Himself."

"What in the world—"

"Quiet, Richard. And hurry up or we'll lose him."

"We?" I said. "You have no business—"

"Letting you have all the fun?"

I'd used the same words to James; but I had the awful feeling Henry meant them. I didn't know what to say. He said, "Hurry."

Curse me a thousand times, I let him push me along. I ought to have insisted, then and there, that he had no part in this, but I was frantic with worry about James, and so I turned, and almost panicked when James wasn't where he should be. But then Henry touched my arm and pointed to him, and we were off again. I tried once more, in a whisper, to demand that Henry leave, but at that moment there was a commotion from James's direction, and the indistinct sound of voices, so I cursed and rushed forward. They were at a place I know well, where a grandfather of an oak stands before an irregular ring

of poplars as if telling them stories. They remain back from
him out of deference; there are only grasses and short weeds,
as well as bare dirt in an oval about twelve feet back from the
oak, and around eight or nine feet wide through the middle.

James had his back to the oak, and confronting him were
Tournier, his sister, and three others I didn't recognize. At that
point, they were supposed to attempt to kill James, and then
the authorities were to emerge and catch them; and just in case
something went wrong, I was there with my pistols.

That was the plan.

Eleanor Tournier's voice broke the silence. " 'He leaned his
back against an oak,' " she recited in a sweet sing-song.
" 'And first it bent, and then it broke.' " James said, "Good
work, Alan. It didn't take you very long." He didn't seem out
of breath; he didn't sound worried. I hesitated at the coolness
of his voice, and stopped, holding out my arm to stop Henry.

"The snow helped," said Tournier. I could see little of him
in the dim light, but from our one meeting all those hundreds
of years and two months ago I remembered him as being rather
a small man, with deep-set eyes and a wide mouth. His voice
was cold. He was holding something that I couldn't quite make
out.

James said, "Where is Andrew with his bow?"

"Chasing around for you. He'll catch up with you eventually. To him goes the kill."

"Not you?"

"No. According to the rules of the game, I haven't the right
to you."

I relaxed on hearing that, and I felt Henry relax beside me.

"That must be a great disappointment to you."

"And a relief to you, since we both know he's no match
for you in a fair fight."

"Why, Alan," said James. "I'm flattered."

His sister broke in then, saying, "That's enough talk, Alan.
Let's get on with it."

"Get on with what?" said James, echoing my own thoughts.

"Making things more even between you and your father,"
he said, raising his hand.

"Christ, Alan, don't be a fool," James said quickly.

I could now see that what Tournier was holding was a large

cudgel, and I had a sudden vision of James with a leg broken, or maybe both legs broken, trying to escape from Andrew. I knew I had to do something, and didn't know what to do. Tournier and those he'd brought with him moved in on James, while Eleanor stood behind, waiting. I kept my hand in my pocket next to my pistol and crept closer.

James said, quite loudly, "Don't you dare," and I froze, again grabbing Henry next to me. Tournier laughed, not realizing to whom James was speaking. I gritted my teeth and gripped Henry's arm so hard I heard him gasp. I missed some of what Tournier said, then, but I think he was mocking James. They grabbed him and threw him to the ground and he said, "Don't you dare," once more, very distinctly, as I saw Tournier's hand, holding the club, rise and fall. I heard the sickening sound of bone cracking, and James cried out very loudly, and someone nearby moaned; I think it was me. The club rose and fell again, and yet again, and James cried out each time. I don't remember if Henry was holding me back, or I was holding him back; I remember being aware of the pulse in my right temple.

Then they stepped away. I couldn't see James, so I didn't know exactly what they'd done; it came to me suddenly that, in spite of their words, they had killed him right in front of me.

"That should even things up," said Tournier. No one else spoke, and I could hear James moaning softly and relief washed over me—relief that my brother had only been maimed while I stood by and did nothing.

Then James said, "Is that in the rules?" in a voice far stronger than I would have thought possible.

Tournier laughed, and turned to go.

James said, "Your family seems to have trouble with rules, Alan."

I saw Tournier stop and turn back. I imagined him frowning, though I couldn't see his face. I discovered that I was moving forward again, trying to be quiet. Henry was next to me, doing the same. A glance at Henry, even in the starlight, showed a very pale face and wide eyes; I suspect I looked the same.

"You probably didn't know that your sister tried to have me shot, did you?"

Tournier looked at him, looked at his sister, and back at James. James had somehow got to his feet, and was leaning against a tree. Whatever they had done, it hadn't been to his legs.

Eleanor said, "Let's go, Alan."

"You'd better, Alan," said James. "You don't really want to learn that your sister has been working all along to get Cauldhurst for her child—not for you."

I saw the shot go home, and so did Eleanor. She said, "Alan—"

James interrupted. "She knew all along I had no right to inherit Cauldhurst. She thought she could wheedle the place out of David. When you killed David, she tried to kill me, and I'm sorry to say she didn't show the least hesitation to shed blood. You've been trying to cut out dear old Andrew and me, and all the time your sister has been trying to cut you out. Now what, Alan? Isn't it embarrassing to have family differences aired in front of strangers? Not that I count myself a stranger anymore, thanks to your sister. Tell me, Eleanor, as a sort of cousin, do I call you Helen after all?"

There was the sound of movement through the woods to our right; either Bankston's men had finally arrived, or another group of stalkers had found the tracks. I hoped for the former and feared the latter.

Eleanor said, "He talks too much, Alan. Shut him up. Kill him now."

"I believe you're right," said Tournier, and stepped forward with his club raised. Henry and I moved, and, from the other side of Tournier, so did Wye and Clayborough. It was fifteen stone of Clayborough who interposed himself between Tournier and James. He did not appear to be armed, but he was still Clayborough, and that was enough. Wye, on the other hand, was armed with some sort of rifle, perhaps a shotgun, and he swung it back and forth in an almost lazy motion covering Tournier, Eleanor, and the others. My pistol was in my hand, but I was shaking so hard I didn't dare cock it.

We all stood there. James said, "How now, Alan?" He was still leaning against the tree, holding his right hand, limp, near his waist. There was something wrong with the shape of the hand, and I now knew what they'd done to him. I think I might have simply killed Tournier at that moment, had we not been interrupted by a group of four more members of the Trotter's Club, none of whom looked familiar. They burst in among us, stopped, and stared. Clayborough still stood next to James; Wye still held the rifle. I was next to Henry, with James about ten feet away. Eleanor Tournier was on Henry's right, Alan Tournier stood in the middle, and the others stood together, staring at Clayborough and James. This left us all in a loose semicircle. It crossed my mind briefly that, if Wye fired, he had a good chance of hitting Henry and me, but it didn't seem important.

James said, "Hello, Richard. You really did call out the troops, didn't you? My compliments."

"Damn you, Cobham," said Tournier, I think to James, and he moved very quickly, diving past Wye and into the trees. Unless he could move as silently as a Red Indian, he didn't go very far. No one else moved, and in the silence, we heard the sound of a pistol cocking. Clayborough moved to position himself between James and the sound. Wye turned to scan the woods in that direction.

James said, "Clayborough, get the hell out of the way."

"No, sir."

"If you don't, someone's likely to shoot a nice hole in you."

"Yes, sir."

James spoke louder, addressing himself to the woods. "That isn't according to the rules, is it? But then, I don't think what your beloved sister has been doing to you is according to the rules good families live by. That's the thing about rules, Alan. When you get caught breaking some, you have to break more."

Eleanor said, also to the woods, "You don't believe him, do you, Alan?"

"Of course he does," said James. "It was just a matter of giving him the key. Now he understands all sorts of things he didn't before. Don't you, Alan?"

One of the robed figures said, "Firearms are forbidden us, Magister. If you use it, you will be cast out from—"

"Oh, shut up, you idiot," said Eleanor.

James kept talking. "You should have some sympathy for

your sister, Alan. She was only acting in the interests of her child. Which child, I'll remind you, makes us relatives. Isn't that amusing? We're both uncles now.''

Evidently, Tournier could move as silently as a Red Indian after all. I heard a whisper of movement, and Tournier was there, five feet behind me, holding a pistol in each hand—the cocking sound had covered another. Clayborough moved to cover James, Eleanor blocked Tournier from having a shot at Wye, which left me and Henry. My pistol was at my side, uncocked; it might as well have been back at Melrose.

The robed figure who had spoken before said, ''This changes nothing. The hunt is still on.''

I risked a quick glance at James, to see his reaction, but he was gone. Bankston's men had not yet appeared, and James had evidently made the calculation that he could still salvage the plan if he could get the Trotter's Club to chase him, even now. I had wanted to give him his Colt's back, but I'd never had the chance.

''The game has changed,'' said Tournier, and raised his pistol.

''No,'' said Eleanor.

''No,'' said Henry, and, for reasons I'll never know, stepped in front of her.

The ball knocked Henry over into Eleanor, and she fell backward, screaming, ''Alan!'' and scrambled out from under my cousin, who groaned and lay still, breathing heavily. Blood erupted from the middle of his chest. I cocked my pistol and raised it. Tournier fired his second pistol, hitting his sister in the throat. My shot came an instant later and it spun Tournier around; he collapsed at my feet. There was the sound of a shotgun, huge and echoing, and someone cried out.

''Find Cobham,'' said the robed figure, and ran off into the woods. Wye looked at me, as if for instructions. His shotgun was smoking.

''Get help for Henry,'' I told him. I knelt down next to my cousin, oblivious of those around me who were running off. But not entirely oblivious. I still had my second pistol. I drew and cocked it.

Henry said, ''Tournier—''

''He's next to you,'' I said. ''Bleeding from the stomach.''

"Good," said Henry.

If Tournier heard this exchange, he gave no indication. He lay still, holding his stomach with one hand, empty pistol with the other, and taking short breaths through his nose. His sister lay next to him, making gurgling sounds as she tried to breathe.

Then someone said, "Here they are," and I raised my pistol in the direction of the voice. A man in a neat, tidy suit and a bowler hat appeared, which was somehow even more absurd than the masks and hooded robes the Trotter's Club were wearing. I lowered my pistol. Three more men appeared beside him as he said, "My name is Cliff, and I'm with the Home Office. I was sent here—"

"This man is injured," I said. "Have you a waggon?"

"Christ Jesus," said one of the others. He was staring down at the man Wye had shot, who was lying perfectly motionless, still holding a cudgel he had probably tried to use on Wye. Idiot. It seemed as if most of his chest was missing.

The one called Cliff looked around and said, "We have one coach. Three of them are still alive. We'll need a second one to get them all to hospital. Go arrange for it, Potter." He looked around, frowning. "Who should we take first?"

I still had a loaded, cocked pistol in my hand. I used it. "No need to take this one," I said. "He's dead."

They looked at me, and at each other; and at Tournier but only briefly. Potter cleared his throat, and Cliff took my pistols from my hands and the Colt's revolver from my belt. He started to speak, but I said, "My name is Richard Cobham. If you want to arrest me, you know where I can be found. I won't be going anywhere. Now let's get these people to hospital."

"All right," said Cliff, nodding brusquely. He seemed confused by the whole thing; not that I blame him. I don't know how long it took for the coach to arrive. I spent the time speaking softly to Henry, but I remember little of what either of us said. Pulling the trigger that last time had done something to me; my memory began to fragment then, just as it had during the fire at the Grey Hound. Perhaps the pistol was pointing in both directions at once, and as the ball went into Tournier's head, something unseen went into mine and cast a grey cloud over everything that was to follow; I know that when I try to think about what happened, I see Tournier, just before I murdered him, and I see my hand holding the pistol; and everything else that happened I see in glimpses around it. To my mind's eye, it is not even my own hand, but I stare at it as if trying to understand how it became joined to my arm.

But even should this journal come to be used as evidence against me, I will not hide behind confusion in the mind. I knew what I was doing when I put a ball into Alan Tournier's head as he lay helpless at my feet, and I did not do so out of hatred, though certainly everything he had done to James, and his shooting of Henry, and all the harm he had caused us all were going through my mind. But it was an act to save Henry, as cold-blooded as anything Tournier himself might have done, and if there is a bill to pay for such an act, I will pay it in whatever coin is demanded, and I am only sorry that it did no good, that my dear cousin could not be saved.

No, I cannot say that. I'm sorry for many another thing besides. I looked down at Tournier before I pulled the trigger, and he looked at me, and he knew what I was going to do, and in that moment he was no longer a conniver who had done great evil to those I love, nor was he a coward, nor was he a brave man. He was just a man who realized he was about to die.

I must close my account here; not because nothing else happened, but because my mind refuses to focus on the rest. I know that, after Wye and Clayborough left with Henry for the hospital, I saw James's footprints in the snow in the light of the newly risen moon and I set off after him, and I know that there were not really drops of blood among the footprints, and I know that I found James, and Andrew, and I have some memories of what happened then, but none of these memories are organized.

Still, even there, I will not deny my guilt. The confusion in my mind occurred mostly after it was over; I was lucid enough during everything that happened. I knew what I was doing, and I even remember a moment of terrible clarity when the only action I could take was laid out for me as if by a voice whispering in my ear. I try not to think about it, because I fear that if I concentrate my memory will clear and I don't want that. My only certain memory after running off following

James's footprints comes hours and hours later, after I had returned to Melrose, though I do not know how I got there; but I know that I was sobbing in Kitty's arms, and she was holding me and rocking me back and forth like a child. That memory is good among all the evil, and I shall endeavour to preserve it.

SUSAN VOIGHT'S JOURNAL

MELROSE HALL
23 DEC 1849

I am writing this

I don't know why I am writing this. So that I know what to say, when I have to tell someone else? Who would I have to tell? Engels; I will have to tell him something. Very well, I shall write down the things that Engels ought to know. Richard? He knows it all, I think, though he hasn't asked me about my part. Why should he? But I might have heard some things that Richard would want to know someday. Very well, I shall include those. No one else would want the entire story, or need it. No, everyone has as much of the tale as he needs, except for a few of us, who have a surfeit of it. Who would want to stand so close to such a thing, given a choice? Obituary notices, discreet paragraphs in lesser journals: CURIOUS TRAGEDY IN KENT, coupled with a sudden grateful thaw and rain to wash away the parts of the narrative more concrete and ruthless than words—those will serve, those will more than serve, anyone who has to ask.

It's difficult to concentrate. I am being sympathized at; I can't think of any other way to put it. Aunt Louisa flutters like a consumptive pigeon, cooing *Poor dear, poor dear*—I wish I knew if I've replied to her. I look at her when she does it, the way cats do when they want you to know that they're trying to be interested in your concerns. Too accurate a mimicry, perhaps. She responds as the pigeon would to the cat. Brian is very manly, and presses my hand, just when I want to use it for something. Even Richard talks, though not to much purpose, seeming to think that we'll all be fine if we can only avoid silence. Only Kitty understands. I don't think I would have expected that—I have lost, for the moment, my ability to expect things, but when I had it I don't think I would have expected Kitty to be the one to see it. She doesn't speak, or pat at me. She tells me what to do when she absolutely must, and leaves me to myself for the rest of it. I prefer silence. I'm listening always, as long as I can stay awake, under the chatter of sympathy callers and family grieving, for silence, and for a sound that will interrupt it that isn't any of the sounds that distract me now.

The worst is the thing that must simply be endured.

24 DEC

I could write no more after that. It was as if every spring of language had gone suddenly dry, and my tongue was rooted in sand, a desert of sand in my mind. Whether it was the memory of a scene (memory—only a word, to be used and let go) in which endurance had been raised to a kind of passionate ritual without intellect, as if it were a vile tarnished mirror-face of ecstasy, I couldn't say. I know I sat fingering the pen as the candles burned low and guttered. One of them went out and sent a thread of smoke into my face; my own cough broke the silence I had sunk into.

It may also have been what prompted Kitty to come into the library. She shut the door behind her with a sharp little noise, and crossed the carpet with a hissing of taffeta skirts, and a step that quivered through the good, tight floor boards and made itself felt even under my chair. She stopped across the table from me and said, "All right. That's enough."

"Not now, Kitty," I told her, with an effort, with a few words wrung back from the desert. I wanted to rebuild the numb peace I had had for a few minutes before the candle went out.

"Now."

I looked up into her face. Her hair was pulled back smoothly, severely; there was no customary halo of gold to soften the sharp chin and straight nose, to make her large blue eyes less penetrating, or to disguise the hard set of her lips and jaw. The black taffeta went up to her collar-bones, and threw

into relief her paleness and the signs in her face of sleeplessness and weeping.

"I don't expect you to turn over all your feelings at once,"
she said harshly. "I don't expect you to fall on my neck and
grizzle like a schoolgirl. I don't expect you to be *shallow*. But
I also won't have you wandering about with all your nerves
exposed, expecting us to dodge around your emotions as if
they were a blind water buffalo in the middle of the road."

"I beg your pardon," I said, and heard my voice come out
soft and level—just as James might have spoken in the early
moments of one of his gathering storms of temper.

Kitty may have heard the same thing, for a strange alertness
flashed across her face and was gone. She let her breath out
in a rush and replied wearily, "No, you don't. You ought to,
but you don't. You're not the only person in this house who's
lost something."

"I never said I was."

"Are you going to talk to me about this?"

I twisted the pen between my fingers and stared at her, wondering what she thought I could find to say—or perhaps we
were thinking of two different things—no, since the early
hours of Saturday there had been only one thing to think about
in this house, whatever anyone actually found to converse
about.

Kitty leaned across the desk and rapped her knuckles on my
brow. "Hullo, Susan, are you at home to callers?"

"Stop that."

"No."

With a great, despairing effort, I fetched out my longest
sentence yet. "Why do you want me to talk about it?"

"Because if I stand back and let you brick yourself in again
... Well, I'd hate to think what Jamie would have to say to
me."

"Very little," I said drily, "just now." I'd meant it to be
dry, at least, but it came out cracked in the middle and sus-
piciously damp, like an underdone biscuit. "Oh, I *can't*, Kit,
not now. I don't ... I feel as if I haven't got *time*. Ask Richard
if you want to know."

"I have. He can't remember."

I replied rudely.

"He can't. He says it's all gone to bits in his head. That half of it's missing, and what's left isn't in order."

On reconsidering, I decided that wasn't unlikely at all. He had hardly looked like anyone I knew, standing on the shore with his shirt-front dark with blood, his eyes narrowed against the light and the bitter air, his wide shoulders rising and falling like some slow piston compressing and compressing an unreleased force. There had been a man at either side of him, gripping his elbows. He hadn't appeared to notice them. I was rather glad, after all, that he didn't have to carry the recollection of the events and his part in them in any coherent form; whatever the outcome, he would not have borne it well.

"I don't even mind if you won't talk about it," Kitty went on. "But I *do* mind if you go on behaving as if we're all a collection of ill-assorted chairs that you keep finding in inconvenient places."

"I'm not so bad as that. Am I?"

"I don't know. You might be more civil to the chairs."

"How could I have been uncivil? Gracious, Kit, I can't recall saying anything to anyone!"

"Just so," Kitty said.

"Oh, God." I got stiffly out of the chair—I'd been there for hours—and went to the window seat, where I knelt on the cushions and pushed the drapery back from the glass. The library was dim enough that I could see out into the night, if I looked through my own dark silhouette. After the straggling, neglected grandeur of the grounds at Cauldhurst, the gardens of Melrose Hall seemed trim and cozy even in winter, even in the dark.

It occurred to me then, rather incoherently, that Cauldhurst was—had been—power, and Melrose was sanctuary, and I could not be comfortable living in either. One needed them, to draw upon as necessary, but to dwell in them constantly required a rare inner balance, a quietness, that I didn't have.

"Earth and water," Kitty said beside me, and I realized that I must have spoken at least some of my incoherent thought aloud. "But not air, and not fire. You're right." She sounded a little sad. "I'd hoped . . . I really had hoped we would all come here in the end, to stay together. But we never will now, will we?"

I turned away from the peaceful night to see the tears running down her face. I let the drapery fall back across the window and held her beside me on the window seat. "You have me for a while," I said.

"Do I, truly?" she asked. Her voice was steady, nothing like her face. "Or do I only have this little bit of you?" She tapped my fingers where they lay on her arm.

"I'll try. Except—no, I'll try to be all here."

And whether because of my resolve, or because of the realization that eventually I will have to go away, it's been easier since then. Not talking, so much as listening with attention; I've been labouring to seem, to be, a part of the household, the circle of grieving that somehow comforts and even tempers those who grieve. The spider sits in her hammocked corner and observes. To join my family in this, I have to forsake the corner, the safe distance, and shut, for now, the door to the windy open places, where possibility and pain are both too big to fit in the rooms at Melrose.

At least now I know who to record these events for, and why. And I have time, as long as I'm waiting. Oh, my poor bludgeoned nerves—thank heaven for mourning, that keeps the world from thinking that we should keep Christmas after any fashion at all!

It was the snow, of course, that held us up, and kept Bankston's men, too, from arriving when they meant to. Cavanaugh, his chosen accomplice

If I manage this at all, it will be a certified miracle, and never mind who I think I'm writing it for. I've left out the doctor already. Nothing else, I think, in London that I need account for. Damn and blast this, anyway.

Cavanaugh met me at the station in London, bearing with him a sturdy-looking man of about thirty in a moderately expensive black frock coat, tasteful hat, and pearl-grey gloves. Also a large glossy leather bag. Thomas introduced him as Dr Paul Gold. I offered him my hand to shake while I took in the large and limpid brown eyes behind his spectacles, the curling black hair under the hat, and the rather brown complexion ornamented with a strictly-pruned beard and moustache, and wondered if I was meant not to guess that he'd changed his first name and dropped off half his last in order to expand his practice in the closed-minded cosmopolitan city of London. I puzzled over how Cavanaugh came to know him, until I remembered the natural allegiance that will develop between artists and medical students over the matter of anatomical studies. Odd to think of C. hovering eagerly over a well-lit, flayed corpse, pencil and sketching-block in hand, but I'd seen a few of his paintings, and could guess that he'd done just that. A man of delicate sensibilities coupled with overwhelming professional thoroughness. Are we all such pieces of unsuspected complexity?

No matter; I'm avoiding my work. So Thomas Cavanaugh, his chosen accomplice, and I went down to Cauldhurst more or less in company with the Whitehall contingent after all, since ours proved to be the only train that arrived that day from London between noon and the next morning. If one had tried it by coach one would not have arrived at all, as the roads were drifted and treacherous, and the light failed completely at six o'clock. But that only meant that everyone with an interest in abridging the proceedings was late in reaching the scene. I know nothing about railways and weather, and perhaps I give the latter too much credit for interfering with the former, but whatever the reason, we reached the station at a little over half-past nine.

I had had the foresight to stable Girasol near the railway station, and to wire the livery to keep a closed carriage, a team, and a good coachman ready for my arrival. Then I distressed Thomas Cavanaugh and Dr Gold by informing them that I was setting off on horseback immediately, while they followed in the carriage. It was not, Cavanaugh said, what he had understood to be the plan; it was unwise; it was, as it turned out, enough to move him to strong language, which made me smile and pat his arm. The doctor, who seems to be habitually grave, was more formal, but no less disapproving. I assured him that if there were any way to get him there on horseback as well, without getting his neck broken in the dark, I would do it.

"It was very clever of you," I said to Cavanaugh as he held my stirrup, "to think of bringing a doctor. I'm sorry, I should have said that hours ago."

"We're going to need one, aren't we?" he replied, as if the question was rhetorical.

I had come down from London in my habit, which was grey wool of the shade that all cats are in the dark, and had a split skirt. I would have preferred trousers, but I'd bled all over my only pair. So I was dressed for it, and Girasol seemed excited about the snow and the dark. Poor Thomas Cavanaugh stood on the carriage step and waved as I turned out of the yard, having no recourse but his dignity, looking rather like the seneschal sending the Duke off to the Crusades.

Which of my intended audience is it that I hear begging, "Get on with it!" I am talking about my clothes, and not talking about the Curious Tragedy in Kent—the stalking-party, with its impressive bag. I'm sorry. In my mind, to arrive at it, I have to ride through the snow as I did then. I've read somewhere about the red Indian medicine-men, who imagine their spirits travelling long hard distances until they come to the place where they can speak to their gods. Like them, I can't seem to come to such a great and terrible place all in a blink.

It was nothing like the ride over the Pennines. The country here is so familiar to me that I think I could have done the trip half-asleep, and at first only my fear of ruts under the snow kept me from pushing Girasol to a dangerous pace. I was two-thirds there before I noticed that the cold seemed to get into the wound in my side in a nagging way, and that I was weary with that, and lack of sleep, and a severe lack of dinner, which I wouldn't have been able to keep down anyway. Weariness narrowed my concentration steadily, until I was hardly aware of anything except my cold hands stiffening on the reins, the ache under my ribs, the numbing pressure of my knees on the saddle, and the dark outline of Girasol's ears against the grey road ahead.

So I didn't see the fire until we were at the lodge gates. It was a red glare like the mouth of Hell behind the elms of the drive and the black wall of the yews at the bottom of the lawn. The wind was full of the ground-pepper grit of ash, and cinders whirled up behind the trees like new red stars.

Very few horses will obey when their riders urge them to race *toward* a fire. Girasol is, of course, exceptional. My world had expanded again, and let in fear and confusion, and finally, the memory of the guns. Of course; the guns had to be got rid of. It was all right, he would have intended this. I got my wits back sufficiently to pull up and dismount on the other side of the yews from the house, and to tether Girasol where he'd be safe from the fire and out of sight.

The noise from the burning house was uncanny. It seemed louder than the Grey Hound had when burning, and perhaps it was; but it might only have been the effect of that isolated inferno set like some threatening and tumultuous clockwork in the cold, blanketed silence of the countryside. Human habitation, burning, should be accompanied by scurrying humans, struggling with water or salvaged items or only wailing over the loss of peace and property. Cauldhurst burned like a sacrifice on a Roman altar—except that it was unattended. Where were the Trotter's Club?

There were wheel-tracks on the drive, to show they'd arrived. No carriages; probably sent off to a discreet and fire-safe distance in the care of their coachmen. I went as quickly as I could through the gardens on the upwind side of the house, and found the marks in the snow where two people had come, running, from the direction of the house, and had stopped in the shadow of the stone wall. Probably to discuss Hegel, I thought irritably at the time. One set of prints, longer and wider, went on along the wall, toward the Home Wood; the other doubled back, toward the line of box hedge that led up to the terrace.

I won't claim that I viewed that second set of prints with an easy mind or a steady heart.

He was not alone, at least. Not for nothing had I made sure to leave James's letter where it would be found and read. Richard would follow, would stick to him, and I was desperately grateful for it, because there was no use my pelting off after them through the wood. I would only be making certain that I arrived too late to do any good.

No, I had to do what I'd told Bankston I was capable of: to use my knowledge of the grounds, to determine where the chase would end before it arrived there. Playacting sorcerers, theatrical murderers, a cool political plotter, Andrew Cobham—where would they be most likely to drive their quarry?

And then, of course, I saw the error in my reasoning. It was the quarry who would pick the ground on which to play out the last scene. James's whole purpose was to steal the direction of the thing away from the Trotter's Club, to rewrite the principals' lines, to twist the blocking to his own ends. I had to assume he was succeeding. I had to find the place he would come to.

Once I realized that, the problem nearly solved itself. The burning house bathed the landscaped grounds in ruddy gold, reaching out and out even to the skirt of the wood. It cast a shuddering light over the unpruned rose-beds, the rough, weedy outline under the snow of the parterre, the brick flank of the stable and the white bars of the paddock gate. It picked out the ornamental water, frozen now and overlaid with snow, and the folly that occupies nearly the whole of the little artificial island at its center, the *faux* ruined tower built of the old abbey stones.

The land slopes steadily from the edge of the wood to the water, forming a shallow cup to hold the little lake and the folly. Whatever happened in that cup would be relentlessly public. Faces and movements would be hard to hide. Voices would carry. The new dramatist would like it for that, and for the deadly irony of the water, where his aged-seven mishap had set in motion the quarrel that had resulted in his mother's death.

I approached it from the side opposite the wood, to keep from leaving tracks where they would be seen immediately. The landscaping of the little island is no more wild than the tower is an authentic ruin; but it was liberally planted to suggest some poetic ideal of wilderness, and neglect has lately assisted the effect. The tower itself is twiggy with ivy and the long canes of some climbing rose, unobtrusively pegged to the stonework at intervals. At its base, on a little arm of land that extends outward toward the house, is a clutter of shrubs, elder, hawthorn, and a thriving rhododendron. I pushed my way in among the leathery evergreen leaves, made myself as comfortable as I could, and proceeded to wait.

Now even I ask, For what? What had I meant to do there, in defiance of his advice and every expectation? I had a pistol I couldn't use and a voice I couldn't raise, not to any purpose, not without risking his whole fragile plot. It wouldn't give him courage to know I was there. It didn't give me strength or hope to be there. If one were feeling generous or poetic (I was neither), one might have said that I was there in the guise of a Valkyrie, hovering above the battlefield waiting for the soul of a hero. I remind the poetically inclined that carrion birds also hover over battlefields.

I suppose it wasn't as long as it seemed. The cold made it longer, and the damp from the skirts of my habit wound around my legs, and the angry throb in my side that was the protest of my half-healed wound. I tucked my gloved hands in my armpits and wondered if the steam of my breath would rise up above the rhododendron leaves and give me away. Then I heard shouting over the animal voice of the fire, from the direction of the wood.

James broke from the cover of the trees as I watched, his head down, his stride uneven. He pressed on as straight for the tower as the snow allowed, and managed to keep his footing on the steep cut of the bank. Then the water played him false one last time; he slipped on the ice and fell to his knees and hands. Or would have; but his right hand failed him, and he came down on his right shoulder with a smothered cry of pain. He scrambled to his feet and arrived at last at the base of the tower, and stood with his brow pressed against the stone, his arms crossed and tight against his body as if he could hold in breath and strength and life itself by force.

He was only a few yards from me, though I was as well-hidden from him as from the shore. I wished I could see his face before I spoke, but I didn't dare wait. I said his name.

He turned against the tower, so that his body was still supported by it, and the strong, changeable light of the burning house fell on his face as his eyes searched the undergrowth. "Here," I said, taking my courage in both hands.

Because it required it. In that face the human had been buried deep, defeated by both animal and angel natures, both the creature at bay and the flaming sword.

I feel as if I owe an apology to someone, and I'm not sure to whom. Me, I suppose. All this tormented flailing of prose needn't be inflicted upon anyone but me, after all, and much better that it not—a good, plain tale of the events in order will best serve everyone who needs my account of them. England is famous for her practical, phlegmatic citizens, and particularly for the *sang-froid* of her female population, as I once heard the length and breadth of France and Italy. I was celebrated as a notable example, to my face. But the English are also, man and woman, famous for harbouring demons. If I have been possessed by the malevolent spirit of Mrs Radcliffe, it can't be a matter for too much wonder.

My intellect defends itself against a perfect descent into pseudo-Gothic excess by enumerating the absurdities that ornamented the business like large and vulgar spangles. The ruined tower built only sixty years before, laboriously asymmetrical and artistically fallen even in its architect's sketch, probably a subject of derision to the masons who did the work. The amateur huntsmen, dressed like the choir from the Church of Questionable Taste, many of them with no more taxing pursuit in their recent pasts than following the footman from parlour to dining-room on the announcement of dinner. The presence of me, damp, shivering, and ineffectual under a rhododendron like a particularly unsuccessful poacher—a comic-opera touch if ever there was one.

But my intellect betrays and is betrayed. The outburst is in the form of anger, not laughter: helpless, bitter anger that the trappings of that night were not tragic but tawdry. And underneath is the primal terror and awe at the centre, before which tawdriness flash-burns to cinders, and which my intellect can get no better grasp of, give no clearer notion of, than can Gothic novelists with their strident excesses.

I was afraid of James's face, because it was both recognizable and strange, but I spoke in spite of it. His gaze found me, and his expression changed only fractionally. He said, "I'm not surprised, you know. Was I meant to be? Stay down, stay down."

"Where's Richard?"

"I don't know. There were shots, back in the wood. I couldn't . . ." He closed his eyes suddenly, and I understood, with a rush of guilt. The human was submerged of intent. I was endangering the self-control that made that possible.

"I don't know," he repeated, and I saw and heard that the breach was filled again.

"I have my pistol," I said, in as commonplace a tone as I could manage. "Do you want it?"

He shook his head. "Wrong tool for the job, now." Then

one corner of his mouth twitched upward; whatever had occurred to him, he believed he was the only person who would consider it funny. "Anyway, I'm a poor shot left-handed."

I remembered his fall on the ice; I assumed he'd sprained his right hand then.

He added quickly, "Stay out of sight. Here we go."

From across the snow, a man's voice called out, like a command. "James!"

James set his back squarely against the stones. His head was lifted slightly; from a distance he might not have looked at all hard-pressed. But I could see his left hand from where I crouched, how it fastened on the stonework as if he wanted to dig his fingers into the mortar, and the rise and fall of his chest.

There was one man on the shore, whom I recognized at last as Andrew Cobham. I recognized him in spite of a quantity of drapery and a gilded half-mask that made the upper part of his face look like Antigone's uncle in a Greek drama, complete with a suggestion of a crown. Behind that was his hair, mostly white as James had observed, and below it his moustaches, likewise. He carried something over his shoulder that I couldn't make out, but decided at last was not a rifle on a sling.

"Good evening, O King. Father." James's voice carried, as I had foreseen. Unexpectedly, it was an orator's voice, strong and pitched to be heard, flexible and expressive. It expressed mild amusement just then. "Does this mean you get the mask and brush? Never mind, you have a mask. You can't be comfortable in that, surely."

"Rather more comfortable than you must be, I think. What happened to your hand?" Andrew's voice was hard and slow, and from the sound, he was smiling.

It was a moment before James replied, "Observant. As a good father should be. Alan Tournier met me in the woods—solicitous for your success, and determined to ensure it." He had not sprained it when he fell. He had fallen because it was already damaged. What had been done to him? "He needn't have bothered, but he's very careful about details. Don't you think?"

"Should I have an opinion about Alan Tournier?"

"Definitely. Every natural human feeling revolts, et cetera.

Pity him, at least. After all, there's his sister, assiduously stabbing him in the back, which interfered so with his efforts to stab *you* in the back.'' James tilted his head with an air of civilized enquiry and added, ''You did know about that, didn't you?''

''As it happens,'' said Andrew, ''I did.''

There were other figures issuing out of the wood, descending the slope to the shore behind Andrew. They were strangely undifferentiated at first, even in the light of the burning (the roof beams had caught by this time, and all the slates seemed edged in gold, with the firelight showing around them, like something out of a fairy tale). I thought there were only five, until I realized that the very large one straggling last into view was really two men, one with his arm over the shoulder of the one helping him to walk.

''But you did nothing to stop him,'' James said.

''Didn't I? How is your hand?''

James was silent.

''Where is he? Did you kill him for me?'' Andrew asked, when it was clear that James was not going to speak.

The answer must have been barely audible on the shore: a line outside the script of the play, delivered with none of the actor's assurance. ''I don't know,'' James said. There was no indication whether he was replying to one question or the other, or both.

James's pursuers ranged themselves along the shore in a loose semicircle, facing the water and James. They all wore masks, I saw, some of them a little askew with exertion, each different, elaborate, and strange. The drapery was also common to all, a short belted robe with a tangle of fabric over the shoulders that must be a hood. They looked from one to the other, shifted self-consciously, and muttered a little. Finally one man, short and broad-shouldered with an incongruously high voice, said, ''Where's Tour—where is Magister Sapientius?''

At that James laughed. It sounded quite genuine.

''We shall begin without him,'' Andrew snapped. ''Iustus, take his part.''

The short man seemed to hesitate. Then he shook himself, and walked around the semicircle until he was next to Andrew, who stood at the center of the arc. He unfastened something from his belt that I had missed entirely, and now thought was a short staff or a heavy wand; but he went down on one knee and fumbled over it, and I saw a little spark of light in his hands which leaped and swelled at the end of the thing. It was a torch, of course. He lifted it, and spoke a phrase of Latin, but I missed the sense of it. Six of the men on the shore had their eyes on the torch and the man who held it. But Andrew Cobham's attention was all on James, and his newly-lit face was like stone below his mask. I saw that the thing I had not been able to make out at first, that hung over his shoulder, was a strung bow, and the strap of a quiver.

I must have moved. James said, barely loud enough to reach me, "I know. Stay still."

The short man seemed to have taken on a little confidence with the lighting of his torch. "Night become day at our will," he said in his high voice, with self-conscious dignity, "that what we do here may be done under the sun without shame." James let that one pass with a flash of his teeth and no comment. The short man turned first to one side, then the other, and I saw that each man carried an unlit torch; light passed down each side of the arc, from torch to torch, until I could pick out the features of every man on the shore. I could see the details now of the robes, the sheen of silk in heraldic red and blue and gold, sometimes torn and stained with the chase; the embroidered edging and ornament, likewise. Light leaped from faceted beads and cabochons on the masks and on bracelets.

"Magister et Regis," said the man who had been addressed as Justice, "why do you come here?"

"To be confirmed in my rule," Andrew answered him.

"Who stands witness to these acts?"

The semicircle of men responded, some strongly, some only muttering, "I do."

There were more questions and replies; there were invocations, in Latin and English. Ritual began to exert its transforming power on everything present. I saw the celebrants—sturdy, well-respected, self-important English gentlemen under their preposterous costumes, a little hesitant, probably embarrassed—slowly forged by solemnity and a growing awe into a unified, purposeful, implacable body. Because, for all the absurdity, the tawdriness, the meanness at the heart of it, the gathering had taken on a strange dignity, a dreadful power. It was wrapped in the night and the elements, and its centre vibrated with Andrew's remorseless purpose.

And at the point of the cone of their attention was James. He didn't protest or plead, or even move; he stood watching as an athlete might watch the approach of his opponents, measuring them, conserving his own strength. To my overstrained fancy, it seemed that between pursuers and pursued there was a kind of circulation, as if some energy passed from them to him and was returned magnified. If I could have believed that the men on the shore were magicians, I would not have identified the man at the base of the tower as their sacrifice.

I watched James, not sure what I was watching for, hoping I'd know it when it came. His breathing was steady. He stood erect, his head high. Steam rose from his hair and shoulders into the cold air, and I saw that they were wet with sweat and melted snow. One lock of hair curved forward unattended over his brow, and a clear drop hung suspended from it, gold as a topaz in the torchlight. It fell, ran into his eye, and made him blink, but I don't think he noticed it beyond the reflex. I don't think he remembered I was there. He was wholly focused on his enemies.

That was the first time it occurred to me to think of him as a stag; because a stag at bay is dangerous, and has been known to kill hounds and hunters. Had that occurred to anyone in the Trotter's Club?

The man officiating in Tournier's absence said, as if in answer to my thought, "Have you been present at the hunt?"

"Aye." A chorus, less ragged now that the spirit of the night had got into the speakers.

"Did the huntsman pursue his quarry without horse or dog, and without any unlawful weapon?"

"Aye."

"Will you witness the kill, and swear the huntsman has the right to the fruits of his hunting?"

Across the respondents' "aye" cut James's voice, like the ringing of steel under a blow. "He has not the right."

It was like being struck. I felt it in all my bones, and judging from the response of the men at the water-side, they felt it also.

I had only looked away from James for a moment or two, but in that time a transformation had been worked. That indrawn, caged power that I had felt around him in the Severn Marshes, in the upstairs passageway of Engels's house, the thing that wasn't anger but rather a weapon for anger to use, that made him speak so softly when it was roused, was on him now.

"Silence!" Andrew bellowed. He was angry, but not, I thought, aware of his danger yet.

"He has not the right, and knows it. I am the illegitimate son of Diana Pearse Cobham and *William* Cobham, and he has known it for over twenty years. Andrew Cobham has pretended to believe as you do, in order to murder me under cover of your beliefs and keep his position among you."

James was not speaking softly now. Every word came down like the thong of a whip, and held us all motionless under the onslaught.

The short man, the spokesman, said, "Can you prove this?" and turning, asked, "Andrew, is this the truth? Do you . . ."

Andrew was not attending; he was staring at James.

"I can't prove it here and now, but I can prove it," James answered. "If what you're doing is sacrifice and not simple murder, you have to let me live until you're sure that Andrew Cobham has a right to shed my blood. Any man who raises his hand to me now . . ." James let go of the sentence as if speaking had become an effort.

". . . is a heretic," finished the short man, with great solemnity and great distress. He must have begun to see the tangle laid out before him, the imperatives of ritual versus the requirements of safety, the presence of a live man who had been hunted and threatened with death, who had to be killed but who could not be sacrificed.

Beside him, Andrew Cobham slowly pulled off his mask and slid the bow from his shoulder. "Lying and faithless like his mother," he said, speaking slowly, too. He was struggling with the quiver, as if it wouldn't slip free. "He is enough like a son to have stolen my power. And I am enough his father to take it back."

In my memory, everything happened at once then, and I know that can't be true. In repeating the events, I can see the ones that had to have touched off others. But when they happened, they happened like motion blur in a daguerreotype, a single smear of occurrence out of anyone's control. Why none of us managed to stop it, I'm not sure, unless James was his own undoing. Had he taken hold of the scene so completely that the Trotter's Club believed themselves helpless, that I believed that nothing could happen without his desiring it? Or were we all simply mesmerized by spectacle, made into mere audience by our attendance on other people's drama?

I say "all". Properly, all but two: Andrew and Richard.

I think I saw the movement at the left edge of my vision first, of a figure coming from the direction of the house, and the struggle that resulted when two of the Trotter's Club broke from the semicircle, grappled with, and eventually subdued the newcomer. I certainly saw it before I understood that Andrew had not been unfastening the quiver. Someone shouted, maybe more than one person, and I was fumbling for my pistol, my hands cold and stiff, as James began to move. Or had he moved when he, too, saw the figure brought down by the two men from the circle? I can't remember seeing Andrew nock an arrow, but if not, why was I trying to get the pistol out?

The next bit is upside-down, I know. I recognized the arrow by the fletching and colour—part of the set kept for games at Cauldhurst, when the grooms would set up straw targets on the lawn for guests and family to shoot at. Not a barbed head like a hunting-point, then, and not even really very sharp. Andrew had usually won at archery on the lawn. But I could not have recognized the arrow until it was closer to me, and had stopped moving. So why do I think of that, before I think of the sound of it striking home, a sound like no other I have ever heard? And why can I not remember any sound at all, at the time when I know James screamed?

That's when I must have identified the arrow, sunk into his body and no longer vibrating. I could see it because James had turned to his left as Andrew loosed, and the arrow protruded from under James's right arm, through his coat, between his ribs. He was still on his feet and leaning against the tower, his head against it as if he were listening to the stones. His face was strangely quiet, except that his eyes were closed tight. His left hand had gone, by some reflex, to the site of the pain. He winced and drew it back, and opened his eyes to look at his fingers, dark with blood. His right arm was bent oddly to keep it clear of the shaft, and his right hand was in view for the first time, crooked, swollen, discoloured.

Exposure to terrible sights can, some physicians say, cause madness, and madness can cause hallucinations. Now that I am no longer mad, I know what I saw: the steam that rose from James's warm, damp coat and hair, and the sheen of wet blood in the torchlight. But for an instant it seemed as if the steam was the shivering in the air that intense heat makes, and the sheen was a line of blue-gold fire on his fingers and on the cloth of his coat.

There was some commotion on the shore. I looked; it was Richard, wild and blood-stained and straining steadily against the grip of the two men, as if they were a pair of stones too narrow to pass between. I couldn't tell which he most wanted to reach, James or Andrew. I grasped, belatedly, that he had been the movement in my peripheral vision; his tracks cut a new channel in the snow from the line of the garden wall. He must have seen Andrew's hand close on an arrow, must have known long before I did that the precarious balance of the moment was lost. Richard shouted something that I couldn't decipher.

Andrew stood at the brim of the steep part of the bank, where the distance from shore to island was shortest. He had dropped both bow and quiver, and stared across the little span of ice, his expression a mixture of dreadful hunger, baffled anger, and fear that came and went and grew like a tongue of flame in kindling.

The man he had named Justice transferred his gaze from James to Andrew and looked long. Then slowly, deliberately, he turned his back to Andrew and began to make his way up the slope through the snow.

Motion drew my eyes back to the tower. Even then I couldn't stir, I couldn't go to him; I couldn't even cry out. In memory, it seems as if I was trapped in a fairy-story or a nightmare. In memory it is bitter, more bitter even than at the time, to be frozen in my hiding-place and forced to play out the role of battlefield crow.

James had his back to the tower again, his chin on his breast, his wet hair fallen forward and hiding his face. As I watched he lifted his head until it, too, was pressed against the stones, and I could see his eyes were closed. He breathed without rhythm, the sound of it like gravel in a metal box. Then his lips parted, and speech came out.

I knew immediately that it must be the language Eileen Coslick had heard, the language James had heard himself speaking to the stallion in the Grey Hound yard. I heard the same echoes of Latin and French, though the inflections and endings and stresses were all strange to me. It was spoken in the voice that had been like a whip; now, I thought, it was like a sword.

I haven't said that James spoke the words, because I was not convinced, then or now, that he did. I will not attribute them to supernatural force. But I don't think they came from the waking mind that usually orders our speech. They may have sprung from wherever words and sounds come from when one talks in one's sleep. Or they may have come from the seat of will itself, a will so driven and thwarted that it burst out in whatever speech it could command.

What seemed supernatural is easily attributed to the state of the observer. I thought I could see that angry power of his, released at last and coiling around him, veiling him lightly like thin smoke. It might have been smoke, except that the wind was blowing too strongly now for smoke to have lingered. James seemed unaware of it; indeed, he might have passed out standing up, by the look of his face.

On the shore, Andrew Cobham shouted—furious, despairing, unintelligible on the wind—and so I tore my eyes away again from the tower. The Trotter's Club had all drawn back from their sacrifice and from Andrew. Some, like Justice, had turned their backs and were walking away, heavy work in the snow and wind. Some had only moved off a few yards and waited, watching, their masks discarded, their eyes wide in blank faces. Two of those were the men who had held Richard back. They had released him.

Richard stood directly behind Andrew, and both were watching James. But on Richard's face was such a fixed look, such fierce attention, as I had never seen there before. I saw his lips move, but couldn't hear what he'd said. Nor, I think, could Andrew, who took two steps back from the water, his eyes still on James.

Richard says he does not remember anything dependably after Henry was shot, and remembers nothing at all of the scene at the water's edge. I remember what I saw, but I couldn't see everything at once, and again, many things happened too quickly to be put in their proper order, or to observe accurately.

I remember seeing Richard's hands close over Andrew's upper arms, and the calm purpose in Richard's face seen over Andrew's shoulder. I know that Andrew slithered down the bank where it was steepest, with Richard close behind him; I think, I cannot help but think, that Richard propelled him down it, however much I might wish not to think so. Andrew may have been trying to cross the water of his own volition. He might have meant to run away from Richard, past the tower where James, dying, might suddenly have seemed less of a danger than the fit and threatening man at Andrew's heels. But as Andrew plunged suddenly, unsteadily, toward the tower, Richard stood behind him at the water's brim, both hands stretched out, and I don't believe it was a gesture meant to draw him back.

Andrew slipped on the ice. He slipped, and lurched forward, and James met him. In James's left hand was the shaft of the arrow, its point shining wet and blue and gold in the torchlight. The motion was almost like a fencer's lunge, but it was clear that the fencer had expended all his remaining force in that single graceless step forward, and would never be able to draw himself back up to a guard position unaided. Andrew himself propped James up, as his own momentum drove his body up the shaft and onto James's breast, and knocked him back against the tower.

I cried out when Andrew was struck. Why that should have been the moment, of all the horrible moments, to free me from my paralysis, I can't say.

Andrew reeled backward onto the ice and sat down suddenly, and his hands folded helplessly around the arrow where it entered his body, on the left side, angling upward and toward the shoulder joint. Even then I remember thinking that it had to have pierced something vital, and wondering if it was the heart or the lung. Andrew coughed, and blood ran shining over his chin; he drooped forward over his legs and toppled by degrees until he lay with his face in the churned snow.

James had slid to his knees at the base of the tower. I caught him in my arms before he fell. "Unless," I said, in a voice that seemed bizarre even to me, "You'd rather lie down after all?"

His eyelids moved, and opened, and he nodded. There was a streak of blood on his face. What property of blood allows it, once let out of its proper course, to appear everywhere without any apparent cause? As I lowered him to the ground, he whispered, "Botched that one. Love. Tell Engels—"

"Shut up," I ordered, "and you may tell him yourself later. Anyway, you didn't precisely botch it."

He grimaced. "Wasn't supposed to *die*."

"You haven't yet." I leaned forward, swallowing against the sudden sharp stone in my throat, and said, "My love, my heart, light of my world. I'm afraid I require your presence rather desperately. Would you please not go quite yet?"

He closed his eyes. "Held it together—with her thoughts," I think he said, though I could barely hear him, and even now can't imagine what he meant. "I'll try. How long?"

"I had in mind another twenty years, but I'll take what I can get."

After a moment he smiled.

I was aware then of the noise and movement across the water. I saw that Bankston's men had finally made their presence known; that the Trotter's Club were being herded together under guard; and that Thomas Cavanaugh was dragging his doctor away from Andrew's huddled form and up to the base of the tower.

"Careful of his hand on that side," I said, as the doctor shifted James's arm. The doctor, poor fellow, was muttering under his breath and looked as if he meant to be ill when he could spare the time.

Cavanaugh asked me if I was hurt. "No," I replied. "Why the devil would I be?"

He flinched a little. "The blood's his, then."

I looked down and found that Cavanaugh's question had not been entirely unreasonable.

Another man came across the ice, a stranger. He knelt to examine Andrew's body; then he looked up at us and called, "Is that James Cobham?"

His accent was London, as were his clothes, the suit good but not top-of-the-trees, the grey bowler respectable but not new. He was clearly used to receiving an answer when he asked a question.

"I think," said Richard behind and above me, "you know very well that it is." I jumped; I hadn't known he was there. Richard stepped out to stand between our little huddle and the man in the bowler, who had to be Bankston's lieutenant.

I had been able to move and speak since the blow that felled Andrew. Now, finally, I was able to think as well, and looking around me, I wondered if I was the only one of us who could. Wishing I had more time and a little more privacy, I leaned close to the doctor.

"You are about to declare that your patient has died," I told him.

"I beg your—I can't do—"

"After which you will whisk him away and produce a certificate of death, and I don't care how you have it witnessed so long as it's convincing."

"Madam—"

"They will never let you take him away from here alive."

I met Dr Gold's eyes, so wide and miserable, until he closed them tight and lowered his head. He took up James's left wrist and held it for a moment. When he looked up at last I held my breath at what was in his face.

"He *was* James Cobham," the doctor said, his voice loud and harsh and a little high. "I'm afraid he's dead."

My smeared fingers lay, as if at random, on the exposed skin of James's throat, and on the faint, unsteady pulse there. Even so, it was easy to react. I had only to show some of what I had felt all night.

The man in the bowler stood up, and I knew he was studying James, studying all of us. One flaw in the tableau and he would come closer, would take James's wrist himself, or produce a cigar-case with a polished surface . . .

"Mr Cliff—sir," another man called from the shore, "there's two carriages has come up the front drive. We're holding the coachmen, sir, but we need to know if they're to be brought in, too."

"I'll be there straightaway," Cliff said, and after a moment I heard his steps receding, crunching in the snow.

"If we don't get him to a place where I can do him some good," the doctor hissed at me, "I won't have been lying, after all. In fact, if we move him, it may well finish him."

I turned to Thomas Cavanaugh. "There's a lane behind the stables. Have the coach brought down it to the iron gate on the right just before the bend. That's as close as it can come in the snow." He sprang to his feet. "There's no rush," I said, my teeth clenched. "You're fetching it for a dead man."

Cavanaugh winced. I wondered how long it would be before he could be considered recovered from his association with this night.

It was raining thinly. I leaned over James and whispered his name.

His lips moved a little. "Understood," he said, so softly that I couldn't feel his breath on my cheek.

"Can you hold on?" I asked him. It seems strange, now, that I should trouble him with a question he couldn't possibly know the answer to. When I asked it, I know I expected a considered, dependable reply.

He did consider it. In the pause that followed his face was still, but I could feel his attention turned inward. Finally his mouth formed a "yes." Nothing else moved. I had asked him for another act of endurance, and he was already settling into it.

The doctor applied a makeshift dressing to James's wound and buttoned his coat over it. "Dead men don't bleed," he explained. "If we leave a trail between here and your damned gate, that man will know it's all bunk. They're government men, aren't they?"

"Yes. Thank you for being so thorough."

"Well, now that I've begun, I have to be thorough, don't I?"

I agreed.

Richard had stood sentinel all that time, watching for any

approach from Cliff's men. His back was to us, to the little struggling knot of conspirators, and to his half-brother lying motionless as the ice on the water, nearly at his feet. Now in the unexpected silence that had fallen he looked over his shoulder at James. In doing so, he turned away from what light there was, and his face was in darkness. "So," he said, in an iron voice. "What's the worst thing that's happened today?"

I saw James's eyes open wide, heard the sharp rasp of his drawn breath, felt the cold skin under my hand pull over tensed muscles. I thought he, too, was straining to make out Richard's expression. I was afraid and angry, and in a moment I would have spoken. Then James relaxed, and I saw he was smiling a little.

"Tell you later," he whispered. His eyes were closed again. "Remind me."

I didn't think the words would have reached Richard, but they had. "I will, you know," Richard replied. Like iron his voice had turned brittle in the cold.

It was impossible to tell if James had heard him; he had sunk down once more into whatever unfrozen depths were left to him, to wait like a trout in a pool for the return of the light.

When Thomas came back, Richard bent as if to pick James up. "No," I said, and laid a hand on his arm.

He looked at me, but didn't straighten up.

"He's dead. If you go with him, Cliff will scent a rat. He's dead. You would let him go."

"No," said Richard, "I wouldn't."

"Cliff doesn't know that. Let Thomas and the doctor take him. We have to stay." I was weeping. I thought perhaps I had been for some time, but couldn't think when I'd started.

I found I couldn't stand without his help; I'd lost the feeling in both my feet, and I was nearly rigid with cold and tension. It was very dark without the torches, without the blaze of the house which had subsided to an angry glow on the hill, and without the promised moon which was shut away behind the rain clouds. There was nothing to see, anyway, besides the blood-stain at the base of the tower, the blood thinned by melting snow at the edges until it faded to white. The hem of my habit had drawn up blood along with the snow-melt; the stain of it was darkest at the top of the line of damp, in the curious way of stains.

"I suppose they'll want to arrest you," I said to Richard. "If they do, I don't know how I'm to get myself to Melrose. I don't think I can ride."

"I told Cliff that if he wanted me, he knew where to come get me. Let's go. Wye will have found a carriage somewhere."

We rescued Girasol from his weary hiding place and tied him behind the carriage that Wye had, indeed, conjured from somewhere. The burden of waiting had already settled upon me, but it was in the carriage that I recognized it for what it was, and that there was nothing to do but carry it.

25 DEC

Just before dinner Wye came to the drawing room with a tray and the look of a man trying to be impassive with his feet on fire. "Miss Voight," he said, and stopped, and held out the tray.

A telegram. I picked it up without daring to look.

"There is a fire in the library," Wye said, so I went there. The waiting was done.

It was from Cavanaugh:

HAVE DONE AS YOU WISHED. RETURNING LONDON 27TH. NO FURTHER NEWS.

C.

James is alive, and out of the country. I laid the telegram on the library fire, and pulverized it with the poker as it burned. So long a wait—they couldn't have moved him without danger, I suppose. But it's done. I can plan again, because I can hope to win myself a future worth planning. I can acknowledge the child I carry, because for the child, too, I will make a future. James is still alive, and if anything I can do will keep him alive and undiscovered, it will be done.

Kitty knocked at the door at last, and I told her. She will tell Richard. Neither will tell anyone else. We have to continue to keep the secret; James is not yet far enough away, and we

are all still being watched by Bankston's people. James will
have a funeral at last, and it must be a convincing one. Our
grief over Henry will, perversely, be a great help there. Poor,
foolish, gallant Henry. If I stop to think of the price of all this,
I don't believe I will be able to live with it. But we have dealt
in things whose value is hard to measure. If one day I see what
I might have done to lessen the cost, I hope I have the strength
to bear the knowledge. Until then, all my strength is required
for other things.

JANUARY 26TH
MELROSE HALL

Dear Susan,

Once again I write to you not knowing when, or even if, this
letter will catch you up, but we both know that sometimes one
must write even if his words will never be read, and even if
you do not hear me thank you for remaining for Henry's funeral, which would have been even more awful without you,
and then James's funeral, so ghastly and so absurd, and I must
thank you even more, because with all of your trials, you were
a pillar of strength to me and to Dick, and even to Aunt Louisa,
and speaking of Aunt Louisa, yesterday she asked me to call
her Mother, but I told her I couldn't until I knew what had
become of Mama, and she asked what I meant by that, and I
told her, which is something I should never have thought of
doing a few months ago, and she said, "Poor child," as if she
meant it, and told me that there were things that could be done,
and she would write a letter at once, and I wondered to whom
she could write, and then I knew so I didn't say anything, but
it may be that I will learn something, after all.

Things are never really over, are they? Dick and I were
talking about what had happened, and he said that every once
in a while he gets flashes of clarity about those last hours, but,
he says, it doesn't matter, it only matters that we are still together, and that I am myself again, which I am, Susan, and
you must not worry about me, I am fine now, promise three
times on the little red leather pony saddle. I think Henry's

death was hard on Dick, but I think he will be all right, he has been reading Hegel, at any rate, which I somehow take as a good sign and I believe I will have to attempt it myself, which Dick approves of because, he says, together we might have some chance of making sense of it. We have also been gathering together all of the letters and documents associated with the entire horrid affair, though to what purpose I do not know, and I know that Dick has lost at least one or two letters he received while hiding at the Grey Hound, but perhaps some-day you will send us copies of some of the letters we wrote you, and we will do the same with the letters you and James wrote us, and we can have everything together to show our children.

Speaking of the Grey Hound, Dick wants to rebuild it and make a gift of it to Mrs Coslick, though we don't know if she would want it, but it can do no harm to ask, so we will do that. Lee is coming to dinner tomorrow and we will ask him to get a message to her.

Wye is still with us, and we have hired Clayborough, though he cannot do much until his leg heals, which saves us from the necessity of deciding what exactly he is to do, and he still will not tell us how he came to be injured, though Dick says he is beginning to remember that he was limping even when he helped poor Henry to the coach, and I said "he" too many times in that sentence didn't I? but you know what I mean because you always know what I mean, and it is no good hiding anything from you so I may as well tell you right out that I am going to find Mama, and I will begin by trying for a Sight, and Dick says he is going to help me, so we have begun putting our heads together about the implements we need, and you must not laugh at us, but I know you won't, whatever you think.

You know who I really want to ask about, and you know why I cannot, but I know that if anything were wrong you would tell us, and I hope somehow, somewhere, we will be able to all be together again, at least for a while, because I dream of someday being able to look back on the horrors as if from a distance, and if I never have the chance to hold my niece or nephew I will haunt you, which reminds me that the day before yesterday I asked Dick, oh so timidly, if he had ever thought about getting an heir and he said he had not the least interest in having an heir, but should not mind at all having a baby, so you can touch the Silk Garter for us, dear, because that is our plan as soon as we know about Mama, and even before that you may as well begin telling me what I ought to expect, which is funny because I had always thought that it should be me telling you first, but nothing ever really comes out the way we expect, but we should be happy, I think, if it comes out to be a way that we can live with, and that permits us to keep trying to make things better, and so I should be happy, and I think I am, and you know very well that Dick and I wish this happiness for you and that you are ever in the thoughts, hopes, and wishes of my husband and his wife who remains your good, true, and loyal friend,

Kitty

ORCHARD HOUSE
PIKESVILLE, MARYLAND
12 NOV 1850

Dear Kitty,

Yes! The miracle happened! Alice came with me! I know I'm being ridiculous about this, but really, if anyone had recited to me the list of implausible things that have so far happened in '50, I *do* think the ones I'd least believe are the ones having to do with Alice. That superior person, paragon of propriety, elevated lady's maid about Town—*voilà*, the draperies are whisked away, and we see a country girl with ten younger siblings who knows *all* about babies and how to expect them. That she condescended to go to Ireland with me I thought startling, even though we were bound for the Talbots' rather grand little pile. (Alice, I'm sorry to say, has no very good opinion of the Irish in London. Imagine my bemusement to find that she has no objection at all to them in Ireland; do you suppose they're ''in their place'' there?)

She dotes on the Pumpkin, of course (as I'm sorry to say pretty well everyone does who sees the awful child—it's witchcraft, I swear, as well as the smile, and it's no use telling them all that the latter is only gas or some such). Still, the world is full of babies; one hardly needs to cross the raging Atlantic and take up residence in the dark primæval forests of America (ahem) in order to have a baby to tend. Well, the sum of it is, she was shocked when I suggested that she didn't have to come along. She seems to have had visions of me starving to death in rags without her, and the baby being raised by wolves. I am *certain* I heard her sigh with relief when she saw Baltimore.

I'm *trying* not to call him the Pumpkin anymore, because I don't think I could face explaining to him that being eight months along is like carrying a very large Rouge Vif d'Étampes in front of you with both hands every minute of the day. Besides, pumpkins have no personality. By the time the crossing was done, I was living in a blaze of second-hand celebrity as Diccon's Mama. "He's such a *good* baby," they'd all say, and I'd smile weakly and think, "Yes, thank heaven!" Though I know very little about these things, he does seem to be quite a good baby. Surely a creature who's only barely got used to being alive on solid ground ought to be put out of temper when asked to accustom himself to seagoing life. But he appears to have thought of the crossing as an enormous rout-party, and himself the guest of honor. I sometimes think he considers crying vulgar; usually when he feels the lack of something he *inquires* after it, with a kind of carrying plaintive gurgle. This may, of course, be because Alice (and sometimes, I) spoils him horribly and leaps to his side if he so much as twitches, and the poor mite never has the *chance* to let out a good yell.

Oh, gracious—*paragraphs* of mother-thought! Are you tired of me yet, dear Kit? When I begin to sound like Dilly Talbot and carry on about measles and molars and nursery-meals, please, please, tell me I'm a crashing bore. Did I properly thank you for your yeoman service as intellectual support, back in August? Not merely thank you, but properly thank you; that is, give you the whole of the credit for my not succumbing to knitting and the more frivolous sort of novel? Well, it's all yours, and not least because you're one of the few people of my acquaintance who wouldn't be puzzled at the notion that a woman should want intellectual support during her lying-in.

You have also stored up heavenly credit for being unremittingly patient with Dilly. How odd, how very odd, to find that one of the lasting wounds of the winter is that I cannot *bear* to watch people amusing themselves by creating troubles and making other people participate in them. It's always been Dilly's favourite hobby, and I used to be entertained no end watching her practice it—so long as she didn't try to include me! Now, well, I never thought I would feel sorry for poor clumping Horace Talbot, married to a woman who can't be sure she's loved unless the man who loves her is miserable and angry. She lives in a Paradise designed for her, the foolish creature, and can only complain about the interminable flow of milk and honey, and the tiresome greenness of the grass. One cannot lay violent hands on one's hostess, however, and you did a really elegant job of removing my temptation to do so whenever it presented itself; I don't think Dilly ever noticed.

She certainly deserves better from me than violence. Perhaps it was only another ploy to cut up Horaces's and her own peace, but she took me in without an instant's hesitation, and never behaved by word, deed, look, or breath as if she expected me to be ashamed of my condition or my unwed state. She knows, I'm sure, that James is Diccon's father; she said something once about it being romantic, having the baby born in his grandmama's country, and then stammered over another few sentences meant to explain that she'd said something else. She probably attributes my situation to James's untimely death. Dilly is the last person to expect a woman to make a hasty marriage for the sake of propriety, if the opportunity exists for her to languish fallen, bereft, and tragically faithful. (What a horrid paragraph. The fact of the matter is that Dilly has a good heart, for all her foolishness, and I am a lucky wretch that she was willing to lavish that goodness on me. Cynicism is childish.)

Dear, you are a proven blasphemer, and I will never again believe anything you swear on the sacred pony saddle. I was shocked at your looks in Ireland, so thin and worn and haunted-looking as you were. I didn't tax you with it then, because I hoped that you'd be the better for not being reminded of your troubles. And you did seem much improved by the day you left; were you? If so, it was the Pumpkin's fault, no doubt, as he had set himself to attach his godmama to him the moment his eyes began to focus.

I have thought since about the discussion we had on the day we went to Drogheda to pic-nic on the beach. (Have I startled you? I believe I have. I'm sure you never considered the possibility that I took any of what we talked about seriously.) If there is anything to the idea that Diccon's patron is the sun, then my child will be dependable in his course and prodigal in bestowing warmth and light from a limitless source. His Aunt Kitty, under Pisces, is as prodigal in her giving—but the source of her strength is finite, and life will always pull her in many ways at once, like the sea between Earth and Moon. Dear Kit, I can't bear to see you take up all our burdens and be devoured by them. Fling them back up on the beach and let us all take responsibility for them ourselves. For yourself, go sun-bathing, at least metaphorically. You're wed to a broad-shouldered, stubborn, unswerving man, just as his stars say he should be. Let *him* hold up the world for a little, while you only rest upon it and grow strong. And though your Virgo cousin may by the dictation of the stars have a great natural reluctance to tell you her heart, remember always that there is nothing in it for you but love, and that for all your life, if there is anything you need that's in my power to provide, you have only to ask.

About another thing we spoke of during your visit, there are no more developments. The child (a boy, baptised Aidan Emrys) *was* born in Wales in January of last year and was sent to live in Brittany, that's certain. But there is no sign of him or his nurse there now, and if there's any person who knows where he was sent, I can't find him, either. We have to accept, I think, that we've done the best we can for now. I've made sure that there will continue to be sharp-eyed men paid to watch for clues to his whereabouts, but I'm afraid the poor little scrap may never surface. I would have liked to let him know that his father's sister doesn't believe in punishing the next generation for the last one's sins.

The past year has been entirely too much, even for me, and I've always favoured a rootless, gipsying life. Though I ought not to blame the travelling; if I'd been gipsying for its own sake, I expect I would have thrived like a weed. I owe more to Tom Cavanaugh than I can ever repay. While I dragged my pretend broken wing all over Britain, Portugal, Spain, and north Africa, he conveyed my money and his wise decisions to the private hospital outside of Paris, and kept me supplied with hopeful reports. Did I tell you that Bankston visited me in London, after I came back from Gibraltar? It was a dangerous moment; I had only just returned, and hadn't heard from Tom yet. If all had gone according to plan, our contested playing-piece was off the board of Europe entirely, sailing for Boston and the care of another set of physicians. But if he'd taken a bad turn and couldn't be moved, then he was still within reach of Bankston, of the French government, of the Prussians. . . .

Bankston offered his condolences to me and to the family on the loss of James and Henry, and I accepted them gracefully. He never let his gaze drop below my shoulders, as if he wanted to be able to say later that he hadn't noticed my condition.

"He was a clever man," Bankston said of James, "a brilliant man. But for all that, it may be as well he didn't survive that last fracas of his."

"Really?" I said, in a style calculated to depress the pretensions of any human being with an ounce of sensibility.

Bankston looked me in the eye, and it was suddenly clear that sensibility was only a weapon in his arsenal, to be used when it served his purpose. I very nearly smiled at him, Kit. In that moment I knew exactly what sort of formidable opponent he was, and that I, *I!*, was up to his weight. Such a rush of excited happiness blew through me that I was afraid I was about to giggle. The immensely *enceinte* woman in black silk was called upon once again to live on her nerves and hang over precipices. I pokered up in civil outrage and added, "You'll understand, Sir George, if his family does not immediately share your sentiments."

"Not immediately, perhaps. But I'm afraid he'd involved himself in some very unsavoury business. If he'd lived, it must have become public knowledge, and caused you all a great deal of pain."

"I find it hard to believe that anything could be more unsavoury than the manner of his death."

"That must have been hard on you and your family. And that, you know, was kept hushed up in some measure, as a kindness to your aunt." (As a kindness to my aunt, was it? Humbug.) "Think of the harm it would have done her for James Cobham to stand his trial, to be hanged or transported."

I stared at him, stretching my neck out and tipping my head like a chicken. "Surely, Sir George, nothing like that would have been considered."

"I'm sorry," he said. "It would have been impossible to consider anything else. You understand now, perhaps, why I say that it is better for everyone concerned that your cousin is dead?"

He was nearly certain, Kitty, that James was alive. I hadn't the time or the tools to convince him he was wrong; but I had to convince him that *I* was sure we had buried James in December. "My goodness," I replied, rather faintly, but gaining force as I went. "My goodness. I really don't see why . . . I mean to say, there's nothing to be done about it now. Is there? If there's no harm in it now that poor James is—gone, it's unkind of you, Sir George, to bring it up at all. Unless there's some problem, in which case, I wish you'd simply *say* so."

He was routed. He wasn't happy about it, but I was so gloriously obtuse on the subject that he had, finally, to settle for a repeat of condolences and an orderly retreat. I was glad that I had nothing else to do after that but trundle myself off to Ireland to have a baby, an activity which I defy even Sir George Bankston to construe as suspicious.

Still, you see why I was worried about the timing of my sailing date. I wanted to leave Liverpool for America almost before anyone could notice that I'd arrived in Liverpool from Dublin—certainly before anyone noticed that I hadn't the least intention of boarding a train headed south. If the weather had been bad and kept us in harbour at Liverpool, I think I would have jumped over the side and begun to swim west. Such a relief when the gangplank was brought up, and the quay slipped away behind us.

And such pain, too, Kitty! I hadn't expected it, fool that I am. I had thought I could go into exile almost cheerfully, re-

gretting only you and Richard, Aunt Louisa and Brian, and
the best of my friends, knowing that even though I would miss
you bitterly, we wouldn't lose each other. I'd thought that England itself was only an island, only another piece of ground.

I held Diccon in my arms at the rail and watched my country
recede, both Liverpool's soot and smoke and the ripe green
and gold of the land beyond the city, and wept until the two
blurred into a muddle of colour. I told Diccon to watch, too,
told him he might never see England again. But of course, he
is an infant, and can't comprehend such nonsense, let alone
care about it. He looked steadily up at me; his allegiance is to
faces and kind hands, not nations or plots of earth. Even so,
it seemed to me in my distress that his steadiness had a sort
of consciousness in it. He is not an Englishman. He is not
Irish, though he was born there. The child in my arms was, if
anything, American, only waiting to come home for the first
time. The idea was sad and strengthening at once. I looked my
last, turned away, and took him for a promenade on the deck,
the first of many that we made. But we never again stopped
in the stern and gazed back at where we'd been.

Kitty, am I a terrible, selfish person? You may answer
"yes"; you should, you want to, even if you don't know it
yet. You had two questions when you laid eyes on the envelope that will eventually enclose this, and I have only answered
the one about the well-being of your nephew. I am selfish, is
all, and silly besides, thinking that sharing a story requires me
to give any of it up, or wears away any of its contents. *Au
contraire*, as a certain person I know will sometimes say. To
share my life with you, good and bad, has been to anchor my
hold on it and to sharpen every colour and detail. The letters
I have written you are copied on my bones and heart, so that
the events in them and all the feelings I poured out to you are
more surely a part of me now than they would have been
locked away in my mind. You were right, after all, to want
me to give knowledge of my heart into your keeping; until I
did so, I didn't know what was in it myself.

The doctor sent his carriage to fetch us directly from the
quayside in Baltimore, which was not only kind but a difficult
kindness to perform; an Atlantic crossing is not a railway journey, subject to strict timetables. We had had some dirty

weather that had delayed us by several days, and that must have required some message-carrying and wasted journeys in order to have the carriage and driver waiting when we arrived. But if he could have known what a pleasure it was to be treated like a welcome friend where one had thought to be a stranger, he must have considered it worth the trouble. Besides, I think black lacquer panels, yellow-varnished wheels, and immaculate brightwork went a long way toward allaying Alice's misgivings.

We trotted through the city with Alice admiring twilled silk pelisses and well-tailored coats, handsome stone row houses and soberly-driven horses, and pointing them all out to Diccon. I pretended to look and admire, but with each mile my mouth was more dry and my palms more damp, and I felt as if I would never be able to move my precisely-placed feet from the carriage floor. I was travelling in the direction I most longed to go, I was closer to my heart's desire than I had been for nearly a year, and every minute brought me closer still. Yet I was nearly speechless with dread.

Does that make any sense, Kitty? But it *had* been nearly a year. I was not sure that what I travelled so quickly toward was anything like what I had lost at midwinter. I had only Tom's kind—over-kind? Over-hopeful?—secondhand reports. I might be riding toward a shut door that would in the end prove impossible to open, or even prove to have been better left closed. Illness, infirmity, long experience of pain can change those they work upon. There are wounds of the body and soul that don't heal, or heal into deformity. Most of all, I feared to find that *I* had changed, during the long months in which I'd had nothing to measure change against. I had very little idea what I was travelling toward, or what I was bringing with me.

The land outside the city was lovely, spread in broad fields and stands of wood like the Shires, broken with sudden bright threads of water bound for the sea. Autumn was on the countryside, in a frenzy of colour that seemed nearly indecent when compared with a staid English autumn. The trees stood green, parrot-yellow, yellow-ochre, red-orange, cherry-red, and a particularly unlikely shade of plum against a sky so blue and far away that I felt as if I could be swept into it if I looked too long. The buildings were mostly grey stone and white-painted wood, and stood marked against the land like drawings cut into chalk through green turf.

Orchard House sits on the edge of the village, closer to the road than I would have expected a house of its size to be. I could see the rows of trees that gave it its name even as we came up the drive, sweeping out behind the buildings like a peacock's tail. A tall, thin man with dense grizzled whiskers and an elegant coat appeared at the door as our carriage stopped in the drive, and descended the steps with the slow self-possession of a heron.

"You must be Miss Voight," he boomed as I came up the gravel. "I had my description of you from a pretty good source. I'm Dan Parker."

I put out my hand and he shook it firmly. It's another measure of the state I was in that I smiled at him with some difficulty. Under normal circumstances, anyone who does not instantly smile on meeting Dr Daniel Parker is probably unconscious or dead.

"Come in," he said before I had time to forestall him, "and have a bite of something. I expect you'll want a little time to settle yourself after the trip. Of course you will," he added a trifle more firmly, when I opened my mouth to protest. I felt a little chill around my heart, but I followed the doctor's housekeeper up to a pleasant room, and Alice followed behind me with Diccon.

Diccon had his wants seen to first, of course, and settled down happily for a nap; then Alice sent me, cleaned, brushed, and changed into wine-red poplin, down to the parlour. There I found the doctor and a sideboard of food and drink. I took a cup of tea to be civil, and sat in a chair that allowed me to see his face. "You want to talk to me before I see him," I said.

He seemed taken aback for a moment; then he shook his head. "Don't know what I was expecting," he muttered. "Yes, I do. I couldn't say what he was like when you saw him last."

"Dying," I answered crisply.

Parker coughed. "You'll find him much improved, then. If you're telling me to take the gloves off, Miss Voight, I'll tell you that they are. But I thought you'd be better off knowing right away that he's not strong, and may never be."

It was what I had been preparing myself for, after all. "Why?"

Parker leaned back in his chair and pressed his lips together, as if he'd had quite enough of the conversation. "Well, now. It may have been the hole in him and the blood he lost, or the infection, or the pneumonia, or sheer physical exhaustion. My opinion as a medical man is that it's all of 'em. If you think there was anything that could have been done for him that wasn't—"

"No. I'm terribly sorry, I hadn't for a moment thought anything of the kind. That your politics happen to march with mine is not why you were recommended to me, after all. I'm not—I'm afraid my manners have been entirely overcome by my anxieties. I apologise."

His expression softened. "No need, no need. Perfectly reasonable."

"Thank you, you're very kind. I only meant, is there a particular reason why you think he might not recover?"

"Because medicine is a little like poker. You hope for a miracle, but you bet with the odds. There seems to be a touch of fever left, though it doesn't trouble him in the usual way. He doesn't always sleep well at night, and sometimes I swear he's fallen asleep with his eyes open in the middle of the day. And whatever happened to his hand is more than either Kappe up in Boston or I can put altogether right. Of course, that he's here at all suggests that he's tough as an old boot. But he's not hale, and I'm telling you so before you see him so you won't be surprised."

"Does he know it?"

I had startled him again. "Oh, yes. I'd say he's accustomed to knowing exactly what he's capable of, physically."

The way he'd put it seemed odd, so I asked, "And other than physically?"

Parker lifted his chin and studied me, his eyes half-closed. "Nobody knows that, does he?"

I didn't understand him, and I doubted he was prepared to explain himself. "May I see him now?"

Parker smiled. "Probably, depending on where he's got to."

"He's not here?"

"Not in the house, anyway. He's not usually, until supper-time. But I don't think he'll have gone far. He might be in his study."

"But you said—"

"The neighbours and I call it that. Back of the house, on a bit of a hill, there's a big maple. He'll read or write there most afternoons if the weather's dry."

"Thank you," I said. I can't recall how I left the parlour, or how I found my way out of the house.

Kitty, I remember what happened next as if it were some-thing I imagined while being read a fairy-tale. I have seen these things and places since that first time, and they are subtly different, both more and less so than twice-seen sights always are. Forgive me for the quality it gives the narrative, because all the lines I want to write seem to have been stolen from the stories we used to tell each other at school, late at night when one of us couldn't sleep.

Behind the house there is a herb garden and a vegetable plot, the latter already turned and ready for winter. Between these and the orchard is a screen of trellised hops and grape-vine; one walks through an arch in the trellis and straight into the ranked company of old apple trees, their trunks heavy, their twisted low branches preventing any good view of the dis-tances ahead. I could only keep the house at my back, and follow the slight slope of the ground.

The plantings of trees stopped where the slope increased. I stood at the edge of a clearing that rose gently before me. The afternoon sun was warm on my face, and the breeze that flut-tered the leaves around me was mild. Somewhere out of sight I heard crows arguing, and behind me in the orchard a mourn-ing dove called, four sweetly melancholy falling notes. The air was scented with windfall apples and dry leaves. It seemed as if I stood on the border of another country entirely, a walled place that no one else could cross into, and that, once having entered, I could never leave.

At the top of the little hill was a tree. Two grown men might have stood on either side of its trunk and reached around, and still not touched hands. Its crown of branches was wide, the lovely half-dome common to maples, and in proportion to its trunk. All the leaves had turned, and many had fallen, so that crown and hillside were clad alike in yellow-gold so bright it seemed to give off heat like a flame. Sitting under the tree, dark and vivid against the yellow and the silver bark, was the slim figure of a man.

The straight shoulders were clad in neat black; the dark hair was full of warm colour from days out of doors. His right leg was stretched out before him, and his left was drawn up, his left arm propped on the knee and his left hand hanging idle in the air, waiting to turn the next page of the book held open in his right. Beside him on the fallen leaves was an untidy sheaf of paper, weighted against the breeze with a stone, and a pencil. The scene was so much like one Tom Cavanaugh might paint—the heart-wrenching light, the unconscious affecting grace of the pose, the indwelling sense of a story half-told, a movement half-begun—that for a single disorienting moment I thought I had invented it. In that moment, literally dizzying, it seemed that the wall of that undefined, unrecognized country had shifted and closed behind me, that I had crossed the border whether I would or no. Then James raised his head and saw me.

He made no other motion. Finally I stepped forward and began to climb the little hill. At that he rose to his feet. I faltered, but didn't stop until I was within a bent arm's reach of him. I could see clearly the clean-shaven chin, the neatly-tied neckcloth; I saw as well the hard marks of past suffering, lines and hollows and the white strands at his temples that caught the light like polished metal. His eyes were wide; they moved as mine must have, searching my face for the familiar and the strange, taking in both and combining them, creating me again in his mind and finding, as I had found about him, that my new self fit that place left empty in him as if it had been grown to it.

He put out his left hand and drew one finger lightly over the side of my face from brow to jaw. "Then you're real," he murmured, and the familiar voice after so many months of silence was like a bell sounded next to my ear.

"So are you," I replied.

He said unsteadily, "That's good to know." His eyes closed suddenly. I stepped forward and found myself held tight in his arms, enclosed by warmth through his clothes, by the smell of clean linen and soap and sandalwood, feeling the rhythmless wracked breathing that eventually released itself in tears into my hair.

I think all my anticipatory dread made that reunion easier for me than it was for him. I'd had the luxury of imagining the worst, and was able to discard my imaginings in a blink when they proved to match nothing in reality. He had known I would arrive soon, but not how soon, and wrenched from waiting to living he was battered by the full flood of fear, hope, and joy so mingled as to be indistinguishable. It seemed a long time before I realized he was relaxed and breathing easy in my arms.

He said, as if he'd heard my thought, "Hegel would have had something to say about that."

I drew back a little and stared at him. "Well, thank goodness he's not here, then."

James laughed, which seemed to penetrate the shadows in his face. It was a promising sign, and in order to urge the process along, I kissed him. I learned by doing so that there are things that, if one doesn't precisely forget them, cannot really be accurately retained in one's memory.

"I like your study," I told him, surveying it from the vantage point of his embrace. I stood leaning back against him, his arms pulled around me like a shawl. "What are you working on?"

"Answering a letter from Richard. No, he was very wise," James said in answer to my quick look and sudden frown. "He waited to write until I was in Boston."

"This one seems to call for a bit of scholarship."

I felt his laugh more than I heard it. "I've got him in a corner. I'm only looking for a suitable quote to buttress the point when I tell him that all he has left to represent his Unknowable is a snippet of non-existent time."

I leaned my head back against his shoulder. "If you were anyone else, I'd tell you it's unbecoming to gloat."

"But you'd tell me . . ."

"That even gloating becomes you. It's a sad thing, an intelligent woman in love."

He held me a little closer. "Dan told you where to find me?"

"No, I simply flew to my heart's delight like a homing bird." That won me a kiss just beneath my ear. "He says you're still delicate."

"Mm. Like crystal, in fact. Perfectly durable under normal circumstances, but I don't do well when dropped. Though now that you're here, I detect an improvement. Why, are you planning any immediate heroics for us?"

"Mere vulgar curiosity, for now. I *do* hope you're fit for heroics by the time our son begins to walk."

I felt him smile. "We'll divide the heroics between us. You may have all the tree-climbing, if you like."

"I would have brought him out with me," I said, turning in his arms to look at him. "But I'm afraid I didn't want to share you yet, even with him."

I could tell from what was in his face that I had done right, even before he spoke. "He and I will have time. You and I haven't had very much, and never any of this sort. You named him Richard."

I wondered if he'd been told, or if it was a guess. "It was the obvious choice."

"It is, isn't it? Will you marry me?"

"No. And anyway, you're a whole month early."

"May I ask you again next month?"

"Suit yourself. I have nothing to fear from a test of my principles."

He laughed. "No, and never will, if I have anything to say about it. Once Dan's finished working on me, where would you like to go?"

"Oh, here and there. Engels has given me a letter of introduction to a correspondent of his in Wisconsin."

"It's all trees and winter up there, I hear. And gloomy Germans and Swedes."

"Well, you'd perk them right up, then. Did you hear I went to Morocco? I brought back embroidered slippers and kohl."

"Did you learn any dances?"

"You're not strong enough yet for those." I stepped away from him and held out my hand. "Come down to the house.

There's a shocking lot of food in the parlour, and I didn't have any of it."

The hand he put in mine was his right one. I held it carefully and, feeling very brave, studied it over. The fingers curved unevenly, the joints of irregular sizes; the set of the thumb was wrong; and the palm was curiously flat.

"It was worse before Kappe got to it," he said, his voice gentle. "Don't worry, it doesn't hurt. It's not as strong as the left, and I can't manage any fine motion with it yet. But I can handle an oar, or reins, or a knife and fork. And my left-hand writing is legible, if not handsome."

"It seems too high a price," I told him, stroking the fingers as if I could smooth them.

"No. Henry was too high a price. And the last ten months were harder to pay than my hand, because they're lost to us. That," he nodded at his hand laid in mine, "is only scars." And he smiled at me.

For most people, scars fade as memory fades, but my tenacious memory allows very little for the action of time. I need another metaphor. And so I tell myself that scars are places where healing has occurred. He's right: one hand, however beautiful, is a small fee for such a crossing. Think of James, after all, twice dead and once buried, alive again in the lands of the West like the hero in an Irish tale. Or perhaps I should think of the Egyptians instead, Isis and her ever-reborn consort, Osiris. They had a son, after all, though with god-like dignity they brought forth between them a hawk and not a pumpkin.

Kitty, you needn't carry my troubles any longer, because I have come to the Land of the Ever-Young and shed them all. I shall spend the rest of my life, with my fond and helpful lover, in causing ripples in other people's calm waters, and swamping lies and hypocrisies in the wake of my passage. Doesn't that sound like ever so much fun?

My love to everyone there, and be assured that I'll write again soon. I think we will go to Wisconsin in a year or so, but I would like to see Philadelphia and New York and Boston first, and James has assured me that it is almost impossible to go west from here without a look-in at Chicago (a beautiful-sounding word, Kitty, magical and strange like so many of the

Indian words). You won't lose me, I promise, however far away I may be.

Yes, the leaf is from the hill. Whenever you find yourself worrying over your absent relations, bring it out to remind yourself that all our wishes have come true. Yours will, too, dear, I know.

Ever your loving
Susan

This second definition of freedom, which unceremoniously slaps the face of the first, is nothing but an extremely shallow rendering of the Hegelian conception. Hegel was the first who correctly presented the relation of freedom and necessity. Freedom is, for him, the insight into necessity. "Necessity is *blind only in so far as it is not understood*." Freedom does not lie in the fancied independence of natural laws but in the knowledge of these laws, and in the possibility which this knowledge gives, of making them work systematically for definite ends. This holds good in respect to the laws of external nature as well as to those which regulate the physical and mental existence of man himself—two classes of laws which we can, at most, separate from one another in thought, but not in reality. Freedom of will, therefore, means nothing other than the ability to decide, when in possession of a knowledge of the facts. Thus the *freer* the judgment of a man is in regard to a definite issue, with so much greater *necessity* will the substance of this judgment be determined; while the uncertainty caused by ignorance, which seems to choose arbitrarily between many different and contradictory possibilities of decision, proves thereby its lack of freedom, its being controlled by the very thing which it should control. Freedom consists then in the mastery over ourselves and external nature, based on the knowledge of natural necessities; it is thus necessarily a product of historical development. The first men who separated themselves from the animal kingdom, were in all essentials as unfree as the animals themselves; but every advance in civilization was a step toward freedom . . .

Friedrich Engels
Anti-Dühring, 1877